Portland Storm: The Third Period

Featuring:
Dropping Gloves
Home Ice
Mistletoe Misconduct
Losing an Edge
Game Breaker

by
USA Today bestselling author
Catherine Gayle

CONTENTS

Dropping Gloves

by
USA Today bestselling author
Catherine Gayle

Chapter One

Katie

CANCER SUCKS DONKEY balls. Great big, ginormous, hairy ones. There's not really a better way of saying it, and I'd long since stopped trying to come up with one.

If anyone should know how bad cancer sucks, it was me. I was diagnosed with leukemia when I was a senior in high school. That was why I was here, at the Moda Center, where the Portland Storm played, staring out the end of the tunnel at the crowd gathered for their annual Hockey Fights Cancer night. If I could do anything to help even one person not have to go through all the crap I'd had to go through, then you could bet I was going to do it.

It might not seem like much, singing the national anthem at a hockey game, but for me it wasn't about the singing or the game. It was about awareness. It was about raising money for research and treatments. It was about being sure everyone in this building right now knew how important finding a cure was.

The teams had already skated out for all of the pregame ceremonies, and the arena crew had gone through all of their music and video programming to get the crowd pumped up for the game. Not that they really needed to do much for that. The Storm had finally made it all the way to the Western Conference Finals last season before falling to the Chicago Blackhawks in seven games, and most of last year's key players had returned for this season. Expectations surrounding the Storm were high, regardless of the rough start they'd had. Tonight they were playing the LA Kings, one of their biggest divisional rivals for the last few seasons. With all that going on, the crowd didn't need any extra pumping up. They were raring and ready to go, whether the team was or not.

But now, the lights dimmed and the music became more subdued, and a video started playing on the Jumbotron. Mom reached over and took my free hand, squeezing. The thing was, this video was about me.

It showed home footage and photographs that my parents and some of the Storm's players had taken over the years, images of me at various Storm events I'd been part of, video of me skating at the team's annual Christmas party, and other things like that.

A song by The End of All Things—a local band that had made it big, not to mention my favorite band of all time—played over the montage. I hadn't heard this one before. It must have been from their upcoming album, which made me wonder how Tim Whitlock, the Storm's in-arena entertainment director, had managed to get hold of it. Then again, there were connections between the team and the band. Brie Burns, one of the players' wives, was a ballroom dancer who had worked with The End of All Things in the past.

The lyrics spoke of holding on to the best parts of life. That, combined with the images that represented some of the best parts of *my* life, had me getting teary-eyed. Not a good thing when I was about to have to get out there and sing in front of a crowd of eighteen thousand or so. Crying and talking was hard enough. Crying and singing? Pretty much impossible.

Now the video started getting to the point where my cancer came in. Me, bald-headed, wearing various scarves to hide the physical evidence of my chemo. I wanted to look away, but I couldn't. This was why I was here. This was why they'd asked *me* to sing the anthem tonight instead of having the in-house singer do it. Looking away wouldn't change anything I had been through. I'd already tried that in multiple areas of my life, and it hadn't worked yet.

Dad put his hands on the backs of my shoulders and started to knead away some of my anxiety. Normally, at this point of the night, he would be behind the bench with the team. Dad was one of the Storm's assistant coaches. He had been since the season after he'd retired as a player. He was my connection to the team, or at least he had been my first connection. But tonight was different. Tonight, he was with me. He'd take his spot behind the bench after this was over.

Just as he started rubbing my shoulders, an image flashed on the screen that choked me up like crazy and caused the whole crowd to *ooh* and *aah*. It was one of my prom pictures. There I was, in my ice-blue dress without anything covering my head, crying while Jamie Babcock kissed me.

I hadn't intended to go to my prom. Not until Jamie asked me.

He hadn't even been one of my classmates. He was one of my dad's teammates at that point, a guy who I'd had a crush on since the first moment I'd seen him. But Jamie had asked to take me, and I would have done anything to be with him, and he'd made it perfect for me even if I was bald and felt like an alien. When I was with him, I'd felt like a princess.

But I'd beat cancer, and I'd moved on with my life—going off to Hollywood to star in an ensemble *Glee*-knockoff TV show called *The Cool Kids*—and he'd moved on with his. I'd broken my own heart when I'd left, and seeing that picture right now brought a torrent of memories and emotions flooding back to life.

"Why did you give them that one?" I hissed at my mom, trying to hold back the massive wave that was threatening to turn to tears.

She arched a brow and shrugged. "I didn't."

"Oh, sure you didn't," I said. I even rolled my eyes. My sarcasm knew no bounds. No one but my mother would have given the Storm that photo. Other than me, only Jamie and my family had copies of it. I definitely hadn't given it to the entertainment people, and there wasn't a chance in hell that Jamie would have done it. I'd broken his heart, too, not just my own. Why would he want a reminder of that flashed in front of his eyes right before he had a game to play?

"I wouldn't lie to you," she insisted. "Not about something like that. I wouldn't have given them any of those pictures. They're too personal."

Which was precisely my point. My mouth was open to argue with her again when Dad squeezed my upper arms from behind. "She didn't. Your mom's telling you the truth."

"Then who did?" I demanded.

"I gave it to them."

"What?" Mom and I said in shocked unison. I spun around to glare at him. Dad had been opposed to every guy I'd ever dated, some of them more than others. He'd just about blown a gasket when Jamie had asked me to prom. Why would he put that memory, that relationship, right up at the forefront of my mind at a time like this?

Dad shrugged. "Tim asked us for pictures that meant something, that would have an impact on the crowd." He nodded his head toward the open end of the tunnel, indicating all the people out there who were watching in rapt silence. "That one meant the most to me, so I thought it would get the biggest reaction from them."

I swallowed hard.

The song finished, the video came to a close, and Tim's familiar voice echoed over the PA system in the cavernous arena. He introduced the Storm's starters for the night, who each skated out to take their positions. The Kings' starting line went out, as well. Then he introduced the Little Starter of the game before taking a moment to talk about the military veteran being honored tonight. Both the Little Starter and the vet were also cancer survivors. They headed out on cue, and the vet stood on his mark. The boy skated over to stand next to Jamie, who patted him on the head and said something that no one could hear but the two of them.

Then Tim introduced me. "Katie Weber has been a member of the Portland Storm family for close to a decade now. Her father, David Weber, played for the Storm for a number of years before becoming one of our assistant coaches. Katie spent her teen years here, and it was here that she was diagnosed with—and beat—leukemia. Our organization was given the task of seeing her through her own personal storm. We watched her grow up, and we watched her leave to become a star bright enough to shine over a much bigger world than Portland. She will always be part of our family, no matter how far away life takes her. Now she's returned, at least for this one very special night. Storm fans, please join me in giving Katie Weber a big welcome back to Portland."

That was my cue. I white-knuckled my microphone with both hands and headed out of the tunnel to the purple carpet that had been laid on the ice. The entire arena was on its feet, applauding and screaming. I'd always loved being in front of a crowd, but I still got stage fright. Being on *The Cool Kids* hadn't helped with that at all. If anything, it had made it worse. For the last four years, I'd been doing all of my acting and singing in front of cameras and crew. But these days when I did something in public, the audiences were bigger, and everyone seemed to think they knew *me*, not the character I'd played. That was clear enough from the number of people in the stands wiping tears from their eyes.

Most of the people in the audience wore the typical purple-and-silver Storm jerseys I'd come to expect during my years here, but a few people had the road whites on, and a smattering had on Kings black and silver. It was easy to spot the pink Hockey Fights Cancer version of the Storm's jerseys in the crowd, like the one I was wearing. The whole crowd was holding up signs they'd been given when they'd come in tonight, bearing the names of people they loved who had cancer, or maybe people they'd lost to cancer.

Mom and Dad followed me to the carpet. Both of their signs had my name on them.

I smiled and waved, trying not to let the turbulence of my emotions swallow me whole, but it seemed like a daunting—maybe impossible—prospect. I felt as if I would fall to pieces the moment I opened my mouth to sing, but this was different from my usual stage fright. It was bigger and more confusing, like a giant ball made up of rubber bands, each one representing a new, massive, devastating emotion, and the bands were contracting in on themselves. It was squeezing the life out of me.

"Please rise and remove your caps," Tim said, not that there was any need for his reminder. Everyone was already on their feet. The rest of his words were drowned out in the unending applause. He was in the scorer's box, the small space across the ice from the team benches that separated the two penalty boxes. I caught his eye across the distance, and he gave me a nod.

Nerves or not, it was time. I took out my pitch pipe, blew into it to find my key, shoved it back into my pocket, and did what I'd come to do. Somehow I got through the anthem without completely shattering, which I considered an absolute coup. Now that I was done, though, all I wanted was to run off the ice and find somewhere I could break down for a minute. But it wasn't time for that yet.

Tonight, the Storm had planned a ceremonial puck drop to go along with all of the other special events, and they'd asked me to do it. Dad took the mic and pressed the puck into my hands. He kissed my cheek before taking his spot behind the bench. Mom hugged me and headed down the tunnel. I wanted to go with her. I wanted to be anywhere but here, doing anything but what I was about to do.

Because it meant I would be inches away from Jamie.

Dustin Brown, the Kings' captain, came out and took his spot on one side of me. He said something, looking right at me, but my head was filled with the buzzing of a horde of bees, and I couldn't make his words out. I couldn't pay attention to him with Jamie skating over to stand across from him on my opposite side. All my attention focused in on Jamie like a laser beam.

In his skates, he was even taller than normal, towering over me despite my Jimmy Choos. His hockey pads only emphasized his muscle, making him seem larger than life. Even with a bit of distance between us, I could see the creases in his cheeks where his dimples always came through. With every year that passed, he looked less like a boy and more like a man, but I hoped he would never lose those dimples.

If this had happened last season, it would have been Eric Zellinger coming out for the ceremonial face-off. He'd been the Storm's captain for over a decade, but there had been an expansion draft over the summer, and both Zee and goaltender Hunter Fielding had been claimed by the league's new team, the Tulsa Thunderbirds. That had left the Storm with an opening for a new captain.

Just before the start of the season, they'd held a press conference to announce that Jamie was it. I'd been in a meeting with my agent, Derek Hatch, in LA when it was all going down. We'd been discussing various auditions he wanted to send me on, the direction he thought my career should take after the end of *The Cool Kids,* but I hadn't been able to focus on anything Derek had said. My phone had kept buzzing with updates about Jamie and the Storm until, eventually, Derek had sent me on my way and told me to get my head straightened out so we could make a plan.

Easier said than done.

So now, here Jamie was, looking at me with that same hurt look in his eyes that I'd seen every time I'd come back to Portland in the last four years.

The look I'd put in his eyes.

The look that ripped me apart.

The pain in his gaze might even be more intense than usual right now. Probably because of that damn prom picture Dad had given them for the montage.

Jamie glanced over his shoulder toward center ice, then looked back at me with a wink. "They're ready, Katie," he said, indicating the slew of photographers and videographers who had lined up opposite us.

I nodded, swallowing down my feelings, and dropped the puck.

He gathered it up while Brown shook my hand and gave me a friendly, cursory pat on the shoulder. Then Jamie handed the puck back to me and wrapped me up in his arms.

I almost let out a sob. Almost. He'd hugged me countless times before, but this was different. He had all of his hockey gear on, the pads and whatnot, and I could hardly feel *him* underneath it all. We were touching, but it felt distant. Cold. I shivered, wishing I could draw closer to him and feel the warmth of his heart.

He pecked me on the cheek, causing an excited titter to run through the crowd, but it was ice that skittered through my veins. I wasn't sure if the coldness was from him or from me, or simply because of the mountain range that stood between us these days.

"I'm glad you're here, Katie," he said, his voice all rough like gravel crunching under Cam Johnson's pickup truck. His words were so quiet I could barely hear him over all the arena noise. He sounded completely unlike what I was used to. He gave me a grin, just enough to make his dimples pop out momentarily, and then he skated away.

"Me, too," I murmured to his retreating form, only I wasn't entirely convinced that he'd meant it. None of this would have felt so detached if he really wanted me here. I was pretty sure—almost positive—he hoped I would be on a plane tomorrow, flying back to LA or maybe to New York like Derek wanted. It had to be easier for Jamie if I wasn't here. I knew that, for me, it didn't hurt as much without the constant, daily reminders of what I didn't have. It was easier when we were apart.

My cheek tingled where he'd kissed me. I locked that up in my mind as tightly as I held the puck he'd handed me, while I walked across that purple carpet and back toward the tunnel. Several of the guys on the team skated over to shake my hand or kiss my cheek as I left, and Dad caught my eye and winked. I didn't hear anything they said to me, though. My head was too filled with fading memories and a confused outlook on the future.

Derek hadn't wanted me to come here at all. *You're bigger than this,* he'd told me as he passed over a stack of scripts and another pile of travel arrangements. He expected me to get on a plane tomorrow, fly to New York, and make my mark on Broadway. To go to all the auditions he'd arranged for me. To follow the path he'd laid out for me, just like I'd done every step of the way for the last four years, despite that I'd hated so many of the things he'd asked of me and that I was still uncertain what I wanted.

Coming here might not have lined up with my agent's plans for my future, but it had accomplished one thing: I was more confused now than I'd been in a long time, and that could only mean that there was something here worth sticking around for, even if I'd end up heartbroken again.

Jamie

KATIE SPUN AROUND and flew past her mom like a flash, racing away from the ice like a winger on a breakaway. I was pretty sure that picture from her prom had hit her as hard as it had hit me, so it didn't surprise me that she was running off like that. There was a chunk of me that wished I could do the same. I didn't have that kind of freedom, though. I had a game to play, so I had to get my head screwed back on straight.

Not such a simple thing to do with the knowledge that Katie Weber was still somewhere in the building. She was close enough I could still feel her essence lingering around me and only hoped that she wouldn't stick around too long on this visit. The longer she stayed, the more of me she would take with her when she eventually left again.

Because she would. Leave. She always left.

I'd told her years ago that she should go and chase her dreams, so I couldn't really blame her for doing the very thing I'd suggested. But fuck if it didn't hurt like a son of a bitch every time she showed up and smiled at me like nothing had changed.

She wanted us to be friends. There was a part of me that wanted that, too—being her friend would be better than not having her in my life at all, or so I thought—but it was hard to do when I saw the way she let her boyfriends treat her.

At the moment, she might not be dating one of the shitheads she'd hooked up with in Hollywood, but it didn't matter. That didn't mean she was kicking them to the curb and making room for me, for the way I *really* wanted things to be between us. The fact was, Katie wasn't going to stay in Portland. She was an *It Girl* now, a Hollywood starlet with people clamoring for her attention, and that meant she needed to get back to Hollywood so they could keep fawning over her. Her show had been cancelled, but it was only a matter of time before she got cast in something else, and then she would be gone again. Out of my life. Probably dating some new asswipe. Leaving me to be the brooding bastard I'd become.

Enough years had passed that, as long as she was away from Portland and not on the news too much, I was able to push her from my mind. I hadn't watched *The Cool Kids* because that was a wound I didn't want to open, and sometimes TMZ left her alone for a stretch. As long as she didn't hit the mainstream news too often, I could almost pretend she had only been a dream. It wasn't too bad, then. Without having her around, I could be the same guy I'd always been instead of the miserable grump I turned into when she was here but I couldn't have her.

Like now.

I tried not to be that guy, but it was hard to brush things off when it felt like someone was stomping on all the broken pieces of me to be sure they were a puzzle I would never be able to put back together.

"Hey," my brother Levi said. He was a couple of years younger than my twenty-four—he and Katie were the same age—a defenseman in his second year with the Storm. He tapped his stick on my shins harder than necessary to get my attention. "Earth to Jamie. Game's about to start. Stop chasing after her in your fucking head."

I gave him a terse nod and took a quick lap around our end of the ice to refocus. We were only a couple of weeks into the new season, my first as the captain of the team, and things had started off badly for us. There wasn't any good reason for it, either.

We'd had some turnover in personnel on the ice from last year, but not too much. Zee and Hunter were with the Thunderbirds now. A couple of guys had changed in free agency, and there'd been a trade involving a few of the younger guys who hadn't fully found their spots on the team. But the core that Jim Sutter, our general manager, was building around was all still intact, the coaches hadn't changed, the systems were exactly the same... Essentially, there was no good excuse for why we'd taken a slide in play to start the year. Tonight, we needed to get back on track, and as the captain, it was up to me to set the tone for the rest of the team.

It was time. The carpet had been removed from the ice, and all the photographers were gone. The officials were in place, and my linemates, Riley Jezek and Aaron Ludwiczak, were already skating to center ice for the opening face-off. I headed over to join them, pushing aside all thoughts not relevant to the game at hand.

The puck dropped, and the Kings won it cleanly back to Matt Greene, one of their defensemen. I was closest to Greene, so I went straight for him and laid a bruising check on him, dislodging the puck so that either RJ or Luddy could grab it and we could get to work.

The crowd went wild as Greene went down hard. He was a big body. Hitting him like that had been enough to rattle the teeth in my head, so I knew he'd felt it more than he'd been prepared for. Luddy stole the puck and cycled it with RJ. I shook off the impact and skated in to join them. After a hit like that, my head was fully in the game. I couldn't afford to think about Katie Weber right now.

I had work to do.

"THAT'S A BAD fucking call," Mattias "Bergy" Bergstrom, the Storm's head coach, shouted as the ref who'd blown his whistle skated by our bench. "You fucking know it, too. Brown was diving."

The ref turned his head and shouted a few choice expletives back in Bergy's direction, neither backing down nor admitting he might have made a mistake. It *was* a mistake, though. We'd been guilty plenty of times tonight, but in this instance, it wasn't our fault. Levi just happened to be near Brown when the guy lost an edge and went down. Guilty by proximity.

The basic gist of the ref's response was that Bergy needed to stop complaining and get his team to play a clean game, or else. There were a lot of implications at play in the *or else* part of that equation. The team could be issued a bench minor and we would have to kill off yet another penalty. Bergy could get fined by the league for abuse of officials. They could probably kick Bergy out of the game if it came down to it. There were lots of ways for this to escalate, and none of them would be good.

"Fucking dive," Bergy said under his breath, but at least he stopped there. He wasn't the sort of coach to lose his cool with the officials, not like our former coach, Scotty Thomas, had always been. Scotty had been more than a little hotheaded. Bergy was the type who tended to calmly let everyone know what he thought, setting the example he wanted us to follow.

He usually reserved his yelling for specific moments and specific individuals. Zee had been on the receiving end of it a lot, but Bergy didn't usually yell at me. He got his point across in other ways, like keeping my ass planted on the bench when I fucked up.

Regardless of all that, right now it didn't matter if the other guy had dived or fallen or what. The only thing that really mattered was that Levi was on his way to the box for a phantom tripping minor, and we had to kill our seventh penalty of the game—a game that we were trailing by a goal. We were only halfway through the game, but we'd already been penalized more times than we should have been in a full sixty minutes, at least if we wanted to keep Bergy happy. Still, there was a lot of time left on the game clock, which meant there was a lot of time for us to either fuck up some more or get our collective act together.

"Keep your fucking head in it, 501," Andrew Jensen shouted across the ice to Levi. "We've got this." Jens clearly thought we were going to be able to straighten up and pull ourselves out of the hole we'd been digging. Or maybe that was just the impression he wanted to give off.

At times like this, there was a part of me that wondered if Bergy and Jim had made the right choice in naming me the Storm's next captain. I never knew what to say to help the boys out. Guys like Jens and Keith Burns were a lot more vocal. They always knew the right thing to say, and Burnzie had even been an assistant captain already for a long time. Shouldn't he have been the new captain? Or maybe Soupy, who had been the other assistant captain for the last few years. Any one of those guys would have made more sense than me, along with at least a half a dozen other players on the team.

None of them were wearing the *C* on their chests, though. I was, and I didn't have the first fucking clue how to lead this team.

We went to a TV timeout, and I made the mistake of looking up at the Jumbotron. Through the whole game, every time there had been a break, they'd been making more tributes to cancer survivors and doing things to draw attention to the warning signs someone needed to be aware of when it came to their own health. This time, they had a camera on Katie up in the owner's box. She was sitting with her mom and several of the guys' wives, each of them holding up a sign with a symptom of leukemia printed on it. Katie looked like she was a lot more relaxed than she had been when she'd left the ice, but the last thing I needed was to start thinking about her again. Not right now.

I turned my head away to stare at the ice in front of me.

"You dated her?" Grant Wheelan asked me. Wheels was a guy Jim had brought in over the summer to mentor me. I wasn't sure he could teach me how to lead this team any better than Zee had in all the years I'd been watching him, but maybe he would surprise me. Mainly Wheels just talked to me a lot. So far, the biggest thing I'd learned was to do things the way I wanted everyone else to do them. *Lead by example.* Wheels had drilled those three words into my head every chance he got. He also liked to remind me I was supposed to be having fun, not taking everything so seriously all the time. I wasn't so good at that one.

"Fuck," I muttered under my breath. Then I shrugged. "Kind of. I guess so." We'd never really technically been a couple, even though I'd taken her to her prom. I'd wanted to, but she'd been so young and had cancer, and then she'd left.

He made a grunting sound next to me. "Bet Webs would be happier if she was dating you instead of the guys she's been all over the news with."

"Fucking right, I would," Webs said from behind us before he moved on to talk to Blake Kozlow about something.

That was definitely a change from all those years ago. I wasn't sure I would agree with that assessment. I'd changed a lot in that time, and I wasn't sure it was for the better. "Doesn't matter what Webs would be happier with," I grumbled. It pissed me off that Wheels was trying to make me talk about this right now when all I wanted to do was pretend Katie wasn't even in the state, let alone in the building. "We aren't together, and that's not going to change any time soon."

"That's too bad," he said.

"I wouldn't be too sure about that, if I were you," Soupy put in. His name was really Brenden Campbell, but everyone except his wife and the Storm's GM called him Soupy—even his two adopted kids. I glared at him, and he shrugged and looked back at the ice. "Just telling you what I see, is all. Up to you to figure out what to do with it."

He had always had a bad habit of doing that—telling me things I didn't want to hear.

The TV timeout came to an end. It was about time. At Bergy's signal, Wheels and Cam Johnson headed over the boards to take the face-off.

"Soupy, Babs," Bergy said once they were gone, his tone returning to normal. "Be ready to go."

I nodded, but I kept my focus on the ice.

"I've got Jonny," Soupy said to me. At least he was back to talking about the game instead of trying to tell me how to handle my personal life.

The Kings had a potent power play this year, always dangerous. They moved the puck well, changing up the point of attack in an effort to get a clear shot in on our goaltender.

Our boys moved as a unit—one guy shifted to block a passing lane, and the other three adjusted their positions accordingly. Jonny dropped down to block a shot from the point, and our *D* managed to get their sticks in the way and clear bodies out from in front of the net so Nicky could see where the puck was coming from. Finally, after almost a full minute of being hemmed into our zone, Wheels poke-checked the puck and sent it flying down the ice, and those guys were able to get off for a change.

Soupy and I piled over the boards as soon as they came off—me about a second behind him since Wheels moved about as fast as molasses in a Canadian winter—and we headed into position.

The Kings switched to their second power play unit and got set up in our zone. They moved the puck back to the point on my side. I dropped to a knee, ready to block a shot, but he passed it to the other point. Soupy tried to get into position to block the shooting lane, but his knee buckled under him, and he went down with an agonized shout.

The shot got past him. Jens got just enough of his stick on it to deflect it away from Nicky's net. I let myself glance over long enough to see that, no matter how hard he tried, Soupy couldn't get himself up.

The Kings cycled the puck back to the point again. I did my best to cover two guys who both had bombs for shots, but there was only so much I could do. One of them pulled his stick back to load up. I went down. A shot blew past my ear and went in the net.

I skated over to Soupy, pissed at myself even though I couldn't figure out why. "You going to be all right?"

"Can't put any fucking weight on it," he said.

"Broken?"

He shook his head. "Felt something snap, but not bone."

That made me think it was something like a ligament. Ken Archer, our head trainer, came over and talked to him for a minute before deciding it was safe to move him, at least. I gave Soupy a hand and helped him up, draping his arm over my shoulder while Archie did the same on the other side so we could assist him off the ice. The whole time, I was thinking I might have just witnessed the injury that would end his career. I hoped I was wrong.

Wheels clapped a hand on my shoulder as soon as I took a seat next to him on the bench. "You know," he said. "You never know what's going to happen. Watching what just went down with Soupy is proof enough of that. If you want something, you should go for it."

"What the fuck are you talking about?" I groused, more agitated than confused.

"You know what I'm talking about."

I did. Apparently, I *still* couldn't hide what I was feeling. Not only that, but I was just as messed up over Katie Weber as I'd ever been. What the fuck could I do about it, though? If she was going to leave, there wasn't anything I could do to stop her…and I knew she would leave.

She always did.

Chapter Two

Katie

"I NEED YOU to cancel those New York auditions for next week," I said to Derek on the phone.

"You mean *reschedule*," he replied, not even attempting to hide his sarcastic tone. "I've already pushed them back once. If you change it again, you could get yourself blacklisted by Broadway, and that's really not what you want to do. I promise you that."

I couldn't blame him for his aggravation. I'd already forced his hand in having him rearrange all sorts of auditions and other things so that I could come to Portland to sing the anthem—despite his repeated assertions that it would do nothing to further my career. Granted, he wouldn't have had to do that if he had listened to me the first time around and penciled my Portland trip in on my calendar instead of brushing my plans off. He'd eventually given in and made the changes—not that he'd been happy about it—and he'd been letting me know just how unhappy he was about the "mistakes" he believed I was making ever since. I'd made plenty of mistakes over the years, and many of them had involved him, but I was one hundred percent positive that this would not be another one to mark down on the list no matter what he thought of it.

I pinched the bridge of my nose, wishing that would relieve the headache I'd had for the better part of a week. It had to be a stress headache. It was one of those that started with tension in my neck and shoulders and worked its way up. I should probably get a massage soon—that would help it more than anything, most likely.

I had never been comfortable with disappointing anyone, and I was definitely letting Derek down right now. Heck, I'd been letting him down ever since *The Cool Kids* had been cancelled, when I hadn't been able to tell him immediately and in no uncertain terms what I wanted to do with myself. I didn't have a plan in place, thinking my career would take care of itself because the popularity of my show was off the charts. I had just been winging it, and he thought that made me flighty and not career-focused. Now I was about to really upset him, and it was doing a number on me, both physically and emotionally.

"I mean cancel," I repeated as firmly as I could. "I'm not going to New York. I'm not going to audition for any Broadway shows. I just can't do it, Derek. I need a break. I need to spend some time with my family. I need to figure out what I want to do next, but I do know that, whatever it is, it won't be on the East Coast. I can't be that far away from them all the time." Being in LA had been difficult enough. My family might drive me bonkers sometimes, but I wouldn't trade them for anything.

"You *have* to go to New York. You're still riding a high after *The Cool Kids*, but if you let yourself drop out of the public eye—"

"I know. It'll be harder to get back in. *I know*, Derek."

What I didn't know was if I wanted to be in the public eye anymore. I wasn't sure fame and fortune were all they were made out to be, and I had been sincerely doubting that I was cut out for that kind of life for a long time. As long as the show had still been in production, I'd been able to push all those doubts aside and focus on my work. But seeing my parents and Jamie yesterday had only reinforced those reservations. Portland was my home; everything about Hollywood felt foreign, despite the fact that I'd been living that life for the past four years.

"Well, if you're not going to take on work right now, you at least need to stay in the news. I could set you up with—"

"I'm not going out with anyone you think I need to be seen with." Not ever again. Derek lived by the mantra that any publicity is good publicity, and I'd played by his rules for a while. Too long. I'd let everyone in my life that I cared about down by doing so, not the least of which was myself.

"So, what exactly are you saying?" Derek asked. In the background, he was furiously typing on his keyboard, probably already firing off emails to cancel the slew of auditions he'd lined up for me. "If you're not going to New York, when are you coming back to LA?"

"I can't answer that."

"What the hell do you mean, you can't answer that?"

"I mean I'm not coming back this week, and probably not next week, and I'm not even sure I'm coming back at all other than maybe to pack up the condo I'm renting and move everything out." I wasn't sure where that had come from, but—to my own surprise—I wasn't in a rush to take those words back. There was some truth to it. A lot of truth, actually.

Derek fell silent for a long time, and when he spoke again, his tone was terse, his words clipped. "If you're not going to actively pursue your career, our working relationship doesn't have much of a future."

I wasn't sure what reaction I'd thought he would have, but I definitely hadn't been expecting *that*. I swallowed the lump in my throat, but another one replaced it almost immediately. This made it feel permanent, as if the decision I'd made on the spur of the moment this morning because of a headache was going to alter the entire course of my future. Just like that. A snap of the fingers. Done.

"Are you firing me?" I finally choked out.

"I don't know that I'd call it firing," he bit off. "It's more that you're no longer willing to hold up your end of the bargain, so there's not anything I can do for you. You've been indecisive for the last four months. You've bombed at the auditions you've gone to, and you've completely flaked out on the others I've managed to obtain. You aren't taking your career as seriously as I am, and I'm not willing to work for someone who isn't willing to work her ass off to have the kind of career you're capable of having. I don't think there's much more to say about it."

I was perched on the foot of my bed in my parents' house, unable to do anything but blink back tears. He was right about everything he'd said, and there wasn't any point in arguing with him about it. "No, I suppose there's not," I forced out, my voice cracking.

We stayed on the phone for a few more minutes, hammering out the details required to dissolve our contract. By the time we hung up, my head was pounding like never before. Had I just completely ruined my chances of having the career I'd always dreamed of? I mean, sure, my first go at it had been everything I'd expected and nothing I'd ever imagined in my worst nightmares, all rolled up in one. But did that mean I should just throw out the idea of ever pursuing it again? Derek Hatch was one of the best talent agents in the world, and now I'd walked away from him.

I tossed my phone on the bed, wishing I never had to pick the damn thing up again, and dug some ibuprofen out of my purse. Then I headed out to the kitchen. Dad was sitting at the bar with an iPad, watching film from last night's game over his breakfast, and Mom was unloading the dishwasher. I took a glass from her and filled it with water from the fridge before tossing back the pills.

Dad glanced up, his brow furrowed. "You sick?"

"Just a headache."

"You look tired." His voice sounded like a bark, gruff and terse. I'd come to understand that meant he was worried. He had worried about me way too much over the years. I'd given him too many reasons to worry, but I wished he would stop.

Especially right now, when there wasn't anything wrong but a stupid headache. "Thanks for saying I look like crap," I quipped, scowling at him. "I *am* tired. I flew in yesterday and headed straight to the arena, and you know how late it was when we got back here." I swallowed some more water and set the glass on the counter across from him, leaning on my elbows. And I grinned, hoping it would help ease his concerns.

"I'm not saying you look like crap. I'm saying you look tired." He shut off the video and pushed the iPad aside. "You look tired like you did when you were sick."

"Dad," I said, hating the whining tone that came out of me. He was hovering, and it made me feel like I was a teenager again. I was twenty-two years old and already a multimillionaire in my own right, thanks to both my work on *The Cool Kids* and taking Derek's advice to hire a financial planner as soon as I'd booked my first job. I'd made as much money in four years as Dad had made in two decades as an NHL player. It wasn't about money, though. The fact of the matter was I wasn't a kid anymore, and I hated that he still treated me like one.

"You're due for your blood work and all that, anyway," Mom said, sliding in next to me to put a cutting board in the cabinet. She gave Dad a look. "Why don't you call Dr. Oliver while you're here and set something up?"

Dr. Oliver was my oncologist. As much as I hated to admit it, Mom was right; it was time for me to get checked and be sure I was still cancer-free. Even though I knew there was no good reason to think there would be anything abnormal about my tests, the thought of going in for them always made me nervous—way worse than stage fright.

Like, puke-up-my-guts-without-being-able-to-blame-it-on-chemo nerves. Getting anxious about something like that would only make my headache worse, though, so I decided not to let that happen until there was a good reason for it, like when I was walking into the doctor's office and they were about to draw half a dozen vials of blood from my veins or something. That seemed like a reasonable time to get nervous.

"Yeah," I said to make Mom happy and to get Dad off my back. And I supposed I would do it to ease my own worries, too. "I'll see when he can get me in."

"But not tomorrow," Mom said, reaching overhead to put away a plastic mixing bowl.

"What's tomorrow?" I was pretty sure I didn't want to know, but I couldn't seem to stop myself from asking. Knowing my mom, she might have set me up on a blind date or a speed-dating event, and anything along those lines was the last thing in the world I wanted. She would never set me up with any guy like the ones Derek had insisted on, but that was beside the point.

"Dani's going to be here," Mom said. "She's coming down for the weekend and wants to spend some time with you."

Dani was my younger sister. She was in her first semester at The Art Institute of Seattle studying fashion design. Our brother, Luke, was off playing college hockey at the University of Minnesota. He hadn't been drafted by an NHL team, but he was starting to really come into his own there and was picking up the notice of a bunch of scouts. A late bloomer, Dad called him. Luke might just turn into one of those undrafted success stories someday. That was what he was hoping for, at least, and even if he'd driven me nuts for so many years when we were growing up, I wanted it for him, too. He was my brother.

It was a lot easier to enjoy my brother and sister now that we were all adults. I hadn't seen either of my siblings in way too long, so there was no chance I would pass up the opportunity to spend time with Dani. "Got it. No doctor's appointments tomorrow." That would give me at least a while longer before the nausea-inducing anxiety kicked in, anyway. I took off down the hall, my glass of water in hand, to get on my doctor's schedule.

My cell was ringing when I got back to the bedroom. Probably Derek. He had likely thought of something else he needed to hash out with me in voiding our contract. I answered it without even looking to be sure it was him.

"What now?" I demanded, sounding harried and harassed, not that I really cared. I *felt* harried and harassed, damn it all.

"Katie?"

It wasn't Derek. I didn't need to look at my caller ID to know that it was Jamie, but I looked anyway to be sure I wasn't losing my mind.

No insanity plea necessary. *Jamie Babcock*, bracketed by a couple of red emoji hearts, lit up on the screen in front of my favorite picture of him. Blue eyes smiling at me, light brown hair in his trademark faux hawk, both dimples peeking out, and the hint of a blush pinking up his cheeks. I'd had that image on my phone since well before he'd asked to take me to my prom. I'd found it on the Internet somewhere during his rookie season. It was one of those iconic pictures, the sort that sums up everything you love about a person in a single shot. This one had all his kindness, his shyness, the underlying confidence that never crossed over into ego. Looking at this shot always sent my heart pitter-pattering. I supposed Dad wasn't the only one who could make me feel like I was a teenager again, although I didn't mind it so much coming from Jamie.

"Sorry," I said, trying to zap the agitation from my tone. I had no earthly idea why Jamie was calling me, though. He hadn't done it in years—not since the day I'd told him I was leaving for Hollywood. At first, I'd looked for this picture to pop up on my phone more times than I could count. But it hadn't happened, so I'd given up on the idea before too long. I could have called him, of course, but I had the impression that he didn't really want to hear from me or else he would have called. "Hi, Jamie," I said once I thought I had my head on straight. "What…?"

"Last night, your dad mentioned he thought you were going to be in town through the weekend," he said after a minute, saving me from figuring out what I wanted to ask him.

"Yeah. I'll be around for a while." I would definitely be here longer than just the weekend, especially now that I didn't even have an agent anymore. But seeing as how I hadn't filled my parents in on all of that yet, I didn't know if I should tell Jamie. Particularly since I wasn't sure what he wanted.

"Can I… I mean, is there a chance I could get together with you sometime this weekend? I could take you out for coffee Saturday afternoon or something like that."

He wanted to get together with me? Coffee wasn't a date, but it was a heck of a lot better than the awkward conversations we'd had when I was in town over the last four years. I didn't have the first clue where this was leading, but I'd be an idiot not to see it through.

"Sure. Coffee sounds good." I wanted to spend as much time as I could with Dani while she was home, but she would understand if I carved out a few hours to be with Jamie.

"You're staying at your parents' house? I can come pick you up at three."

"Three's great."

We finalized our plans and hung up, and I was in a much better mood when I called Dr. Oliver's office. They were able to work me in for Monday morning—soon enough to appease Dad but not so soon that I would start panicking until after I'd gotten together with Jamie, an event that was likely to cause a bit of panic in and of itself. I should be able to push it all from my mind until after my sister left on Sunday afternoon. It should work out for everyone.

I was already confused about what I wanted before Jamie had called, though. Now... Now I feared I would never be able to separate *what I wanted* from *Jamie*.

Although I wasn't so sure that was a bad thing.

Jamie

THE LAST TIME I parked in this driveway to pick Katie up had been the night of her prom. Sitting here with the engine running and my hands in a death grip on the steering wheel, I couldn't help but replay that night over and over in my mind. It was already at the forefront of my thoughts and had been ever since the game on Thursday, when she'd walked back into my life, as she had so many times before.

Ever since then, I'd been attempting to prepare myself for the moment she walked out of it again.

It was coming. It always did. She showed up here and there to visit her family, but her life wasn't in Portland anymore. And that brought up a harsh truth: I wasn't part of her life. Not really. I might have been at one point, but these days I was just one of the guys on the team her dad coached. She was friendly enough to me when she came. She smiled at me and talked with all the animation and enthusiasm for life that she'd always had, and she kissed me on the cheek the same as she would with just about any of the boys. But then she always returned to her other life, to the glitz and glam of Hollywood and the lure of a career doing the things she loved. The things she was meant to do.

I couldn't blame her for that, for wanting to live out her dreams. I was doing the same thing here. There'd never been anything in my life I'd wanted more than to play in the NHL. When I was a kid, it had always seemed like a pipe dream, something that would prove to be out of my reach. Yet here I was, in my seventh season with the Storm and my first as the team's captain.

I had a great life. I had a job that half the guys growing up in Canada wished they had, I got to play on a team with one of my brothers, another brother might get a chance to play in the league at some point this season—albeit with a different team—I had a fantastic family who loved me, I earned more money than I would ever know what to do with… The list of things that made my life seemingly perfect went on and on.

Yet the only thing I could focus on since Katie had showed up a couple of days ago was the one thing I *didn't* have.

Katie.

I'd tried dating other girls in the last few years, but I couldn't seem to put my heart into it. That wasn't fair to them or to me. It *really* wasn't fair when I was dating one of them and Katie would pop up somehow. I always got sullen and sulky at those times, enough that I could tell it for myself without someone pointing it out to me, and I wore my broken heart on my sleeve. It wasn't their fault I was unable to love anyone but Katie, but I took it out on them. Then she would waltz back to Portland, like she had a few days ago. Sometimes she would have an asswipe boyfriend on her arm; other times it was just her. Either way, she would tell me she wanted us to be friends. She wanted us to go on like nothing had ever happened between us. Like she didn't have her hand circled around my heart. Like she wasn't squeezing the life out of it every time she left.

That was why I'd asked to see her today. Not to get her back—that ship had sailed a long time ago—but to find a way to get my head on straight again. I couldn't afford to have my focus divided every time she showed up in Portland or I saw her on TMZ and it took me by surprise. I needed to put a true end to whatever we had once been. I didn't know if I could be her friend when something as simple as seeing her, talking to her, hurt like a son of a bitch.

My cell buzzed on the center console. I glanced down to see a text message from Webs.

You coming in, or are you waiting on a personal invitation?
Should I send someone out to escort you?

I didn't know if he had any idea why I was really here. He hadn't said anything at practice about me taking Katie out for coffee. He'd acted as if nothing was out of the ordinary.

Ours was a very different relationship these days, Webs and me. He never gave me shit about Katie anymore. If anything, he was always lamenting the fact that I hadn't had what it took to keep her with me. The two of us tended to see eye to eye when it came to the guys she dated of late, particularly how they weren't good enough for her. There wasn't anything I could do about that, though.

If he knew I was sitting in the driveway, though, odds were high that Katie knew, as well. I shut off the engine and headed to the porch. Dani opened the door before I could ring the bell, throwing herself into my arms and giving me a kiss on the cheek.

"Home for the weekend?" I asked after disentangling myself from her.

"Drove down last night. Mom and Katie and I went for manis and pedis this morning, and Katie said she was going out for coffee with you this afternoon." She peeked over her shoulder and dropped her voice. "She's sticking around for a while this time, you know."

I didn't know that, actually. And while I was sure Dani thought I'd be pleased to hear it—maybe thinking that our coffee date was meant to be a *date*—instead it made my heart sink. How the hell was I going to tell Katie what I needed to tell her if she wasn't going to leave soon after? I didn't want to hurt her in any way, but especially not if I would have to see her every now and then.

Before I had a chance to come up with an appropriate response, Katie came down the stairs and smiled at me, and my gut twisted.

"Ready?" I asked, holding out a hand. I shouldn't have done that. I shouldn't have done anything that would lead to touching her without being able to really hold her.

Sometimes, I could be my own worst enemy.

She took it, slinging her purse strap over her other shoulder, and smiled at me. "Ready."

Her palm was warm and soft against mine, her hand barely larger than a child's. Katie was tall and slender, with blue eyes I could get lost in, if I let myself. But really, it was her hair that did me in lately. It was long and a rich mahogany brown that fell in silken waves down past her shoulders. These days, it looked exactly as it had before she'd had cancer, rich and full of life. When I looked at her hair, all I wanted to do was bury my nose in it, run my fingers through it, hold on to it with all I had in me as a reminder that she was still here. Even now, a light citrus scent wafted up to me, and I knew it was from her shampoo. She'd used the same kind as long as I'd known her. In my mind, that scent had come to be part of her.

Dani winked at me as I headed out the door with her sister, which only made me realize just how much I might be throwing away if I went through with what I intended. If I told Katie I couldn't be her friend anymore, the whole Weber family would have it out for me. I could deal with Webs, even though he was the one I had to see the most often. I'd finally figured out he was all bark and no bite. Katie's mom, Laura, had been like a mother of sorts to me since I'd first arrived in Portland, and Dani and Luke had treated me like I was a sibling.

I opened the passenger door and waited for Katie to get in before closing it and heading around to my side. Now I wasn't sure I could go through with it at all.

"You look like you're about to get sick all over me," Katie said once I sat behind the wheel and shut my door.

I quirked a grin at her. "I'll be sure to roll down the window and do it outside the car. Wouldn't want to get anything on you." I hit the brake and pressed the button to start the engine.

"If you're going fast enough, the wind could send it all back in on us."

I was gripping the wheel so tight that she reached over and touched the back of my hand. That touch made me flinch. She removed her hand, and I instantly missed the warmth of her skin.

"Spill it," she said. "Whatever it is. It can't be as bad as all that."

I backed down the driveway and pulled into the road. "Spill what?"

"Don't pretend you aren't upset about something. I know you."

She did know me. She knew me as well as just about anyone, which only made this worse, somehow.

"You don't want to wait until we get to the coffeehouse?"

"Not if you're this worked up about it. I want to know. Even if it's something I'd rather not know."

The huge knot that had started in my gut had worked its way up to my throat. I tried to swallow it down, but that didn't exactly work out.

We came to a stoplight, and I glanced over at her. It was the first time since she'd been back that I'd really, truly looked at her, not just skimming the surface. She had grown up a lot in the years we'd been apart. There was a worldliness in her eyes now, a sense of having learned things both her father and I would have preferred she hadn't. I knew bits and pieces of what that new knowledge might have been because of what had ended up splashed all over the gossip sites.

The first guy she'd dated in LA, Jesse Carmichael, had been busted for drugs more than a few times while they'd been together. Nothing too bad with the next couple of guys, other than pics of them on vacation when she was wearing a hell of a lot less than she should have been in my opinion. But it was the last guy who really set my blood boiling. Beau Brunetti. He was famous more because of family connections than anything he'd done himself. When she'd been with him, I'd started to notice a different sort of look in her eyes. It was a look that spoke of the kinds of knowledge that could only come from the wrong sorts of life experiences, and it was one that had haunted my sleep.

Now here she was, looking at me with those eyes, wanting to know what was wrong with me. And there wasn't a goddamned fucking thing I could do protect her from whatever had put that look there. I couldn't turn back time. I couldn't go back to the day at Zee's and Soupy's weddings, when she'd told me she was leaving for Hollywood, and beg her to stay with me. I couldn't bash the fucker's face in for whatever it was he'd done to her. I couldn't do anything but say, "I can't do it anymore, Katie."

She blinked a few times, and she shook her head, but her smile faded. "Do what?"

"This." My voice cracked, which only served to piss me off. "I can't keep trying to be friends with you when it's not enough. It's not what I want. I don't want to be just your friend. And you keep dating these sons of bitches who—" I cut myself off before I told her they weren't good enough for her. If she couldn't see that, then there were bigger issues at hand. The light turned green, and I clenched my jaw, hitting the gas. "But then you leave, and you break my heart all over again every time. I can't keep doing this. I can't watch you with them and accept being nothing but your friend. Not when I still love you as much as I ever did."

I don't know why I told her I loved her. It wasn't something we'd ever said to each other before, but it was the absolute truth. It was one of those simple facts of life: the sky was blue, gravity kept our feet firmly on the ground, and I loved Katie Weber even though she had trampled all over my heart more times than I could count.

I turned into the Starbucks lot and found a parking space, then put the car in park. When I looked at her, she had tears pooling in her eyes, which made me feel like as big of an ass as the guys she'd been dating.

"What are you saying?" she asked quietly. She didn't turn away. A few years ago, she wouldn't have been able to look anywhere but down at her lap, but now she was staring straight at me as those tears slowly spilled over.

"I guess I'm saying that I can't handle trying to be your friend."

"All or nothing, huh?" Katie's expression was completely unreadable, but she stared straight through me, not even blinking. Tears were still wetting her cheeks but no longer fell from her eyes. I nodded, not trusting myself to speak without attempting to take it all back, and she pursed her lips together. "All right. I understand. I may not like it, but I understand. It hasn't been very fair for you, has it?"

"Do you want me to take you home now?" I asked in lieu of answering her. I hadn't brought her here to point out all the places we might have gone wrong over the years, and I didn't think it would do either of us any good to make it out to be all her fault. It was mine as much as hers. I'd allowed myself to fall head over heels in love with a girl even though we'd both known all along that she was going to leave. That just made me an idiot, I supposed, or maybe a masochist. At some point, I had to staunch the wound. I had to make the bleeding stop if I was ever going to move on.

She didn't answer immediately, which took me aback. When I stopped studying my death grip on the steering wheel and faced her, it was to find her still staring at me, appraising me. It was such a different sensation from when she had looked at me in years past. Before, she'd seemed to think I was perfection personified. It was overwhelming, to be honest. No one could live up to the sort of image of me she'd seemed to have. She'd always seemed to think I was so much better than I ever could have been. Now, though, maybe she was starting to see I was human.

"You promised me coffee," she said after a minute. "For old time's sake? And then you can take me home, and we can move into this next phase."

"One last cup?" A final moment to be her friend, to let myself think of all the things that could have been. And then I could hit the button on a restart. I could finally attempt to move on. I tried to force myself to smile, even though that was the last thing in the world I wanted to do. "Yeah, let's do that."

This could be my closure, something that had been a long time coming.

Chapter Three

Jamie

I STILL HADN'T gotten used to going home and not having anyone there with me. I'd grown up as the oldest of seven boys, so there had been no such thing as having time to myself, let alone peace and quiet, in my childhood. When I'd gone on to play junior hockey, I'd lived with a billet family who had three kids of their own. As a rookie with the Storm, I'd lived with Zee. After that, I'd always had a guy or two on the team for roommates—Soupy, Liam Kallen, Luddy for a while, then Levi last season—other than brief stretches when one of them moved on, right up until this season.

Over the summer, I'd finally bought a house. I'd signed a big, new contract with the team, and Jim Sutter and Bergy had named me captain. With all that, they'd made it clear I wasn't going anywhere any time soon, so I'd figured I might as well put down some roots. I'd offered Levi a room if he wanted it, but he had opted to go in on a swanky downtown condo with Koz, one of the new guys.

I wasn't sure how I felt about my brother getting close to Koz. Mainly because the guy had come to us with a less-than-stellar reputation after his first few seasons in Anaheim. Living in So Cal had made it easy for him to get mixed up with the wrong people—kind of like what had happened with Katie—and he'd developed a reputation as a wild child who missed practices because of his hangovers, spending all his spare time at strip clubs and partying with porn stars.

Everyone said that was the reason the Ducks had given up on him so easily, trading him away as a twenty-two-year-old center who had the potential to be a top scorer in the league. It was like Tyler Seguin, part deux, or at least I was pretty sure Jim was hoping for similar results to what the Stars got with the Seguin trade.

Jim was always giving guys chances that no one else would, so the fact that he'd pulled the trigger on that trade hadn't come as a surprise to any of us in the Storm organization. So far, Koz had been settling in all right and hadn't gotten into any trouble, but I wasn't sure he wouldn't before too much longer. Portland was the strip club capital of the US, and there were bars all over the place. Still, I was willing to give him the benefit of the doubt as long as his behavior didn't get out of hand. It was a reflection on the team, after all.

But my brother was a different concern entirely.

I'd always felt the need to look after Levi, but he was all grown up now. He and Koz were the same age, and they were both young guys getting their start in a new city, and so I supposed it only made sense that they would hit it off together. The only other really young guys new to the team this year were European and were hanging out together. Levi and Koz were two young North Americans striking up a friendship.

My hope was that Levi would be a good influence on Koz and help him straighten his shit out; my fear was that Koz would be a bad influence on Levi, and then I'd have to figure out a way to help them both climb out of the holes they might dig for themselves.

Anyway, the point was that Levi hadn't come to live with me. I'd thought maybe there would be a young guy I could take in and mentor the way Zee had done with me, but that hadn't happened, and here I was. Alone. And it was weird. Maybe I should get a pet. But if I did that, I'd have to figure out what to do with it when I left on road trips with the team. I couldn't just leave an animal alone here for a week or more at a time.

After taking Katie home, I'd come back to my place and gone through my fridge to figure out what I would eat for dinner. I'd never been much of a cook. A few years back, I'd finally learned how to make coffee that didn't burn, overflow the coffeemaker, or kill someone. That had been a first step. These days, I had a small arsenal of things I could make using one of four appliances—a Keurig, a microwave, a waffle iron, and a toaster oven. A couple of years ago, I'd asked Will Archer, the team chef, to teach me how to feed myself in the easiest ways possible. He'd tried to convince me he could teach me to use the stove and oven, but I figured it was safer to start small and work my way up. Those were the appliances we'd settled on, and he'd given me some lessons and basic recipes to follow. I actually ate pretty well, even if my cooking skills were limited.

The guys all laughed and teased me about why I'd bothered buying a house with a big chef's kitchen if I was afraid of most of the things in it. If you were cooking for one, though, there wasn't any good reason to heat up a whole big oven when the toaster oven could do the job.

I took out some fresh asparagus, a lemon, and a jar of already-minced garlic, grabbed a couple of tilapia fillets from the freezer and tossed them in the sink to thaw, and set to work preparing my meal. After I had the fish and veg in the toaster oven, I put couscous in a bowl under the Keurig spout and got that cooking. In less than twenty minutes, I had a full, balanced meal—and I'd made it all myself.

I'd just sat down in front of the TV with my plate, ready to eat while catching up on *Black Sails*, when my phone buzzed again. I dug it out of my pocket and swiped a thumb over the screen to find another text from Webs.

> *What the hell did you do? Why is Katie holed up in her room and crying?*

Well, fuck. I'd known that telling her what I had would hurt her, and I'd been fully aware that it would land me on the wrong side of her father's ire, but knowing it and being prepared for the guilt turning my stomach to lead were two very different things. It would have been easier to deal with if I didn't know she was crying. Webs probably realized that. Hell, it might be why he'd told me, hoping to make my guilt match his helplessness. I wasn't going to take back any of the things I'd said, though, regardless of her tears or anything he might try to do to punish me for whatever crimes he thought I'd committed against her.

I set my plate on the coffee table and typed a response on my phone.

> Me: *I didn't do anything wrong. I swear.*

> Webs: *You think I'm going to take that as an answer and be okay with it?*

Me: *Seriously. I just told her I couldn't hang out with her and act like everything's all right anymore. I'm not okay.*

Webs: *Well, damn.*

Me: *Well, damn?*

Webs: *I hoped she would figure out she wants to be with you before you decided not to let her string you along anymore. That's all.*

I didn't have the first clue how to respond to that. Maybe it didn't need a response at all.

My doorbell rang, and I tossed my phone on the coffee table next to my dinner before getting up to answer it.

Levi came in as soon as I opened the door. He sniffed the air. "Smells good. Have enough for me?"

"If you make your own." I followed him down the hall.

He veered into the kitchen, opened the fridge, stared for a moment, shook his head, and then headed to the pantry to get the fixings for peanut butter sandwiches.

I left him to it and went back to my meal.

A minute later, he joined me with three sandwiches on a paper plate. He plopped down on the sectional and put his feet up before taking a bite.

"You should get Willie to teach you how to make a few things," I suggested. "Peanut butter sandwiches are okay sometimes, but you need to get better food in you."

"Koz and I go in early enough to get Willie to make us breakfast. We have lunch with the boys. It's just dinner I have to worry about."

"And you should worry about it. Your body needs more than peanut butter." I'd been on him about eating better for at least a few years, once I'd started to really focus on my diet and seen the difference it could make on the ice.

"I know." He scowled at me over the top of his sandwich, but he took another bite.

I went back to my tilapia and asparagus. "What's Koz up to tonight?" I asked, trying not to sound like I was fishing for information even though that was exactly what I was doing.

"On a date. Some chick he met at Amani's the other day."

Amani's Family-Style Italian Restaurant was where most of the guys went for lunch on game days. It wasn't exactly the kind of place I would expect to find a date, but I supposed it wasn't entirely out of the question. If he was on a date, maybe he was staying out of trouble.

"Oh, I love this episode," Levi said, mouth full of bread and peanut butter. "It's the one where Billy Bones—"

"Are you here for food or something else?" I interrupted before he could tell me everything that was to come in the show I was about to watch. I never managed to keep up with TV shows I liked when they were airing. I set my DVR to record them, and then I would try to watch a few episodes at a time when I got the chance. With this show, I was almost a full season behind. He knew that, but he'd always been bad about spoiling what was to come. It was one of his quirks that drove me crazy. I loved all my brothers, but we were definitely brothers in every sense of the word—able to get on one another's nerves without even the slightest effort. It was a talent.

He raised a brow at me, but he took the time to swallow before answering, at least. "I'm here because you were with Katie this afternoon."

"I was. And?"

"And I thought maybe it was best if you weren't alone."

I grunted in lieu of coming up with a coherent response. That was the other thing about being one of the Babcock brothers—I could always count on each of them to know exactly what was needed even if I didn't know myself.

"Oh, this part is the best," he said with his mouth full again. He kicked his shoes off and put his feet up on the coffee table, settling in for the long haul. "I love it when Flint..."

He kept talking, but I didn't take any of it in, too busy thinking how grateful I was to have a brother who would come over and annoy the shit out of me so I wouldn't wallow in my own thoughts.

Levi might drive me crazy, but he was a pretty good guy when it came down to it.

Katie

I ALLOWED MYSELF an hour for my pity party, but that was all the time

I could spare. Dani was only here through tomorrow, and I was wasting time I could be hanging out with her.

Once I got my tears under control, I headed into my bathroom. My tears had streaked my makeup, and I looked an utter wreck. I washed my face and ran a brush through my hair, trying to remove the traces of crying before I went back out to join my family. Not that I thought I could fool any of them. Mom, Dad, and Dani had all been in the living room when I'd come through the door and started sobbing before racing up the stairs and locking my door. They might not know what had caused my upset, but they knew *something* had happened. They could definitely deduce that it had to do with Jamie. I only hoped they didn't expect me to tell them about it.

The thing was, I still wasn't sure how to feel about it, myself. I mean, yes, Jamie had told me he couldn't really bear to be my friend anymore. That sucked. It hurt. It made me want to punch my pillow as much as it made me cry into it.

But he'd also said he loved me.

Maybe he hadn't realized he'd said it, maybe he hadn't intended to let me know how he really felt about me, but I had definitely heard it come out of his mouth. It wasn't me imagining things. It wasn't me wishing for something so hard until I convinced myself that it was real. *Not when I still love you as much as I ever did.* Those were his exact words. They might as well have been branded on my brain because I doubted I would ever stop hearing them filter through my mind.

He loved me.

He loved me, but it hurt him when I kept leaving. Totally understandable. Completely made sense. I mean, hell, it hurt *me* every time I left, and it wasn't just because I was leaving my family. It was because I was leaving him, too.

I'd dated a few guys over the last few years, and every single one of them had been a mistake. Derek had pushed me into it, and I'd told myself that if I couldn't be with Jamie, I could still be with *someone*, and maybe I'd come to love one of them as much as I loved him. Or even more than I loved him. I suppose that was what I'd been hoping for, but what had really happened was so far from my ideal that it was laughable.

But Jamie loved me. And I loved him. And I was pretty sure I'd fucked up any chance I might have once had of being with him. Now I had to figure out what I was going to do about it. It was only fair for me to give him what he'd asked for, to stop trying to be his friend when it so clearly caused him pain every time I left.

But what if I didn't leave again?

The idea was crazy. I mean, singing and acting were the things my life was supposed to be about. I'd been studying vocal technique since I was a child. I'd taken acting lessons starting in my early teens. My parents had put me in a private high school that was known for the performing arts. I'd gone to Hollywood, gotten the representation of the best entertainment agent out there, landed my dream job, and started what should have been a long and lucrative career.

Should have been.

Probably would have been, if not for the fact that I'd already screwed myself over on that front after yesterday's conversation with Derek. I honestly wasn't sure what I was going to do now, but I didn't *have* to leave. I could stay here. With Jamie. I could do whatever it took to make this work, if he would give me one more chance. I could figure out a new direction for my life and be sure it included him.

Yes, it would mean leaving behind all that I'd thought I wanted. I'd been learning that sometimes life had a funny way of showing you that what you'd once thought you wanted and what you really wanted didn't always line up. In fact, sometimes they were complete opposites.

I didn't yet have a plan as to what I would do from here, but there was no point wallowing in my bedroom anymore. I was on my way to join the rest of my family when there was a soft knock on the door and Dani's voice saying, "Katie? Can I come in?"

I opened the door, pasting a smile on my face even though I knew she wouldn't buy it. Sure enough, she furrowed her brow in concern.

There wasn't any reason to let her worry about me, especially since we had less than twenty-four hours left before she'd have to drive back to Seattle, so I drew her in for a hug. "I'm okay."

"Promise?"

"Promise."

"Well, you'd better put some makeup on to hide your crying if you want Dad to believe you." She stepped back and shut the door, then headed into my bathroom. When she returned, it was with a tube of concealer in her hand. "Let me help."

I sat on the edge of the bed and allowed her to perform her magic tricks on me.

"Close your eyes," she said.

I did as she ordered, and she smeared some of it on the sensitive skin all around my eyes. "Would you think I was crazy if I said I was going to stay in Portland?" I asked. "Instead of going back to LA?"

She took a moment before answering, going back into the bathroom for something else from my arsenal. "You're not going to get any acting gigs around here other than community theater work," she finally said once she returned and started putting foundation on my skin. "But would that make you crazy? No, I wouldn't say so. I think it would just mean you're reevaluating what's important to you."

I nodded and let her dust powder and bronzer on my cheeks.

"Are you thinking about staying because you're over the whole Hollywood thing, though, or is it because of Jamie?"

I shrugged, popping my eyes open so I could look at her. "Maybe both? Is one a better reason than the other?"

"I guess that depends on you and what you decide to do with yourself, doesn't it?" She added a bit of blush and handed me a tube of mascara. "A bit of mascara and some lip gloss, and you're good as new."

I got up and went into the bathroom so I could see myself. "Thanks, Dani."

"Don't thank me for that. It's what sisters do." She grinned at me in the mirror, hitching a hip against the doorjamb. "If you want to know what I *really* think, though, I think you would be crazy to leave again."

"Why do you say that?" I tossed the mascara tube back in my kit and rummaged for my favorite lip gloss.

"Because if you can still get this worked up over Jamie, there's something there worth fighting for, and you're not an idiot. You know what's really important in life." She backed out of the bathroom. "You'll figure it out. You'll make the right choice. See you out there in a few," she said just before leaving my room.

I was pretty sure I had already made my choice. Now I just needed to figure out how to implement it.

I SPENT THE rest of the weekend with my family. Dad had to leave for team practices and things like that, but otherwise he hung out with us girls. We had meals together, talking and laughing, all the while wishing that Luke could be here with us, too. Ever since I'd left for Hollywood, it was extremely rare that we were able to have the whole family together. It made me yearn for the old days, when we were kids and griped and complained all the time about being forced to be together.

The three of them were plainly curious about what had happened between me and Jamie, but none of them pressed for details. I would probably talk to Mom after a while, once I knew what I was going to do, but I wasn't ready yet.

Late Sunday afternoon, Dani packed up her bag and gave us all hugs, and then she got in her car to make the drive back to Seattle. That was when I remembered about my appointment with Dr. Oliver the next day, and my panic started to creep back in. At least I'd been able to keep it in check while she was here. There was no good reason to let anyone else worry. Hell, there was no good reason for me to worry.

I couldn't sleep Sunday night, even though I knew the results of my tests wouldn't come back right away. Some of them might not come back for a week or more. That knowledge wasn't enough to stop my anxiety from ratcheting up to the nth degree.

As I was coming to expect, I got up to find Mom puttering around in the kitchen while Dad sat on a barstool with his iPad propped up in front of him. Mom poured a fresh cup of coffee and handed it to me when I came in.

"Thanks," I said, going to the fridge for some half-and-half.

Mom took out a pan and set it on a burner. "I can make a veggie omelet if you want."

"I'd be happy with a bowl of Cheerios."

"You should have a solid meal," Dad said, glancing up from the video playing in front of him.

I grabbed a banana from the fruit bowl and raised my brows at him. "How about oatmeal and fruit?"

He'd been insanely vigilant about everything I put in my mouth since my diagnosis years ago, thinking that maybe if I only ate organic foods, nothing processed, I could stay healthy. No doubt there was some truth to it, but he took it over the top sometimes. His mouth screwed up in something between a grimace and a scowl, but he went back to watching the screen.

Mom went into the pantry and came out with the oatmeal. "Want me to come with you today? I could—"

"I'm a big girl, Mom. I don't need you to hold my hand when they stick the needle in my arm anymore." As many times as I'd been poked and prodded over the years, I didn't really feel the tiny pricks when they went in to draw blood and the like anymore. Or at least not as much as I would have before having cancer. They'd even put a port in me and left it for months, when I was getting chemo. I'd had to have surgery for them to implant it, and then they'd done another procedure to remove it once I was cancer free. A brief stick to give them some blood was no biggie compared to all that.

Mom looked miffed, though. She nodded and kept quiet, but that was only further proof that I'd hurt her feelings. If she wasn't talking, there was no doubt it was because she didn't trust herself to speak without blowing up about something.

I finished making my oatmeal and sat down next to my father.

He finished off his coffee and shut down the iPad. "Better get out of here." He pushed back from the bar and kissed me on the cheek. "Tell me everything later."

"There won't be anything to tell for days."

"I know." He winked before heading over to kiss Mom, as well. "Tell me anyway."

Once the garage door had closed behind him, Mom took down a wineglass and opened a bottle of her favorite merlot. "Want some?"

"At this hour of the morning?" I shook my head.

"Might help steady your nerves."

Which was definitely the reason she was getting started this early. She had always loved her wine, and she tended to break it out for just about every occasion. I gave her a wry smile. "How about when I come home?" I suggested. By then, I would definitely need something.

"All right." She swirled the wine in her glass, staring at the circular movements of the liquid.

I got busy eating my breakfast while ruminating. I still felt like an ass for hurting her feelings. And when it came right down to it, no matter how much of an old pro I might be at letting doctors poke and prod me, she was still my mom, and I would always need her to hold my hand. So I reached across the bar and took hers, squeezing until she met my gaze. "You want to come with me?" I asked.

"Are you sure?" she said, the words gushing out of her like a pent-up breath of air. "Because I know you're an adult now, and I don't want to invade your privacy or anything, but I really just—"

"Finish your wine and let's get ready," I cut in. "But I'm driving."

Mom smiled so wide she could have been the Cheshire cat's twin. "Good. Then I can have some more before we go." She grabbed the bottle and topped off her glass.

I finished my breakfast, showered, and dressed. Mom was waiting for me in the kitchen by the time I finished getting ready, another glass of wine in her hands. She finished it off, and we left together.

My doctor's appointment went exactly as it always did. The phlebotomist drew several vials of blood. I talked with Dr. Oliver about everything going on with my health. I didn't think my headaches and stress and being tired lately were worth mentioning, but Mom interjected to let him know. I glared at her, and she raised a brow at me in return.

He just nodded and marked a few things down on my chart, not acting as though that were anything to be concerned about. Once we got through all his questions, he shook my hand and told me someone from his office would be in touch in about a week so we could discuss the results.

And that was that. As usual, it really wasn't anything to have let myself get worked up about.

After I checked out at the receptionist's desk, Mom and I headed home, and she poured us both a glass of wine.

"Thanks," I said when she handed one to me.

She sat next to me on the sofa and tucked her feet up beside her. "Now that that's over and we're alone, want to tell me what happened with Jamie?"

I'd been afraid this was coming at the same time as I was impatiently expecting it. My tears started up almost immediately, and I settled in to lay out for my mother everything that had been going through my head since Saturday afternoon.

"Well," she said once I'd recounted every detail, including my thought that I might stick around Portland. She refilled both our glasses and set the empty bottle down on the coffee table. "You know your father and I will be behind you, whatever you decide to do, right? Your dad may not always like the decisions you make, but he respects your right to make them, and he loves you no matter what. We both do."

"I know that."

She grinned and held up her glass. "Then you should also know that there's no one who would be happier than your father if you stick around and give it another go with Jamie."

"What?" My mother had to be on something to say anything of the sort. Dad had hated everything about the thought of me being with Jamie. If he could have his way, he would keep me and Dani both under lock and key until we were forty. Mom was losing her mind if she thought he'd changed his tune on that.

She sipped and lowered her glass, eyeing me astutely. "Why do you think he gave Tim that prom picture, Katie? Why *that* picture, when there were dozens—hundreds, even—he could have given them that would have elicited a big reaction from the crowd?"

That was an excellent question.

Chapter Four

Jamie

TO MY SURPRISE, Webs didn't treat me any differently that week than he ever did, at practice, in games, or anywhere else. I must not have pissed him off as badly as I'd thought I had. I'd been bracing myself for the worst, whatever that might turn out to be, but he acted as if nothing out of the ordinary had happened.

He had always been full of threats as far as Katie was concerned, but he'd never actually acted on any of them. At least not with me. I was pretty sure he never had with any of the other asswipes she'd dated over the years, either, despite the fact that some of them definitely deserved it. Maybe I deserved it, too. But…nothing. Nada. No reaction at all.

That said, I would never put it past him to change his mind about torturing me. As soon as I convinced myself I was in the clear, he was bound to follow through, and then my dick and balls might not be where they'd started out anymore, or at the very least, they would no longer be in usable condition. To be safe, I'd been keeping my distance as well as I could manage, considering I still had to go to all the same team functions as him.

We had back-to-back games involving a short trip out of town, and we were going to be without Soupy for the foreseeable future. The doctors were still determining how serious his injury was, but the coaches had let us know we wouldn't be seeing him for a while. They kept throwing around the term *ACL*, which could mean Soupy was done for the season. That meant we had a young guy called up from our American Hockey League affiliate, the Seattle Storm. Austin Cooper was the lucky twenty-year-old getting the chance to make an impression. I had volunteered to be Coop's road roommate. I didn't have to have one anymore, but I figured it would be a good way to get to know the guy and make him feel welcome. If he stuck around for a while, maybe he could come and stay at my house. I'd made the offer, but he still didn't know how long he'd be with us, so nothing had been settled.

The first game was against the Panthers at home, followed by a match against the Wild on the road. We pulled off a hard-fought win against Florida, partially due to Coop scoring on his first NHL shot, and we came out of Minnesota with an overtime loss. Immediately after that game, we headed to the airport and flew to Dallas for the second and last game on this brief road trip.

After eating the chicken parm and salad the flight attendants served us, I spent the rest of our time in the air playing Texas Hold 'Em with RJ, Burnzie, and Ghost. Or maybe *losing my ass to Ghost* would be more accurate. The guy's face never gave a fucking thing away. By the time we touched down at Love Field, I was pretty sure he had bluffed me out of at least a few hundred dollars, and both RJ and Burnzie were definitely lighter in the pockets, too, but there was no chance Ghost would admit to any deception.

"If you think I'm bluffing, call me on it," Ghost said, slinging his carry-on bag over his shoulder before heading up the aisle.

Burnzie filed in behind him. "Every time I stayed in, you took all my money," he grumbled.

Ghost laughed.

The second I stepped out on the stairs coming down from the plane, the heat hit me like a slap shot to the gut. It was about three in the morning, but it had to be close to ninety degrees out even though we were getting close to Halloween. I wished I had taken off my suit jacket and tie before getting out in the Texas air, but at least I didn't have on a bulky coat.

Mom had texted me a day or two ago that it was already snowing back home. I imagined that for the guys who played on teams down south, there had to be a bit of a shock to the system. Well, at least for most of them. These days, there were starting to be guys drafted who'd grown up in Texas, California, Florida… They were still the exception, though, not the rule. Most guys in the league came from places where snow was a lot more common than triple-digit temperatures.

We all headed to the waiting bus, which took us to our hotel. I was on my way to the front desk to get the envelope with my room key when Webs came up alongside me and took my arm, hauling me to a stop. He didn't say anything, only nudging his head to a quiet hallway off to the side of the lobby, but there was something familiar in the crease of his forehead that turned my dinner to concrete.

I followed him until he turned and faced me.

"Katie's cancer is back," he said without preamble.

He might as well have punched me in the gut. His words hurt as bad as that would have. Worse, even. Much worse. The concrete that had replaced my stomach had bubbled up into my throat. My lungs were collapsing on me, and that fucking cement block in my throat wouldn't budge no matter how hard I swallowed.

"Laura left me a message to fill me in. She knew my phone would be off but I needed to know."

Laura was his wife, Katie's mom. I nodded, then wished I hadn't because that small motion was all it took to melt the concrete and turn it to bile.

Webs's voice crunched over every word, and his fists kept clenching and releasing at his sides. "They have to run a bunch more tests, figure out exactly what we're dealing with this time. Figure out a plan. Katie didn't—" He dragged a hand through his hair before punching the wall and pressing his forehead to the same spot.

I might have done the same if I thought it would help. I knew better, though. There wasn't a fucking thing I could do that would make it feel better. Nothing I could do would help.

After a moment, he turned to me again with shining eyes. "Katie didn't want me to tell you, but I thought you needed to know. I just— I thought you should know."

I might have nodded. I couldn't be sure because after the debilitating blow of his words, everything in me went numb. Maybe I was in shock. Maybe my body was shutting down my ability to feel because pain on that level was more than I could take, and something in my brain knew that better than I did. "Thanks," I croaked out, but I didn't know why I was thanking him.

Because I'd told Katie I couldn't be in her life anymore.

Because loving her hurt too much.

And all this did was make everything else hurt worse.

"I'll keep you informed," Webs said. "Once the tests come back. Once we know."

"Okay," I forced through clenched teeth, but what I wanted to say was *no*. I wished he hadn't told me. Not any of it. If I didn't know Katie's cancer had returned, then I would have been able to go on nursing my broken heart. Maybe one day it would have healed enough that I could have moved on.

But right now, all I could think about was going back. Back in time. Back to Portland. Back to Katie.

"She's going to be all right." His voice cracked over the words, the crunching giving way to emotion like water bursting through a dam. "Right? She's beat it before, so she—" He couldn't go on, but there was no need to.

I was torn between the desire to punch something until my knuckles bled and the feeling that I should try to comfort him.

Webs didn't exactly give me the chance to figure it out, either. He muttered, "Fuck," and closed the distance between us, tugging me in for a bear hug. He was just as strong as he'd been back when he was still one of my teammates. His arms were like a vise around me. There was no escape.

Out of instinct, I put my arms around him and patted his back.

That was when Burnzie and Ghost ambled into the hall, busting a gut laughing about something. Webs released me almost immediately, but I knew my face would give away my embarrassment at being caught like that. I had always blushed way too fucking easily, which only embarrassed me more than I already was. Pissed me off. Blushing was something that people normally associated with teenaged girls, like the ones who were always following me and Levi around and gushing over how cute we were. I was a twenty-four-year-old man, for Christ's sake, and I still blushed as bad as I ever had.

"Shit," Ghost said. "Sorry, we, uh…"

"We were just heading the other way," Burnzie said, physically turning Ghost around and dragging him back toward the hotel lobby.

"What—" Ghost started.

"None of our fucking business is what," Burnzie muttered right before they turned the corner.

"Sorry," Webs said, clearing his throat once they'd disappeared.

"Don't be," I said out of habit.

He sniffled, and his facial muscles twitched as he tried to get himself back under control. "You should head up," he said. "Try to sleep."

"Yeah." I shoved my hands in my pockets, wishing I had a rock to kick around with my toes. "You should, too. Sleep," I clarified.

He gave me a wry half smile. "Not a lot of chance that's going to happen."

Not for me, either, but if anyone understood that, it was Webs. I nodded and shuffled off down the hall. Instead of turning for the elevator bay, I followed the signs to the hotel's gym, stripping off my jacket and tie and rolling up my sleeves as I went.

There wasn't a punching bag, which was what I really wanted now that I was here, but maybe that was for the best. Bruising my hands probably wouldn't be my best move at the moment. Regardless of what was going on with Katie, I still had hockey to play and a team to lead. In the end, I got on a bike and tried to wear myself out to the point that I couldn't think. Letting myself think only led me back to Katie. Should I call her or try to talk to her? The idea of taking back everything I'd said to her about no longer being her friend was weighing on me, and I was afraid I might end up doing just that. And then where would it leave me? She was still going to leave. She'd beat cancer again, and she would go back to Hollywood and date some asswipe who could never deserve her, and I would be left here to nurse my broken heart once more. That was the only sort of leaving I could let myself contemplate; the other possibilities threatened to rip my heart out just by allowing them to flit across the corners of my mind.

I cycled harder in an effort to rid my mind of any thought of her. I don't know how long I was on that stupid stationary bike. Long enough that I had sweated through my clothes and would have to send them off for cleaning. Long enough that my muscles were screaming for relief. Long enough that I should have stopped thinking about anything but getting off the fucking thing, taking a shower, and going to bed, but I could still think of nothing but Katie. At some point, the gym door opened, and Levi, Burnzie, Ghost, Coop, and half a dozen of our other teammates came in. They should have all been in bed. I should have, too, but that was beside the point.

Levi picked up my tie and jacket from the floor, where I'd tossed them before getting on the bike. "Come on," he said.

I shook my head. "Go up to bed."

Ghost grabbed the handle of my carry-on bag, ready to haul it off. "Not until you come, too," he said.

"Why the hell are you guys even down here?" It had to be four or five in the morning by now, and we had a mandatory meeting and film session scheduled for after breakfast. That was going to be here far earlier than I would want to be up.

Burnzie came over behind me and gave me a cuff on the backside of my head, something he'd been doing since my rookie season. "Because you are, you dumb fuck, why do you think? Ghost and I got Webs to tell us what was going on when he came through the lobby. We were still debating how long we should let you sulk when Coop came wandering around like a lost puppy and said you still hadn't picked up your room key or headed up. That was when we all got together and decided to figure out where you were."

"Well, you found me," I bit off, wishing I had bothered to grab a towel. Sweat dripped down my forehead and got in my eyes, stinging. "Mystery solved. Fuck off."

I sounded like an ass, and I knew it. I was reacting like a damn toddler, minus the kicking and screaming. It was definitely a toddler-worthy temper tantrum I was throwing, at the very least. My teammates didn't deserve that kind of treatment, but I didn't know how to stop myself when everything inside me was twisting into knots. I couldn't very well kick and scream at the universe and expect it to do any good.

Jonny frowned at me, his arms crossed and his feet planted like two tree trunks making roots in the floor. "You boys go on up," he said quietly. "I'll stay with him."

"Yeah," Burnzie said, backing out of the gym while the other guys followed, Ghost and Levi hauling my shit along with them. Burnzie caught Jonny's eye and nudged his head in my direction. "Feel free to bust his face in for being a dick."

If there was anyone on the team who could—and *would*, considering I deserved it—it was Jonny. He grunted in response, which Burnzie and the boys seemed to accept as a suitable answer. They trickled out of the room.

When the door closed behind them, Jonny crossed over and sat backward on the weight bench across from me. He ran a hand over his shaved head and stared at me. "So you can keep cycling if you want, or you can talk if you want. Whatever. I'm not leaving until you do, though, and Sara will tell you I get really cranky if I don't get my beauty sleep."

"Beauty sleep, huh?" I couldn't help but chuckle, and I raised a brow at the yellowish bruise around his eye and the fresh set of stitches on his cheek. I knew better than to think he would get up and go just because I told him to. I was pretty sure the only person I'd ever met who might come close to him on the stubborn scale was his wife, Sara.

"It takes a lot of work to look this good." He stretched his legs out in front of him, crossing them at the ankles. "Point is, I don't think you need to be alone right now, and I don't intend to let you be."

I mimicked his earlier grunt.

"So what are you going to do about it?"

"I guess I'm going up to bed so I don't have to sit here with you staring at me like that all night."

"I meant about Katie."

Hell if I knew.

Katie

IN ORDER TO keep my mind occupied while I was waiting on the results of my latest barrage of tests, I had decided to go house hunting. Mom and Dad wanted me to just move back into their house, now that I didn't have any good reason to go back to LA, and especially now that I *did* have a good reason to stick around in Portland. If I was going to have to go through cancer treatments again, there wasn't a chance in hell I was going to do it under anyone but Dr. Oliver.

That didn't mean I wanted to live with my parents and have my mother hovering over me constantly until I was cancer-free again, though. It only made sense, she said, because I was already living here at least temporarily. I hadn't forgotten what it was like, going through radiation and chemotherapy and all that jazz. I remembered everything about it, not the least of which was the emotional toll it had taken on my family. I needed at least some space of my own, some distance between us without completely going away, if I was going to get through it again without going completely berserk. I wanted to be able to hang out with my mom when I felt like crap but to not have her watching me so she could pick out every minuscule change I went through before I noticed it. There had to be some sort of balance there, and I intended to find it.

I had more than enough money set aside that I could get a reasonable place of my own without it hurting my bank account, whether I was going to be working in the near future or not, so I didn't see any reason to put it off. Chances were pretty high that I'd be starting some treatment plan or another pretty soon, and once that happened, I would have a lot less energy for things like house hunting.

When I headed into the kitchen for breakfast, Dad was there eating a bowl of oatmeal and some fruit, but this time he didn't have his iPad playing video. I'd been at my parents' house at breakfast more than enough times since Dad had started coaching to know that he *always* watched game footage on his iPad over breakfast, but the tablet was nowhere to be seen.

By the time he and the team had gotten in after their loss against the Stars last night, I had long since gone to bed. I'd still been awake, though. I'd heard him come in, his footsteps careful in the hall as he made his way to my bedroom and opened the door. *Katie?* he'd whispered. *You awake?* I hadn't answered him, lying there with my eyes closed, hoping he would close the door and make his way to his own bed.

He hadn't done that. He'd crossed over to me and sat down on the edge of the bed, and he'd kissed the back of my head. I could tell he was crying. That was what I'd been trying to avoid, the reason I'd pretended to be asleep. I wasn't ready for all this again—to have everyone hovering and crying all the time. That didn't help me. It just made me feel as if I was the one responsible for everyone's lack of emotional well-being. I had hoped he would wait until the light of day before starting, but my hopes were in vain.

He'd stayed there for a few minutes, stroking my hair, and then he'd sniffled and shuffled out of the room, pulling the door closed behind him. Only after he was gone did I allow myself to break down in tears. I hated crying. I really fucking hated it, and I'd allowed it to go on so long that I ended up with a massive headache that kept me awake for hours after he'd left my room.

And now, here he was, looking up at me with red-rimmed eyes over his breakfast, and it took everything in me not to break down again. We'd talked on the phone some in the last couple of days. He knew everything I knew at this point about my test results. Which, admittedly, wasn't much. It was just enough to know there something to worry about but not enough to know how worried we should be.

"What time did you get in?" I asked, pretending I didn't know. I just needed to talk. To keep myself from bawling again. I took down a mug and brewed a cup of coffee.

"Late." His voice was rough. "Your mom has a meeting with the women's league this morning. You could go with her."

Mom had been getting involved with all sorts of clubs and groups ever since Dani had graduated from high school. She'd been a stay-at-home mother the whole time we were growing up, but now that we had lives of our own to lead, she'd been getting restless. She'd always been involved in things with whatever team Dad played for or coached for, of course, but apparently that was no longer enough to keep her appropriately busy.

"I could," I hedged. I'd already told Mom I didn't want to go with her, but I hadn't broached the real reason *why* I wasn't going with either of them. "If I didn't already have other plans."

He set his spoon down and met my eyes. "What other plans? More tests?"

"Not today." Hopefully not any time soon. They had stuck me more than enough over the last couple of days to last me for a while, thank you very much. "Actually, I have an appointment with a realtor."

"A realtor?"

"Yes." I took out a bowl and started fixing my own breakfast, copying his.

"Here in Portland?"

I rolled my eyes. "No, I thought I'd fly to Timbuktu and go house hunting there. Yes, of course here in Portland."

"So you're going to stay? You're not planning to go back to Hollywood?"

"Not in the near future, at least. Maybe someday." Of course, if I was going to be able to return to Hollywood, I'd have to still be alive to do so. For some reason, airlines aren't really fond of transporting dead people. And then there was the small matter of no longer having an agent or any real desire to live that lifestyle anymore. I wasn't ready to close the door on that part of my life completely, but that didn't mean I needed to walk through it any time soon. "Even when I'm working on a show, I still come back and spend quite a bit of time here. This is home. I might as well act like an adult and really make it home, right?"

"Did you tell your mother?"

I shook my head, biting my lip. Mom wouldn't take it as well as Dad, so I'd been keeping it a secret, hoping maybe I could get him to break the news to her instead of me. I hated having to tell her things that she wouldn't like. "Not yet."

"And this has nothing to do with you not wanting Mom to be up in your business all the time, right?" He chuckled, shaking his head. "Who's your realtor?"

At least he understood. "Sierra Firth," I said, letting out a breath.

Dad picked up his spoon and went back to his oatmeal with a nod. "She's the one who helped us find this house."

"I know. I remember. I was fourteen, you know." With my breakfast prepared, I took the stool next to his at the bar. I'd been a teenager when we'd moved to Portland. Dad had played in Toronto, New York, Carolina, St. Louis, Edmonton, and Detroit before signing on with the Storm, so we'd moved around a lot. That's just how it is sometimes for a pro athlete. It had been rough on me as a kid. As soon as I'd grown comfortable somewhere and settled on who I wanted to have as my friends, we were on the move again. Portland had been the one place he'd really stuck. It was the only place I wanted to call home.

He shoved the sugar dish in my direction so I wouldn't have to reach for it. "Never thought you would have paid attention to things like that when there were boys to be ogled."

"They were at school, not in the empty houses we were looking at."

"So where are you going to look? I just saw a *For Sale* sign on a house around the corner. The one with the blue shutters."

I couldn't help but grin at him. "Not around the corner."

"Too close to your mom?" He finished off his coffee and pushed the cup aside. "Yeah, too close to your mom. I get it. Not too far away, though, okay? She—*we*—need to hover at least some."

"I know." That was going to be one of my biggest decisions—how close was too close, and how far was too far. "It'll be in Portland. I don't know where. Sierra said she had some ideas that she thought I'd like."

"Fair enough." He reached in the fruit basket for a banana and started peeling it before passing it to me and taking out another for himself. "I told Babs."

I swallowed hard, blinking back tears. I'd told both Mom and Dad that I didn't want Jamie to know. Jamie had made it clear that he couldn't be my friend anymore, and I had no intention of doing anything to hurt him worse than I already had. I wanted to give him a clean break. No contact. Nothing more than the knowledge that we both existed and were in the same city. I could give him that, couldn't I? I owed him that much. "I didn't want—"

"I know you didn't want him to know, but I thought he should, and I told him. You can be angry at me if you want. You can yell at me and curse me. Hit me, if you think it'll help. But I told him, and I'm not sorry I did, so you're just going to have to accept it."

It wasn't *me* accepting it that I was worried about, though. It was Jamie.

Chapter Five

Katie

"NOT ONLY IS it a great location for you while you're undergoing treatments, but it's right in the heart of things for when you're healthy again," Sierra said, opening the door to the backyard and stepping aside so I could go out before her.

It might as well have been a private garden out there, with various trees, bushes, and flowering plants lining the fence, making it seem like a sanctuary. A swinging bench hung under one of the bigger trees on one side looking toward the mountain view over the tops of the greenery, and a pond was situated off to the side, with rocks and plants arranged around it so it looked as if it had always been there even though it surely must have been installed after the house was built.

My parents lived in a classic Tudor-style house in Grant Park on the east side of Portland. I'd asked Sierra to show me houses on the other side of the river, claiming it was because I wanted to be close to all my doctors downtown. She'd already taken me to more than half a dozen houses today, mainly in Beaverton and Lake Oswego, because they were close enough to downtown for what I needed but with enough distance to still feel as if I had some privacy. She'd caught on pretty quickly that privacy, a place where I could just be away from it all, was a big factor for me.

This house, though, was just outside of downtown in the Northwest District. It hadn't been on the original list we'd discussed; she'd suggested it after we'd been out looking for a while, once she had a better sense of my likes and dislikes. I hadn't seen any more than the front entry and the path through the house to the backyard, yet. It didn't matter. Unless the place was completely gutted and would need a ton of work, I was pretty sure I wanted this house to be mine because of nothing more than the peace and solitude I would have in this backyard.

I strolled to the swing and took a seat, imagining being out here on a nice night at sunset. For the first time in days, a feeling of stillness settled over me, starting at my head and trickling all the way down to my toes.

Sierra sat next to me and cocked up a brow. "You want to take a look at the inside?"

"I should probably do that before making an offer, huh?"

"Might be a good idea."

"Right." I sighed and pushed myself up from the swing. "I guess we should do that, then."

We went back inside and she took me on the grand tour.

"They recently renovated the kitchen and the master bath," Sierra said as we moved from room to room. "All stainless appliances in the kitchen. Separate shower and a garden tub, which might come in handy when you aren't feeling well. They also tore down a wall between what used to be two smaller bedrooms and turned it into a really good-sized home office with room for some built-ins and a nice view out back. I don't know what you might use it for, but I bet you could come up with something."

The second I stepped into that space, I had an idea. I could turn it into a music studio of sorts. Ever since I'd ended my representation with Derek, I'd been trying to think of what I could do to remain in the entertainment business but do it from Portland. The one thing that kept coming to mind, even though it sounded crazy, was songwriting.

I'd never written a song before. I'd only sung them. It seemed like something I should at least *try*, though, because it would give me opportunities to continue my career but do it on my own terms, not those of an agent who was going to push his own agenda. Having a studio in my house would be perfect.

I followed Sierra through the rest of the house, taking it all in. Even after the remodeling the owners had done, there were still two bedrooms and two bathrooms in addition to this big office. I didn't need a ton of space, but it would probably be a good idea to have a guest room in case…well, in case I got so sick that I needed someone living with me to take care of me.

"Can I wander around for a few minutes and think?" I asked her.

"I'll be in the kitchen. Take all the time you need."

I did just that, moving from room to room and imagining myself living here. It wasn't brand new, and there were a few things I would want to change right away, not the least of which were paint colors. The people who owned it were apparently fans of dark, bold hues. Not me. I wanted it to be light, warm, and airy, like the colors you'd expect to see in Tuscany or Greece. Paint was an easy fix, though, and there weren't any major changes I could see needing to make as long as there weren't any structural issues.

The real deciding factors for me were the oasis in the back and the studio. Between those two things and the fact that I would be far enough away from my parents without being too far, I knew—this was the house for me.

I meandered back to the kitchen and leaned against the bar.

"You still like it?" Sierra asked.

"Like it? Love it, more like."

"I thought so, but it's never a good idea to make assumptions."

"So how does this work? How do I make an offer?"

"You don't want to think about it? Bring your parents or a friend over to see it?"

"No need for that." I wasn't going to let anyone or anything change my mind. Not on this.

"Well, then." She grinned and pulled out a file from her briefcase. "Let's talk numbers."

Jamie

"YOU'RE NOT SERIOUSLY going to keep calling him Spanky, are you?" Levi asked. "Of all the things to name a cat…"

"Maybe? I don't know. He already knows it's his name."

"He's three months old, if that. He doesn't know you mean him when you say that. He's just responding to your voice. He seems to like you, for whatever reason."

The scruffy silver tabby in question squirmed free from my brother's grasp again and sunk his razor claws into my sleeve—and beyond—to climb up to my shoulder. The people at the shelter said they were pretty sure he was about three months old even though he was about half the size he should be at that age. He'd been rescued from near a dumpster at a convenience store a couple of weeks before, malnourished and sick, and they hadn't been sure he would make it. He had a clean bill of health now, though, even if he was still kind of scrawny. This little guy was a fighter, in more ways than one, as he was reminding me at the moment. Now that he was up on my shoulder, he dug his claws into my skin so he wouldn't slide off.

"Ouch. Can't you hold him still for three more minutes?" We were almost back to my place, and the kitten was tiny. Levi was probably a hundred times his size. He ought to be able to restrain the kitten at least long enough to get home.

"You try making a kitten do what you want it to do," Levi grumbled. "You should have taken them up on that cardboard box thing they offered. They said this might happen. Clearly, he likes to explore. And he likes you. There's no explaining taste."

Whether I should have or not, it was too late now. Once Spanky got where he wanted to be, he curled up in a ball, mewling in my ear with the same pathetic sound he made that had convinced me I needed to take him home with me. That's where he'd hung out the most while we were playing with him at the shelter. Or at least he'd been up there a lot when he wasn't otherwise occupied with climbing my pants and making flying leaps at feather toys and chasing balls and wrestling with the bigger kittens. But then after all that playing, he got tired, and he'd sought me out again to snuggle with during his nap.

I hadn't really intended to come home with a cat. I'd been looking at a dog that was some sort of beagle mix when a huge chocolate Labrador had caught my eye. The second I walked over to the Lab's kennel, this tiny kitten had pranced through the door from the cat area and sprinted up my legs and back to perch on my shoulder. When I'd tried to pull him down, he'd given me that pathetic mewl, and he'd dug in his claws, making sure he wasn't going anywhere without turning my skin to ribbons. Then the purring had started, and I was a goner.

"What do you want a cat for, anyway?" Levi asked, his voice mixing with the kitten's purrs in a very odd manner. "Do you even know how to take care of a cat?"

"Do you even know how to take care of yourself?" I countered instead of trying to explain that I was lonely without having someone to come home to. On our day off in Dallas, I'd offered a room to

Coop since it looked like he'd be sticking with the team for a while. Apparently Wheels had gotten to him first, so I still had no roommate. Between that and the news Webs had given me about Katie's cancer, I'd decided that I needed a companion of some sort, human or otherwise. I didn't know a better way of making that happen than by bringing home a pet.

Levi shrugged and tried to pry the kitten free, but Spanky was having none of that. Those tiny claws dug into my neck again, and I let out a series of expletives.

Levi let go. "Guess he's staying there until we get back to your place."

"I guess so."

Spanky resettled and started purring again, a warm, fluffy ball right where my shoulder and neck met.

"You should call him Tiger," Levi said.

"Why Tiger?"

"Why Spanky?"

"Because I don't know him well enough to know what else to call him." I made the turn onto my street. There were two cars parked in the drive of the empty house next door to mine. Probably a realtor showing it. That had been happening a lot as long as I'd been living here. I pulled up in my driveway and hit the button for my garage door to open.

"Um, Jamie?"

I turned my head toward the cars in the driveway next door, since that was where Levi was staring. Then I wished I hadn't because Katie was staring back at my car, standing next to one of the realtors I'd seen a time or two. She looked as thunderstruck as I felt.

"Fuck," I muttered. This really couldn't be happening. I couldn't handle having her move in next door to me. And what the hell was she doing, looking at buying a house here? If she was going to stick around in Portland to go through whatever treatments she needed, she should stay with her parents. She'd need help, someone to look after her when she wasn't feeling well, someone to take her to all her doctor's appointments and hospital visits and God only knew what else. Cancer wasn't something she should try to deal with on her own, and she knew that better than most since she'd already been through it once.

I would tell her so if not for the knowledge that she didn't want anyone to tell me she was sick again. And then there was the small matter that I'd told her I needed her out of my life. Not to mention the fact that the second I opened my mouth to try to speak to her at all, I would probably break down and take everything back.

It was the only thing that had been racing through my head for the last few days—telling Katie that I hadn't meant it, that I would be her friend, if that was what she wanted, or her boyfriend, or whatever the hell she needed me to be. That I needed her in my life and didn't care what corner of hers she put me in, as long as I could hold on to some piece of her.

God knew I was a fucking glutton for punishment, but I couldn't give in and do that. She'd flattened my heart so many times she might as well have run over it repeatedly with an eighteen-wheeler. Someday, I wanted to be able to give it to someone, and I couldn't as long as she kept ripping it to shreds. I had to stick to my original plan and stay as far away from her as I could.

Levi opened his door and climbed out. He was crossing the lawn and heading over to talk to them before I could make up my mind about what I ought to do—like pull my car into the garage, go inside the house, and pretend I hadn't seen her.

Katie had seen me, though. There wasn't any doubt about that, based on the way her jaw had dropped when she'd looked at the car. I figured I had to at least go and say hello. Maybe once she knew I lived here, it would help her realize this wasn't the house for her and she should move on.

I undid my seat belt and put a hand over Spanky's back so he wouldn't take a tumble, and then I followed my brother.

"So you live here?" Katie asked as soon as I reached them. She blinked a couple of times, staring at the fuzz ball on my shoulder. "You have a kitten?" As soon as she remarked upon that realization, her voice had gone all soft and sweet, like women tended to do around babies. She reached out for the little guy, and he surprisingly allowed her to pick him up without leaving me a bloody mess. The next thing I knew, she had him cradled against her chest and was cooing to him.

Which drew my eyes there. Where he was. Or really more to what was under him.

Her breasts.

Which were amazing.

They were perfect and perky, just the right size for me to cup in my palms. The top she was wearing had a vee at the neck, lining the small amount of cleavage she had showing with a bright turquoise fabric that lit up everything about her. And my kitten was hanging out there.

Enjoying himself immensely, it seemed, based on the way he was purring. I could hear his purr motor working like crazy. The tiny bastard.

Levi cleared his throat, and I forced my gaze up to Katie's face. She was watching me with a bemused grin, one of her brows raised in question.

"Oh. Yeah, the house. I bought it over the summer. Figured it was time to set down some roots. I've been here seven years so far, and it doesn't look like I'll be leaving any time soon." Unlike her, which made the idea that she was looking for a house, not only in the city but right next door to me, fishy. Not that I said as much. Was she looking at houses near mine for a reason? Portland was plenty big enough that she could live any number of places that weren't in my immediate vicinity. But that should be a private conversation, if we had the discussion at all.

The whole time I was talking, she kept petting Spanky, drawing my eye down over and over, and leading me to thoroughly inappropriate thoughts that had nothing to do with that kitten.

"I had no idea you lived here. I just put in an offer on this house," Katie said, and I was pleased to hear that she did sound at least a tiny bit hesitant about making her revelation. Granted, I could barely hear her reticence over the sound of my jaw grinding. "If I had known…"

"Speaking of your offer," the other woman said, "I'd better get back to the office and see whether we have a response from the seller yet. I know he's anxious to get something done." She smiled and nodded, and within moments, she'd climbed into her car and backed down the drive.

"Right," Levi said. "Well, I should probably get out of here, too."

His departure wasn't unexpected since I knew he had plans for tonight, but I shot him a look anyway so he'd know I thought he was acting like a damn traitor. He didn't have to leave for hours, and the guy never took longer than seven minutes flat to get ready for anything.

"Got a date tonight," he said, winking at Katie and ignoring me. "Double date with Koz and some twins he met last week."

She grinned at him. "Sounds like fun."

"Fun doesn't even begin to describe what I expect it to be." He backed away, waggling his brows suggestively, and headed into my garage for his car before I could stop him.

"Don't stay out too late," I called after him. "And don't let Koz—"

"Are you coming along to babysit us?" he shouted just before disappearing in the garage. "Who'll take care of Tiger?"

"Aww, is his name Tiger?" Katie asked. The kitten was gnawing on her finger and making adorably ferocious sounds, as though trying to prove himself worthy of a name like Tiger. Instead of pulling her hand away, Katie gave him another finger to chew.

"They've been calling him Spanky." Admittedly, I felt like an idiot saying that name, particularly saying it to Katie.

Levi backed his car down my driveway and waved as he turned onto the street. *Asshole.* He could have stuck around until Katie was gone. Now that we were alone, I wasn't sure how to go about this. Not any of it. I hadn't been prepared to run into her today. I had hoped I wouldn't have to bump into her at all, other than maybe at the occasional Storm event, since she might pop in now and then. But here, at my house, when I'd just come home with a kitten who had a ridiculous name? Absolutely not ready for that.

Katie laughed. "Who would give him a name like that?"

I dragged a hand through my hair, realizing too late that I'd just messed it up worse than it likely already was. "They said he was always beating up on all the other kittens when they wrestled even though he was the smallest of the bunch. Runt-of-the-litter syndrome or something." I shoved my hands in my pockets so I wouldn't fuck anything else up with them. "He's an energetic guy."

"I can tell." She held up the fingers that the kitten had been chewing on, which were now pinkish on the tips. Not bleeding, at least. Just irritated.

"Sorry." I don't know why I apologized to her. Not really. I mean, she was the one who had given him her fingers to gnaw on, so it was her own damn fault. Still, *sorry* was one word that had been burned into me from a very young age. I grew up in Canada. Canadians tended to apologize for everything. It was a habit that seven years in the States hadn't cured me of.

"It's fine. Jamie, I—"

She averted her eyes for a moment, staring down at the kitten before raising her gaze again and looking at me full on. Her eyes were this clear blue, lighter than the summer sky and a hell of a lot deeper than the ocean. Her eyes fucking killed me. Always had. I was pretty sure I'd fallen in love with her eyes well before I'd fallen in love with the rest of her. And I had to stop thinking about how much I loved her. It would only do me more harm than good.

"I meant it. I honestly didn't know that you lived here, or I never would have— Do you want me to see if I can take back the offer on the house? I don't want to make you uncomfortable."

I had been growing increasingly more uncomfortable the longer we'd been standing here, but it had a hell of a lot more to do with thinking about moving that kitten away so I would have a better view of her cleavage than it did about the likelihood that she'd be moving in next door.

I shook my head. "If you want the house, buy the house." It wasn't like she would be living with me, just next door. I never really talked to my other neighbors, so she could be like the rest of them. We could wave in passing and leave it at that. Somehow, I could find a way to pretend I didn't know the taste of her lips or the softness of her fingers when she would touch me. Couldn't I? And even if I couldn't, that didn't mean I had to act on anything.

She smiled, but it didn't reach her eyes. "You'd tell me if you didn't want me here, wouldn't you?"

"Your father told me," I blurted out instead of answering her question. Then I wished I could take it back. "That the cancer is back," I finally added.

"I know. He came clean this morning." She swallowed visibly and pushed the kitten back toward me, almost apologetically.

As soon as I took him, he scrambled up my chest and settled into his preferred position on my shoulder, purring up a storm. Katie crossed her arms in front of her. That pushed her breasts in and up.

I had to force myself to meet her eyes. "Why didn't you want me to know?"

"Trying to keep that separation you asked for. That's all."

She shivered, and it was only then that I realized she wasn't wearing a jacket or sweater. Then I felt like an ass.

"Come on," I said, putting a hand over the kitten's back again so I wouldn't jostle him. "Come inside. It's cold out here." I turned and crossed the lawn, heading for my house.

"Jamie…"

"Come inside," I repeated, glancing over my shoulder to find her exactly as I'd left her. "Please."

She looked back at the house she was buying, but then her feet fell into motion, and she followed behind me, a frown creasing her forehead.

It was only once she came into my kitchen that I realized I was doing exactly what I couldn't afford to do—I was letting Katie back into my life, welcoming her in with open arms, and inviting her to beat my heart to a bloody pulp.

Katie

NORMALLY, I DIDN'T have a tentative bone in my body. Yeah, I got stage fright, but that was a different sort of beast. It had never kept me from getting up on the stage and doing my thing. It was just that adrenaline coursed through me in those moments, and the sensation just made everything *different* in some way, more than anything. I knew that about myself, and I could recognize it for what it was, and so I just powered through whenever stage fright hit me. But right now, following Jamie into his house, my feet were as heavy as those Acme anvils that were always dropping on *Looney Tunes* characters.

Ever since Jamie had pulled up with his brother and I'd realized I was buying the house next door to his, I'd been in a state of intense emotional turmoil. It was like having vertigo; I couldn't figure out which way was up, and everything was spinning, and I had no sense of my bearings. He kept looking at me the way a man looks at a woman he wants, but the only thing Jamie wanted from me was to get out of his life.

Supposedly.

I was pretty sure we both knew there was still more there, but it was buried underneath a lot of hurt, and I wasn't sure he was willing to let me unearth it.

Yet here I was, walking into his kitchen while he brought his new kitten home.

He shut the door behind me, and I set my purse on the counter and took a glance around. It was a state-of-the-art kitchen, very similar to the one in the house next door. Jamie's counters were covered with a few small appliances that were surprising, at least if you knew much about him.

"Don't tell me you can use more than a coffeepot and a toaster now," I teased. It wasn't all that long ago that he couldn't do more than make a peanut butter sandwich, at least without running the risk of needing assistance from the nearest fire department.

"Maybe a bit. Zee always told me a guy has to be able to feed himself. I guess I finally listened." Jamie bent over and set the kitten down on the floor, not that it did any good. He'd barely let the kitten go when it let out a pathetic meow and raced back up to his shoulder, causing Jamie to hiss in a breath with his eyes pinched closed. "Those claws are intense," he said when he looked at me again.

"I think he feels safe with you." When I'd held the kitten outside, it had been shaking, and I wasn't convinced that it was just because of the cold. Now he was in a big new house where nothing was familiar. Nothing but Jamie.

"I guess he's going to be my parrot, then."

"You should name him Blackbeard."

"Better him than me." Jamie laughed, and warmth bubbled up inside me. At least I could still make him laugh. "You're sticking around for a while, then?" he asked. He took a couple of glasses out of a cabinet next to the refrigerator and filled them with water before offering me one.

"For a while." I took a sip and eased onto one of his barstools. "Probably for a lot longer than a while."

He nodded. "Because of your treatments."

"Because I think I'm done with Hollywood," I corrected. "At least done with everything I've tried so far." Not that I was ready to go into the particulars. Some things, I wasn't sure he ever needed to know— the things I'd been keeping buried so no one would realize just how badly I'd fucked everything up. They were all disappointed in me enough without knowing the full truth.

Jamie shook his head. "It's what you've always wanted. What you were born to do. You can't just give that up."

"Already have. Derek's not my agent anymore. I don't have anything in the works, and I have no desire to be on a new show or audition for a film. I thought it was for me, but I was wrong."

He bent over the island between us, resting his weight on his forearms. The kitten apparently didn't like that angle, so he hopped down onto the granite countertop, dashing over to attack my fingertips again. Jamie wasn't watching the kitten, though; he was staring at me. Through me. "You come alive when you sing, though."

"Well, maybe I can figure out a way to sing but do it from here. I don't know. I was thinking that I could use the office in that house for a studio, maybe write some songs." I fluttered my fingers, and the kitten leaped for them, sinking a claw into one momentarily. I probably shouldn't be teaching him that fingers were toys, but I didn't have anything better on hand. "Something like that, anyway. Whatever I end up doing, I'm done with LA." The finality of it, of saying it that way, felt good. It felt comfortable, and there wasn't a whole hell of a lot that had given me a sense of serenity in the last few days. Nothing but putting an end to my career in Hollywood and settling on buying that house. It could only mean I was making the right decision.

"So you're staying in Portland?"

I could tell he was trying to make it sound casual, but it came across as anything but. I looked up and held his gaze. "Yeah. I'm staying."

While I wasn't watching him, the kitten made a flying leap for some of my hair that was apparently swinging and looking like prey.

"Not so fast, little guy." Jamie caught him midair just before he latched on to my face with all those razor-sharp claws, and the kitten squeaked in indignation. "I should probably bring in the box of things they sent home with me for him. Food, toys, all that stuff."

"Tell you what," I said. "You keep him in here and figure out something you can make me with one of your fancy new appliances, and I'll go bring it all in so we can get him set up."

"Yeah?" He smiled—a true smile, one of the ones that made his dimples pop out. It gave me hope that maybe—possibly—he would give me a chance to prove I wasn't going anywhere this time.

Now that I had that tiny glimmer of hope, I knew there was nowhere I wanted to be and nothing I wanted to do unless he was there. I'd hurt him a lot, though. I knew it, and there was no easy way around it. I was going to have to fight and claw my way back into his life if I was going to have any chance at getting what I wanted. But at least now, I knew what it was.

I didn't want fame and fortune.

I didn't want Hollywood—the long hours, the intense scrutiny, the sense of never being able to be *enough*.

I didn't want to live my life under a microscope and have every mistake I made blasted out to the world even before I could recognize the implications of what I'd done.

I didn't want guys like Jesse Carmichael, who was more into the high-rolling life that fame could grant him than he was into me. I didn't want guys like Beau Brunetti, who only cared how I looked on his arm when we were in public and who did things I would never be able to speak of when we were in private.

I didn't want a life that would force me to be apart from my family, my friends, the people and life that I'd always known and loved.

I didn't want any of that.

I wanted Jamie Babcock.

"Yeah," I said, trying to impart with that single word all the things I was only starting to understand myself.

"All right, then." Jamie put the kitten back up on his shoulder and headed back toward the fridge. "The box is on the backseat. Blackbeard and I have work to do." When he turned around, he had his arms full with more ingredients than I would have ever imagined he could name, let alone use.

I bit my lower lip, a renewed energy making it next to impossible to keep from grinning. "Be right back."

One thing life had taught me was that a person only had so many opportunities to get the things they really wanted. I didn't yet know how I would do it, but there wasn't a chance in hell I would let this one pass me by.

Chapter Six

Katie

WHILE I SET up Blackbeard's food, water, and litter box—all the while thinking he would *have* to have a different name, even though I'd been the one to suggest it, because Blackbeard was no better than Spanky—and played with him to keep him out of the way, Jamie made us a complete meal using nothing but a waffle iron and a toaster oven. I kept stealing glances at him and what he was doing while he worked, and in all honesty, I was both intrigued and impressed. He was actually cooking! Not only that, but there were enticing smells filtering through the air, and it didn't seem as though the smoke detector was in danger of going off.

After about twenty minutes, he carried two plates to the dining room table. "Ready to eat?" he asked.

I unhinged the kitten's claws from the front of my shirt, set him down on the floor, and joined Jamie. I couldn't hide my shock when I saw what he'd made: ham-and-veggie omelets done in the waffle maker, waffled hash browns, and a cucumber and bell pepper salad. I looked across at him, wide-eyed and slack-jawed.

He gave me a sheepish grin, one that revealed a hint of pride. "I thought breakfast for dinner sounded good. Hope it's all right."

I sunk down onto a chair and put a napkin on my lap. "It looks really good, Jamie." It looked absolutely fantastic, actually, and smelled ten times better than it looked now that it was right under my nose. It might as well have been a full gourmet meal, considering only a few years ago he couldn't make coffee without potentially burning down the building or causing a monumental flood.

Jamie had barely taken his seat when the kitten climbed up first his pant leg, then his shirt, and took up his favorite position. Blackbeard perched himself sitting upright on Jamie's shoulder, staring down at the plate with blue-gray eyes almost as big as his head.

"I think he wants some," I said.

"Not sure if I should give him any. Shouldn't he stick to kitten food?" Jamie craned his head around to look at the kitten, who mimicked his action in reverse. In a flash, Blackbeard nipped the end of Jamie's nose, growling something fierce and pulling back, like he was trying to rip the nose free from Jamie's face.

I cracked up into uncontrollable laughter.

"Oh, you think that's funny?" Jamie rubbed a hand over his nose and looked down at his fingers, as if searching for blood.

"Yes, actually. Hilarious."

He was obviously fighting to hold back his own laughter, pinching his lips into a thin line, but his dimples were peeking out at me. Eventually, he gave in and chuckled, too, trying to re-situate the kitten so it wasn't quite so close to his face. Every time he moved Blackbeard a few inches, though, the kitten just edged closer and dug in harder. There wasn't a chance Jamie would win this battle of wills.

"You might as well just give up and try to eat," I said. "He's not budging."

Jamie let out a beleaguered sigh and, with a final narrowed-eyed glance at his new companion, picked up his fork. "This should be interesting."

It was, at least for me. I couldn't stop myself from watching the show. Blackbeard focused in on Jamie's plate, his nose working overtime as the smells wafted up to meet him. Each time Jamie moved his fork up to his mouth, Blackbeard's head moved right along with it, his neck straining forward in a comical attempt to steal a bite.

Jamie didn't seem inclined to talk, so I followed his lead, paying more attention to my food and watching the kitten's antics. By the time we were about halfway done with our meal, the excitement of the day seemed to catch up with Blackbeard. He ended up lying down across Jamie's shoulder, paws hanging down in the front and back, and his head dangling down Jamie's chest.

"I think he's going to sleep like that," I said.

Jamie twisted his head around and snorted in laughter. That wasn't enough to bother the kitten. Blackbeard's ears twitched, but that was the only sign he wasn't completely lost to the world. "I don't know what it is about my shoulders."

I knew *exactly* what it was about Jamie's shoulders. They were broad and strong enough to carry more than just his own burdens. They were a safe place to lay your head. They were home. But that wasn't something he would want to hear, at least not from me, so I ducked my head down and took another bite, trying to smother my smile so he wouldn't ask me about it.

"Why are you buying a house?" he asked after a minute.

"Is it such a strange thing? You bought a house. It's what people do."

"That's not what I mean. Why aren't you staying with your parents while…" He let his voice trail off, apparently not wanting to speak the words aloud.

"While I go through whatever treatment I have in store?" I finished for him. There wasn't any point in avoiding the issue. Whether either of us was prepared to deal with it or not, cancer was very much back in my life. I flickered my eyes up to find him staring through me again. He'd always had a way of making me feel as if he could see all of me, right down to the thoughts running through my mind so fast that I couldn't catch them and make sense of them. "You remember how Mom was last time. I just need some room to breathe."

"She's just like that because she loves you. Like—" He cut himself off and shook his head. That jostled Blackbeard enough that he slid forward. Jamie didn't reach out to grab him in time, so the kitten tried to slow his fall in the only logical manner—he dug his claws in to Jamie's chest, eliciting a stream of curses and a thin streak of red blood staining his butter-yellow T-shirt.

Jamie went to the sink to clean himself up, leaving the kitten on the table. Blackbeard immediately went for the plate, so I scooped him up, Jamie's words echoing in my head. *She's just like that because she loves you. Like*—like what? *Like your father does?* Or had he been about to say, *Like I do?*

"I'd better put some Neosporin on this or something," Jamie said.

I'd been paying attention to keeping the kitten out of our food, but I looked up when Jamie spoke. He had taken off his shirt to rinse the blood and clean the cut, and was standing there in nothing but his pants. I couldn't make myself look anywhere but at his chest. I'd known it was muscled and defined, but there was no comparison to actually seeing it in person. I wanted to lick it, but I sincerely doubted he would let something like that happen, so I forced myself to look away. That didn't do anything to slow my pulse or stop heat from flooding through my body.

"Probably a good idea," I murmured. I hugged Blackbeard to my face so I could nuzzle my nose in his fur, hoping that would keep Jamie from discovering where my thoughts had gone.

"Careful," Jamie said, winking when I allowed myself to look at him again. "He's vicious. He might bite your nose off." He flicked a finger over the end of his own. Then he disappeared down the hall, leaving me and his kitten to entertain each other.

Blackbeard didn't bite my nose, though. He just purred and closed his eyes, getting comfortable to continue the much-needed nap that had been interrupted.

Jamie had a clean shirt on when he returned, much to my disappointment. He sat down and started eating again. "You can put him down, you know," he said after a couple of minutes.

"I know." I just didn't want to. Blackbeard had fallen asleep in my arms. I carefully lowered him to my lap, keeping one hand around his back to support him so he wouldn't slide. No point in both me and Jamie ending up bloody today. Then I finished my meal, eating with just one hand.

He didn't say anything else for a long time, so I didn't either. He kept staring at me in the way he had that drove me crazy, and I kept staring down at my plate and trying to figure out how I was going to convince him to give me another chance.

"I'm glad you're not leaving," he said quietly.

I lifted my gaze. His eyes were as warm and intense and perfectly serious as ever. "Are you?"

He chewed a bite and swallowed, taking his time. "I am. You should be with your family. You should be with people who love you at a time like this." He set down his fork.

"People like you?" I asked before I could stop myself.

He didn't answer. He just kept staring into my eyes so long that I got self-conscious and had to look away. After a few moments, he picked up his fork again and resumed his meal.

What was I thinking, asking him outright like that? I was still shocked that he was speaking to me and letting me into his house, allowing me to play with his kitten. I might not have a full plan in place for how I was going to earn that chance with him, but I was pretty sure I'd just skipped over steps two through seven hundred forty-three.

When he was done, Jamie got up and cleared away the dishes. "In the mood for dessert?" I couldn't discern anything in his tone, couldn't read anything in his expression. It wasn't like him to put on a mask like that. Or at least it wasn't like how he used to be. I'd changed a lot over the last several years, and Lord knew he had to have changed, as well. He was still Jamie, but there were so many things about him I didn't know now. Things I didn't understand and wasn't sure I ever would.

"Don't tell me you have that in your arsenal, too," I said, trying but failing to keep my tone light and teasing. Instead, my voice cracked with emotion.

He didn't let that faze him, quirking up a grin. "No one makes a microwaveable chocolate mug cake quite like mine." At least that was still the same Jamie I remembered. Nothing ever threw him.

I did my best to return his smile. "Now this I have to see."

He set to work, taking out flour, sugar, cocoa powder, and a half dozen other ingredients. He measured things out in two coffee cups, stirred it all up, tossed in a few chocolate chips, and set the mugs in the microwave. While they cooked, he took some fresh raspberries and a can of whipped cream out of the fridge. He rinsed and dried the berries, put them on top of the chocolate cakes when they came out of the microwave. A shot of whipped cream later, they were ready.

He brought mine over and set it down in front of me, then handed me a spoon. Our fingers brushed in the transfer—accidentally, I assumed, but before I could jerk my hand back, he closed his fingers around mine. They were warm and strong, not to mention familiar. I'd always felt safe in his hands, protected and cherished in his arms.

Right now, I only felt vulnerable. "Jamie?"

"You should be with people who love you," he said, repeating his words from earlier, his voice as strong and sure as his touch. "People like your parents. People like Luke and Dani. People like your friends—your true friends, the ones who've stuck by you through everything, not the ones who just showed up when there was something they thought they could get from you."

I couldn't look at him when he was talking like that, when I felt so open and raw and exposed. I'd laid it all out there for him when I'd asked him my crazy question, leaving no doubt as to where I stood on things between us. On the fact that I still loved him. If I dared to look in his eyes, I would be able to see whether it was the truth or not, no matter what he claimed about his feelings for me. I couldn't bear to know the truth if it wasn't what I wanted to hear. It would hurt so much worse than anything I'd ever been through, and I'd been through a hell of a lot.

But he tipped my chin up with his other hand, and he waited until I looked up into his eyes. "And yes, people like me."

There was no dishonesty in his eyes. They were painfully clear, as pure and sharp as ever. My heart was pounding so hard it was a wonder it didn't burst through my chest, but it was more because of the apologetic tone of his words.

He loved me and he would never lie to me about that.

But he didn't want to love me.

So while he might not ask me to cancel the offer I'd made on the house, and while he might be willing to spend an hour or two with me, cooking and talking and playing with his kitten, he didn't want what I wanted. He didn't want there to be an *us*. He didn't want me. I knew better than to think that would have changed in such a short amount of time, whether I was sick again or not. But I'd still allowed myself to hope.

I eased my chin from his grip, removed my hand from his, and passed his kitten over to him, pushing the chair back so I could stand.

"Katie," he started.

I shook my head, fighting back tears and heading for the door.

"Don't leave. You don't have to go."

"That's just it. You don't want me to *leave*, but you don't want me to *stay*, either." I needed him to want me to stay. Needed it more than I knew how to handle.

I was already at the door, but I'd forgotten my purse. I turned around and grabbed it off the counter. Jamie put his hand on my upper arm, and that was when my tears started.

"I want you to be okay," he forced out.

"I know." I nodded, batting at my tears and backing toward the door. "I know you do." There wasn't a malicious bone in his body. No matter how badly I had hurt him—and I absolutely had—he would never hurt me in return. At least not intentionally. I reached behind me and placed my hand on the knob. "But do you know what I want? I want you to want me again. I don't know if that will ever happen, but if it doesn't, I don't think I will ever be *okay* again."

He cursed beneath his breath and pressed his eyes closed.

"I'm not telling you that to make you feel responsible for anything,"

I said. "I just need you to know. I need you to understand exactly where I'm coming from and where I stand. I'm not going back to LA. I'm staying here, and I am as in love with you as I ever was. I want a chance. I want us to be like we were before."

Blackbeard squirmed out of Jamie's grasp and climbed up to his shoulder perch.

"It doesn't work that way, Katie. We can't go back in time." His voice was rough, like Dad's tended to get when he was all choked up. Jamie was as affected by all this as I was.

"Not backward," I said. "You're right. We can't go back to what we had before. We've both changed. We've been through a lot. We aren't the same as we were before. But I want a chance to go forward. With you." I turned the knob and headed outside. "Think about it," I said, moving toward the house next door and my car. "I'm not going anywhere. I'll be around."

Jamie

I WATCHED KATIE get behind the wheel of her car, but the urge to stop her was one of the most intense internal battles I'd ever waged.

I want you to want me again, she'd said. I'd never stopped wanting her, no matter how hard I'd tried. *I am as in love with you as I ever was.* I might be more in love with her now than I was before, something I had never thought possible. *I want a chance.* Even though I knew I shouldn't, that it was absolutely the wrong choice for me to make, I wanted to give her that chance. I wanted it more than my next breath, but I forced my feet to stay where they were, forced my lips to remain closed so I wouldn't call out.

Blackbeard nipped my earlobe. I tried to jerk my head away from him, but he was having none of that. He put both his front paws up on my face and held me in position, making sure I didn't move by digging in slightly with his claws, and then his rough sandpaper tongue rasped over my cheek repeatedly.

Katie turned her head and watched for a moment. The ghost of a smile came to her lips, probably because of Blackbeard and his antics. Even that wasn't enough to keep her here, though. She backed out to the street, and I tried to dislodge Blackbeard's claws from my flesh without ending up bloody again. But she didn't drive away; she turned in and parked behind my car. She climbed out with the engine still running and left the door open, and she came up my sidewalk like a woman on a mission.

When she reached me, she plucked the kitten free and carried him through the door, setting him on the floor of my front entryway. I followed, bemused. When she straightened, she put her hands on either side of my face, pushed me back against the wall, and stretched up on her toes.

And she kissed me.

It wasn't a sweet kiss, like the ones I'd given her in those months before she'd left to chase her dreams. It was hungry. Needy. Almost violent in intensity. Her lips surged against me. She angled her head, tugging on my hair. Her body fit with mine just like I remembered— breasts tight to my chest, hipbones bumping, my dick coming to life and pulsing against the softness of her belly.

I tried to keep myself from responding, from kissing her back, but it was no use. Touching her again, holding her, was as close to heaven as I would ever be. Her arms went around my neck. I wrapped mine around her waist, picked her up, spun around so the wall could help support her, and I kissed her the way I'd wanted to for years.

She drew her legs up and locked them around me. Her teeth nipped my lower lip. Hard. I sucked in a breath, and her tongue slipped inside to tangle with mine. She wriggled, edging closer, grinding herself against me in a way that felt so fucking good I wanted it to never end.

I ran my hands up her sides, grazing my fingers over her ribs. With the tip of my thumb, I stroked the underside of her breast. She urged me on with a mewling sound coming from deep in her throat.

An inch at a time, I shifted my hand higher, skimming that perfectly soft mound with my palm. Her nipple was a hard nub straining against the center of my palm. I wanted to close my hand over her. To squeeze and knead and mold her to fit my hand. To slip her shirt over her head and strip off her bra. To take her into my mouth.

She arched her back, driving her breast into my palm until I did close my hand over it. She was a perfect fit, just like I'd imagined. I squeezed her softness and nearly lost it.

"Jamie," she said, her mouth by my ear. Just my name. Nothing more. Panting. Or was that me? She kissed my neck. Flicked her tongue along my jaw. Her hands went up under my shirt, and she splayed them over my abs. If she went lower, if the tip of her finger even so much as swept over my cock, I would lose it then and there. I was painfully hard, hard enough to cut diamonds.

But her hand didn't slither any lower, and Blackbeard chose that moment to climb up the inside of my pant leg and sink a claw into my sac through the layers of my clothes. Then he squirmed to get free, which only made the claw go deeper somehow.

"Fuck," I shouted. I mean, there was pain, and there was *pain*. This definitely belonged in the latter category. I lowered Katie and reached down to disengage the kitten that was dangling from my balls by a claw.

Katie looked dazed, at first, but then she glanced down and started giggling.

"Oh, you think that's funny, do you?" I finally worked Blackbeard's claw free and pulled him up so we could see each other, eye to eye. "Not okay, dude," I grumbled, but I couldn't put much heat behind it. Not when Katie was still cackling so hard. The kitten let out an annoyed meow and swatted at my face, so I figured I'd better not let him stay so close to his target. I lowered him to my chest, and he curled up in the crook of my arm, apparently content for the moment to stay there if I measured his comfort by the volume of his purring. I sure as hell wasn't content, though. That wasn't exactly the direction I'd intended for that to go.

"I guess I should say I'm sorry," Katie said through her snickers. "At least for laughing, if nothing else. But I'm not. That was hilarious."

"I doubt you'd think it was so funny if he'd been dangling from your—" I cut myself off before I said something so rude my mother would have washed my mouth out with soap. Using a word like *pussy* was not something I had any business doing around Katie.

She stopped laughing finally, but she was still grinning. "No, I don't guess I would." She leaned in, resting one hand on my chest, and kissed my jaw. "I should go. I just... I just needed to do that."

I reached for her hand as she retreated. I needed to hold on to her even if it was only for a moment longer, which just served to prove that I'd already allowed her back in to my life far more than I ever should have. I was a fucking wreck. She let me hold her fingers for a moment before withdrawing them. Her eyes were filled with just as much heat and lust as her kisses and touch had been, but she was still backing away.

How the fuck could she do this to me all the time, and why in the hell was I letting her do it again? But I was, as sure as the sky was blue. I'd invited her into my house. I'd made her dinner and let her name my damn kitten and watched her play with him, all the while working her way back into my heart. I'd let her come in and kiss me like she meant it.

And now she was walking away again.

What kind of masochist must I be?

She headed out the door again, glancing over her shoulder at me just before getting in her car.

She wanted me to want her? Mission accomplished.

This time, I closed the door and locked it. I didn't know what kind of game she was playing, but at the moment, she was winning. She had me in check. I was pretty sure she wasn't far from checkmate. If I was going to have any chance at coming out ahead, I needed to pay more attention to both her moves and my own.

Chapter Seven

Katie

IT DIDN'T TAKE long at all before I got word that the seller had accepted my offer on the house. Sierra called to fill me in on my way back to Mom and Dad's place after I left Jamie's. The seller wanted to move quickly, and I was paying for it outright instead of taking out a mortgage, so the rest of the process was going to happen fast. "You can start furniture shopping whenever you want," she told me.

We didn't talk long this time, as she needed to get some paperwork started to push the sale through. We were disconnecting the call by the time I parked in front of my parents' house. They were in the living room when I came in, Dad with his feet up on the ottoman, looking as relaxed as could be, and Mom beside him, sitting straight as an arrow and already working on her wine. It was only about seven o'clock, so that probably meant she was seriously upset about something. Dr. Oliver's office would only give my test results to me, not to her, so I had a feeling it was because I'd been out looking for a place of my own. Dad must have filled her in, which was what I'd wanted, but it still made me feel like a chicken coming home to find her like that.

"So?" Dad said when I flopped down on the chair opposite them. He sounded downright chipper. "What did you think about that house in the Northwest District?"

I narrowed my eyes at him. "How do you know I looked at a house over there?"

"Because I suggested it. I knew the house next door to Babs was empty. I texted Sierra and tipped her off that there was a house you might be interested in. Gave her the address and the MLS listing number just so she wouldn't misunderstand exactly which house I meant."

That had Mom leaning away and giving him an oh-no-you-didn't look. I completely understood the sentiment behind her look. "Why would you do that?" Mom demanded, setting her wineglass on the coffee table. There was a lot of hurt in her voice. "She should stay here with us. So we can help her. And you're trying to make it easier for her to leave us? What if she needs—"

"I'm not leaving town or anything," I argued. "You can still help me out." I'd known she would be upset that I wasn't going to stay here, in this house, where she could hover over me constantly, but it seemed to be hitting her even worse because of Dad's involvement. Maybe I shouldn't have filled him in on my plans this morning. I could have told both of them about it now, together, after the fact.

Granted, I probably wouldn't have looked at the house that was soon to be mine, seeing as how Sierra likely wouldn't have thought to show it to me today if not for my father's interference.

"But that would be easier if you were *here*," Mom insisted.

"I did it because I thought they needed a bit of a nudge," Dad said, totally deadpan, redirecting the conversation back to where he wanted it.

"A nudge," I repeated. And he'd said *they* needed a nudge. Not just me. This clearly was not about a house.

"To get back together."

My father was matchmaking. Christ on a cracker, what the hell had gotten into him? "You never wanted us together before."

"Better the devil you know…" Dad let his voice trail off, as though that should be a sufficient answer for his complete about-face. "What I want," he said emphatically after a long moment, "is for my little girl to live a happy, healthy, long life. I want you to have everything you want. I want you to love and be loved, and not just by your mom and me. I want you to know the love of a good man."

He was tearing up, and Mom and I were both openly crying, but he didn't let any of that stop him. "Now we all know that no one can guarantee you the healthy, long life part of it. But you can damn well have love. You love him. And I know, whether he likes the idea of it or not, he loves you. I might not have liked the idea of him a few years ago, but you're an adult now and can make your own decisions. Your heart decided on Babs. That happened a hell of a long time ago. There aren't many men in this world better than him, and there are a lot of things I can overlook if it means you have a man like Jamie Babcock in your life."

I wasn't so sure he'd still be singing that tune if he knew I'd basically just mauled Jamie in his front hall, but it was probably better if I didn't mention things like that. What Dad didn't know wouldn't hurt Jamie, and I had no doubt Dad meant things of that nature when he mentioned the *things he could overlook.* He had threatened every guy I'd ever dated to within an inch of his life over things as simple as chaste kisses and holding hands. I knew it had been hard on my father when TMZ and the other paparazzi and gossip sites had followed me around with the guys I'd dated in Hollywood. Every time I'd come home to Portland, I'd gotten an earful of it myself, Dad griping about everything from the clothes I wore in public to why I would allow any man to objectify me in the ways that some of them had. He didn't even know the worst of it, and it was best if it stayed that way.

The fact was, Jamie couldn't be more different from those guys. He was kind and sweet and thoughtful. When he'd touched me a while earlier, and I'd put my hands on his flesh, that had been the most intimate we had ever been together. Years ago, he'd never done more than kiss me, and even then, his kisses had often been of the tender and chaste variety. Everything had been aboveboard and proper. He never would have touched me like that before, putting his hand on my breast. Even today, he'd been cautious about it, at least in comparison to me. If Blackbeard hadn't interrupted us like he had, I might have attempted to take things a whole lot further.

At least I knew Dad and I were on the same page when it came to Jamie now. I got up for a tissue, and I brought the box back with me, passing it over to Mom. She took the box, but Dad plucked out a couple of tissues for himself and settled me against his side, the way he used to hold me when I was a little girl. I tucked my feet up alongside him, resting my head on his shoulder.

Dad's shoulders were safe, too—like Jamie's—but they weren't home. Not anymore. They were still a comfort, though.

"Are you mad at me?" Dad asked.

I shook my head, still crying too hard to speak.

Mom didn't let him off so easy. "David Weber, I have been underestimating you. That's the kind of move I would expect to come up with myself. Not you." She wasn't kidding about doing things like that. Mom tended to use a heavy hand when it came to getting people to do her bidding, always sticking her nose in other people's business and convincing them she was right. She usually was, but that was beside the point.

I was still stuck on the fact that my father was butting in to things that he would normally steer clear of. I dried my eyes and blew my nose, and then I inched back enough that I could look him directly in the eye. "Did you know anything about that house other than Jamie lived next door?"

"Not a thing, until after I'd looked up the listing," he said, grinning like a proud papa, despite the tears still making his eyes glisten. "The pictures online are nice. That home office could be fun. Did you like it?"

"Loved it," I said, narrowing my eyes at him. "I put in an offer for it."

"Did you?" he replied, not even attempting to hide how pleased he was with himself.

"I did. And it's been accepted."

"Imagine that."

Jamie

THE NEXT FIVE games on our schedule were all at home. We came away with a divisional win against the Vancouver Canucks, almost solely due to our goaltender, Nicklas Ericsson, standing on his head through the whole game. We only managed to put up two goals, one of them seriously flukey, and we gave the Canucks more opportunities to score than they should have had in a week of games. Nicky didn't bat an eye, though. He stopped every shot they sent his way, and he came off the ice with a smile on his face, telling us all what a good job we'd done in front of him.

It was a bald-faced lie, and he knew it, but I was just glad he was keeping his head on straight. He'd been in and out of the net over the last several years, even getting sent down to the minors for a full season, because of some addiction problems. That all seemed to be a thing of the past, or at least he was being diligent about his sobriety.

Lately, he had been a rock in goal. Good thing, too, because the rest of the team? We had been an utter wreck all season, and in particular tonight. We'd been lucky to come away with any wins so far this year, considering how we'd been playing. We couldn't let it keep going like this, either. The luck that had been following us around would eventually give out, and we would start losing, maybe even in some games that we ought to win. That was just how it went in the NHL.

Players-only meetings tended to happen after a really bad loss, usually in the middle of a stretch of other bad losses. It wasn't common to call for one after a win, especially when it seemed like the team just hadn't found a groove in the new season. But we were a team with a lot of expectations for being a contender for the Stanley Cup this year— from ourselves, our fans, the media—and we couldn't afford to fall into a slump. Tonight, the Canucks should have won by a mile. At this point, something needed to be said, and nothing the coaches or team executives had to say to the guys had been getting through.

So after we left the ice and everyone bumped heads with Nicky, congratulating him for his shutout that saved our bacon, I went over to Bergy. He was about to give his postgame speech to the boys, but what I had to say needed to come first.

"Can you give me a few minutes with them?" I asked.

He gave me one of his intense appraisals that used to make me twitchy. The guy had a hell of an evil eye, but I'd come to understand that he wasn't trying to kill me with laser beams or anything when he looked me over like that. Instead, it was more that he was attempting to get a read on my thoughts. Kind of like he was discerning the things I didn't say so he could piece the whole puzzle together. "It's your team," he finally said. "You do what you think is necessary."

He gave Webs and Adam Hancock, the other assistant coach, a nod, and all three of them filed out of the locker room. Webs had an odd look in his eye, and his lips were pursed together all wonky, and I didn't have the first clue what that was about. I wasn't really in the mood to explore it, either, considering it likely had something to do with Katie. Had she told him how I'd had my hands all over her? He might be plotting my death at this very moment, or if not that, something equally unpleasant. Still, he left with the other coaches, so I figured I had at least until I was done talking to the boys. After that, I might need to get Levi to act as a lookout for me. Or maybe Coop. Coop was still a wide-eyed rookie, so he was easier to boss around. Levi always acted like I'd lost my mind for thinking he would do what I told him to. That was the problem with brothers.

Time to get on with it. I closed the door behind the coaches and locked it.

When I turned around, Wheels caught my eye and nodded, similar to the look Bergy had given me. I glanced over at Burnzie, who gave me a get-on-with-it wave, and then I caught the eye of Marc "Danger" d'Aragon. Danger was another older guy, like Wheels, who'd been with the Storm for a few seasons now. He'd been wearing the other *A* since we'd found out Soupy had definitely torn his ACL and wouldn't be back the rest of the season. Danger's face was an expressionless mask right now, which I knew meant he felt exactly how I did about the shitty way we'd played this game. He was always joking and smiling, unless things weren't going well. Checking him for a grin was the easiest way to tell where he stood.

I cleared my throat, and the boys all focused in on me. Once the guys realized the door was closed and it was just us, all the talk and laughter died off pretty fast. Everyone took a seat at their stalls, still stripping off their gear but doing it without the usual chatter. Some of the guys looked sheepish, probably because they recognized their own shitty play. Others looked rebellious. Koz, in particular, looked like he wanted to blame someone else even though he'd been one of the biggest problems out there tonight. Yes, he had a ton of offensive skill, but he'd completely ignored the idea of helping out on defense.

"We won tonight," I finally said, choosing my words carefully. "But we shouldn't have, and I think every guy in this room fucking knows it."

Koz let out a snort, and a few guys, including Levi, shot him looks from all around the room. I kept going, doing my best to ignore his interruption.

"The whole fucking season so far, we've been playing sloppy hockey. We're making stupid passing through the middle without looking up to see the forward from the other team who's streaking in. We're trying to make pretty plays with the puck instead of just dumping and chasing or trying to get a greasy goal. We're getting completely away from Bergy's system. We're putting too much pressure on our goaltenders, and we're forgetting the idea of five guys playing as a unit in every zone. Turnovers in the neutral zone. Forwards hanging out up high waiting on the *D* to get the puck out of the zone instead of backchecking. *D* giving the other team too much time and space instead of playing them hard. And there's no fucking excuse for any of it. It ends now. Everybody pulls his fucking weight. We're going to forget all about playing a *pretty* game and just focus on the basics. Anyone who can't do that, who tries to get too fucking fancy and screws things up for the rest of us, is going to have to answer to the room."

"Answer how?" Koz demanded, as surly as I'd ever heard him. Probably because he knew he was one of the biggest offenders. At least half the things I'd listed, he'd been guilty of tonight. "You might be captain, but you're not God. You can't make us do shit."

"If you were paying more attention to what's happening on the ice than flirting with that girl in the front row, maybe we wouldn't be having this talk," Burnzie shot back at him. "If Babs says you're going to answer to us, you're going to fucking answer."

"Says who?" Koz demanded. "You? Yeah, let's see you make me."

"Come on over here. I'll be happy to." Burnzie cracked his knuckles.

Jonny stood up, slowly taking off his gear. He could have done that sitting down, but I got the sense that he was trying to send a message. I wasn't sure who he was sending it to, though—Burnzie or Koz.

I should have thought this through better before speaking up, and I needed to figure things out fast, before animosity completely took over the room. Should I have guys put money in a till? A set amount would hurt some more than others because of the huge differences in contracts from one player to the next. Extra reps in the gym? That could end up helping the team even if it sucked for the guy having to do them, I supposed. But no matter what I settled on, how was I going to enforce any of it? The whole thing was going to fall on my shoulders, since I was the one instituting it. I was still racking my brain for the best solution when Wheels spoke up.

"Suicides after practice, ten percent of your earnings for that game to the charity of your choice, and taking over rookie duties for a week sounds fair. Maybe on a sliding scale, depending on how many times you fuck up in a game."

Sounded brutal to me, but maybe something brutal was called for before our season went down the drain. Suicides—skating from one line to another and back repeatedly—were guaranteed to make your thighs and lungs burn. Ten percent of a guy's pay for a game, no matter what kind of salary he earned, was enough to make a dent in his wallet. And most guys were glad to be done with being a rookie as soon as possible because of how much they got razzed. When it came right down to it, we put them through a bit of hazing. Nothing horrible.

They had to carry bags for the veterans, pick up pucks after practice, things like that. Once a guy got past his rookie season, though, he never wanted to be stuck handling those tasks again. In fact, the idea that Wheels was the one suggesting it made me do a double take. He had to be willing to do those things himself or he would never have suggested it as a blanket rule. He wasn't perfect; he fucked up in games just as much as the rest of us.

"No fucking chance I'll do any of that," Koz said. He laughed, too, and nodded at Levi with a cocky grin. "Right, 501? That's bullshit."

"What's bullshit is the way you played tonight," Burnzie said. "If you would stop prancing around out there—"

Koz jumped to his feet and was halfway across the room, eyes bulging. "Who the fuck is prancing?"

Burnzie was on his feet in a flash. Fists flew before I knew what was happening. I rushed in to break them up, but everyone else had the same thought and someone landed a punch right on my nose. Well, not quite everyone. Wheels and Danger grabbed me and dragged me back, with Wheels saying, "Let them go at it. Koz needs to have his ass whipped."

I put a hand to my nose. No blood, at least, but it was fucking sore.

Everyone was shouting over each other to be heard. A few more guys than just those two started throwing punches. This was absolutely not what I'd had in mind. Not even close.

But then someone whistled, high and loud, and guys started to back off. Jonny was in the middle of the room, standing over the Storm logo, with both Burnzie and Koz trapped in headlocks, one under each arm. They were still trying to get at each other, but Jonny wouldn't let go until he was good and ready to. "You two dipshits want me to crack your skulls together? There's nothing I would enjoy more, I can promise you that. Cool your fucking jets."

The rest of the guys helped him separate the two, and everyone gradually settled back into their stalls. Koz had a red welt over one eye that was bound to leave him with a nasty shiner. Burnzie was holding his hand funny like maybe he'd hurt it when he'd busted Koz's face.

I turned to Wheels and Danger, hoping for some wisdom. "Now what do I do?" I asked, keeping my voice down.

Danger grinned. He fucking grinned, like he was enjoying this. "Let it work itself out. Teams need something to bring them together. Sometimes it's bonding on road trips. Sometimes it's overcoming a bunch of injuries. And then there are the times like this."

"This doesn't seem like something that'll bring anyone together," I muttered. "Seems like something that'll drive a wedge in the middle of us. Guys'll pick sides. I don't know."

Wheels just crossed his arms in front of him and nodded. "Maybe. There's always that risk. But I've seen it happen. Let things settle down, and we'll see where we're at." He reached overhead and tugged his shirt up and off from behind. "I bet that was all it'll take to keep from having guys skate suicides and all, though."

My stomach soured. Maybe he was right, but I had a strong sense that he was wrong and I'd just fucked everything up for the whole team. I should have just kept my damn mouth shut.

Jim and Bergy never should have made me the captain. The guys deserved better than what I was able to give them.

I'D BEEN LYING in bed, thoughts racing through my mind, for almost an hour when my phone dinged. When I shifted to grab it off the nightstand, I dislodged Blackbeard. He gave me an irritated meow and a sleepy scowl before circling his spot three or four times and resettling on my pillow. Even when he slept, he liked to be curled up on my shoulder, or more specifically, on the pillow, nestled in the space where my neck and shoulder met. I waited until he was cozy again and then unlocked my phone screen to see who was texting me at this hour.

It was from Ray "Razor" Chambers, a guy who had been my best friend since our rookie season, even though he could be an ass. We'd been nearly inseparable in the early part of our careers. After two years, though, he'd been traded for a draft pick—the same pick that Jim Sutter had used to select Levi. Razor had gone off to play for the Sabres, and over this past summer, he'd been picked up by the Thunderbirds in the expansion draft. The only reason he would be up this late was that the T-Birds were on the road right now, playing on the West Coast. They'd be here in Portland in a few days. I had promised to buy him dinner when they got to town.

I debated ignoring his message until morning, because it was probably just about that dinner, but decided against it. With everything that had happened after the game tonight, plus the fact that I couldn't get Katie and the way she'd kissed me out of my mind, there wasn't a chance in hell I'd be sleeping any time soon. I opened his message.

What the fuck kind of captain are you to call a meeting and then let the guys come to blows?

I'd hoped that we would be able to keep all of that in the room. Bergy and the other coaches hadn't said anything when they'd come in, although there was no doubt they knew *something* was up. But the media had been just outside that door, waiting for it to be opened up for their scrum. They must have heard.

Me: *What do you know about it?*

Razor: *Polanski and a dozen other reporters were live-tweeting while it went down, whatever it was. It's bad, Babs. It's all over the blogs. Mom said TSN talked about it on-air tonight. What the fuck is going on in there?*

Me: *You know I'm not going to tell you. These things stay in the room.*

Razor: *It's me, Babs. You know I won't say a fucking word to anyone.*

Me: *Exactly. It's you, and you're not part of this team anymore. No fucking chance.*

Razor: *Fine. But if there's anyone you want me to go a round with when we get to Portland, you just say the word. I'll gladly bash someone's face in for you.*

Me: *You're my fucking hero.*

Razor: *Apparently you need someone to play the hero. Can't keep your team in line. Jim should have tried harder to keep Zee around. No chance anyone would pull that shit with Zee as the captain, and then I wouldn't have to deal with him here.*

Me: *Ha fucking ha.*

Razor: *Seriously, I will break someone's face for you. Just say the word. It'd be my pleasure to sort out your team's personality issues since you can't seem to do it. Think about it.*

Me: *Yeah, playing the martyr. Shocker.*

Razor: *Hey, it's not like anyone'll think anything's out of the ordinary. Since we can't seem to fucking score, let alone keep anyone else from scoring, guys are fighting every game. Trying to prove their worth or some shit. Hunter's about to go ballistic.*

Me: *I'm sure all that fighting's helping you score more.*

Razor: *I'm scoring more with the ladies.*

Me: *Never would have thought that was an issue for you.*

Razor: *Because I'm not fucking hung up on a girl? One who isn't just as hung up on me as I am on her?*

Me: *You don't know anywhere near as much as you think you do.*

Razor: *You going to deny the fact that Katie Weber has you completely pussy whipped? I bet you still haven't been laid. Jamie Fucking Babcock, the millionaire fucking virgin All-Star who all the girls are ga-ga over. They don't even know they'd be breaking you in.*

Me: *Like I'd tell you if I was? Besides, I meant you don't know as much about Katie as you think.*

Razor: *You think Katie's still a virgin? Not fucking likely. Anyone with an Internet connection or a smart phone has seen her plastered all over TMZ with all sorts of douchebags, and I promise you, she's been tapped. Multiple times. Who the fuck do you think you're saving yourself for?*

Me: *Shut your fucking mouth, talking about her like that.*

Razor: *If that's not it, then what the fuck did you mean?*

Me: *I meant I'm not the only one still hung up.*

I don't know why I would tell him that. Hell, I don't know why I'd ever let him in on the fact that I was still a virgin years ago. He knew, and Levi knew, but that was it. I was just lucky he hadn't said anything about it to the guys, and I had to skate a fine line with Levi all the time to be sure he didn't open his big mouth and blab. Things like that get around a locker room really fast, and I had always taken enough heat from the guys just because I had a baby face that girls liked. I had dimples, I blushed easily, girls screamed for me at games and whatnot like I was in a damn boy band... Add *virgin* to that, and they would torture the ever-living shit out of me until I buried my head in the sand and retired.

Regardless of all that, there was no reason for me to tell Razor about Katie. About how she wanted to be with me again. No reason to let on about any of it. I wasn't planning to act on her suggestions, and I'd already allowed her to take things further than I should have. What purpose would filling Razor in serve?

Razor: *She still wants you? If she's sticking around and you don't figure out a way to put a ring on her finger, you're a bigger fucking idiot than I thought you were.*

Who knew Razor could be philosophical?

Chapter Eight

Katie

TODAY WAS TURNING into one of my busiest days in recent memory. It was barely after lunchtime, and I was already exhausted. In the morning, I'd gone in for the closing on my house. I was officially a homeowner now, and at the moment, I was sitting on the empty floor of my house. I had a bunch of stuff being delivered tomorrow morning, and I wanted to have a plan in place. I was trying to get a good visual formed in my mind for furniture placement when my phone rang, interrupting my solitude.

I dug my phone out of my purse. Dr. Oliver's office was calling. Nausea swamped me almost immediately upon seeing his name flash up on the screen. I pressed my eyes closed, flopped down to lie on my back, and answered the call.

"Hello?"

"Katie? It's Dr. Oliver."

Not one of the nurses or a receptionist, even. He was calling me himself. That couldn't bode well for whatever he had to tell me. Every part of my body tensed in preparation to hear the worst, even though I knew there was no chance he'd tell me over the phone. That wasn't how doctors worked, typically.

"I take it my test results are back?" I said, sounding a lot more put-together than I felt.

"Just got the last of them this morning. I need you to come in so we can discuss what we've found and come up with a treatment plan."

That definitely wasn't a surprise. We already knew it was cancer, so at this point, *any* result would be in-person-appointment worthy.

"Okay. Tell me when, and I'll be there."

"Can you be here at two? I'll have my receptionist move my schedule around."

Two o'clock. Meaning today. I glanced at my watch. Meaning in just over an hour.

Meaning no time to prep myself for the news I'd been dreading.

"Yeah," I said, my tongue thick from the effort of holding back my tears. "Two o'clock. I'll be there."

We hung up, and I pressed my hands to my stomach, wishing it would make the churning stop.

I probably should have someone go with me in case I had an emotional breakdown and couldn't drive. That seemed like the smart thing to do, but who?

Dad was still up at the practice facility, surely. He rarely got home before mid-to-late afternoon these days. He had a job to do, so I shouldn't call him and ask him to go with me.

I *should* call Mom, but I wasn't sure I could handle her being with me for getting the news, whatever it might be. It would be easier to deliver it to her if I knew what was going on and decided how best to fill her in. At home. On *my* terms. Nope, definitely not calling her right now.

For a moment, I tossed around the idea of looking up one of my high school friends. They all had jobs, though, and couldn't just take off in the middle of a workday with no notice. They had their own lives to lead, and they couldn't just drop everything to come with me and hold my hand for a doctor's appointment. This wasn't an emergency. It wasn't life or death...well, not *immediately* life or death, at least.

In the end, I decided I'd just go alone. If it was too much for me to handle by myself, I could call someone to come and get me or take a cab. Something.

I dragged myself up from the floor, grabbed my purse, and headed out the front door. I'd just put my key in the lock when Jamie's car stopped in his driveway. Not only that, but he opened his car door and got out instead of driving into the garage. Under normal circumstances, I would be glad that he'd gotten out instead of pretending he hadn't seen me. This wasn't normal, though. This was as far from normal as possible.

My hands were shaking so badly that I fumbled with the lock. I tucked the stray hair that had slipped out of my ponytail behind my ear and tried to slow my breathing and my pulse so I could get the shaking under control. No go. The keys dropped out of my hand and hit the porch. "Damn it."

"You all right?" Jamie asked. He was right behind me, close enough I'd step on his foot if I took a step back. Close enough I could feel the warmth of his body all along my backside.

"Fine." I bent down to get the keys.

When I straightened, he reached for them. Or for me. His hand closed over mine, steady and strong. "You're shaking," he said. He put his other hand on my waist, drawing me back toward him. "You're not cold. What's wrong?"

"Why does something have to be wrong?"

"Because I know you." He said it so matter-of-factly. And it was the truth. He knew me, maybe better than I knew myself sometimes.

His body heat enveloped me, even though we were barely touching. He was like a protective shell around me, guarding me from whatever life might throw at me. Or maybe that was just what I wanted him to be, and he was letting me believe in the fantasy for a while. I wanted to lean back against him. I wanted to press my length against his and allow myself to pretend, for a little bit longer, that he could be my harbor in the storm I was about to face.

"You're crying," he said, his mouth just behind my ear. "It kills me when you cry."

"Would you believe they're happy tears? I just bought a house."

"But you're shaking too hard to lock the door."

I supposed that meant he didn't believe my excuse.

He released my hand, easing the keys into his grip. Then he locked the door for me and nudged my arm until I faced him. His eyes were deep wells of concern, searching me, and he brushed a tear from my cheek with the backs of his knuckles. "Tell me. Whatever it is. You said you want another chance. You want me to want you. So tell me." He chucked me under the chin with his other hand, keeping me from turning away again. "Talk to me."

"I don't even know if it's anything worth crying over." That was a lie. Cancer was definitely a cry-making kind of thing, and saying even that much only made my tears kick into overdrive.

Jamie's eyes traveled over me, probing as though he could ferret out the answers he wanted with nothing more than his gaze. I couldn't handle the scrutiny. I felt as though he were peeling away all the layers of secrecy I'd built around myself over the years. If there were ever anyone I could feel safe opening up to about it all, someone I could trust to share my fears with, it was Jamie, but I couldn't bear the thought of what he might think of me when he knew the truth.

I tried to shrug away from him, but he slipped an arm around my waist and held me close, and his lips pressed against my temple. And I was toast. I was putty in his hands, his to mold in any way he saw fit.

"You're not shaking anymore," he murmured, his lips still touching my skin. "Tell me, Katie. Let me help."

It just wasn't in me to deny him anything. Not right now. "I have to go get my test results from my oncologist," I forced out.

He nodded, his jaw brushing my forehead, and both his arms tightened around me, cocooning me and giving me a safe haven, at least for the moment. I let my head fall forward, nestling it on his shoulder, even though I would make a mess of his shirt with my tears.

"When?" he asked.

"Now. He's fitting me in at two."

"Is your mom meeting you there?"

I shook my head.

"Your dad, then?"

I tried to answer, but another sob came out instead.

"Damn it, Katie. You haven't told anyone, have you?"

"No."

"You can't do this alone." He smoothed a hand over my hair, brushing it back from the tears on my cheek. "Come on. I'll take you." He took my hand and led me to his car. I let him because right now, I needed someone to take over. Someone had to take charge, tell me what to do, and make sure I did it. I allowed myself this moment of weakness because conserving my strength was an absolute necessity right now, and would continue to be for a long time to come.

Kicking cancer's hairy ass out of my life the first time had taken more than I'd thought I had to give. I didn't get the sense that this would be one of those things that got easier with practice. I was going to need every bit of strength I could muster and then some if I was going to come out on the other side of this.

Jamie opened the car door and waited until I was situated. Then he closed the door and crossed to the driver's side. He put his key in the ignition and started the motor, but instead of shifting into reverse, he reached for my hand.

I shot my gaze up. His expression was fierce and caring at the same time.

"I do want you, you know," he said. "I want you more than I know what to do with. I've never stopped wanting you. I don't think I ever will, either, and I can't handle losing you again."

I blinked back a couple more tears. He was going to give me another chance. "I'm not going anywhere, Jamie," I said. "I already told you that."

"No, you're not leaving. And you're not going to die on me, either. You got that?" He squeezed my hand so hard it almost hurt. "I'm not going to let you. So you just need to get it in your head right now that you're going to fight this with everything you have and then some. Anything less isn't going to cut it. All right?"

I sniffled and put my other hand over the top of his, my insides tingling from all the feelings racing though me. I nodded, never breaking eye contact. "I've got it. I'm ready to fight." If he stayed by my side, I could do anything.

"Good." Then he kissed me so hard I felt it all the way down to my toes. He sucked my lower lip into his mouth briefly before breaking off and putting the car in gear.

My face was still drenched from my crying. I dug around inside my purse to find some tissues. "How is it that I'm always crying when you kiss me?" I finally fished out my tissue pack and took one out to blow my nose.

He quirked up a grin, glancing at me with a heated expression before backing out of the drive. "Not *always*. I seem to recall a recent kiss that didn't involve tears."

"Well, there was that one," I conceded. Still, there needed to be more kisses and fewer tears. It looked like I might finally get my way, too.

Jamie

"THYROID CANCER," KATIE repeated after the doctor.

I clutched her hand tighter, unsure if I meant to reassure her or myself. Now that I'd made up my mind that I couldn't *not* have her in my life, the last thing I wanted to do was sit here in a doctor's office and listen while he told us all the things that might take her away from me. I'd rather be at home with her. Holding her. Showing her how much I wanted her in ways that proved how words failed. That was going to have to wait, though.

I was just glad she'd let me in to meet with her doctor. This was something she shouldn't go through alone, not any part of it.

Dr. Oliver nodded. "Right now, the tumor is small. It doesn't appear to have spread at this time, but we won't know for certain until we get in there—"

"Get in there," she interrupted. "In my throat." Her panicked gaze flickered over to me and back to the doctor. Her eyes glistened with unshed tears again. She'd had all sorts of procedures before, so I wasn't sure why she was freaking out so badly this time.

He gave her an appraising look. "Yes. You know how this works. We have to remove all traces of the cancer or it will only grow and spread."

"I know, but… How close is the thyroid to the vocal chords?"

Fuck. It hadn't crossed my mind. If anything went wrong…

Over the next hour or more, the doctor answered all Katie's questions and mine as well as he could. Yes, there was a possibility her vocal chords could be damaged in the surgery. No, it wasn't likely. They eventually settled on radiation first, then chemo, hoping to shrink the tumor as much as possible in order to minimize the risk of complications during surgery, even though that wasn't standard procedure for this type of cancer. I got the sense that he was changing it more to appease her than anything. No, he couldn't guarantee that she would be able to sing again.

With every question we asked and with every answer he gave, Katie's tension grew. She was close to falling apart at the seams, and I was the one who would have to catch all the pieces and stitch her back together again.

I tried to absorb everything the doctor was telling her about the treatment plan he thought was best and the time frame for each component of her care. No matter how clearly he laid it all out there, I doubted she was taking much of it in. She kept going back to the thyroidectomy that would have to be performed. Back to the thought that she could lose the ability to speak or sing or do any of the things that had been her dream since well before I'd met her. Back to the notion that she might lose herself, or maybe the idea of herself that she'd been holding on to for so long.

We finally finished up. Dr. Oliver handed me a manila folder full of paperwork detailing the treatment plan. I tucked it under my arm and shook his hand, and Katie headed up to the receptionist's desk to pay for today's visit.

"She's going to need help," he said once she left the meeting room. "Going through radiation and chemotherapy isn't easy for anyone, but it seems to be more debilitating in cases like this, when the patient has already been through it before. She thought she'd put it all behind her, but now it's happening all over again. She's going to need people to keep her spirits up."

I nodded my understanding, still processing everything that had happened in the last few hours.

"Depression is common in cancer patients," he added. "And if it becomes severe, it can derail any treatment we can give her."

"Are you telling me I need to keep her happy? Because I don't know if that's something I have any control over." In fact, I would wager the opposite was true. There were a hell of a lot of things I didn't know about life, but I did know that no one could force anyone else to be happy. Life just didn't work that way.

"I'm telling you that you need to keep a close eye on her emotional health, not just her physical health. It's just as important, and just as deadly."

"All right." That I could do. I was already going to be doing it, but it wouldn't hurt to have it spelled out explicitly like that. "And if she needs help?"

"Make her get it."

Those words were still echoing in my mind twenty minutes later when I parked in front of Webs and Laura's house. Katie had asked me to come with her and help her explain everything to them, and I didn't think it was the best idea to let her drive herself anywhere right now, anyway. She kept spontaneously bursting into uncontrollable tears, which I doubted would make for easy or safe driving.

It felt weird walking up the sidewalk and going through the door with her hand in mine. Weird didn't even begin to cover it when her parents both looked up from the living room.

Laura took one good look at her daughter and was instantly on her feet and crossing to us. "What is it? What's wrong?" She reached for Katie to draw her in for a hug, but Katie inched closer to my side. She shook her head, her eyes flashing over to me in a plea, and Laura visibly blanched.

"Katie met with Dr. Oliver," I explained. I worked my hand free and held Katie's waist, drawing her in as if I could shield her from the world. If only it were so simple.

Laura's eyes filled with tears as Katie nestled into my arms. She crossed her arms in front of her since she couldn't put them around her daughter. "What…" Her voice cracked, and she looked away and put a hand over her mouth.

"Why don't we all go sit in the living room so we can talk about it?" I suggested.

Webs was still in there, his feet up on an ottoman. He shut down the iPad he'd been watching game film on and followed me with his eyes every step of the way as we joined him, Laura trailing behind me and Katie. I was pretty sure Laura had gotten her feelings hurt when Katie had chosen me for comfort instead of her. Maybe because I'd been the one with Katie at the doctor, too. I never wanted to hurt Laura, but I had to admit that it had made my chest puff up a bit when Katie had burrowed in to me.

Katie and I sat on the love seat across from her father.

Webs had his eyes zeroed in on me. I suppose it was more us than just me. He focused on how she leaned into me. Was he back to trying to intimidate me? I had gotten past that years ago. Katie was shaking again, like she had been when I'd gotten home from practice this afternoon, so I put a hand on her waist and nestled her closer to my side. When I looked up, I thought Webs gave me a nod. But that couldn't be. Could it?

Laura's banging kitchen cabinet doors drew his attention away from me, at least for the moment. She had gone in there before joining us, and when she returned, she had a bottle of wine and a bunch of glasses on a tray. "Figured we might need it," she said. "Or at least I will." She poured a couple of glasses and offered them around, but no one took her up on it. I figured she would need it more than I would, knowing her as I'd come to over the years. Laura wasn't an alcoholic. She tended to have a glass or two every evening, for the most part, nothing excessive. But there were definitely times that she used wine to help keep her calm. Once we'd all turned her down, she curled up on the sofa next to Webs, both wineglasses still in her hands. "More for me, then."

Webs put an arm around her shoulders as she drank from one of them. Once she was settled and had guzzled about half a glass, he nodded across at us. "All right. What's the deal? Do we have a plan?"

Katie swallowed hard enough I could hear it, and her entire body tensed at my side.

"It's thyroid cancer this time, not leukemia," I answered for her, and she softened so much that she melted into my side. Dealing with her parents—her mom in particular—about anything to do with cancer had always been hard for her. I could do it, though. I could take that responsibility from her and let her save her energy for the much bigger fight she had ahead. "Dr. Oliver wasn't surprised it was a different type of cancer than before. He said that isn't uncommon after chemo."

Laura finished her first glass and set it on the coffee table, bringing the rest of the bottle back to her lap. I kept going, laying out the finer points of everything the doctor had told us. Surprisingly, Laura still had half a bottle left by the time I finished my recitation.

"So radiation again, then more tests, then maybe chemo, then more tests, then surgery," Webs said, boiling it all down to the basic parts.

"And probably more radiation after surgery," I said, nodding.

Laura sat up, placing the wine bottle back on the table. "How long are we looking at before surgery?"

"Not long enough," Katie choked out.

"Too long," her father countered.

"But what if—"

"*What if*, nothing," Webs cut in. "The tumor has to come out. From what you've told us, they're going to try to shrink it first with the radiation and lower the risk of complications."

"Which are rare," I added. "Less than two percent, so you have a ninety-eight percent chance that everything will be perfectly fine with your vocal chords after the surgery is complete and you have time to heal."

Katie turned her head to look up at me, mountains of hurt forming tears in her eyes. "You're supposed to have my back on this."

"I do have your back." Which meant I would do everything in my power, including gang up on her with her parents, to make sure she had the best chance at living. She could be mad at me all she wanted, but I wasn't going to budge on this. Katie was too important for anything less. "You remember what you promised me?" I asked, dropping my voice so her parents wouldn't overhear.

She pressed her lips into a thin line instead of answering.

"You promised you would fight with all you had," I reminded her, "and I promised I would do everything I could to make sure you came out of this on the other end. I meant it. Did you?"

This time, she glared at me, but there was some heat behind it. It was a bit of the fight she would need to get through this, I hoped, and not just Katie putting up her back and digging in her heels.

Webs straightened himself, taking his feet off the ottoman and setting them on the floor. He bent over his knees, his fingers laced together, and met Katie's eyes. "All surgeries come with risks. The risk of leaving the cancer in there is so much higher, though, baby girl."

She turned to face her parents again, extracting herself from my arms. "I don't want the surgery. I'll do the radiation and the chemo, all of that. I'll do it as many times and for as long as it takes, but I don't want the surgery. Maybe we can shrink the tumor enough that it just disappears."

That seemed like a huge leap to me, but she was holding on to the idea with both hands, not letting go.

"I can't— I can't lose that part of myself."

"You can if it means you'll live," Laura said.

"What kind of life will it be if I can't do the things I love?"

My gut twisted at the anguish in her voice. I pressed my thumb and fingers to my temples, trying to imagine a future in which Katie couldn't sing. Just the thought of it was as bad as a future without hockey for me.

But a life without Katie was so much infinitely worse that it was unfathomable.

"It would still *be* a life," I argued.

For what felt like an eternity, Katie didn't say anything. She looked from one of us to another, seemingly searching for an ally to support her argument. But we *were* her allies. We were on her side.

She just couldn't see it.

"Well, there's time before we have to worry about it," Laura said. She got up and took her half-full bottle of wine and all the glasses back to the kitchen, putting the kibosh on the rest of the discussion. "I'm going to start dinner," she called out from the kitchen sink. "Jamie, will you stay?"

Webs nodded at me. Whatever he thought was going on between me and Katie, he was on board with it. Laura was, too, but she had always been agreeable. I angled my head so I could see Katie. She was so mad she might as well have been fuming like a cartoon character with smoke coming out of her ears. I supposed that meant she wasn't quite as amenable to the idea of me staying as her parents were.

"Yeah, I'll stay," I said loud enough for Laura to hear but never taking my eyes off Katie. "Thanks, Laura."

If looks could kill…

There wasn't a doubt in my mind that the three of us—her parents and I—were in agreement with Katie's doctors. She needed the surgery. The tumor had to go, even if it meant that she couldn't sing anymore. The benefits far outweighed the risks.

Now we just had to convince Katie.

She'd found a bit of scrappy attitude, at least, which she was definitely going to need for the battle that lay ahead of her. I just wished her visual daggers weren't all aimed squarely at me.

Katie

FEAR IS AN ugly thing. It eats at you from the inside, gnawing away organ and muscle and bone, leaving nothing but skin behind, the shell of the person who'd previously inhabited it. Fear makes you do things you would never do under normal circumstances, makes you say things you don't mean, makes you lash out like a wounded animal.

Right now, it was coming at me from multiple directions.

I didn't want to die. Absolutely. Did. Not. Want. To die. But I also couldn't bear the thought of no longer being able to do what I'd been born to do. Yes, I had decided to walk away from Hollywood, but that was the sort of decision I could change my mind about at any moment, should the right opportunity present itself. I didn't think I would ever go back and act again, but that didn't mean I ought to close the door completely.

Acting had never been my true love. It was just one of those things that I *could* do in addition to singing. All through the years when I was a kid, I'd done musical theater because it kept me busy all the time. When I'd first gone to LA, I'd tried to convince Derek that singing was where my heart was, that it was what I wanted to devote myself to, but he'd convinced me his plan was better for my career in the long run. *There's this show*, he'd told me. *Like* Glee *or* Fame, *acting, but also lots of singing and dancing. You can make use of all your skills at once, and if it takes off like I think it will, it'll pay you better and open more doors for you.*

He'd been right about the show taking off and it opening doors for me. And maybe, if what I'd truly been after were fame and fortune, starring in *The Cool Kids* would have been worth it. But it had come at a great cost, too. It had introduced me to Jesse Carmichael and his crowd, who had introduced me to drugs and partying and the uglier side of fame. It had put Beau Brunetti into my path, a man who had been silky and seductive, trapping me into thinking he cared for me as much as he cared for the image we presented to the world. A man who had introduced me to the sorts of depravities I wished I could burn from my mind. There was no erasing these things from my past, but I could damn well keep them from being part of my future.

If I was going to have a future at all.

I wanted one. I didn't just want any old future, either, but one with Jamie. I'd probably always loved him, from the moment I'd first met him, but other things I'd thought I wanted had proven to be far different from what they'd been in my dreams. Maybe I was incapable of knowing what I truly wanted. Maybe I didn't understand myself well enough to make these kinds of decisions about my life. That was yet another fear that was closing in on me, squeezing the life out of me. What if it was just a ginormous gaffe, another one to add to the long string of errors in judgment I'd already made? But it was Jamie, so could it *really* be as bad as all that?

All of these fears kept growing and expanding, overwhelming me with their intensity and mass. They made me feel small and inconsequential. Like I was sinking in quicksand, and darkness was surrounding me, enclosing me. Suffocating me. I didn't know how to climb out of it. I didn't know if I would ever be free from the memories of the massive blunders I'd made over the years in the name of furthering my career.

All of this was racing through my head as I cleaned up after dinner. Jamie had offered to help, but I'd waved him away and told him to stay with my parents, preferring to have a few moments to myself. The monotony of rinsing plates and putting them in the dishwasher was a perfect escape, allowing me to sort through the uncomfortable reality my life had become.

I added some detergent to the washer and set it to run, then put some soap on a wet cloth to wipe down the stove and counters, nearing the end of my peace and quiet. For a moment, I debated cleaning the fridge or the oven, just to prolong my respite, but Jamie walked in before I could start on either of those projects.

"Hey," he said gently.

I glanced up, brushing my hair behind my ear, to find him leaning his hip and shoulder against the doorframe and looking good enough to eat. "Hey," I replied, scrubbing the countertops hard enough to wear a hole in them.

"I should…uh… I should go. Get out of here. Let you have some time with your parents."

"You don't have to go." I didn't want him to leave. I wasn't sure I wanted him to stay, either. I was as confused about him all of a sudden as I was about everything else, and all because he wanted me to have the surgery that we all knew I had to have or else I would die. I was a damned mess. I rinsed my cloth under the faucet, wrung it out, and hung it on the rack under the sink to dry, then turned to face him.

He had his arms and his ankles crossed, his head cocked slightly to the side. It made me wonder what he thought when he saw me. Did he undress me in his mind the way I did with him? But every time I did it, I felt as if I were using him the way Beau had used me. In my head, I knew there was a ton of difference between the two. I was just an object to Beau; Jamie was as good as salvation to me. My heart was having a hard time catching up with my head, though, and I felt unclean for thinking about Jamie in that way.

"I mean it," I said. "You can stay, if you want."

"What I want is to clear up what's going on between us."

My heart went all fluttery. It had been a long time since I'd felt anything like that—nerves zinging and everything turning floaty and light as air, but there was nothing solid for me to get a grip on. No man had ever been able to do that to me but Jamie. I backed up to the counter, gripping the edge of it to ground myself. "Meaning what, exactly?"

"Meaning I want to put words to it. I want to give it a name. I'm not okay with kissing you and holding you, being by your side for all the things a boyfriend would be there for, without it being understood in no uncertain terms that that's what I am to you. I want us to be a couple. I want to be by your side through everything that's coming, to hold your hand when you're scared and pick you up when you're weak. I want to know that you're not going to run to some other asshole when we disagree or when I try to make sure you do what we both know is for the best for you. I want you to run to me, even if I piss you off. Because I will piss you off. Because I love you. And because you love me. And because I can't go one more day without being able to tell you that as often as it comes to mind, which is about a dozen times a minute."

Somewhere around the second or third word out of his mouth, my legs had felt like pudding, so it was a good thing I was already holding myself against the counter. If I let go now, I'd probably end up on my face instead of in his arms, which was the only place I wanted to be.

"I do love you, Jamie," I said, gripping the counter so hard my fingers hurt. "I love you, and I'm furious that you would go along with my parents against me even if it's for the best, and there's no one else I would rather run to, and I'm scared. God, I'm so scared." The last bit of that came out through blubbering tears, but it didn't matter because Jamie crossed the room and put his arms around me. I rested my head on his shoulder, tucking it into that special space that seemed to have been designed to carry burdens, big and small. And he held me.

"I'm scared, too," he whispered in my ear. But then he held me tighter, and some of my fear lifted because he was there. With me.

Chapter Nine

Jamie

I STUCK AROUND for a few hours after dinner. We watched *Dancing with the Stars* because Zanna McQuaid, one of Katie's co-stars from *The Cool Kids*, was competing and paired up with a Russian dude who acted like he was God's gift to women. Judging from the reaction of the women in the audience, not to mention Laura, maybe he wasn't the only one to think so.

I wasn't so sure about that. He came across as a demanding ass to me. One look at Katie when the guy yelled at her friend for screwing up in practice was all I needed to know we were in agreement on that. She visibly cringed and burrowed more fully into my side. That only made me wonder what, exactly, had gone on with the guys she'd dated over the years. I sure as fuck wasn't going to bring it up in front of her father, though, whatever it might have been. That was something that we could talk about when it was just the two of us. And we would. Soon. There were things I needed to know, even if hearing it ripped me to shreds.

Zanna and her partner danced a rumba to the same song that had played over Katie's video that night she'd sung the anthem. It was a sensual dance, full of sexy moves that looked like they belonged in a bedroom more than on live television. At first, I watched and wondered how Zanna could dance with him like that when only days ago he'd been berating her, but then my thoughts shifted. To the song.

Or more specifically, to the band. It was by The End of All Things, one of the biggest rock bands in the world these days. They were Katie's favorite band, too, or at least they had been a few years ago. But they just so happened to be based out of Portland. Not only that, but I had a connection with them. Burnzie's wife, Brie, was a ballroom dancer who'd starred in one of their music videos and had helped to choreograph a few dances for their latest tour. My thoughts took off in a thousand directions at once, trying to come up with something I could do for Katie to make her decision easier. Maybe if she could do something with them, one final big moment when she could see some of her dreams come true...maybe then she would be willing to go through with the thyroidectomy. It was certainly an idea worth exploring.

I'd been lost in thought for a few minutes when Katie elbowed me in the ribs.

"Ouch," I said, rubbing the spot she'd hit. Considering I got slammed into the boards and worse on a regular basis by guys easily twice her size, you'd think I would be immune to something like that.

"Get your phone out and vote," she said. She rattled off the number. "Seven times," she added once I'd disconnected the call. "And then seven texts, and seven votes on the website with your email address."

"Got it."

Webs chuckled to himself, but I couldn't help but notice he was doing exactly as Laura had ordered him to do, too.

Once I had sufficiently voted according to Katie's instructions, she settled against me again, tucking her feet up under her and letting me put my arm around her. It felt cozy and perfect, and I didn't want it to end. Before long, though, the show was over and I needed to get home. We had practice tomorrow, and then I had to do a couple of radio spots and things like that. Plus the Thunderbirds would be getting into town, and I was buying Razor dinner, and Katie would be moving in to her new house. It was going to be a busy day, to say the least.

All I wanted to do was stay right where I was. Or maybe take Katie home with me, but I didn't think that was going to happen. Not at the moment, at least. I didn't want to rush anything, particularly not since she had so much on her mind right now. Some things were worth waiting for and doing right.

"I should get home," I said, straightening myself away from her.

"Don't want to show up to practice tomorrow without getting enough rest."

"You probably need to go play with Blackbeard, anyway," Katie said.

Webs popped up a brow. "Blackbeard?"

"Jamie got a kitten."

"And named it Blackbeard?" Webs's shoulders shook with the effort of containing his laughter.

I shrugged. "He perches on my shoulder."

"You two realize Blackbeard was the pirate, right? Not the parrot?"

"Nobody remembers the parrot's name," Katie said defensively.

Webs snorted and turned to me. "The boys will give you shit when they find out."

Considering how much shit they'd give me if they found out other pertinent information, I wasn't too worried about the teasing I'd get over a kitten's name.

"Well, they don't have any reason to find out about that, now do they?" Laura said with a meaningful look at her husband.

"Guess it depends." He eyed me as I stood. "Depends on how you treat my little girl."

And we were back to the threats I'd come to know and expect from him. I nodded, holding back a grin. We were on familiar footing again, and that made me a hell of a lot more comfortable with the situation.

"See you in the morning," I said to him, but he was already pulling up his iPad to look at more game film. He just nodded and gave me a brief wave. Then I turned to Laura. "Thanks for dinner."

"You're welcome anytime. It's nice to have other people over. Feels more like when the kids were growing up, like we're a family."

I thought she might be skipping a few steps, saying it felt like family, but that was definitely the direction I wanted things to go.

Katie followed me to the entryway, taking my hand to slow me when we reached the hall. I stopped just inside the door, pivoting to face her because it seemed as if she had something she wanted to say. Her hair was down, obscuring her face, so I tucked it behind her ear. I wanted to see her clearly, see everything going on in her eyes.

There was a tumultuous storm there. Understandable, given the events of the day. Hell, the last week or more, even. She nibbled on her lower lip before finally spitting it out. "Sometimes in life," she said cautiously, "you think you know what you want, and you want it with a fire that consumes you to the point that you're willing to give up just about anything to get it. So you do. You give up everything, and you work, and you sacrifice and compromise, and then you get it. You finally get your hands wrapped around that elusive thing that has been eating you alive. But then, only after you have it, you realize that it's not what you thought it would be. It's empty and hollow, and what you really wanted—what you needed—is exactly the thing you gave up to get it."

"Don't know what you've got till it's gone," I said, cracking a grin.

She smiled, too, but the smile wasn't as bright as usual. There was a sadness to it that might bring me to my knees if I wasn't careful.

"Right. Exactly," she said.

"I know you gave up a lot to go to Hollywood. I understand it. I always did. I might not have wanted to let you go, but I understood why you had to. But now you're back."

"I am." She wrung her hands together, giving me a moment's pause. "Because it wasn't what I really wanted. What I really want is you."

She'd already made that clear, so I wasn't sure why she felt the need to explain it again. I nodded for her to go on.

"But I need to be able to sing, too."

"Ah. I see." I wasn't enough. Not that I wanted her to give up everything for me. I needed to remind myself of that and not let it hurt my ego. I loved Katie because of everything about her, all the disparate parts that made up the whole. I didn't want her to give up pieces of herself in order to be with me. I would hate it if she felt she had to. If she *wanted* to, that was another story entirely. "Will I see you tomorrow?" I asked.

"Furniture's coming in the morning. Mom's going to bring me over and then I'll be there getting settled most of the day. You could come over whenever you have time."

My time was definitely going to be limited tomorrow, but that didn't matter. "Want to come to dinner with me and Razor? We can celebrate your new house."

She laughed. "You're still friends with him, huh?"

"He's good for me. Keeps me from being too serious all the time."

The arch of her brow underscored her laughter. "Okay. Dinner it is." She stretched up on her tiptoes, putting both arms around my neck to draw me down for a kiss.

I was completely on board with kissing her again—as often as possible—but after a moment, I remembered we were in her father's house. I separated myself before things got too heated. "I don't think your dad would be very happy if he came around the corner right now and saw this going on."

"Why wouldn't he be?" she asked. "He's been trying to set us up since the day I came back to Portland."

"He might be all right with us getting together, but I wouldn't go so far as to say he's setting us up."

"Then you haven't been paying attention. The prom picture. My realtor showing me that house. Dad telling you about my cancer being back even though I'd told him not to. That was all him, and it was all done to give us a nudge."

"That doesn't make any sense." Not at all.

"Better the devil you know," Katie replied. I shook my head, not following. She quirked up a grin. "That's his explanation. He likes you. He wants me to be happy. To be loved."

That might be, but I still doubted he would be very forgiving about seeing me with my hands on his daughter. It'd be best to save that for times when we were alone, or at least not in his foyer. "Tomorrow," I said. "I'll kiss you all you want tomorrow." When we were alone.

"Promise?"

I met her gaze and held it. "Promise." Not that it would be a difficult promise to keep. "Spend some extra time with your mom," I added. "She needs it."

Katie nodded. She kissed me again before I left, and it was all I could do not to beg her to come with me now. But I didn't. She needed some time with her parents, and maybe some time by herself to sort out how she felt about everything. And I had something I needed to do.

I got in my car and headed across the river. I wasn't going home, though. Not yet. The lights were still on at Burnzie's house when I drove up, and Jonny's pickup truck was there. I probably should have called before coming over, or at least texted to be sure it was all right, but I didn't think of that until I was getting out of my car. Too late now.

I rang the bell.

A chorus of barks sounded almost immediately, followed by, "Shut the fuck up already." The porch light flipped on right before Burnzie opened the door looking harassed, his three large dogs barking excitedly behind him. He glared at me. "What the fuck do you want at this hour?"

"Actually, I was hoping I could talk to Brie about something." I dragged a hand through my hair.

"Your hair's a fucking mess. What do you need to see my wife for?"

"It's about Katie."

Burnzie eyed me for a second. Then he stepped back, body-blocking his dogs to give me room to follow. "Come on. She's in the living room."

Jonny and his wife, Sara, were there, along with their three-year-old son, Connor. Sara was in the late stages of pregnancy and had her feet up. Brie was apparently pregnant, too, not that you could tell it yet. Burnzie had filled us in during training camp. Jonny was on the floor acting as a jungle gym for his son. As soon as the dogs returned with us, though, Connor decided to climb the German shepherd instead of his father.

Based on how calm the dog stayed, I got the distinct impression that he was used to it. Not that it should surprise me. A lot of the guys had kids around that age these days, and Burnzie's house was so big that he often hosted parties for the whole team. It made more sense than trying to rent somewhere that could accommodate us all.

They all looked up when I came in.

"Babs thinks he needs my wife more than I do," Burnzie said.

"Shut the fuck up," Connor said. Then he cackled, and Jonny glared at Sara.

"What?" she said. She pointed at Burnzie. "He's the one who said it."

"This time," Jonny mumbled.

"He needs to stop saying it so much," Brie said, patting a hand over her belly.

Burnzie threw his hands up. "I'm working on it. I have time." He picked up an ice bag from the counter and held it to his hand before sitting next to his wife. Not a good sign.

Jonny was about to open his mouth when Sara said, "I'm working on it, too."

"He's three years old," Jonny muttered. "I think you should have figured it out by now that he's going to repeat everything you say."

"Obviously, since that's how I learned it all," Sara said. "I spent my whole damn life surrounded by hockey players who think fuck can be used as every part of speech."

"Fuck fuck fuck," Connor chanted.

Brie shook her head, trying to stifle a laugh. She nodded in my direction. "You wanted to see me about something?"

I took a seat in an armchair. The smallest dog jumped into my lap almost as soon as I was down—possibly because I was as far away from the toddler as possible. Calling her the smallest wasn't really saying much. She was still way too big to be a lapdog, making me appreciate more than ever before how tiny Blackbeard was, even if he did have some wicked claws. She licked my face, and I petted her out of instinct. Then Brie's fluffy white cat jumped up on the back of my chair, purring.

"Right," I said, overwhelmed by the menagerie I'd walked into and how fast my world had changed today. "I need a favor."

Katie

THE FURNITURE I'D ordered was all in position. I'd brought my suitcases from Mom and Dad's house with me when Mom drove me over so I could meet the delivery guys. After that, I went to the grocery store and stocked up, so now my fridge and pantry were fairly well sorted out. After I'd returned from that, Mom came over with a few odds and ends—lamps, framed family photos, some vases and fresh flowers. She hung around for a while, letting me show her around. We talked about the colors I wanted to put on the walls, what kinds of artwork I was thinking about putting up, and who to call if I had various problems that sometimes come up for homeowners. But then she left, claiming she had a women's league meeting even though we both knew that was a lie. I was pretty sure it was just that she was trying hard not to butt in too far, trying to give me some space.

But now she was gone, and it was just me and this empty house, and I wasn't sure what to do with myself. Dr. Oliver had scheduled my first radiation session for Monday, so I had a few days to figure things out before it all started.

In LA, I rented a condo, but I was almost never there. I was on set, or out with Zanna and some of my other friends from the show, or doing something with whomever I was dating at the time. My place was just a place to store my things. It wasn't really somewhere I did anything other than sleep. Hell, I barely had more in my kitchen than coffee and cereal since eating at home was something I only did in extremely rare circumstances.

Now I had a house of my very own, and no job, and no friends who were home in the middle of the day. I had a boyfriend, but he had a life that kept him busy a lot of the time. I couldn't count on Jamie to keep me from boredom at all hours of the day, so I was going to have to figure out a way to occupy myself a lot of the time.

I flipped through a few channels on the TV, but nothing really caught my attention, so I turned it off. I dug my phone out of my pocket and checked my email. There was another long one from Derek, griping about how the *perfect* audition for me had just come up—the kind of gritty role he'd been grooming me for by having me hang out with guys like Beau—but he'd had to tell them I was no longer his client. That was exactly the sort of thing I didn't need to see at the moment, so I shut it down, tossed the phone on the coffee table, and headed into my office space.

I hadn't bought any furniture for this room yet. I was still trying to get a feel for it and settle on exactly how I wanted to use it. The idea of a writing and recording studio was still very appealing, but I needed to figure out what sort of equipment I'd need before I did anything else. The late afternoon sun was pouring in through the windows looking out over my backyard, casting everything in warm light that spoke to my soul.

I lay down on the floor in the middle of the room, soaking it in and making plans. The wall of windows would be perfect for a desk on one side and some sort of cushy chair on the other. I'd need to build in some soundproofing. Not that it was loud around here, but I didn't want to be in the middle of recording something and have a car horn blare in the background. I could do a wall of built-in shelving on one side, and the other could have all my recording equipment. Once I decided on what I would need, at least.

My eyes were getting droopy from lying there for so long with the sun shining on me. If I didn't get up and move around, I'd end up falling asleep down here on the floor, and I would definitely regret that. The view out that window was fantastic, though, so I pulled on a sweater against the chill and made my way into the backyard to my swing. I don't know how long I was there—long enough that the sun was starting to set behind the mountains and the only thing keeping me awake was the back-and-forth motion—but then Jamie's voice startled me out of my ruminations.

"There you are."

I swung my head around and found him smiling at me across the fence. Blackbeard was perched on his shoulder, nibbling his earlobe.

"Here I am," I replied.

"I rang your bell and tried calling your phone when you didn't answer. Thought maybe you'd changed your mind about dinner with me and Razor."

"Not a chance. Just forgot my phone inside when I came out here."

"Mind if I come around?" he asked.

I shook my head.

With Blackbeard in position, Jamie went through his gate and then mine. He took a seat next to me on the bench, and the kitten jumped from his shoulder to mine before coming down to settle on my lap. Not to take a nap, though. His little sniffer was working overtime. I couldn't blame him. All these sights and smells must be new for him.

There was a lot new for me, too, like the way Jamie casually put his arm across my shoulders and drew me closer to him. The way he treated me was so different from any of the other guys I'd dated. With them, every touch was possessive and done for an audience to see or to send a message of sorts. With Jamie, every touch was gentle and meant for only the two of us. I could get used to his kind of touches.

We sat there for a while, telling each other about our days and chitchatting. It was easy to imagine doing this every single day, coming home to one another and sharing the ups and downs, however large or small, we'd experienced since the last time we'd seen each other.

Before long, Blackbeard was antsy to move. I set him down on the ground, and he raced around the yard, leaping at invisible enemies and wrestling a blade of grass.

"It's not fair, leaving him to play all by himself," I said.

"You think I need another kitten? A playmate for him?"

I laughed and shook my head. "I was thinking maybe we should get down there, too."

I should have moved the second the words left my mouth, but I didn't, and then it was too late. Jamie picked me up and dragged me to the ground, rolling us over until I was on top of him. My breasts pillowed between us. My lips were only inches from his, close enough I could smell his cinnamon breath mints.

"Like this?" he asked, breathless and laughing.

I answered him by bracing my knees on either side of his waist, resting my arms on the ground beside his head, and kissing him with every ounce of love I possessed. His lips were spicy and sweet when my tongue traced the seam. He opened, inviting me in, and his hands settled on the small of my back. Tender. Tentative. I could feel how much he wanted to be with me—his erection came to life in about 0.28 seconds—but he was still so cautious about caressing me. It was as if he was worried my father would walk up at any moment.

I kissed the line of his jaw, moving down to his neck. "Touch me, Jamie. I want to feel your hands on me."

He lifted one hand, sliding it up to my head. He threaded his fingers through my hair, drawing it down to his face. "Did I ever tell you how much I dream about touching your hair?" He sniffed a few strands, letting them fall in waves against his skin. "It's so soft. Like silk."

With all the things he could choose to touch, he chose my hair. I didn't know what to make of that.

But then he rolled us over until he was on top. A layer of leaves blanketed the ground beneath me, and he had me pinned below him, his weight supported by his arms. I drew my knees up, holding him between my thighs. Breathless, heart pounding, I waited for his next move.

And waited.

He stayed like that, gazing down at me in awe, as if he was memorizing every detail. The colored light of the setting sun outlined his face above me, a wash of pastels painting the sky. Finally, he lowered his head, placing a kiss on the bit of exposed skin on my chest.

I sucked in a breath, squeezing my eyes closed in anticipation of his next move.

His phone rang in his pocket, and he raised himself away from me again.

"Don't answer it," I said. I wasn't ready for this to end.

"It's Razor."

I pouted. We'd been getting so close to a moment I'd been dreaming about for years, and now he was going to pass it up for his buddy. "Can't you tell him you're busy? I'm sure he'd understand."

But Jamie was already getting up and taking the phone out. I supposed that answered my question.

Blackbeard loped over and replaced him, curling up right over the spot where Jamie had just kissed me. It was sweet, but he was a poor replacement.

"Hey," Jamie said into the phone. "No, I haven't forgotten. I was just picking up Katie first." He fell silent for a minute. "Just working on doing what you told me to, asshole. We'll be there in ten minutes."

He hung up the phone and reached down to help me stand.

"What did he tell you to do?" I asked, brushing the leaves from my butt.

Jamie blushed, and his dimples popped out. He didn't answer me, though. He just took my hand and tugged me in for another kiss, the kind of kiss that made my toes curl. "Come on," he said when he broke it off. "Let's drop Blackbeard off at home and go pick up Razor."

He might have tried to deflect my question, but I went along with him. For now. I was almost positive I knew someone who would answer it for me, and we were on our way to see him.

Chapter Ten

Jamie

WHEN KATIE AND I got to the Thunderbirds' hotel, we walked hand in hand into the building. It was unreal how easily we'd fallen into doing what felt natural—talking about our days, holding hands, playing around with each other. I could get used to this really fast.

Razor was waiting for us in the lobby, along with Hunter and Zee. As soon as she saw them, Katie raced across the foyer and kissed Zee on the cheek. That was just Katie. She'd known Zee longer than she'd known me, and all the guys who'd been part of the Storm over the years had become like older brothers to her. Well, all except me, but I was glad she didn't think of me that way. She did the same with Hunter and was moving on to Razor by the time I got there.

He was apparently anticipating it, and he swept her up off her feet and planted a kiss on *her* cheek before she could kiss him. By the time he set her down again, she was trying to catch her breath from laughing so hard.

I held out a hand for Zee's.

He shook it but with his eyes narrowed at me. "Everything all right?" he asked.

"Everything's fine." I had no doubt his curiosity came down to the leaked reports of the locker room incident after the last game. Not that he wanted dirt on us or anything like that. He had been part of that locker room a long time, and he still had a lot of friends there. Most likely, he just wanted to offer up some advice or something else of that nature. I wasn't going to involve him, though. I meant what I'd told Razor. Those things needed to stay in the room, and no matter how long Zee had been part of it, he wasn't now.

He had always been the kind of guy who would respect that sort of decision, and sure enough, he let it go. He pulled an envelope out of his pocket and handed it to Katie. "Dana sent me with these to show you."

She raised her brows in question but opened the envelope to find three photos, one of each of Zee and Dana's two kids, and a sonogram. "Again? You're having another baby?"

"Another boy. He'll be here in May." Zee didn't even attempt to hide his pride.

We spent a few more minutes catching up with Zee while Razor cracked jokes here and there. Hunter didn't really say much. He just sulked a lot, occasionally interjecting something slightly more coherent than a grunt. I wasn't sure what was going on with him other than maybe feeling like his talents were being wasted on a team he didn't want to play for—he'd made that much clear over the summer when he'd found out he'd been claimed in the expansion draft—but he didn't seem inclined to talk about it.

"Do you guys want to come to dinner with us?" Katie asked when we were getting ready to leave.

Zee shook his head. "Soupy and Rachel insisted on a family dinner for me tonight." That didn't surprise me since Dana was Soupy's younger sister and Zee had been his best friend since they were kids. "Rachel's picking me up on her way home."

"And Hunter's going to a meeting of the goalie guild," Razor put in cheerfully, ignoring the glares coming from Hunter's corner. "Nicky, Bobby, and Jacks are planning to spend time with his hostile ass, for some reason, so we might as well go."

Katie handed the photos and sonogram back to Zee, and we headed out to my car.

I got on the highway, heading toward the Old Town-Chinatown District. "What's under Hunter's skin?" I asked Razor.

"You mean besides his wife?"

I did a double take as I exited the highway. "He's married?" The last I knew, Hunter hadn't even been dating anyone.

"Yep. Miss Oklahoma or something. They're fucking disgusting together, nonstop PDA and shit, but he's surly all the time now. Well, surlier than normal. You'd think that if they're all over each other like that, he'd be getting laid all the time. And you'd think that getting laid all the time would improve his disposition. I don't see that one lasting, but what can you expect when a guy marries a piece of ass he's only known for five seconds?" He looked over his shoulder at Katie, in the backseat. "Sorry. Language."

"It's fine," she said. "I can promise you, I've heard worse."

That wasn't the point, but I decided not to say anything about that. I was just glad Razor had corrected himself this time before I'd had to. Maybe he wasn't always going to be a complete asshole. I scanned the side roads, searching for a place to park. "So he met this girl and married her? Just like that?" I finally found a spot not too far from the Davis Street Tavern and took it before someone else could come along and snag it out from under me.

"As far as I could tell. And he's been a fucking bear to deal with ever since. Well, more so than normal."

I took Katie's hand as we crossed the street to the restaurant. When we got to the front door, she surprised me by stretching up on her tiptoes to kiss my cheek. I was almost positive I was blushing, but I didn't give a shit. Not only that, but I wasn't satisfied with a kiss on the cheek. That might be good enough for Zee, Hunter, and Razor, but I wanted more. I drew her in for a real kiss.

"Fucking surrounded by it everywhere I go," Razor muttered when I let her go. "You two should get a room."

The hostess seated us in a booth almost immediately. I slid onto the bench next to Katie, and the hostess passed around menus. Once she left, Katie set her menu down in front of her and focused in on Razor.

"So, what is this advice you gave Jamie?" she asked.

"Nothing," I said, shooting daggers in his direction in case he thought it would be a good idea to give her a solid answer.

"Advice?" He quirked up a brow and cocked his head to the side, eyeing me. I shook my head. He chuckled and turned back to Katie. "Oh, *that* advice. I just suggested Babs listen to the words of one of the greatest thinkers of our time."

"And who's that?"

"No o—"

"Beyoncé," he said, cutting me off. "You know. The part in 'Single Ladies' about what he should do if he likes it."

"Put a ring—" Katie stopped short as soon as she understood, her cheeks turning almost as pink as mine. She picked up her menu again and hid her face behind it, but there was no hiding how embarrassed she was from me. "I see."

We'd barely decided we were dating again, so it was way too fucking soon to start talking about getting married, no matter how much I might want that to be the end result.

The waitress dropped off glasses of water and took our orders, scratching things down on a notepad before collecting the menus.

"And I think we all know he likes it," Razor added as soon as she walked away.

I kicked him under the table.

"What? It's not like it's a secret." He shifted down the bench so he was across from Katie instead of me, not that it would do him any good. I could still kick him if he deserved it, and chances were high that he would. He caught Katie's eye and winked. "Maybe once he's getting laid on a regular basis, he won't be so tetchy. But then again, he might end up like Hunter and be more unbearable than ever."

I was already pulling back my foot to deliver another solid kick when Katie smiled and said, "I guess there's only one way to test your theory." Her eyes flickered over to me for a fraction of a second before fluttering away, but there wasn't a chance in hell I could have missed the invitation in that glance.

I froze.

The waitress returned with a bottle of wine and a basket of bread, and Razor caught my eye during the exchange. The corners of his lips twisted up in a shit-eating grin.

Holy hell.

WE ENDED UP spending hours hanging out with Razor before taking him back to the hotel, but Katie didn't seem to mind. Actually, with the way she talked and laughed with him, the two of them ganging up together to tease me, I was pretty sure she had enjoyed it immensely. So had I. Today was the first time I'd spent quality time with Katie since she'd come back to Portland that had been free from either her tears or us talking about cancer. I just hoped we were going to be able to keep it up without him around, because he definitely would *not* be around for this next part.

We had barely left the hotel's parking lot when Katie turned in her seat and asked me, point blank, "Do you have condoms back at your house?"

I nearly lost control of my car in shock. "No. Why?" Then I mentally berated myself for coming across as an idiot.

"We should stop at the drugstore and get some," she said, ignoring the most senseless question to have ever crossed my lips.

"Are you— I mean, aren't we… Don't you think we're rushing into things?"

"We don't have to use them tonight if you think it's better to wait," she said, as calm and collected as ever. "I think we should have some on hand, though. For when we are ready. There's nothing worse than being in the middle of things and having to stop to go to the store because no one has a condom on hand."

"Nothing worse," I repeated, hating myself for it. But I couldn't stop myself. There were things I needed to know, and Katie had been the one to broach the subject to begin with. She'd opened the door. I might as well go through it. "So you've had that happen? You've been about to have sex with some guy and had to stop so you could go buy condoms?"

There wasn't any way to hide the jealousy in my tone. No way to mask the fact that it hurt me that she'd been with someone else. If she had stayed in Portland, I was sure we would have been together by now, and God knew the girls I'd dated since her had done their best to get me in their beds. I wasn't even entirely sure why I hadn't slept with them other than it hadn't felt right. I'd wanted them plenty bad enough, at least from a purely physical standpoint. My body had responded. My heart just refused to catch up. With Katie, my body was there, and my heart was fully in it. The only problem was my head kept telling me I needed to slow everything down.

We were coming to an intersection, and the light turned yellow, so I braked and stopped. Then I turned so I could really see her when she answered me.

"Yes," she said. "I stopped him because we didn't have condoms, and I went to the store to get some."

"He didn't go? Why didn't he go with you?" Or better yet, instead of her.

She shrugged and looked down at her lap, where she was toying with the bottom of the zipper on her jacket repeatedly. "He was mad I made him stop over something like that. He said I should have thought to be sure we had condoms before things ever got as far as they did. So

I went and got them, and I brought them back. And we had sex."

"Which one was this?" I asked, trying to keep my anger in check. I wasn't just mad at the asswipe who'd treated her like that; I was mad at Katie for letting him, for not standing up for herself and refusing to let anyone act that way toward her.

"Does it matter who it was?"

The light turned green, so I adjusted my hands on the wheel and eased onto the gas, chewing on my frustration. "I don't know," I finally said. "You tell me. Does it matter who he was?"

Katie spun her head and stared out at the city as we passed it by. "It was Beau. With Jesse, his drugs were more important to him than I was, but he at least bothered to...to take care of me when we were in bed. The other guys I dated, it never got serious enough for me to sleep with them."

"But Beau acted like the ass he is when you were alone together," I finished for her.

"You have no idea."

There was a part of me that wanted to leave it at that, to stop probing for more information when everything she told me made me want to drive to LA so I could force these guys to answer for how they'd hurt her. It might not have been them, though, but *something* had put that haunted look in her eyes. I couldn't go hunt them down, anyway, and it didn't have a thing to do with thinking I needed to know every detail of what had gone on in her life. Katie didn't owe me anything. She didn't need to explain herself to me. But I had a sinking suspicion that *she* felt the need to tell me, before we took things further.

The drugstore was about a block away. I changed lanes to turn in.

"Do you hate me?" she asked quietly, once we were in the parking lot.

"There's nothing you could ever do to make me hate you." I shut off the engine and sat there, waiting for her to look at me. When she finally did, I said, "I might not always be happy with every decision you make, but I love you. That's enough."

"But you don't— I know how TMZ and the other gossip sites made me seem. They made me out like I was easy. A slut going from guy to guy. It was what Derek wanted. He wanted me to have some edge, so I could get different sorts of parts, and I just...I went along with the publicity stuff. I trusted him to know what was best for my career, and I shouldn't have. When something felt wrong, I should have put my foot down and said I wouldn't do it."

I agreed wholeheartedly, but telling her so wouldn't solve anything. "You can't go back and change things," I said. "It happened. What matters now are the choices you make moving forward." Like the fact that she wanted to buy condoms to use with me. My hormones had been working in overdrive since she'd kissed me in her backyard earlier, and thoughts like these weren't helping to cool things down.

Her hair had fallen into her eyes again, so I brushed it back, letting my fingertips trail over her cheek before I tucked the tendrils behind her ear.

"Promise me something," I said.

"What's that?" She blinked a couple of times, as if she were trying to hold back tears again. I didn't want tears to have any part of things when I finally took her to my bed.

"Promise me that if I ever treat you as anything less than the princess you are, you'll break my nose and then be sure your dad finishes me off."

"How can you possibly think I'm a princess, that I deserve to be with someone as good as you, after—"

"Promise me," I interrupted. "Don't you fucking dare sell yourself short. Not ever again. I can live with a lot of things, Katie. I can accept that you did things you regret, that you made choices I would rather you hadn't. But I can't handle you thinking you're not good enough. For anything or anyone. That's not even close to all right. That's the kind of thinking that leads to you accepting the kind of treatment those guys gave you. So you promise me you won't ever put up with me treating you as anything less than perfect, because that's what you are. At least to me, and if anyone thinks otherwise, then they need their thinking adjusted."

I didn't know where these speeches kept coming from when I was with Katie. There was a part of me that wished words would come to me like that when I was with the team because that was what they needed from me as their captain. It never seemed to happen with them, though. Only with Katie, who at the moment was looking at me with the most thunderstruck expression I'd ever seen.

"So are we buying condoms or what?" I asked. My face felt hot. I had to be fucking blushing again. I opened my door and got out, slamming it behind me because I was so damn pissed at my own embarrassment I could hardly function.

By the time I got around to Katie's side, she'd already gotten out on her own.

"Sorry," I said. "I shouldn't have gotten upset like that."

"It's okay."

"It's not okay." Losing my temper with her over something that was my own damn problem would never be okay. "That's one of those things you're not supposed to let me get away with. You should be breaking my nose right about now." I shut her door and pressed the button on my remote to lock the car.

When I turned around, Katie stretched up on her toes to kiss me.

"Why did you do that?" I asked.

"Because you can't even imagine half the ways I've screwed up, and you still think I'm perfect." She reached for my hand. "Come on. Let's go buy some condoms."

Katie

"Do you have a type you prefer? Or a brand? There are those condoms that claim they enhance sensitivity. That could be good." A box caught my eye, and I picked it up, holding it out to Jamie. "Ooh, or those super thin ones. They're supposed to feel like they aren't even there. That's what the advertising says, at least, but I can always tell there's something there. Can't you? Or we could go with colored, flavored, *magnum*..." I intentionally left that last query hanging between us to see if he would bite.

He didn't.

I'd seen him blush a lot over the years, but I had never seen him as bright red as he was right now. He looked like he would rather be anywhere but here, which made sense when I thought about it. Jamie had always been a private kind of guy. He never seemed to have a hard time talking to me about anything when we were alone, but I doubted he wanted his private life spread all over the news. I couldn't say I blamed him for that. I'd had enough of the paparazzi to last a lifetime, and then some. That was another good thing about staying in Portland. I doubted TMZ would be hanging around here to catch me doing something they could twist into a scandal.

"Whatever you want," he said quietly, keeping his head down. "You choose."

I raised my eyebrows, a grin stealing over my lips. "You sure? I'm not terribly particular as long as it's covered."

"Same for me," he said through gritted teeth.

If he wasn't going to be picky, I might as well be adventurous. I grabbed a few boxes, just for fun: flavored, glow-in-the-dark, and another that claimed to be ribbed for her pleasure. I'd never known a condom to enhance my pleasure before, but for the most part, they didn't diminish it, either. The *diminished pleasure* I'd experienced tended to fall squarely on the shoulders of the man wearing the condom, instead of the protective gear itself. Beau had never bothered to see to my needs, worrying only about his own. Every aspect of our relationship had been like that, but nowhere had it been more pronounced than in bed. We did things when he wanted, how he wanted, and as fast as he wanted, and tough if I didn't enjoy myself.

There was no chance it would be anything like that with Jamie. He was so caring in everything he did, I knew without a doubt that it would carry over into the bedroom.

Once I was satisfied with my selections, we headed up to the checkout counter. I reached in my purse for my wallet, but Jamie beat me to the punch, handing over a wad of bills. The checker bagged everything up, doing his best to hide a knowing smile but constantly peeking up at me, and handed over the receipt. We left the store and got back into Jamie's car.

Jamie didn't start the ignition, though. He had put on his seat belt, but he was staring at the guy who'd rung up our purchases. When I glanced up to find out why, I could see him through the store windows with his phone in his hands as he leaned over the counter.

"What do you think he's doing?" Jamie asked.

"Texting his friends that he just saw us buying more condoms than we could use in a month. Maybe tweeting it, but hopefully texting. And he could be adding something else to our purchases, like blindfolds and handcuffs. Something to make it seem worse than it is. That's just what people do." They always exaggerated the truth, whatever the truth was. I'd come to accept it as simply part of being somewhat famous.

"You think he knows who we are?"

"You think he doesn't?" I gave Jamie a dubious look. "Maybe he doesn't watch hockey, so you might be in the clear, but he definitely knew who I was. You saw the way he was looking at me."

Jamie undid his seat belt. "I'm going back in there."

"What? No." I put a hand on his arm to stop him. "Why would you do that? Going in there again will only make things worse."

"Because someone needs to tell him that what he's doing is wrong!"

I flinched and let go of his arm, folding my hands on my lap. "Fine. You're not the one who's been dealing with this for four years, but surely you know best. Go on. I'm sure it'll make everything better if slutty Katie Weber's latest man goes in and threatens the guy who's just letting the world know how slutty Katie still is."

"I wasn't planning on threatening him."

"No? Then what? Skipping that step and going straight for the throat punch? Sounds like something Dad would do, not you, but maybe you've been paying attention and taking a few notes about how to be sure you draw *more* attention to the things you want to hide."

A few more moments passed in silence. Then he put his seat belt on again and started the car. "I'm sorry," Jamie said, driving out of the parking lot. "I wanted to make things better for you, and what I had in mind would have only made it worse. You're right. I didn't think it through." He pulled up at a stoplight and held out his hand between us, open to take mine.

I hesitated, but then I put my hand in his. "I'm sorry, too. I'm sorry I've done things to make you think I'm a slut. But I'm not, Jamie. I'm really not. I know how things seem, but that's just what they wanted the world to see. For some reason, it's easy to believe the worst of people and hard to believe the best, but no one is either as good or as bad as the media paints them. No one."

Jamie dragged his other hand through his hair, mussing his faux hawk so some of it was standing on end. "I don't think you're a slut."

"No?" I still sounded pouty and petulant. "Well, you're one of very few, then. Even Dad fell for everything the media tried to sell about me." And thanks to how well Derek cast me in that role, it hadn't even been a hard sell.

A couple of minutes later, Jamie parked the car. He closed the garage door behind us.

I grabbed my purse and the drugstore bag, ready to go home. To my house. Alone, because I wasn't really in the mood to fool around with him after the argument we'd just had. I wasn't used to disagreeing with Jamie, and I didn't like it. There was a hollow ache in my stomach that had nothing to do with hunger and everything to do with conflict. I really fucking hated conflict.

"Come on," Jamie said as we got out of his car. He waited by the door leading into his kitchen, holding out a hand for me. "Blackbeard'll be frantic for company by now."

"You sure you want me to come in?" I hedged. "I could go home if you'd prefer that. Since…" I wasn't sure how to put into words that maybe he wasn't in the mood right now after we'd been arguing and talking about what a slut the world thinks I am. And honestly, even though he said he didn't think of me that way, the only thing he had to go on to the contrary was my word. Maybe he needed more time to think about all of this.

He gave me an overblown suspicious look and pointed to the bag in my hands. "You sure about that? Because it seems wasteful not to put those to use."

"You think you can use them all, huh?" I laughed. "They do have expiration dates, but I think they'll last a while. We don't have to rush into anything."

His whole face dropped. "I'm not going to rush you, Katie. Not ever."

That much was painfully evident, since I was the one making almost every move. I smiled and crossed over to take his hand, kissing him on the side of his jaw. "I meant *I* wouldn't rush *you*."

A frisson of hope flitted between us, and I couldn't tell where it started and where it ended. It just was. Tangible. Nearly physical.

He threaded his fingers through mine. "So you'll come in?"

I stepped ahead of him and opened the door. Blackbeard raced through it, making a flying leap straight for Jamie and landing halfway up his thigh. Within seconds, he clawed his way up and made himself at home on Jamie's shoulder, amid a stream of curses.

I tried to stifle my laugh. "Just be glad he only weighs about a pound right now. Wait until he's a full-grown cat and still doing that."

Jamie sent a half-hearted glare in the kitten's direction. "We'll see if he makes it that long."

Blackbeard nipped Jamie's nose in response before licking all over his face.

I went inside and tossed my purse and bag on the kitchen counter. A moment later, the door closed, and I felt the heat of Jamie's body behind me. He touched my upper arm, his strong fingers gently circling my skin. I leaned back, allowing myself to sink into him.

"You're not rushing me," he said. "And I meant what I said. I believe you. I don't think you could possibly be all that they would have the public believe. But there are things I need to know first. I need to know where that line falls between what's true and what's not. I need to know if any of them…if they hurt you. I need to know that *you* believe what's going to happen between us will be…untainted, I guess I mean. Not dirtied by things that someone else has done to you or by all the things you're afraid I believe."

I squeezed my eyes shut, willing myself the courage to tell him everything he was asking for. "I know. It's only fair for you to know exactly what you're getting into with me before...well, *before*." I allowed myself to revel in the shelter of his embrace. He would still want me once he knew, wouldn't he? I had to believe it or I would never be able to tell him. I hadn't told anyone the worst of it, not even Dani or Mom. There was too much shame, because like Jamie had said—there was a line between the truth and the fabrication. The media hadn't made things up out of thin air. They'd taken what I'd given them and run with it to make up their wild stories, to cast me in a light that wasn't true but wasn't wholly a lie.

"And there's something I need to tell you, too," Jamie said.

I really didn't want to hear about the girls he'd dated while I was in Hollywood, but I supposed it was only fair since he was about to hear a whole lot he likely didn't want to know. I just hoped he didn't feel the need to give me too much detail. "All right," I said. "Whatever you need to tell me, I can take it. I'm ready." It couldn't be any worse than what I had to tell him.

He backed away and went around the kitchen island, heading for the living room with Blackbeard enjoying the ride. "Come on. Sit with me."

I followed, sitting beside him on the sofa but with a bit of space between us. He might want that distance once I started talking about what life with Beau had been like.

"You first," I said once we were both settled.

Jamie reached up and petted the kitten's back, looking thoroughly nauseated. Maybe it was worse than I'd imagined? But he was still *Jamie*, so it couldn't be that bad.

Finally, he took a breath and blurted out, "I'm a virgin."

Chapter Eleven

Jamie

I FELT LIKE I might puke after admitting that to Katie, but she didn't laugh or do anything to make me feel like I was a sad, pathetic excuse for a man. Not that I believed that about myself over something as stupid as still being a virgin, but still. People could be weird about a man having never proved his virility by doing the deed. That was why I tended to keep it a secret. It was a total double standard, too. Me being a virgin? Pitiful. Katie *not* being a virgin? Somehow that made her a slut, according to everyone with a social media presence and an axe to grind. Pissed me off, but I didn't know what I could do about it.

But Katie didn't react. She didn't crack a joke. She didn't get up and run out. She didn't do anything at all, actually, but sit there and stare at me, one brow slightly raised in question.

I didn't know what she was asking me, so I followed her example. I sat there exactly how I was and waited for her to respond.

"That's it?" she said after one of the most pregnant pauses I'd ever lived through. "That's what you needed to tell me? That you've never had sex?"

"Well, you don't need to sound so underwhelmed."

She blinked a couple of times. "I don't— I just thought you were about to tell me all your deep, dark secrets about all the girls you've slept with over the last few years. That's all." She pushed some hair back from her face, but it immediately fell forward again. "I was expecting you to air your dirty laundry like I'm about to do, and you hit me with the fact that you're even more impossibly perfect than I already thought you were."

"I'm not perfect," I grumbled. "And that's exactly what I did tell you. I let you in on every single girl I've fucked, all zero of them. It wasn't like I didn't have the opportunity, either. I just—" I nearly bit my own tongue forcing myself to shut up before I revealed more than I was ready for.

"You just what?" Katie asked.

"Nothing."

"It's not nothing. I'm about to fill you in on all the sordid details you want about my sex life. You owe me the same if we're going to move forward with this."

"You've already got all the details. There *are* no details. It's just me, my hand, and my imagination. That's it. That's all I was going to say."

She frowned, in a way that made me think of her mother—the sort of I'm-not-buying-for-a-second-that-you're-telling-me-the-whole-story frown that all moms must learn to do the moment their first child comes out of the womb. Or maybe sooner than that, since Katie could already do it. The way she was scowling left me squirming in my seat. I shifted, and I dislodged Blackbeard enough that he woke up and circled before settling down again.

"Fine," I said. "All right. I just couldn't take any of them up on what they were offering because they weren't you. Which is stupid because you were *gone*, and you clearly weren't waiting around for me, so I might as well move on with my life, right? Take what I could get when I could get it. But I couldn't."

Katie blinked again, but this time she was blinking back tears, making me wish I'd had the decency to talk to her without all my frustration coming through in my words. "You've never had sex because you were waiting for me?" she said, awed.

"Maybe. Kind of." I reached up to shove my hand through my hair again but stopped myself just in time. That wouldn't do anything but prove how nervous I was, talking to her about this. About sex. About all the things I'd been lying in bed at night thinking about for years but had never gotten a chance to do anything about. But now here she was. With condoms. Wanting me. And I was so fucking worked up about telling her this shit that I might blow my chance. "I just thought it should mean something, you know? I didn't want to go to bed with some girl I didn't love just for the sake of having sex. I wanted to know there was a future there. I wanted to be in love and have it matter. It should be a big deal, right? It should be important. And none of them mattered because they weren't you."

Her lips twitched a couple of times, and then the smile I'd loved since the first time I'd ever seen her crossed her face. It was a shy smile, one that lit up her eyes and turned her cheeks as pink as mine, but she ducked her face down as though that would hide any of her beauty from me.

"You were saving yourself for me," she said when her eyes fluttered up to meet mine again.

"Well, not necessarily for you. Just for someone I could love like I loved you. Like I still love you."

She pursed her lips together and shook her head. "Stop while you're ahead. Tell me you were saving yourself for me."

I laughed hard enough that Blackbeard dug in his claws and grumbled. "Fine. I was saving myself for you."

The kitten was sleepy enough that he let me bring him down from his roost. I set him on the sofa, right beside my hip, and he let out a sound that was half sigh, half snore. He must have been running himself ragged all over the house while we were gone to be this tuckered out.

"I know you don't want to hear this," Katie said, drawing my attention back to her instead of the kitten. "But that just reinforces the idea in my head that I don't deserve you. You say I'm perfect for you, but you're *perfect*, Jamie. You don't have any flaws. None."

"Not even close to true. I can't figure out how to lead my team even though they made me captain. I'm scared to use the stove, much less the oven, because I'm bound to start a fire. I think too much and act too little. My hair's a damn mess all the time, which Burnzie is all too happy to remind me of, I blush at the drop of a fucking hat, and I can't grow out of these dimples that make me look twelve—"

"The dimples and the blushing are assets, not flaws," she cut in. "And I think you'll recall how I feel about your hair."

I did remember that. Back when she'd had cancer the first time, when the chemo had caused her hair to start falling out, Webs had shaved his off in support. I was about to do the same when she'd flipped out and begged me to keep it. So I had. I'd do just about anything she asked of me—then and now—if it would make her happy.

Still, I rolled my eyes. I'd heard that part about my fucking dimples and blushing way too many damn times, since I was a kid. The only thing that made it slightly easier to deal with was the fact that my brothers—all six of them—suffered from the same affliction. I wasn't totally alone in it. "The point is, nobody's perfect. But that doesn't mean you're not perfect for me. And maybe I can be perfect for you, too."

"I don't think you need the *maybe* in that statement," she said with a smile that would have knocked my feet out from under me if I'd been standing.

Her hair had dipped in front of her eyes again, and I reached over to slip it behind her ear. Briefly, she turned her head in toward my touch, kind of how Blackbeard would do when he wanted affection, only without the same determined feline insistence. Her skin was as smooth as satin as I let my fingertips glide along her cheek. Pinpricks of electricity shot between us, jolting my pulse and leaving it stuttering to catch up.

"Why don't you think you deserve me?" I asked, dropping my hand down to her shoulder. I couldn't seem to make myself stop touching her in some way.

She inched closer. "Are you sure you're ready to hear it all?"

No. I wasn't even close to certain, but I said, "Yes."

Katie took a breath, scanning my eyes. "Okay. I'm not sure where to start, though."

"Start at the beginning."

"The beginning." Her lips twisted up in a grimace that I wanted to kiss away. "Right. So Derek sent me on a few auditions when I first arrived in Hollywood. The general consensus from casting directors was that I was adorable and sweet and way too pure for the roles they were casting, but they'd keep me in mind if a part I was suited for came along. He wasn't thrilled by their reactions. Then he arranged for me to read for *The Cool Kids.* The part he sent me to audition for was the one Zanna ended up playing—a little edgier storyline than mine—but they ended up offering me the role of Courtney. I was perfect for Courtney, they said. Sweet, adorable, and pure, exactly like all the other casting directors had described me and what they used as the reason I wouldn't fit their parts. I accepted, and Derek was thrilled for the exposure I would get from this role, but he was worried that I was going to be typecast by taking on a part so similar to who I was in person. He didn't think I'd be offered anything with more grit, more edge, unless we did something about my public image."

"So he suggested you date Jesse Carmichael?" I filled in.

"Yeah. He'd been trying to get me to hang out with a group of some of his other clients who were often in the news, but I didn't really know them, and I wasn't comfortable. Jesse was in the cast, and he'd been flirting with me on set. When Derek saw that, he decided that was the course I needed to take. At first, it wasn't anything serious. I just went to red carpet events with him, things like that to keep Derek happy. But then Jesse wanted it to be more than just for show. I wasn't so sure about it. I was still hung up on you, and I had already caught on to the fact that he was into some things I didn't really want to get messed up with. But they both pressured me, and I gave in. I gave in on a lot of things."

She wrapped her arms around her stomach and backed away from me, tucking her feet up under her. It felt like she didn't want to be too close to me. Like she was ashamed of herself and didn't want it to rub off on me. The urge to go to LA, find Derek Hatch, and bash his face in was as strong as my desire to draw Katie into my arms and convince her there was nothing she could do, then or now, to make me stop loving her. But I stayed put. There was a lot more story she needed to tell, and I was determined to let her get through all of it.

"Jesse and I were good together, even if I didn't love him. The physical attraction between us was off the charts, and we had great chemistry in"—she stopped and gave me an apologetic look—"in bed. But he got high a lot. Pot just about all the time, acid at least a few times a week… He liked cocaine, too, though. When I was with him, I felt pressured into using the same things he did. I never used much, and I hated the way I felt when I did."

My stomach churned, thinking about all the things that could have happened to her when she was high. Bashing Derek Hatch's face in was too good for him, and there were no words for the anger I felt for Jesse Carmichael.

"Drugs and I didn't get along," Katie said. "Not at all. People who get high don't like being around people who don't, though, so I caved. It was only when he got busted one time and I was with him—and of course, TMZ was all over it—that I decided I couldn't do that anymore. I had never used enough that I'd developed an addiction, and I decided to quit using altogether. But then Jesse decided that he didn't want to be with me anymore. Said I wasn't fun, that I wasn't willing to have a good time with him, so we broke things off. I stopped hanging out with him and his crowd."

"He never— He didn't hurt you?" I wasn't sure exactly what I meant by that, but leaving it open-ended was probably for the best. She could answer that however she saw fit.

Katie shook her head. "No, I hurt myself by going along with him, but he never did anything to hurt me. I cared about him as a friend but never anything more than that. Still do. I worry about him. I was surprisingly okay about it after we'd ended things, but Derek wasn't so happy. He kept trying to get me to go out with other guys like Jesse, other men who ran with that same crowd. I didn't have any desire to do that, even if he thought it was best. Zanna and I hit it off, though. She had a lot more edge in the public eye than I did, so he was happy about that. She introduced me to a couple of guys who I used to satisfy Derek's desire to have me seen in public with the edgier crowd, but there was never anything to it. We were friends, and we went to red carpet events and whatnot together, and we made nice for the camera. But since I never really dated them, we weren't in the news as often as Derek wanted. He wanted me to constantly show up in magazines and on all the entertainment shows, and the profile I was keeping was too low for him. That was when he introduced me to Beau."

And this was the part where I was sure my blood was going to boil over. It was only after she'd started dating Beau that I'd noticed the haunted look coming into her eyes in photos. Before, anytime she'd been caught by one of the paparazzi with a guy, she'd looked like the Katie I had known and loved for years. She'd still had that innocent look, a certain sweetness that her agent had deemed troublesome. When she was with Beau, everything about her had changed.

I picked Blackbeard up and shifted him to my other side so I wouldn't squash him, and then I slid over close enough I could put my arm around Katie's shoulders.

She immediately tensed. "What are you doing?"

"Holding you," I said. "So you'll know I'm here. And that I love you. And that it won't change no matter what you tell me next."

"Don't you think you should hear it before you make promises like that?"

"No, I don't."

"Oh. Well." Then she started to tell her story again, but she didn't relax against me. "Derek convinced me to go out with Beau. I wasn't sure it was a good idea, because the Brunettis are a lot like the Kardashians. The kids are all famous because they've got rich, famous parents, and that usually leads to trouble."

"You've got rich, famous parents and you came out all right," I argued.

She rolled her eyes. "Dad's fame and fortune don't even come close to the Brunettis' and you know it. But that's beside the point. The point was, Beau wasn't into drugs, so I decided it couldn't hurt anything to go out with him for a little while."

Except it had hurt, and in ways I knew she had never imagined.

"In the early days, he was great. He spoiled me rotten with extravagant gifts and taking me on romantic vacations when I had time off from filming. I even let myself start to think I could fall in love with him. But then things changed. If I wasn't dressed right in public, or if I tried to shy away from him when he was groping me for the cameras, he went into rages. He started yelling at me, railing about how I needed to stop flirting with Jesse even though I never flirted with Jesse anymore and hadn't since we'd broken up. He flipped out any time I talked to another guy in public. He wanted me to do things in front of the cameras that I would never do because I didn't want my friends and family to see me like that. I didn't know how to make Beau stop yelling at me. I tried to defuse his anger, and that just made things worse. He would scream awful things at me when we were alone, telling me I was a cheating whore and he would ruin me if I didn't change. It got so bad that I would do anything to make him stop, and usually the only thing that he wanted was to take me to bed and—"

She choked off for a moment, and I squeezed her shoulder, drawing her closer to me as a reminder of my presence.

"He wanted to take me to bed and essentially screw me into submission. He could be rough at the best of times, but when he was worked up like that, he lost all sense of caring about me. The time I made him stop so I could go buy condoms, he just about threw my purse at me as I ran out the door. He was furious that I would make him stop over something like that. I'm just glad he did eventually stop. I wasn't sure he would."

I was having a hard time keeping my breathing even, keeping myself seated on the couch instead of pacing the room or looking for something to hit. But the same as with cancer, hitting something right now wouldn't do anything to help. This had all happened in the past. I couldn't go back in time and undo it. I couldn't erase it from Katie's memory, or my own now that I knew the extent of it.

"Do I want to know what happened when you came back?" I asked. I really didn't want to know, because I was fucking positive that once she'd returned with condoms, he'd forced himself on her. And if that was what he'd done…

She shook her head.

"Do I *need* to know?"

"I think you already do. At the very least, I bet you're close."

"He raped you," I said.

She scooted over, easing herself out of my embrace and leaving a void where she'd been. "I don't know if I'd call it rape," she said.

"Did you want it? Did you give consent? Did he force you?" I tried not to let my anger come through in my voice because it wasn't Katie I was mad at. I wanted to follow her to the other end of the couch, to draw her into my arms again. To hold her. But the last thing I would ever do was push her into something she didn't want. It took a hell of a lot of willpower, but I stayed where I was, my hands itching to caress and comfort her. I grabbed hold of my thighs to make sure I didn't do anything to cross a line, whether it was one I could see or not.

She shook her head. "It just happened," she said. Excusing it. Brushing it off. "I let it happen. We were together, and I let it happen. If anything, it was my fault."

"It wasn't your fault," I said. There was no fucking excuse for what he'd done to her. And based on everything else she'd said about it, I doubted that was the only time he'd raped her.

She shuddered, as if she could shake it off now. Or maybe she was trying to shake off the truth of what I'd said.

"That was after we'd been here at the holidays," she said. "He said I'd flirted with you, and maybe I'd fucked you while he wasn't looking—although don't ask me how he thought that would have happened—and he was pissed off that I'd pushed him into doing the Light the Lamp event for New Year's. And he took it out on me."

"Was that the worst?" I asked, my voice cracking on the words. "Please tell me that was the worst he did to you."

She shook her head. "But it's bad enough. I don't think I need to go into detail. Do I?"

If she went into any more detail, I would end up either puking or breaking my hand. Maybe both.

"No. That's enough as long as you think it is."

She looked up, her beautiful blue eyes streaked with red and glistening with unshed tears. "So here's the part where you tell me you were wrong. That you see me differently now, and maybe I'm not good enough for you." She scoffed. "This is the part where you cut ties and move on. Where you come to your senses."

"No, it's not." I trailed a hand down her arm, seeking her hand. She let me take it. Her skin was warm and soft, and goose bumps pricked up along the path I'd followed. I raised our hands to my mouth and kissed the backs of her knuckles. "This is the part where I finally get to prove that I may not be perfect, but I'm perfect for you."

Katie

JAMIE SHOULD BE disgusted by the way I'd allowed my agent to manipulate me and then so easily caved in to peer pressure in order to be accepted by Jesse. He should be furious about how I'd been so weak-willed that I had let Beau treat me the way he had. If Jamie had any sense at all, he would be sending me on my way, back to my own house, and telling me he'd had second thoughts about me and I needed to stay out of his life, that he deserved better. Because he did. He deserved to have a woman who was as good and kind and pure as he was. Not someone like me.

But he wasn't doing any of those things. He was caressing my hand and kissing my knuckles, and I was at a loss as to how he couldn't see that it was wrong.

"I don't deserve you," I said.

"I thought we agreed you weren't going to say bullshit things like that anymore."

"But that was before you knew. God, Jamie. Your deep, dark secret was that you've never slept with someone before, but mine—"

"Isn't a secret any longer."

I shot my gaze up to meet his. He looked back at me, as steady and sure as ever. There wasn't even a hint of hesitation in his expression or the way he held my hand.

"Now we both know where we've been," he said. "We can move forward with both eyes open. We're not jumping into anything blind without checking to be sure there's a safety net in place."

"I haven't had a safety net in years." Not since I'd left Portland. I hadn't had my parents there to help me find my way. I hadn't had Luke and Dani around to rely on.

I hadn't had Jamie.

"Now you do," he said. "That's what I can be for you."

It's what he'd always been. I'd just been stupid enough to leave him behind.

"You still want to?" I asked. I knew I'd hurt him with the things I'd done. Hell, I'd hurt myself. How could he forgive me so readily when it had been months since I'd gotten up the gumption to leave Beau behind, but I still hadn't forgiven myself?

"Still," Jamie said. "Always." He closed the distance between us, the heat of his body far headier than any drug I'd ever tried. He tipped my chin up, met my gaze. "I've never stopped wanting you, Katie. I only want you more now. I want to love you the way I should have been all along."

"Oh," I whispered just as his lips pressed to mine and stole my breath.

The kiss started out gentle and indulgent, a luxuriant tease. I put my hands in his hair and held him to me, my tongue slick against his as he leaned over, angling me against the arm of the sofa. But then our pulses went spastic and our breathing became ragged, and everything kicked up a few degrees on the intensity scale.

I tugged on his shirt, dragging it free from his pants so I could splay my hands on his abs. They were muscled, defined, and taut to my touch. I spread my palms up and out, lifting his shirt as I explored his chest and shoulders.

He sat back on his knees, straddling me, and impatiently jerked it the rest of the way over his head. His eyes were dark with lust when he looked down again. I reached for the fly of his pants, my hand brushing against his hardness as I unzipped him. He pulsed against my fingers, heat and straining need.

I finally undid his pants enough that I could lower them some. His dick sprang free.

"Oh God." He slammed his eyes closed. "Maybe we should slow down. I need— Tell me...tell me what you need. Tell me how to make this good for you."

That was when I knew there was no chance he was going to last long—not this first time—but that was okay. This time couldn't be about me. I pushed back on his chest so I could climb out from under him. "Stay right there."

He fell back onto the couch cushions, a dismayed look in his eye, as I rushed into the kitchen for the bag from the drugstore. I dug through it, found the box of flavored condoms, and came back, ripping a foil wrapper open with my teeth. He reached for it, but I shook my head and kept it away from him. Then I kneeled on the floor between his legs and placed it on the tip. He moved his hand in as if to unroll the condom over his length, but I swatted him away. I took him in my mouth, using the pressure of my lips to properly position the strawberry-flavored thing.

I should have tried the strawberry ones years ago. They were a little sweet and a little tart, and best of all, they didn't taste like latex. Who knew?

When I pulled back, pointing my tongue to drag along the underside of Jamie's cock, he let out a ragged breath, his hands fisting in the cushions on either side of him. I drew back and licked my lips, then looked up. His face was red with strain, and his eyes had turned so dark they were almost black.

"Did you like that?"

"So fucking much I can't even..." The rest of his words fell off into nothingness because I swirled my tongue around his head. "Ahh."

"Let me know when I do something you like."

"I like everything you're doing."

I grinned, bracing myself with a hand on each of his thighs. "You can put your hands on my head. Direct me where you want me." Then I bobbed down again, taking as much of his length in as I could.

He didn't talk to me at all, but after a bit of exploration and gauging his response based on the way his hips nearly jerked up off the couch, I figured out what was working for him so I could do more of it. Every now and then, he let out deep, growly sounds that let me know I was absolutely figuring him out.

I added a hand to the mix, stroking his shaft and gently massaging his balls while I focused on his crown with my lips and tongue.

"Oh. Oh fuck." He put his hands in my hair, getting a good grip, and I knew he was about to come. "Katie, I—" His sac tightened, and his hands tightened against me as his hips came up almost involuntarily.

I kept doing as I had been, seeing him through his climax, until he relaxed his hands and ran them through my hair instead of holding me by it. I turned my head to the side, resting it on his thigh.

When I opened my eyes, it was to find two gigantic feline eyes, almost solid black and so big they were about to burst out of Blackbeard's head. He had his front paws on the same thigh and was sniffing like he meant business, too, apparently wide awake after all the activity on the sofa he'd been using as a bed. I burst into laughter.

Well, there was a first.

Chapter Twelve

Jamie

IT FELT INSANELY awkward to get up, clean myself off, pull my pants on, and move around the house as if nothing earth-shattering had just happened. But it had. My whole world had changed in the moment that Katie had put her lips on me. Even now, I felt it all the way to the ends of the messy hairs on my head, and I could see it in the way her eyes fell on me every time I walked by her. Both of us knew nothing would ever be the same between us again, and that was a good thing.

What kinds of things should we talk about after what had just gone down, though? How the hell was I supposed to move from something like that into whatever came next? She'd just given me my first ever blow job, and I hadn't done a fucking thing for her, and that wasn't even close to fair. I was almost as much of an ass as fucking Beau Brunetti, but she acted like she didn't mind me being so selfish. In fact, she'd seemed as though she'd enjoyed it. Was that normal? I didn't know. I mean, I completely understood why men loved it because, holy hell, that had been amazing and mind-blowing and a thousand times better than anything involving nothing more than my hand, but I wasn't sure I followed how a woman could be into it.

Maybe I should talk to her about it, but the idea of asking something along the lines of *Hey, did you enjoy having my balls up in your face, because I did?* seemed even more uncomfortable than pretending our world hadn't just tilted so far off its axis that it fell through space. I'd better just zip it for now. My mouth and my pants, both.

I went into the kitchen and put fresh water in Blackbeard's bowl, then grabbed a can of his kitten food. I left the dry stuff out for him all the time, but the people at the rescue had insisted I should give him some of the stinky wet stuff every day, too. He was still on the couch. Katie had joined him again there after she'd gone off to the bathroom for a minute, and he was gnawing on her fingers. But the second he heard the can pop open, he raced into the kitchen and climbed my pants. Thank God I'd put them on again and hadn't just pulled on some boxers. I should have put on a shirt, too, but it was too late for second thoughts since he was sinking his claws into my skin to get to my shoulder.

I hissed in a breath. "Fucking hell, dude."

Katie joined us just in time to snicker. "Should you be using language like that in front of him?"

"I doubt he'll start repeating everything I say anytime soon." Not like Connor Johnson. So many inappropriate things had come out of that little boy's mouth the other night that I hadn't been able to stop myself from laughing out loud. My reactions had only made Jonny glower at Sara more than he already had been, until she'd thrown up her hands and said, *What do you want to do, wash my mouth out with soap for every bad word he picks up?* I was pretty sure Jonny was debating it, but chances were he would come up with a better solution. Granted, she might not agree his idea was better. What I wouldn't give to be a fly on the wall in their house sometimes... The battles of wills had to be epic.

"I don't know," Katie murmured, tapping her fingers on the table even though Blackbeard was *not* willing to be distracted by something silly like playtime right now. There was food coming, after all. "He's more parrot than cat, at this point."

"Just don't tell me I need to start feeding him birdseed. I have no doubt he'd eat it because he eats everything, but I'm guessing this is better for him."

"He might not mind it if you got a parrot," Katie said, grinning. "They could be buddies and entertain each other when you're gone."

"He'd probably try to kill and eat the parrot."

"As small as he is, the parrot might eat him first."

"Not so sure about that," I said, extracting Blackbeard's claws from my skin so I could set him on the counter now that his food was ready. "I don't think birds are carnivores."

He flailed, frantic to grab on to me again, until I got his nose right in front of his dish. Then he devoured his food in about two and a half seconds. By the time he finished it, his belly was big and round, and he had a sleepy look on his face again.

Blackbeard settled those huge blue eyes on my shoulder. I picked him up and put him there to avoid more claw marks in my skin.

"He looks fat and happy now," Katie said.

I grinned. "You want to join him?" As soon as I said it, I realized how that might come across. Too late, though. The words were already out of my mouth. Heat raced up my neck and face.

She arched a brow. "You want my belly pooching out like his? Not sure I'll be able to gain much weight once I start radiation and chemo. I'll probably lose weight then because of all the nausea. And there's no telling if I'll ever be able to...well, that's not what you meant, anyway."

Her cheeks were pink and she wouldn't look at me. She meant being pregnant. She meant she might never be able to have a baby. I really hadn't thought anything through when I'd opened my fucking mouth. I didn't mean to turn the conversation back to cancer and chemo and all the ways it would hurt her even though it might save her life. I didn't want to bring all that sadness and pain back into this moment. I wanted to keep things light and playful, to give her a place where she could escape from the harsh realities of her life for a while. I wanted to be her safety net.

"I meant I could make you something to eat. Dessert or something," I said, recognizing how feeble it sounded in comparison to what she'd initially interpreted it to mean. "I fed you once, and you didn't immediately keel over and die from food poisoning. You never did eat the chocolate mug cake I made for you."

She smiled without looking up, tracing the patterns of the swirls in my marble counters. "If I ever turn down chocolate, that's when you know there's something to worry about."

"Two chocolate mug cakes, coming right up."

I disengaged Blackbeard again, passing him over to Katie. Then I took out two coffee cups and the ingredients, and I set to work. She put him on the floor and got him to chase a feather toy on a bright yellow fishing pole for a while, but I doubted he would keep it up for long. Not after a big meal like that. When I took the cakes out of the microwave, I turned around to find him making a flying leap at me...only it was really the feather he was going for. It was just heading right in my direction. I dodged out of the way just in the nick of time to avoid claws sinking into my balls again. Once was more than enough for this lifetime.

"Sorry," Katie said, but she was laughing and didn't look remotely apologetic.

"Did you swing that thing my way on purpose?"

"Not really. Maybe." The look in her eyes said *absolutely*.

"So that's what I get for making chocolate cake for you, huh?" I set them on the counter to cool, put some raspberries in the mugs, and topped them off with whipped cream.

"Can you put some more in mine?" she asked.

"After you sent that killer flying straight at my nuts?" I scoffed. "You should be glad I'm not going to keep it all for myself." But I still put more whipped cream in her cup. I set the can on the counter, grabbed two spoons, and carried everything into the living room.

She followed me, Blackbeard chasing the feather toy behind her. When she sat down next to me, she set the can of whipped cream on the coffee table.

"Still not enough?" I asked, laughing.

"Never enough." She gave me a seductive smile that heated my blood. It was too soon after I'd just come, wasn't it? But I was already starting to get turned on again.

Blackbeard swatted at the feathers a few more times, but Katie wasn't swinging it anymore, and he was absolutely pooped. He curled up on the area rug, wrapping both front paws around the feathers to keep them close, like a child would hold a teddy bear, and was asleep in no time.

Katie took one of the mugs and a spoon and dug in. I waited to see what she thought, not that I had to wait very long. She swallowed and glanced up at me. "How on earth is this so good?"

"Oh, you're surprised, eh?"

"Well, not that you made it," she clarified. "I already figured out you've learned a lot in terms of making your way around the kitchen. I'm more surprised that something that can be put together so fast could possibly be this good."

I shoved my spoon in my cup and came up with a big mound, making sure I got cake, berries, and cream, too. Katie reached for the can, but instead of spraying it in her cup, she shoved the dispenser between my lips and shot some cream in my mouth alongside my bite. In shock, I laughed so hard I snorted, which was apparently the wrong thing to do with a mouthful of chocolate, raspberry, and sweetened cream; it went everywhere.

"What did you do that for?" I asked, trying to catch what was falling from my mouth but failing miserably. It dripped down my chin, dribbled all over my chest, and some even landed on my lap.

Katie had a mischievous gleam in her eye. "So I could do this," she said. Then she took my mug from me, set them both on the coffee table, and licked some of it from my chest.

That was all it took for me to go from laughing to harder than steel. I'd been uncertain a few moments before if I could get another erection so soon, but there it was, plain as day, tenting my pants. I leaned back against the cushions, watching her in wonder. "If you wanted your cake and mine, too, you could have just asked," I said. My voice shook because she was working her tongue up the cleft in the center of my abs, the same way she'd done to my cock earlier. "I would have given it to you. Made you another. Whatever." I'd give her anything she wanted.

"I could have," she said when she dipped her head lower and flicked her tongue around my belly button in a way that made my stomach quiver. "But I wanted to do this more than I wanted cake."

I leaned back, eyes locked on her every move, trying to get myself under control. I couldn't exactly complain about what she was doing, either. I couldn't do much of anything but watch, hope that I could hold out long enough to actually make love to her this time, and clench my hands on the couch cushions.

She still had the can in her grip, and she sprayed a dollop on one of my nipples. Her lips closed over it, and she sucked so hard she might as well have been doing the same to my dick, because it jerked in response.

"Does it—" I cut myself off, trying to get my thoughts in line. Not an easy task since now she was swirling her tongue around that nub, and her hands were gliding all over my ribs and abs, and I was about to completely lose my shit.

"Does it what?"

"Does it feel like this for you? If I— If I touched you like this, would it feel this good?"

She didn't answer right away. She kept licking my skin and leaving a trail of wet kisses in her wake as she came up my neck to my mouth. Her thighs straddled my lap, and she ground herself against me. She kissed me, tasting sweet and chocolaty and perfect, and I put my hands on her hips to bring her closer to me.

But then she straightened, set the can of whipped cream aside, and tugged on the hem of her shirt. I watched in wonder as she stripped it up and over her head, tossing it to the floor behind her. "Why don't we find out?" she said.

She had on a pink, lacy bra, delicate fabric cupping her flawless breasts. My mouth watered, my eyes hungrily taking her in. I wanted to see every bit of her. To touch every inch of her skin. To discover all her scents and tastes and learn the sensitive places she liked to be touched.

She had a mole on her left shoulder, and there was a pink blemish on her skin over her right breast. I lifted my hand to touch it, tracing the scar with a fingertip. She shuddered slightly, an almost imperceptible tremor, and I looked up to meet her eyes.

"Chemo port," she explained. "They put tons of makeup over it any time they dressed me in something where it would show on *The Cool Kids*."

"Is it tender?"

"Not now. It itches sometimes."

An overwhelming urge to kiss her scar hit me, so I did. I pressed my lips to the raised bit of flesh. Her breathing sharpened, her lungs lifting her breasts closer to me. Feeling bolder, I kissed her lower, slipping my tongue out to taste. Her skin was smooth as satin. The flesh of her breast was warm and pliable, giving way ever so slightly to my pressure. I kissed the other, just above the top of the lace, and could feel her heartbeat pounding as fast as mine against my lips.

"Touch me," she said, velvety and low.

She didn't need to ask me twice. I cupped her breast with one hand, the other dropping from her hip to explore her ass through the denim of her jeans. She was supple everywhere, soft curves and delicate dips, so different from me. Her body was hot against my hands, and she drove back into my touch, arching to push into me with a quiet sound coming from somewhere deep within her. I squeezed gently, and her nipple hardened beneath my touch.

She sucked in a breath, and I met her gaze. Her eyes had turned an intense blue, bright like flame. "More, Jamie." She placed one hand over mine and crushed it against her. "I need more of you."

"I don't want to hurt you."

"You won't." Her smile was as silken as her skin. "I promise."

She sounded so certain, but she was so small. And she was sick again. When she'd had leukemia, she'd bruised so easily I'd been afraid to do much more than hold her hand. It wasn't leukemia this time, but I was still afraid to touch her in the ways I wanted to. She was precious to me, someone I wanted to protect. Someone I wanted to love with all the reverence and care that had been lacking in all that she'd known before.

Reaching both arms behind her back, she unclasped her bra and drew it forward. I released my hold on her, and the lace scrap dropped to the space between us. Those beautiful, perfect, intoxicating breasts jiggled for a moment before settling, still perky, and practically begging for me to kiss them. Should I? I didn't know, but she'd licked and sucked on my nipple, so it only seemed fair. She drew her arms free from the straps and tossed the bra behind her, but I couldn't look anywhere but at those orbs of softness.

Katie leaned forward, and I froze, unsure what she was doing. She grabbed the can of whipped cream, sprayed some on her breast...and then everything happened at warp speed. I couldn't think anymore. I closed my mouth over her, sucking up the cream and rasping my tongue over her tit. It just got harder, bigger, swelling under my ministrations. She fisted a hand in my hair and put more cream on her other breast, and I greedily lapped it up as she held me to her.

Her breathing was shallow and frantic. The heartbeat thundering behind her ribs was loud enough it almost echoed through the room. She ground her hips into me, heat building upon heat, and then shouted, "Ah!"

I reared back, instantly concerned. "Too much?" I should have trusted my gut. I was being too rough with her. Hurting her.

But she locked both hands in my hair and kissed me so hard, so desperately, that I forgot all about anything but kissing her back. I ran my hands over her back, her sides, her arms, trying to memorize every minute detail. When she came up for air, she said, "Take me to bed, Jamie. I want to be with you."

No need for a second invitation. I was on my feet, Katie in my arms with her legs wrapped around my waist, in about two seconds flat.

"Don't step on Blackbeard," Katie said. She put her arms around my neck, helping to hold her weight.

I glanced down to gauge where he was and took a different path around the coffee table.

"And condoms. We need the condoms."

Right. Condoms. Good thing Katie was capable of thinking about things like protection, because that ability had left me the moment she'd removed her shirt. I made a detour through the kitchen, slowing down long enough that Katie could grab the plastic shopping bag off the counter, and then headed down the hall. As soon as we reached my bedroom, I flipped on the light and kicked the door closed behind us, because I didn't want another repeat of what had happened earlier with Blackbeard trying to help out, and set Katie on her feet.

She tossed the bag on the bed and started stripping off her skintight jeans right away. She still had shoes on, though, so I was able to whip my pants down and kick them to the corner of the room before she finished. I grabbed the bag, dug out the first box I laid my hands on— "Not the flavored ones," she said, still struggling with her jeans— glanced down to see that I'd grabbed the wrong box, tossed it back, and dragged out the next one I found. I tore open the lid and fumbled for a foil packet. By the time I'd ripped it open with my teeth and unrolled it over myself, Katie had gotten free of her jeans.

She slid to the center of the bed, reaching out a hand to me. Nerves turning my legs to jelly, I had to sit down unless I wanted to make a fool of myself and fall on the floor. She touched my arm as soon as I sat, tugging until I relented and lay beside her. I tried to remember how to breathe as my skin met hers.

Every inch of her body was as silken as her breasts. I locked my gaze with hers and trailed my fingertips down the center of her chest to her belly. Her muscles jumped to life beneath my touch.

"Are you sure about this?" I asked, straining to form words. Hell, I was straining to form coherent thoughts. I knew *I* was sure. I'd wanted Katie for years, and now, with her lying here beside me, I could hardly believe it was happening.

"Yes. I want you, Jamie. I want to be with you now, before I have to deal with radiation and chemo and surgery again, before I feel like crap all the time. I want to feel you inside me. To experience this with you without anything else in the way. I want this."

Even hearing her words and knowing them for the truth, I still couldn't seem to make the next move. There was a part of me that wanted to freeze this moment in time and make it last forever. Maybe I was putting off taking the next step because I knew at some point it would come to an end. Maybe I didn't want to face what would come afterward because the future was a giant mass of uncertainty.

Katie must have sensed my hesitation. She took my hand from her belly and edged it lower until my fingers skimmed the liquid heat of her curls. "Touch me," she said again. "I'm ready. I love you, and I want this. I want to experience this with a man I love and respect, and who loves and respects me, too."

So I touched her. I slipped a finger through the slick folds of her flesh. She lifted a knee and moved it to the side, opening herself to my exploration. I found a nub near the top of her private place and traced circles around it. She gasped and moved her hips to meet me.

"Good?" I asked.

She bit her lip and nodded. "That's my clit."

I might not be experienced in the bedroom, but even I knew enough about female anatomy to realize I'd just struck gold. I concentrated my efforts on that small spot, varying my pressure and changing up the tempo until her eyes went unfocused and she couldn't hold still. She had to be close to orgasm.

"Move lower," she gasped. "Don't stop."

So I lowered my hand, keeping my thumb on her clit, until I found her entrance. She was so soft and wet, and my finger slipped inside without any resistance. Katie moaned and bucked her hips, driving my finger deeper. I added another, shocked at the sensation of having her flesh surrounding me, accepting me, clutching to keep me in.

"Jamie," she rasped, and I glanced up to meet her gaze.

She hooked a hand under my shoulder, tugging gently until I came up above her. I braced my weight on my arms on either side of her, and she opened her thighs wider to allow room for me to nestle between them. My cock was straining to reach her, as though it had a mind of its own and could sense the proximity of her pussy.

With a gentle scrape of her nails, Katie moved her hands down my back, stopping when they were on my ass. She gripped my cheeks hard, drawing me closer, even as she locked her legs with mine. "Please." Just one word. Almost inaudible and full of need.

I held my weight on one arm and used the other hand to guide myself inside her. She took me completely, stretching to accommodate my size but fitting as tight as a glove. She squeezed my ass again and shifted, and then primal instinct took over.

My forehead against hers, eye to eye and nose to nose, we moved together until she clenched me tighter and let out an unintelligible shout. Every muscle in her body had been tensing, clasping, reaching for this moment, and now they all gave way in the sweetest, most exquisite explosion imaginable, like a coil releasing. I kissed her, increasing my pace until I came, too, wrapped up in her love.

"I don't think I could ever love you more than I do right now," I murmured, my nose buried in her hair that was splayed over my pillows.

She relaxed her legs so they were tangled with mine but not holding me in place, and she ran her fingers through my hair, her nails scraping my scalp in an oddly comforting manner. "Why do you love me?" she asked.

Why did I love her? Talk about a complicated question. I let it roll around in my head before propping myself up on my elbows and looking down at her. "I love you because I don't know how to not love you. Because I can't imagine my world without you, and I don't ever want to have to face that again. Because you are sweetness and light and life, and you see me as the man I could be, not as the man I am."

Katie shook her head. "You are that man. You just haven't learned how to see yourself that way."

I rolled off her, drawing her along with me to hold against my side. "You make me want to be better than I am," I said gruffly. Then I couldn't seem to stop kissing her. Every time I thought I was done, she would smile again, or her eyes would take on this lazy, sated look, and I would have to kiss her again. I kissed her hair, her forehead, her nose, her cheeks, her lips. I couldn't get enough. I wanted to bottle this moment and the way we both felt right now so we could return to it whenever life got to be too much to bear.

Because that was coming. She knew it and I knew it.

I had never been the praying sort, but I said a silent prayer right now. We'd had this one perfect moment; I asked for it not to be the last.

Chapter Thirteen

Katie

I ENDED UP spending the night with Jamie instead of going home. He let me sleep in a pair of his boxers and a T-shirt that were easily two or three sizes too big for me, but at least I didn't have to go back over to my place to find anything. Once we had cleaned up and were fairly sure there wouldn't be any more sexy times for the night, Jamie had opened the door and let Blackbeard join us.

As tiny as he was, that kitten didn't have any problems at all getting into the bed on his own. Not that either of us found that surprising, considering the way he was always climbing up to Jamie's shoulders. Jamie slept on his back, one arm holding me to him. I used his chest as my pillow, and Blackbeard nestled in the space between Jamie's neck and shoulder, hanging out above my head. None of us moved a muscle the whole night, it seemed, until sometime after dawn, when Blackbeard started chewing on my hair and attacking it as if it were his feather toy.

Needless to say, I woke up laughing.

Jamie jerked awake, stretching once the initial shock wore off. "He should be eating my hair instead of yours."

"Not a chance in hell I'd go for that."

"Hmm." He rolled his head to the side and glanced at the clock on his nightstand. "Morning came way too early today."

I felt a tiny bit guilty since I'd been the one to keep him up later than he should have been when he had a game the next night, but not too guilty. "You already have to get up?" I asked, yawning and snuggling closer to him. I wasn't ready to let go of the flawlessness of the night.

"I've got a meeting with the coaches before morning skate." He inched out from under me, despite my pouting, and Blackbeard let out a whining sound that suited my mood perfectly. "What are you doing today?"

I blinked at him, still trying to wake up. The sun streaming in through the windows lit him in a golden glow. He'd only put on a pair of boxers before we'd gone to bed, so I could see every detail of the muscles my hands had explored last night. That only made me want to do some more exploration, though, and it was going to have to wait if he had to leave for a meeting soon.

I frowned, not ready to move yet, and Blackbeard came down from the pillow and circled a couple of times before curling up in the bend of my elbow. I drew him closer to me, nuzzling my nose against his. Then I regretted it, because he yawned right in my face. His fur might smell sweet, but his breath left a lot to be desired. "I guess I'll go shopping for some art to put on my walls this morning," I said. "Mom wants to have lunch. Then I've got that appointment with the radiation team in the afternoon before coming to the game." I hadn't wanted to think about my upcoming meeting with the doctors. I'd rather just forget all about that, pretend I was perfectly healthy and didn't need to go through this again, but I doubted anyone would let me get away with it.

"You're coming to the game, then?" He stretched his arms over his head, pulling them from side to side to work the kinks out. Probably also in an effort to hide the hint of a blush and the way his dimples had come out. I guessed that meant he wanted me to be at the game, even if he didn't want to show it.

"Unless you'd rather I didn't," I said. "I might not be able to come to games once I start radiation." For that matter, I might not be able to be around Jamie and Blackbeard much for a while. It depended on what type of radiation they'd settled on, but some types of therapy would leave *me* radioactive for a while. I really hoped I didn't have to go through that. Some of the other kids in the cancer center when I'd been treated before had been stuck in the hospital, isolated, for a week or more at a time. Others were allowed to go home, but they'd had to limit their contact with the people they loved and couldn't be around children or animals. I didn't know if I could handle that kind of treatment plan right now. I forced myself to stop thinking along those lines. No point in worrying until they gave me something to worry about. "I don't know if you'd rather we took some time letting people in on the idea that we're together now..."

With all the talk, Blackbeard was starting to get a spurt of energy. Instead of snuggling with me, he was chasing his tail, racing so fast that he was making me dizzy.

Jamie shook his head. "Pretty sure all the guys already know after you came along for dinner with Razor last night. I don't care if anyone knows. I'll even call my mom and tell her if you think word might get out publicly soon."

My heartbeat kicked up a notch, now that he was already thinking about telling his mother about me. This was what I'd wanted, of course—for us to really be an official couple—but to have it happening so fast along with all the other changes in my life was leaving my head spinning as fast as Blackbeard.

"If we were in LA," I said, trying to keep my excitement in check, "I'd tell you to call her on your way to the rink. No paparazzi here to worry about, though. Tell her when you're ready for her to know."

A memory from a few years ago hit me and caused a brief twinge— news about Cam Johnson and Sara Thomas being an item getting back to Jonny's sisters in Canada before the two of them were ready for anyone to know—but this was different. That was at a point when Jonny and the whole team were surrounded by a ton of controversy, so the media had been hounding them. There was no reason to think that any of the hockey media would latch on to this right now.

"Go shower," I said, brushing that thought aside. "Want me to make you breakfast?" It was only fair, after all. Jamie had cooked for me a couple of times now.

He grinned. "I would love for you to make me breakfast." He bent over me on the bed and gave me a peck on the cheek.

Then I remembered how he went about his cooking. "Do you own any pots and pans, or..."

"Nope. Just small pans that'll fit in the toaster oven. Need me to help?"

I waved him toward the bathroom. "I'll figure it out." And I would probably do that by going back to my house and dragging some of my new pans back with me so I could christen them and his stove.

Jamie didn't hurry off to shower, though. He gave me a solid kiss, this time, shoving Blackbeard to the side and settling himself over me, nearly pinning me to the mattress. He took his time about it, too, leaving us both breathless and wanting more.

"You could come and shower with me," he said hopefully when he finally came up for air.

"I could." I laughed. "Not sure Bergy would be too thrilled with you if you're late, though."

"Probably not the best idea, huh?"

"Probably not." This time. We could save that for another day.

Jamie

I COULDN'T STOP thinking about Katie all day even though I didn't get to see her. I had my leadership meeting with the coaches, morning skate, a media scrum, a film session, lunch with the boys, and my afternoon nap before I had to head up to the arena for the game. She'd been at her doctor's appointment when I got home for my nap, and she'd left me a text message saying she would meet me in the owner's box once I arrived, and that she loved me. Nothing more. No word about what the doctors had told her. Needless to say, I was on edge from the moment I saw that message until I got to the arena.

Usually I headed straight for the locker room so I could get started on my pregame routine. The other guys often stopped by to see their wives and girlfriends and kids before getting ready for the game, or they dropped off friends and family from out of town to be sure they were well looked after. I didn't often have someone here, though. I couldn't help but feel nervous as I made my way up the elevator to the suite level.

"Hey, if it ain't Captain JB," said Davey Hearne as I walked up, holding out a hand. He was one of the regular security guys at the Moda Center. He'd been working here since they'd built the place, apparently, and during Storm games, he worked at the owner's box, making sure no one entered who didn't have clearance.

I shook his hand. "Hey, Davey. Is Katie Weber here yet?" I poked my head through the door to look around.

"Sitting up front with her mama."

The room was already jam-packed with not only the guys' wives and girlfriends but their kids, too. Tons of kids of every age, along with all the noise you expect with a veritable nursery. I couldn't see Katie through the mass of toys and toddlers, but if Davey said she was up front, then that was where I intended to go. Not that I had a clue how to get through the maze in front of me.

I thanked him and headed in, and Connor Johnson immediately toddled over to grab my leg. I picked him up because it was easier than trying to walk with a massive growth on the top of my foot, and I assumed Sara would be with Katie and Laura, anyway.

He put a hand on the side of my face, turning me to look at him, his expression as serious as a heart attack. "Razor is a asswipe."

I didn't laugh this time, but that took a gargantuan effort on my part. I tried to look as serious as he did. "Is he? And who told you that?" I asked, cautiously making my way through the room to avoid stepping on any children or toys. I wasn't going to argue with the little guy on that score. I'd called Razor an ass and worse so many times myself that Connor might have picked it up from me without me realizing it.

"My mommy."

"I see." So maybe I was in the clear. I hoped for Sara's sake that Jonny hadn't heard the latest from his son, though. He might go ballistic on her, not that he would ever hurt her. They would just argue, which would cause her stress, and that was not something she needed right now. She'd had two miscarriages before, and carrying Connor hadn't been easy for her, either. She'd spent almost two months confined to bed rest with him. This pregnancy was the only easy one of the bunch, not that it had been easy, but I doubted it would help anything if they got into another argument over something like Connor picking up on bad language. "How about we don't say that in front of the other kids, okay?"

He pouted at me, but he said, "'Kay 'kay."

Soupy and Rachel's twin two-year-old daughters were camped out on the floor with their dolls right in the middle of the aisle I was trying to traverse. They weren't identical, but close to it, with Rachel's bright red hair and a smattering of freckles everywhere you looked. I stepped high to go over them, but I felt little hands grab on, and they giggled. I cautiously put my foot down, and then they each claimed a leg to ride.

Before I'd settled on how I would get out of this mess, their older half brother, Tuck, came up to me. I loved this kid. He had the same hair, same freckles, but a devious streak that would rival Connor's, but in a ten-year-old's body.

"Let Mr. Jamie walk, Peyton." He bent down to pick up one of the girls.

I held out my free arm, and he passed her over to me. "Ginger Ninja to the rescue once again. Thanks for the assist." I'd been calling him that since I first met him years ago when he was five.

He blushed a ferocious shade of red, but then he pried Sidney, the other twin, free. "They like to climb Mr. Soupy's legs, too. They make him carry them around while they ride his feet and stuff. Mom isn't letting them do that right now, though, because he's hurt, and I'm too little. They still try sometimes." He grinned. "But you're as big as Mr. Soupy, so I guess they saw their chance and took it."

"Not quite as big as Soupy." I shouldn't have opened my mouth because the second I did, Peyton shoved her fingers in there and giggled. I wasn't sure what she'd been into, but at least whatever sticky stuff was all over her tasted sweet.

"Close enough."

Sidney was too heavy for Tuck to carry very far, but he didn't let that deter him, coming along beside me as we headed for the front where the women were congregating.

Sure enough, Katie and Laura were there with Sara, Rachel, Brie, and Mia Quincey, Q's wife. Katie's brows were pinched and her lips were thin, so I knew she was worried or upset about something, but the moment she looked up and saw me carrying the two toddlers, her whole face lit up.

"I see you come bearing gifts," she said, and all the other women glanced over.

I winked. "Something like that."

"Did they try to ride you over here?" Rachel asked, rolling her eyes.

"They tried to. Might have succeeded if the Ginger Ninja hadn't come along."

She took her daughter from me, and Laura reached for Connor, who was squirming to go in the opposite direction of his mother. Sara had a hand on the small of her back and looked like she was absolutely miserable. Mia patted her lap for Sidney, and Tuck passed over his sister right as Jessica Lynch, Nicky's fiancée, came in with his niece and two nephews. Elin found Tuck's older sister, Maddie, in her usual spot in the other corner up front. The two of them huddled together, probably waiting on Danger's wife and kids to get there since Elin and Étienne were kind of a thing lately. The boys, Hugo and Nils, were right around Tuck's age. His face lit up when he saw them.

"Later, Mr. Jamie," he said, racing away.

"Homework, Tuck!" Rachel called behind him. I had a feeling he was going to feign deafness on that one.

Katie got up to join me, but Brie caught my eye before we took off to find somewhere quiet to talk.

"When you get a chance, I need a word."

"After the game?" I asked, taking Katie's hand. Brie nodded, and I wound my way through the obstacle course of kids and toys to a corner near the back, leading Katie along with me.

"What's up with Brie?" she asked me, eyeing me suspiciously.

"Just a thing for Burnzie she asked me for help with." It was a bald-faced lie, and I *hated* lying ever. Especially because I was really fucking bad at it. I searched Katie's face to see if she was on to me, but I thought this time I might have gotten away with it. This was all supposed to be a surprise for her, though, so I was going to have to get used to lying, and in very short order. "So what happened with the doctor? And why are you upset?"

"I really hate how you can always tell when I'm upset."

"I'd be a bad boyfriend if I couldn't."

She perked up a bit at the word *boyfriend*, and her lips quirked up in a grin. "You looked really hot carrying those kids in."

"Thanks." Now I was blushing again. "Stop avoiding the question, though."

Katie's smile turned to a pout. "Party pooper. The good news is they're not going to force me to stay in the hospital for weeks at a time. The bad news is they want to do systemic radiation this time, so I'll have to be pretty much isolated while I'm going through it." She sounded upbeat, like she was trying to laugh it off, but her eyes told another story.

"Isolated how?"

She shrugged. "Stay at my house. Not be around pregnant women, kids, or animals at all. Limit my contact with anyone else to less than two hours a day. Oh, and any clothes, bedding, dishes, and whatnot that I use while I'm radioactive will have to be tossed later." No matter how hard she fought to give off an air of nonchalance, she couldn't pull it off. Not with me.

"For how long?" I was trying to wrap my head around the fact that she would be right next door to me but I wouldn't be able to hold her, to comfort her when she felt bad.

"A few days each time. Four rounds of this, about a week apart, before moving on to chemo."

"But more tests first," I reminded her. "You might not need chemo." The radiation might shrink it enough to go ahead with the surgery without going through that step.

She let go of my hand and crossed her arms in front of her. "I'm getting chemo if there's even a remote possibility it will get rid of that tumor before they decide to cut me open."

I wrapped her up in a hug because there wasn't much to be said. Sometimes, touch was the best comfort to be had. Which only made it worse that she was going to have to spend so much time completely isolated from everyone she loved. I squeezed her close. "Less than two hours a day? But we could break that up, right? So you could be around your mom for a while, and your dad, and me…"

"It's not much."

"It's not much, but it's something."

"That's not even the worst news I got today, though."

My stomach dropped. What was worse than learning about her treatment plan? "No?" I asked.

"I don't guess you've taken a look at Twitter today, have you?"

I *knew* I should have gone back in to the drugstore last night and confronted that douchebag who had checked us out. "It's not something I feel the need to do every day," I said cautiously.

Katie backed away so she could look up at me with shining eyes. "I thought I was safe from paparazzi here."

"Paparazzi? So not just the dude at the drugstore?"

She shook her head. "I don't think Mom and Dad have seen it yet, but it won't be long. You should probably talk to your family. Tell them what's going on before they see it. I'll figure out how to explain it to Mom and Dad, but I don't want your family thinking…" She shook her head, lost for words.

"Seen what?" My blood pressure was going through the roof, and I didn't even know exactly what I was mad about yet. "Explain what?"

She slipped her cell phone out of her pocket, pulled something up, and handed the phone to me. The TMZ headline read *Katie Weber Caught with Not One But Two New Boy Toys*, and it had a picture of her surrounded by two guys who were clearly me and Razor even though our faces had been blurred out. It was from last night. I clicked on it to get to the main article, which was riddled with photos from dinner. No blurring here. A lot of the pics had me holding her hand or with my arm around her waist, but the photographer hadn't missed Razor dipping her to kiss her on the cheek at the hotel, or when she'd kissed him again afterward when we were dropping him off. With the angle of the shots, though, those kisses looked like *real* kisses. We might be lucky that they hadn't caught her planting one on Zee's cheek when we first got to the hotel. But then again, maybe they had, but since he hadn't come to dinner, they hadn't used it. *Yet.* When I scrolled down to the bottom, I found the tweets from the guy at the drugstore, and they were every bit as offensive as I had imagined and worse. He'd even snapped a pic of us when we'd been in the condom aisle, multiple boxes in hand. The whole article made out that we'd gone back to the hotel with Razor and had an orgy or something.

I handed her phone back to her, my rage barely held in check.

"You should probably fill the team in if they haven't seen it already," she said, tucking it away in her pocket. "Jim, the coaches. They might need to get PR on damage control. And Razor, too. He should probably let his parents know what it really was, and he'll need to explain things to the Thunderbirds brass."

I'd be sure Razor knew, but I doubted his parents would react like mine would. I'd never met his father, or even heard him talk about the guy, and his mother seemed to take everything in stride as long as he was happy and healthy. He did everything he could to make her life easier, but I didn't think he would need to do too much to explain himself. My parents would believe whatever I told them, especially since they knew I would never lie to them, but I doubted they'd be thrilled about having to explain this to my youngest brothers if they got wind of it. And then there were their neighbors and coworkers to think about, and the parents of kids my brothers went to school with, and former teachers who would wonder where I'd gone wrong. The list of people my parents would have to deal with seemed endless.

"This is what they've been doing to you all along, isn't it?" For the first time, I really thought I understood how damaging her years in Hollywood had been. It had gone far beyond Jesse Carmichael and Beau Brunetti. The ways those two had hurt her had only been the tip of the iceberg.

She nodded, hugging her arms to her chest. "Pretty much. They sneak around, following everything you do, take a pic, find a way to make it incriminating in some way, and ruin your life."

Several of the other guys had already come and gone from the owner's box, and I knew I was running out of time before I needed to get down to the locker room. I kissed her on the forehead. "I'm not going to let them ruin your life," I said.

She nodded, but she didn't seem as if she believed a word out of my mouth. I couldn't blame her. I didn't have the first clue how I would prevent the paparazzi from doing anything, and it might not even be possible.

But I'd be damned if I didn't try.

Katie

THE GAME AGAINST the Thunderbirds turned out to be an absolute blowout. Nicky had a shutout, the Storm put up eight goals, and the T-Birds were an utter wreck throughout. I felt bad for Zee, Hunter, and Razor having to play for a team that had zero chance of getting to the playoffs, and likely wouldn't for years to come. They said all the right things to the media, of course—well, *now* Hunter did, even if he'd let a few choice sound bites fly when he'd first been claimed in the expansion draft—but it wasn't hard for anyone who knew those three to realize they would rather be playing for any other team in the league.

Jamie must have filled in the Storm's head honchos on the TMZ stuff before the game, because Rachel sat down next to me midway through the third period. She wasn't just Soupy's wife. She was also Jim Sutter's assistant.

She dropped her voice and leaned in close. "Does your mom know yet?"

I nodded. "Filled her in during the first intermission."

"Good. Jim's already got PR working on it in conjunction with the Thunderbirds. We're going to do everything we can to squash it as what it was—completely innocent."

I wrung my hands together. I'd been doing a lot of that today. "I just hate that Razor's being dragged into this. I mean, he just wanted to hang out with Jamie for a bit. They never get to see each other."

"He's a big boy. He can take it." One of the twins waddled over and held up her arms, and Rachel instinctively drew her onto her lap. "I can see if Jim can sneak you in to talk to him for a minute after the game without the media around, if you want."

"Could you?" I owed him an apology for involving him in my screwed-up life, if nothing else.

A few text messages later, it was all arranged. When the final horn sounded, I went with Davey through some back hallways and a private elevator, and he took me straight to an entrance to the visiting team's area. I'd been all over this building through the years, but only on the home team's side. It felt strange to turn right instead of left at certain points. Another security guard stopped us at the double doors leading to the locker room and went inside, and a couple of minutes later, Razor came out. He was covered in sweat and still had on his skates, breezers, and all of the lower half of his equipment, even though he'd removed his jersey and shoulder pads.

The two security guards stepped a discreet distance away and started up a conversation, leaving us to talk.

"Hey, Katie," Razor said, rubbing a towel over his face and bare chest.

"Hey," I said, blushing. "I guess you know about…" I caught myself trying to read some of the tattoos on his naked skin that I'd never known he had, and snapped my head up. His tats were none of my business, nor was his chest or any other part of his body.

He had a cocky grin at the best of times, but it was cockier than ever right now. No doubt he'd caught me gawking at him. "About the TMZ shit?" he finished for me.

I nodded.

"Yeah, that's all kinds of fucked up. Sorry they're screwing you around like that. No pun intended."

I had no doubt he'd meant every bit of it. That was just Razor.

"I'm the one who's sorry," I said. "If I'd thought they would find me here, I would have stayed home and left you and Jamie to hang out without me."

Razor let out a snort. "You think I'm worried about it? When the girls back in Tulsa find out that I'm open to a threesome, they'll be all over me whether it's true or not. I'm sure this will only help me score more than I already am."

I scowled up at him. "Charming."

"It was a joke. I'm not in need of *that* much de-douchifying. De-douchification? Whatever." He waved a hand, dismissing his attempt at coming up with a real word.

"I come down here to apologize to you, and this is what I get." I laughed. "You're something else, Razor."

He winked. "That's why the ladies love me. But seriously, there's not a fucking thing you need to apologize for. Don't worry about me. I can handle it. I'm just worried about you and Babs."

"I don't want your family to think you've done anything wrong."

"I can promise you, my mom's seen and done much worse than anything some tabloid thinks they can peg on me. This won't even faze her for a second. Now, Mrs. Jernigan, on the other hand? She'll throw a shit-fit." He grinned at me, the kind of wicked grin I recognized as meaning he was up to no good, as usual. Mr. and Mrs. Jernigan were the husband-and-wife ministry team who'd made a fortune with their massive church, televised sermons, and Bible-study books. They'd decided to invest their earnings by buying a hockey team, for some reason. I couldn't even begin to imagine how a guy like Razor was getting along with them at the helm, let alone how a couple of morally upright people were putting up with him and his shenanigans, but he seemed like the same Razor I'd known when he'd played in Portland—no concern at all for what anyone else thought. He was always himself, no matter the consequences.

"But while you're down here and Babs isn't around," he said slyly. "Did he finally get some? He fed me some pansy *I don't kiss and tell* bullshit and threatened to break my nose when I asked earlier, which makes me think he got laid. So did he?"

"I have to go," I said, rolling my eyes and spinning on my heel before retreating down the tunnel.

"He did! I could kiss you for that, Katie. I could totally fucking kiss you."

I kept walking but called over my shoulder, "You already did. Just check TMZ if you don't remember."

Chapter Fourteen

Katie

THE STORM'S WIN against the Thunderbirds might have been a positive sign of the team coming together, finally, working out their differences and figuring out how to play together as a cohesive unit. That was certainly what everyone hoped, but it didn't prove to be the case.

In their very next game against the Toronto Maple Leafs, the Storm couldn't score at all despite getting more than forty shots on the Leafs' goaltender, Jonathan Bernier, and Nicky let in three Leafs goals in the first period alone. Bergy sat him on the bench and sent in Sean "Bobby" Roberts, the Storm's backup goalie, when the teams returned for the second. That didn't work out much better. They lost the game five to nothing thanks to stellar goaltending from Bernier and a hat trick from Joffrey Lupul.

The script flipped on the Storm again in the next game when they played the Winnipeg Jets. Nicky might as well have stood on his head, making all the "easy" saves alongside a number of spectacular ones, and the Storm's offense was clicking like they rarely had all season so far. The problem that night was that they completely forgot how to play defense—a fact the Jets took advantage of at every turn. The Storm squeaked out a win, but they didn't deserve it. Not by a mile.

They couldn't seem to play a solid game unless they were up against a team that was in shambles, and that was the talk every night in the owner's box between the wives and girlfriends. Apparently now I was one of them instead of one of the kids. I'd been hanging out with them for years, but things seemed different now.

One thing I'd learned in my time with these women was that while each of them had her own life and interests, they all very much lived and died right along with their men during these games. Whatever was happening with the team inevitably came home with the guys, and that meant the women spent a lot of time trying to sort out how best to help them.

That extended to helping each other, too. Last season, when Nicky's sister had passed away leaving him with his niece and nephews to look after, these women had dropped everything in order to help Nicky and Jessica find their footing. That was just the latest in a long string of events where they'd all banded together to support each other, proving Jim Sutter's mantra that the Portland Storm was a family. Weddings, births, illnesses, deaths, injuries, birthdays—the fact was, with the guys on the road so much, sometimes the women of the Storm family saw each other more than we saw our guys.

They'd banded around me before, when I'd had cancer the first time. That was back before my reputation was in tatters, though, so I could understand that.

They'd done it again a few days ago, though, when all the news outlets started putting out their crazy stories about me, Jamie, and Razor. They were sticking close to me, never letting me be seen anywhere alone. It was like they were putting up a front around me, trying to show the world that whatever might be said about me, they were with me. I wasn't sure how well it was working so far, since I still saw more vicious rumors and innuendo every time I flipped on the TV or cracked open the Internet, but at least the girls were helping to prevent anything new from showing up there. Through it all, I felt more and more…confused. Seriously confused. I didn't get why they would put their own reputations on the line by being seen with me if they could avoid it.

And if that wasn't enough, I could tell they wanted to rally around me again over the cancer returning, too. I hadn't told anyone but my family and Jamie that I was sick again. I wasn't ready to deal with the sympathy and well wishes and whatnot. It sometimes felt stifling, smothering, especially when there wasn't a damn thing they could do that would help.

But they knew.

It was clear because of the way they were treating me when we were all together. It wasn't the kind of girl talk and giggling I would have expected when they'd figured out Jamie and I were finally a couple. It was more like they were treating me with kid gloves, scooching over to be sure I was in the center of things, getting up to grab a drink for me instead of letting me get it myself, asking if I was warm enough or if I needed to borrow a sweater.

They knew. I hadn't told them, but they knew. At this point, it didn't even matter how they had learned or why someone had thought it necessary to tell them. I was just resigned to it, and I figured I might as well come clean so they could stop pussyfooting around the issue.

It was Sunday night during the first intermission of a tie game against the Chicago Blackhawks. The score didn't even come close to telling the whole story of the game so far, as was becoming a trend with this year's team. The Storm hadn't been playing well at all, and a few of the guys were making the kinds of mistakes with the puck that would undoubtedly get Bergy's blood boiling. I had a feeling they were in the locker room right now getting an earful from him.

I was set to start radiation tomorrow morning. Mia and Rachel had gone down to the locker room because Q had gotten hurt a few minutes ago, but the rest of the regular crew were here. I steeled myself for fending off whatever help they tried to insist on giving me and dove in. "So I guess you all know by now that my cancer's back," I said, and they stopped talking and laughing almost instantaneously.

Mom looked like she was about to burst into tears, even though I'd barely said a thing, and Jessica closed down the laptop she'd just opened and pushed it aside. Brie nodded, like she'd been waiting for this. Sara was sitting right beside me, Connor curled up and sleeping on the bit of lap her pregnant belly wasn't covering. She took my hand, which was a big deal for Sara Johnson. She'd never been the touchy-feely sort.

"I'll be starting radiation tomorrow." I was doing my best not to get choked up but failing miserably.

"Tell us what you need," Brie said.

I shook my head. "There's nothing you can do."

"Bullshit," Sara said. "We can hold your hair back when you puke. We can bring you movies and chocolate and soup. We can drive you to doctor's appointments or the hospital, or pick up groceries, or take you to the damn pharmacy. We can help you get out of the house when you're up to it. We can fucking cry with you when you need to cry. Don't try to push us away, Katie. I think you should fucking know by now that we won't let you."

I looked to Mom for help. She knew. She understood. But she just nodded for me to go on with tears in her eyes.

I clenched my hands into fists, digging them down between the arms of the chair and the cushion. "I know you want to help. All of you. I get it, but you can't this time. I can't be around any of you. The doctors said I have to be completely isolated for a few days with every treatment."

"*Completely?*" Jessica asked. "No one can be near you at all?"

"No one who's pregnant. No kids or animals."

"So that rules out the kids, animals, Brie, and Sara," Jessica said, being her usual, logical self. "But not your parents. Not me. Not Rachel and Mia and anyone else we can get involved. Not the guys."

The others nodded.

"But you have to go home to your kids and pets. What if you get exposed to radiation and don't get it all washed away before you go home?"

"We'll be really careful," she said. "You've got an extra bathroom at your house, right? So we can bring extra clothes and towels, take a shower in the bathroom you're not using before we leave, and make sure there's no trace of anything harmful."

My jaw dropped. "That's crazy. There's no reason for any of you to go through all that."

"There's every reason for it," Brie said. "You're the reason. You can bet if I wasn't pregnant, I would be there."

Jessica nodded. "There are enough of us around that we can make sure you're never alone unless you want to be."

"I do—"

"You don't get to call us off yet," Mom interrupted. "Not until you've given us a chance to overwhelm you with love."

"And Brie and I can call you and text you and drive you batshit crazy on FaceTime since we can't be there," Sara added.

Brie gave a decisive nod. "Exactly."

"Exactly what?" Rachel asked as she and Mia came back in. She plopped down in the seat on my other side. "Are we finally planning for cancer treatments? Jim's been asking me how things were progressing with that, so he could help sort out what the team can do."

"The team can't do anything," I said, throwing up my hands.

"You really think that's going to fly with them?" This time it was Julianne d'Aragon, Danger's wife. She'd been keeping an eye on Elin and Étienne to be sure they didn't sneak off alone somewhere, but now some of the older kids were coming over to join us, so she came, too. Julianne took a seat facing me and pinned me with the sort of mothering look she'd perfected probably around the same time Mom had. "Some of these guys have known you since you were thirteen years old. They think of you as a kid sister. Jim and most of the front office think of you as a daughter or a niece. They're not going to let you shut them out. None of us are."

Maddie Campbell was one of the kids who'd just joined us. She was thirteen now, but she'd been wise beyond her years for as long as I'd known her. She sat cross-legged on the floor nearby and gave me the shy smile I'd come to be very familiar with, and it took me back to nights sitting in this box with her, sharing her blanket and letting her surprise me with her insights. "I don't think Mr. Jamie's going to stay away no matter what you tell him, so I think you're just going to have to accept that everyone else is going to help, too. Wherever he goes, the rest of them eventually follow."

And with that, the part of the discussion in which they allowed me to argue effectively came to an end. Whether I wanted their help or not, I was going to get it. I could live with it, but I wished I felt better about accepting it.

Throughout the rest of the game, they discussed safety measures they'd have to take and worked out a schedule, and I waited until Jamie was done so he could take me home. Right now, he was the only thing I wanted.

A THOUSAND THOUGHTS were racing through my head as Jamie drove us back to his house. It felt good to be cared about so much that the Storm's WAGs weren't going to let me go through it alone, but I wasn't sure I deserved that sort of concern again. Being associated with me right now shouldn't be on any of their to-do lists, because the firestorm of gossip mag fodder still hadn't died out, and there were a lot of risks they would be running in terms of their health if they were with me. I didn't know how to stop them, though, and I wasn't sure I had the energy for it, anyway. Even if I did right now, as soon as the radiation kicked in, it would knock me on my ass and zap any energy I had left. I supposed I would just have to go with the flow, but that wasn't something I was very good at.

Over the previous few days, I'd done a lot in order to get settled in my new house. In the mornings and early afternoons, while Jamie and Dad had been busy with practices and other team functions, I'd spent a lot of time with Mom. We'd gone shopping for different knickknacks for the house and planned how to put together my studio.

Dad had come over in the afternoons to help me paint the walls and measure the space. He wanted to do a built-in for me along one wall, even though I'd told him I could hire a contractor to do it. *I'm your father*, he'd said. *Let me do this one thing for you.* He hadn't always been able to do the sorts of father-daughter things he'd wanted to over the years, so I'd given in, despite my reservations about his construction skills. He'd been tinkering with things in the garage lately, Mom had told me. She hadn't seen anything he'd made yet, but maybe he would surprise us all.

Most days, if he wasn't busy with some call-in radio show or community involvement arranged for by the Storm, Jamie had come and helped, too. Occasionally he brought Levi or Austin Cooper along and put them to work. The guys had all painted together side by side, bickering and bantering while Dad grumbled orders, and it had started to feel normal.

Every night, though, I ended up next door at Jamie's instead of sleeping in my own house. It didn't seem to matter that I was a homeowner now. Not once had I slept without him since that first night, and I was dreading the fact that tomorrow, I would have to. Not only was I going to be radioactive but the team's home stand had come to an end with tonight's game. They were due to fly to Philadelphia tomorrow afternoon.

My new normal was about to be stripped away from me. The loss of normalcy was already weighing heavily on me, and it hadn't even started yet.

The team had lost three to one, and only a handful of players hadn't made several glaring mistakes in the course of the loss. Jamie had been as quiet as I had the whole way home, but then he reached across the console for my hand. "It's going to be all right," he said.

"You don't know that. No one knows."

"You're right. No one knows, but I believe it."

I laced my fingers with his, and that was when I noticed his knuckles were red and swollen. I pulled his hand up so I could see it more clearly in the streetlights, which made it even more obvious that he'd used his hand to throw punches at someone or something. There were a couple of splits in the skin that had been closed with butterfly bandages instead of stitches. I'd been around hockey players my whole life, so I knew what this meant. There was no possibility of misunderstanding.

"You didn't get in a scrap tonight," I said. "You haven't fought once all season. What happened?"

"It's nothing."

"Don't brush me off, Jamie."

"It was just me being stupid. That's all. No big deal."

"You could have broken your hand." For that matter, I wasn't convinced that he hadn't broken something. I turned it palm up and scrutinized it, but that didn't really help. No X-ray vision. "It is a big deal. Who did you hit?"

"The wall." He drew his hand free from mine and placed it back on the wheel. "I punched the fucking wall in intermission, not that it did anyone any good. I hurt my hand, I let my teammates see me lose my shit, and we still fucking lost the game."

"Why did you punch a wall?"

"It was either the wall or Koz, and I figured it would be better if only one of us got hurt instead of both of us."

"Do you want to talk about it?" I asked even though I knew he would say no. It didn't matter how many issues hockey players had with their coaches or teammates, they never talked about it outside of the locker room or the coach's office. Maybe behind closed doors with a wife, but I wasn't his wife, and even that could sometimes be shaky ground because there had been more than a few cases of players' wives cheating with a teammate. They seemed to all live by the rule of handling issues within the organization, not spreading things to the media. That was just part of the deal in the hockey world. What happens in the room stays in the room. It was the complete opposite of Hollywood, where one person's business becomes everyone's business in a flash.

"Not really, unless you know a good way to get an asshole to stop being an asshole and start acting like he isn't a one-man show," Jamie said.

That was a lot more of an answer than I'd been expecting.

We were on our street. Jamie hit the button on his garage remote and waited for the door to open. I took a moment to think about how best to respond. Once we were in the kitchen and Blackbeard was climbing Jamie's suit, I said, "You know, you could try to think of him like you do Razor."

"Koz and Razor aren't even in the same ballpark of assholishness."

That was debatable, but I chose not to argue the point. "I'm just saying that they both have some issues when it comes to how they come across to other people, and maybe you could draw from your arsenal for dealing with Razor in order to tackle Koz."

Jamie took out a spoon to transfer a can of Blackbeard's food to a dish. "That's what Levi's supposed to be doing. They wanted me to be a good influence on Razor. I knew that. I tried. Not sure how much it helped, but maybe some. Levi's supposed to be the good influence on Koz, but I think it's having the opposite effect."

Blackbeard didn't waste any time getting onto the counter to snarf down his meal.

"So Levi's turning into an asshole?" I quipped. "Should we let Mama Babcock know so she can have a word with him before it's permanent?" I found a mixing bowl in the cabinet and filled it with ice water, shoving it in Jamie's direction.

He raised a brow.

"Ice your hand. You know the drill."

Jamie scowled, but he took off his jacket and rolled up his sleeve before dipping his hand in the water. "Levi's not turning into an asshole. He's just…"

"He's just not you and he's making different decisions than you would, and you don't know how to feel about it because you feel responsible as his older brother and as the team captain and as simply being Jamie Babcock. That's just how you are, Jamie. But sometimes, people need to make their own mistakes." I knew that better than anyone.

"Are you better off for the mistakes you made?"

That stung, and he had known it would before he ever let the words out of his mouth. "Maybe not better off, but at least now I know what I want. Levi is still Levi. He's still your brother. And I bet he's having more of a positive effect on Koz than you think he is. For that matter, maybe the influence Koz is having on Levi isn't *all* bad."

"You don't think so?"

"Has Razor's influence on you been *all* bad? Nothing good has come from that friendship on his end?"

"I never said that. But Levi and Koz—"

"Levi and Koz aren't you and Razor. I know." I picked up

Blackbeard's dish, since he'd finished eating, and washed it in the sink. "But even you have to admit there are an awful lot of similarities."

"Fine. There are similarities. Tiny, infinitesimal similarities. So now what do I do with them? How do I use that to get Koz to act like a decent human being sometimes or, at the very least, play like he wants to be part of a team instead of a solo act?"

I set the dish on a towel to air dry and wiped my hands on my pants. "I don't know. That's the part that you've got to figure out. My part was helping you see the direction you should head in."

I turned around to face him, and he flicked his ice-cold, wet fingers in my direction, flinging drops of water in my face. I squealed and ran. Jamie chased me. I didn't run fast, though. Tonight, I wanted to be caught, and I got my wish. When he put his arms around me, I melted into him, all the fight draining out of me at his slightest touch.

"Come to bed with me?" he said, his mouth by my ear, laughter mixing with the heat of his words.

I laughed, too. "Yes," I said. There was nowhere else I would rather be.

Jamie

WEBS HELD ME up when the boys were leaving the ice after practice, jerking his head toward the other end of the ice. Bergy was waiting for us.

I didn't want to be here right now. I wanted to go home and see Katie, to spend the allowable two hours with her before we had to get on a plane and fly across the country. But I was here. And she would probably try to kick me out if I was there, anyway.

"How's the hand?" Bergy asked when we got over to him.

I shrugged. "Hurts. I can deal with it. I've played with worse."

Bergy nodded. "I'm thinking about benching Koz tomorrow. Having him watch a game or two from upstairs. You have any thoughts on that?"

I had at least a few dozen thoughts on that, and most of them would fall somewhere in the range of *Absolutely, yes, sit his fucking ass down because he's hurting us more than he's helping us*, but Katie's arguments from last night kept ringing in my head. I still didn't know how to treat Koz as if he were Razor, but I wanted a chance to figure out a way to get through to the guy on my terms. If the rest of the team and I could get through his thick skull, it would probably have a hell of a lot more lasting impact than watching a game from the press box.

So I nodded. "It might not hurt him to sit, but I'm not sure it would help, either. Give me this road trip to figure something out. I'll talk to Burnzie and Danger, maybe Wheels. We'll come up with something."

"All right. It's your team, so if that's what you want, I'm willing to wait." He drew the cord with his whistle up over his head and shoved it in the pocket of his tracksuit. "We can't wait forever, though, Babs. We have to get everyone heading in the same direction, and right now Koz is a big part of the problem preventing that from happening."

I nodded my agreement, and Bergy skated off to meet with the team doctors and get a status update on Q for the road trip. Webs didn't go with him, though, so I stayed, too.

"Laura should have Katie back at her house by now," he said. "I thought I'd stop by there on my way home to pack. And I'll make sure Laura comes with me when I leave, so if you wanted some time with her…"

"Yeah. I do, thanks." I'd held her all night long, not getting anywhere near enough sleep because I'd kept making love to her. Every time I'd thought I could stop, that I could keep my hands off her and let her rest, I'd proven myself wrong. She'd been just as needy as I had. We both knew that it was going to be a long time before we could really have a night together like that again, and I supposed we were trying to fit everything in up front. It was probably going to backfire on me, though, because all I wanted to do was hold her again.

And I couldn't.

I couldn't even go near her. The doctors said we were supposed to stay six feet away from her. No touching. Definitely no kissing. It was going to be absolute torture to go over to her house this afternoon and force myself to keep my distance, but I couldn't leave without at least seeing her again first.

"I've gotta be honest with you, Babs," Webs said, and my gut clenched in anticipation of whatever it was he intended to say. "I almost went to Jim to see if I could stay behind on this trip, or at least for a few days. I don't know how I'm going to get through this. I really don't have a fucking clue how you're going to do it."

"Me, either." I let out a snort. "At least I'm not the only one who thought about trying to stay behind."

He kicked up a grin. "I'd want to bash your face in if you hadn't at least thought about it."

"I'm still not convinced that going with the team is the right thing even though I have a job to do and I know it."

"You're going to make a hell of a son-in-law someday, you know that?" Webs slapped a hand on my shoulder, which didn't even come close to erasing the jolt of his words. "I know, I'm way ahead of you. It's all right. But you know, Laura and I were already married and starting our family by the time we were yours and Katie's ages. Anyway, I'd better get out of here so I can see Katie for a bit and drag Laura out of there."

He skated off, leaving me to pick my jaw up off the ice. I'd realized that Webs had turned over a new leaf as far as I was concerned, but I still expected him to come after me with a pitchfork all the time. Now he was dropping less-than-subtle hints about marriage. I didn't know how to take this change, but I supposed I should be thankful he wasn't trying to stuff my balls down my throat after chopping them off with a dull skate blade.

WHEN I GOT to Katie's house after lunch with the guys to give her parents some time with her, Laura was alone in the living room, and Webs and Katie were nowhere to be seen. She let me in and then sat on the couch, anxiously tapping her feet against the hardwood floor.

"The nausea's already started," she said. "Dave's trying to help her get comfortable enough that she can take something to calm her stomach. I've already been near her longer than I should have been."

I didn't have a clue what to say, so I just sat across from her and nodded.

"Do you have any idea how hard it is to see your little girl so sick and not even be able to hold her?"

"Pretty sure I'm about to get a sense of it," I replied.

She gave me a tired, sad smile. And to think, this was just the beginning of it. We had a long way to go from here.

A few minutes later, Webs came down the hall to join us. He stripped off a pair of latex gloves and tossed them in one of two garbage cans. I looked closer and saw that this one was labeled as radioactive. He washed his hands twice and used a paper towel to dry them, once again pressing the foot lever to open the same can.

Laura got up and looked at a schedule that was attached to the fridge with a couple of magnets. "Julianne d'Aragon's coming over before you'll need to leave," she said when she turned around again.

"Remember not to get too close," Webs added. "Not unless you have to. And wear gloves if you do touch her or something she's touched, or if you have to clean anything up. Use the other bathroom. And get her to drink. She needs a lot of fluids to flush all this shit out of her system."

"Ginger ale might be best today because of the nausea," Laura added.

I let them know that I understood, and eventually Webs got Laura out the door. Then I went down the hall and knocked on Katie's partially open door.

"You shouldn't come any closer," she said, her voice muffled by the pillow she had her head buried in.

I ignored that and moved to sit in the armchair by the window. She turned her head to look at me. Her skin was already a pasty-white color and clammy, and her hair was sticking to her scalp in places.

"I look like shit," she said, tearing up.

"You look like you feel like shit," I corrected her.

"I don't want you to see me like this."

"Tough. You're going to have to deal with the fact that I love you, and that means I love every part of you. Even the cranky, feeling-like-shit, trying-to-send-me-away part."

Katie rolled over to her back, tucking her arms over her chest. "Dad said you'd thought about trying to stay behind."

"Yeah. I have. I'm still not convinced I should go."

"You can't sort out the mess with Koz if you're here trying to keep my puke bucket clean." She indicated a paint bucket on the floor by the bed with her eyes. I supposed that was why Webs had been wearing gloves when he'd come out.

I laughed, which caused her to send a glare in my direction. I pointed at her bucket. "I don't know," I said. "Sending him in here to deal with that might improve his attitude by a mile."

I could tell she was fighting it, but a small smile finally forced its way through to the surface. "You're ridiculous. Do you know that?"

Yeah, I knew it. I would be as silly and outrageous as I had to be if it meant keeping her spirits up, and the truth of how next-to-impossible a task it might prove to be was sinking in.

"Drink some ginger ale," I said, pointing to the disposable bottle on her nightstand.

She drank, all the while giving me a pathetic pout that could rival a toddler's.

Chapter Fifteen

Jamie

INSTEAD OF PLAYING cards with some of the guys like I often did, I spent my time on the flight to Philly having a meeting with my leadership team. I brought Burnzie, Danger, Wheels, Jonny, Nicky, and Q together at the back of the plane so we could hash out a plan for moving forward with the Koz issue, as well as for bringing everyone together. There was no better time for some serious team bonding than on a road trip because we were going to be forced to spend time together whether we wanted to or not. I just didn't have a sound idea for how to do it.

Katie had proven to me that two heads were better than one when she'd pointed out the similarities between me and Razor, and Levi and Koz, so I figured bringing in more guys than just my assistant captains could only improve our odds of finding a solution. Jonny and Nicky had spent their entire careers in Portland, and Wheels and Q had both been around the league a long time. The more experience I could pull together, the better. I wasn't too proud to admit I needed help.

"So here's the deal," I said once I had everyone together. "We're more than a full month into the season, and we can't keep our heads out of our asses long enough to blink, let alone play like we have a shot at the playoffs. Bergy's ready to start benching guys, but I got him to give me a shot at pulling everyone together first. As much as we might enjoy having someone like Koz getting splinters in his ass, that won't help us as much in the long run as having him on the ice and scoring goals. At least it won't as long as we can convince him to play within the system. We need to figure out how to do that, though, and nothing so far has worked. Punishing him for fucking up is having the opposite effect from what we wanted."

The guys nodded and grunted their agreement.

"I think we all know what the fucking problem is, Babs," Burnzie said. "Too many guys out there thinking they're fucking perfect. Not enough guys pulling their weight. How the hell do we fix it?"

I grinned, since he'd given me exactly the opening I needed. The thing was, Burnzie and Razor had a lot in common. Burnzie would fall on the other end of the spectrum from Koz, with Razor landing somewhere in between the two of them. "You're a good example, Burnzie. You're a cocky son of a bitch, right? How do you respond when someone tells you you're doing something wrong?"

He chuckled. "I punch him in the fucking nose and keep doing what I'm doing."

"Exactly. But then look at guys like Q and Jonny," I said. "What happens if someone comes along and tells one of them they're screwing something up?"

Danger crossed his arms and leaned back in his seat. "They put their fucking heads down, work ten times harder, and sort their shit out on their own."

"And think about punching the guy in the fucking nose," Q added with a grin.

"But we're role players," Jonny said. "That's what we do. We don't get shit handed to us on a silver platter. We work for every fucking thing we get."

"You're never going to convince a guy like Koz to just bury his head and work harder," Wheels said. "He's not built that way. He's been told his whole life that he's the best there is, so he doesn't think he needs to change a fucking thing."

"That's my point," I said. "Koz is built like Burnzie. He knows he's one of the best in the game. He's got all the skills in the world and he knows how to use them, and he's never had anyone tell him he couldn't have anything he wanted. He works hard when it's something he wants, but otherwise, you can go fuck yourself, as far as he's concerned. But Burnzie, what would happen if instead of telling you you're doing something wrong and need to fix it, they told you what you're doing right and then asked you to step into a bigger role, but to do that you'd have to improve a few things? What would you do then?"

"You mean if you stroke my big, fat ego before breaking the news that I'm shit?" He laughed. "Telling me I'm awesome always helps."

"Massaging the confidence does wonders for everyone, as long as you don't go overboard," Wheels said.

"Right," Q said. "So what the hell do you want us to do? Go fawn all over his ass? He's already had enough of that for this lifetime."

I shook my head. "We massage his ego in a different way. We've got Wednesday off. No practice. We'll be in Raleigh, and I know there's this team-building place. It's a puzzle-solving escape game. You have to work together to figure out how to get free before you run out of time. I say we do some team bonding."

IN THE GAME against the Flyers, you could say that we had been the better team for fifty-five minutes of play. We'd been winning face-offs, getting plenty of offensive zone time, making crisp passes, scoring a couple of goals, staying out of the box, and receiving solid goaltending with Nicky in the net.

But then, with just under five minutes to go, Koz tried to make a fancy pass up the middle of the ice to Ghost instead of skating it out of our defensive zone. Flyers captain Claude Giroux cut off the pass, and then he was off to the races. Levi tried to defend him, but he lost an edge when he tried to dig in. Levi fell and couldn't get back up in time to be of any use. His partner, Ilya Demidov, was out of position. Demi couldn't get back in time. Koz got caught flat-footed in neutral ice and wasn't even thinking about backchecking, and Giroux pulled Nicky out of position before roofing the puck with a sick backhander.

We were still up by a goal. No cause for panic.

Once he got off the ice, Levi went down the tunnel with Drywall Tierney, our head equipment manager, to get the edge on his skate fixed. Bergy sent me, RJ, and Luddy out for the next face-off, along with Burnzie and Cole Paxton on defense.

"Let's lock this shit down," Burnzie said as we got into position.

The puck dropped, and RJ lost the face-off to Sean Couturier like he had been all fucking night long.

I busted my ass getting back into defensive positioning, with

Burnzie directing traffic. The Flyers dumped the puck into the zone, and I headed in to help Colesy dig it out of the corner. I finally got it free, but Couturier snagged it away from me, and when I tried to steal it back again, my stick got loose. I ended up high-sticking him right in the nose.

Blood started gushing right away. Double minor. I was going to be in the fucking box for nearly all the time left on the clock. Well, I would be if I was lucky. I'd get released early if they scored on either of the ensuing power plays, so at this point, the best scenario I could hope for was being released at the end of my penalty.

I didn't even attempt to argue with the ref over the call. No fucking point. I skated to the box and took a seat, and hoped the boys could bail me out of this one.

Thirty seconds into the penalty kill, Cody "Harry" Williams took a shot to the head and hit the ice like a fucking bag of bricks. He was able to skate off with the trainers on his own power, but they had to take him back to the quiet room for evaluation because of concussion protocol. That meant we were down to five defensemen.

Play resumed. Levi was one of our *D* out there. A shot headed his way, and he got his foot over to block it. Instead of hitting the plastic protective piece, it knocked the blade clear off his skate. He couldn't do anything but hop around on one foot. They cleared the puck, and Demi put an arm under his shoulder to help skate him off to the bench, but he had to go get his skate fixed. That would probably take longer than the rest of the game.

A new set of penalty killers went over the boards, but the Flyers brought off a tic-tac-toe play that ended with the puck in the back of our net and Nicky flat on his face with a hand on the back of his thigh, like he'd pulled his groin.

It was a tie game, and I was still stuck in the box for another two minutes of penalty time. I could only sit there and hope the boys held out long enough to get us to overtime.

They helped Nicky off the ice so he could be seen to by the trainers. Bobby went in along with fresh penalty killers. The puck dropped, the Flyers controlled it, and my team was scrambling.

Colesy went after the puck carrier, who turned at the last second, which led to Colesy slamming him hard into the boards. The ref put up his arm and blew his whistle, and then Colesy was joining me in the box for boarding even though it wouldn't have been boarding if the Flyers player hadn't turned his fucking back.

Needless to say, Colesy and Bergy and everyone on our fucking bench were livid. Bergy climbed up onto the players' bench and was screaming obscenities at the refs. Both Webs and Wheels were physically restraining him, keeping him from jumping out onto the ice. I'd never seen him lose his shit like that. Not in person, at least. Back when he'd been a player, he went wild more than a few times, but he'd retired before I ever got into the league.

Colesy was still trying to argue his case when the linesman skated him over to join me, but it was no use. They'd made the call, and they were sticking with it. Now we had to deal with nearly a full two minutes of five-on-three penalty killing, and we were down to only three defensemen and our backup goalie, who hadn't been granted a chance to warm up before being thrown to the wolves.

"It'll be all right," I said when Colesy flopped down next to me. "They're going to fucking get us out of this mess, and then we'll get to overtime, and it'll be all right." I wasn't sure if I was trying to convince him of that or me, but it didn't matter. Neither of us believed a fucking word out of my mouth right now.

RJ didn't usually kill penalties, but he was our best guy on the dot, so he usually went out for a five-on-three kill. Sure enough, that was who Bergy sent out. We watched helplessly as Giroux beat RJ on the face-off, and the Flyers set up their power play. A few sharp passes pulled Jens and Burnzie both out of position, and a slapper from the point went in the net. The fans in the building were going wild as I made the eighty-foot skate of shame across to the bench.

It felt like we were finding new ways to lose every game instead of finally figuring out how to win.

Webs thumped me on the back of the head. "Game's not over, Babs. Keep your head in it."

It might not officially be over, but it might as well be.

Katie

TRUE TO THEIR word, the WAGs had hardly left me alone at all other than overnight when the only thing I was doing was sleeping, anyway. Monday had been miserable, made worse because both Jamie and Dad had to leave with the team. By the time I'd awakened today, though, the worst of the nausea was gone, and Mom was at my door with breakfast.

Every two hours throughout the day, someone new showed up to be with me. Jessica brought some work with her from Light the Lamp. While she was over, Sara called me wanting to talk about girls' names that started with the letter C, so she could stick with the theme that was running in Jonny's family. Julianne brought over a stack of movies and told me to pick whichever one I was in the mood for. Mia had dropped her kids off with Brie for a playdate, and she had her camera with her when she arrived. *Come on*, she'd said, *outside with you. You need some fresh air, and I want to shoot you in your garden.* No amount of arguing had been able to convince her I was better off staying cooped up in the house, and by the time we'd come back in, I *was*, admittedly, starting to feel a little better.

Just before the game started, Soupy showed up with a pair of crutches under his arms and a takeout dinner bag hanging from one hand. Mia excused herself to shower before going to pick up her kids, and Soupy brought me a disposable tray of my favorite Chinese food and some plastic ware. "Rachel informed me that since I am currently of no use to her in terms of taking care of the twins by myself and she already has to send them to daycare while she works," he said, "I get to be on Katie-sitting duty for the game. I figured you wouldn't mind watching with me."

"I don't mind. How did you know I would want General Tso's chicken?" Not to mention the brown rice that I always got.

"Called your mom to ask." He dutifully washed his hands and took a seat on the opposite side of the room before digging into his own meal.

A few minutes later, Mia was done showering and cleaning up, and she left promising she'd see me again tomorrow. So here we were, Soupy and I watching the Storm fall apart in the third period over the brownies he'd made me swear I wouldn't tell Rachel about.

"Babs looks like he's about to implode," Soupy said as Jamie skated from the penalty box to the bench after the Flyers had taken the lead in the game.

The Storm were still killing a penalty, too, and there was only a minute and forty-three seconds left on the clock. Not much time for them to do anything in terms of tying the game and taking it to overtime, and it was a game they should have won handily based on the early play.

"He's got a lot going on," I said feebly. Soupy knew that perfectly well, but I guess I'd just felt the need to defend him.

"He needs to channel it. Bergy needs to send him out there and let him bang some bodies." Apparently, Bergy agreed with Soupy even though he was all the way on the other side of the country.

It seemed that Jamie didn't get the memo about banging bodies. Instead, he kept bumping the puck out of the zone and chasing after it, trying for a short-handed goal. After the third time he did that, the other Storm players followed him, and the goalie headed to the bench for an extra attacker. The clock kept ticking down, and Colesy was released from the penalty box. He skated straight to the bench so Luddy could go on to replace him.

Jamie and the rest of the guys put a furious flurry of shots on the Flyers' net, but it wasn't enough. The final horn sounded, and they left the ice with a loss in a game they should have won.

Jamie was the last guy to leave the ice. The camera zoomed in on him, making his frustration evident even through the distance.

"Do you think he'll figure out how to get the guys on board?" I asked. Then I wished I hadn't. Team dynamics weren't anything Soupy needed to be talking to me about, whether Jamie had brought them up or not.

But he surprised me by answering. "I think he's already figured it out. He just needs to believe in himself enough to really take charge of this team. I think there's some part of him that still thinks it's Zee's team, but hell, even Zee knew for the last year or two that he was just filling in until Babs was ready."

"Did he?" I'd never gotten that impression from Zee, but then again, I'd been busy in LA and hadn't seen everything going on here as closely as I used to.

"Oh, yeah." Soupy stretched his legs in front of him, grimacing when he moved the knee that had recently gone under the knife. "He knew. I think all the guys who really paid attention could see how they were grooming Babs to take over. Except Babs, but he's so damned humble that he doesn't notice those things."

"You think he's close to believing in himself enough?"

He narrowed his eyes at me from all the way across the room. "I think having you in his life again is helping with his confidence. In more ways than you could possibly know. He was a fucking wreck the whole time you were gone. Every time you popped up on the gossip shows, he lost his shit for a while." Soupy leaned forward in his chair all of a sudden, resting his elbows on his knees. "There's a way you could help him out some more, you know."

I knew enough to be suspicious. Soupy didn't get that kind of look in his eye unless he was being devious. "How?" I asked slowly.

"Well, you two can't…you know…for a while." He waved his hands in a crude gesture that left nothing to the imagination. "But you could *call* him. No radiation through the phone."

Call him. That was one way of putting it. "You mean phone sex?" I didn't blush all that often these days, but right now I had to be tomato-red.

"Don't tell Rachel I mentioned that. Or Babs, either. But sex can fix a lot of problems with a guy's confidence." Soupy's phone buzzed, and he looked down at it. "Finish your brownie. Rachel's on her way to trade out with me, and I have no intention of letting her know I've been eating this."

I laughed. It felt good to laugh, not to mention surprising considering how down in the dumps I'd been leading up to my confinement. "Will she be jealous? It's not nice to have chocolate and not share."

"I'm sharing with you," he said, shoving another bite of his into his mouth. "But no, she won't be jealous. She's got me on a diet."

I raised a brow.

He scowled. "It seems that when you aren't burning a ton of calories every day, skating and playing hockey and working out in the gym, you can't eat the same way or you start packing on the pounds." He nodded toward my paper plate with the half-eaten brownie. "I'd ask you if you were done and if I could have that, but sharing food with you is a big no-no right now. So eat it or I'm going to have nightmares about a brownie gone to waste."

I laughed, but I finished my brownie.

Jamie

NICKY DID HAVE a minor groin pull after last night's game, so we left him out of the day's activities so he could get treatment. A goalie from our AHL team would be coming to fill in as backup for Bobby until Nicky was cleared to play again, but he wouldn't arrive in Raleigh until sometime tonight. Harry's concussion tests had all come back normal, and he was symptom-free, so he *would* be taking part in everything.

I'd filled the guys in on the plans for today after we'd boarded the plane for the flight down to North Carolina. A few of the boys weren't exactly thrilled to have their day off taken away from them, Koz in particular, but they were just going to have to deal with it.

When we'd gotten to the hotel, I'd texted Katie to see if she was up, but she hadn't responded. I knew she needed her rest, and she had left me some messages earlier in the night about how Soupy was over to watch the game with her, but I couldn't help but be disappointed. I missed her. I missed seeing her smile and hearing her laugh, and I missed the softness of her hand sliding over my skin. In only a few short days, I'd gotten so accustomed to sleeping with the warmth of her body pressed against mine that I had a great deal of difficulty getting to sleep. Coop's snoring in the other bed didn't help, either.

Koz was late coming down for breakfast, and when he showed up, he glared at everyone who dared to look at him. This definitely wasn't a good start to the day.

Burnzie cuffed me on the back of the head and sat down next to me. "You sure this is what you want to do?" he asked, angling his head in Koz's direction.

I wasn't sure at all, but I didn't think it was a good time to back down. I nodded. "I'm sure."

"Well, I hope you're right."

The bus I'd arranged for arrived at the hotel at nine thirty, and we filed out to board it.

"This is a fucked up way to spend a day off," Koz said loudly to Levi as he walked past me. "I could still be sleeping."

"Or you could be shoveling shit at a farm," Levi said, snickering. "Pretty sure that's what he would rather send you to do, and there are plenty of those around."

Danger winked at me. "It could still be arranged."

Koz didn't let up with his complaints the whole way to Cipher Escape. We finally pulled up in front of a brick building hidden behind a row of trees. I was glad to get inside just so I wouldn't have to listen to Koz's bitching anymore.

"Right," I said once we'd all assembled in the parking lot. "We're going to break up into three teams of seven. I want Koz, 501, and Coop to be the team leaders."

A few of the guys made comments under their breath after I'd named the team leaders, but they kept it to a low rumble.

"It'll be a schoolyard pick. No choosing linemates, *D* partners, brothers, roommates, or countrymen to be on the same team, until and unless you have no other options available to you."

"What the fuck are we even doing?" Koz demanded. "How do I know who I want to have on my team if I don't know what the point of this whole fucking mess is?"

I shrugged. "Pick and then we'll figure out if you made good choices or not. Coop barely even knows everyone's names, so this puts you on more even footing."

"And if I don't want to do this?"

"I'm sure I can arrange for you to go shovel some shit somewhere."

"Already found a farmer looking for cheap labor," Danger called out, holding up his phone. "Can't get any cheaper than free."

After a lot of eye rolling and cursing, not to mention quite a bit of good-natured ribbing when Harry was picked last—*Gingers have no souls*, Levi had explained—we finally had our teams. I was on Koz's team, which I'd fully expected after giving the rules for the selection process. We also had Colesy, Radek "Radar" Cernak, Harry, Bobby, and Axel "Jo-Jo" Johansson. That should make for an interesting mix for the task ahead.

We went inside, and the owners explained what would happen. Each team would be locked in identical rooms that had been filled with pictures, boxes, objects, and other sorts of clues that would require logic, problem solving, and teamwork in order for the team to escape within the one-hour time limit. The first team to finish would be rewarded with getting to select the first recipient of the thunder hat. It would go to the guy who best helped the team as a whole to win a game, and it was hideous. It looked like a thundercloud, and it boomed every time you turned your head. The last team to finish would be buying the rest of us lunch. If any team failed to escape, they'd be funding a night out for the team once we got back to Portland.

Once everyone understood the rules, we headed into our separate rooms, and the game was on.

"Bunch of fucking idiots on this team," Koz muttered.

"You chose us," I pointed out, shrugging when he shot a glare in my direction.

I started looking around, trying to sort out what we were working with but not trying too hard. I wanted Koz to take charge. I wanted him to pull this team together and get us all working toward the same goal.

He didn't. He found a chair and sat down, sulking like a child.

The rest of the guys spread out, everyone opening boxes and turning objects over, trying to sort out the clues. No one was helping anyone else, though. After a couple of minutes, Colesy came over to me with a bottle in his hands that had some markings on it. "What do you suppose this is about?" he asked.

"No clue," I said, even though I'd already discovered a notepad with similar markings on it. Those markings might lead us to deciphering a code of some sort, but I wasn't leading this team. This wasn't my show. I knew I might be shooting my team in the foot, but I wasn't going to give in. I couldn't, or my plan would backfire. Koz was going to have to bring everyone together or we would be party planning soon.

Even though I kept going through the room, checking things out, more than anything I was watching to see what Koz would do. A few of the guys took things over to him, and he brushed them off at first. But then I could see it starting to get to him. Around fifteen minutes into our hour, Jo-Jo had the bottle Colesy had brought me and was showing it to Koz, and I could practically hear the battle going on inside the kid's head. He had figured something out, but he didn't want to be part of the team.

"Radar!" he called out after a very pronounced moment of silence. "Bring me that notepad you had a minute ago. And Harry, what did you do with that thing that looked like a compass?"

"Why should I bring it to you?" Harry grumbled.

"Because I'm the only guy in this room smart enough to fucking decipher this code."

I had to give him credit. Koz might not have a lot of tact, but he was probably right about being the only one of us able to sort out the code. I had followed the other guys over, and none of it made any sense to me, but within minutes, Koz had grabbed a pen and was making notes on his arm.

"Twenty-two, forty-seven, three," he said. "Babs, try that on the lock."

Lock? I hadn't seen a lock. I'd been too busy trying to figure out how Koz's mind worked to worry about looking for clues and figuring out how to get out of here. "What lock?" I asked.

"The one on that box right behind you." Apparently I didn't move fast enough for him because he got up and shoved me aside. "Just let me do it all, then." He spun the dial a few times and put in the combination he'd come up with.

Sure enough, the lock opened. He removed the lock and lifted the lid off the box, taking out a photograph. "The teddy bear. The fucking teddy bear." He looked over his shoulder. "Bobby, what the fuck did you do with that teddy bear?"

Bobby led him to it, and my plan was starting to come together. I took a moment to sit back and be proud of myself for figuring out what made our newest asshole tick. I didn't take too long, though. We were still locked in this room, and the clock was ticking.

I might have been willing to lose if it meant getting through to Koz, but now that it looked like we might get through to him *and* we could possibly win, there wasn't any point in sitting on my ass.

"I think I've seen the umbrella in that picture, too," I said.

Koz's head popped up. "Where? Did you open it to see if it said anything?"

I hadn't. It wasn't something I would have ever thought to do, but Koz had. Within four or five minutes, he'd solved another logic puzzle and gotten the first clue for the next part, and he was directing the rest of us to sort out the things he needed. That was the first time I felt as though I understood the guy. We might be dealing with a fucking genius, or at least with someone whose thought pattern worked in a different way from most of us. I tended to think in straight lines, but Koz saw things as a bunch of spatter drops that made up a bigger picture. That meant I was going to have to talk to him in a different way if I was going to get through his thick skull.

I may not have solved this team's problems in one day, but I was definitely a hell of a lot closer to getting everyone on the same page than I had been before. Not only that, but I never would have come up with any of this if Katie hadn't steered me in the right direction.

I couldn't wait to talk to her once we were done here. More than that, I couldn't wait to surprise her with what Brie was helping me plan. I only wished I could give her the surprise as soon as she'd been able to help me sort through my issues with Koz.

One thing at a time.

Chapter Sixteen

Jamie

KATIE ANSWERED ON the first ring. "Took you long enough to call me today. Dad said you guys had the day off," she said without any sort of normal greeting. She sounded sleepy even though it was the middle of the afternoon. I might have interrupted a nap, which made me feel guilty, but only for a second.

"We had the day off from anything the coaches were involved in," I said. I was in my hotel room. Coop had gone out with a few of the other guys to enjoy the sunshine since it was a gorgeous day in Raleigh, so I was alone for once, and fully prepared to take advantage of it by talking to my girlfriend.

"Oh. You called a captain's practice?"

"No practice. We went to a place where we got locked in a room and had to escape."

"That sounds…odd," she said. And she laughed. "Did you enjoy it?"

"I enjoyed being on the winning team."

"You don't like to lose."

"Nobody likes to lose." But she was right. I *really* didn't like to lose. Most professional athletes were the same in that regard. "What have you been doing today?"

"Thinking about you." There was a heaviness to her voice that I hated. I wanted to smash it, but it wasn't something real and physical and tangible. It was just there. "I went out back for a while. Sat on my swing under the tree with a pad of paper and a pen. I thought maybe I could try writing a song, but nothing happened. I couldn't come up with anything to say."

"So then what happened?"

"I fell asleep on the swing for a bit. Then I woke up with Julianne yelling for Blackbeard to come back."

"What?" I nearly choked on my laughter.

"She ran into your cat sitter when they were both showing up. She thought maybe Blackbeard would like to see me from the other side of the fence, but he apparently didn't understand he was supposed to stay over in your yard."

"Did he climb you?" I had no doubt that was what he'd intended. He liked curling up on Katie's breasts as much as I liked playing with them. A whole fucking hell of a lot.

"The cat sitter caught him before he got to me. He was about three or four feet away, which was closer than he should have been, but it was only for a second. We called a vet to be sure it wouldn't hurt him. They said he should be okay since it was such limited exposure."

She stopped talking for a minute, and I thought I heard her sniffle.

"You all right?" I asked.

"Would it be bad that I wanted him to come snuggle with me even if it was dangerous for him? Just that little bit of contact would— Never mind. I'm fine."

She wasn't fine. She wasn't even close to fine, and it had only been a few days. I didn't know how she was going to get through a month of this. I didn't know how *I* was going to get through a month of not being able to touch her, to hold her and comfort her, to tell her everything was going to be all right and know that what I was saying was the truth.

"What are you doing right now?" I asked, hoping to move her thoughts away from her loneliness.

"I told Mia I was tired and needed a nap. I'm alone in my bed. Thinking about you. What are you doing right now?"

"The same. I'm alone in my hotel room and thinking about you."

"Coop's not there?"

"Out with the guys," I said.

"When's he coming back?" She sounded devious. No, that wasn't quite right. She sounded sexy.

I groaned, already getting hard just from thinking of all the things that couldn't happen right now. "Not for a while," I said.

She made a quiet humming sound. "Lock the door."

"What?" I sat up in the bed, sure I was hearing things.

"Lock the door so he doesn't walk in on you while you're...while we're... Just get up and lock the damn door."

I got up and locked the damn door. "Okay. Done. Door's locked." Now what?

"What are you wearing?" she asked.

"Jeans and a T-shirt."

"I'm still in my pj's. I never got dressed today since I knew I wasn't going out. It's a satin shirt that buttons down the front and reaches almost to my knees, and it slides over my skin like butter."

I imagined her gliding her hand down that material. Without conscious thought, I rubbed my hand over my cock. "Are you touching yourself?" I asked, lying on the bed again, one knee bent and the other leg stretched out.

"No. Do you want me to?"

Fuck, yes. But I said, "If you want."

"My nipples are hard, Jamie." Not only that, but her breathing was heavy.

"Are you touching them?"

"Yes. I'm pinching my nipple and rolling it between my thumb and fingers, and it's straining for more."

"Are you wearing a bra?"

"No."

I swallowed hard. "Panties?"

Silence. A lot of silence that stretched into forever. Then, "Not anymore. Are you touching yourself?"

"Yes." My voice cracked.

"Are you hard yet?"

"Hard enough to crush stone."

"Take off your pants, Jamie."

"I'm on it." I held the phone in place with my shoulder and lowered my jeans and boxers to my knees.

"Did I tell you that I'm wet?" she asked. "I'm already so wet. My fingers can just slip and slide wherever they want to go."

"Dip a finger inside," I said. I stroked myself, eyes closed, imagining it was her mouth on me.

"I have two fingers in there. And my thumb is circling my clit, and it feels good, Jamie. It feels almost as good as having you touch me."

"I wish I could touch you right now."

"What would you do if you could?" she asked.

"I'd push your knees apart and put my mouth where your hand is, and I'd lick you. I'd lick your pussy until you came, and then I'd roll you over on top of me so you could ride me, and I'd play with your breasts until you came again with me inside you."

"Are you rubbing your cock?"

"Yes. Pretending it's you instead."

"What are you seeing me do?" she asked.

"Your mouth is on me."

"On you how?"

"Your lips are around me, squeezing, and you're taking as much of me as you can. Hot and wet. You're using your hand, too."

"Teasing your balls?"

"Yes. Massaging and tugging on them."

"I'm pretending it's you inside me."

"Oh God."

"Yes. You're in me, and you're so big and hard, and you want me so much that you're filling me all the way. It hurts, but it's a good hurt, you know? The kind that is about to give way to the best feeling ever."

"Am I moving?"

"Fast and hard. So hard. Almost bruising, but not. Just enough to leave me tender tomorrow. The kind of tender that makes me think of you every time I feel it, and then I want you all over again."

"I always want you," I said. My mouth was dry from wanting her.

"Are you close? I'm close, Jamie. I'm so close."

She was. I could hear it in the way her breath was hitching and in the soft, whimpering sounds she was letting out.

"Yes, I'm close," I said.

"Close your eyes."

"Already closed."

"Mine, too. Can you see me? In your mind? Do you see me there?"

Always. I would never be able to see anyone but her. "Yes," I rasped.

"I see you, too. I see you, and I hear your voice and the harshness of your breath in my ear, and I can almost feel you, Jamie."

Almost. This was as close as we were likely to come any time soon.

I was past the point of no return. "I'm going to come," I said.

"Do it. Come, Jamie. I'm so close, too."

So I did on a groan, stroking my length until after the spasms stopped.

"You always sound the same when you come," she said. "Did you know that?"

Was that normal? Did some people sound different? I shook it off, preferring to focus instead on helping Katie to join me in at least that one way. "If I were there right now," I said, "what would you want me to do?"

For a long moment, there was nothing on the other end of the line but an occasional gasp or whimper. "Hold me," she finally said, but this came out as far more than a whimper. It was a plea. A prayer. "Just hold me."

It was all I wanted to do.

Katie

WITH EVERY DAY that passed, I felt better than I had the day before. I had been expecting that, of course, since I'd been through this whole rigmarole recently enough that there wasn't any chance I would forget it. That being said, the effect on that first day had been more intense than I'd remembered, but this was a different treatment plan than what I'd gone through the first time. Same side effects, different severity.

When Friday finally rolled around, my first forced isolation came to an end. Now, at least for a few days until my next treatment, I was allowed to have limited contact with other people. I was still supposed to avoid children, pregnant women, and animals as much as possible, so no hanging out in the owner's box at Storm games, but at least I could hug my mom again without worrying about causing her harm.

Jamie and the rest of the team weren't due to return until early the next week. He and I talked every day, as often as possible. Our first experience with phone sex had turned into a way to connect on a physical level—even though we weren't truly touching each other—at a time when I wasn't allowed any physical contact with anyone. I hadn't been so sure about it when Soupy had initially made the suggestion, but I was glad I'd given it a shot. In some ways, it was helping to keep me sane.

The other thing keeping me sane was my garden out back. I spent more and more time there, especially in the late afternoons and early evenings. Sunset was the time that called to me. I took my notepad and a pen, sat, and listened to the sounds of the world passing me by. I'd started jotting down a few lines, scattered and fragmented phrases, much like my thoughts. I could always make sense of them later, but for now it was enough just to get them out of my head and put them on paper.

Now that my visitors weren't limited to two hours of contact at a go, Mom was spending most of her time with me. Well, more *at my house* than *with me*. I couldn't get her to stop cleaning. She was constantly going around my house with her protective gloves on, wiping down surfaces and throwing bedding and towels into the laundry, dealing with all the things that could be contaminated with radiation. She wouldn't stop no matter how many times I asked her to just sit with me.

I understood it. She needed to *do* something, and right now the only thing she felt as though she could *do* was take care of things so I wouldn't have to. Still, I wished she would just sit next to me and talk to me about things that were going on outside my little house. I was feeling more and more cut off from the world.

Over the weekend, we went shopping for furniture and equipment to put in my studio. Dad was going to finish the built-in once the team got back to town, but I wanted to go ahead and get everything else in now, particularly since this first week of cancer treatment had proven to me just how isolated I was going to be. I needed an outlet. I needed a way to channel all the things I was feeling instead of keeping them all bottled up inside me, and it was worth trying to see if I could do that by creating music.

I paid extra for Sunday delivery because I wanted it all set up before the next round started, and a few of the WAGs came over to help Mom and me get everything installed properly. Julianne even brought her kids with her—all teenagers, old enough that we didn't have to worry too much about radiation—and Elin and Maddie tagged along, too.

Maddie brought a huge stack of books with her. "Romance novels," she explained, carrying them into my bedroom to put on the nightstand closest to the window. "Mom sent them. She likes to read them when she doesn't feel well. Sometimes I sneak one of them off to my bedroom to read at night and put back in the morning before she notices. Don't tell her."

"Our secret," I murmured.

She pulled a fancy notebook out, as well, setting it beside the books. "For songwriting."

"How'd you know I was thinking about writing songs?"

Maddie shrugged. "Why would you be making a studio in your house if you weren't going to be singing? And a lot of singers write their own songs. It just makes sense."

I supposed it did. I picked up the book on the top of the stack. *Lord of Scoundrels* by Loretta Chase. "Have you read this one?" I asked. Maddie had always been an avid reader, but I supposed she'd grown up a lot in the last few years if she was reading books like these. I was used to seeing her with the Percy Jackson series or the Harry Potter books.

She nodded, eyes wide with excitement. "That's one of my favorites. Mom's too. That's why she put it on top. She said to start with that one." She looked around my room, her brows puckered. "You need a reading chair in here."

"I hadn't thought of that yet," I murmured, tossing the book back on the pile.

"Which one is the most comfortable? From the living room?" Maddie was already on her way out. "We can move one in here for now, and then sometime you can get one that'll go with the rest of your furniture in here better. But if you're going to be shut away in your room a bunch, you need a good chair."

I followed her and picked one out. As soon as I did, she hollered for Étienne and his older brother, Patrice, to come and move it, directing them as to exactly how it should be placed.

"You take after your mom a lot," I said to her. "Did you know that?"

Maddie rolled her eyes. "We all look like Mom."

"I wasn't talking about the way you look," I said, winking. "I meant the way you just get things done."

She blushed, but she kept working. She found a warm blanket and draped it over the back of my chair, and she relocated a floor lamp so it was behind the chair. In no time, she'd created a cozy reading corner.

It wasn't long before everyone else had my studio set up and functional. Soupy came over after a while, claiming that Rachel had kicked him out because he was a nuisance. I suspected she just wanted a quiet evening without having to watch the game, though. She worked for the team, and she was married to one of the players. I had a feeling she couldn't escape it. Anyway, Tuck had gone over to play with some friends for the afternoon, and Soupy said the twins had come down with something they'd picked up at daycare and were napping. I figured she didn't want the game—or Soupy's reactions—to wake them up.

I ordered pizza, and everyone dug in while we watched the Storm's game against the Washington Capitals. The guys played much better this time, and I couldn't help but notice that even though Koz still liked to showboat a bit out there, he was at least starting to make an effort at backchecking when the play headed the other direction. That was a huge improvement. Maybe Jamie's plan was starting to work.

They still lost the game, but it wasn't for a lack of effort this time. It was more that the Caps' goalie was a beast in the net tonight, and he wasn't letting much of anything past him. That happened sometimes. They could play well but run into a hot goaltender who would essentially steal the game. We all knew Nicky had done that on more than a few occasions himself, so you couldn't curse the hockey gods for it. All signs were starting to point toward the guys turning their season around, though, so my guests went home in a more relaxed mood than they would have a week or two ago.

Soupy and Maddie were the last to leave. I followed them out to be sure he didn't catch one of his crutches on something in the dark. Maddie got into his SUV and dug a book out of her bag—I had to wonder if it was one of her mom's romance novels—but Soupy held back for a minute.

"You ready for tomorrow?" he asked.

"No." I would rather not think about tomorrow at all.

"You'll get through it all right. I'm on afternoon Katie-sitting duty. Rachel said I get to be there for the puking-up-your-guts part this time. Something about men being disgusting pigs anyway so I should be able to handle it." He laughed. "It can't be any worse than changing explosive diapers, right?"

I didn't feel like laughing.

"Hey," he said, "lighten up some. There's more than enough time later to be down about it."

I smiled for his sake even though I was on the verge of crying again. Those tears seemed to always be just under the surface these days. I was like a ginormous ball of anger and anxiety and fear lately—mainly fear. Always fear. "I'm trying."

"I know you are." He let go of the handgrip on one of his crutches and waved me closer. "Come here."

"I shouldn't get too close right now." They said some contact was all right, but how could they be sure? And how much was too much? Soupy had a family who needed him healthy and whole, and he had enough issues of his own without adding whatever my radioactive body might add to the mix.

"I promise I will avoid touching you at all costs for the next few days and I'll follow all the damn safety rules while I'm around you, but right now you need a fucking hug. So come here."

He was right about that. I needed a hug. I needed human contact. I was so desperate for it that I didn't know what to do with myself. That desperation finally won out, and I crossed over to him.

Soupy gave good hugs. He was a big, strong man with arms that felt safe, and I let him enfold me in a brotherly embrace. He held me a lot longer than I should have allowed, and he kissed my cheek when he finally backed away.

"Better?" he asked.

I nodded. "At least for now."

"All right. I'll see you after lunch for cleanup duty."

I wandered back inside, not sure what to do with myself now that I was alone. Jamie would probably call me after a while, but not until they got to the hotel in Tampa. I thought about reading one of Rachel's books, but I wasn't in the mood. Instead, I picked up the notebook and pen, and I headed out to the backyard to sit on the swing, thinking I could give songwriting another try. It hadn't worked out so well the first time, but I wasn't ready to give up. There'd been a lot on my mind lately, which surely had an effect on my ability to be creative.

The light of the moon combined with the streetlights around the city were just enough that I could see what I was writing. At first, I just scribbled a few words that didn't make any sense. But then the emptiness I felt from seemingly being alone even while I had people surrounding me started to take shape in words, and I filled the page. As I moved farther down the page, some inner sense took over. I realized some of the lines I'd written early on were wrong, they merely skimmed the surface of what I'd meant to say, so I went back and scratched through them, scrawling in the margins to put down what I really meant.

I got so caught up in what I was working on that I completely lost track of time. It was only when my phone rang and I realized it was Jamie calling me that I had a clue how many hours had passed. I answered, gathering up my notebook and pen so I could go back inside.

For a while, we talked about the game and other things going on with the team. He told me about a prank Coop and some of the other guys had played on Levi, and he filled me in on the fact that Dad had done a face-plant coming off the plane and busted his nose so badly that he looked like he had been in a fight. I walked him through my day in much the same way.

"Sounds like you had a bunch of company all day," he said.

"Yeah." But I'd still been lonely. How did that work? I'd been surrounded by people all day, people who obviously cared about me because they'd given up their time to help me out, but I had still felt as if I were on an island of one.

"You alone now?"

"Yeah. Soupy stuck around for a bit after the game, but he had to get home and help Rachel with the kids. Mom's coming back at the butt crack of dawn to take me up to the cancer center." And then the whole process was going to start all over again. I got choked up just thinking about the isolation that would be upon me in less than half a day. "Jamie, I don't know if I can do this! I can't handle it."

"You can. You will." He sounded so certain, but I was on the verge of a total meltdown. "I'll be back late on Tuesday. I'll come over when I get home if you want."

"You can't stay with me then."

"I could stay in your guest room."

"Blackbeard needs you."

"So do you."

I did, but he couldn't give me what I needed right now.

Jamie

"IT'S BULLSHIT. IT'S absolute fucking bullshit." Soupy was barking into the phone, spouting off more obscenities than I could keep up with, and I still didn't have a clue what the hell he was talking about in the first place.

"Slow down," I said over the latest string of curses. "What's bullshit? What's going on?"

"You haven't seen the pictures of me and Katie?"

Apparently not. "What kind of pictures?" I asked warily. I knew better than to think anything had happened between the two of them. Soupy was as head over heels in love with Rachel as I was with Katie. Plus, Katie had been dealing with cancer treatments, for fuck's sake. But I was quickly learning that there was no telling how sick and twisted the media could make something innocent seem.

"I hugged her last night out in front of her house," he said. "She needed a hug, and I was there, and I gave her a fucking hug. They've apparently been camping out down the street all week, taking pictures of me every time I come and go so they can talk about how often I'm coming over to fuck her or some shit. And then last night, they got their money shot when I hugged her. Like it's fucking proof of anything."

"They don't need proof," I said. They just needed some fodder to work from and then they were off to the races.

"What the hell do we do about it?"

Punching things wouldn't help, I reminded myself. "Does Katie know yet?"

"I doubt it. I hope not, at least. This is the last thing she needs right now. Laura's got her home now, but I doubt she's feeling up to doing much."

"Well, for now, just keep doing what you're doing. It doesn't matter what people think. What matters is keeping Katie's spirits up enough that she can get healthy again." And in the meanwhile, I needed to up my game on figuring out a way to combat the paparazzi.

That was just the way my life was lately—solve one problem and another would crop up to replace it.

WHEN WE FINALLY got back to Portland, Blackbeard had nearly doubled in size. Or at least it seemed that way. He hadn't forgotten me, though. As soon as I walked through the door, he made a flying leap for me and climbed the rest of the way to my shoulder. I tried to pet him, but he bit my finger and butted his head against mine, rubbing all over me so hard that he would have fallen off if not for my hand holding him steady.

I texted Katie to see if she was awake. No answer. Even though I was desperate to at least *see* her, despite the fact that I couldn't *touch* her, I stayed at my house all night. She needed her sleep. Not that I got any. The whole night, I tossed and turned, going crazy being this close to her again and not being able to talk to her or touch her, to let her know that I was here and do whatever I could to make her feel better. Blackbeard wasn't a fan of my insomnia. Every time I rolled over, he grumbled at me and readjusted, sometimes nipping my nose or my ear to be sure I understood the gravity of his displeasure.

Morning finally arrived. I felt like shit from lack of sleep and having flown all the way across the country after yet another loss, but it didn't stop me from texting to see if she was up. Still nothing. I took a shower, made my breakfast, and played with Blackbeard for a bit, waiting for her to wake up.

She didn't respond, though.

I needed to leave for practice soon. Bergy had told me I should take the day off. He and Jim were willing to call it a maintenance day for me even though I didn't have any injuries that needed to be rested. I didn't feel good about that, though. Yeah, the guys all knew that Katie had cancer again, and I needed to be with her, but we were finally starting to play like a team even if we were losing. Skipping out on practices didn't seem very captain-like, so I wasn't going to go there.

With about ten minutes left before I had to head out the door, I thought maybe I could look across the back fence to see if I could get a glimpse of her through one of her windows. Right now, anything would help to ease my worries. I went out back and walked up to the fence to find her swinging under the tree.

"Hey," I said, and she swiveled her head to look at me. I propped my arms on top of the rails and rested my chin on them, staring. Just staring. I couldn't get enough of her.

"Hey," she said, her sweet voice cracking.

"I texted to see if you were up yet."

"My phone's inside. I came out to watch the sun come up. Haven't moved since."

She had on a checkered shirt with a soft, fuzzy blanket draped around her shoulders. It wasn't cold out, but she was shivering hard enough I could see it from here. All I wanted to do was go over to her side of the fence and hold her close until she stopped shaking. We both knew that wasn't possible right now, though.

"Why don't you go inside and warm up?" I suggested.

She turned her head again, looking off into the distance. "Why? So I can turn on the TV and see the latest headlines and figure out what they're accusing me of next? *Katie Weber bought a house across town so she can screw every guy in the NHL right under her father's nose!* Next thing you know, they'll be saying I'm screwing Dad, too. Or maybe that he's my pimp. I bet that's it. He's sending you guys my way so he can take a cut of the profits, and Mom's working as my madam. Maybe I'm busy training up all the other WAGs so they can prostitute themselves, too. I bet that would make for a great headline."

"Have you thought about revealing that you have cancer again?" I asked. I didn't want her to have to do that if she wasn't ready for it, but I was grasping at straws to figure out a way to get them to leave her alone. "Maybe if you let the world in on what's really happening, the gossip sites would leave you alone."

"Or maybe they'll just find a new way to twist it into something worse than it already is," she bit off. "*Breaking news! Katie Weber is funding a radical, costly, and dangerous cancer treatment by whoring herself out to everyone with a cock and two pennies to rub together.* Thanks, but no thanks."

I wished she would look at me. I wished I could see her face and know she was looking in mine, so I could reassure her in some way. But there wasn't much I could say, and it felt as if there was even less that I could do to actually help.

"I'll figure something out to get them to leave you alone," I said.

"Good luck with that. For all we know, they've found some way to tap our phones. They've probably been recording our calls, and they're saving that to broadcast sometime soon, when the latest bit of gossip has died off. *Sordid phone sex with Katie Weber is just a button away...for the right price!* Just wait. It's coming."

But it wasn't. Not if I had anything to say about it.

Chapter Seventeen

Jamie

"NEW YEAR'S EVE?" I repeated after Brie, glancing up at her, Jessica, and the guys from The End of All Things to be sure I'd heard correctly. They nodded. It seemed so far off even though it wasn't all *that* far at this point.

It was a day off for the Storm, and Katie was with her mother at the cancer center to get another round of radiation. She'd refused to let me come with her. *All I have to do is drink some nasty shit and wait for it to start working. And by the time it does, all I want to do is puke, and you can't be around me then, anyway.* I'd still go over to spend my couple of hours with her later, but this had given me the perfect excuse to get together with Brie and see where our plans stood. She'd set up a meeting with the band and Jessica so we could all be together at the same time and hash out the finer details. We were at the Light the Lamp offices, and Jessica's assistant was manning the phones while we talked over coffee and Voodoo Doughnuts.

"That's the soonest we can possibly get something put together," Spencer Braddock, the lead guitar player, said. "We've got the final leg of our tour to finish up. While we're doing that, we can have Brie, Jessica, and some of our people back here doing the legwork."

"But what about the Light the Lamp event that night?" I argued, adding cream to my coffee. Every year, Jessica put on a big event on New Year's Eve for her foundation, a party where addicts and anyone else who wanted to join in could come and hang out for a sober good time. It acted as a fund raiser for Light the Lamp, too, since she got local hotshots to be celebrity drivers for the night. If we were in town, she usually wrangled a bunch of the Storm players to take part. Katie and Beau had done it last year since they'd been in town. People would bid on the opportunity for us to drive them home afterward. It didn't seem fair to take that night away from Light the Lamp in order to do something for Katie.

"We're going to figure out a way to combine it all into one big night," Jessica reassured me. "This is actually going to work out great for Light the Lamp because if we can get the band involved, the turnout will be through the roof."

"We'll pay for the production costs for the concert out of the ticket prices," Brie said. "Everything that's left after that is going to be split equally between Light the Lamp and the Katie Weber Foundation."

"Laura and I should be done getting the new foundation set up in the next couple of weeks, so it'll all work out," Jessica said.

"And you guys don't care that you'd be working for free?" I asked the band.

"It won't be the first charity gig we've done, and it won't be the last," Emery Johnson said. He was the keyboard player for the band, and the one who did most of the songwriting. He was the one I wanted to get Katie involved with more than any of them.

"Our agent says it's good to do one every now and then," Spencer added.

"And it only helps them to increase their presence in the local community," Jessica put in. "It's the same thing as when you guys get involved in something local. You don't have to donate your time or your money, but you do it anyway."

We did, but hockey players were small potatoes compared to The End of All Things. They were up there in the stratosphere with The Beatles and Elvis and shit. These guys couldn't go anywhere without their security guards at their sides. It was even worse than what Katie had been dealing with, and her ordeal was more than enough.

"If you're sure," I said.

"We're sure," Emery said. "So then it'll be up to you to get Katie to stay at the arena after the game."

"Exactly," Spencer said. "You get her to stay, and we'll take care of the rest."

I half laughed, half snorted. "Right." That would be easier said than done. By then, she was bound to be in the midst of chemotherapy. I wasn't positive she would want to come to the game that night to begin with, but even if she did, she would probably want nothing more than to go home and go to bed once it ended.

"You can convince her," Brie said. "They're her favorite band. It'll be something fun she can do, and we all know she hasn't had much fun lately."

That didn't even begin to cover it.

THIS TIME WAS worse than last time. Maybe not the nausea part of it, but just in general. I could tell she ached everywhere from the soft moans she let slip every time she rolled over in her bed, the notebook she'd been writing in knocked to the floor, splayed open at the spine with pages crushed due to falling from her bed. Standing here in the doorway and watching her made me feel so fucking useless. I should be holding her. I should be rubbing her aches away or keeping her wrapped up in my warmth so she wasn't lying there—alone—with her teeth chattering from the cold. But instead I was here, leaning against the doorframe to her room, and I couldn't do a fucking thing to make her feel better.

The doorbell rang, and she didn't even look up. Not that we would let her get out of bed to answer it anyway. Soupy and I were both here, and Jim Sutter had dropped in for a bit to check on her, as well. That was one of the things I respected most about Jim. He cared as much about the friends and family of his players as he did about the players themselves. When he said we were a family, he meant it.

I headed down the hall in time to see Soupy crutching toward the front door. Levi came through when he opened it. And Koz, surprisingly, who was carrying a vase with white and yellow Gerbera daisies. This was the first time Koz had ever voluntarily done anything with me outside of the rink, and he'd brought flowers. I didn't know what to think of that.

They both had notebook-paper-sized bits of poster board in their hands that had charity information scrawled on them. I'd stolen the idea from a few other celebs who'd been hounded by the paparazzi. I had handed out the poster board and permanent markers, told the guys what to write on them, and to hold the signs up and make sure any pics the fucking hidden cameramen decided to take of us as we went into Katie's house would have the messages included. It meant they were less likely to post shit about her online, and even if they did, at least we were sending out a good message. I was sure they weren't ready to give up on their current obsession, anyway, especially since even more of the guys were coming over and giving them more gossip fodder, but there wasn't a whole hell of a lot else we could do, short of staying away. I didn't know about the rest of the guys, but they would have a hell of a time keeping me away when I could be here.

"How's she doing?" Levi asked.

I shook my head. "Not well." There wasn't a hell of a lot to say other than that.

"Can I…" Koz held up the vase and angled his head toward the hall.

"Just be sure you keep your distance," I said. I had no clue if he'd been paying attention when I'd told everyone who wanted to come see her how far away they had to be.

"Got it," he said, and he took off toward her room.

Levi and Soupy followed me into the living room, and Soupy plopped down on the sofa, putting his injured leg up on the coffee table.

"You could go home now," I told him. "I'm not going anywhere."

"Can't do that. Rachel's orders."

Jim chuckled. He was in the dining room at the table with his laptop open, doing Lord only knew what. The guy was always working.

"Rachel's orders?" I repeated.

"I'm supposed to be sure you don't stay too long, you don't get too close to Katie, you don't touch her, and you absolutely don't kiss her under any circumstances. If I fail to uphold my end of things, my wife is going to withhold certain privileges that I have no intention of giving up on your account. So I'm staying."

"She would never have to know," Levi pointed out, and I agreed wholeheartedly.

"Rachel knows everything," Jim said. He looked up at us over the tops of his bifocals. "That's why I can't do my job without her. I wouldn't advise putting that to the test."

"And I don't intend to," Soupy said, smirking. "Sometimes I'm on Katie-sitting duty. Today, it's Babs-sitting duty. But if she pukes, you get to clean it up."

"Levi can do that."

"No fucking chance." He shuddered.

"Point is," Soupy said, "I'm looking after you as much as you're looking after her today. That's just how it's going to be, so you might as well accept that I'm going to be here until you go back over to your place."

I rolled my eyes, but I left it alone. We all sat around talking for a while, but then I realized that Koz still hadn't returned from taking Katie the flowers. I excused myself to investigate. The door to her room was open, and I popped my head in. She was sitting up in her chair by the window, the flowers on a table next to her and a book in her hands. Koz was on the other side of the room on the floor, knees bent and arms stretched out across them.

The thing that surprised me most, though, was to find Katie smiling and Koz laughing. She glanced over at me and her smile got even brighter.

"Did Koz show you these?" She pointed toward the flowers.

"He did," I said, still feeling wary because I didn't understand what was going on or how he'd gotten her to mood to lift in such a short amount of time. I mean, he'd just brought her flowers, for fuck's sake. Anyone could do that. I hadn't, but that wasn't the point.

"He's been telling me how he used to take flowers to his grandma every day when she was going through radiation and chemo."

"I didn't know your grandmother had cancer," I said.

He shrugged and gave me a fuck-you look. "You never asked."

That was true. I had never bothered to learn much of anything about the guy. I knew what everyone had been saying about him when he'd come over in the trade, and I'd assumed it to be the truth. It was the same thing people had been doing to Katie, and it was bullshit.

"I never did," I said. "You're right." I had always just assumed the worst about the kid, and I figured it was all rubbing off on my brother, and I didn't like him because of it. The room-escape activity had helped me to learn a lot about him just through observation, things I never would have realized otherwise. But now I was coming to understand that maybe there was even more to the story than I ever would have imagined. I sank down to the floor just inside the doorway, taking up a position much like his.

"She loves daisies. Always has. They made her smile when there wasn't a hell of a lot worth smiling over. She said it helped her get through the worst of her treatments. She knew she would always have fresh flowers in the house. I figured it couldn't hurt to see if it would help Katie smile, too."

And apparently, it had. She was still beaming. "How's she doing?" I asked him.

"She just bought a motorcycle," he said, and he actually grinned at me. "And over the summer, she asked me to go with her to the tattoo parlor. We got matching ink."

"Which tat?" I asked.

"The one on my left shoulder."

I did a double take. "Your grandma got a tattoo of giving someone the finger?"

"Giving cancer the finger, because that's what she'd just done." He sobered. "She raised me. My mom was still a kid when she had me, so Grandma took over."

Which served to prove that you never really knew someone's story, even if you thought you did. I'd pegged him as a spoiled rich kid who'd never been told no his whole life.

For the rest of my time with Katie that day, the two of us got to know more about Koz. Even though it was very obvious that she still felt like hell, she was smiling when the guys and I left. A real smile, not one she'd pasted in place so we wouldn't worry.

I WASN'T SURE if the signs the guys and I carried with us as we came and went from Katie's house were helping, or if it was just the fact that she was staying out of the public eye. Whatever was behind it, the media was finally easing up on her and finding some other celebrities to feed their addiction.

That was one positive thing.

The way the team had been playing of late was another positive. Whether Koz was starting to feel more like he belonged or we were treating him more like he was one of us, there had been a huge change in the way he was playing. He was listening more and talking less, but when he did speak up, he usually had something constructive to say. He saw the ice differently than most of us, almost like he could see a play forming from up above. He realized not only where the guys on the ice were at the moment but could see where they were heading. Now, when he said something, the rest of us listened.

Our puck luck was starting to change for the better, and everyone was playing a lot looser. Well, almost everyone. I hadn't been playing my best. I hadn't scored a goal in nearly two weeks, and I'd hardly even gotten any assists. Those I had gotten had been due to luck more than any of my own efforts. My aim and timing were off, and I didn't know what to do about it. I tried not to let it get to me, but it was. I felt as if I wasn't holding up my end of the bargain, and that didn't make me a very good captain.

In my weekly leadership meetings with Bergy and the rest of the coaches, we always discussed the things we could do to keep the team moving in this direction, keep the guys focused on the big picture and our overall goals. Bergy was a huge proponent of goals, big and small, short-term and long-term.

Even though I knew my game was suffering, it surprised me when, during our most recent meeting, Bergy wasn't happy with the short-term goal I'd written down: *Spend a day on the road with Koz to get to know him better.*

"That's not a good goal for you," Bergy said.

"Why isn't that a good goal?" I asked.

"Because you've already done what you needed to with Koz. Now you need to trust the rest of the guys to pick up where you left off. He's being a team player now. He's found his voice in the room and on the ice. He doesn't need to be your focus anymore."

I must have been giving him a confused expression because he scowled, crossing his arms. "You need to make goals about your own game. Not the team. You need to figure out what's going on with your own shit instead of worrying about everyone else's for a while."

"It's easier to worry about them than to deal with what's wrong with me."

"I think you know what's wrong with you." Bergy handed me another three-by-five index card. When I didn't immediately start writing, he said, "Tell him what he needs to focus on, Danger, because he's not getting it."

"If your personal life isn't in order, your game is going to suffer," Danger said. "It's a simple fact. Right now, your focus shouldn't be on the team as much as it should be on your life away from the game."

My life away from the game. Right now, that was just Katie. Nothing more and nothing less. And obviously, the ways I worried about her had probably been affecting my play.

"It's only normal to worry about the people you love, Babs," Burnzie said. "That's what we do. You need to find ways to channel that when we're off the ice so that during games, you can think about what's happening there."

I chewed on that for a while, and then I remembered what Koz had said about bringing his grandma flowers every day because it had made her smile. He had done it because it was something that lightened her load, even just for a moment, and that made living his own life slightly easier. He couldn't cure his grandma's cancer any more than I could cure Katie's, but he could bring her flowers. He could make her smile, even if it was only a brief respite. I could do the same thing.

I wrote down a new goal: *Make Katie smile every day, no matter what it takes.*

Bergy looked over my shoulder, and then he nodded and walked away. "I think that's good enough for this week, boys. Let's get ready for practice."

Katie

"THE TUMOR IS definitely shrinking," Dr. Oliver said.

I grasped on to that like it was a life buoy. "Then no surgery."

He glanced up over the top of my chart. "It's shrunk, but not enough to rule out surgery. It's not gone, and I doubt it will completely disappear until you have the thyroidectomy. You're skipping over steps, Katie. Important steps."

I sighed like a deflating balloon, and Jamie took my hand. We'd hardly had this much contact in a month, and I let his warmth cocoon around me.

For the last couple of weeks, he'd been bringing me flowers every day and having them delivered while he was out on the road. My house was starting to look like a spring garden. Daisies, tulips, roses, lilies, carnations…he'd given me every flower under the sun in every color imaginable. I kept running out of vases and having to send someone out to buy me more so I'd have room for them all. That wasn't what had touched me the most, though. He'd given me a soft, stuffed cat, a toy like you'd give a five-year-old. *So you'll have something to hold when you're not allowed contact*, he'd said. I'd felt silly at first when I'd snuggled that cat close to me at night, but eventually the thought had faded and I'd been glad for something to hold.

But now, he was next to me. Holding my hand. Helping to settle me through the simple act of touching me. I doubted he understood just how healing his presence could be, but it was a balm to my soul at a time when I felt as alone as I'd ever been in my life.

"Radiation has definitely helped things along," the doctor said. "It hasn't helped enough, and I don't think this is something we want to just keep throwing radiation at. I think we definitely need to move on to chemotherapy, as we discussed previously."

I bit my tongue to keep from throwing a fit. Radiation had been awful, and chemo was worse, but at least chemo wouldn't keep me in isolation nonstop. I would be allowed to touch people again. To touch Jamie, like we were doing now. To let him hold me. Maybe we could even make love sometimes, as long as I felt up to it and he wasn't disgusted by my bald head and all the other fun things that came with the territory.

"Okay. Chemo next, and then maybe the tumor will disappear."

The doctor grimaced, and Jamie squeezed my hand, and I almost lost my shit.

"I know!" I said. "I shouldn't get my hopes up about that, and I know that I'm probably going to end up having surgery. But I have to have hope that I can avoid it. Don't take that one small thing away from me." My damn tears were back, and it pissed me off. I batted them away with the back of my free hand. "Please. Just let me hope, even if you know that there is absolutely zero chance in hell that it'll go the way I want, at least have the decency to leave me with some hope." I took a shuddering breath, bracing myself for him to tell me the same shit he'd been telling me all along and squash my plea and my spirit in a single blow.

Dr. Oliver set the chart aside and fixed me with his professional stare. "There is always hope," he said.

I took those words in and held them tight to my heart.

We spent some time hashing out all the details for my upcoming chemotherapy regimen. I would go in to have a port implanted in a few days, and I'd start the first round of chemo in a week. Dr. Oliver said I could start getting back to being around people like normal, as long as I was up to it. I needed to still limit the time I spent touching kids, pregnant women, and animals for another week or two, but I could have sex again—thank God—and have fairly normal contact with Jamie other than spending a full night together. The doctor said that should wait a week, as well, but we could gradually build ourselves up to the type of physical relationship that we wanted.

Once all of that was arranged, Jamie drove me home. It wasn't a game night, and he'd already finished everything he was required to do for the team for the day, so he was mine until I had to go back to my place and sleep.

As soon as he opened the door from his garage, Blackbeard made a running leap for him.

"He's so big!" I said. In a month, that kitten had to have doubled in size.

Jamie grinned. "Over two pounds now. He's still underweight for his age, but he's catching up as fast as he can."

He headed into the living room, Blackbeard going along for the ride, and I followed. The fishing pole feather toy was on a table, up out of the kitten's reach, so I took it down and gave it a swish. That was all the enticement Blackbeard needed to turn into a rabid feather hunter. He leaped and twirled, doing backflips, twisting in midair, and generally contorting his body in ways that left me and Jamie in stitches. I had to stop because I was laughing so hard it hurt, but Blackbeard acted as though he could have kept going forever.

I collapsed on the floor, flopping on my back until I could catch my breath. Four tiny paws ended up on my chest, and two wild, gigantic kitten eyes stared right at me.

"Oh, you haven't had enough, have you?"

"Never," Jamie said.

I flushed with heat from the promise in his voice. "I didn't mean you."

"I know." He lay down on the floor beside me, stretching his body out so that we were touching at so many different points.

Then I couldn't catch my breath, but for an entirely different reason.

He propped his head up on an elbow and looked down at me, tracing the lines of my face with his other hand. "Do you have any plans for New Year's Eve?" he asked.

"Beyond coming to the game? After this last month, I'm ready for some human contact, at least where I can get it."

"I mean after the game."

I shook my head. "Are you not doing the Light the Lamp event this year?" I would do it, too, if not for the fact that I was bound to be bald alien-girl again by then, and I wasn't really keen on having that plastered all over the entertainment news. Besides, chemo zapped the energy right out of me. Staying up for much beyond the Storm's game was probably more than I could commit to doing.

"Jessica hasn't told you?" he asked.

I shook my head, confused.

"It's going to be different this year. She got together with Brie and managed to get The End of All Things on board."

"What?" I was so excited by that news that I would have sat upright on the floor if not for his fingers tracing lazy patterns on my skin. Maybe I *could* convince my body to play along for that one night, if it meant a chance to hang out with my favorite band in the history of ever. "Aren't they still supposed to be on tour then? Oh my God, they're going to be celebrity drivers for the night? Do you think I could talk Jessica into letting me just be a guest for the night? I would make a huge donation if I could get Emery to drive—"

"Slow down." Jamie laughed and placed a fingertip on my lips to silence me, and I kissed it. "Like I said, it's going to be different this year. It's going to be at the Moda Center after the game, and the band is going to put on a concert. The tickets they sell will raise money for Light the Lamp. I think she might still be doing the celebrity drivers afterward, too. Not sure on that part. So do you want to come with me? We don't have to take part in anything official. I just know you love their music—"

"Yes. Yes, yes, yes, yes, yes." And a thousand more yesses where that came from.

"Okay. I'll make it happen. I can probably even convince Brie to figure out a way for you to get backstage and meet them. Maybe you could even watch the show from back there if you didn't feel up to being out with the crowd." His fingertips were still touching my lips, dancing lightly over them. "It's been forever since I've kissed you."

"Yes," I said again. My voice was a harsh whisper against his touch. The excitement of his revelation combined with my longing for him made my heart feel like it was breaking through my ribs, it was pounding so hard.

He didn't kiss me right away. At least not in a way where I could kiss him back. He pressed his lips to my temple first, holding them there for an impossible length of time before kissing the bridge of my nose. I held my breath, anxious to discover where his kisses would lead him next. He took his time, ramping up his efforts at such a gradual pace I thought I would go insane. I was so deprived of his touch that every ounce of contact left me feeling drugged, but in the best possible way.

Blackbeard had curled up on my chest and started purring, but he wasn't alone. I was almost positive that I was purring, too.

"I need to make love to you," Jamie said. "I need you so bad I can hardly stand it."

He couldn't need it as much as I did. I fisted my hand in his hair and drew him down to my lips, and I almost cried when they finally touched.

He kissed me slow and deep, his tongue exploring every hidden area of my mouth. He dislodged the kitten and rolled onto his back, bringing me up on top of him and cradling me against him.

I rested my head on his chest, savoring the sensation of him drawing his fingers through my hair—hair I wouldn't have soon.

He buried his nose where his fingers had just been and drew in a deep breath. "Have I ever mentioned how much I fantasize about your hair?" he murmured.

He didn't need to tell me. I knew.

"I want you to take me to bed, Jamie," I said. "I want your hands on me, and I want to feel you inside me so that every time I get scared and lonely and can't have your touch to calm me down, I can reach back in my mind and remember. I need your touch seared in my memory. I need it burned into my skin so it will never leave me."

So he did. He got up and carried me to his bed, and we made love as though it were the last chance we would ever have. Having him inside me, looking into my eyes as though they were the key to my soul, allowed me to feel again. I'd been fighting to numb myself, not wanting to experience the emptiness that had surrounded me. But it was the moments afterward—when he held me like I'd been dreaming of for weeks on end, his fingertips methodically untangling my mass of hair—that I truly savored. Those moments allowed me to breathe again for the first time in weeks. He tenderly eased apart the knots in my hair, and I filled my lungs with life.

Chapter Eighteen

Jamie

AS THE WEEKS PASSED, leaving Katie behind while the team went on road trips was getting to be more and more difficult. I honestly didn't know how the guys with wives and kids could stand it, especially when someone they loved was sick. But throughout the league, players did it all the time. I never heard any of them complain about it, so I had to do it, too, and bite my tongue if I had to.

It was easier for me than it might have been, since I had Webs around to commiserate. He'd been leaving Laura and their kids behind for as long as I'd been alive. Not only that, but he cared about Katie as much as I did, so he understood the emotional toll it took on me each time we had to get on that damned charter plane. He helped keep me focused when we were out on the road.

Being able to talk to Katie every day—even if it was just a quick chat through text messages—helped me even more than having her father around did. I still spent a hell of a lot of my time worrying about her, though, and I didn't know if that would ever ease up. At least not until the doctors gave her a clean bill of health again, which we all knew would be a long time coming.

I was still sending her flowers every day. Sometimes I'd throw in a teddy bear or a box of chocolates, anything I could think of to make her feel better even if it was just for a moment. In return, she sent me a selfie every day. It was something I'd hounded her for, even though I wasn't sure what I was going to do with them.

We started on the day that she went to the cancer center to have the chemo port put in. She took the picture on her cell phone from her hospital bed, hair covered by a cap and tubes connected to her. She looked more resigned than scared that day, despite her smile.

One by one, she sent me more pictures of herself, even on the days when the team was in Portland and I was with her. Some days, she was laughing and being goofy. Every now and then, she would pull Blackbeard into the shot, and he would be a blur of movement trying to get free or rubbing noses with her. Sometimes she would have her pen and notebook in hand, ink smudged on her cheek. Other days, her pain and fears came through in every aspect of her appearance.

The one that stabbed me in the gut came when we were in Winnipeg for a game against the Jets. She took a shot of her bare feet with teal-blue toenails—Brie and Mia had been over that day and they had given each other pedicures—with piles of her hair everywhere, and a message of only two words: *It's starting*.

Years ago, I'd been there the day that her hair had started to fall out. She'd come to the locker room and had Webs shave the rest of her hair off with Jonny's clippers because she couldn't bear the thought of waiting on it to fall out bit by bit. This time, we were all miles and miles away. I got choked up thinking of how she would handle it. This time, Jonny had just flown in to join us after going home for the birth of his daughter, Cassidy. He went with me to the hotel's gym that day and held a bag still so I could punch the shit out of it. Not that it helped.

When we got back to Portland, I went straight home. She was in my bed, as bald as the day she was born, with Blackbeard snuggled up by her shoulder. I stripped off my suit and got into bed with them, and I kissed every inch of her head while she cried.

AFTER BEING CLEARED to be around kids, Katie had started to come to some of our home games when she wasn't feeling completely miserable. Once she lost her hair, though, she stopped coming.

At first, I didn't understand. I mean, she had been through this before, and she hadn't let losing her hair stop her from living her life back then. She'd thought about it, at first, preferring to hide at home instead of going to her prom or any of the other things she normally would have done. But then she'd gotten over it. She'd worn a wig or put on a scarf and gone on with her life. Hell, when I'd taken her to her prom, she'd gone without a fucking thing covering her head.

Not only that, but she'd just spent an entire month where she had been essentially a prisoner within her own home. Her contact with the outside world had been so limited, I didn't understand why she would put herself through that again voluntarily. It was only when I realized that every time she left her house for any reason, she looked up and down the street, searching for photographers hidden in bushes or behind cars. Once I picked up on that, I got it.

Katie wasn't ready for the world to know that her cancer had returned. She was waiting for the paparazzi to pounce again.

As soon as I connected the dots, I called up Brie. "I think this is a mistake," I said the second she answered the phone. "The concert, getting her up on stage with them, proposing in front of the crowd, the whole shebang. I think I fucked up. Really, truly, royally fucked up."

"It'll be all right. You're overreacting."

"I'm not overreacting. We have to cancel it."

"We can't cancel it now," she said. "It's in two weeks. Everything's booked. Jessica and Laura already got the foundation set up in Katie's name. The show's almost sold out. We've had dancers preparing for it for weeks, and the band has been pimping it out all over the place. There are too many wheels in motion, Babs."

I knew all of that as well as I knew the back of my hand, but I couldn't shake the feeling that I had made a huge blunder in putting this together without explaining it to Katie first. Without seeing if she was even *interested* in performing with them. What if she didn't want the world to see her as she was? What if she wouldn't go out on the stage and sing with them? Everything we'd been planning would go up in flames, just like that.

"People will find out sooner or later anyway," Brie said. "She can't hide the fact that she's sick forever. And she shouldn't. There are a lot of people out there who would want to support her through it, and she's not giving them the chance."

"I don't disagree, but shouldn't it be on Katie's terms?"

"Are you chickening out of proposing? Because that doesn't seem like you."

"I'm not chickening out. I want to marry her." I just didn't want to traumatize her in order to do it. She'd already been through enough without me adding to it.

In the end, I'd accepted that things had already gone too far for me to change any of it. I would just have to hope for the best and figure out a way to minimize the damage if Katie didn't respond well.

KATIE'S TREATMENTS PROGRESSED as expected. Most of the time, she felt like shit and wasn't up to doing much. She was tired a lot, and she ached. I tried to help by giving her gentle massages when I could, but most of the time she just wanted me to cuddle her. Her sex drive was almost non-existent these days, but I didn't imagine I would want to get it on, either, if I were going through what she was.

The days immediately following her treatments were the worst, but after a bit of time passed, she would get up and start doing things. Webs and I had finished setting up her studio, and sometimes I would find her in there with headphones on, picking at the keyboard or strumming a guitar, humming a melody. Other days, I would come home and she would be on the swing in her backyard with her notebook, writing down lyrics or completely lost in thought. Even in this time, which for so many people would be the lowest point of their lives, Katie was figuring out who she was and who she wanted to be.

Usually, when I found her like that, I smiled to myself and backed away, leaving her to her work. Sometimes she looked up and saw me before I could escape, though. She would smile and pat the seat beside her, and she would play me a bit of what she was working on or sing a few lyrics for me. There was a lot of sadness in her music, but always with an underlying sense of hope. That gave *me* hope, too. I locked those moments away in my mind. I didn't want to lose them.

The entire Weber family got involved in the preparations for the big night. Laura had been working with Jessica on setting up the foundation, of course, but it didn't stop there. She was the one making sure Katie was occupied whenever I needed to get together with someone for planning some aspect or another of the big night.

When Dani came home from school for a weekend, she and Webs went ring shopping with me—Dani because she knew Katie's style and the two of them wore the same ring size, and Webs to be sure whatever I chose was good enough to be worthy of giving to his little girl.

Luke and his teammates at the University of Minnesota filmed a video, getting everyone on the team and in the stands at one of their games to do a dance that Brie choreographed to a song called "Summer Stars." She and Mia flew out together to teach everyone the dance and film it, claiming they were each going to visit relatives so Katie wouldn't suspect anything. The song was Katie's favorite by The End of All Things, and the one that the band would bring her on stage to sing with them. The video would be played on the Jumbotron while they performed.

My family was trying to get involved, too. My birthday fell just before Christmas, but since all my brothers played hockey, my parents tended to pick which of their kids they would be with for the holidays. This year they were coming to Portland and bringing my three youngest brothers—Seth, Isaac, and Jack—with them. It was supposed to be Cal's turn to have Mom and Dad for Christmas, but he said he would be more than all right hanging out with the billet family he was living with in Oshawa, and Reece was going to spend Christmas on the road with the Binghamton Senators in his first year as a pro.

The contingent of Babcocks arrived in Portland one day before my birthday, just in time for a home game against the Sharks. I offered to set them up in the owner's box, along with most of the other relatives who were in from out of town, or get tickets for regular seats, but Mom had other plans. They decided to watch the game at my house with Blackbeard and Katie, since she still wasn't going out much other than to her doctor's appointments and hospital visits.

Katie texted me her selfie for the day just before I shut down my phone prior to the game. She had Blackbeard in a grip he was frantically trying to escape from, and my parents and three teenaged brothers were all surrounding her. Isaac, a sixteen-year-old with arms as long as I was tall, held the phone out to fit them all in the shot, and he had his head turned like he was going to kiss Katie on the top of her head if not for the kitten claws zooming straight for his nose. I laughed and powered off my phone, setting it in my stall.

"At least we know one thing about tonight," Koz said over the hip-hop music playing in the background and all the talk as everyone got ready.

"What's that?" Burnzie asked. The two of them were on much better terms lately, but that wasn't saying a whole lot. Burnzie still thought Koz needed an attitude adjustment and wanted to be the one to give it to him. I had decided to let those two sort their differences out themselves.

Koz finished taping his socks and tossed the roll of tape to Levi. "The best fucking captain in the game tonight's going to be playing for the home team," he said.

I snorted. "Not sure it means much when the other team doesn't have a captain."

Burnzie gave me a disbelieving look and shook his head. "Take what you can get, Babs. Take it and run."

Katie

I'D NEVER SPENT much time around Jamie's family before other than Levi until the last couple of weeks. Mom and Dad had invited them over for a big Christmas dinner. Levi and Koz joined us, too, as well as Ghost, Harry, RJ, and Luddy, a few of the other young, single guys on the team. Luke and Dani were both home from school for the holidays.

My parents' house wasn't big enough for the whole clan, so Jamie suggested we do it at his place. We could have overflow and an extra kitchen with my house, and we could open up the gate between the two backyards for everyone to easily move from one place to another. It worked out great, with Mom and Mrs. B taking over the food prep.

I spent most of the day curled up in a ball on one of Jamie's recliners. I'd had my latest round of chemo a few days before Christmas, and while the nausea had passed, my whole body ached. I didn't have the energy to do much, but I didn't want to be shut away from everyone in my room, either. Sometimes, Jamie would pick me up and steal my chair, drawing me onto his lap to cuddle with me. Other times, he was off keeping the guys entertained, playing pool or video games or something similar. That was when Blackbeard would jump up for a snuggle session. I was surrounded by people I loved the whole day, though.

When everyone else left to go home for the night, Jamie took me back to my house, carrying Blackbeard along with us. He handed me a small box that shook as he passed it over.

I gave him a wary look.

"Just open it," he said, laughing.

As soon as I untied the ribbon, the lid popped off and a black-and-white tuxedo kitten climbed out.

"You didn't." I had to blink back tears of surprise and awe.

"I figured it couldn't hurt for you to have one of your own, even though Blackbeard sometimes prefers you over me." Jamie picked the new kitten up and set it in my palm. "She's a snuggly thing. I thought, since I can't be with you all the time when you need someone to hold you, maybe you needed another cat to curl up with. And it couldn't hurt for Blackbeard to have someone else to play with, right?"

"She, huh?"

He frowned and picked up the kitten again, holding her to the light so he could check the appropriate parts. "Unless I'm mistaken. So I guess you'd better come up with a name for her before Levi gets any bright ideas."

"Why don't you name her since I named Blackbeard?"

"Yeah?" he asked.

I nodded.

"What about Oreo? She's about as sweet as one, at least, and it fits her coloring." He set her on the floor to join Blackbeard since she was squirming to go explore, and then he sat next to me on the couch, drawing my legs over his lap.

"Oreo works for me," I said. So did the way he was kneading the muscles of my forearm, working all the tension out.

For his Christmas gift, I'd given him a hand mixer and a promise that I'd teach him how to use it while making sure he didn't burn down the house. All of a sudden, that felt wholly inadequate in comparison to a kitten who would keep me company for years and years to come.

The two kittens ran around for a bit, but it didn't take long before they were as worn out as I was. Oreo climbed up on the sofa and curled up on my lap for a nap, and Blackbeard headed straight for his traditional perch. I decided he had the right idea and copied him, resting my head next to Blackbeard on Jamie's shoulder. That was one of their many uses, after all.

THE BABCOCKS STAYED in Portland through the holidays, even though the team had to go on a brief road trip between Christmas and New Year's. "We want to go to the concert," Mrs. B explained when I questioned her about it. "The boys *love* The End of All Things. And it's a great opportunity to get to know you and your family without Jamie and Levi getting in the way."

Mom and all the WAGs helped me keep Jamie's family entertained while the team was gone. Nicky's two nephews, Hugo and Nils, planned some pickup hockey games for all the kids, and the Babcock boys were a welcome addition to the regular crew.

A couple of days before the big concert, I went back in for more tests. The primary one I was concerned with was the MRI that would show how much my tumor had shrunk. I wanted that sucker to be gone. Zapped. Kaput. Finished.

"Well?" I asked the radiologist as soon as I came out of the tube.

"Dr. Oliver will fill you in once he and I have a chance to go over the results," she said. I'd known she would say that, but it still sucked to hear it.

Jamie came with me the next day to get the news.

"No change," Dr. Oliver said, and I nearly slammed my way out of his office in frustration.

"None?" I demanded. "Nothing at all?"

"Nothing, which is actually a good thing," he said, nodding enthusiastically. "That means it hasn't grown. We've kept the cancer from spreading. But you can't spend the rest of your life on chemo and radiation in the hope that it will remain contained."

I didn't want to hear it. I didn't want to hear anything more he had to say, and if not for Jamie squeezing my hand, I would have mentally checked out right then and there.

"So how soon will she need to have surgery?" Jamie asked.

Hot tears pricked at the backs of my eyes. "I'm not having surgery." In the last few weeks, the songs I'd written had finally started to come together. They were still really raw, and the lyrics were maybe a bit too emotional and honest, so it might be better for me to work on making them a little more vague and generic. But the fact was, they were *good*. They were something I could envision myself singing in front of a crowd, and the more time I'd spent writing them, the more it was something I wanted. I didn't know if simply writing the songs would be enough. I wanted the chance to perform, to get up on a stage and use the voice that I'd been born with in order to touch people.

Jamie turned to me with a pained look in his eyes, the same sort of expression he used to have before we'd gotten back together. "You have to," he said. "You remember what you promised me? That you'd fight with everything in you."

"I have been," I forced out. "I still am."

"And now it's time to ramp up the fight," he said. "You've got to do this. You know it. We're not just trying to push you into something because we're sadistic fuckers who want to torture you."

Hot tears splashed on my lap. The way I saw it, I had two choices. I could follow my dreams or my heart. I'd already followed my dreams once before, and everyone knew how that had turned out. I supposed that meant I knew what I had to do next.

I swiped the back of my hand over my cheeks, brushing away the tears, and looked across the desk at Dr. Oliver. "So when can I get on the schedule for surgery?"

WHEN NEW YEAR'S Eve finally rolled around, I pulled out my most natural-looking wig and even put a bit of makeup on. I hadn't been bothering with trying to make myself look decent lately. I didn't *feel* decent, so what was the point? But for this? I figured I ought to make myself presentable.

My thyroidectomy was scheduled for the following Tuesday. I didn't know if I would ever be able to sing again after that, so I was determined to make the most of tonight. I was going to have fun at the game with all the other WAGs and Jamie's family. Then I was going to the concert, and I was going to sing to my heart's content in the audience. And damn it all, I was going to look good while I did it.

I tried on about a dozen different outfits before settling on a blue A-line dress that had just a hint of sparkle. I used to sparkle all the time, but there hadn't been much point in wearing glittery things lately. Getting to see The End of All Things was a good enough reason to glam it up some.

Jamie did a double take when I answered my door, his eyes moving up and down in an appreciative sweep.

"Too much?" I asked, slipping my coat on as he held it up for me.

He kissed my forehead. "Never."

The whole way to the arena, he kept glancing over at me every chance he got, his expression heated in a way that made my previously dormant tingles of awareness come back to life. There was a part of me that wished we could turn around and go home again so we could just be together. He had a game to play, though, and I wasn't about to give up all that I had planned for tonight.

I kissed him and wished him good luck before he headed for the bowels of the arena and I made my way up to the owner's box. Mom and some of the other girls were already there, so I headed over to join them.

The Storm were playing the Oilers tonight, and the crowd in the building was raucous. Jamie got the team out to an early lead, scoring on a breakaway only two minutes in. The guys didn't look back from there, running over the Oilers to the tune of a six-to-nothing shutout, with a hat trick for Jamie.

By the time the game was over, my exhaustion had given way to the excitement coursing through the building. Brie and Jessica headed downstairs as soon as the game ended so they could oversee getting everything switched out from a hockey setup to a rock concert layout. I waited with Mom until Jamie came to collect me. His eyes were still shining with postgame intensity as he took my arm and we headed down to ice level.

The crowd had dispersed after the game, but the arena was already starting to fill up again. Excited fans pushed their way through the concourses, but Jamie expertly guided me to a back hallway where we wouldn't be jostled.

"Brie arranged for you to meet the guys," he explained.

A few more turns, and then we were being ushered into the dressing room, where the band was getting ready to go on stage, and I turned into a blushing, gushing, twelve-year-old girl again.

Brie was in there, too, in full dance costume for one of the numbers she'd be performing in later tonight. She tapped Emery on the shoulder and brought him over to me, and my knees nearly buckled underneath me.

"Hi, Katie," he said. He reached for my hand, smiling, and all I could do was gape like a fish out of water and let him take it.

A few of the other band members came over, shaking my hand and greeting me like I was an old friend. I felt woozy, probably from too much excitement, and they led me to a chair and helped me sit down. Jamie hovered nearby but not too close, letting me enjoy the moment.

I had almost gotten my nerves under control when Kellan Davies, the lead singer, sat down next to me and said, "So do you want to come on stage and sing with us? We were thinking about doing something special with 'Summer Stars' tonight, and I thought you could help us out with that."

I picked my jaw up from my lap and put it back in place. I mean, yes, I was something of a celebrity and people knew who I was. I'd done quite a bit of singing on *The Cool Kids*, but that didn't mean I had any business getting on stage with The End of All Things. Their fans hadn't paid good money to hear me. They wanted to hear Kellan.

"You're joking, right?" I said.

He took a moment and then looked up at Brie. "You weren't kidding when you said it might take some convincing, were you?"

Chapter Nineteen

I WATCHED THE show from the wings, still in awe of the fact that this was even happening. Kellan Davies from The End of All Things really *had* asked me to come on stage and sing with him, and the rest of the band was on board, and none of this was a joke. It was all so surreal that I kept pinching my arms, and it hurt every single time.

"You're going to end up with some hard-core bruises if you don't stop that," Jamie said, laughing beside me.

"Just trying to be sure I'm awake and this is really happening."

"It's really happening," he said in my ear. He put his arms around me, drawing me against him. I leaned back and let him bear the burden of keeping us both upright. He didn't appear to mind.

Even though it seemed too good to be true, and I had just decided it made so much more sense to follow my heart than my dreams, this wasn't the sort of opportunity I could pass up. I wasn't deluding myself into thinking anything would come of it. It was one night, one song. A blip on the radar that would be quickly forgotten. If I *was* going to make a career for myself in music after my surgery, it was going to be the result of a lot of hard work, not some fluke opportunity like this.

They played through several of their newer songs, including one that had been getting a ton of play on the radio in the last few months. The audience was on their feet, singing along at the tops of their lungs. Every now and then, Kellan would cut away and hold out his microphone to pick up the voices in the crowd.

That only increased when they started playing "Open Spaces," one of their biggest hits of all time from a few years back. It had a slinky, seductive beat, and soon the whole arena lit up with the lights of thousands of cell phones. When they got to the chorus, Brie and another dancer joined them on stage, performing the dance they'd choreographed for the music video. She was far enough along in her pregnancy now that she was showing, but she didn't let that stop her from doing all the lifts and other intricate moves that were called for. Their movements were just as intoxicating as the music. When that song came to an end, the band dropped the volume but kept playing, and Kellan spoke over the applause.

"On behalf of The End of All Things, I just wanted to thank everyone for coming out tonight. We love Portland!" Massive cheers filled the arena. "Portland has always been our home, but these days we have to spend a lot of our time away from here. It's always good coming home, though. We know a lot of you would have come to see us even if we weren't donating all the money raised tonight to a couple of very worthy causes."

A couple? I glanced up at Jamie, but he shrugged, as lost as I was.

A video popped up on the Jumbotron overhead, showing some highlights from events Light the Lamp had been part of in recent years.

"For a few years now, the Light the Lamp Foundation has been helping to turn around the lives of a lot of people in this community who've fallen victim to drugs and alcohol. They're putting addicts in touch with people who can help them, and they're giving addicts a way to give back—through building homes, cleaning up parks, serving meals to the homeless, and dozens of other projects that most of us would never think of. As a band, we're proud to support them in their efforts. And we're also proud to be supporting the Katie Weber Foundation."

It was a very good thing I was already letting Jamie hold me up because I would have been on the floor otherwise.

"There is no Katie Weber Foundation," I hissed at Jamie.

"There wasn't," he said in my ear. "There is now."

"Katie is another product of Portland," Kellan said as the video on the Jumbotron switched to the one the Storm had put together for Hockey Fights Cancer night a few months ago. "She may not have been born here, but she calls Portland home, and you can be damn sure we claim her. She was only seventeen when she was *first* diagnosed with cancer. Katie's friends and family have set up a foundation in her name to support cancer research and to monetarily aid families of children with cancer."

"How much of this did you have a hand in?" I asked Jamie.

His arms tensed around me. "All of it."

"How much more is there?" I needed to know. I needed to get a grip on myself or I would never be able to go out there and sing. I'd barely gotten through the Star-Spangled Banner back in October after watching this video, and that was before I knew the cancer had returned.

"A decent amount," Jamie said.

There wasn't much hope of avoiding all these tears, then. I just hoped my makeup would withstand it. I forced myself to watch the video, determined not to fall apart. This was my life on that screen. It was filled with the people I loved and the moments that had brought me to this place. Kellan kept talking, but I didn't hear him. Not now. A thousand memories drowned out the sounds of the present.

I had braced myself for the prom picture, but nothing could have prepared me for the images that came after it. All the selfies I'd been taking and sending to Jamie over the last several weeks popped up in a montage. They flashed across the screen in chronological order, showing the almost twenty thousand people here tonight all the things I'd been attempting to hide from myself, even, not to mention the world.

Taking those pictures had required a hell of a lot of acceptance—of myself, my appearance, the reality of my health and present situation. But it had also forced me to love myself exactly as I was. Because Jamie loved me. He didn't give his love to just anyone. For him to love someone the way he loved me, you had to be worthy of it.

Not so very long ago, I hadn't been so sure that I deserved his love. I'd made a lot of mistakes over the years, and he had been here being his flawless, perfect self. He hadn't stopped loving me, though, and that had to count for something.

In my book, it counted for a whole hell of a lot.

"Is this why you wanted them?" I asked. "For this video?"

He squashed me to him, holding me so close I could hardly breathe but couldn't bring myself to care about that. Because it meant he didn't want to let me go. "I wasn't sure what I was going to do with them when I asked for them. I only figured it out later."

"Hmph," I said, but I couldn't put any heat behind it.

"Are you mad at me?" he asked, pressing his lips to the wig.

I shook my head, realizing too late that it would knock the wig askew, and I was about to have to go out on that stage in front of all those people, not to mention their cell phones and cameras and Twitter accounts. But that was all right, because they'd already seen the truth of the situation. They knew I had cancer again. They knew I was the bald alien-girl I'd been at my senior prom, so there was no point in pretending I wasn't that person. She was me, and I was her, and that was that.

Within a few moments of that happening, the band starting playing the opening strains of "Summer Stars," and Kellan turned to the wings of the stage and held out a hand to me, urging me to join him.

I took a breath and squeezed my eyes against the tears that were attempting to fall. Then I stepped out of the protection of Jamie's arms. My wig slipped out of place, so I reached up and took it off, pressing it into Jamie's hands. He met and held my gaze, and I nodded—maybe to reassure him, or possibly to reinforce the surge of confidence bubbling up within me to fight off the stage fright and fears.

I stepped out into the spotlight, moving toward Kellan. The crowd roared over the strains of music pulsing through the sound system, but I couldn't see them. The lights left me blind to anything but what was immediately in front of me, but for whatever reason, that soothed me. Because I knew what my future held now. A life with Jamie. A life, however long, of a love so pure and steadfast and honest that it filled me with peace in a world that seemed bound and determined to threaten me at every turn.

And I knew that what Kellan had said was right. This was my home. Whatever life held in store for me, I would experience it here with the people I loved.

Sometimes in life, dreams aren't all they're cracked up to be. When they're not, though, there's usually another dream—a better dream— waiting for you in the wings.

Jamie

THERE WAS SOMETHING about the stage lighting that made Katie look like an angel. It seemed appropriate, considering how she fit within my life. She always said she looked like an alien without her hair, but she was wrong.

She took the mic Kellan held out for her and held it up to her mouth. It was as if the roof opened up to let the sun pour into the arena when she sang. The video her brother's team and school had put together started playing, and Kellan tapped Katie on the shoulder to point up at the Jumbotron. She kept singing as she looked up, and then she laughed into the microphone, shaking her head in disbelief. "My brother has some serious moves, people," she said in a break between the verse and the chorus. "Watch out. He'll be the next big thing."

Behind me, our families quietly moved into place, along with just about every guy from the team and all of their loved ones. I handed the wig to Laura. Levi came up to stand next to me. He fished out the jewelry box from his pocket and handed it to me. I nodded, shoving it into my own pocket.

Kellan joined her to sing the second verse, and the crowd went wild. The lighting changed when they got to the chorus again. Everything went a deep blue, except for a spotlight hitting the disco ball overhead, giving the effect of stars twinkling in a perfectly clear night sky.

Everything picked up for a big push to the end, but then the band members dropped out one at a time, until it was just the drummer keeping a rhythm along with Kellan and Katie. Two voices and a simple beat, thumping like a heart. By the time they came to a finish, there wasn't a single person in the arena still in his seat.

A cameraman focused in on the two singers, and that image replaced the video her brother had made.

Kellan grinned at Katie. She smiled and waved at the crowd, and she made to hand the mic back to him, but he shook his head. "Keep that. You'll need it."

She shook her head in confusion, and that was when he caught my eye and waved me onto the stage. "There's someone here who needs to talk to you," he said.

It took a second—and a none-too-gentle shove from Burnzie, along with a cuff to the back of my head and, "At least you bothered to fucking comb your hair after you showered this time"—to get my feet moving.

The spotlights blinded me, and I blinked a few times as I crossed the stage. By the time I reached the pair of them, my eyes had adjusted. Kellan handed me his mic, but my hands were shaking so badly I didn't know if I could hold on to it. The crowd was so quiet that you could hear every time someone shifted in his seat or coughed, which only made me more nervous. What the hell was I thinking? Katie was used to getting up on a stage in front of people. She had cameras on her all the time, and she knew how to say what she wanted to when the spotlight was on her. I couldn't even figure out what to say in front of twenty fucking teammates, though.

Yet here I was, with twenty thousand people waiting for me to make an ass of myself.

I bit the inside of my cheek and forced myself to start talking even though I wasn't sure what was going to come out of my mouth. "This is kind of weird for me. Usually when I have this many people watching me in this building, they don't care what I have to say as long as I put the puck in the net."

"Why don't you try scoring four next time, you slacker?" some guy shouted from one of the front rows, and everyone who heard him laughed.

"I know," I said. "A hat trick's not enough. I'll work on that." The interruption threw me off for a second, but it did at least loosen me up some.

I focused in on Katie, trying to tune everything else out. She laughed, but the tears she'd been trying to hold back since this whole thing had started were streaking her cheeks with mascara.

"I still remember the first time I ever saw you," I said. "You were sixteen years old, and so full of life I couldn't help but watch you across the room all day. We were at an Ice Breaker event for the Storm, and I was an eighteen-year-old rookie who was scared to death and intimidated as hell to be around these guys I'd been trying to emulate my whole life. But then I bumped into you. Literally." The crowd laughed, but I kept powering through. "You blushed and stammered an apology, but I blushed harder and couldn't figure out how to say a damn thing because you were the most beautiful girl I'd ever seen. You said something about my dimples, which embarrassed me more than ever. I think I fell in love with you in that exact moment. But then you walked over to your dad and planted a kiss on his cheek. That was when I realized who you were. He looked back at me with one of those threatening looks he always seemed to give me, and I was pretty sure I'd already earned a spot on his shit list just for accidentally bumping into you."

Even with her tears, Katie chuckled. She ducked her head down, and I caught a glimpse of Webs standing in the wings. I was pretty sure he winked at me. I still hadn't gotten used to the fact that he was not only okay with this but encouraging me.

"I didn't think it was possible, but I only love you more now," I said. "Every day, I love you more than the day before. I used to be scared of your father." More laughter from the crowd. "Now I'm just scared of a future that doesn't have you in it. We don't know what's going to happen. There's no crystal ball that will show us exactly where we'll be in a month or a year or ten years or even fifty. But I know this. However long we have, you and me, I want us to spend it together. I want to be right by your side through it all. I want to hold your hand when you're scared, and I want to carry you when you can't go on. And no matter what, when it's our last day together—whenever that may be—I want to know that I loved you more on that day than I did any day before it."

I dug the ring box out of my pocket, but my hand was shaking so badly I dropped it on the stage. I bent down to retrieve it, and Katie said, "Yes," into her microphone, loud and clear. The word echoed in the arena.

I laughed. "I haven't even asked the question."

"So get on with it," she said. Her tears hadn't stopped flowing. "Ask me so I can say yes, because I can't stand it."

I dropped down to a knee, and I tried to open the box, but I kept fumbling with it. She tucked her microphone under an arm, opened the box, set it back on my hand, and gave me a get-a-move-on look, waving her hand for further emphasis. The audience roared with laughter.

I couldn't help but join them. "Katie Weber," I said, choking on my laughter. "Will you marry me?"

She drew the mic out again and put it right up to her mouth. "*Now* can I say yes?"

Shouts of "Yes!" came from all around us, including more than a few from our friends and family.

She raised a brow in question.

"Go on," I said.

"Yes!" She dragged me to my feet and kissed me so hard I dropped the mic, but then everything else faded away, and it was just the two of us.

By the time we finally broke it off, Kellan had apparently retrieved the microphone.

"Well, I'd say that was well worth the price of admission, wouldn't you?" He winked at us. "You all be sure to put pictures up on Twitter and Instagram and whatnot, okay? This is the kind of news that should be shared with the world. How often do you go to a rock concert and end up witnessing a proposal?"

Katie put the ring on her finger and took my hand. She led me off the stage to the wings as the band started playing the next song. Everyone circled around us, offering congratulations and hugs and handshakes.

Webs caught my eye and angled his head off to the side for me to follow. Since some of the women had already dragged Katie in the other direction so they could gush over her ring, it was easy enough to follow him. I just had no idea what he wanted this time.

He crossed his arms, taking up a familiar, threatening stance. I'd given up on trying to figure him out. He'd been trying to get me and Katie back together for months. He'd told me I would make a good son-in-law, and he'd helped to pick out the ring. Now—*now*—he wanted to rip my balls off again? What the fuck was I supposed to do?

"For almost twenty-three years," he said, "Katie has been my little girl. She's been my responsibility. Mine to protect. Mine to guard her heart. I haven't always done a good job of it. I've failed her more times than I care to admit, and she's been the one to suffer the consequences. Now it's your turn. You'd better do a much better fucking job than I did. You understand me?"

For once, I understood him perfectly well. I nodded. "I might need help sometimes, though. I don't think she'll ever stop needing her father."

His lips twitched, and I knew he was fighting either tears or a smile. He slapped me on the back. "Good man. Go make my little girl happy." Then he turned and walked away.

I made my way back into the melee of friends and family, looking for Katie. She was easy to spot in the center of it all, her bare head shining like a beacon. She beamed up at me when I reached her. But then she grabbed on to my arm and pulled me away from the crowd.

"Mom wants to talk wedding dates already," she said.

I laughed. "She doesn't mess around."

"Never has, never will."

"Do you want to start planning?" I asked.

Katie shook her head. "I am not going to have a naked head in both my prom pictures and my wedding pictures. That's not going to happen. No setting a date until we're sure I'm done with chemo for good, so we can know that I'll have hair."

"Fair enough." I kissed the top of her head. "But can we do it while your hair's short and spunky?"

"You like it like that?"

"I love it like that. Because it means you're healthy."

"Oh." The single word was marshmallow soft.

She put her arms around me, hugging me close. As soon as I did the same, she melted against me.

"I always love your hair," I murmured, my lips against the smooth skin of her head. "Long, short, thick, thin, any color you want it to be. I even love it when you don't have any. Because I love you."

"Have I ever mentioned you're perfect?" she murmured against my chest.

I opened my mouth to argue with her, but she cut me off.

"Perfect for me."

She got that right. We were perfect for each other.

Epilogue

Katie

THE INSTANT JAMIE opened the door, both kittens came racing for us. Jamie had his arms full with the overnight bag I'd had with me at the hospital and the prescriptions they'd sent home with us. Blackbeard had made it halfway up Jamie's body before he realized I was the easier climb. He leaped from Jamie over to me, catching his claws on the fabric of my coat before shimmying the rest of the way to my shoulder.

At least I was wearing a coat.

"Is he all right?" Jamie asked, his voice full of concern.

I nodded. At the moment, my throat hurt too much to talk unless I had to, so I was trying to use more nonverbal cues for communication.

Jamie closed the door behind us and carried everything away, leaving me to deal with the kittens. I headed into the kitchen, Oreo doing her best to trip me up as I walked, and took out a dish and a can of the stinky kitten food. As soon as I popped the top, Blackbeard's nose went into overdrive, and he jumped down to the counter. Oreo started crying, so I picked her up and set her beside her buddy to wait while I scooped it all out for them.

Once they were happily munching away, I took off my coat. Jamie had returned by then. He took it from me and kissed my cheek before turning to hang it in the hall closet.

The thyroidectomy had been successful. They'd gotten every bit of the tumor, taking every bit of my thyroid along with it. I was going to have to take meds for the rest of my life to replace it, but that wasn't such a big deal. At this point, taking a few pills was the least of my concerns.

I was cancer-free again. No more chemotherapy. No more radiation. My hair should start growing again sometime in the next few weeks, so there was nothing to stop me from making wedding plans with Jamie.

Not only that, but I ended up as part of the ninety-eight percent of successful surgeries, not the two percent. Which meant no damage to my vocal chords. Which meant I could still sing, if I decided that was the path I wanted to take.

After the concert on New Year's Eve, Kellan and Emery had both sat down with me for a few minutes, offering to spend some time writing songs with me. I'd been floored. It was a good thing I'd already been seated when they'd made the offer, because there was no chance I would have remained standing.

They were heading back out to finish up their tour next week, but we'd arranged to get together once they returned to Portland in February. By then, I should have fully recovered from surgery and be well on my way to being normal again. I didn't know what kinds of doors this would open for me, but it only made sense to explore it. Songwriting might not end up being the right path for me. Singing might not, either. The only thing I knew for certain was that no matter what I decided to do, Jamie would be by my side.

"How's the throat feel?" he asked me now, leaning on the counter and watching our fur babies shoving one another out of the way so they could each get to their meal more easily.

I scrunched up my nose. "Sore," I mouthed, careful not to let any actual sound escape.

"Would ice cream help? It's chocolate. I remember you telling me once that if you ever turned down chocolate, that's when I need to worry about you."

I grinned and nodded.

He winked. He took out a couple of bowls and spoons, then headed for the freezer. It wasn't a store-bought ice cream tub, though. It was a reusable plastic container, the type that people used for storing leftovers.

I gave him a questioning look.

"I made it," he said, waggling his brows. "With the hand mixer you bought me."

I shook my head, wishing it didn't hurt to talk. I wanted to tell him that you couldn't just mix up ice cream and pop it in the freezer, that you needed an ice cream maker to churn it while it slowly dropped to the right temperature, or else you'd end up with frozen, icy chunks that were not what anyone would call ice cream. That was way too much to attempt saying, though, so I just watched, baffled, as he scooped out what appeared to be perfectly smooth, creamy ice cream.

He put some in a bowl and passed it over to me with a spoon. "It's fine," he said. "I tested it out last night when I got home. It's a recipe that Archie taught me. Just try it."

Dubious, I dipped my spoon into the bowl and put a small bite in my mouth. It was perfection. Smooth as velvet, rich and sweet but not overpoweringly so. It was so good I let out a moan, which I regretted because it hurt. I winced.

"That good, huh?" Jamie leaned over the counter and kissed me, licking his lips as he backed away. "Yep. That good."

I went back for more, sighing in pleasure as the cold hit the aching spot in my throat. There was no way he'd made this. Not without an ice cream machine, at the very least, and even then he would have had to cook the custardy stuff before putting it all in the machine.

"Where's the machine?" I forced out, hating the raw, scratchy sound of my voice almost as much as the pain of forming the words.

He was still scooping out some for himself. He set the spoon down in his bowl, turned to the cabinet, and took out the mixer I'd given him for Christmas. "Right here."

I shook my head. "You couldn't have made this"—I pointed at my bowl—"with that." I followed up by pointing toward the handheld appliance.

"Oh, ye of little faith," he said. He put the mixer away and finished getting his ice cream. The kittens had finished their meal, so he eased them down to the floor before carrying his bowl and spoon to the living room.

I followed, curling up against his side, still as perplexed as ever.

He kissed the tip of my nose before taking a bite of his dessert. "Two ingredients," he said, mouth full. "Heavy cream and sweetened condensed milk. That's it. Toss it in a bowl, whip it up, and freeze. This is what you get. I added cocoa since you love chocolate."

"Seriously?" I said, grimacing at the pain. I was going to have to try harder to avoid talking.

"Seriously. Have some faith in me."

I had more than just *some* faith in him, but he continued to surprise me at every turn. One thing was certain. No matter how many years we had together, and I hoped there were so many that most couples would be sick of each other before it was over, there was no chance I would ever get bored.

I took another bite, letting the frozen goodness soothe the aches in my throat the same way that Jamie soothed the aches in my soul.

I'd told him once before that sometimes a person didn't understand what they really wanted until they'd lost it. Well, I'd lost him, and I'd gotten him back again. No matter how many wild and crazy hairs I got about things I wanted to do with myself, I would never forget that *he* was better than any dream I could conjure up. He was perfect—for me. And he was mine.

Good thing I was smart enough to learn from my mistakes. I'd left him before and gotten burned. Now I could be with him and know there was no place I'd rather be.

Portland wasn't my home; Jamie was.

There is nothing in this world that feels as good as being completely at home. Not even chocolate.

Roster

Name	Position	Nickname	Number
Dominic Medved	Defense	Bear	2
Cole Paxton	Defense	Colesy	3
Andrew Jensen	Defense	Jens	4
Levi Babcock	Defense	501	5
Keith Burns	Defense	Burnzie	7
Cody Williams	Defense	Harry	8
Brenden Campbell	Left Wing	Soupy	11
Blake Kozlow	Center	Koz	14
Radek Cernak	Center	Radar	15
Austin Cooper	Center	Coop	16
Ilya Demidov	Defense	Demi	18
Jamie Babcock	Right Wing	Babs	19
Axel Johansson	Right Wing	Jo-Jo	20
Grant Wheelan	Center	Wheels	22
Marc d'Aragon	Right Wing	Danger	24
Otto Raita	Left Wing	Otter	27
Cam Johnson	Left Wing	Jonny	28
Mitchell Quincey	Right Wing	Q	29
Nicklas Ericsson	Goal	Nicky	30
Sean Roberts	Goal	Bobby	35
Aaron Ludwiczak	Left Wing	Luddy	43
Jiri Dvorak	Right Wing	Devo	44
Jared Tucker	Center	JT	51
Nate Golston	Left Wing	Ghost	83
Riley Jezek	Center	RJ	91

Home Ice

by
USA Today bestselling author

Catherine Gayle

Chapter One

Paige

"OH MY GOD." My eldest daughter, Zoe, stopped dead in her tracks, her face completely pale as though she'd just seen a ghost.

Her sudden halt caused a pileup of my girls, all screeching to a standstill right beside her. The huge crowd surrounding us in the concourse at the Moda Center—all here for the Portland Storm's StormSkillz Competition, the same as we were—nearly ran our little group over in their quest to get food and drinks and get to their seats for the day of family fun.

Clueless as to what led my girls to cause a traffic jam, I took a cursory look around, but all I could see was the ocean of purple and silver jerseys jockeying for position. Nothing stood out as being anything that should cause that kind of reaction in my sixteen-year-old daughter. "What?" I asked, since I didn't have the first inkling what was going on.

Zoe looked like she might have stopped breathing.

Her younger sisters had figured it out, though. Evie, my fifteen-year-old, clutched her older sister's hand and let out a squeal, her face turning twenty-seven shades of pink and red with excitement. "It's Levi Babcock! Right there."

Well, that explained it. My girls were seriously boy crazy—all four of them—and Levi Babcock was their obsession du jour. Zoe was even wearing a Storm jersey that had "Future Mrs." as the name and 501 as the number. Apparently, everyone called him 501 because of his name and the jeans, or something like that. I had a hard time keeping up with all the preoccupations kids talked about these days. There was just too much on my plate.

I spun around, and that was when I found him—tall, broad, dark-haired, wearing a designer suit. A few other men in suits were around him, which made them stand out among the jersey-clad fans filling up the building. They were probably all players, or at least involved with the team in some way. Why else would they be in suits? My girls didn't have eyes for any of them but Levi, though. In recent years, I had come to learn that female teens had a certain type of hormone that produced single-minded determination in a way that I didn't quite recall experiencing. Surely I couldn't have been too different from my girls, though. Maybe I'd just blocked it all from memory due to embarrassment.

The young Storm defenseman should probably run away, and fast, because I didn't know if I would be able to control all four of my hormone-riddled daughters, and if they got their hands on him... I shook my head. I'd probably be doing good to keep any *one* of them in check, but all *four*? The end result could be disastrous for the young man.

Zoe's jaw was hanging open, her eyes popping out of her head in a way that was downright comical; Evie was practically hyperventilating, her skin flushed; Izzy, my thirteen-year-old, had started bouncing in circles and was talking in a nonstop stream of high-pitched babble that sounded like *oh-Mom-can-we-go-meet-him-and-get-his-autograph-and-kidnap-him-right-now-please-I-promise-I'll-take-good-care-of-him-he-can-be-my-first-brother-husband-then-we-just-have-to-kidnap-Kaner-and-Seguin-and-Torey-Krug-too.*

And then there was my youngest, eleven-year-old Sophie. As with everything in life, Sophie was a special case. She stopped alongside her sisters long enough for it to seep in that her crush was standing not twenty feet away from us, and then she was off like a shot.

"Shit," I muttered beneath my breath, taking off after her and calling out, "Sophie, stop right this second! Help me with your sister," I added over my shoulder to the other three, in the hope that they could pull themselves together enough to do what needed to be done.

I needed all hands on deck, because when Sophie had her mind set on something, it was next to impossible to veer her off her intended course. A mean stubborn streak went along with the territory with my youngest, as was common in kids who had Down syndrome. Not that she was mean; she was just obstinate about getting what she wanted. She was actually one of the sweetest, kindest, most loving and loveable kids I'd ever known, but at the moment, she wanted to give all of her love—whether it was welcome or not—to an unsuspecting Levi Babcock.

"Levi!" she shouted as she raced toward him, ducking between people traveling in every direction around her. She only had eyes for her prey, though, oblivious to everything else going on.

Levi swiveled his head around, trying to determine where the voice had come from, and caught sight of her just in time. He broke into an easy grin, but I doubted he understood that he was her intended target and was about to get pummeled with affection. Sophie launched herself at him, and he barely got his arms out and ready to catch her in time, his grin disappearing in exchange for wide-eyed surprise. Being smaller, stronger, and far more determined than I was, my little girl had made it through the crowd in a flash.

I pushed my way through the throng, desperate both to get to my daughter and to apologize for her overzealous behavior. A lot of people in this world just didn't understand, and some weren't very forgiving. I had no way of knowing which category Levi might fall into. Zoe, Evie, and Izzy were right on my tail, which was good, since I might need backup.

We arrived just in time to hear Sophie ask him, "Levi, will you marry me?"

A genuine smile lit up his features and brought out a dimple in his left cheek as he held my daughter high up in his arms. Hers were wrapped so tight around his neck that she had to be making breathing difficult, but he didn't seem to mind. No wonder my girls were all head over heels in puppy love with this guy. I probably would be, too, if I were their age.

He winked at Sophie, and then he nodded over at me. "I'm not so sure your mom is ready to give you up just yet," he said, deftly brushing off her proposal without doing so in a way that would hurt her feelings. "How about we see how things stand in a decade or so? You might meet someone you like better than me by then, you know. I might get old and fat and lose my hair."

"I'll never love anyone better than you." Sophie put her head down on his shoulder, her expression as blissful as I'd ever seen it.

"I'm sorry," I said, trying to pry her death grip free, but she was on him like duct tape with no intention of letting go. "Sophie, honey, we have to let Levi go get ready to skate."

"Actually, no, you don't," one of the other men in suits said. He had a deep, accented voice that rumbled through me, and I shot my gaze up to his, fully ready to give him a piece of my mind about telling my kid something that directly went against what I'd just told her. It was hard enough to get her to listen as it was, sometimes, and the last thing I needed was someone giving her the wrong impression.

Then I started suffering from a case of the same hormonal chaos that had taken over my daughters. I had no idea who this man was—huge, muscled, with a strong jaw and a full head of salt-and-pepper hair that was perfectly styled, not to mention blue-gray eyes that had no business being anywhere but the bedroom—but simply looking at him stole my ability to form a more coherent thought than *unh* at the same time as it made my knees suddenly go weak.

This was trouble. I had too much on my hands already to deal with jumping back in time to my own teen years.

Then he smiled at me, and I feared I might thoroughly disgrace myself in front of my girls and let rapid-onset jelly-legs syndrome take over my life. I hadn't gone gaga over a man in years, but apparently I wasn't immune to it.

"Mom, I *told* you I was gonna marry Levi," Sophie said, her smile bright enough to light up Times Square at New Year's.

That was all it took to remind me I was the grown-up here, and I had a job to do. Sophie still had a death grip on Levi's suit jacket, but he wasn't acting anxious to be rid of his ardent and very much too young so-called fiancée.

I steeled my spine for the task at hand—figuring out a way to extricate her without either ripping his jacket or instigating a temper tantrum—and reached for her again. "Maybe someday," I said, trying to pry her stubby fingers free. "But it's going to have to wait. He's got to do work today."

"That's what I was saying," the drop-dead gorgeous older man said.

He gently eased Sophie's grip open and lifted her out of Levi's arms, setting her down on the ground. More than that, she *let* him do that. Sophie didn't let anyone get away with something like that so easily. There was something about this man that made her trust him, and I wasn't sure if that was a good thing or a bad thing. My hormones were leaning toward the good thing part, but trusting *them* to make decisions for me wasn't something I could—or should—do.

"What were you saying?" I asked, mentally telling my hormones to

242

get in line, or else. Ha. Like they'd ever paid attention to my threats.

"There's nothing he has to do today except cater to you and your girls," the older man said, grinning at Sophie.

That smile? The way he was looking at my baby girl? That was a panty-melting move for me, only I wasn't positive he meant it to be one.

I shook my head. "I'm sorry. My head's in the clouds and I'm not quite following."

"I'm not either," Levi said. "What am I supposedly doing today?"

My girls all tittered nervously, blushing up a storm, just because he'd opened his mouth. He could speak gibberish, and their response would be the same. Still, he was as lost as I was about this whole thing. At least I wasn't the only one confused.

That amazing smile turned to me. Cue panty explosion.

"Sorry. I'm Mattias Bergstrom, the Storm's head coach." He held out a hand, but I was too nervous to shake it.

"Paige Calhoun," I spluttered. "And my daughters, Zoe, Evie, Izzy, and Sophie."

Then he kept going, dropping his hand back to his side as though I hadn't just been exceedingly rude. "In our last game, 501 got tripped up and hit his head on the goal post. He had some concussion symptoms that night, so we've got to hold him out of all activity for at least a week. That means he can't take part in any of today's events…which means he gets to be your personal companion for the day. All day long, he's going to take care of you five ladies. He'll take you up to the press box to show you around. He'll sit with you through the different events and explain whatever you want him to explain. After it's over, he'll bring you back down to the locker room and introduce you to the boys so you can get autographs. He's going to make today special for you and your girls."

"He is?" I spluttered at the same time as Levi said, "I am?"

I shook my head. "There's got to be some sort of mistake here, some confusion." I reached for Sophie's hand, determined to corral my girls and head toward our seats without any further boy issues. "We've just got regular tickets for the event. Nothing special. We should go." I tugged on Sophie's hand, but she didn't budge.

"Mom," she said in the long, drawn-out way that was unique to her when she was annoyed with me. "We're spending the day with *Levi*."

"There's no mistake," the coach said. "The other coaches and I will help him out where we can, but I want to make this happen." He looked off to the side at a gray-haired man with glasses, another one of the suits who'd been listening with a good deal of interest and a slight smile. "We can make this happen, can't we, Jim?"

"I don't see why not," the older man said. "Rach—"

"Not to worry. I'm already on it," a petite redheaded woman said, stepping into our circle. Even with only those few words, I could hear her thick Southern accent. She definitely wasn't originally from around here. She fished through a messenger bag for a moment and came up with a handful of passes on neck straps. She counted off five and handed them over to me. "Be sure you're wearing these at all times. Just keep them around your necks. They'll get you access to wherever Bergy wants 501 to take you." She smiled at me, then at each of my girls. "I think y'all are going to have a great day."

With fierce determination, Sophie released my hand, took her badge, settled it around her neck, and reached for Levi's hand. The whole time, she was grinning from ear to ear.

I supposed that settled that. With a sigh of resignation, I handed the other girls their badges and put one around my own neck. "I guess we're getting the royal treatment today, girls."

Not that I didn't want to give them the world. I did, and they knew I would do everything I could for them. I didn't make a ton of money as a massage therapist, though, and I worked hard for every penny I earned. Their father paid child support, but that money only went so far. The only reason we were here at all today was because he had won tickets in a raffle at work, but he had to be out of town this weekend. He couldn't bring the girls. That left it to me to corral them and herd them in the direction of our destination without veering off our course too far, as usual, and so here we were.

Coach Bergstrom winked at Sophie, and my knees almost gave out on me. There was apparently something about a man looking after my little girl like this that did me in.

"Let me have a word with 501, ladies, and then I'll leave you in his hands."

Mattias

I JERKED MY head to the side for Levi Babcock to follow me a few steps away from Paige Calhoun and her daughters. He came, but not without a stowaway attached to him at the hip. Sophie, the little girl who reminded me so much of my sister, wouldn't release his hand, leaving my young defenseman with a comically bewildered and anxious expression. Not that I could blame him for his nerves.

Much like most hockey players, Levi was better known by his nickname, 501, than by his given name. He was a lot like his older brother, Jamie, a guy everyone called Babs. They both had the sort of youthful good looks that brought out screaming teenaged girls in droves, like they were in a boy band or something. Babs was engaged to be married now, so he could always use his fiancée as an excuse to get away from his more overzealous admirers, but 501 didn't have the same luxury. He was fair game, as far as they were concerned.

That meant he had to be careful. I understood that even if I'd never experienced anything like it myself. Some of those girls might try to trap him, and then he'd have a world of problems to sort out, both personal and potentially legal. Not something he needed to add to his plate right now. Our general manager, Jim Sutter, and I had already given him plenty to work on as soon as he was medically cleared to return to the ice. He didn't need to add any off-ice issues to his agenda right now.

This girl was not one he needed to be wary of, though, and I didn't need to know her personally in order to be certain of that fact.

I smiled at Sophie. She gripped 501's hand harder and hugged her cheek to his arm, oblivious to the look of panic in his eyes or the fact that, for as much as she was holding on to him, he was doing his best not to touch her in any way. The look on her face was one of pure bliss. I doubted she would stop smiling for a week, which made it difficult to suppress my own smile.

"Are you excited to spend the day with him?" I asked.

"Mom didn't say we would get to meet Levi," she said. "Best surprise ever, Mr. Coach."

"Sounds like it to me. But you can call me Bergy." I dug out my wallet and removed a few bills, then passed them over to my young defenseman. "I've got a few things I have to see to before I can help you out. Take them up to the press box. Show them around, introduce them to whoever they want to meet up there, buy them some snacks and drinks. Just be yourself." Then I thought to add, "But watch your language. I'll be up to join you before everything gets started."

"But...I..."

The kid looked like a lost puppy, to the point I was tempted to pet him. Something told me Sophie might take care of that for me if the idea came to her. I knew better than to be the one to plant the idea in her head.

"You'll be fine," I promised him. "They're just girls. Besides, they've got their mother with them."

Based on what I'd seen so far, I had no doubt Paige Calhoun was the sort of mother who would prevent her daughters from doing anything that would put 501 in harm's way. Even now, she was watching Sophie like a hawk, not that there was anything to worry about. She should be more worried about me and 501 doing something to Sophie, since she didn't know us at all, but her focus was squarely on making sure her daughter didn't do anything she shouldn't.

I understood it better than most. Growing up with a younger sister born with Down syndrome gave me a good grasp on the single-minded determination those kids could have, not to mention the fact that they often missed social cues that other kids would pick up. But I also knew they tended to have hearts of gold.

The thing was, underneath it all, they were just like the rest of us. They were just people, and that meant Sophie was just a girl like any other her age in so many ways. She had hormones and would experience crushes and love and heartache the same as everyone else. And right now? She had the opportunity to spend the whole day with her crush. I'd be damned if I didn't do whatever it took to make it a memorable day for her and her entire family. If I could have done something similar for Linnea when she was this age, I would have done it in a heartbeat.

"You're sure, Bergy?" 501 said, looking at me like I was a madman. And maybe he was right about that. "I mean… This is… I don't—"

"Positive," Sophie responded, despite the fact that he hadn't asked her anything at all. She tightened her grip on him. "You're my date."

I arched a brow and nodded. "I think Sophie's got the right of it." I clapped a hand on 501's shoulder in encouragement and nudged him in the direction of Sophie's mother and sisters. "All right," I said once we were next to them again, unable to stop myself from looking in Paige's direction. Paige's allure was far different from Sophie's but no less magnetic. I needed to watch myself around her. For all I knew, she was married. Even if she wasn't, that meant she was a single mother. Either way, she had a hell of a lot more in her life that needed her focus than me finding her attractive. I smiled for her. Couldn't stop myself, actually. "Looks like you're all set. I'll be up to help out in a bit, but in the meantime, you're in good hands."

The oldest of the daughters looked like she was about to pass out, but she couldn't tear her eyes away from 501. One of the others was having the opposite reaction to being near him, nearly bursting out of her skin with the sort of exuberance and overabundance of energy that could only come from teenage hormones.

But even though her girls certainly drew my eye momentarily, it was Paige who held my attention. She had the most amazing long hair that fell straight down her back, almost pure black in color and as thick and luxurious as I'd ever seen. She was petite and fit, and she seemed to know that she was gorgeous exactly as she was, not bothering with more than a light dusting of makeup.

Her uneasiness over the current situation appeared to be getting the best of her, as she shifted from foot to foot and reached up to resituate the strap of her purse over her shoulder. That action drew my eye to her hand. More specifically, to her ring finger. Which was bare. I wasn't sure why I'd bothered to notice that, but I had. And she saw the recognition hit my face, too, if her sudden blinking was any indication.

But then she shook her head, as if that would be enough to brush whatever was bothering her aside. Her expression was as apologetic as I'd ever seen, which was saying something. My own mother had spent years apologizing for Linnea, even though there'd been no damned good reason to apologize, before she'd finally broken the habit. Something told me Paige hadn't managed that feat yet. She opened her mouth, but I cut her off before she could tell me she was sorry. That was the last thing she needed to say, and I definitely didn't need to hear it.

"My sister has Down syndrome," I said.

I wasn't sure why I told her that other than it was the first thing that came to mind and the only thing that came to my lips in time to stop her apology. And it worked. She snapped her mouth closed, and everything about her appearance changed in an instant. Her hazel eyes softened, and she dropped her hand to her side instead of attempting to force Sophie to release 501's arm.

"Does she?" Paige asked.

Sophie lit up. "You have a sister, Bergy? Where is she? I want to meet her."

I chuckled. "She's in Sweden. I don't think you'll be able to meet her today."

"Okay. Maybe tomorrow."

"I don't know about that," Paige said. "You have to go back to school on Monday."

"Can Levi come to school with me? I want to show him to my friends."

With that, 501 tensed up.

"I bet we can get some pictures to show your friends," I said, and he started breathing again. I glanced at my watch. "But for you, I think you should go have some fun with him."

"Okay," Sophie said. She took off walking in the wrong direction, dragging 501 alongside her. The rest of the Calhouns followed in their wake.

Somehow, 501 must have convinced Sophie that he knew a better way of getting to their ultimate destination, because they turned around and shuffled past me heading in the appropriate direction.

"Give me twenty minutes," I called out as they passed me by.

501 nodded, wide-eyed, but it was Paige's expression that once again drew my eye. She seemed completely and utterly perplexed as her head swiveled so she could take me in.

And now, whether it was a good idea or not, I really wanted to get to know her.

Chapter Two

Paige

IT WASN'T MUCH longer before we were given the royal treatment ten times over. Levi took us up a private elevator and led us through a series of halls we never would have been able to see otherwise. Every now and then, a security guard would ask to see our badges, which Sophie would lift up high in the air and wave around for them, but then they would wave us through. We stopped at a concession stand and Levi bought the girls drinks and snacks—despite my attempt to pay for them myself—before showing us around the press box. He introduced us to the Storm's television crew as well as Axel Johansson and Jiri Dvorak, a couple of other players who, like Levi, were currently injured and ineligible to participate on the ice today.

Now he'd found us all seats together near the front of the box. Axel and Jiri joined us, spreading out between my girls, who giggled and tittered nervously. Well, all of them but Sophie. I'd never seen my youngest so confident. She hadn't released Levi's hand once since she'd first latched on to him, and I was positive I would have to pry her fingers loose later. The poor guy would have to go to the bathroom sometime, at the very least, and she couldn't very well follow him in there. Not that she wouldn't try. I knew her better than to think she would voluntarily release him any time in the next decade. He'd be lucky to find his freedom within a century or two.

I sat down a couple of rows behind them all, close enough to be certain that none of my girls did anything they shouldn't—always a concern, considering the sheer number of hormones wreaking havoc on my household these days—but giving them enough distance so they wouldn't feel as if I were breathing down their necks.

The lights in the arena dimmed, the music cranked up, and the stage lights started to flash. A video came up on the Jumbotron overhead at the same time as I felt someone take a seat next to me.

Based on the hit of expensive cologne that wafted over to me and tickled my nostrils, I had no doubt that *someone* was actually the coach. He smelled good enough to eat, a realization that made my belly flutter like it hadn't done in years. Not since well before Dan and I divorced, actually. The spark had gone out years before we'd given up on the marriage, fading in the strain of countless specialist visits and oodles of therapist appointments that had been necessary for Sophie's development.

They say there aren't many marriages that are strong enough to withstand the strain of raising a special needs child. I now had the firsthand knowledge to be able to say that they, whoever *they* might be, were absolutely one hundred percent right.

But now I had butterflies in my belly for the first time in well over a decade, and it was because of this man sitting to my left, close enough to me that his body heat melded with my own.

The truth was there simply hadn't been time for attraction or lust or a fling. There hadn't even been time for *me*. All my energy had been put into making sure my daughters had everything they needed, and when I got as close to meeting those needs as I possibly could, I collapsed in a heap and attempted to get what sleep was possible. No matter what, I always felt inadequate and stretched too thin. I worried that I wasn't giving Zoe, Evie, and Izzy the support they needed because I was so fixated on Sophie. I *knew* that no matter how much of my focus I gave Sophie, it wasn't enough. There just wasn't time for any sort of romantic relationship, and if I couldn't make the time to sleep, then I definitely didn't have time for sex. I hadn't even thought about it in years because the simple act of thinking about sex required energy I couldn't muster.

But all of a sudden, being in Mattias Bergstrom's presence had parts of my body coming alive that had long since been dormant, and I couldn't say I minded. At the very least, it served as a good reminder that I was very much still a woman, not just a mother. It was good to know I hadn't completely lost that side of myself.

"I didn't mean to be pushy," he said quietly. The girls and his players were all busy talking and laughing and watching the spectacle below us, so I doubted they would have heard him anyway. "I just thought of my sister when I saw Sophie, and I wanted to give her an experience she wouldn't otherwise be able to have. It was instinct."

"I wasn't positive you recognized you might be stepping on my toes," I said. The fact that he realized he was overstepping, considering we'd only just met, was a point in his favor. Those only seemed to be adding up. I needed to keep an eye on my response to this man before I got myself into trouble. "It's not that I don't appreciate—"

"You don't need to explain."

I glanced over at him and locked on to his blue-gray eyes, which seemed to see straight into my soul, but that was enough to convince me to take him at his word. I seemed to put so much effort into explaining things, because most of the world didn't really understand what Down syndrome was, that it was second nature. It was nice to be around someone who simply understood. I smiled. I couldn't help it.

"I promise I won't offer your girls anything else without talking to you first," Mattias said. The way he looked at me when he said it left me breathless, almost trembling. He might as well have told me I was the most beautiful woman he'd ever seen, because that was what his eyes were saying to me. Those words had a decidedly more profound effect on me than anything he could have said about my appearance might have, anyway.

"Thank you for that." Belatedly, I realized I was staring down at my hands in my lap, my sudden shyness similar to Zoe's when she'd seen her crush across the concourse, and I forced myself to meet his gaze again. Good grief. I was thirty-nine years old. I should be able to look in a man's eyes without falling apart like my teenaged daughter at my age, and I'd be damned if I wouldn't manage it.

He smiled. Heaven help me, he had the most amazing smile. It was bold and confident but nowhere close to being cocky.

"I thought hockey players were supposed to be missing half their teeth," I joked. But then I remembered that he was the coach, not one of the players, and I wished I could take it back. Not that you could tell he wasn't a player based on his size.

He was every inch as big and strong as the three younger men seated in front of us. Maybe even bigger. There was no hiding the muscle filling out his frame, not even under the impeccable suit he wore, and their builds were closer to those of teenaged boys. It took years to build up the kind of muscle mass Mattias had. I knew muscles as well as I knew the back of my hand. I worked with them every day. Even with my eyes closed, I could tell so many things about a person just using my sense of touch.

But Mattias winked. "Now that I'm not playing anymore, I got permanent bridges put in." Then he flashed that smile at me again, not that I could tell the difference between the real teeth or the fake ones.

Yeah. That was a panty-melting smile if ever there was one. Poof! My panties might as well be gone. Which meant my brain had already all but disappeared.

If I had to spend too much time in this man's presence, I was due for some serious trouble.

"So you played before you coached?" I asked, trying to bring everything internal back under control.

"Nearly two decades in the National Hockey League. I grew up playing hockey in Stockholm. My grandparents made a lot of sacrifices so I could play, especially once my sister came into the picture. She needed so much of my parents' time and their resources, it was the only way I would have been able to play."

I didn't know what social services were like in Sweden, but I knew all too well what they were like here. Dan and I put every penny we could into Sophie's trust. She'd be able to get a job someday, but it wouldn't be the sort of job that would support her. At least she would have her sisters once the two of us were gone, but the more we could have already in place for her, the better.

But, as tempting as it was to talk to him more about his sister, I ended up putting my foot in my mouth again.

"How many teeth did you lose?"

"A dozen?" He gave me an odd look, as if he thought I could confirm or deny his response. "No, maybe it was thirteen."

"That's a lot of teeth to lose."

"Yes, but it was a small price to pay to be able to build the career I had. Actually, the one I have," he corrected himself.

"I suppose you must love hockey. It's nice to be able to make a career out of doing something you love."

"You sound like someone who has experience doing exactly that."

I arched a brow. "Do I?"

"Like recognizes like," he replied, a knowing tone coloring his words.

And he was right. I did love my work. Massage therapy was

physically exhausting work but as rewarding as anything I'd ever done outside of being a mother. "I suppose you're right," I finally conceded after he continued to eye me with a hint of a smirk.

"So, tell me, Paige," he said. "Is it all right if I call you Paige?"

"Yes." At the moment, I was fine with him calling me anything, as long as he would keep talking. He had a smooth, rich voice, and the hint of his Swedish accent was just enough to present some spice, like chocolate with a hint of cinnamon.

"Paige. I like that name. You can call me Matti if you want."

"Matti? Is that what everyone calls you?"

"Not everyone," he said. "Just my sister. But you can call me that if it fits for you."

"Oh." The word came out sounding soft and dreamy. Sitting here and talking with him made me *feel* soft and dreamy. But he didn't look like a Matti to me. He seemed much too dignified for that. Too hot. "I think I'll stick with Mattias, if you don't mind."

"I don't mind." The corners of his eyes crinkled. It didn't make him look old, just insanely handsome. "Tell me what it is you love to do, Paige."

I didn't even pause to think. Before I could stop myself, I said, "To look at you." I could have shot myself for blurting that out, but there was no taking it back.

And there was no deluding myself into thinking he might have missed it, either. Not with the way he chuckled. "I love to look at you, too," Mattias said. "I think I'm enjoying it a lot more than I should."

I should have kept my mouth shut. I should have turned to check on my girls, or looked to see what was happening down on the ice, or done any number of things other than what I did next. But, just like the teenager in a thirty-nine-year-old's body I'd apparently become, I did the exact opposite of what I should do; I let my hormones win.

"Why shouldn't you enjoy looking?" I asked, sounding much saucier than I felt. Inside, everything was roiling and jumbling and taut, like Izzy's bowstring during archery practice.

Mattias angled his head, taking me in more fully. Not to mention appreciatively. "Well, if you put it that way."

Not only had I put it that way but I didn't want to take it back, as long as he was going to continue looking at me that way.

It had been too damn long since anyone had flirted with me. I wasn't fooling myself. This wasn't going to last any longer than just today, but that didn't mean I couldn't enjoy myself for a little while.

It wouldn't mean the world was ending.

No harm would come to my girls just because I decided to let myself feel like a woman for a few hours.

Maybe a little flirtation was exactly what the doctor ordered. After today, life could go back to normal. But for now? A sexy-as-sin man was looking at me like there was nothing else he would rather be doing, nowhere else he would rather be, and I was determined to let myself enjoy it.

Mattias

I COULDN'T SEEM to help myself. I'd initially been drawn to Sophie, but now that she was happily latched on to 501 for the foreseeable future, her mother was drawing all my focus.

She was blinking at me. I couldn't decide if she was wishing she hadn't returned my flirtation or surprised that she had. Either way, I didn't mind. I liked the effect I seemed to be having on Paige. In fact, I might like it a bit too much. Wedding ring or no, she probably didn't have time to get involved with someone, let alone a man as married to his work as me. It had always been my biggest flaw. I couldn't keep track of how many times Linnea had told me to *Loosen up, Matti.* I worked so hard in order to be sure she never went without anything and everything she needed, of course, but Linnea never saw that. She only knew she rarely got to see me other than on a TV screen and for a few weeks in the summer, which wasn't nearly enough.

I'd thought about bringing her to the US with me. In fact, I'd talked it over with our parents multiple times, but we'd always concluded it was best to keep her in Sweden. While she was there, she had our parents, she had her friends, she knew the language, and she was receiving excellent social services. If I brought her to live with me, we would have to go through a mountain of paperwork and red tape to get her the same benefits, and then what would happen if I ended up working for a team in Canada instead of the States? It was a definite possibility, so we'd decided to keep Linnea in Sweden as long as our parents were able to continue giving her the aid she needed. After that, I'd have some tough decisions to make.

That was yet another reason for me to avoid getting involved with someone. In fact, I'd sworn off starting up new relationships with women years ago. I'd dated a few women back in my playing days, but it had never lasted long. They didn't understand why I chose to live modestly, driving a Toyota instead of a Mercedes and living in a reasonable house instead of buying a multimillion-dollar house. They were gold diggers, plain and simple. They wanted me to spend lavishly on them, and when I refused—stating I had other, more important uses for my money—things came crashing to a halt. After a few repetitions of this same pattern, I'd decided it wasn't worth my while to keep putting myself through it, and it definitely wasn't worth potentially losing anything I intended to set aside for Linnea's future.

Something told me Paige would more than understand where I was coming from, which only encouraged me to keep up the flirtation we'd already started. This might not be my brightest move ever, but I couldn't seem to stop myself.

The blaring music from the opening of the event finally came to an end, and they brought up the lights again. The team was split in half, one group wearing the home colors and the other group wearing road whites. As captain, Babs had made the executive decision as to who would be coaching each of the two teams today. He'd brought in kids from some of the local peewee teams to take over that job, giving me and the rest of the coaches the day off, essentially. Tim Whitlock, the Storm's in-arena entertainment director, came over the PA system to announce the first event would be the fastest skater competition.

"Fastest skater," Paige murmured. "Any chance this would have been your event?"

"Not in this lifetime. Skating was never my strength." I'd been lucky to make it into the NHL at all, actually, but I'd found ways to make my shortcomings work for me. "I would have been in the hardest shot competition."

She passed appraising eyes over me, letting them hold longer than necessary on my biceps. "I suppose I can see that."

"This should be interesting, though. The whole team right now is built on speed and skill, other than a couple of the older veteran players. There are a few guys who are faster than others, of course, but I think the winner could surprise some people."

"My money's on Jens," 501 said, looking over his shoulder at us.

"Jens?" Jo-Jo said incredulously. "Not a chance. It's Koz all the way."

Devo let out a cross between a snort and a chuckle. "Coop young and fast. Too big energy. He leave them in dust." His English was broken and heavy with his Eastern European accent, but there he got his point across well enough.

The three they named were certainly among the top contenders, but I had someone else in mind who could potentially run away with it. I thought Nate "Ghost" Golston had an opportunity to make a big impression today.

Paige's daughters tittered and giggled, each of them naming a player she thought was the fastest. They still hadn't settled down by the time the competition began.

After the two goalies raced each other in full pads—which was a complete debacle but got the fans involved when Nicky just barely beat Bobby by a skate blade—they ran five heats of regular skaters. In the end, it was Ghost for the white team and Koz for the purple team who turned in the fastest times. They were all set to race each other to determine the winner when Paige leaned over.

"You don't seem at all surprised," she said quietly in my ear. Her breath tickled my neck, turning my thoughts entirely away from the action down below.

"Ghost was my pick from the beginning," I said.

"Ghost was? Really?" 501 gave me a look of pure skepticism.

"Yeah, Ghost. Maybe you should think about why that is." Ghost was easily the smallest guy on the team, so a lot of times he got overlooked by guys like 501 and other defensemen like him. They thought that because they had longer legs and weighed more, they would have the upper hand. I knew from experience, though, that the smallest guys out there were also the best at evading the big guys like me, and it had a lot to do with speed. When Ghost wanted to turn on his jets, he could really fly across the ice. I hoped he would choose to do so today, actually. I wanted to use it to convince him he could give more than he'd been giving in games in order to be a more effective player.

I'd never been the kind of teacher who would spell everything out for someone, though. I liked letting my players learn things on their own, only giving them a nudge in the right direction when necessary. That was what I hoped to do with 501. He let out a grunting sort of sound and turned his attention back to the ice, while the crew changed the setup for the next event.

"I bet you would win," Sophie said adoringly to him.

"Not likely," Jo-Jo said. "501 would trip and slam headfirst into the goal post again or something." Which was exactly how my young defenseman had ended up with concussion symptoms. It was worse than that, even. Somehow, he'd gotten himself called for a tripping penalty in the process of chasing the opposing player back to the goal, and he'd almost knocked the puck into our net at the same time.

The boys had been giving him shit over it ever since.

The coaches and I had been, too, to be honest, but in a different way. We'd been using this time while he was forced to sit out to remind him to slow down and that he had more time to make his moves than he seemed to think. Sometimes, it was better to take a step back, especially for a young guy like him. Being up here right now might not be fun for him, but it was far better for his future in the league.

Sophie didn't pay Jo-Jo any attention. Her eyes were only for 501. "You would win," she repeated.

One of her sisters, who had previously been just as smitten with 501 as Sophie, was now making gaga eyes at Jo-Jo, though.

I said a silent prayer that all my players would remember that these were teenaged girls and, therefore, well out of bounds. Then I chuckled and got up to get a drink, nodding at my assistant coaches, David Weber and Adam Hancock, as I passed them. I'd barely gotten to the back of the room, where we had a buffet table full of drinks, sandwich fixings, and the like, when Paige caught me, stopping so close she almost brushed up against me.

She smelled like sunshine—warmth and fresh air combining into a state of perfection. I'd noticed it earlier, but it nearly knocked me on my ass now. "Can I get you something?" I asked. I should have asked her before I got up to begin with. I just hadn't been thinking.

She shook her head. "I just wanted... I wanted to thank you. It's really rare that anyone thinks to do anything for Sophie, let alone for the rest of my girls. I wanted you to know how much I appreciate it."

"I only did what anyone would do," I said, but even as the words left my mouth, I knew them to be untrue. She was right. Most people wouldn't have done what I had, whether they had the opportunity to do it or not. They would look right past this young girl, assuming that they'd offend by offering help where it wasn't wanted or simply not having a clue what help they should offer. Too many times, I'd seen people completely look past Linnea, ignoring her or pretending they didn't see her. And it always made me mad. It made me feel inadequate, because no matter how big or strong I was and no matter how much money I made, I couldn't protect her from the cruelty she'd faced every day of her life, whether she recognized it as what it was or not. It made me hurt for my sister, who was so sweet and always thought the best of everyone she came into contact with, whether they deserved her sweetness or not.

People apologized when I confronted them about it. They were always quick to make excuses. They just didn't realize they were making assumptions about her, whether they recognized it or not. They assumed Linnea was less than they were. They assumed she wouldn't fit in or couldn't do what they were going to do. They made plenty of assumptions.

Because of that, the only thing I would ever assume about Sophie was that she would most likely surprise me at every turn.

"I suppose that's not exactly true, is it?" I said, once again letting a slight grin creep to my lips. I couldn't seem to help that when it came to Sophie, the same as when I was with Linnea. The surprising thing was that Paige was starting to have a similar effect on me.

"No." The look in Paige's eyes was one I couldn't quite place. Curiosity, maybe? "No, it's not the case. Far from it. So thank you. It means more to me than you could ever know."

"I think I do know," I said. "If someone had done something like this for my sister, I would have done anything I could to be sure they understood what it meant to me. But regardless of what anyone else would do, I felt it was only right."

She didn't say anything, picking up a small dessert plate and putting a few grapes and bits of pineapple on it. My eye once again fell to her hand. Still no wedding ring, not that I'd expected one to appear out of thin air.

"So if there's anything else I can do for Sophie, anything you and your husband can think of..." I intentionally left the suggestion hanging in the air, waiting to see if she'd answer the question that was eating me alive.

"My ex-husband, you mean." Not only did she answer me but her eyes fluttered up to meet mine. She was flirting with me as much as I was flirting with her.

I had to hold myself back from doing a victory dance. That wouldn't be appreciated right now. "Your ex," I repeated after her. "Just let me know."

"Why are you doing this?" Paige asked, popping a grape in her mouth. "Are you really just a good guy, and this is exactly what you say—that you were drawn to Sophie because she reminds you of your sister, and that's it? Nothing more?"

"There might be something more." Fuck, it had been a long time since I'd tried to banter with a woman I was interested in. I was seriously out of practice. With everything else I did in life, I had all the confidence in the world. I knew what I was doing every step of the way before beginning step one, and I never stumbled or fumbled my way through it. But with this? I felt like a gangly fourteen-year-old boy again, with feet that had grown faster than the rest of me that had me tripping over them with every step I took. "There is something more," I corrected myself.

"Which is?" She picked up a napkin and folded it, slipping it beneath her plate.

"The truth is, I'm drawn to you every bit as much as I'm drawn to your daughter," I forced out. "I want to get to know you, Paige."

A smile crept to her lips despite her obvious effort to keep it at bay. "I'm not sure how I feel about that."

And that was as good as a punch in the gut—further proof that she already had her hands full without adding a man like me to it. I had no business chasing after this single mother, and I knew it, but damn if I didn't want to convince her it was a good idea.

Then, picking up a glass of water, she turned to go back to her seat.

I put a hand on her shoulder, stopping her, before I could think through what I was doing. In fact, I didn't want to think it through. I'd acted without planning every tiny detail when I'd invited her and her daughters to join us for the day, and so far it had turned out better than I could have imagined even if I was faltering at every turn. Maybe I needed to be spontaneous more often. Maybe it would be good for me.

Maybe Paige would be good for me. And maybe I could be good for her.

She glanced up at me, her brow arched. "Yes?"

"Do you and your girls have plans tomorrow?" I asked. Her lips formed a perfect O, but she didn't immediately turn me down, so I pushed through. "It's still the weekend. We've got an afternoon game. I'd like you to come as my guests. If you want. And if you don't have other plans. We could maybe have dinner after."

"I…" She looked as lost as she sounded, as if she was as out of practice was I was.

But then one of her girls—probably the oldest one—came over to the buffet table and started fixing herself a plate. She glanced up at me. "Did you just ask my mom out on a date?"

"I did." I kept my eyes on Paige while I answered her daughter.

"What she means to say is *yes*. And by the way, she likes tulips. Yellow ones."

"*Zoe*," Paige said in a very mom-like voice.

"What? You do like tulips." Zoe gave me a cheeky grin. "Can we hang out with 501 during the game?"

Chapter Three

Paige

WITH MATTIAS'S HELP, I managed to extricate Levi from Sophie's exuberant grip and guide all of my girls toward the parking garage after the StormSkillz event came to a close. Mattias came with us, actually, walking along beside me while my daughters raced ahead in a torrent of squeals pitched so high that only a dog should be able to hear them.

"You think they had a good time?" he asked me, the deep rumble of his voice a pleasing contrast to their excited chatter.

I chuckled. "I doubt they'll stop talking about it for a month." Even as I said it, Sophie turned her head to look at us over her shoulder, her smile as sweet as I'd ever seen it. Her eyes were all crinkled up, and her cheeks were flushed with exhilaration. She looked like she might never be able to stop smiling.

"That's good."

"Good, yes, but they might drive me insane with it before the month is out." In a good way, though. Sometimes I complained about how excitable they could be when it came to boys and their crushes, but really I wouldn't change it for anything.

"I guess I'll have to make that up to you," he said, and my butterflies returned.

They kept coming back, each instance stronger than the last, when he did even the smallest thing. Sometimes it was when he would smile at me with that panty-melting look in his eye. Once, they'd fluttered to life when he'd entertained Sophie while Levi escaped for a few minutes, answering every question she put to him as though it was the most important question he'd ever heard. Another time, the flutters caught me unawares when he took the time to explain what icing was to Izzy.

How pathetic was it that this man could turn me on simply by taking an interest in my daughters? But it was the truth. He'd paid as much attention to each of the four of them as he had to me over the course of the afternoon, and he'd even taken a few moments to talk to his players and give them instruction for their own play based on some of the games and drills taking place on the ice below us. If I wasn't careful, I might find myself falling for this man, and that wasn't something that fit well in my plans.

"They're growing up too fast for me," I admitted. "When they were little, there were times I couldn't wait for them to grow up. Three was always a rough year. Whoever decided the twos were terrible must never have met a three-year-old. I didn't think I would escape their threes with all of us being alive and intact."

Mattias chuckled. "But here you are."

"But here we are, and they're teenagers. I think I blinked one day and they were practically adults. Now I regret all those moments I wished they would hurry past those difficult stages, and I'm praying they'll slow down."

"Sadly, I don't think it works that way."

"No, it doesn't." I glanced up at him and caught him staring at me in the way he had that made my heart race, and I quickly looked ahead again. "What about you?" I asked to deflect my own attention away from the overwhelming *awareness* he brought out in me. "Do you have kids growing up too fast? Or maybe already grown?"

"No kids. Just my sister." His arm brushed against mine, and I broke out in gooseflesh. He didn't react to the contact. "Linnea has a boyfriend, my mother tells me. He's got DS, too. He works in the mail room with her and asked her out for ice cream after work one day. Now they're talking about how they want to live together."

"Oh, wow. Have you met him?"

"Many times. They've worked together for years. They've been friends for a long time."

"And do you like him?"

"As a man? Sure. As a man my sister is living with?" He laughed and shook his head. "It's hard to wrap my head around it, is all."

Since the thought of Sophie dating someone gave me hives, I could understand that. "Has she dated before?"

"There was one," he said cautiously, making me wonder what had happened with that first boyfriend. "It's been a while, though. And I want her to be happy and have love in her life, but I can't help but worry. I mean, it was only a few years ago that she moved out of my parents' house to live in a group home."

"But she's done that," I said. "And she's fine. Right? She has a job. He does, too. You don't think he's trying to take advantage of her, do you?"

"No, it's nothing like that," he rushed to say. "I just never thought she would live on her own, let alone with a man. She keeps surprising me. In good ways."

The girls were already halfway down the escalator. Mattias put his hand on the small of my back as I stepped onto it in a slightly protective yet somewhat possessive move, and I had to fight the urge not to inch closer to him.

I swallowed hard. "Sophie surprises me every day," I forced past my thick tongue. "In good ways, too. She's exactly like her sisters in some ways."

"Like with having a crush on 501," he said, chuckling. He was on the step directly behind me, his body heat warming my backside.

"Yes, like that." I spun so I could see him, but looking up at his face, with him being a step above me, left me dizzy.

He tightened his grip on my waist, steadying me, but that didn't stop me from reaching out to grab on to him, as well, my hands resting on his torso. My fingers could feel every single muscle underneath them. Six-pack? He probably had eight. He was solid and unmovable, and my knees were weak.

"You all right?" he asked.

I was fine except for the fact that I might have a crush on Mattias Bergstrom even bigger than all the girls' crushes on Levi Babcock combined. The way he was holding me upright, acting as if I were as light as a feather and it was simply what anyone would do, robbed me of all thought. Including my purpose in turning around to look at him to begin with. All I could do was hold on and hope he didn't care that I was suddenly sixteen again.

"Fine," I finally managed to breathe.

"Fine enough to walk? Because we're almost to the bottom." He laughed, but not in a way that made me feel as though he were laughing *at* me.

I turned around and managed to step off the escalator without tripping over my own feet, but that wasn't saying a whole lot. Mattias kept an arm around my waist, and I was happy for him to leave it there.

We didn't say anything the rest of the way to the parking garage. The girls were huddled together by my SUV when we got there, still giggling and chattering so much I doubted they'd settle down before midnight at the very earliest. There wasn't a chance they'd let me get much sleep tonight. Add to that my nerves about this supposed date with Mattias tomorrow…

Sophie spun around and headed our way, arms outstretched. I thought she was coming to hug me, so I opened up to accept it. I wasn't her target, though. She walked straight into Mattias's arms and gave him a bear hug. He gave back as good as he got, even lifting her off her feet and swinging her around while she giggled. His smile was as wide as hers.

And that was it. I was a goner. There wasn't any chance I would be able to stop myself from falling for this man. I didn't know him very well yet, but in these few hours, he'd shown me everything I needed to know.

My eyes stung, and I put a hand up to cover my mouth, as if that would be enough to stop me from crying. Not that there was any realistic chance of that happening.

"Thank you, Bergy," she said when he set her back on the ground.

He winked and took a knee, dropping down to be on her level. "You're welcome, Sophie."

Zoe dug a tissue out of her purse and brought it over to me. I wiped my eyes with it but gave up after a few tears. They weren't going to stop any time soon if Mattias kept being this sweet with my baby.

"Can I meet your sister someday?"

"Maybe," he said. "We'll have to see if we can work that out."

"How come she can't just come over to my house?"

"Well, she lives a long way away."

I heard a sniffle and glanced over to my other girls. They were all three crying, just like I was. I made a mental snapshot of this moment, not wanting to let it slip away too soon.

"How far?" Sophie asked, turning the palms of her hands up and shrugging. "She could come over tomorrow. Mom won't mind."

"Halfway around the world."

Her eyes went wide. "That's a *long* way, Bergy. Maybe she can come on Friday."

He laughed and said, "Maybe. I'll have to see what I can work out."

"I need you to help me," she said, her tone as serious as it ever was. I didn't know what she was about to ask him for, but I started mentally preparing myself to dig him out of whatever hole she tried to drag him into. I knew this tone of voice, and she wasn't going to give up on whatever it might be very easily. In fact, I was afraid it had something to do with a certain young man named Levi.

"If it's something that's okay with your mother and something I can help you with, I promise you I will." And he sounded as sincere as she was determined.

"I want to play hockey like Levi. I want to skate fast."

Instantly, my mind started turning over every reason I'd ever been told she'd never be able to do X, Y, or Z. From the moment my OB-GYN had told us that my unborn baby had Down syndrome, they'd been trying to pound into my brain all the things she couldn't do. Things she would *never* be able to do, no matter how much she wanted to and no matter how hard she tried.

I'd never fallen into the trap of letting those impossibilities become reality. I'd always encouraged Sophie to follow her heart, to try to do anything she wanted to do. Dan and I both had spent eleven years telling her she could do whatever she wanted if she just tried hard enough, and we'd held her hand through it all. We'd taught her sisters to treat her exactly the same way we did because letting her believe she *couldn't* do something would simply prove it true.

Sophie had participated in the school choir even though they'd told her she couldn't sing. She'd run in track meets even though they'd told her she was too slow. She'd learned to read—albeit at a level far lower than her actual age—even though they'd told her she would never do more than learn the alphabet, if that. She'd proven them wrong so many times, and I knew she would many more. But this time, as her mother, I was afraid.

I was afraid they were right. And I was afraid that she would try, and fail, and try, and fail, and try, and fail…and maybe, eventually, she would just stop trying altogether. And it broke my heart.

Skating, the act of keeping herself upright on those tiny blades… I didn't see how it could be possible.

The older girls' sniffles got louder, and I knew they were thinking along the same lines I was. None of us wanted to see Sophie hurt, but we also didn't want to fall into the trap of telling her she *couldn't*, because we'd always told her she *could*.

Mattias didn't pay our crying any mind. He focused in on Sophie, his expression serious. And he nodded, which made something in my belly flip even as I wanted to stop him from saying whatever was about to come out of his mouth. "You want to skate? To play hockey? That's what you really want?"

"Yes. Just like Levi."

"All right," he said, and my heart sank down lower than my toes, because no matter how much I tried to convince myself that Sophie could do anything she set her mind on, I knew it wasn't really true. And skating? Playing hockey? That would be as close to impossible a task as she could set for herself. But Mattias didn't let it deter him, and I didn't stop him in time to prevent him from making her a promise that he would never be able to keep. "I'll make you a deal."

"What deal?"

"You convince your mom to let me kiss her after our date tomorrow, and I'll find a way to make it happen. I'll help you learn to skate and play hockey. It might take longer than tomorrow, though."

"Deal!" Sophie said.

Done. That was that, even though I knew she was in for a huge disappointment when he couldn't find a way to make it possible for her. The balance necessary to stay upright on skate blades, the coordination required to stay on skates while attempting to hit a puck with a stick were outside the realm of her skill set, no matter how much she wanted it and no matter how hard she tried. Whether I was ready for it or not, my sweet little girl was going to try to skate.

And apparently, I was getting a kiss tomorrow.

Mattias

I'D GIVEN THAT little girl a promise I wasn't at all positive I could deliver on, but I'd be damned if I didn't exhaust every resource I had before admitting defeat. And not just because I wanted to kiss her mother, either. I was reasonably certain I'd be able to get the kiss from Paige whether I helped Sophie learn to skate or not.

Playing hockey was something that Linnea had wanted, too, and I'd never been able to give it to her. I had always felt like a failure on that score, like I'd let my sister down. But if I could make it happen for Sophie, taking into account all the technological advances that had taken place in the last few decades and with the hockey minds involved with the Storm organization at my disposal, then maybe I could make it up to Linnea in some way.

Yes, it was an illogical thought, but I didn't care. I was determined to find a way for Sophie Calhoun to learn how to skate and play hockey. And when I made up my mind to do something, there was nothing that would stop me from reaching my goal. I might have some stops and starts. There would likely be failures along the way. But I would only truly fail when I gave up and admitted defeat.

The next morning, well before any of my players were due to arrive, I was already holed up in my office with my laptop open, Googling everything under the moon remotely related to assistive devices for skating to get my ideas flowing. I needed something that would help her stay upright but which would leave her arms free so she could hold a stick, and so far I was coming up empty. I kept coming to devices similar to a walker only with skis on the bottom, but she would have to hold on to something like that with both hands.

David Weber, one of my assistant coaches, poked his head through the door after I'd been working for well over an hour. "Wasn't expecting you here so early," he said. He came in carrying two cups of coffee and set one of them in front of me. "This have anything to do with your hot mom from yesterday?"

I shot him a go-to-hell look. "Her daughter, actually. Sophie wants to skate and play hockey."

"Sophie is the one with Down syndrome?"

I nodded, scrolling through page after page of search results, paying more attention to my computer than I was to him.

Webs gave a grunt of some sort, sounding as sober as I'd ever heard him. That moment of seriousness didn't last long; in no time, he snorted out a laugh. "You could find a way to strap her to 501's legs so he would be doing all the work. Wouldn't hurt him any. Probably be good for him."

"Not going to happen." I wouldn't put 501 through that, and I didn't think Paige would go for it, anyway. "Besides, Doc hasn't cleared 501 for anything physical yet."

"You planning on having him do it today?" Webs demanded. "It'll take us at least a week or more to set up the rig."

"Not today, no. Doesn't matter. That's not the solution I'm looking for."

Adam "Handy" Hancock came through the door, tossing his gym

bag on the floor along the wall. He raised a brow. "What kind of solution do you think you'll find that's better than that?"

I supposed he'd heard quite a bit of our conversation. Either that or it wasn't too difficult to interpret.

"I'm going to find a way for her to do it on her own," I said. I needed to find something that would let Sophie do all the work but give her support while she built up her core strength. If she was serious about it and really worked hard, she could probably eventually skate on her own, but I wanted to know she'd be safe while she worked on getting there.

And while she was working on that, I could work on finding a hockey program she could participate in, one for kids with special needs and developmental difficulties. I knew they existed. I just wasn't sure if there were any of them around Portland. If there were, I would find them and do whatever it took to get her involved.

Webs plopped down in a chair across from me and dug out his iPad, propping it up across from me. "Sounds like you've got it bad."

I glanced up from my screen again. He was giving me a knowing look, the sort that said he knew exactly what was behind my actions, and he assumed it had everything to do with Paige and not her daughter. "I'm not denying that I'm very interested in Paige Calhoun—"

"Good," Handy said, doing the same thing Webs had just done. "Because we'd see straight through it."

"But," I added with a hell of a lot of emphasis, "that's not why I'm doing this." Not that they needed to know about Linnea. I'd played in the NHL for twenty years and had been coaching ever since, and not once had I said a word about my sister to any of my teammates or coworkers. I wasn't ashamed of her. Far from it. In all honesty, it had a hell of a lot more to do with not wanting anyone to see what I was like with her.

Around the league, I had always been known as a hard-assed son of a bitch. In my playing days, I'd been a big, skilled defenseman with a mean streak. These days, I was a sullen coach with a crusty exterior, more likely to grumble and grouse than to crack a smile. My sister, on the other hand, was all sweetness and light. Simply thinking about her or talking about her was all it took to put a grin on my face and melt away the façade. No one but Linnea needed to see that side of me, or so I had thought until little Sophie had leaped into 501's arms yesterday. That was all it had taken to chip away at my crunchy exterior in front of people I'd never let see that part of my makeup.

And now, here I was. At the moment, I didn't care how many of them had seen my smiles. I didn't give a damn who had noticed the cracks in my armor. All I wanted to do was make one of Sophie's dreams come true.

My two assistant coaches nodded and grunted their assent, but it was clear from the look that passed between them that they weren't buying my denial. Which was probably for the best. Let them think it was all about Paige if that was what they wanted. Maybe that way no one would realize the truth, and I could go on being the hard-ass they'd all come to expect.

We all fell quiet then. They were probably watching film from the Flames' last game, since we were scheduled to play them this afternoon, or otherwise preparing to do their jobs. Unlike me. I never shirked my responsibilities, but I supposed everyone got a free pass for that every now and then. I'd be ready for the game whether I watched more film or not.

After a few minutes, Webs shot his head up. "What if we could fashion something ourselves?"

"Like a walker on skis that we could strap her into so she wouldn't have to hold on to it," Handy said. He was squinting at his screen, reading something. Not watching film.

Neither of them were watching footage. They were both doing the same damn thing I was, and now Jim Sutter and Drywall Tierney—our GM and the head equipment manager—were coming into my office as well.

Webs nodded, eyes narrowed in thought. "If we set it up to be behind her, she'd have full use of her arms and legs. We could make some sort of harness like you'd use for zip-lining or parachuting."

"Would a walker be sturdy enough if her legs couldn't support her on skates?" Jim asked, crossing his arms and legs and leaning back against the wall.

"It would if I built it," Drywall said.

Before I knew what was happening, half the team executives were gathered in my office, and we were brainstorming ways to help Sophie Calhoun skate.

I still didn't know how we were going to make it happen, but that didn't matter.

Because we were going to make it happen.

Chapter Four

Mattias

NOT WANTING TO keep Paige and her girls waiting any longer than necessary, I headed up to the owner's box at the Moda Center as soon as I'd released the team after the game. We'd won, but it hadn't been easy. The Flames were a young, exciting, well-coached team. There'd been a lot of back-and-forth action and way too many turnovers on both ends of the ice, but my boys had pulled through in the end.

I'd decided to give them a light, optional practice tomorrow. We were already through the first half of the season or so, and things were running along well. There wasn't any need to reinforce systems or anything like that, and we had several guys who had been playing through injuries for a while—Cam "Jonny" Johnson and Grant Wheelan, in particular. A couple more had come off the ice with minor issues in the course of the game, too. It would be better for all of them to get some rest, take maintenance days, so they'd be ready for the grueling push toward the playoffs.

But now, I was gathering up Paige and her daughters for our *date*, if you could call it that. I wasn't positive that I would, but I hadn't been on a real date in years. Did it count if you had four giggling teenaged girls with you? Probably not, but I wasn't going to argue with it.

Sophie was the first to see me when I came through the door. She lit up like a Christmas tree, her smile as wide as I'd ever seen it when 501 wasn't in the room. "Bergy, we *won!*"

"We sure did," I said, holding up my hand for the high five she ran over to give me.

She and her sisters had been sitting with some of the older kids among the players' families. It didn't surprise me at all to find Maddie Campbell, Rachel's oldest daughter, right in the center of them. Rachel was Jim's assistant and the wife of one of my players, Brenden "Soupy" Campbell, who had been out with an injury nearly all season long. Maddie tended to be quiet but perceptive and incredibly thoughtful. She gravitated toward the damaged and the broken, or anyone who needed an extra dose of compassion. Not that Sophie was broken, but it warmed my heart to know that Soupy's shy, sweet girl would have taken Sophie under her wing with all the strangers around.

Paige gathered up the other three and brought them our way in time to hear Sophie ask, "Can Levi come on our date, too?"

"I think Levi has other things he needs to do," Paige answered before I had the chance.

Izzy deflated like a balloon, and Evie's disappointment was tangible. Zoe looked so relieved I almost laughed.

"You don't want him to come?" I asked the oldest girl.

"Nope." Zoe shook her head vigorously. "I turn stupid the second I get near him. I don't think I said more than three words all day yesterday."

"Oh, you said *plenty* once we got home," Paige said, laughing.

"Well, I had to make up for all the time I couldn't speak at all!"

"I don't think you need to have any fear you'll forget how your tongue works," Evie said, giggling. Then she took off out the door, and the rest of us followed behind her, all three of the older girls taking jabs at each other and laughing at such a high pitch that I thought I might lose my hearing if I spent too much time around them. Sophie rushed to keep up with them, once more leaving Paige and me trailing in their wake.

"You've given them quite a weekend," she said after a reasonable distance fell between us and the girls. "I don't think they'll stop talking about it for quite some time."

"I'm glad." More than glad. I might not know these girls very well, let alone their mother, but there was something about being with them that felt *right*, in a way that few things in my life ever had.

"Are you sure you know what you're getting into with this?" Paige waved a hand in front of us, indicating the girls who seemed to be skipping across the air rather than walking. "You can still back out of taking us all to dinner, you know. I'll find a good excuse."

I glanced over at her, taking in the long stretch of her neck. She had her hair all piled on top of her head today, in a sort of bun that looked at once haphazard and elegant.

"Are you trying to get out of that kiss? Because I'm doing everything in my power to follow through with my end of the bargain."

"No!" She looked down at my chest instead of meeting my eyes, though, and I got the distinct sense she was fighting a blush. "No, a deal is a deal."

There was no denying the boost my ego got over the fact that she wasn't telling me to go to hell. But still... "I made that deal with Sophie, not with you. And her part of it was simply to *try* to get you to agree."

"Mattias, she's never going to be—"

"Don't tell me that she won't ever be able to skate. Not you. Not her mother." Even as the words left my mouth, I had to wonder if I meant them more for Paige in dealing with Sophie or if I was thinking of my own mother and Linnea. Either way, I meant it.

"But the kind of balance that would require? The strength to keep herself up on those blades?" The same worried look Paige had taken on last night when I'd first talked with Sophie came back into her eyes now. "I just don't want to see her fail so many times that she stops trying. I don't want to see her give up."

"What if she doesn't give up? What if she doesn't stop trying?" I argued.

"But—"

"I can't promise that she'll ever be able to do it on her own, but what's the harm in trying? Technology has advanced so much in recent years. I think I can find a way to at least get her out on the ice, and then we can see what happens. If we can devise something to help her balance at first, there's no telling what she'll be able to do down the line."

"You're talking like you're still going to be involved when it gets to that," Paige said, frustration punctuating her words.

"And you're talking like I won't be."

She stopped cold, and I had to stop, too, or I'd completely pass her by.

"Look, Mattias," she said, using the same tone my mother had always used when she was trying to protect Linnea as best she could. "I know you mean well. I do. And I appreciate it more than I could ever say."

"But?" There was no point trying to hide from it, since we both knew the *but* was coming.

"*But* you and me? We're adults. We can handle disappointment. We understand that you're a good man trying to do something nice for my little girl, but you're probably getting yourself in deeper than you initially intended. You probably didn't realize all of the implications of what you were suggesting. Maybe you do now. I hope so, at least. But Sophie doesn't always understand when people back away. She gets attached, and then they leave before they're able to keep their promises, and then she gets hurt. And my girls and I are the ones left to pick up the pieces. We're the ones who have to listen to her ask, over and over again, where Dad is and why he isn't with us, or why her friends stopped coming to play, or why she isn't able to move on to the next grade in school when all her friends are."

"So what are you saying?" I asked cautiously. Although I probably didn't really need to ask. I could tell where she was going with this. She was trying to kick me out before I got too close, before my leaving could hurt too much.

Maybe she was right to do that. Not because I wouldn't follow through with helping Sophie learn to play hockey but because there wasn't a ton of job security as a coach in the NHL, and I had responsibilities to take care of in Sweden. I had to go wherever the work took me, and that might mean stepping out of Sophie's life at some point down the line.

Paige put her arms over her chest in a self-protective gesture. No matter how big a game she talked, I could see through it. She wasn't just trying to protect Sophie in all this.

"I'm saying," she said after a protracted silence, "maybe it's for the best if you step away after tonight. She hasn't latched on to you too much yet. You're still just in the *maybe we can find a way to make this work* phase. You haven't yet made her any official promises that you'll have to break eventually."

"Why would I have to break them?" I asked, even though I knew all the answers she would likely come up with, and then some that wouldn't even cross Paige's mind. But she didn't know me very well yet. She didn't know that I was the most determined son of a bitch she'd ever met. She didn't know that once I set a goal for myself, there would be no stopping me. Now I needed to make her understand, or at the very least give her a hint.

She was looking at me like trees were sprouting from my ears.

I raised a brow. "Like you said, a deal is a deal. I told Sophie I would do whatever I could to help her out. I meant it."

The corners of Paige's lips quirked up, despite her efforts to fight off the smile. "I'd let you kiss me even if you didn't hold up your end of it," she said. Then she bit her lower lip, and I couldn't look anywhere else.

"And why would you do that?"

She shrugged. "Because it's been too long."

It'd been too long for both of us, then.

"Mom!" Zoe shouted from well ahead of us, and Paige whipped her head in that direction. "You can kiss him later. We're hungry." We were too far away to see it, but an eye roll was overly evident in Zoe's tone.

Paige pressed her eyes closed for a moment before glancing up to meet my eyes. She pinched her lips together in a thin line, and a gorgeous blush stole over her cheeks. "Sorry. We should— We should go." Then she took off heading toward her daughters with a determined stride.

I turned to keep up with her. Reaching out to put a hand on the small of her back, I tried not to laugh. At least not too much. "It's fine. Don't want to keep them waiting."

Once we caught up with the girls, Sophie reached for my free hand. I let her take it, my other hand settling into the curve over her mother's hip while the older girls rolled their eyes and hurried ahead of us...giggling and snickering as they went. They kept peeking over their shoulders at us, though, nearly tripping over their own feet because they weren't paying attention to where they were going.

And it felt good. I only hoped Paige liked it as much as I did. Because, now that I realized how much I enjoyed spending time with her and her girls, I didn't simply intend to follow through with my promise to Sophie; I was starting to think of ways I could make other promises, as well.

Paige

MATTIAS HAD TO be bored out of his mind. He'd brought us to the Old Spaghetti Factory for dinner. Since it was a Sunday evening and we were a party of six, we'd had to wait almost an hour before they had a table big enough to seat all of us together. The whole time we'd been waiting, my girls hadn't been able to stop chattering.

For that matter, they *never* stopped chattering, not even in their sleep, it seemed. I was used to it, but Mattias was a single man with no children. He spent his days surrounded almost exclusively by grown men, and I sincerely doubted their talk ever came close to the inanity that came out of my daughters' mouths.

By the time the hostess had seated us, the girls had already gushed over who was cuter among Austin Cooper, Blake Kozlow, and Axel Johansson (no need to add Levi into the mix, since everyone already knew he was the cutest of the cute); debated the likelihood that the four girls could end up married to the four cute hockey players; informed Mattias that they'd added Cooper, Kozlow, and Johansson to the brother-husband list ("It's like sister-wives in reverse, and they're all hockey players," Izzy explained patiently upon seeing Mattias's confused expression); and hatched a plan for the four of them to split up, travel to the various NHL cities around North America, and snatch the wayward brother-husbands who didn't play in Portland. After hearing all that, *I* was exhausted. I could only imagine that *he* was rethinking his plan to take us all to dinner and trying to come up with a good excuse to get out of it.

But he came with us, and once Sophie claimed a seat on one of the booth's benches, he inched in beside her. The other three girls gave me giggling glances and piled into the bench opposite them, leaving me to take the final spot next to Mattias. He was so large that I had to be right up against him or else I'd be practically falling out of the booth. I did my best to calm my nerves as I slid in beside him. As if it were the most natural thing in the world he could possibly do, he put his arm around my waist, his hand resting on the curve between my waist and my hip, and drew me as close to his side as I could possibly be.

His body heat was intoxicating, but nothing could have come close to his scent in terms of making me want to get even closer. He smelled like heaven, and it was all I could do to keep myself from burying my nose against his chest and sniffing my fill. It was a good thing the girls were here and we were very much in public, because otherwise I might be hard-pressed not to do my best to crawl up on his lap. That would be taking things way too far, way too fast, particularly since tonight was going to be it.

Not that I'd gotten Mattias to agree to end things after this one *date*, but he had to see the reason behind it. His sister had Down syndrome. He understood, even if he didn't want to admit it.

"Balloon!" Sophie squealed, pointing toward a man making balloon animals a few tables away from us. Then she was bouncing on the bench, unable to contain her excitement. I hid a smile, hoping she would never lose her childlike enthusiasm.

"Do you want him to make you something?" Mattias asked, chuckling.

She was too excited to do anything more than nod, and I was impressed by her restraint in staying seated where she was. Under normal circumstances, I would expect her to crawl under the table, bumping her head and knocking into legs as she went. But with Mattias beside her, she stayed relatively in place and let him wave the balloon man over.

The man smiled at Mattias and me before zeroing in on Sophie. "How about a crown for the little princess?" He was already in the process of filling a pink balloon with air.

She bounced in her seat. "Can I have a dog? I want a dog."

Pink could lead to a meltdown. I'd never figured out why, but Sophie couldn't stand the color. She didn't want it anywhere near her, typically throwing a fit of epic proportions if someone gave her a pink anything. I started to tell the balloon man that maybe pink wasn't the best color, but Mattias stopped me with a big hand enveloping mine. I shot my gaze up to meet his.

He shook his head. "Let her tell him," he mouthed at me. He didn't even know what I was about to say to the man, but he must have sensed my intent.

I bit down on my tongue. Maybe he was right. I couldn't always do everything for her. Someday, I would have to let go. She was already eleven years old, not to mention fiercely independent. She wanted to do everything she could by herself. She wanted to be as grown-up as her older sisters. She was starting to discover her wings; I needed to let her fly, even if sometimes she might fall.

The balloon man winked at her. "A dog it is, then." In no time, he was twisting the pink thing into shape.

"Not pink. No pink." Sophie's tone bordered on temper tantrum, and my blood pressure started to rise.

Mattias squeezed my hand.

"Not pink?" the balloon man repeated. In a smooth move, he shoved his half-finished project into the bag slung over his shoulder and took out a plastic bag filled with balloons of every color imaginable. "Tell me what color you want, then."

"Purple," she said emphatically, surprising the heck out of me. Purple was often her second most dreaded color. But she grinned up at Mattias and plucked at her Storm jersey. "He needs to match," she explained.

"Good call," Mattias said. "That'll make him look like he belongs with us."

With us. The way he said it made it sound like there was an *us*, Mattias included.

"Can you get me a real puppy, Bergy?" she asked, all sunshine and innocence.

"I think you'll have to ask your mom about that," he replied, cleanly deflecting her question so he wouldn't end up as either the bad guy or the hero.

"Mom?" she asked, and her sisters chimed in with promises of how they'd be the ones to feed and water and walk and wash, all of which they'd tried leveraging against me time and again.

"We'll talk about it later," I said as the waiter came over to take our orders.

The balloon man finished her dog. He stuck around until the waiter was done, so he could make her a matching purple crown even though she hadn't asked for it. They both walked away around the same time, and Sophie was grinning from ear to ear with her crown on her head and her balloon dog tucked in beside her on the bench.

"What's his name?" Mattias asked, angling his head in the balloon dog's direction.

"Levi," Sophie said emphatically.

He let out a silent chuckle, one I could feel rather than hear, and I fell for him a little harder.

THE INSTANT HE parked in my driveway, all four of my girls barreled out of his SUV and rushed straight for the door.

"Kissy-kissy time," Evie said in a sing-song voice amid their chorus of giggles, and I let out a groan.

Zoe took her keys out of her pocket and let them in, and then Mattias and I were alone for the first time. She slammed the door closed behind them. Within seconds, I saw the curtains flutter. Which meant they were peeking out at us.

"They meant to say thank you," I said on a sigh. I turned to find him staring at me with those intense blue-gray eyes. They should have frozen me, like icicles boring into me, but there was so much heat in them I burned instead. I couldn't look in those eyes very long or I'd melt into his floorboard. I hurried to speak again before I forgot how. "So thank you. For everything. This whole weekend..."

My words trailed off, along with my ability to think, because he took my hand in his again, lacing our fingers together and sending jolts of electric awareness through my veins at breakneck speed.

"I should be the one thanking you," he said. "And your girls, too."

I shook my head, unable to process it. "What? Why?"

With the pad of his thumb, he traced lazy circles on the back of my hand, raising goose bumps all up and down my arms. I shivered, but not from cold.

"Because you showed me I could be the man my sister loves even when I'm not with her."

I still didn't follow. I hadn't known Mattias very long, but he'd repeatedly shown himself to be kind, thoughtful, and entirely too much man for me to ignore. But now it was time for me to give him that kiss and get out, before I fell too hard. Before Sophie fell too hard. Before we all got too attached. It was happening, faster than I'd been prepared for, and I was already dreading the damage control I'd have to do once he walked out of our lives. I'd let him in further than anyone since Dan and I had split up under the pressure of raising a daughter with special needs. Ever since then, I'd been cautious to keep enough of a barrier between us and the rest of the world that no one could cut us too deeply, but with Mattias I'd let down my guard.

He cleared his throat before my thoughts were coherent, and I forced myself to meet his gaze again.

"I've got to head out of town in a couple of days with the team. We have a short road trip. We'll be back on Friday, though, so I was wondering—"

"I meant what I said earlier," I cut in. I tried to tug my hand away, but he tightened his hold, keeping me firmly in his grasp—exactly where my body wanted to be, and maybe my heart, too. The only part of me not on board with that was my head, which was the part I needed to be listening to. "I really appreciate everything you've done for my girls, especially for Sophie, but I think we should just end this—

"

"I wondered if you had plans next weekend," he continued, as though I hadn't tried to give him a brush off. "You and the girls, I mean. Friday is Valentine's Day, so I thought—"

"The girls— It's their father's weekend with them, so it would just be me." And as soon as I said that, I realized I shouldn't have. I should have told him I had to work. Or I was going out of town. Or anything but what I'd said, really, because now he was looking at me with that panty-melting smile again, and I couldn't make myself look away. Hell, I didn't even want to. I wanted to keep staring into those eyes and feeling the jittery sensations he made me feel for as long as possible.

"So I could have you all to myself for the weekend?" Mattias said, and his smile turned into this wicked, sinful, delicious expression that made me want things I hadn't even thought about in years.

"I..."

He brushed the backs of his knuckles along my cheek, and my nipples pebbled in response. Then his lips were on mine, soft and smooth, gently coaxing me to open for him. I did, fisting my hand in his thick hair as his tongue met mine and drove me to a frenzied ache I'd thought dormant.

He hooked an arm around my waist and dragged me across the seat until I was practically in his lap. In fact, that seemed like a good idea, so I raised myself up on my knees and straddled him, steadying myself with a hand on his strong shoulder and the steering wheel pressing against the small of my back. My fingers itched to explore more of the muscles beneath them, but reason returned before I did anything stupid. My girls were watching every bit of this.

When I broke away, his breathing was as labored and ragged as mine, and he looked at me with an expression of wonder.

This had been a bad idea. A very bad idea. I should have kept it to a simple kiss, nothing more. For that matter, I should never have let it get this far. Yesterday, when we'd first encountered Mattias and Levi in the concourse, I should have wrangled my girls and gone to our regular seats. If I had, then I wouldn't be feeling so torn right now. I wouldn't be debating how I was going to come out of this with my heart intact, let alone how I would protect Sophie and my other daughters from getting too attached to this man who had his own responsibilities to worry about. I wouldn't be staring down into the eyes of a man who looked like he wanted to toss me over his shoulder and carry me back to his cave to do sweaty, dirty, amazing things to me. I wouldn't be thinking I wanted to let him.

"I should go in," I forced myself to say. I needed to get off him, but my body wouldn't cooperate, and Mattias didn't seem inclined to let me go, anyway. He had both hands on my waist, strong and steady. Big. The longer he left those hands on my body, the more I wanted to feel them.

"You probably should," he said, without even blinking.

"Yeah. I definitely should."

"All right." But he gripped my hips more tightly and drew me closer to him, until my chest was pressed up against his. He dipped his head, and I thought he was going to kiss me again. I tried to prepare myself for the sensual assault, only to have him rest his forehead against mine, both of us taking in labored breaths. "Can I pick you up when I get back into town on Friday?" His breath smelled like the spearmint mints he'd passed out to each of us as we'd left the restaurant.

I should have said no. But I didn't. I didn't even come close. "Yes," I said. Then I forced myself to climb off him, ease over to the other side of the SUV, and get out, grabbing my purse as my feet hit the concrete.

"Seems like a long time away." He winked, and my chest squeezed. "I'll give you an update on what we can do to help Sophie skate then."

I nodded, biting down on my lower lip. Then I turned and headed inside, doing my best to keep my feet moving forward. When I opened the door, I heard him back down the driveway at the same time as all four of my girls raced away from the window, giggling and leaving the curtains fluttering like my heart.

Chapter Five

Mattias

PAIGE ANSWERED THE door wearing a cream-colored dress that fit her body like a glove and made my mouth water. Her hair was swept off her neck in some sort of up-do that made it look simple but was probably really complicated and time-consuming. I didn't care about that. All I cared about was the fact that it gave me an excellent view of her long neck, and it made me want to kiss her in that spot just under her ear.

I hadn't seen her since I'd dropped her and the girls off at her house on Sunday evening, but I'd talked to her every day since. After I was done with whatever work I'd had to get done for the evening, or following the night's game when I was back in my hotel room, I'd sent her a text message to see if she was still up. Every night, she'd responded by calling me almost as soon as I'd hit send. It was as if she wanted to hear my voice as much as I needed to hear hers.

During those calls, she'd told me stories about the girls and their time at school, or bits and pieces about the clients who came to her house for massage. I'd told her about the places we stopped on the road, or the tribute the Rangers had put on for a soldier who surprised his overly pregnant wife by showing up at the arena instead of being on a video call like she'd expected. The shock had been so great that she'd gone into labor. They'd rushed the couple off to the hospital, and the baby was born before the second intermission.

Our calls had always been easy like that, a simple recounting of our days. It was as if we were old friends, like we'd known each other for years.

I'd never had that sort of relationship with any of the women I'd dated before. They'd always been so self-absorbed that all they cared about was what sorts of presents I'd bring home for them when I came back. With Paige, it was the complete opposite. I had to encourage her to tell me about herself, because she wanted to hear about me or tell me about her girls. It was as though she was lost in the mix, and I hated the thought of allowing that to continue. So I asked about her every chance I got, and she slowly started to tell me.

In all those calls, I'd never completely lost my mind and told her that I was falling for her. It seemed too soon for that, besides the fact that it wasn't the sort of thing that should be said over the phone. But everything about being with Paige felt right. It was one of those things like playing hockey, something that had come as naturally to me as breathing. I wanted to know everything there was to know about her daughters, her life, her day-to-day goings-on. I wanted to tell her everything there was to know about mine. I wanted to hear her voice and learn the sounds she made when she was surprised or overwhelmed. I wanted to ease some of her burdens. I didn't understand it, but I couldn't deny it.

And now, with her standing just inside her doorway in that dress, with her neck bare and a nervous smile lighting up her face, I couldn't seem to form a coherent thought. I held out the vase of flowers I'd brought her—yellow tulips, like Zoe had told me her mother liked—and stood there like an idiot.

With a hint of a blush, she reached for the bouquet. "Hi," she said, sounding as breathless and anxious as I felt. Because, whether the first date, when her girls came with us, could really be considered a date or not, tonight would be. I hadn't been on a date in so long I didn't know what to do with myself. It appeared I wasn't alone in that.

"Hi," I repeated.

She held up a finger, silently begging me for a moment. I nodded, and she waved me inside before setting the vase down on a cabinet just inside the door and disappearing up the stairs. I took the time while she was gone to explore. Her house wasn't simply a house; it was a home. The furniture looked cushy and comfortable. The walls were painted in warm colors and covered with family photographs and artwork surely brought home from school by the girls. The short, wide cabinet where she'd set the tulips was littered with ponytail holders, lipsticks, notes, device chargers and cords, and colored paper and markers. A row of backpacks, purses, and coats hung above it in a sort of organized chaos. It all reminded me of my parents' home, not perfectly neat and tidy but well lived-in and loved.

I was poring over a group of photos from a family vacation when Paige came back down the stairs with a piece of gray construction paper in her hands.

"From Sophie," she said, thrusting it into my hands. "She made me promise I'd give it to you when I saw you."

I glanced down and found her childlike handwriting in purple marker.

> *Dear Bergy,*
> *Thank you for teachen me hokey. Thank you for Levi.*
> *Thank you for diner. You are real nice. You mad me smile. You*
> *mad Mom smile. I hope you kiss Mom again. A lot. I like you.*
> *Zoe Evie and Izzy like you. Mom likes kisses.*
> *Love,*
> *Sophie*

She'd drawn a stick figure family of six, one much larger than the others. They all had long hair and skirts except for the big one. She'd drawn something small next to the littlest stick figure, which I assumed to be her balloon dog, Levi. Her handwriting was difficult to interpret, but I understood her meaning even if she had some problems with spelling and grammar.

"She's already attached," Paige said when I looked up. She had tears in her eyes, which I brushed away with my thumb. She shook her head and stepped away, not allowing me to comfort her. "I worried this would happen."

"Is that so horrible? I'm not going to hurt her, Paige." That was the last thing I would ever want to do.

"You won't mean to." She shrugged and gave me the most pathetic look imaginable. "Why couldn't you have been mean and horrible? All of this would have been so much easier if you were awful, you know."

I laughed. "Depending on who you ask, they'll tell you all about how mean and horrible I am. Burnzie might have a few choice words to say after the way I laid into him last night, for one, and I lost track of how many guys have called me the meanest son of a bitch they ever played against a while back."

She shook her head. "But that's… That's not you. It's not the real you."

I wasn't sure who the *real* me was. It probably depended on whom I was with. There was the version that Linnea saw…the one that came out when I was with Paige and her girls. And then there was the other version, the one that everyone else saw.

Arguing about it wasn't going to change anything, though. I held out a hand for her. "Come on. Let's go have some fun and worry about all of this later." Not that I expected her to ever stop worrying. It went with the territory when you had a daughter with Down syndrome. Still, she had the whole weekend free from her kids, and I intended to make good use of that time in getting to know *Paige*.

She picked up her purse and put her hand in mine. "Fine. No worrying, at least for now."

Little did she know, I intended the *for now* part to last the entire weekend.

Paige

MATTIAS TOOK ME to dinner at El Gaucho for our Valentine's Day date, an upscale steak restaurant downtown that I would never consider going to under normal circumstances. Granted, *normal circumstances* meant having all of my girls with me, since Dan only kept them one weekend a month, on average. He was supposed to have them every other weekend, but his job prevented that from happening. With tax season coming up, he might not be able to keep them at all after this weekend for at least the next couple of months, so I was determined to enjoy this one with Mattias, whether my girls were with us or not.

Fun, bright places were always better when they were along—Sophie, in particular—and El Gaucho was dimly lit, elegant, and exceedingly romantic.

It was easy to fall right back into the trap of falling for Mattias in that sort of setting. There were candles and more flowers on our table, and he kept leaning in closer to me, resting his chin on his hand and staring so deep into my eyes it felt as though he could see all the way down to my soul.

A Latin band was playing off in the distance, and our waiter flambéed parts of our meal directly beside our table. I oohed and aahed more than I expected I would, but how often could I experience something like this? Not very. As a single mom, I had more academic meets, soccer games, and laundry days on my calendar than dates. But I couldn't imagine anywhere I'd rather be or anyone I'd rather be with.

Once the waiter left us with our meal, Mattias leaned in again, thoroughly invested in me in a way that made me feel heady. "You've never told me how you got into massage. Did you always want to do it?"

I shook my head, sipping from the robust red wine he'd ordered for us. "Not always, no. I came to it in a roundabout way."

He raised a brow, a silent encouragement for me to continue.

"I was in college when I met Dan. We were both accounting students. We got married when he graduated, in the summer after my sophomore year. I was pregnant with Zoe before Christmas break in my senior year, and I never ended up finishing my degree. We decided it would be better for us both if I was a stay-at-home mom, at least while the girls were little. By then, he was getting ready for his CPA exam, and he was already making a decent living. But then Sophie came along, and she needed a lot of extra care—like daily massage. When she was a baby, her therapist taught me to massage her little body, to help with her blood flow and to increase her muscle tone and awareness. It was a sensory thing, too—a way for me and Sophie to connect. It was something I did for her three times a day, every day, for the first few years of her life. By the time she was three, Dan and I were both so stressed with all of her appointments and visits and therapy sessions that we just…fell apart. We didn't know each other anymore. There was no time for us to be a couple. The stress of it all drove this huge chasm between us, and we were never able to recover from it. But when we divorced, I knew I needed a job of some sort. Preferably something where I could set my own hours and work either at home or close to home, and massage seemed like a good fit. I started my training as soon as Dan moved out of the house, and the rest is history."

Mattias hadn't looked away the whole time I spoke. He had been eating some, but honestly he'd paid far more attention to me than he had to his meal. It was a very rare thing for me to have someone's undivided attention. I was far more used to having my own attention split multiple ways, trying to make sure each of my daughters had everything they needed and none of them felt neglected.

He reached across the table and let his fingertips fall on the back of my hand, sending electric jolts up my arm. I bit down on my lip, and he grinned, like he knew he was the cause of my nerves. "No regrets?" he asked. "You don't wish you'd gone back to college to finish your degree? I can tell from the way you talk about your job now that you love it, but…"

"No regrets. I don't believe in them. And I do love my job. Actually, I'll be taking some continuing ed courses next month that you might be interested in. I already do deep tissue work, trigger point, that sort of thing, but I'm going to learn about sports massage."

He made an appreciative humming sound and raised a brow. "If you ever need a guinea pig to practice on, I'm sure it wouldn't take much arm twisting to get some of the boys on board."

"I'll keep that in mind," I said, winking at him.

In truth, I was slightly shocked and more than just a bit disappointed that he hadn't volunteered himself. I'd been dying to get my hands on him—*really* explore his muscles—ever since I'd first seen him last weekend. Having watched his players and spent some time close to Mattias, he seemed as fit as any of them, and likely a heck of a lot stronger than many of them. There was a certain sort of strength that came to men as they got older, and I had no doubt he had it in spades.

I speared a piece of roasted potato with my fork and popped it into my mouth. Then I almost melted from how good it was. "How do they make something so simple taste *so good?*" I asked, still chewing.

"Something tells me they won't be giving us their secrets."

"Too bad. I could teach the girls to make it, and then we could make a killing out of my kitchen."

"I doubt the government would look too kindly on slave labor," he joked.

"No slaves involved. We'd call it their chores and pay them an allowance. It'd be all aboveboard."

He laughed. Mattias had a rich, deep laugh, much like his voice. It rumbled through me and made me want to be closer to him, to feel it beneath my touch. Once I started thinking along those lines, though, I doubted I'd be able to stop anytime soon. I bit my lower lip again.

"If you don't stop doing that, I'm going to have to join you," he said.

I arched a brow in question.

"Biting your lip."

"Be careful not to hurt yourself."

He lifted his wineglass and tilted it in my direction. "I meant I'd bite your lip."

I downed a large swallow from my own glass to hide the rush of heat that flooded my face, not that it was likely to do any good. Besides, I wasn't fifteen. I was a grown woman. I could flirt and tease and talk about adult things without blushing like my daughters would, couldn't I? Determined to prove I could, even if only to myself, I met his gaze. "Try not to draw blood when you do."

"Is that an invitation?"

"More like a promise of things to come."

He sipped and let the wine roll over his tongue for a moment before swallowing, taking his time to answer. "I like promises," he finally said. "Maybe as much as you like kisses."

So apparently keeping myself from blushing was going to be next to impossible. As soon as I'd seen what Sophie had written in her letter to him, I'd known he was going to pounce all over that one. Good to see he didn't intend to let me down on that score.

I cut into my steak, searching my brain for any topic I could turn to in order to deflect the attention away from me, at least for long enough that I could refocus my thoughts. With Sophie on my mind, the first safe subject that came to me was Mattias's sister.

"So, does your sister ever come to visit you?" I asked, taking a large bite of steak so I wouldn't have to talk too soon.

A soft expression came into his eyes the second I mentioned his sister, but he shook his head. "Not often. Linnea lives in a group home in Stockholm, and our parents are close by. I spend as much time with her as I can when I'm home in the summers, but it never feels like enough." He stopped there and shook his head, as if he didn't want to go on.

"What?" I asked.

He shrugged. "I told you she has a boyfriend and she wants to live with him now, didn't I?" When I nodded, he said, "His name's Johan. He was the one who helped hold her together when her first boyfriend died about five years ago. I was here, coaching. I couldn't be there to help out, and my parents were at a loss about how to help her understand and grieve. But Johan took Linnea under his wing. He brought a book to work one day. *Adjö, herr Muffin*, it was called. *Good-bye, Mr. Muffin.* It's meant to help kids understand about death and grief. He took her aside on their break and read it to her, and he let her cry on his shoulder. That started a routine. Every day, he would bring some children's book or another to read to her. They had been coworkers for a long time, and they'd been friendly before that, but they started getting a lot closer because he brought his books to read and share with her."

"And then he took her out for ice cream," I said, smiling as his voice trailed off.

"And then he took her out for ice cream," Mattias repeated, nodding with a sheepish chuckle. "And now she wants to live with him."

"Sounds like he's a good guy." Maybe a lot like the man sitting next to me and staring at me like he never wanted to look anywhere else. My belly flipped at the unwavering look in his eyes.

"He is. He's a very good man."

"Does it ease your mind at all to know that?" I asked. "I mean, she could have fallen for someone who would have been the worst sort of influence on her, and then what?"

"Is your mind ever going to be at ease when it comes to your girls?"

"Good point. As boy crazy as they are…"

"But they know a good man when they see one," Mattias said emphatically. Like he knew them well enough to know that.

I shook my head, my brows pinching together.

"501's a good man," he explained. "Way too old for them, but he's a good man. I think they can sense it. They've got good instincts when it comes to their hormonal crushes." He reached across the table. I thought he was going for the saltshaker, but he took my hand instead, and he winked. "Like their mom."

My earlier belly flips couldn't hold a candle to what was going on internally now. I was seriously melting. So were my panties. They were all, *poof*, gone. Just like that.

Or they would be if we weren't sitting in the middle of a crowded restaurant.

Chapter Six

Paige

AFTER A DINNER filled with the most intoxicating mix of heady flirtation, banter, and soul-baring conversation, Mattias took me to a play at Portland Center Stage. It was over, and we were on our way back to my house, but I honestly didn't know if the play had been any good or not. The whole time we'd been there, I'd been so caught up in the sensation of Mattias's arm draped casually over my shoulders and the heat of his body warming me down to my toes that I couldn't pay attention to anything happening up on stage.

In fact, even now as we made our way through Portland's neighborhoods, I couldn't make my brain cooperate. No matter how hard I tried to think like a rational adult, my recently acquired reverse-aging process was raging, and my hormones were in complete control. All I wanted to do was take him inside my house the second we got there and jump him. I couldn't even remember the last time I'd been this out of control with lustful urges. Years. Maybe more than a decade.

I couldn't do a damn thing about it while he was still driving, though.

My cell phone beeped with a text message. Probably Zoe. She was always good about checking in with me when the girls were with their father or otherwise not with me. I assumed it had something to do with her being the eldest.

I dug around in my purse for my phone. It beeped again, and then a couple more times before I finally pulled it free. As soon as I wrapped my fingers around it, I unlocked the screen as I drew it out.

Then I burst out snort-laughing at Zoe's series of messages.

Are you having a good time with Beefy? Getting kissy-faced yet? You should totally take him inside and make out with him on the couch like you're a teenager. We promise we won't walk in on you and ruin the fun, like you would do to us. We're cooler than that.

OMG. Beefy! Beefy. BEEFY.

Stupid phone.

B E R G Y. I meant Beefy.

Gah! Autocorrect is killing me.

Just make out with him, 'kay? You deserve a good make-out session. And pretend you never saw this. I'm going to go crawl under a rock and die now.

Mattias angled his head toward me, attempting to hold back a laugh of his own. "That good? Do I want to know?"

I shook my head and tried to stop laughing, but it was no use. *Beefy.* Every time I read it, my mind changed it to *Beefcake*, which was way too appropriate. Not to mention inappropriate. That wasn't something anyone needed to know other than me, not even my girls. If I let it slip to one of them? They'd be chanting it every chance they got, and he would be bound to find out at some point. No chance I wanted him to see it because then I'd have to find a way to explain without putting my foot in my mouth, and that didn't seem even remotely likely.

"If it's that funny, I need to know. Fair's fair."

"Just a text from Zoe," I forced out between snorts and guffaws.

"Mm-hmm. *Just* a text. Your phone went off at least five times, and now you're laughing so hard you can hardly breathe."

I needed to deflect him, and fast since he wasn't giving up. "Autocorrect issues."

"Those are the best. Now you *have* to tell me." He smiled, and my pulse kicked up a notch or two.

"Just something that happened to her today at school," I hedged, angling myself so he couldn't accidentally read what was on my screen.

He came to a red light and stopped the car, turning more fully to face me. Based on experience, the light at this intersection would be a long one, too. Crap.

"If it's something from school, why are *you* blushing so hard?"

"I'm probably purple from laughing until I was out of breath."

He narrowed his eyes. "I think it's about me."

"It's not about you," I lied, even though I knew I was a horrible liar. Always had been. I should have taken acting classes in school or something. Anything to help me put on a mask and convince him I was telling the truth.

Not that I wanted to make a habit of lying, but it would be a good skill to have on occasion.

"So it is about me, then." He grinned, that sexy, panty-melting one again. It made me want to crawl back into his lap, and I didn't want to stop with just a kiss this time. He looked like he knew exactly what I was thinking. In fact, he looked like he would be completely on board with doing exactly that if we weren't sitting in the middle of an intersection. "I swear, I won't let on that I know, whatever it is. I won't ask you to take a screenshot so we can post it all over the Internet. I wouldn't embarrass you or your girls like that…"

"She would *die* if I let you see it. And then she'd murder me."

"If she was already dead, she couldn't do anything to you," he pointed out, invoking reason—something that had escaped me the second he'd walked into my life.

"Then her sisters would kill me."

He shook his head, clearly fighting back another laugh. "What did she say? You can't keep it from me."

I was reaching for my purse to hide the evidence when he made a grab for my phone. He was lightning fast, snatching it out of my grip before I could rip it away from him.

"Beefy? That's…"

"Awful," I finished for him.

"I was thinking more along the lines of hilarious, but we can go with awful if you want."

I pressed my eyes closed, sinking down in my seat. "If she finds out you've seen this…"

"Our secret." He tossed the phone back to me just as the light changed.

I punched in a quick response for her and hit Send before shoving the phone back in my purse.

"So what did you tell her about the whole getting kissy-faced on the sofa idea?" he asked, not even attempting to make the question casual. His words were heated. Needy. Somehow, there was still a hint of humor in it but not enough to outweigh the sensual quality it had taken on. The deep tone of his voice rumbled through my body, jump-starting my sex drive like nobody's business.

I couldn't seem to catch my breath. For once in my life, I didn't mind that I couldn't. I nibbled on my lower lip. "I told her she needed to worry about herself and her sisters and leave me alone."

"You and Beefy, you mean. To leave us alone."

In my mind, I turned it to *Beefcake* again. I let out a nervous laugh and bit my tongue to keep from saying it aloud. "Yes, me and Beefy."

He turned onto my street and rolled into the driveway, but he didn't turn off the engine. He put the car in park and turned in his seat to face me, that same panty-melting smile on his face, and he trailed the tips of his fingers up the back of my hand. Every touch, no matter how seemingly insignificant or barely there, had my body buzzing like an agitated beehive.

"I'm not going to lie," he said after a long minute. "I want you to ask me to come in. I like the idea of testing out Zoe's suggestion. I think she's onto something, and I think we should explore it. But if you aren't on board with that or if you think we'd be rushing things, I'll walk you to your door and then go."

"Without even a good-night kiss?"

He winked. "I would hope you'd allow me that, at the very least, but I'd understand if you didn't want it."

I wasn't inclined to let things stop with a simple good-night kiss. I mean, how often would a chance like this present itself? I was almost forty, and most of my evenings were claimed by my daughters. They would be for a long time to come, too, even though they were growing up far faster than I would like sometimes. I probably wouldn't have another kid-free night for at least a couple of months. It had been an eternity since I'd been with a man, and there was no telling how long it might be until the next opportunity presented itself.

I screwed up my courage and decided to go for it. "I'm not sure I'll be satisfied with just a kiss."

"No?"

"No. Why don't you shut off the ignition and come in with me?"

"Oh, thank God."

Mattias

WE BARELY HAD the front door closed when Paige was practically climbing me, like she was trying to crawl inside my body. And damn if I didn't want to let her. We both removed our coats, tossing them on the hall cabinet along with her purse to join the array I'd discovered earlier.

I leaned back against the door and dragged her forward by her hips until she was nestled right up against me. I couldn't get enough of her curves. Every time she'd allowed me to guide her with a hand on her back, I'd been dying to really touch her, to explore her body.

Paige was petite and fit. Some women who worked hard to stay in shape lost most of their curves, toning until they were almost as straight and angular as me. Not Paige. She had the sexiest ass, one that her dress hugged and accented in a way that made my mouth water. I slipped my hands down and back, exploring how tight it was, its perfect shape, and she burrowed closer to me. My cock came to attention then, more urgently than it had been to that point, pressing into her belly. We fit together seamlessly, soft against hard, her curves molding to me in an addictive way. It was like we were made for each other.

"I want to feel your hands on me," she said, breathless, tugging my shirt up from my pants. "Everywhere. On my skin. And I want to touch you. I want to learn everything there is to know about your body, to memorize the feel of you."

When she freed my hem, I still hadn't processed the fact that the very thing I'd been unable to stop thinking about for the last week was really happening. Her fingertips teased my abs as she slid them up my torso.

"Weren't we supposed to be taking this to the couch?" I asked.

She popped open a couple of my buttons. "We could take it straight to the bedroom."

I fought down a groan. "No point wasting time?"

In lieu of an answer, she took my hand and took charge, leading me up the stairs and down the hall. She didn't leave me any time to take in my surroundings. She spun me around and pushed on my chest with both hands, and I fell back onto the bed. I reached for her as I collapsed, gripping her thighs and drawing her up so she straddled me. That forced her dress to inch upward. Starting at the backs of her knees, I teased her sensitive skin as I began my study of her—learning what she liked; discovering her erogenous zones; discerning if she preferred soft or hard, fast or slow, rough or gentle.

As I trailed my fingers up the backs of her thighs, my eyes never leaving hers, she made short work of undoing my shirt and pushing it back over my shoulders. She raked her eyes over my chest, and then she followed the same path with her hands.

When Paige touched me, it was unlike any other woman's touch I'd ever experienced. It was as if her hands were an extension of her soul, and she was using them to find mine. I'd had plenty of massages in my day, but this was as different as night and day. She followed a path her hands knew well, even though she'd never had those hands on me before, exploring the way the various muscles came together.

Then she dropped her head and used her tongue to follow the same trail her fingers had just blazed. I sucked in a sharp breath.

Paige lifted her head enough that she could look in my eyes, her tongue on my skin. I propped myself up on my elbows so I could watch, content for now to let her do as she would.

She traced the lines of my pecs with her tongue, lazily moving closer to my nipple and driving me out of my mind with need. When she reached it, she flicked her tongue a couple of times before taking it into her mouth and sucking, and my cock jerked as if *that* was where she had her mouth. With a lusty laugh, she wiggled her hips.

That was enough to brush the heat of her center over the tip of my cock. Never mind the fact that we were both almost fully clothed. I was practically desperate to get inside her, but at the same time, I hated the thought of putting an end to her ministrations. Paige Calhoun was a woman who knew what she wanted, and I'd be damned if I didn't let her have it.

She inched upward, focusing her attention on the hollow at the base of my neck.

"You're killing me," I ground out.

"You want me to stop?"

Hell no. But I wanted to give as good as I got. "Tell me what you want. Show me what you like."

"I want you. Naked. And I want to get my hands on every hard inch of your body."

"I think we can make that happen." I put a hand on the small of her back to support her as I flipped our positions, momentarily crushing her to the mattress.

She let out a sharp gasp, but a needy moan soon followed. I kissed her chin and straightened away from her so I could get up and strip. With her eyes taking in my every move, devouring me as I bared myself to her, she bit down on her lower lip. She was so fucking sexy when she did that. It made me think about her using those teeth to nip my flesh. With those thoughts racing through my head, I couldn't get my clothes off fast enough.

I tossed them all in a heap on the floor and crawled back into the bed, supporting myself above her with my arms. She still had every stitch of her clothes on, right down to the slinky heels she'd worn tonight. My hands were itching to peel that dress off her body, but I was just as anxious to see what she would do next.

Starting at my wrists, she slid her hands up my arms, a painstaking inch at a time. Good thing I still worked out as much as I had in my playing days, because she wasn't in any rush to move on to the next bit. When she got to my shoulders, she put one hand on the back of my neck and drew me down to kiss her.

As soon as our lips touched, her mouth was open and waiting. I slid my tongue inside to meet hers, and they tangled together the way we'd done that first time, both languid and urgent at once.

She didn't stop there, gliding her hands down the expanse of my back and opening her legs so I could settle between them. If not for her dress and panties, I could already be where I wanted to be—so deep inside her that her toes would curl. I groaned against her mouth when she reached my ass and gripped each cheek like she meant it, drawing me closer still to her heat. When she rolled her hips, I nearly lost it.

I broke off the kiss and ground out, "I need to be inside you." It had been too damn long since I'd been with a woman. I didn't know how much longer I could hold out, especially with the sensual torment she was putting me through.

She gave me a sultry, slinky grin. "Roll over."

It was about time. I did what she told me to, bringing her with me and trying to figure out how to get her dress off her as soon as she was no longer trapped beneath my weight. I tugged at the hem, attempting to peel it up and over her head, but that didn't work very well. It only moved a bit.

She shook her head, though, and slipped out of my grasp.

I was a patient man, normally, but Paige was seriously trying it right now.

Kneeling on the edge of the bed, she resumed her careful survey of my body by inching her way up my legs. By the time she reached my knees, I broke out in a sweat, desperate for more. When she lowered her head and licked the inside of my thigh, it was all I could do to fist my hands in her bedding instead of her hair.

She worked her way higher slowly. Meticulously. A brief touch of her tongue to the vee line of my oblique muscles. Then I couldn't help it. My hips bucked up, an involuntary reaction to her being so close to where I wanted her. I could feel her smile against my skin. She settled herself between my thighs. Lowered her head. Took me in her mouth.

I was in heaven.

Paige

MATTIAS KEPT FISTING and releasing the comforter. I thought about telling him he could grab hold of my hair and direct me where he wanted me, but that would require taking a break from what I was doing.

He was reveling in it too much for me to stop my efforts now. His enjoyment gave me supreme satisfaction, so I focused on giving him the best blow job of his life. It was one thing that, in all the years I'd been married, Dan had never gotten bored with. I knew how to suck a man off. Until I'd gotten Mattias down on the bed and put my hands on him, I hadn't realized just how much I'd missed it. I got my hands in on the act, gently massaging his balls with one as I used the other to assist me in covering more ground.

I dipped down again, and he brought his knees up on either side of me, straining with the effort to let me pleasure him without grinding his hips up into me.

"*Ja*," he said, his voice rough and husky, cracking from exertion even though I was the one currently doing all the work. He'd have his turn soon enough. "*Det är så bra, sötnos.*"

The fact that he was speaking in Swedish only reconfirmed the idea that I was rocking his world, even though I didn't have the first clue what he meant. I ramped up my efforts, swirling my tongue around his head before taking him in as deeply as I could manage.

Then he did put a hand on the back of my head, gently urging me to bob. If that was what he wanted, that was what I'd give him. Relaxing so he could take control of things, I allowed myself to exult in the sensation of his hot, hard erection filling me in this way.

"Paige," he said, easing me up and off his length.

I shot my eyes up to meet his.

He caressed my face, his thumb gliding over my cheekbone. "I can't wait anymore. I need to be inside you." He'd already said that to me before, but this time there was a sense of urgency to his words that I knew better than to ignore.

I fished through my nightstand drawer for a condom. I'd bought some while the girls were in school one day, on the off chance I'd have the opportunity to make use of them—better safe than sorry—and squashed them between the pages of an anatomy book, in case one of the girls went searching through my things for tweezers or a particular shade of fingernail polish. It took me a minute to get my hand on the little foil wrapper, but as soon as I did, I tossed it Mattias's way.

While he opened it and prepared himself, I reached over my shoulders and unclasped my dress, then eased the zipper down. Once it was loose, I allowed it to slide off my shoulders and drop down my arms, pooling at my feet. Mattias's eyes never left me. He rolled to his side and propped himself up on one elbow. When I stretched my arms behind my back to unhook my bra, he reached for himself and stroked. My breasts jiggled when the bra fell away. I fixed my thumbs in the waistband of my panties and started lowering them.

"Wait," Mattias said harshly.

I froze. "What?" Had I done something wrong? Or maybe he'd changed his mind now that he'd seen me mostly naked. Talk about making a woman self-conscious. "What's wrong?" I asked, since he didn't immediately answer.

"Sorry. Nothing's wrong." He pumped himself a few more times. "I just...I just wondered. Are you ready? Wet? You've been taking care of me, but I've hardly touched you at all."

Wet didn't even begin to cover it. As long as he wasn't having second thoughts, I decided to finish lowering my panties. Once they hit my ankles, I stepped out and toed them aside before crossing back to him.

"I'm more than ready," I said as I sat on the edge of the bed again. "But I won't try to stop you from touching me in any way you want to."

He reached for me as soon as I was close enough, tugging me down beside him. Leaning over me, he traced a finger from my collarbone to my hip, letting it whisper over my flesh. My already taut nipple juddered as he tweaked it on his meandering journey south. However much I wanted him inside me, I couldn't complain. Turnabout was only fair, and I had taken my time and then some in teasing him to a frenzy.

I brought my knee up in invitation and anticipation, dropping my head back onto my pillow. Gradually, he edged his exploration down, lower, lower, closer to where I wanted him to be. Mattias touched the inside of my thigh and pressed it toward the bed, opening me for him to discover what he would.

With only the tip of a single finger, he outlined my lower lips. "Very wet," he murmured.

"I told you." My entire body was trembling, not from cold but from need.

One finger slipped inside me, then another, and I arched my back in bliss.

"I can't wait much longer," he said.

"I can't, either."

He pumped his fingers inside me a few times, my hips rising to meet him of their own volition. The heel of his palm brushed against my clit, and I let out a moan.

"Yes, *sötnos*," he said. "You're going to come for me, Paige. But I want it to be while I'm inside you."

I wanted that, too. More than I could say. I nodded, moaning as he removed his fingers from my channel and repositioned himself. Mattias raised himself over me again, placing his cock at my entrance. He rocked his hips a few times, only sliding an inch or two inside me at first. But then I wrapped my legs around his waist and put my hands on his shoulders, and he drove all the way home, nearly splitting me in two.

I bit down on my lower lip to keep from crying out, but I couldn't stop myself from tensing at the sting of his entrance.

"Am I hurting you?"

I shook my head, trying to buy myself another moment before answering. "It's just been so long," I finally forced out. "Give me a minute and I'll be fine."

He held himself still, resting his forehead against mine, and kissed me tenderly. "I don't want you just be fine."

The sting eased to a dull ache as my sex stretched to accommodate him. I rolled my hips to let him know I was ready. He groaned, but then he started to move within me, gentle thrusts at first that gradually increased in speed and intensity. He lifted his weight off me, staring down into my eyes as we moved together, a slick glide that felt as natural as breathing and as exhilarating as skydiving.

My body tensed as I approached orgasm. I slipped a hand between our bodies to rub my clitoris. A few more thrusts and I splintered, shuddering and burying my head in Mattias's shoulder.

He shifted our positions, lifting my legs and spreading them wider, which somehow allowed him to drive even deeper into me. Then he collapsed against me, his cock jerking inside me as he came. "*Det känns som om jag är hemma, sötnos,*" he said next to my ear.

We lay there with our limbs tangled, too done in to move despite our sweaty bodies starting to stick to one another, until our breathing returned to normal and our pulses slowed to a mere gallop. I relished the weight of him pushing me down into the mattress, the heady scent of his cologne mixing with the musk of our efforts.

I didn't want it to end.

And it wasn't just because I didn't know when the next time I would have an opportunity like this might be. I had to be honest with myself. Yes, I'd asked Mattias to come in, and I'd decided to take him to my bed *initially* because I'd wanted to indulge myself. But that was far from the whole truth of what was behind it.

I was falling for Mattias—hard—and even though I still had a thousand reasons not to humor the selfish idea of getting into a relationship, it appeared to be too late for that. Now I just had to figure out what to do about it.

He rolled off me after a long while, and I immediately felt the loss of him. I turned on my side, following him so I could rest my head on his shoulder. He trailed his fingers through my hair, an action that felt both familiar and right.

"Mattias?" I asked after a few moments.

"Hmm?"

"Tell me what you said."

He looked down at me with a question in his eyes.

"The Swedish a minute ago."

He thought for a moment. But then he said, "It was just heat-of-the-moment nonsense. Something like *I feel like I'm home, sweetie.*"

Something warm and pure bubbled up in my heart. "I don't think that's nonsense at all."

Chapter Seven

Mattias

MY INTENTION WASN'T to spend the night—I would never have been so presumptuous—so I hadn't come prepared for that. After Paige and I got up, showered, dressed, and had breakfast, I had to go back to my place for clean clothes and the like before practice. I promised her that as soon as I could, I'd be back to pick her up and we could continue with our weekend together.

When I left—following a few lingering kisses—I told her to rest up and dress comfortably. The comfortable part of that was an absolute necessity because of what I had planned. We were going hiking in the Columbia River Gorge. I'd been out to Multnomah Falls a few times since I'd been in Portland, and they seemed like the perfect place for an active date. Lucky for me, the weather had cooperated today. It was cool but not too cold, considering it was February, and the sun was shining.

It was 501's first full-contact practice with the team following his concussion, and I pushed him hard. I *always* pushed 501 hard, actually. He reminded me a lot of myself when I'd been his age. He had all the potential to be one of the best defensemen in the world, but he was still making a lot of rookie mistakes, even though it was his second year in the league. He seemed to go back and forth between sitting back and trying too hard, though, so he wasn't getting the kind of ice time he and I both knew he was capable of handling. I'd already decided that for the rest of this season and likely all of the next, he was going to be my special project. I was determined to get every ounce of effort I could squeeze out of him. He might not like it while it was going on, but he would thank me for it down the road. After practice was over, I sent him off to see Doc for another evaluation before he was cleared to play in our next game.

Then, for the first time in my career as a coach, I took off early. Webs and Handy were perfectly capable of handling all the game prep that needed to be done. Jim was always telling me I needed to take some time for myself so I wouldn't burn out, and I never took him up on it. Today? I planned to take full advantage of that.

When Paige answered the door, she was blushing and shoving her phone into the pocket of her jeans.

"Zoe checking up on you and Beefy?" I asked.

"You think I'd tell you that?" She winked, grabbed a rain jacket and her purse, and locked the door.

We spent the drive talking about my plans for helping Sophie learn to skate. Drywall had already drawn up a blueprint of sorts for the first rig he intended to build, and now that we were due to be home for a long stretch, he thought he could get at least an initial attempt put together within the next week or so.

There weren't too many cars in the parking lot when we reached the lodge at Multnomah Falls, which meant we shouldn't be overrun on our hike.

"Ready?" I asked as we climbed out of my SUV.

Paige slung the strap of her purse across her body and reached for my hand with a smile filled with trepidation. "So I guess I never mentioned my fear of heights, did I?"

I shook my head, lacing my fingers with hers. "I'll keep you safe."

Her fear didn't stop her from hiking up the trail with me. We completely bypassed the primary viewing area. That was where most of the small crowd would be, so getting out on the hiking paths would give us more privacy.

When we reached the Benson Bridge, I slowed down, not wanting to assume anything. "You up for it?" The bridge spanned the space between two halves of a ridge and looked down over the lower cascade.

She gripped my hand tighter but nodded.

We made our way to the center of the footbridge and stopped, turning toward the gushing water. A chilly spray hit our faces, and

Paige nestled herself in front of me, taking both my arms and wrapping them around her waist. She was shaking, but I wasn't sure if it was fear or cold behind it.

"You're not scared?"

"I'm fine as long as I only look up, not down."

"Do your girls know you're scared of heights?" I asked.

"They know. It's too hard to hide it when they want to go on roller coasters and sky trams and God only knows what else."

"So what would they think if they could see you now?"

She waited a moment but then laughed. "They'd think you'd brainwashed me."

I took my cell phone out of my pocket and nudged her to turn so we were facing the other direction. "I think we need to send them a selfie so they can see you facing your fears."

"Oh, please don't make me look that way," she said, stiffening.

"Look up, not down. I've got you." I tightened my other arm around her, drawing her closer to me.

She waited a beat, but then she nodded resolutely.

I got us in position and held my phone out so it would catch us, the falls in the background, and at least a bit of the bridge. "Are you smiling?"

"I'm squeezing my eyes closed."

I laughed. "That's not what you want them to see, is it?"

"Maybe not, but it's as good as I can do."

There was something else she could do that I was sure would work much better. I put a finger under her chin and tilted her head up toward me, and I kissed her. When I broke it off, she said, "Oh," and blinked up at me a few times. That was when I snapped the shot.

"Give me Zoe's phone number, and I'll let her see how kissy-faced you're getting with Beefy."

"Only if you swear not to mention Beefy at all."

I pecked her on the lips again. "Done." Right now, I would promise her almost anything. I put the number in as she rattled off the digits and hit Send.

"There aren't many people in the world I'd do that for, you know," Paige said.

I spun her around in my arms so I could see her eyes. "Do what?"

"Get up here. Face my fears. You bring things out of me that I didn't know were there."

She and her girls did the same for me. Well, not exactly. I knew this side of me existed, thanks to Linnea. But until Paige and her family had come into my life, no one but Linnea could bring out that side of me, and I'd been happy to keep it that way.

I kissed her on the forehead and took her hand. "Should we keep going up, or are you ready to go down?"

"Up," she said at the same moment as my phone dinged with a reply.

Mom and Beefy, sitting in a tree. K I S S I N G.

And then my phone went crazy with more replies.

OMG. Beefy.

No. B E R G Y. Not Beefy.

I am so sorry.

I hate my phone. Stupid autocorrect.

I'm going to go crawl under a rock now. Please forget I ever existed. Tell Mom I love her.

I burst out laughing so hard and so loud it echoed through the valley.

Paige

MATTIAS SPENT THE night at my house again. We hadn't exactly had a huge conversation about it or anything. It felt right, so we let it happen.

I was already getting used to waking up in his arms, and it had only been two nights. This could only spell trouble for me, but I didn't know how to stop it. For that matter, I wasn't sure I needed to stop it anymore. He cared about my girls—enough that he was going to all sorts of trouble to keep a promise to Sophie—and they seemed to like him. This weekend, we were doing things with just the two of us, but all of our plans for the future were things that would include my daughters, and he was the one making the suggestions.

He wasn't asking me for things I wouldn't be able to give him. He didn't expect me to drop everything and be with him, and he wouldn't drop everything to be with me, either. We both had our own lives, but that didn't mean we couldn't find a way to share parts of them with each other. Did it?

Oh, and then there was the small matter that—despite the fact that we'd now had sex several times—he could still make my panties melt with nothing more than a grin. If anything, that had only increased.

I was a mess over him, but for some odd reason, I couldn't seem to make myself mind.

While he was gone to deal with practice and other work with the Storm on Sunday, I used that time to clean my house, try to make a dent in the massive piles of laundry that had built up over the course of the week, and go grocery shopping in preparation for the week to come. There was a brief moment when I debated taking a nap, but I brushed that aside. I could nap when my girls were grown and living on their own. I didn't often have time to myself like this, and I knew better than to let it go to waste.

There was still a Mt. Everest-sized pile of laundry waiting to be washed when the doorbell rang, signaling that my time alone was at an end. The instant I opened it, Mattias put his arms around me and gave me a toe-curling kiss, as if he hadn't seen me in months instead of hours. I wouldn't have minded continuing with what he'd started if not for the fact that Dan's weekend with the girls was at an end, and I needed to go pick them up.

Mattias came with me to get them. "I'll stay in the car if you think it would be better," he suggested once he'd parked in Dan's driveway.

I shook my head. "No need for that." In fact, it was better for my ex to meet Mattias now, because I had made up my mind that I wanted to take things further. I wasn't sure what it would look like, and I was even less positive what the girls were ready for, but I wanted to make things as smooth as possible for my kids. That meant their father needed to know there was a new man in my life.

Zoe answered the door and let us in, giving Mattias a wide-eyed look. "Just so you know, that was all my phone's fault."

She'd barely gotten that out before Sophie came running, arms wide for a hug. But instead of jumping into my arms, she made a flying leap for Mattias. She hugged him hard, nearly strangling him with her grip around his neck.

It was too much for me. I stepped back, blinking down the tears stinging behind my eyes. My baby girl had decided he should be part of her life, so who was I to say otherwise? Even if I hadn't already been leaning toward making this relationship with Mattias more official, I would have given in upon seeing this.

Once Mattias extricated himself from Sophie's exuberant display of affection, he shook Dan's hand and exchanged a few pleasantries while I helped the older girls pack up the last of their things so we could head home.

We were in the SUV heading back to my place when Sophie piped up with, "Bergy?"

"Yes, Sophie?" He glanced at her in his rearview mirror.

"Good job on kissing Mom. Zoe showed me the picture."

Everyone burst out laughing, including Mattias. Everyone but me. I bit down on my lower lip, unable to decide between snort-laughing along with the rest of them or burying my head in the sand like Zoe kept threatening to do.

"Well, we had a deal, right?" he said after the laughter died down.

"Right. So when can I skate?"

He turned onto my street, smiling like he'd just won the lottery. I wasn't sure what to make of that, but he answered her before I got the chance to overanalyze it. "Soon," he said. "But first, we need to start doing some exercise so we can build up your muscles."

"Like what kind of exercise?"

"Do you know what crunches are?" he asked.

"Yep."

"Well, we'll do things like that. You'll need strong core muscles to be able to skate."

"We can all do it together," Izzy said. "So we can all skate."

"Sure," he replied, and his grin just kept getting bigger. "We can call it Workouts with Bergy or something like that."

"Can we work out with Levi?" Evie asked.

Mattias chuckled. "Not sure I can make that one happen, but maybe we can get some of the guys involved when we're ready to skate."

That was apparently enough to get the girls chattering and giggling. *Hormones.*

Sophie wasn't taking part in it, for once. She sat quietly for a moment, but I had no doubt she wasn't finished with her questions. Her mind was working a hundred miles an hour. When he parked in my driveway, she said, "Can we start now?"

Mattias

MORE THAN HALF the team had come to the practice facility today, including a few of the guys who didn't have families.

Like 501.

He was here as a favor to me—there wasn't any point in trying to think he'd come for any other reason—but the fact was, he was here.

It was a Saturday afternoon in early March. With the playoffs only a little over a month away, the other coaches and I had decided the guys needed a break. A day with their families would do a lot more for how they played each night than another tedious practice going over the same systems and strategies we'd been pounding into their heads all season.

Soupy was still recovering from ACL surgery much earlier in the season, so he couldn't get out on the ice, but he and Rachel had brought all their kids. Rachel was busy suiting their twin toddlers up to go out on a sled that one of the young, single guys would pull around. Soupy had his bad leg propped up on a bench and was helping tie the skate laces for one of Dominic "Bear" Medved's kids. Tuck and Maddie Campbell were already out on the ice, as were Nicky Ericsson and his adopted niece and nephews, Marc "Danger" d'Aragon's teenagers, Grant "Wheels" Wheelan and his teens, and Mitch and Mia Quincey with their two little ones.

Babs and 501 were over on the other side of the ice, along with Webs and Drywall. All four of them were huddled up and bent over, no doubt putting finishing touches on Sophie's rig.

I'd carried in a bag of skates for Paige and the girls, and I dropped it on the bench next to Cam and Sara Johnson. Sara was bouncing their newborn in her arms while Jonny sat on the floor tying three-year-old Connor's skates. Connor, meanwhile, was bopping a Minion toy on his father's head. It kept saying unintelligible things with every hit, but then it said something that sounded distinctly like, "What the fuck?"

Connor giggled maniacally and repeated it. "What the fuck? What the fuck? What the fuck?"

"What did I tell you about not using Mommy's bad words?" Jonny said.

His son laughed even more fiendishly than before.

I did my best not to laugh out loud while I bent over to unload skates and other gear for my crew, but I saw Jonny calmly take the toy out of his son's hand, put it in their diaper bag, and give his wife a look that had her rolling her eyes.

"Don't blame that one on me," she said. "It's a toy."

When I handed Zoe the skates in her size, she was fighting the urge to bust up. I shook my head slightly, and she put a lid on it and took her skates.

Once Paige started helping the older girls get ready, I turned to Sophie.

She was bouncing on the balls of her feet and staring out at the ice. "Do I really get to skate, Bergy?"

"You really get to skate," I said. "So that means we need to put your gear on." I picked up her skates, kneepads, and helmet and took a seat. When she turned to look at me, grin a mile wide, I patted the spot on the bench next to me. She raced over and sat down.

By the time I had her properly outfitted, Babs and 501 were on their way around to join us with her rig.

Her older sisters giggled and made their nervous sounds, but not Sophie. She looked up and beamed at him. "Hi, Levi."

"Hi, Sophie. You ready to skate with me?"

She nodded emphatically and tried to stand up, but she wobbled on the skates.

I took her by the waist and steadied her, and the two brothers and I got her all strapped in. Drywall came over to be sure we had her situated right and all his measurements had been correct.

"Told you I could do this," he said, slapping me on the back after he'd completed his inspection.

"So I can skate?" Sophie squealed.

"You can skate," I said. I took one of her hands and 501 took the other, and we helped her walk cautiously to the door with her backward walker on skis coming behind her. When we got there, I picked her up and set her on the ice.

Then 501 took over. He took both her hands and skated backward, pulling her along with him. "You've gotta bend your knees," he said to her. "Get down low and push your skates into the ice."

In no time, they were too far away for me to hear them anymore. I could hear the other girls coming up behind me thanks to their giggles. Evie and Izzy stepped onto the ice and almost fell. They decided to take the easy path around the boards so they'd have something to hold on to.

Zoe stopped by my side before joining her sisters, though. "Hey, Bergy?"

I kept my eyes on 501 and Sophie to be sure that her rig was supporting her the way we intended it to. So far, so good. "Yeah?" I replied.

"I was just wanted to tell you that I've been talking to my sisters."

I chuckled. "No surprise there."

"Yeah. But we all agree."

Now I was curious. To my knowledge, they never agreed on anything but the fact that they needed to kidnap 501 and convince him to stay with them forever. "Agree about what?"

"Well, you know about the whole brother-husband thing?"

I nodded, internally cringing.

"Well, we think you should be Mom's brother-husband. Only there should just be you."

I definitely hadn't been expecting that one. "Don't you think that's moving a little—"

Before I could finish my question, she was rushing to catch up to the group of teens congregating on the opposite end of the ice.

I stayed in place for a few minutes, watching 501 and Sophie skate circles. She wasn't doing much of the work, letting him drag her along with him, but she lit up the entire rink with her smile. Even better, though, the rig was doing its job. It was supporting her weight while she found her legs and gained her balance. She might not ever get to the point that she could skate without it, but I wouldn't put it past her. Not when she was clearly having the time of her life. That would only make her want to work harder to make it happen.

Paige came up behind me and put her hand on my arm.

"She's doing great," I said.

Paige sniffled.

I spun around to face her and used my thumb to brush away the tears falling down her cheeks. "Hey," I said. "What's this about?"

"I didn't think this would ever happen," she said, shaking her head and waving her hand toward Sophie and 501. "She's doing things even I thought would be impossible, and it's all because of you."

"Not because of me."

She laughed through her tears. "Okay, fine. All because of Beefy, then."

I wrapped my arms around her and held her close, resting my chin on the top of her head. Not that I agreed with her assessment, but it wasn't worth arguing over. I was just glad to hold her for a while.

Over the last several weeks, I'd spent more and more time with Paige and her daughters whenever the team was in town. We weren't shy about showing physical affection for each other in front of them, but we kept it all on a PG level. The girls had started giving me hugs and acting like I was a normal fixture in their lives instead of an outsider they had to be on their best behavior for, and there had even been a few nights when, after the girls had gone to bed, Paige had snuck me up to her room before sending me on my way. I wasn't about to spend the night with the girls in the house. That seemed like stepping way over the line. But I couldn't deny that I liked the thought behind Zoe's suggestion even if it might be too soon to take that kind of step. It was something to think about.

Something to talk to Paige about, but preferably not when we were surrounded by half my team and their families.

She broke away from me and angled her head toward a quiet corner. I took her hand and followed her, trusting that 501 and Sophie's rig would be enough to take care of her, and that the other girls were fine with the rest of the teens.

When she came to a stop, she stretched up on her toes and kissed me.

I laughed out loud. "I didn't realize it was kissy-kissy time."

"I think it's always kissy-kissy time when I'm around you. I think about you all the time. About how you don't just care about me but you care about my girls, too. About how you take time out of your life to be with all of us. You're like a dream, Mattias, except you're real."

"You're my dream," I said, looking down into her rich, hazel eyes. She still had tears in them, but there was something else, too. Something deeper. It was as though I could see all the way to her heart just by looking in those eyes, and that heart was smiling back at me.

She bit down on her lip. "I just… I wasn't prepared for this."

"Prepared for what?"

"For falling in love with you. But I have."

She could have blown me over with that, because I was in love with her, too. And her girls. And her life. The more time I spent in her house, surrounded by her family and the way they loved and supported each other, the more it felt like exactly where I needed to be. I'd thought it would take more to convince her we were meant to be together. I'd expected to have to work harder to find a way to fit within her life, and to convince her to let me in since she had to think about her daughters as well as herself.

But she loved me.

"That's good," I finally said, unable to wipe the goofy grin off my face.

"Why is that good?"

"Because I think I've been in love with you since not long after I met you. And I know I love your daughters."

"I know you love them. I think that's why I finally stopped fighting it. Because you're so good to them, and you're so devoted to Sophie. You work harder to make her life better than even her own father." Paige's tears started up again, so I drew her into my arms and held her to me. "He's a good man, but he just doesn't take the time to be there for her. But you do. All the time. I've spent so many years feeling like her sisters and I were the only ones fighting for her, and now it feels like a huge weight has been lifted."

If I wasn't careful, she was going to bring out some emotion in me that I'd kept locked away for a very long time. The last thing I needed was for my players to see me cry, so I put that under lock and key. It was one thing to laugh and smile in front of them; it was something else to let them see me being so vulnerable.

Once I thought I had it under control, I said, "I've got big shoulders, Paige. I can carry a lot."

"Mom!" Sophie screamed. My blood turned to ice, and we both spun around in panic.

But it was a good scream. A happy scream.

Because she was skating all by herself. Yes, she still had the rig holding her up. Yes, she was moving slowly and awkwardly, and if she didn't have the rig, she'd be on the ice in a heartbeat. But she was bending her knees and digging into the ice, and she was propelling herself forward, chasing 501, who was a few strides ahead of her.

"Oh," Paige said, and her hand shot up to cover her mouth as a fresh flood of tears streamed down her cheeks. "My baby's skating."

She wasn't the only one crying, either. As soon as I felt a hot tear blaze a trail down my own cheek, I brushed it away with the back of my hand. So maybe it wasn't the end of the world if my players saw me cry. Not if it was for the right reason, and this was definitely the right reason.

Epilogue

Paige

"WHY ISN'T BERGY here yet?" Sophie asked. "He's late."

"He's not late," I replied, glancing at the clock on the wall. In the months he'd been in our lives, he had never once been late, and I doubted that would change today. He still had ten minutes before he was due to arrive.

"But he's not early, Mom," my youngest complained, and I laughed.

"Just because he's not early, that doesn't make him late," Evie pointed out.

"It does for Beefy," Izzy said.

I was inclined to side with Izzy on this one, not that I would say so in front of the girls. If Mattias said he would be somewhere at eight, you could count on him to show up at 7:45. It was just part of his makeup. So, like Sophie and Izzy, I wondered where he was and what had held him up.

Zoe tossed a throw pillow at her sister's head, her face bright red from the effort to stop a laugh combined with her continued embarrassment. "Stop calling him that."

The girls were on Spring Break, so I had taken the week off. It was the last week of the regular season, and the Storm were finishing things out at home, so Mattias was in Portland for now. He'd promised to pick us up after he got done with practice because he had a surprise for

Sophie.

A surprise he hadn't even told me about, no less.

Before an argument broke out, the doorbell rang, and all four girls raced to open it.

"Bergy!" Sophie squealed as I rounded the corner and saw him for myself.

He had Sophie wrapped up with one arm and was holding another bouquet of yellow tulips with the other hand, and he winked at me over the top of them. "Sorry I'm late," he said. "I just remembered I hadn't brought your mom flowers since we got back in town."

The older girls giggled and took care of getting the tulips in water while Mattias and I gathered up purses and Sophie's backpack.

"You don't have to bring me flowers every time you come back from a trip, you know."

"I know," he said. "I like bringing you flowers, though."

"Why's that?"

"Because you light up with the prettiest smile when you see them. Almost as bright as Sophie's."

I laughed. "Well, that's saying something."

Within a few minutes, we were all in his SUV and he was backing out of my driveway.

"You still won't tell us where we're going, Bergy?" Izzy asked.

"I guess I could tell you now." He gave me a look I couldn't interpret. "I'm taking you to an ice skating rink where a kids' hockey team practices."

"A hockey team?" Sophie repeated, her excitement creeping into her tone.

"Yeah. For kids your age, Sophie."

I caught his eye and shook my head. She'd been skating with her rig every day for weeks, as often as either Mattias or I could get her to the Storm's practice facility. And she was definitely making improvements, but that didn't mean she was ready for something more. She still needed the supportive structure to hold her up. Her core wasn't strong enough for her to balance on skate blades.

"I'm going to play hockey?" She was bouncing so hard in her seat that I could hear it.

"We're going to talk to the coach and find out if you can play next year," he said.

"But *you're* the coach, Bergy."

"Not for this team, I'm not. Coach Carlson is a special coach, and he works with extra special kids."

Special kids. Meaning kids with special needs. I caught the hidden meaning even if Sophie might not have, and I decided to reserve judgment until I could see what this program was all about for myself.

And once I saw what they were all about and heard the coach tell Sophie all the things she would have to do between now and next October if she was going to be able to play with the rest of the special needs kids? I nearly started crying.

Coach Carlson let Sophie put on all her gear, including strapping into her rig, and get out on the ice with the rest of his team. He gave her a hockey stick, and the rest of us watched from the stands as one of the other kids taught her how to shoot the puck toward the net.

"She's really going to play hockey, isn't she?" Zoe said, sniffling.

Mattias nodded. "Yeah. I think so."

I was too overwrought to do anything but take his hand and squeeze.

For the next half hour, we sat there and witnessed Sophie beginning to realize her dream. Once the kids started to leave the ice, Mattias climbed down the bleachers and helped the coach get Sophie out of her gear.

"Mom?" Zoe asked once he was well out of our hearing.

"Hmm?"

"I think he's a keeper."

I laughed, still sniffling. "Oh, you do, huh?"

"Yeah," Izzy said.

"Definitely," Evie added. "He's not the kind of guy you let get away from you. So you need to do something about that."

I got the distinct sense that my girls were ganging up on me, and I wasn't sure what to do about it. "Do something about it like what?"

Izzy shrugged, and Evie said, "I don't know."

But Zoe didn't brush it off. "Something like asking him to come live with us."

"What?" I didn't even attempt to hide my shock. That wasn't something we'd ever talked about, whether my girls were around or not. "Why do you think he should come live with us?"

"Because you love him. So do we." Zoe gave me a look that clearly said I was being slow. "It just makes sense."

"What makes sense?" Mattias asked when he and Sophie clomped back up the stairs.

"You coming to live with us," Izzy answered.

He nodded, looking at her before turning his gaze to each of my girls in turn. Then he settled that gaze on me, and I nearly melted into the aluminum bench I was sitting on. "Is everyone on board with that?" he asked cautiously.

"Yes!"

"Absolutely."

"Mm-hmm."

My daughters were going to be the death of me.

Sophie was still holding his hand, and she tugged on it until he looked down at her. "Will you come live with us?" she asked.

He squeezed her hand and winked before looking over at me. "I don't know. I guess it depends on what your mom has to say about that."

"Oh, please, Mom!" she said. "I need Bergy to help me skate. I got to get a lot better by next year so I can play hockey."

Her sisters chimed in with a chorus of "Please," not that it would have made a difference. I already knew what I wanted, and I already knew what I thought would be best for not only myself but also my daughters.

I narrowed my eyes up at him. "I say," I said slowly, "that if Beefy wants to come live with us, he can. But only if he keeps bringing me flowers every now and then. And maybe if we can arrange to meet his sister sometime this summer."

He laughed. "It's a deal."

And we all knew how Mattias felt about deals. Once he made a deal with someone, he followed through on his end of it.

Mistletoe Misconduct

by
USA Today bestselling author

Catherine Gayle

Chapter One

Jim

EVERYONE DESERVES A second chance. Maybe even a third chance. That was the primary tenet by which I'd been living my life for decades. As the general manager of the Portland Storm, one of the most successful teams in the National Hockey League during my tenure, giving people new opportunities to turn their lives around had been a hallmark of my term. Not only with my players but with the people who worked under me, like my assistant, Rachel Campbell.

The reasons for my need to give a helping hand instead of turning my back on people went deep. I'd been the oldest child of a single mom, and I'd seen how many people had left her—and therefore *us*—out to dry. But I'd also seen firsthand what a difference it had made in all of our lives when someone offered a helping hand and gave me my first pair of hockey skates.

Then there was my hockey career, which should have been over almost before it began. A very long time ago when I was just starting out in the National Hockey League, one of the GMs I'd played under had given me a second opportunity to prove myself as well as my dedication to the team and my future, and he'd done so at a time when I'd least deserved it. That simple act had changed not only my career for the better but my life.

Something told me he might not understand the impact he'd had on me, but I'd never forgotten the ways his decision had altered my trajectory for the better.

Those reasons, and many others, were why I made such a point of offering second chances where I could and it made sense to do so. Sometimes, those decisions turned around and bit me in the butt. More often, they worked out for the best for everyone concerned. And since things usually came out better for everyone involved, I had no intention of changing my ways.

If I could offer someone the possibility of turning things around, I would do it.

I had to. It was the only way I could live with myself.

That was why, with the Christmas break and the holiday roster freeze breathing down my neck and my team in a serious bind on defense, I was contemplating yet another second-chance scenario.

More than contemplating, actually. I'd already made up my mind, and I'd talked it over in detail with my coaching staff. Everyone was on board. This was the move we needed to make, and I wasn't about to let it pass me by. If I didn't snap this guy up now, some other GM would before I could blink. The second half of the season usually separated the wheat from the chaff, and every team in the play-off hunt would be looking for reliable, experienced bodies to fill holes on the blue line. They'd snatch Hammer out of my grasp, and then we would be back to the drawing board.

Chris Hammond sat across from me in my office. The guy everyone called Hammer was a thirty-six-year-old defenseman who'd been there, done that. Once upon a time, he'd won the Stanley Cup with Pittsburgh. He'd been through countless play-off battles over the years, coming out of them bruised and bloodied but usually on top, as long as his team had him situated in the right spot.

The guy had never been top tier. He'd never been in consideration for the big NHL awards. That said, he was solid and dependable, and I needed him.

But he'd had a rough go of it over the last little while. He'd been a victim of the system, more or less.

Three years ago, Hammer had a monster of a season, putting up more points in one year than he had in the previous four combined. It had turned out to be perfect timing for him, since he'd been eligible to become a free agent immediately following that. He'd signed a huge contract with Winnipeg. They'd brought him in, essentially hoping he could fill the role of their top defenseman—never mind the fact that he hadn't been the top D on his previous team during that best year of his career, or any of the others before that—and the deal hadn't panned out for the team.

After a couple of years during which his play had regressed to his usual level of production, the Jets had bought out the rest of his contract. And, since he was an older defenseman who was seen by some as being too slow to be relevant in the modern, fast-paced, high-octane NHL, not a single team had signed him as a free agent.

I hadn't signed him because, at the time, I hadn't had a spot open for him to fill. Now I did. He'd been keeping himself in playing shape by helping coach his son's pee-wee team over the last few months, just in case someone called in need of his services.

I was glad to learn I'd been the first to make that call.

"Here's where we stand," I said, taking off my bifocals and setting them on the desk between us. I leaned back in my chair and laced my fingers in front of me. "Cole Paxton had an emergency appendectomy yesterday and is out for at least a couple of weeks, probably longer. Andrew Jensen took a puck to the head two weeks ago, and the doctors can't give me any indication as to when he'll be cleared. My guess is it could be a while. He might not be back before the play-offs, if then. He hasn't shown any sign of improvement yet. Keith Burns is playing through a hairline fracture in his foot, and it could deteriorate to the point that he can't play through the pain at any moment. Whether that happens or not, he's not nearly as effective right now as normal, and he can't play as many minutes as he usually does for us. Dominic Medved has had recurring groin issues all season, and I don't think the doctors are convinced he's in the clear. That means we're completely without two of our top three defensemen, the third is only able to give us about fifty percent of what he could if he was healthy, I've got an aging role player who may or may not come up lame at any moment, and my healthy D are young, inexperienced, and being asked to fill roles they aren't ready for. That's where you come in."

"You just tell me what you want me to do, Jim. I'll do it. I'm ready." If his words weren't enough to convince me, the eagerness in his tone would have done the trick. A motivated player could make a world of difference in our current situation.

These days, we were in the hunt for the Stanley Cup every year. In fact, last season, the boys had taken it all the way to Game Five of the finals before crumbling to the pressure put on them by the Lightning. The three seven-game series that had come before the finals might have had something to do with our eventual collapse. The Lightning had gone into that last series well rested, having swept two of their three series and only needing five games in the third of them.

All those extra games my guys had played in the summer had meant they didn't get as much recovery time before this season started as they needed. I knew that had a lot to do with the current injury issues we were facing, but there wasn't much I could do about it. You had to play all those extra games if you wanted to win the Cup, and if you weren't fighting tooth and nail to win the Cup, you had no business being in this league.

My guys wanted to win.

Chris Hammond had won before, he wanted to win again, and he could help us do exactly that.

"The coaches and I have talked about it a lot," I said. "We aren't going to ask you to do anything but what you do best—defend well and provide a voice of experience. Right now, we want you to come in and help keep the younger guys calm on the ice, so they don't make stupid decisions with the puck. You've got years in this league under your belt. You've played in all the toughest situations and on the biggest stages. I know they say you've lost a step, but I just want you to come in and be a steadying presence on the blue line, a reassuring voice on the bench."

A ghost of a smile crossed his face. "I can do that. You just give me a chance to prove it."

I nodded, giving him another once-over to be sure my instincts still told me what they'd been telling me about him all along. Then I leaned forward and put my elbows on the desk, making a steeple with my hands. "All right. Let's get your agent on speakerphone and work out the details of your contract, then."

Twenty minutes later, the Storm had a new veteran defenseman, and I could breathe a bit more freely. Amid the jingling of bells from the wreath hanging from my office door, I walked him out to my assistant's desk so she could have him sign on all the appropriate lines of his new contract, but when we got there, I stopped short.

Rachel wasn't alone at her desk like I had expected to find her. She was surrounded by some of my players' and coaches' wives, and they all looked up at me with guilty expressions and backed away from Rachel's desk as soon as they saw me.

Well, not all. David Weber was one of our assistant coaches. His wife, Laura, gave me an appraising look as she slowly stepped back. She'd given me that look several times before, usually when she was trying to get people involved with the team to allow themselves to be auctioned off for charity or to walk a runway to raise money for some cause or another. I'd come to expect her frankness and the way she volunteered people to do what she wanted without asking them first. It was definitely something I could respect and appreciate.

"What project are you signing me up for this time?" I asked, letting out a lighthearted chuckle. I knew better than to think I'd be thrilled about whatever she had planned for me, but I also knew I would go along with it. Everyone did, eventually. Laura had a magnetic personality and an authoritative manner that brooked no argument.

She pursed her lips and narrowed her eyes at me, then gave the other women a victorious smile. "You'll see," was all she said. Then she turned to Rachel. "So we're all set?"

"All set," Rachel said, and the rest of them scurried off down the hall toward the stairs, leaving me with Rachel and Hammer.

"Do I want to know?" I asked my assistant.

Her freckled cheeks turned pink, which wasn't uncommon. It was a curse of being a redhead, I'd come to learn in the years she'd been working for me. In lieu of answering my question, she reached for the stack of papers that I'd just sent to her printer and motioned for my new defenseman to take the seat across from her.

"You're not going to tell me?"

"Consider it our Christmas gift to you," she replied.

That could either be a good thing or a very bad thing, and based on the wink in her tone, I was leaning toward the *bad* end of the spectrum.

Elaine

SOME PEOPLE MIGHT call it a midlife crisis. I wasn't one of them.

Yes, I was starting all over again at the age of fifty. Yes, it scared me to death and made me think maybe I'd lost my mind. The truth was that I hadn't lost my mind, though. I'd just finally come to a point in which I was determined to be exactly who I was and nothing else, to treat myself right, and let the chips fall where they may. Everyone in my life might not agree with or approve of my choices, but I wasn't going to let insecurities or the opinions of others rule my life anymore. If I was being completely honest with myself, I just plain didn't have time for that.

Granted, it had taken a kick in the pants from my twenty-four-year-old son, Dillon, to convince me.

"You deserve to find a good man, Mom," he'd said to me at Thanksgiving as he'd squeezed his girlfriend's hand. "And he's out there. I know he is; you just have to open yourself up to finding him."

"I am open to finding him."

He'd given me *the look* over the top of our turkey—the same look that reminded me so much of his father and caused my heart to squeeze every time the recognition hit me square in the chest.

"Okay," he'd said, "so maybe you're open to *finding* him, but you're not so open to *letting him into your life*. For years, you used me as an excuse for shutting yourself off from having a man around, but I'm all grown up now. You don't have to keep protecting me. It's time for you to look after yourself. I don't like that you're all alone."

"He's right, Elaine," Kelsey said, nodding and giving me a sympathetic smile. She was his girlfriend. In fact, I was beginning to think she might be *the one*.

Point taken. As hard as it might be for me to admit it, my little boy was right. And he wasn't a little boy anymore but a man, the same age as his father had been when we'd first met.

After Jim had admitted to an extramarital affair, I'd taken Dillon and left. Jim had sworn it had only happened once. That it would never happen again. But the fact was, he'd cheated. He had been an adult, and he'd made a choice, and that choice had devastated me.

Not once in all those years had I seriously entertained the thought of letting another man get close enough to hurt me or my son so deeply. I'd also never been able to forget the man I'd loved and given my heart to only to have it flung in my face.

But it had been twenty years. Two full decades. Dillon was a man now. He was a *good* man, too. He had a career he loved, a steady girlfriend who—I hoped—would soon be my daughter-in-law, and he was thriving, despite not having his father in his life since he was only four years old.

So, to fulfill my promise to Dillon and Kelsey that I'd try to find the good man who they swore was out there waiting for me, I'd set up a profile on Match.com the day after Thanksgiving. That was how the two of them had met, after all, and their relationship was flourishing. She was absolutely perfect for my son, and I loved her to bits for it.

In the intervening weeks, there had been dozens of men who'd contacted me through the web service. Most of them were as skeevy as

I could imagine and then some. A few had seemed decent enough that I'd agreed to go out for coffee, but once I'd met them I'd realized they were miles away from being the sort of man I'd want to spend more than an hour with, let alone the rest of my life. None of them had the same ready smile that Jim had always had, or the huge, giving heart, or the desire to help others the way he always had. No matter what, it all kept coming back to Jim.

I was on the verge of giving up, in all honesty. Maybe online dating worked for some people, but I seemed to only find creepers.

But then last week, Kelsey had convinced me to expand my net. She'd encouraged me to search through profiles of men who might be long distance instead of localized to the Minneapolis-St. Paul metropolitan area, and see whom Match might pair me up with.

I hadn't had time to take a look since I'd made the change until now. There wasn't any point in denying that my nerves were through the roof when I logged in to my account.

The first few Match suggestions I came across were as squicky as the men I'd encountered in the early weeks of my endeavor. I checked the boxes to delete them and moved on down the list. There was one man in his early sixties who lived near Chicago and sounded promising. He'd been married for over thirty years and was a widower looking to connect with someone. Three kids, two grandchildren, and, best of all, no dick pic in his profile. I moved him to my maybe list and scrolled down to see who else there was before making a decision as to whether I should contact the widowed grandpa.

And then my heart stopped. Completely quit beating. My chest tightened around it, sending tears to my eyes before, slowly, my pulse kicked back into gear. Because there, smiling back at me through my computer monitor the way he always had in person, was Jim.

He was older, sure. His hair was all gray now, and he wore glasses, but it was definitely the man who still owned my heart. Everything always seemed to point me back in his direction.

I knew what he looked like these days, even without the photo reminder. After all the years he'd spent playing in the NHL, he'd gone on to become a team executive. It had been easy to follow his career since he'd spent so much of it in the limelight. I wouldn't deny it—I still stalked him online sometimes, keeping up with the teams he'd worked for and watching interviews so I could hear his voice. No matter how many wrinkles he might have, and no matter how gray his hair had turned, his voice was still the same.

He'd hurt me deeply—there was no point arguing that fact—but I still craved the sound of his voice. Sometimes, twenty years later, I woke up in the middle of the night and felt for him in the bed next to me, my heart breaking all over again when my hand came up empty.

Because that's how I had felt without him all these years.

Empty.

In the twenty years since I'd left, the hurt had lessened and forgiveness had blossomed in my heart, even though Dillon still held the sort of grudge that only a boy who'd been deprived of his father could hold. Even though I'd forgiven Jim, though, I wasn't prepared for the kind of gut-wrenching, heart-squeezing response I was currently experiencing over finding his profile on a silly dating site.

I knew I shouldn't do it, that putting myself through this was only asking for trouble, but I couldn't stop myself. I clicked on his profile and read every single word.

It turned out it wasn't Jim who'd created the profile, even. Some of his players' wives had covertly put it together. They'd written: *For years, we've watched as Jim has given dozens of people—players and otherwise—a second chance, but we've never seen him do it for himself. We know he was married once. We don't know what happened to bring that marriage to an end, but at this point it doesn't matter. He's the kindest man any of us know, and he deserves to have someone in his life who will love him the way he loves every single person he's come into contact with. And because of that, we want to help him out. Maybe give him a little shove in the right direction. If you think you might be that woman—if you want to be treated like a queen by a kind, considerate, caring, loving, giving man— then send us a message. We would love to talk to you.*

My phone rang, and I glanced down to see Dillon's name and photo flashing at me. I swiped my thumb over the screen to answer. "Hello?"

"Mom?" He waited a beat. Then, "Why are you crying?" he demanded.

Was I crying?

I reached up to my cheek with my other hand and came away with salty tears on my fingertips. How was it that my son could tell that from only hearing a single word from my mouth, and I didn't even realize it was happening? And how long had I been sitting here with tears falling down my cheeks? I glanced down to find dark, wet spots on my shirt. Big ones. I must have been at it for a while. It might have even started the instant I'd seen Jim's picture pop up on my monitor.

"Mom?" Dillon repeated.

"I'm fine." *Fine* probably wasn't the right word, but I wasn't sure what would be better.

"You don't sound fine."

"Well, maybe I'm not right this minute. But I will be."

"What's going on?"

I rested the phone between my cheek and my shoulder so I could use both hands to type a response to the women who wanted to set up my ex-husband. "I think I'm about to reconcile with your father."

Silence met me on the other end of the line.

Chapter Two

Elaine

TWO DAYS BEFORE Christmas, I stood at baggage claim at PDX, luggage in hand, and searched the sea of faces for Laura Weber. She'd texted me a picture of herself so I'd know who I was looking for, but I was shaking so hard I wasn't sure I'd recognize the back of my own hand. I hadn't been this nervous since the day of my wedding. Lucky for me, she tapped me on the shoulder before I'd found her.

"Here," she said, passing me a brown paper bag that undoubtedly held a bottle of wine. She took the handles of one of my suitcases. "Can't drink it in the car, but there's no law that says you can't drink it before you get in."

I took a breath, and then I took the wine.

She passed me her keys, which had a corkscrew attached.

"How did you know this was exactly what I'd need?"

"Just a guess. I've always got some handy." She headed out of the building toward the parking lot.

"You're an angel." I followed her, taking a long swallow and hauling my other bag behind me.

"Be sure to tell my husband that when you meet him, because when he finds out that I've been meddling with Jim's love life…" She shook her head.

"You're meddling for good reason, though."

"I don't think Dave will see it that way, but we'll run with your suggestion for now. I like it better than reality." She stopped behind an

SUV and clicked the remote so the back end would open. We loaded the bags in, and she glanced at her watch as she closed it. "We've got time before the game tonight to get you checked in at your hotel if you want, or we can head over to meet up with the other girls and introduce you around. Some of them can't get to the arena until later, but my daughters are both there already, and Paige Bergstrom said she and her girls would probably be there early, too."

As much as heading to the hotel first sounded appealing, I knew it was a bad idea. It would only allow me more opportunities to chicken out, and I didn't leave Dillon and Kelsey at Christmas in order to get cold feet. I had to do this. I shook my head. "Let's just go to the arena."

"Whatever you want," she said. She took the wine, replaced the cork, and packed the bottle in the back with all my things before we climbed into our seats.

On the way, she chitchatted about everything under the moon *except* digging to find out details about what had happened between me and Jim. I'd been expecting her to grill me about the reason for our split the second I landed, since she hadn't delved into it when I'd first contacted her, but she was avoiding that subject like stinky feet.

It preyed on my mind, though. Would Jim want to see me? Would he be amenable to trying to get back together again? While it was true that he'd been in the wrong when he'd cheated on me, the intervening years had opened my eyes to some of my own faults. Like the fact that I hadn't believed him when he'd claimed it had only happened once, despite all the evidence pointing toward his words being the truth. Or how I hadn't given him the benefit of the doubt when he'd promised it would never happen again. Then there was the fact that I hadn't thought twice about ending the best thing that had ever happened to me after one single—albeit devastating—bad decision. And I couldn't ignore the fact that I'd indirectly deprived a good man of a relationship with his son, and my son of a relationship with his father, all because of one single mistake.

A huge mistake, yes.

But it was just one. And no one was perfect—certainly not me—so it wasn't fair of me to expect perfection from Jim. That hadn't stopped me from expecting it, or from being furious when he'd proven himself to be human. The least I could have done at the time was agree to talk it out with him, or to go to counseling. To see if we could have found a way to work through it. But I hadn't given him—*us*—a chance. There was no excusing what he'd done, but in recent years I'd started to think about all the what ifs. What if I'd stayed?

All of this kept racing through my head as Laura nattered on and drove us to the arena. The effect of it all combined with the wine she'd given me left me nauseated.

"I might have made a mistake," I interrupted her.

She stopped talking and kept her eyes on the road ahead of us. I turned in my seat to see her more fully. She had the look of a woman weighing her words.

"You want to go to the hotel first?" she finally asked me, although it was clear from her tone that she hadn't missed my meaning.

I shook my head. "I think I should just go home. Pretend I never came out here. Forget I ever saw Jim's profile on that stupid website."

"But you *did* see it, and you *came*. I understand being nervous, but why not let this play out and see what will come of it?"

My tears were back, and this time I was fully aware of them. I blinked against the sting, trying to keep the silly things at bay. No use. They spilled over my cheeks, surely ruining my makeup.

"Now don't go getting yourself all worked up until you know if there's a good reason for it. Here," she said, rummaging in the console between us. She took out a tissue pack and handed it to me. "I'm all for having a good cry sometimes, but you've got to get the timing right. This isn't it."

"Thank you," I said through my sniffles. I took out a tissue and dried my eyes. Then I flipped down the sun visor. There was a mirror on the back, thank goodness. Apparently I hadn't completely destroyed my makeup.

Yet.

The arena loomed large to the right, and Laura turned that direction. Before I had completely fixed the damage I'd caused to my makeup, she was being waved into the parking garage by the attendant.

"If you're going to puke, please wait until you're out of my car."

"Trying," I forced out. "You don't think there's any chance Jim won't be around tonight, do you? Maybe he's sick? Or what if he decided to travel early to go check out the World Juniors or something?"

"Keep dreaming, hon. He's going to be here. Rachel made sure of it. And everything's going to be fine. I'm sure of it."

By the time she'd found a spot to park, I'd reined my nerves in enough to put on a brave face, despite the anxiety doing a tap dance in my belly. She opened the back and took out the bottle of wine. When I came around to join her, she thrust it in my hands.

"For courage. Drink some more. It'll help."

I'd never been much of a drinker, but now seemed as good a time as any to follow her advice. I took a long swallow before tucking it beside my luggage and nodding that I was ready.

She took me by the elbow and guided me into the building. Almost a dozen women and their kids turned with excited smiles when we walked into the owner's box on the suite level. They swarmed over to embrace me, each of them drawing me in for a hug and gushing about how perfect it all was and what a great surprise my arrival would be for Jim. Completely numb, other than the buzz from drinking my wine too fast, I could do nothing more than smile and nod as they welcomed me.

Until a young girl with Down syndrome put both arms around my waist and hugged me tighter than anyone but Dillon had ever done before. She took my breath away with her sweetness, both literally and figuratively. When she finally let go, she held up a sprig of mistletoe with a red bow tied around it and handed it to me.

"This is for you and Mr. Jim. I told Mom you needed it because it would help. It worked for Q and Miss Mia. They told me all about it."

"Well, thank you..." I fingered the bow, debating whether I should hold on to it or toss it and run as fast as I could back to Minnesota. Because, while I'd forgiven Jim for everything he'd done, I wasn't sure he was ready to forgive himself. Or me. How could he forgive me for taking his son out of his life? That was at least as egregious as the fact that he'd cheated. I wasn't going to make excuses for him, but I couldn't make excuses for myself, either.

But I couldn't run. I'd already argued about what I was doing with Dillon enough. The last thing I needed was to disappear before I'd seen it through.

Jim

"A PROBLEM? WHAT kind of problem?" I barked into my phone, already racing toward the elevators on the press-box level at the Moda Center before Rachel could answer.

"Just get down here quick," she said. Then she hung up the phone, not giving me the chance to get any more information out of her. Or any information at all, actually.

The game was as good as over, and going well, thanks in no small part to Hammer's steadying presence on the back end. Medved had gone off early in the first period, limping like he'd pulled his groin again, so we'd only had five *D* out there for the majority of the game. But none of them had panicked. Burnzie and Hammer kept their cool, and that rubbed off on 501, Harry, and Demidov. It didn't matter who'd gone out there without his regular partner; they'd just gotten the job done. And even though it had been a low-scoring game, we'd gotten two quick goals in the second period—only twelve seconds apart—and Nicky Ericsson was working on his third shutout of the season.

There were only five minutes left in the third, but anything could happen in that time. Our two goals were proof enough of that. Rachel knew how fast things could change in this game as well as anyone. She wouldn't have called me away from watching the boys unless there was a damned good reason for it.

Maybe someone was hurt. Or somehow someone got past security and was in there with the guys' wives and kids when they shouldn't have been. I didn't know what was going on, but it was definitely *something*, not to mention important. Which explained why I was out of breath and more than halfway to full panic by the time I rushed through the doors of the owner's box.

Then I couldn't breathe for an entirely different reason.

Instead of chaos greeting me, it was Elaine.

My ex-wife.

The woman who still owned my heart, even all these years later.

The woman whose heart I'd broken in a moment of youthful weakness and utter stupidity.

It had been nearly twenty years since I'd last laid eyes on her. I'd talked to her over the phone in that time, making sure she and Dillon had everything they needed, getting reports about him once he'd become a teenager and refused to have anything to do with me, but phone calls weren't the same as seeing her in the flesh.

Her hair was still blond, her eyes a beautiful moss green. She had on a sweater that matched her eyes and looked as soft as silk. The last time I'd seen her in the flesh, she'd had the most perfect, flawless skin. It still glowed today, but there were a few wrinkles around her eyes and mouth. Not anywhere near as many as I had, and somehow they only made her more beautiful to me.

My arms ached to hold her.

But Elaine wasn't mine, and she hadn't been for a long time. She never would be again. I'd lost her and my self-respect in a single act. I'd been working to regain my opinion of myself ever since, but I knew better than to think I could ever win my wife back.

Some hurts dig too deep. Some scars never fade.

"Hi," she said, sounding as breathless as I felt. Her voice had changed. It was a bit lower than I remembered. Rougher around the edges. Sexy as all hell.

I nodded, my tongue too thick to respond to her, and forced my mind back to figuring out what Rachel had called me down here for. I spotted my assistant's bright red hair in the crowd and gave her a questioning look, since I couldn't make my mouth work.

"Merry Christmas, Jim," Rachel said. She waved her arm toward Elaine, as if that was enough explanation.

And it hit me.

This was what she'd been up to with Laura Weber and the other wives last week.

This was the surprise.

Not *this*—Elaine.

I didn't know how they'd managed to get her here. Couldn't fathom what they might have told her to convince her to come. All I knew was it would backfire. Go up in flames.

Because I'd cheated on her.

There wasn't anything I could do to change the past.

There wasn't a damned thing I could do to be worthy of Elaine's understanding, and without that, there was no point in them bringing her here.

"I'm sorry," I said, first to Rachel and the other wives. But then I met Elaine's eyes and held her gaze. "I'm so sorry," I said again.

She shook her head, and a soft look came into her eyes.

It wasn't enough. It would never be enough, but it was all I had. It was the only thing I could give her. Then I spun around and headed out of there before I made a fool of myself, begging her for the forgiveness I would never deserve.

Chapter Three

Elaine

I SHOULDN'T HAVE come. I shouldn't have been stupid enough to think that he was ready for us to move on from the mistakes we'd made in the past.

That much was clear from the fact that Jim would rather walk away from me than say more than three words, let alone hear what I had to say to him. The way he'd apologized, his voice filled with intense anguish and his eyes full of regret, had ripped me to shreds as much as everything that had happened all those years ago.

The only thing I'd accomplished by showing up here was to rip open an old wound for both of us. For Dillon, too. And maybe I'd tossed some salt on all three of those wounds while I was at it.

My heart in my throat, my feet cemented to the floor, I watched Jim walk away. The last time he'd gone, I'd been a sobbing, screaming mess, throwing things at his retreating form to hurry him along. This time, I was desperate for him to stop. To turn around. To come back. But I couldn't seem to find the gumption to tell him.

"If you don't go after him, I will," Laura said from somewhere in the sea of women and children behind me. "We all will."

"This was a mistake. The whole thing. I shouldn't be here."

"Then why did you come? Why did you get on a plane and fly halfway across the country—away from your son at Christmas—if all you're going to do is say hi and let him turn his back on you?" Laura took my arm and turned me to face her. A scowl marred her otherwise flawless features. "Look, I'm not going to sit here and pretend I know what happened between you two. I don't know what split you up or kept you apart for so long. I don't know why you came back now. I don't have the first clue what it is he's so sorry about. But I do know this. You clearly still love him or you wouldn't have made the effort. He still loves you or he wouldn't be beating himself up like he is. And you know what? We all adore Jim. Every single person in this room, and all of his players. Everyone involved with this organization. We love him. We want the best for him. Now, maybe that's you. But if you don't chase after him, if you don't stop him and make him talk to you, then I doubt it. He deserves someone who's willing to insist he take a dose of his own medicine, even if he's fighting against it."

I hadn't gotten to know Laura very well in the brief time we'd been acquainted, but I appreciated her frankness. She was right. Absolutely one hundred percent right. No matter how nervous I might be, and no matter how my doubts might be screwing with my head, there was a lot of truth to what she said.

So I took a breath.

I squared my shoulders.

And I took off after my ex-husband, only to be stopped by a small but strong and insistent hand on my elbow.

"You almost forgot your mistletoe," Sophie said, pressing the beribboned bundle into my hand.

I fingered the satin ribbon and forced an anxious smile to my lips. "Wouldn't want to forget that." Or would I? If Jim was running off, he probably wouldn't be inclined to fall prey to a silly holiday tradition, even if I worked up the nerve to try to make use of it. Still, I thanked her and hurried on my way.

Jim was well ahead of me in the corridor, but I could still make out his retreating form. There wasn't much time left on the game clock, though, which meant that the jam-packed arena would soon be emptying. I had to catch him before the final buzzer, or I wouldn't have a chance. The crowd would make it impossible.

I couldn't remember a time in my life that I'd run in pumps, but there was no time like the present to start.

"Jim!" I called out. The noises from the ongoing game drowned out my shout, submerging my voice under the excited chatter, the hustle and bustle of almost twenty thousand people on the edges of their seats.

He didn't even flinch. My shouts didn't have a chance in hell of carrying through all of this. I increased my pace to match the frantic beat of my heart, but he was getting close to the elevator bay. If he got on...

"Jim!" I shouted once more, sounding desperate even to my own ears.

He didn't hear me, but the security guard standing next to the elevator did. He said something to Jim and pointed in my direction. Thank the Lord for small blessings. That held Jim up enough that I was able to reach him, puffing and panting and clutching at the stitch in my side.

He looked at me with the same pained expression of moments ago and shook his head. "Why are you here, Elaine?"

I fumbled with the mistletoe in my hands, staring down at the ribbon and smoothing it between my thumb and forefinger. Then I shrugged. "I'm not sure." I glanced up at him as I said it, gauging his reaction.

He shuffled his feet, glancing back at the security guard still within earshot. Then he nodded his head toward a quiet corner near the window overlooking the highway below.

I followed, tempted to reach for his hand. It was too soon for that. Way too soon. Especially if I couldn't even articulate the thousands of emotions that had been racing through me for days. Hell, for years. I wasn't even sure how long ago it was that I'd forgiven him.

He shoved his hands in his pockets, taking that choice away from me. "You've traveled a long way to not know why you came."

The horn sounded in the distance, making the floor reverberate beneath us. Within seconds, thousands of fans poured out of the stands into the concourse, their voices flooding the air. They all headed straight for the escalators, though, leaving us alone in our corner. I glanced over my shoulder at the sea of happy faces, many of them wearing red Santa hats and other holiday gear to complement their purple-and-silver Storm jerseys.

Contemplating my words carefully, I met Jim's gaze head on. I still didn't know how to articulate everything that had been keeping me up at night. "The girls said you didn't know they were trying to set you up," I said, since I had to start somewhere.

His jaw dropped. "With you? How did they find you? Why would...?"

"They didn't. Not exactly." I twirled the ribbon around one finger, slowly unwrapping it. "I found you."

Jim shook his head, not following.

"They listed you on Match.com."

He dragged a hand down his face in embarrassment.

"That's where I found your profile. And I... I knew I had to contact them. Because if I didn't, I would regret it for the rest of my life."

"Regret it? I don't—"

"I want another chance, Jim."

"You're not the one who needs another chance. You're not—"

"I do need another chance," I cut in, tears suddenly making tracks down my cheeks. I should have gone without makeup. It was a rookie mistake, and I was way too old to be making slipups like that. But it had been so long since I'd dated, since I'd been with a man at all, that I felt like a complete novice where all of this was concerned. "You made a bad decision. I'm not denying that. But I did, too."

"You left because I cheated on you," he said, without even a hint of humor. The lines in his face deepened, like cuts digging into his flesh. "You didn't cheat. You made the only decision that made sense."

"That wasn't the only decision I could have made. And I'm not convinced it was the right choice. We could've gone into counseling. We could have tried to make it work."

"You deserve better than that. I didn't honor our vows."

"I'm not saying you're a saint. You screwed up, and nothing can change that. But you know what I deserve? I deserve to love and be loved. I think we could have that, if you're willing to try. You said it was a mistake that would haunt you for the rest of your life. And it *has* haunted you, hasn't it? Have you—" I stopped, shaking my head.

"Have I what?" His voice, usually so steady and sure, cracked and dissipated.

"Have you ever even dated since I left?"

He shrugged, like it wasn't a big deal.

"Because I don't think you have," I said. "I've been watching you all these years. Following your career. Stalking you in my own way, I guess you could say. Never once have I seen a woman on your arm at an event. There's never been mention of one in an interview. Nothing."

"Have you been dating, then?" This time, it was Jim giving me *the look*, like Dillon had at Thanksgiving. "It's been just as long for you. How well have you moved on?"

"Not well. I'm trying, though. That's why I'm here."

"Maybe I'm not ready to try."

"Not ready?" I asked. "Or is it that you don't think you should?"

"Some things you just can't ever come back from. Some mistakes are too big."

"Says who? The man who gives everyone under the moon a second chance?"

He rolled his eyes.

"I've been paying attention. You're constantly taking on guys everyone else has given up on. Brenden Campbell."

"I played with his father. You remember that."

"He's far from the only one," I said. "Blake Kozlow. No one wanted to touch him. They all said he was a lost cause, full of talent but bound to flame out, but you brought him on. You made him part of the team. You gave him a place to belong. Rachel told me she was one of your hard luck cases, too. And you just did it again with Hammond."

"That's different."

"It's not."

"It's hockey."

"It's your *life*," I insisted. "It's what you do every day. Every time you see someone who seems down on their luck, you find a way to give them a helping hand."

"I'm not down on my luck."

I swung my arms in frustration, trying to come up with an argument he wouldn't immediately shoot down. His eyes followed my hand.

"Mistletoe?" he asked, his tone lightening slightly.

"Sophie gave it to me. She thought it would help."

"Sophie?" Jim chuckled slightly, shaking his head. "They're really all in on this, aren't they?"

"I think so. At least most of your players' wives, and several of the coaches' wives, too."

"And the kids."

"Yeah." I went back to twirling the ribbon around my finger.

"That's what I get for trying to make this thing like a family. They all gang up on me."

They were the only family he had, since I'd left him and Dillon had cut him out of his life. I knew why he worked so hard at making things a family atmosphere with this team, whether anyone else knew or not. That was something that had become abundantly clear to me during the game, when I'd been up in the owner's box with the family. Every person here cared about everyone else. And him. Especially him. "They love you, Jim," I said. I doubted they could help it.

He shook it off. "It's just because I'm the GM."

"It's not. It's because you're you."

Everyone had always loved him, as long as I'd known him. It'd been easy to fall in love with him. He had a smile for everyone he met, and he had such a big heart. The day we first met, I'd known right away that I was in trouble. He'd been out at the bar after a game with a bunch of his teammates. I'd been there with some girlfriends from college. I'd been underage. The girls had snuck me in with a fake ID, but I hadn't been brave enough to order a real drink the whole night.

At one point, the other girls had all been off flirting with various men, leaving me alone. An overly drunk guy from my school had come on to me and wouldn't back off. I was trying to figure out a way to get away from him when Jim had come along. He'd put an arm around the guy's shoulders, told a few jokes, and led the guy to the bar—well away from me. When Jim had returned, he'd brought a Shirley Temple for me, since the bartender had told him what I'd been drinking all night.

Thank you, I'd said. *For the drink* and *for getting rid of him.*

No big deal. I signed his arm and made sure his buddies would get him home safe. And then he'd smiled at me. *Do you have anyone making sure you get home safe?*

I'd held up my Shirley Temple, as a reminder. *I'm the designated driver tonight.*

So I guess that means you won't let me drive you home and walk you to your door, huh?

Do guys still do that? Walk a girl to her door? Seems kind of old-fashioned.

He'd grinned, a smile that had lit up his blue eyes like the sky on a clear spring afternoon. *Maybe not all guys. But I do. I guess you could say I'm an old-fashioned kind of guy.*

Old fashioned is good, I'd said. And I'd melted a bit.

He'd hung around and talked to me the rest of the night, staying right by my side to make sure the creep wouldn't return. When the time had come for me to drive the other girls home, he'd followed me to each of their apartments and then followed me to mine. And he'd walked me to my door, waiting to hear me click the lock into place. He didn't walk away until I'd given him my phone number, though, having me slip it under the door on a torn-off scrap of notebook paper.

That was all it had taken for me to fall in love with him. And over the years, I'd watched as he'd worked the same magic on countless others. He'd always had a ready smile and a heart too big to fit in his chest, which worked as a magnet. Everyone was drawn to him.

Yet somehow, he'd always had a hard time showing himself the same compassion that he gave freely to everyone around him, whether they deserved it or not.

It was time for that to change. Jim needed a dose of his own medicine. And apparently, it was up to me to be sure he got it. I'd forgiven him long ago; now I needed to help him find a way to forgive himself.

Chapter Four

Jim

IT'S BECAUSE YOU'RE *you*. Elaine's words kept rolling through my mind on repeat, and I wished I could believe them. But so did other words that had once come from her lips, and they were much louder and more insistent. *How could you? I kept waiting for you to call so Dillon and I could tell you happy birthday, but you were too busy with some puck bunny slut to bother with your wife and son.*

In twenty years, I'd never been able to get those words out of my head. I might be able to push them aside briefly, but they always came back to haunt me.

I'd been on the road with a new team after being traded at the deadline. Elaine and Dillon had stayed behind in Hartford, since she hadn't been able to pack up everything and come with me at the drop of a hat. I hadn't seen her or my son in weeks, I didn't know or like my new teammates yet, and I was lonely. Insanely lonely. So instead of doing the smart thing and going back to my hotel room to call them, I'd ended up at a bar on my birthday, and I'd had way too much to drink, and I'd made the biggest mistake of my life.

Admitting it as soon as possible didn't absolve me from what I'd done. Nothing could erase the past.

Since Elaine had already been busy packing up our entire house, it had been easy enough for her to put it all in a moving truck headed back to her hometown in Minnesota instead of going all the way across the country to join me in LA.

And that had been that.

I'd screwed up, so I had to be a man and accept the consequences. Those consequences weren't supposed to include my ex-wife standing in front of me two decades later and asking for another chance.

The noise around us seemed to press in even though we were still well away from the crowd. Elaine folded her arms in front of her, tucking the mistletoe away and holding herself as if a chill had taken hold of her. It wouldn't be a surprise. She'd always gotten cold easily, and they kept it nice and cool in the arena for our games. So many nights, she'd burrowed up against me, trying to absorb as much of my warmth as she could. Out of instinct, I took off my suit jacket and put it around her shoulders.

"Thank you," she said.

"We should..." *We shouldn't be doing this.* "Can we go somewhere and talk?"

I wasn't sure where that had come from, but she was here. It seemed like the least I could do after she'd made this kind of effort.

"How about a coffee?"

"I can do coffee. Let's go get your purse."

She made a face.

"What?"

"I haven't checked into my hotel yet. My bags are still in Laura's SUV. She was going to take me. I don't want—"

"Let's get your bags, then. I'll make sure you get to your hotel safe." But then I thought of the first time I'd met her. That had been a bar and me following her to her apartment, but the similarity was undeniable.

A soft smile came over her face, and she looked down at the floor. No doubt she was remembering the same thing I was. "You never change, do you, Jim?"

"I've changed a lot."

She chuckled. "Not really. Not in the important ways."

I didn't know what to do with that, so I started walking back toward the owner's box so we could get Laura and go down to the parking garage. Elaine came alongside me, her fingers clutching the lapels of my jacket.

I couldn't seem to help myself. I put my hand on the small of her back like I'd done so many times before.

My heart hurt with wanting.

Christmas was always difficult enough for me, because I had to spend it alone. But this… This was too much.

Elaine

"I MADE A mistake," I said, warming my hands on my cup of vanilla latte. The bit of mistletoe Sophie had given me rested on the table between us, safely within reach but also *not* over either of our heads. Most of the employees had on Santa hats, and someone had painted Santa and his reindeer on the windows. Holiday tunes came over the sound system to go along with the festive air the staff had created.

In the Starbucks he'd brought me to, the air was warmer than the arena had been, but I was still chilly. He hadn't asked for me to return his jacket, not even when we'd gone outside in the almost-freezing air. Not only that, but he'd bought my coffee, opened doors for me, and held out my chair to help me sit. It only made me believe what I'd told him more than ever before. He was still exactly the same in all the ways that mattered. Now I needed to convince him of that.

"*I* made a mistake," Jim interrupted.

I scowled and held up a hand. "Let me finish, please. You've had twenty years to beat yourself up over your mistakes. But you weren't alone."

"I haven't been beating myself up over it all this time."

"Haven't you? Tell me why it is you're so intent on helping everyone you come across who's made a mistake, then?"

"Everyone makes mistakes."

I raised my brows to make a point. "Right. Everyone makes mistakes. You did. And so did I, because I gave up on you. I didn't give us a chance to get through the bad times. *For better or for worse, for richer or for poorer, in sickness and in health.* All marriages go through tough times. When I married you, I promised to stick by your side when we hit those tough times. But I didn't. I walked away, even though I loved you more than I loved anyone but Dillon, even though it ripped my heart to shreds to leave you. I *know* you, Jim."

"You *knew* me."

I shook my head. "No, I *know* you. I know you'll do anything in your power to make someone smile. I know you're always looking out for everyone around you, often to your own detriment. I know you beat yourself up when you make a mistake and then work ten times harder than everyone else to be sure you'll never make that same mistake again. And I know I was wrong to not give you another chance, because if things were reversed—if I were the one who'd cheated—you would have given me another opportunity to prove myself. Because that's who you are. It's what you do."

Jim stared out the window for a long time, and I could practically see the wheels spinning in his head. Which meant I was starting to get through to him. I was chipping away at all the doubts that had been eating him from the inside for years. He took off his glasses and folded in the earpieces before meeting my eyes.

"So what are you saying?"

"I'm saying it's my turn. You give everyone a second chance. I want mine. And I want you to take yours, for once."

"I gathered that much," he said. He fumbled with his glasses before finally setting them down next to the mistletoe. "I guess what I mean is *why?* Why now?"

And that was the question I'd been asking myself ever since the moment I'd told Dillon what I planned to do. I took a sip, stalling for time. The hit of warmth and caffeine gave me courage, and I decided to spit it out before I could change my mind. "Because I love you. I've never stopped loving you, and I don't think I ever will. And I think you still love me, too."

Tears started pricking at the backs of my eyes again. Because I was afraid. What if I was wrong? What if Dillon had been right when he'd told me I'd lost my mind? What if Jim really *did* have some other woman in his life, but he kept her out of the public eye? What if I'd just left everything out there on a whim, laid my heart on the table between us, and it was all for nothing?

The truth was, he might not love me anymore. I hoped he did. I'd taken a huge risk on that hope, and it could come back to bite me in the butt. When I'd left and taken our son with me, it had to have hurt him as deeply as his infidelity had hurt me. Was it too much? Or the time? Had it been too long?

He hadn't said a word since I'd made my declaration. Seconds kept ticking by on my watch, counting down to the moment he would either hand my heart back to me—carefully, of course, because this was Jim—or he would accept my olive branch. And I didn't have the first clue which it would be.

The longer he took to answer, the further my heart dropped. If he had to think about it this long, it couldn't be good. Could it? Or was it just my anxiety getting in the way of thinking clearly? The music switched to the Frank Sinatra version of "I'll Be Home for Christmas." A sign? Or a slap in the face? I wasn't sure. I finished off my latte and got up to toss the cup in the garbage, but Jim reached for my hand when I would have walked past him.

"Elaine?"

My pulse skipped a few beats from his touch and the torment in his voice. "Yes?"

"What about Dillon?"

Our son was absolutely the last thing I wanted him to ask me about right now. I swallowed down the lump in my throat. "What about him?"

"What does he think about all of this?" He looked up and held my gaze as firmly as he held my hand. His grip was so warm I didn't want to break contact.

"He thinks I'm making a huge mistake," I finally said. "But he refuses to see that I forgave you for your mistakes a long time ago, and I'm trying to mend fences with you now. He's stubborn like that, kind of like his father."

The corners of Jim's lips quirked up for a moment. "Glad he's like me at least in some ways."

"He's like you in a lot of ways. Every day, he does or says something that makes me think of you."

Now, a full smile took over his face. Except for his eyes. It wasn't quite there yet. "I bet he hates that."

"He might if he knew how much alike you two are." I bit my lip, pondering my next move. "He blames you. But he should blame me just as much. It takes two to make a marriage, and it takes two to break a marriage."

"I don't want him to blame you." He teased the pad of his thumb over the back of my hand. "A man needs his mother."

"Dillon needs his father, too. He doesn't want to. But I think he'll come around."

"Do you? What makes you think that?"

I shrugged. "Just a hunch. Because I don't have any intention of walking away again. Maybe you don't want me to stick around. If you tell me to leave, to go back to Minnesota and Dillon, I will. But you're going to have to tell me to go. Otherwise, I want to make this work. And if we manage it, he'll have to get over the grudge he's holding if he wants to keep his relationship with me."

"Why would you do that?"

"Our son is a good man, Jim. But he's a man now. He's making his own decisions. He doesn't need me the way he once did." I threaded my fingers with his, and a shot of adrenaline coursed through me because he allowed it. "You know, he's dating a really sweet girl. I think he's going to ask her to marry him soon."

"Yeah?" Jim's eyes filled with both joy and sadness over that.

"Yeah. And he thinks he knows what marriage *shouldn't* be. I think we need to show him what a marriage *should* be. He needs to see that marriage is hard work. That sometimes you make mistakes in your marriage, but when you do that, you need to fight to make things right instead of running away from the things you've done wrong, or the wrongs that have been done to you. Because when you love someone the way I love you, it's not always easy. But it's still worth it."

He blinked a few times, weighing his words. "Is it really?"

"You know it is. And more than that, you're worth it."

Chapter Five

Jim

MY HEAD STILL reeling, I wheeled Elaine's suitcases behind me as we walked into the hotel lobby to the strains of Elvis's "Blue Christmas." That was one I related to all too well. Even if I spent the holidays with the family of someone on my staff—I usually got invitations from no less than a dozen people to join them—it wasn't the same as being with my own family. The holiday season was always rough on me. It would be easier if the NHL didn't shut down for those days, but I couldn't begrudge my players and coaching staff the time off.

Family is the most important thing in this world. I knew that better than anyone.

I waited while Elaine got checked in, the whole time rethinking my decision to bring her here. Why not just take her home with me? Before we'd left Starbucks, we'd agreed to spend as much time together as possible until she went back to Minnesota after the New Year, trying to work through all the decades of hurt between us so we could make a decision about the future. We hadn't so much as kissed each other yet, though, so taking her to my house felt like skipping over a bunch of crucial steps.

Tucking her wallet back into her purse, she crossed over to me and reached for the handle of one suitcase with a shy smile, shrugging her way out of my suit jacket.

I shook my head to stop her before she got the jacket all the way off. "I've got them."

She tugged on the lapels again, tightening my jacket around her body. It looked good on her, taking me back to our early days together.

"I just—I thought maybe you'd be ready to go home for the night. This has been a lot to take in. For both of us."

"It has been, but that's not a good enough reason for me to leave you until I'm sure you're safe in your room."

She chuckled and shook her head in a familiar way, but then she headed toward the elevator bay. When we got in, she pressed the button for the eighteenth floor. The strains of "I Saw Mommy Kissing Santa Claus" filled the space as we rode up. Elaine kept fingering the piece of mistletoe she'd been carrying around all night, staring down at it in her hands. It made me want to be Santa right now.

We'd held hands earlier, and she'd let me put a hand on her waist as we'd walked. But we hadn't come close to a kiss. Taking her home with me might be moving too fast, but a kiss couldn't be a bad thing. Could it?

I hadn't decided yet when the elevator doors opened and she led the way to her room.

She opened the door and held it for me to follow her in with her bags. I lifted the heavier one onto the luggage rack so she wouldn't have to struggle with it later.

She was smiling when I faced her. "See? You haven't changed a bit. Not in the ways that matter. You're still getting me safely to my door and doing all the heavy lifting."

I couldn't stop myself from smiling right along with her. This felt good. Being with her again. Talking. Hearing her voice and remembering how good we'd been together before. "Old habits die hard," I finally said.

"We're really getting old, aren't we?"

"I am. I don't know about you." To my eye, the years hadn't been as hard on her as they had on me. There was still that youthful excitement in her eyes that had initially drawn me to her, and even though tears had come easily to her eyes tonight, they hadn't stopped her from smiling and laughing.

"We were really stupid to let so many years pass," she said, sighing as she sat on the edge of the bed. She kept playing with the ribbon on the mistletoe, tangling it between her fingers and unfurling it a moment later.

Now or never. "Are you just going to play with that all night, or are you going to put it to use?"

Her eyes flickered up to meet mine. "Sophie gave it to me with a specific purpose in mind."

I raised my eyebrows in question, waiting for Elaine to take the lead. She'd been doing a good job of it all night long.

She patted the spot beside her on the bed. "Come here, Jim."

I didn't waste any time taking the seat she'd offered, heart in my throat and blood roaring through my veins.

Her chest rose and fell with shaky breaths when she tipped her face back to look at me. "We weren't this awkward the first time, were we?"

I shook my head. "It didn't mean as much then. We didn't know any better."

The first time I'd kissed her was after the first real date I'd taken her on. It was fall, and we'd gone to a park people liked to take their dogs to. Back in those days, there wasn't any such thing as a dog park, but this was as close as you could come to it. Neither of us had dogs, but it hadn't mattered in the least to either of us. We'd gone, and we'd played with other peoples' dogs in the massive piles of autumn leaves, laughing until our stomachs hurt too much to laugh any more but unable to stop.

The sun had still been out when I'd walked Elaine back to her apartment, both of us out of breath from laughing so hard. She'd nearly tripped on the steps leading up to her door, and when I'd caught her, she'd fallen into my arms. The only natural thing to do was to kiss her. So I that was exactly what I did.

I think I knew in that moment that my life was about to change for the better. But I'd only realized it once my lips were on hers, once she was in my arms.

Now, sitting next to her in this hotel room, it felt even more momentous than that first kiss had. This was it. My second chance— the only one that would ever really matter, because it was with the love of my life.

I didn't want to screw it up.

Elaine made her move at the same time I did. We bumped noses, and she laughed, the same way she had that day in the park when she'd been buried in a mountain of leaves.

There wasn't a more beautiful sound in the world.

I changed the angle of my head and tried again.

This time, I got it right.

She was still laughing, but she put a hand on the nape of my neck and tugged me closer. I might have laughed, too. But then I slid my tongue along the seam of her lips, and she opened, and our laughter got lost in a kiss.

I DIDN'T SLEEP much at all that night. My brain wouldn't shut off. It had always been a problem for me, since I'd been a little boy trying to take care of my mom after my father died. I would lie in bed for hours with thoughts racing through my head—analyzing things I could have done differently, waffling over what I needed to do next—all sorts of things that an eight-year-old boy shouldn't be thinking about. But I'd done it then, and I still did it today.

For years, I'd spent hours each night replaying the moment I'd taken that woman in the bar back to my hotel room, trying to undo what I'd done. Other nights, it had been the conversation with Elaine that had haunted my mind and kept me from sleep. Should I have pretended it hadn't happened and kept it to myself? There'd always been a Guys' Code in the league, so I doubted any of my teammates would have said a word to her. I could have kept it hidden, but it would have eaten me alive. I wouldn't have been able to live with myself. But maybe there was something else I could have done or said to convince Elaine to give me another chance. To stay with me.

The truth was, I hadn't fought for us. I'd admitted what I'd done, and I was so upset with myself over it that when she'd said she was leaving and taking Dillon with her, it had made absolute and total sense to me. I loved her too much, and at the time I'd hated myself so much for hurting her that I didn't think it was worth putting up a fight over.

I was wrong. She was right. And that was that.

But now she wanted us to try. To fight for what should have been, not for what was.

After tossing and turning in my bed for hours, wishing she was there with me so I could hold her—she'd always had a way of soothing me to sleep when I got like that—I knew there was only one thing I could do.

Fight with her, for us. When I dragged myself out of bed on Christmas Eve, still groggy and not nearly rested enough, that was the only thing in my mind. Before going to the hotel and bringing Elaine over that morning, I had a couple of things to take care of.

The first was a call to Mattias Bergstrom, the Storm's head coach, to let him know I wouldn't be joining his family for dinner after all. I supposed he'd lost the annual lottery and was stuck with babysitting me for Christmas. Granted, he probably wouldn't have described it in quite those terms, but that was how it always felt to me when someone from the Storm organization shared their holiday and their family with me.

Once I'd backed out and apologized for the short notice, I dug through my kitchen catch-all drawer until I found what I was looking for and made a trip to the mall. Leaving the jewelry store armed with a small gift-wrapped box, I headed over to pick up Elaine.

She breezed out to my car, smiling bright enough to make me forget about all the clouds that had blown in overnight. The weather forecast was calling for snow, but I wasn't sure I believed it. Not with how brightly Elaine shined today.

When she got in the car, she handed my suit jacket to me. Our fingers brushed in the transfer, sending a jolt of electricity between us. Her lips parted in an O, so she'd felt it, too.

I'd forgotten all about my jacket last night, since I was so flustered after kissing her for the first time in decades. She was making me feel like an awkward boy instead of a grown man in the wrong half of my fifties.

She gave me a sweet smile that had my heart racing. "You didn't sleep last night, did you?"

I shook my head.

"Good thoughts or bad this time?"

"A bit of both."

Once she'd tossed her small bag in the backseat and fastened her seat belt, I pulled out of the hotel parking lot.

"So… Tell me. What did you solve in your midnight ponderings?"

"Just that seeing you now, after all this time, I still love you more than I know how to handle." When I glanced at her before turning to enter the highway, she had a soft look in her eyes. She was staring at me like she was trying to see into my mind.

"Is that the good or the bad?" she asked after a moment.

"The good."

"Well, I guess I can breathe again, then. And I suppose I can guess the bad."

"You think?"

"You spent hours beating yourself up and trying to figure out what you could have done differently all those years ago, so we wouldn't have lost all this time."

Despite my better intentions, my lips quirked up in a grin. "Maybe not *hours*."

"Oh, really? So how much sleep did you get?"

I tried to pull off an apologetic shrug. "Maybe not hours," I repeated.

"Mm-hmm." She set her hand on my knee as I drove, stealing my ability to think. Good thing getting home was like going on autopilot. Her long fingers curled over the kneecap. "Jim?"

"Hmm?"

"I love you more than I know how to handle, too."

That was good. That was really good.

I wasn't one to break down in tears very often, but I felt them pricking at the backs of my eyes. "So now what?"

She stared out the window, watching the city pass by. "So now we figure out how to make this work."

Chapter Six

Elaine

GETTING TO KNOW each other again after all this time was proving to be an adventure.

There were some things that hadn't changed. I was still cold all the time. Jim always did everything he could to be sure everyone around him was comfortable and smiling, having a good time. He still did better steering clear of the kitchen, whereas cooking was one of my favorite things to do.

But there were differences now, too. The whole time I was in the kitchen making our Christmas Eve dinner, he was right by my side. Not getting in my way, though. Years ago, if he'd come into the kitchen while I worked, I usually fussed at him to move because he was slowing me down. This time, he was reaching for things before I realized I needed them and handing them to me so I could keep doing what I was doing.

And we talked. The whole time I worked on our glazed ham, mashed sweet potatoes, and roasted Brussels sprouts, we got to know each other all over again. I filled him in on all the Christmas traditions Dillon and I had followed over the years. Jim wanted to know every tiny detail, right down to when we hung the stockings over the mantel and how many presents I allowed him to open on Christmas Eve.

"Your gifts for him had to wait until Christmas Day," I said, sliding the butcher knife down the center of a sweet potato.

"Why's that?"

"Because that was when we opened the important presents."

A certain sadness came into his eyes when I said that.

"He didn't think they were all that important, did he?"

"He will someday. And I wanted to be sure there was a distinction." I tossed the sweet potatoes into the steamer and set the butcher knife down on the counter. "I never wanted to keep him from you, Jim. I always tried to be sure he had a relationship with you. That you had one with him."

"I know that."

"Do you?"

He chuckled and grabbed a handful of toasted nuts from the bowl at the edge of the counter, chewing a pecan before answering me. "You said he's a lot like me?"

"So much that it broke my heart all over again every time he picked up another of your habits. It was like you were with me, even though you weren't."

"Well, if he's a lot like me, then he probably tends to internalize things. Keep it all bottled up inside. And then blame whoever it's easiest to blame."

"You only blame yourself, though."

"Which makes it really easy for Dillon to blame me, too. Clearly, I already agreed with him, right?" He picked out a walnut and held it out for me to eat from his hand, bringing a bit of flirtation into our conversation. "So what do you think he's doing now, without you there?"

"He's starting up a new set of traditions with Kelsey, I'd imagine." The realization hit me like one of Jim's players slamming me into the boards and brought a new sort of ache to my heart. Dillon was all grown up now. He was starting his own life. Which was what I wanted for him, of course, but at the same time, it left a piece of me hollow. Dillon was all I'd had for so many years. He was my world, and now he was making his own.

That was even more reason for me and Jim to find a way to repair the relationship as best we could. He'd been alone all this time. He'd had this same hollow ache inside his chest every Christmas, wondering what sort of things Dillon and I were doing without him.

"Were you lonely?" I asked, putting the steamer on the stove. "All those Christmases without us?"

He shrugged it off. "I was never alone. My teammates always made sure I had somewhere to go while I was playing, and since I've been working in the front offices, there've always been families inviting me along. I got to experience countless family holiday traditions over the years."

"But they weren't yours."

"No. Well, I suppose they were in a sense."

"But not the sense you wanted."

"Not in the sense I wanted. No."

"I'm sorry, Jim. I'm sorry I took all of that from you, and no amount of apologizing can ever make it better."

"But you're here now." He smiled at me when he said it, a real smile that wiped away his earlier sadness.

"I'm here now."

"So what do you say we start a new tradition? Since we're giving this a real shot, I mean."

I washed my hands and dried them on a dishtowel, pleased as punch that things were going as smoothly as they were. I honestly hadn't been sure it was going to work out for us at first. I loved Jim with everything in me, but he was stubborn when it came to carrying the whole world on his shoulders and not wanting to share the load.

"What kind of new tradition?" I asked cautiously.

"You said that with Dillon, you always saved the important gifts for Christmas Day?"

"Yes…"

"I want the two of us to always give the most important gift on Christmas Eve." He grinned, and his whole face lit up. "I know you might not have something—"

"I do," I cut in. "I have something I want to give you." I just wasn't sure it would go the way I'd been hoping for. All of a sudden, my insides all knotted up with nerves again, like they had been when I'd first arrived in Portland.

"Yeah?" He raised his brows in question.

I bit my lip and nodded. "Yeah."

"Come on." He took my hand and led me into the living room. The fire in the hearth had the room lit up in a soft glow, and the first few snowflakes were starting to fall outside.

"We're getting a white Christmas," I murmured.

He turned to look out the window. "Well, look at that." Then he took a seat on the sofa and tugged me down beside him, reaching for something behind one of the pillows. "This is turning out better than I could have planned it. Me first."

When he brought his hand out, he held what appeared to be a small black jewelry box with a simple red silk bow tied around it.

I shook my head. "You didn't have time to go jewelry shopping."

"Just open it."

With shaking fingers, I loosened the bow and slid the ribbon off. Nerves zinging and leaving me jumpy, I opened the lid.

A single, silver house key lay in a bed of red satin.

I jerked my head up to meet Jim's gaze.

"A key to my house. I know—I don't want to rush you into coming to stay if you're not ready, and I know you've got a whole life in Minnesota. Dillon and Kelsey are there. But you came back into my life, and you said you wanted another chance. For us. To make this work. And I want it, too. I want it as much as I want my next breath. So whenever you're ready, I want you to come home."

"Home?" My eyes fluttered to hold back tears, not that it was any use. And I'd made the same rookie mistake again today. Mascara was sure to be steaking down my cheeks any moment. Damn if I didn't want to look as good as I could for him.

He brushed a tear from my cheek with his thumb and then cupped my face in the palm of his hand. "Home. And not just for the holidays."

I took the key out of the box and fished in my pocket for my set of keys. My hand was still shaking too much for me to get the key on the ring, so Jim took it all from my hands and finished the job for me, grinning as he pressed the set into the palm of my hand. He moved to kiss me, but I stopped him with my palm to the center of his chest.

"Not yet. I have something for you first."

He nodded.

I returned my keys to my pocket, digging my phone out of the other one. I dialed Dillon's number. He answered on the second ring.

"Merry Christmas, Mom," he said, sounding happy and healthy and perfect.

"Merry Christmas to you, too. Are you having a good time with Kelsey's family?"

"They're great. We're about to drive around town and look at all the Christmas lights everyone has up."

"That sounds great." I glanced over at Jim, noting the crease in his brow. Anxiety. He'd figured out what I was planning to give him. I reached over and took his hand, holding it firm in mine to reassure him. "Listen, Dillon, there's something I need you to do before that."

Jim shook his head and tried to back away, but I wouldn't let go.

"You know I'll do anything for you, Mom."

"I know you will. So I want you to talk to your father."

"I... Really?"

"Do it for me, Dillon. I love you."

Before my son could argue with me, I passed the phone to Jim and got up to return to the kitchen. Their first conversation in a decade should be private, and I needed to check on dinner.

Twenty minutes later, Jim brought my phone to me in the kitchen. Crying. I couldn't remember the last time I'd seen him cry. Maybe not ever. He'd always had a heart twice the size of a normal man, but tears weren't part of his usual repertoire.

I bit down on the inside of my cheek to keep mine at bay. "Good tears or bad tears?" I really hoped they were good, but there was something in my gut telling me bad was more likely.

He set my phone on the counter and nodded. And kept nodding, like he couldn't get words out.

I opened my arms, and he came straight into them, wrapping me tight in a bear hug that might just rob me of my breath, but I didn't care. He buried his face in my hair.

"Good," he whispered against my ear. "Really good."

I held him until his tears stopped and my ability to breathe returned. And then I heard something.

Singing.

"Carolers?" I asked as Jim backed away, drying his eyes on his sleeves.

He raised a brow and looked toward the front door. "Sure sounds like it."

The familiar strains of "Silent Night" gradually became clearer. Whoever was caroling, they were doing it here, at Jim's house.

He reached for my hand, and we went together to the door. He opened it, and we stepped out on the front porch to find Coach Bergstrom and his family all dressed in white gowns with red sashes. An older couple was with them, too, as well as a man and woman who had Down syndrome like Sophie. The girls had wreaths on their heads lit up with candles, and little Sophie was holding a tray filled with cookies as everyone else sang.

The snow was coming down a lot heavier now, and I shivered. Jim wrapped his arms around me from behind and held me close, warming me all around.

"*Pepparkakor*," the coach explained, nodding at Sophie's tray. "They're gingersnap biscuits. Mom and Linnea taught the girls to make them. We're honoring St. Lucia by bringing them to you. It's a Swedish tradition," he added, winking. "And caroling is something Paige and the girls do every Christmas."

"A bit of the old and a bit of the new," Jim said.

"That's right."

They finished their song, and Sophie lifted her tray toward me. "Merry Christmas, Miss Elaine."

I took it from her. "Thank you so much. And Merry Christmas to you, too. All of you," I added, nodding at each of them.

Sophie curled a finger for me to come closer.

I took a step out of Jim's arms and leaned in.

"Did you use the mistletoe with Mr. Jim?" she whispered.

"I did."

"So it worked like Miss Mia said it would?"

I laughed. "Yes. It worked."

She nodded so hard the force blew out a couple of her wreath candles. "Good. Because Mr. Jim needs someone to love him. He shouldn't be alone at Christmas."

"He's got that, sweetheart. He's not alone anymore." And I'd be damned if he would ever be alone again. I finally had my second chance, and I had no intention of squandering it.

Losing an Edge

by
USA Today bestselling author

Catherine Gayle

Prologue

MY OLDER BROTHER, Jamie Babcock, had the puck on his stick, racing toward the Team Sweden goal and our Portland Storm teammate, goaltender Nicky Ericsson. Jamie had a clear breakaway, and the only chance Swedish defenseman Peter Nylund—a former teammate—had to stop him was to trip him.

Which was exactly what Ny did. The ref's arm went up for a penalty shot. Not something you normally expected to see in the Winter Games.

But Jamie—being the impossibly perfect guy he'd always been—somehow got off a backhand shot while his feet flew through the air. Nicky grabbed a piece of the rubber with his glove, but not enough. The puck bounced off his glove, then the crossbar, and then it went in. The goal negated the penalty shot and put Team Canada up three goals to one late in the third period.

This was the final game of round robin play. The quarterfinals were up next. Talking to Jamie and the other guys, it was obvious Team Canada could practically taste them already.

There was nothing I wanted more than to be out on the ice with my brother for a moment like this. For the majority of my life, I'd dreamed of being at the Winter Games. Those dreams had always included me *participating* in them, though, not being forced to watch from the stands as my brother and several of our friends and teammates represented their home countries out on the ice.

Jamie's fiancée, Katie Weber, was currently on her feet and screaming her head off while waving a Canadian flag in the air, all wrapped up in scarves and hats and whatnot. But at least I had one of my other teammates sitting up in the nosebleed seats with me. Cam "Jonny" Johnson and his family had all made the journey halfway around the world to watch his sister, Cadence, skate for the gold medal in the pairs figure skating competition. In between her events, he was hanging out with me. We were *watching* hockey instead of *playing* it, for once. Not exactly what either of us would prefer, but we weren't the sorts of players who often got chosen to represent Canada in international play these days.

I used to be. Back when I was playing in juniors, I was one of the best. Something had happened when I made the leap up to the NHL, though. Now I fucked things up more often than I got them right. There were only so many spots for a defenseman in these things, and the competition was crazy tough. So these days, I was on the sidelines, watching my older brother earn all the glory.

Play started up again, and Jonny glanced down at his watch.

"Time to head over to watch Cadence?" I asked.

"Yeah. Mom and Sara are holding a seat for me, but if I don't head that way soon…" There wasn't any need to finish that sentence. Figure skating was one of the hottest tickets at the Games, and just because he had a ticket for entry to the event, it didn't guarantee him a particular seat.

He slipped his arms into the sleeves of his coat. "See you after a while," he said, already halfway down the steps toward the exit.

Even though the only reason I'd come was to watch my brother compete, at the moment I had a bad taste in my mouth. Envy—it tasted like bile. Jealousy wasn't doing me any damn good, though. All it did was pry open a wound that had been festering for decades…at least as long as I could remember. I glanced up at the game clock on the Jumbotron overhead. Four minutes left. The Swedes were good, so there weren't any guarantees that Team Canada would win, but I didn't want to sit here and watch any more of my brother's heroics. Twenty-three years of seeing him be the best had already been more than enough.

I leaned over so Katie could hear me. "I'm gonna go with Jonny and watch his sister." Once she nodded her understanding, I grabbed my coat and darted down the stairs to catch up with him. By the time he got outside, I was keeping stride with his determined pace.

He raised a brow. "Not staying?"

"I think watching some figure skating will do me good. Besides, Cadence is going for gold tonight. This game doesn't matter in the long run. None of them do until the medal rounds."

He nodded and let out a grunting sound. "I don't have an extra ticket for you, so you're going to have to figure out how you're getting in on your own."

"Someone will be hawking them."

That had been the case so far at every event we'd been to, with the scalpers' prices often being five times the face value. I wasn't worried about the money. I could more than afford whatever they demanded. My bigger concern was escaping the shadow my brother always cast over me, even if only for a while.

Jonny texted Sara to see if she could wrangle a second seat, since I was coming, too. We got in Jonny's rental car to head across the city to the figure skating venue. The event had been going on most of the day already, with the pairs who'd received lower scores in the earlier round taking the ice well before we arrived.

Sure enough, I found someone scalping tickets outside the rink. I forked over an astronomical sum and hurried inside after Jonny. Sara and Mrs. Johnson had their hands full with Sara and Jonny's kids, not to mention holding on to a couple of seats for the two of us, but they looked up with massive smiles.

"Just in time," Sara said, plopping her two-month-old daughter, Cassidy, on Jonny's lap. "The final group is coming out for warm-ups."

Three-year-old Connor climbed up my back and flung himself over my shoulder, trusting that I'd catch him before he catapulted himself to the ground and giggling like a maniac. Then he tugged on my shirt to pull himself upright to stand on my thigh. As soon as he could reach, he held out some sort of snack and shoved a couple of fingers into my mouth. They tasted like applesauce and Cheetos.

I glanced over to Jonny for help.

He didn't give me any. "You wanted to come. You hold the kid for a bit."

"I hope Jamie and Katie don't get any bright ideas about making babies any time soon," I grumbled, trying to readjust the little boy since he'd taken a step and landed his foot firmly on my junk. Something as tiny as a toddler's foot shouldn't hurt like a motherfucker, even if it was on the most sensitive part a man had. Who knew I needed to wear a cup to watch figure skating?

"You know they're going to try soon," Sara said. "At least once Katie's doctors have given her the go-ahead."

Before too much longer, the skaters all cleared the ice, and an American couple was announced. They skated to some classical piano concerto or another and performed very well right up until the guy tossed his partner for a jump and she fell on the landing.

Mrs. Johnson made a tutting sound next to me. "This might knock Whitby and Young out of it. They were already behind…"

I didn't know the first thing about figure skating other than the fact that their toe picks tore the shit out of the ice, leaving all sorts of holes all over the place, so I nodded for her benefit.

Falling wasn't good. Got it. The judges' marks made no sense to me when they popped up on the scoreboards, but Mrs. Johnson pursed her lips together and nodded like she'd seen them coming.

A German pair followed. They were far enough out of sync on some spins that even I noticed, and they had a few other bobbles.

"They were starting from a lower base value, so I think they're out of it," Jonny's mom said. The score they received was higher than the Americans', but only by a couple of points.

Then a Chinese couple took the ice as Connor's fingers discovered the lobe of my ear. He yanked hard.

"And *that's* why I don't wear earrings anymore," Sara said from behind me.

To my eyes, the Chinese couple skated an almost flawless routine. That wasn't saying much, given my lack of knowledge of the sport. The judges scored them much higher, and Mrs. Johnson white-knuckled the armrest of the seat between us. She didn't say anything this time.

Then Cadence Johnson skated out to the center of the ice along with her partner, Guy Archambeault.

Mrs. Johnson seemed to take a breath and hold it.

Cadence was tiny next to her partner. He had to be close to my size—I was six foot three and a hair over two hundred pounds—but she was like a brown-haired pixie out there. A crazy-hot pixie, but I kept that thought to myself. I didn't need to be thinking like that when it came to Jonny's sister. Not if I wanted to keep the body parts his son was currently mashing where they belonged.

"After the short program," Jonny said, leaning in toward me in an odd move likely designed to keep Connor's sticky fingers off him, "they're behind the Russian pair by slightly under two points, and they were barely ahead of the Chinese. And considering how well the Chinese pair just did, there's no room for error."

"At all," his mother said, even though I was positive she wasn't breathing.

The crowd hushed except for Connor, who had started bouncing up and down on my lap and laughing to himself. I held on to his waist and attempted to keep him from propelling himself down a few rows. The strains of a familiar tune from some ballet or another filled the arena. Cadence and Guy slipped into motion, fluid and powerful, all at once. He lifted her overhead and she soared through the air. They did side-by-side jumps and joint spins and all sorts of other things I couldn't possibly name and would never in my lifetime dream of being able to do. Then Guy picked Cadence up by the waist and threw her the same way as the other couples had all done, only she went higher, faster, farther as she spun.

She landed on two feet, and Mrs. Johnson cursed under her breath.

"Damn it," Connor repeated, only to have Jonny hush him.

"That wasn't good?" I asked Jonny, clueless. "She didn't fall."

"She needed to land on a single foot," he explained. "They'll deduct some points for two-footing it."

It felt like forever waiting for the scores while the judges viewed replays of the performance to verify whatever they needed to be certain of. Finally, the scores flashed up on the screen, and Mrs. Johnson leaped out of her seat, screaming her head off and waving a Canadian flag with a massive grin on her face.

Cadence and Guy had come in a few points ahead of the Chinese couple, but the Russian couple had yet to take the ice. No matter what, these scores guaranteed at least a silver medal in the biggest competition of their lives.

A shot of Cadence and Guy flashed up on the Jumbotron. They ought to be elated after their performance. Tonight's effort had been the culmination of years of hard work and sacrifice. But even though I couldn't hear what they were saying, I could tell he was giving her an earful about something.

She listened to him, a smile still plastered on her face for all the cameras trained on them, but the usual glitter wasn't in her eyes. I'd seen enough pictures of her over the years to know she was always smiling, always laughing, happy as could be. She was Jonny's exact opposite in that way.

Jonny, Sara, and Mrs. Johnson were all still cheering and screaming. I didn't get the impression they'd noticed what I'd seen. Hell, maybe her reaction was all in my head.

Before I could overanalyze it the way I tended to do with most things, the Russians took the ice and skated an almost flawless piece. Their performance was so perfect, in fact, that I had no idea they'd done anything wrong until Mrs. Johnson grabbed my hand and squeezed all the blood out of it.

"She doubled the lutz," she said hopefully. "They've got a chance. A tiny chance, but we'll take it."

Once again, the judges took an enormous amount of time before settling on a final score for the Russians. The whole arena was so quiet I wouldn't have been surprised if everyone in the place could hear little Connor singing to himself—something about smelly farts—on my lap.

But then the scores flashed on the screen—and they were a whole 2.03 points behind Cadence and Guy. Jonny was instantly on his feet, tucking Cassidy securely over his shoulder and covering her ears to protect her from the sudden noise. The crowd erupted as the cameras landed on his sister and her partner.

This time, there wasn't a doubt in my mind. Not only was she *not* floating somewhere up on cloud nine where she ought to be, but Cadence Johnson was almost in tears. And not the good sort of tears. The sort that made me want to bash her partner's face in, because there was zero chance in my mind he wasn't the one behind it.

Maybe I should have stayed to watch hockey.

Chapter One

ALL AROUND THE National Hockey League, there are guys who have reputations for being *clutch*. They're the sort of guy who, when his team reaches overtime of Game Seven, everyone in the stands and on the team wants the puck to be on *his* stick. Those guys score huge goals in even more important games. They lay jaw-dropping hits that change the tone of not just a game but an entire series, maybe even instigating a rivalry with another team that will last for years to come. They fight the right guys at the right times to drag their teams back into the fray. They're the ones who always seem to play their best when the stage is at its biggest and the stakes are at their highest.

My older brother was one of those guys. Jamie was the golden boy, the one who could do no wrong. He was the captain of the Portland Storm, the team we both played for. He was the guy who, whenever our team needed a spark, found the perfect moment to put the whole team on his back and carry us to the finish line. Hell, he'd just done it last postseason. We wouldn't have gotten to the Stanley Cup Finals if not for the way he'd dragged us along with him. Jamie got shit done. He made people believe—in him, and in us.

His life was about as close to perfect as humanly possible. This past summer he even married Katie Weber, one of Hollywood's darlings from a couple of years ago. In almost every area of life, Jamie could do no wrong.

But me? Clutch? Don't make me laugh.

I was not that guy. Or at least I wasn't any longer, now that I was a pro hockey player. The scouts had all thought I was clutch. That was why I'd been drafted so high a few years back. Bet they regretted their decision now. My whole life, I'd always felt as if I were a step or two behind Jamie, but once we got to the NHL, the distance had grown. Now the gulf between us stretched for miles.

Instead of being clutch, I was the guy who'd had the puck on my stick when my team was up by a goal with seconds left in Game Five of the Stanley Cup Finals. We were down three games to one in the series, so we *had* to win. The Lightning had pulled their goalie for an extra attacker. I had a clear path to the net and no one was close enough to catch me. But instead of shooting it in, I'd lost an edge, tripped over my own two fucking feet, and fallen on my ass. I couldn't get up again in time to stop Stamkos from sweeping the puck away from me, skating it into the zone, and putting it past my goaltender to send us to overtime.

Where we lost.

Which meant it was over.

The series-clinching goal had even bounced in off the blade of my stick.

We hadn't simply lost the game. We'd lost everything we'd worked for the entire season. Eighty-two games in the regular season. Twenty-six more in the playoffs. All gone.

Yeah, that was me these days. My brother was a hero, but I was a fucking goat.

None of the guys ever gave me shit over it, especially not Jamie. I doubted he had any clue just how fucking jealous I was of him. Even if he was aware, he didn't do anything to make my resentment worse beyond being himself.

Those are the breaks, the guys would say to my face. *Shit happens. We'll be better next year.* I knew better than to think they truly thought that way or said things like that when I wasn't around, though. The fans weren't anywhere near as discreet about their thoughts on my ineptitude. Hell, #damnit501 trended on Twitter nearly every time we played this season, especially in the Portland area. There was no escaping the truth: I was the guy always letting everyone down, and I didn't know how to deal with it.

I'd never been as good as Jamie, despite spending every waking minute of my life trying to live up to his hype, but I'd never sucked so bad before.

There was nothing I wanted more in life these days than to be better than him at *something*. I didn't even care what, right now. Underwater basket weaving. Filling up a gas tank and stopping with zeroes in the cents columns. Fastest balloon animal creator. It didn't matter, exactly.

Part of me wished Jim Sutter, the Storm's general manager, hadn't made a trade on draft day in order to claim me, even though that was crazy talk.

The hockey media spent hours reminding me and the rest of the world that my draft class had been a hell of a lot thinner than the year he'd been drafted, too, as if that was the reason I'd been drafted higher than he had. They all thought if we'd been drafted in the same year, I might not have even gone in the first round.

If my older brother and I played for different teams, maybe he wouldn't constantly be in my head. Maybe I wouldn't feel the need to prove myself, to find my own niche where I could excel.

But that wasn't how things had worked out.

The Storm had drafted me, and instead of finally stepping out from under Jamie's shadow, I now doubted I would ever have an opportunity to be anything other than the second-best Babcock brother.

I had hope—slim hope, but still—that tonight would help me escape from the bullshit running on repeat in my head, at least for a bit. If nothing else, at least there'd be plenty of beer around for me to drown my sorrows in.

All my inadequacies were fresh on my mind as I headed in for Keith Burns's big New Year's Eve party, because my bad puck luck had reared its ugly fucking head in tonight's game, the same as it always did.

I'd tried to clear a puck out of Nicky's crease, but instead I'd nudged the damned thing into our goal to put the Sharks up, when it *had* been a tie game. Jamie had come through for us about five minutes later. He'd tied the score and, once again, saved the day.

As if that weren't enough, he'd scored the game winner in overtime, just for shits and giggles, I supposed.

He and his now-wife, Katie, had arrived at Burnzie's enormous mansion on the river well before me. Usually for New Year's Eve, a lot of us got dragged into doing a charity event for the Light the Lamp Foundation. This year, they'd bumped the festivities back due to the founder's wife, Noelle Kallen, giving birth a few days ago in Sweden and the foundation's local vice-president and our goaltender's wife, Jessica Ericsson, being on bedrest and due to pop with Nicky's first baby within a few weeks. Instead, the big event had been moved to St. Patrick's Day, and Lord knew what Jessica had in store for us then. Nicky said she was constantly on her phone and her laptop, even in bed.

So much for getting rest.

I parked behind Jamie's car on the overcrowded street out front. When I reached the sidewalk, it was to find Jonny and Sara already at the door, along with some petite blonde with curves that went on for days. I'd almost missed the blonde because Jonny's massive frame blocked her from my view, but she shifted and I caught a glimpse of her adorable smile as she looked up at him. Jonny's shiny bald head reflected Burnzie's Christmas lights. But I didn't have a clue who she was. Sara didn't have any siblings, and Jonny's sisters all had dark brown hair similar to mine. I did know she was a hot little package.

There weren't any kids with them tonight. Jonny must have hired a babysitter. At least Connor wouldn't be jumping up and down on my balls all night.

It had been almost a year since that night at the Winter Games, but he still stomped on my nuts every time he could land his sticky little hands on me, giggling the whole time like it was the highlight of his four-year-old life. I'd be lucky if I could ever have kids of my own after all his rough treatment, not that I was in any big hurry to start a family.

I got the sense that Jonny encouraged his son, but he'd never admit it.

The bit of snow still on the ground from last week's freak snowstorm crunched under my feet as I made my way across the lawn, and all three of them spun around to look at me. Jonny grunted, Sara grinned, but the blonde didn't make any outward sign of recognition. She looked insanely familiar to me, though. I could swear I'd seen her before.

It was the eyes. She had wide hazel eyes, seemingly too big for her face.

Then it hit me. They were a hell of a lot like Jonny's eyes, only bigger. Softer. Filled with a sort of sweetness—a word I'd never in a million years use to describe her older brother—that was as addictive as candy.

She was the fuck-me-sideways-and-hang-me-up-wet kind of hot that always got me in trouble, too—perfectly cute as a button one minute, and the next moment it was as though she'd flipped a switch and morphed into a seductress. Fit, with exactly the right amount of curves in all the right places, all wrapped up in a tiny, perky package.

I wouldn't ever admit the truth to Jonny, but copies of magazines she'd been in were all over my apartment. Including the one from *ESPN: The Body*. Yeah, the important bits had been covered in that one, but it didn't take a whole lot of imagination to fill in the missing details. I'd fantasized about her more than a few times.

But this was no fantasy.

Cadence Johnson had apparently bleached her hair, but she was very much *here*, standing only a few feet in front of me. After she and her partner had won the gold, her gorgeous grin had been everywhere back home. She was all anyone could talk about for months. They'd offered her reality TV shows and dozens of endorsement deals like the one for ESPN. Canada couldn't get enough of Cadence.

She smiled at me, and it was like she'd flipped that switch. Bedroom eyes. Holy fuck, were those ever bedroom eyes, and they were locked right on me. I froze. Couldn't help it. There was something about her that left me staring, absolutely tongue-tied and probably shit-faced.

But what was Canada's darling doing in Portland? Just visiting Jonny and Sara for the holidays? That didn't sound right to me. The figure skating world operated on a similar schedule to hockey. At this time of year, I would expect her to be too busy training for competitions to travel, so it seemed more than a bit odd.

"Hey, fuck face," Koz called out from the street, slamming the door to his Ferrari. *Fuck face* was Blake Kozlow's current favorite name for me. I wouldn't bother to guess what he'd be calling me by next week, since he changed his mind about as often as he changed his boxers. We'd been roommates last season, but over the summer he'd decided to buy a place downtown. He liked to flash and make a splash; I preferred a quieter life. At least I did most of the time.

"Fuck off," I groused as Koz joined us.

"Watch your language around my sister," Jonny said.

Koz snorted. "You brought your sister to the wrong place if you don't want her hearing shit."

"I've heard plenty of it before," Cadence said. But she blushed as she ducked her head.

"Including at our house," Sara added with a wink in Cadence's direction. "From your son, even."

"And whose fault is that?"

"It doesn't matter," Cadence insisted. "I can handle myself tonight."

Jonny grunted, but then Burnzie opened the door and ushered us all inside out of the cold. He had a naked baby—his eight-month-old son, Garrett—freshly bathed but not yet diapered in his arms. All three of Burnzie's big dogs barked at us as we passed, and the baby waved his arms in their direction and giggled.

"Everyone's spread out. Toss your coats in there," Burnzie said, pointing toward a room that never got used for anything at these parties. The place was enormous, so there was no need to fill every room. "Food and booze in the kitchen. I'll be a better host once this little guy is in his bed."

Right on cue, the little guy in question peed all over Burnzie's shirt and cackled even louder than before. Koz burst out with a snort-laugh, and even Cadence fought to hide her grin behind her hand, since Burnzie was holding the baby out like he was a ticking bomb. He didn't spare us another thought before taking off up the stairs to finish tucking him in.

We all took off our jackets and added them to the existing pile. Jonny said something quietly to his sister, and she nodded and shooed him away. Then he and Sara made their way to the living room, where several of the older, married players had gathered. Cadence headed toward the kitchen. I couldn't seem to stop myself from watching her go, focusing on the sway of her hips a lot longer than was good for me.

Koz caught my eye and nudged his head toward the game room downstairs, where I expected most of the younger, single guys on the team to be congregating.

I shook my head. "Later." No doubt I'd end up down there at some point tonight, but not yet. It wasn't like they were going anywhere.

He flipped me off on his way down, calling out, "Screw you, fuck face."

"Not tonight," I muttered under my breath, but he was already gone.

Before I could think better of it, I headed toward the kitchen.

Cadence was standing in front of the island, filling a red Solo cup with ice cubes from a bowl. She glanced up at me and smiled again. It went all the way up to her eyes. I couldn't help but think about the tears shining in her eyes right after she'd won gold in the Winter Games, but my moment of reflection didn't last long—not with the sexy curve of her lips as she stared at me.

No one else was in the kitchen, but talk and laughter filled the air all around us, making it seem as if we were surrounded. I smiled, too. There was no way to stop myself from grinning, with the sweet, sinful, and slightly embarrassed way she was looking at me. Everything about her seemed to be a contradiction, which only made me want to know more.

"Does he always call you fuck face?" she asked, moving to the fridge to add water to her cup. "Or is that something special for New Year's Eve?"

I shrugged. "He'll probably have something else to call me by tomorrow or the next day. Likely something more colorful. Koz likes variety."

"So fuck face is a term of endearment, then."

She didn't state it as a question.

"Something like that." I wasn't entirely sure Koz held anyone or anything in that kind of esteem.

"I'm Cadence," she said.

"I know." God, I felt like a fucking teenager around her. "I'm Levi. Levi Babcock."

"I know, too. Cam said the guys all call you 501. Like the jeans." She blushed and crossed over to me, holding out her hand. I took it, but I held on to her palm rather than giving a proper shake, letting the warmth of her skin travel up my arm and wrap around my heart. She tugged her hand away. "I shouldn't have come. It should've only been the team. I told Cam maybe it would be best if I stayed with the kids tonight instead of—"

"It wouldn't have been best for me," I interrupted.

She blinked at me in surprise.

She couldn't be any more surprised than I was. The crazy thing was, I meant it, even though I didn't understand a lick of all the shit going through my head.

For one thing, I was thinking a hell of a lot more about myself than I was about her—wondering if she'd mind helping me forget all about my woe-is-me attitude of late, among other things. For another, Cadence was Jonny's sister—not someone I needed to involve myself with by any stretch of the imagination if I valued my life and keeping my balls in their present location. And finally, I wasn't even sure I wanted to get involved with *anyone*, let alone her. I'd only been on my own for a few months, and I kind of liked it. Yeah, I was lonely sometimes, but I also had more freedom than I'd ever known in my life. Growing up with six brothers, not to mention twenty-some-odd teammates every year who might as well be my brothers, left me with very little time by myself.

But there was something niggling at the back of my mind. Something that felt a lot like guilt, and I didn't have a clue what I had to feel guilty about, beyond finding Jonny's sister hot as hell.

Except…

Cadence Johnson wasn't just Jonny's sister. She was the belle of the ball as far as Canada was concerned. Hell, most of America and the rest of the world had fallen for her in the Winter Games, too, and they hadn't let her go. Her smile was infectious, and she seemed as sweet on the inside as she appeared on the outside. At the moment, she was a bigger deal than Katie had been at the height of her popularity, and Katie's shine kept fading as she spent more and more time in Portland writing songs instead of in Hollywood being a starlet.

And there was a part of me—an ugly, petty part of me, which might be better kept under tight wraps—that thought maybe I could finally be the better Babcock brother, at least in one way, if I managed to snag Cadence Johnson as my girlfriend.

I usually managed to keep that part quiet. I used the less generous side of me as fuel to work harder, to improve myself in whatever ways I could. Right now, he was screaming to be set free.

I crossed over and grabbed a beer from the fridge, my eyes settling on her again when I leaned against the counter and popped the bottle top. For the briefest moment, I thought there was something wary flashing through her eyes, but that something was gone as soon as it had appeared.

She should be wary of me. Lord knew I was.

Because I couldn't seem to stop myself from acting out of jealousy, even though it was the last thing I should do.

I took a swig of my beer. "I don't know how long you'll be in town, but is there any chance you'd let me take you out one night?"

Before she could answer, Jonny came into the kitchen and headed for the fridge, glaring at me. He very well should glare at me, especially if he had any idea at all of what was going through my head. Which he almost definitely did. He was a guy. He had to know how hot Cadence was, even if he didn't think of her in those terms.

I didn't think he'd hit me. Not yet, at least. But I wasn't about to take my eyes off him just in case.

He held out a hand for the bottle opener. I gave it to him, and he opened the two beers he'd retrieved.

"I like you, 501," he said slowly. "Don't do anything to make me change my mind."

There wasn't anything I could say, so I shook my head.

He grunted again and headed out with the beers. By the time he was gone, his sister was, too.

For a moment, I thought about finding out where she'd gone. Then I thought better of it. Jonny had warned me off, and even though she hadn't said a word after I'd asked her out, her answer had been clear enough.

Cadence Johnson wasn't interested in me. Smart girl.

Instead, I headed down the stairs with my beer to join Koz and the other single guys. There were a lot of ways I could spend my night that would be a hell of a lot worse than hanging out with them. They were my brothers, after all, almost as much as Jamie and the rest of my biological brothers.

Koz shot his head up from the pool table when I came around the corner. "You could've brought us some fucking beers, too."

"I could have," I said, smirking in an effort to forget the huge mistake I'd almost made. "I just thought you were already wasted, after the shit way you skated tonight."

Then I ducked to avoid the cue chalk he tossed at my head.

Chapter Two

Cadence

"I THINK THAT'S good enough for today," Ellen Simpson—the woman I'd recently chosen to be my new figure skating coach—said. She glanced down at her watch. "Why don't you two spend the rest of our time practicing your stroke, trying to match each other? They'll want their ice back soon."

Anthony Young squeezed my hand and winked down at me, his every movement reassuring and comforting.

I steeled my spine and nodded. I'd made it through everything else to this point. There was no good reason—none at all—why I couldn't handle a few more minutes skating at Anthony's side, even if we might be a bit too close for my comfort.

Together, we took a breath. Then we pushed off as one, heading toward the opposite end of the ice from where my brother's team would soon appear.

It was New Year's Day, so the ice rink where Anthony usually skated was closed. Cam had made special arrangements with the Storm for us to use their practice facility for today's tryout skate, but they had practice coming up shortly. If Anthony and I chose to work together beyond today, we'd do it at his regular rink and not at Storm headquarters.

"You feel as good about this as I do, don't you?" he asked once we were out of Ellen's earshot. "Please tell me you do. I mean, don't get me wrong. Part of my certainty has to be due to the fact that I *want* this pairing to work out, but there's more. There has to be more. Don't you think?"

"It felt right within the first couple of minutes." As right as I believed myself capable of feeling with a new partner, at least. But Anthony didn't need to know my insecurities. There was no reason for me to let on precisely how anxious I'd been about the whole thing, or that my nerves went a heck of a lot deeper than typical new partner discomfort.

Anthony sighed and gently nudged my hand, drawing me in front of him so we were skating in a closer hold. He settled his right hand on my waist, taking my left in his as we continued striding in almost perfect sync. It wouldn't take us long to learn one another's tendencies, to breathe in time with each other. Not as long as I was able to let go of the past and remember that Anthony was not Guy. They weren't the same man. I couldn't put the years of Guy's behavior on Anthony's shoulders. He wasn't meant to carry it.

Besides, I already knew Anthony's skill level was on par with mine, and he knew the same about me. The two of us had been opposing each other in international competitions for years. We were each aware of the areas in which the other excelled and those where the other struggled. We could come into our new partnership with both eyes wide open.

When I'd heard through the grapevine that Anthony's partner, Tamara Whitby, was retiring to start a family but Anthony wanted to continue with a new partner, I'd picked up the phone right away and called Ellen to set something up. I couldn't run the risk of someone else reaching him before me, and he would be in high demand. Everyone involved was aware there were issues we'd have to work through, not the least of which was the problem of my citizenship, but none of that would matter at all if we weren't compatible as partners. The skating had to come first; the rest would follow.

"We can make this work," he said now, gently squeezing my hand.

"We can. We absolutely can. And we will." I had to. No matter what, I wasn't going back to Guy. Not ever. I would give up skating completely before I would do anything as drastic as that.

After we made a turn around one end of the ice, Anthony released my hand to pick me up in a lift. I settled my hands over his and tried to focus on keeping my core strong, but it wasn't any use. This was the first time in months that anyone had lifted me on the ice. The first time since the *last* time I'd skated with Guy. A thousand painful memories raced in front of my eyes, making it impossible to breathe. Something chemical inside me caused me to shake, and I couldn't make it stop.

Faster than I expected, Anthony had me safely back on my skates. "Too soon?" he asked, spinning around in front of me so we could look at each other. "I just... Never mind. I shouldn't have tried that yet."

I wouldn't pretend I didn't understand what he was asking me. He was aware, of course. At least, he knew as much as anyone did. Some parts of the situation, I'd kept to myself. But word of these things had always traveled fast in our world. When a partnership like I'd had with Guy came to an end, whatever was public knowledge about the breakup—true or not—spread like wildfire. And since we were the reigning gold medalists, there was no hiding the fact that I'd decided to move on. I only hoped the whole world didn't know the full truth about why I'd made my decision.

Still, if Anthony and I were going to make a go of this, I had to get over myself and learn to trust him. A line my sports psychologist had repeated again and again for the last several months hit me now: *trust is a choice*. In both my head and my heart, I knew Anthony was not Guy. I had no reason to distrust Anthony, and every reason to give him my trust. I simply had to choose to do it.

Simply. Ha ha.

So I would. Right at this moment. I bit the inside of my cheek to focus on the here and now. Then I squared my shoulders as I looked up at him, shaking my head. "It's all right. We're going to have to do this a lot if we're going to have any shot at making this work, aren't we?"

"That's no reason to rush you."

"It's fine, Anthony." I took his hand again to emphasize my words. "Really. *I'm* fine. I'm not a crystal vase, ready to shatter at a moment's notice. You don't have to be so careful with me."

"That's where you're wrong," he said, but his smile softened the words. "Ellen beat that into my head years ago. My partner and her safety are in my hands. I've got to treat you with the utmost care."

I blinked a few times to ward off the tears threatening to fill my eyes. Crying would only prove he was right, that I was delicate and fragile. That I was one fall or missed hand connection away from breaking. Shattering.

That couldn't happen—I couldn't fall apart, and I couldn't let him think I was on the verge of it, either. I refused to allow it.

The big double doors at the other end of the rink banged open, and deep, rumbling, masculine voices flooded the space. Time for us to clear off so the Storm could have their practice.

I'd hoped we would be finished and well off the ice before the team arrived. I didn't mind running into Cam, but I wasn't so inclined to see Levi Babcock right now. Not after the way I'd sprinted away from him without explanation last night at Keith Burns's party. The thing was, Levi had smiled and flirted with me the same way Guy had done so often early in our partnership, and the similarities gave me the heebie-jeebies.

Only I didn't know if my gut instincts where Levi was concerned were warranted or if I was putting my prior experiences with an abusive ass on him for no good reason. I needed to talk to someone about him. Someone who knew him—but not Cam. My brother would likely murder his teammate before there was any good reason to do so. That was one of many reasons I'd never told Cam anything about all that had gone on between me and Guy. He was aware of my injury, and that I'd decided to make a change at the same time. That was all.

The team started to come out on the ice, and Koz cursed—something about all the holes in the ice from our toe picks. Without another word, Anthony and I headed for the door Ellen was holding open for us. I took a seat on the aluminum bleachers near the ice. Anthony sat next to me, and Ellen stood in front of us, leaning back against the boards as we undid our laces. More laughter than cursing filled the arena as my brother's teammates headed out for their practice.

Cam caught my eye and winked at me. I nodded at him, trying to smile, but then Levi skated up alongside him. He said something to my brother, but then he waved at me. I ducked my head. This was *not* what I wanted to happen. I wasn't ready for it—for deciding if I could trust my instincts about men. Yeah, six months had passed since I'd made up my mind and left Guy, but six months wasn't too terribly long. Was it? Could I learn to read a man's intentions, to see into his heart, in such a short amount of time?

I wasn't so sure.

Ellen zipped up her sweater and crossed her arms, shivering. "So, I think it's a good idea for the two of you to spend some time together off the ice, too, getting to know each other. And then I'll talk to each of you—separately—in a few days, so we can see where everybody stands."

I'd already opened my mouth to tell her that wouldn't be necessary, that Anthony and I were a good fit and we could go ahead and move forward with things, when he spoke up beside me.

"I think it's a great plan." He turned to me, tossing his skates in a duffel bag. "Do you have plans tomorrow afternoon?"

"I promised Sara I'd help her take the kids to an indoor park—"

"Perfect," he cut in before I could finish putting words to my excuse. "Sounds like a fun way to hang out together. And we'll have your sister-in-law and the kids as a safety net. Should I meet you at your brother's house, then? What time?"

A safety net. He was determined to protect me in every way. I couldn't exactly say I was surprised, since his protectiveness and general kindness had as much to do with why I'd chosen Anthony to be my new partner as his skill level, but his determination still took me aback. I wasn't used to men treating me this way. Not anyone other than Cam. And he was my brother. I was his youngest sister, the baby of the family. He *had* to treat me like that. It was written into family law or something.

Five minutes later, Anthony and I were finished removing our skates and had our plans for tomorrow all worked out. He and Ellen headed out, but I wanted to make my way up to see Mr. Sutter and thank him for letting us use the ice today before leaving.

In order to go upstairs, I had to walk past the side of the rink where the team was congregating next to the benches. Cam skated over as I passed.

"So? Is he the one?" he asked.

"Maybe. Probably." I shifted my gym bag from my left shoulder to my right and hitched my hip against the boards. "We're getting together tomorrow afternoon to hang out. Get to know each other, that sort of thing."

His forehead creased over his nose. "He'd better not try anything."

"We're going to be with Sara and the kids," I said, rolling my eyes. Cam could go from docile to murderous in 0.18 seconds. I appreciated that he wanted to look out for me, but there was no call for him to go all caveman. Especially not over Anthony. "You do realize he's gay, right?" I added, just in case.

Cam raised a brow. "You're sure?"

"One hundred percent positive." I couldn't count how many times I'd caught Anthony holding hands backstage at various competitions with his longtime fiancé, Jesse Schwartz. Jesse was a men's singles skater, so he was always around at the same competitions. "Anthony's gay, and he's been with his fiancé for close to forever. Frankly, I'm shocked they haven't gone ahead and tied the knot yet, since gay marriage is legal all over the country. And even if he weren't gay, he's just as overprotective of me as you are, already, and we aren't even officially partners yet."

"Good."

"Good for you," I said in a huff.

"And for you, too."

I rolled my eyes.

"I worry about you," he said. "About you getting hurt again." The tone of his voice made it clear he didn't only mean physically. Of course, he and the rest of the family knew that Guy and I had been a couple, not strictly an on-ice partnership, but I'd done everything possible to keep the whole truth from them. There were some things it was better they didn't know.

"I know you do." I stretched up on my toes and tugged on his arm so he'd bend down enough for me to kiss him on the cheek. "You don't need to, though."

By that point, the coaches had made their way out onto the ice, and several of the guys were starting to skate drills and shoot pucks at the goaltenders. But not Levi. He was skating toward us, which made me antsy to get the hell out of Dodge.

"You should probably start warming up or something," I said, inching back to make my exit.

Cam glanced up at the clock on the scoreboard. "Still have ten minutes before practice officially starts."

Damn. I took a full step back, starting to turn. "Well, I should—"

"501 tells me he asked you out last night," my brother interrupted, reaching for my hand to stop me. "He said you didn't answer. You just disappeared."

"Yeah…" I shifted my gym bag to the other shoulder again, glancing past my brother. Levi had been held up by one of the other guys. Thank goodness. But I didn't know how long this reprieve would last.

Cam glowered at me. He should know better than to think looking at me like that would make me nervous. I knew him too well. Underneath all the muscle and bravado, he was as soft and sweet as a marshmallow.

He kicked his skate against the boards. "So he was doing what I thought when I came in."

"Wait a minute. You mean you weren't sure what was going on, but you threatened him for the heck of it?"

"I'll threaten anyone who steps a toe out of line around my baby sister."

Didn't I know it. He'd already proven that by having a minor freak out moment about Anthony.

"Why didn't you tell me one of my teammates hit on you?" Cam demanded, turning into a surly, growly papa bear.

"He didn't hit on me. He asked me out. There's a difference."

"Not much."

"Enough."

"You're splitting hairs, Cadence."

I shifted my bag again, not because it was heavy but because it gave me something to do with myself. Which I needed. Desperately. Anything other than to sit here under Cam's scrutiny.

"If he didn't hit on you, why are you so nervous?"

Because Levi wasn't talking to the other guy anymore. He was about half a second away from us, and I wanted to skedaddle before the uncomfortableness of this conversation swelled to mammoth proportions. But instead of hightailing it out of the rink, I did the stupidest thing I could have possibly come up with. I looked up at my brother, stared straight into his eyes, and told a bald-faced lie.

Levi

"BECAUSE YOU GOT it wrong," Cadence said, right as I skated into earshot. "He did ask me out, but I didn't disappear before answering him. I said yes."

"You *what?*" Jonny roared at the same time as I said, "You did?"

Jonny turned on me, eyes blazing like he was about to bash my nose in.

"She did," I said, putting a bit more distance between us, just in case.

Only she hadn't. I would have known if she'd said she'd go out with me. It would have made the rest of the night a hell of a lot more interesting, because I would have spent the time trying to get to know her better instead of drinking as much as possible to ignore the fact that I'd struck out, proving once again that my brother was the better Babcock.

The look in Jonny's eyes was enough to pin me in place. Then he spun around to face his sister again. "You're not going out with him."

"I am if I want to. I may be your baby sister, Cam, but let me remind you. I'm all grown up now. An adult. I can make my own decisions."

"Not if those decisions have anything to do with dating some asswipe teammate of mine, you can't."

"It's a date. One date. That doesn't mean we're *dating*."

"What the fuck kind of screwed up definition for the word do you have in your head?" he bellowed, and half the team turned to see the show.

"Watch your fucking language in front of your sister," Koz shouted from the other end of the ice. "Fucking douche canoe."

"One date," Cadence reiterated, undeterred by the way the guys were acting. Jonny had never been much of a practical joker. He was quiet and kept to himself, for the most part, so I wasn't sure how much of this kind of behavior she would have ever been exposed to before. Still, it was a good sign if she wasn't letting the guys' crudeness sway her now.

"When is this supposed to happen?"

Cadence looked at me, her expression one of pure sweetness as she shrugged and raised her brows in question.

Holy hell. Maybe this was actually going to happen. After the way she'd run off, I'd convinced myself she wasn't interested. But maybe it wasn't that. Maybe she simply hadn't wanted to hash it out in front of her brother last night. And if that was the case, I couldn't say I blamed her. It was damned uncomfortable trying to do this with him standing between us in the present.

"Tomorrow," I spit out. "Tomorrow night."

"Exactly," she said. "You're picking me up at eight, right?"

I supposed that meant I was. "Yeah, eight."

The way she looked at me then, gratitude mixed in with her undeniably adorable charm, was all I required to breathe easier.

"I'll see you then," she said. Then, like a spring breeze, she floated past us and took the warmth of the sunshine with her.

I started to skate back over to my new defense partner, Chris "Hammer" Hammond, but Jonny grabbed a fistful of my jersey and stopped me.

"Everything you do to her, I will do to you. Got it?" His voice was quiet but as intimidating as anything I'd ever heard.

"Everything?" I tried to swallow but choked on my tongue.

"Everything. And I'll make it hurt a hell of a lot worse than you hurt her."

"What makes you think I'm going to hurt her?" I asked. That probably wasn't the right thing to say when he might as well be breathing fire through his nostrils.

He took so long answering me I started to wish the fire were real, so he could melt the ice beneath my feet and I could disappear through the floor. But then he said, "No, 501. I don't think you're going to hurt her. Because you're not stupid. You're a smart kid, so you know better than to do anything that would hurt her. Which is why you're going to take her on a date tomorrow, and you're going to be perfectly fucking nice but as interesting as a bag of rocks. You're going to keep your fucking hands to yourself. You're going to bring her home safe—early—and then you're going to move on with your life and let her move on with hers. You got it?"

Before I could answer, the coaches called us out to the center of the ice for practice to start.

I was in a daze the rest of the day. I didn't have the first clue what had happened last night, when Cadence had run off after I'd asked her out. I had even less understanding about what had happened this morning or why she wanted to go out with me now.

All I knew was that if Jonny could come up with a way to be a fly on the wall during this date tomorrow night, he would do it—so I needed to be on my guard and make sure I didn't do anything I'd regret. I had no doubt he'd meant what he'd said.

Chapter Three

Cadence

"YOU HAVE TO help me," I said to Sara the second I walked into the house. I tossed my gym bag on the floor just inside the door and put my purse and coat in the hall closet.

"Do I, now?" my sister-in-law said, sarcasm dripping from every pore of her being as she held out Cassidy toward me. "*I* have to help *you?*" She scowled to add further emphasis when I raised a brow in question, then she inclined her head toward everything around her. She was standing in the middle of the living room, surrounded by what appeared to be a flour explosion, a mess I had completely missed in my panic. Connor was nowhere in sight, which likely meant he was the cause of her current catastrophe. That little boy caused more mayhem than all the Allstate commercials combined, and he could cause his damage in the blink of an eye. And he usually giggled about the destruction afterward, too, the little stinker.

I took my niece without hesitation. Playing with Cassidy while Sara cleaned sounded a heck of a lot better than trying to figure out how to remove all that flour, and besides, I could never get enough baby time. But I regretted my decision almost as soon as the squirming, gurgling girl was in my arms. She stunk to high hell. I scrunched up my nose, in a vain attempt to prevent the smell from making its way into my senses.

Sara rolled her eyes at my response. "Cassidy needs to be changed,

385

and as you can see, I'm in the middle of cleaning up World War III."

Diaper duty wasn't a foreign concept for me, but it wasn't exactly my favorite way to interact with Cassidy. Granted, changing diapers was still better than cleaning up Connor's latest art project. Two minutes, tops, and I'd be done with the nastiness. Sara would probably be busy for another hour or more. Quickly weighing the two options, I carried Cassidy upstairs and took care of her own form of tiny, but disgusting, explosion.

Connor came in around the time I was fastening the new diaper in place. "Is Mommy mad?" he asked tentatively. White powder covered him from head to toe. What the heck had he done, roll in the stuff?

I gave him my best effort at a stern look. "She's trying to clean up a bunch of flour in the living room. Do you know how flour got all over the place? Flour is supposed to stay in the kitchen."

He shrugged with an I-don't-know expression, his lips turning down dramatically. "I think Cassidy did it."

"Hmm," I said, tugging the little girl's ruffled pants back into place. "I wonder how she's so clean, then."

"You just cleaned her up!"

"All I did was change her diaper, buddy. And if Cassidy did it, how come you're the one who's covered in flour?"

"She throwed it on me!" he said, as adamant as ever.

I picked up Cassidy and put her over my shoulder. Almost immediately, she grabbed a fistful of my hair and started chewing on it. *Note to self: always keep my hair pulled into a ponytail around her.* Too late this time.

"You know," I said slowly, facing Connor fully, "you should think long and hard about what you're going to say to Mommy when she asks you about the flour. Because you don't want to tell her a lie. Lying is bad." I should know, since I'd flat out lied to Cam not so long ago.

"I was just trying to help her make some damn cookies," he said, tossing his hands in the air. Bits of flour dust floated all around him in a cloud, and he sneezed, which only kicked up a new dust cloud.

I had to bite down on my tongue not to laugh. "I'd suggest you not use that word when your daddy asks you about it later."

His eyes went wide. "Don't tell Daddy! Please, CayCay."

"Oh, Daddy's gonna find out," Sara said from the doorway, Roomba in hand, causing her son to spin around in a panic. "The only question is if you're going to tell him or if I will."

The next thing I knew, Connor raced over to me and threw both arms around my thigh, covering me in his flour.

"I think maybe you should tell Daddy," I suggested.

"But I'm not asposed to help in the kitchen."

"No," his mother said dryly. "You're not. At least not without adult supervision. Never mind the fact that you weren't even *in* the kitchen."

"Can I bake cookies with CayCay?" he asked, attempting to redirect the conversation.

"I don't know if your aunt will want to bake cookies with you after this," Sara said.

"We can," I said. Connor gave me a white-faced grin, and I ruffled his hair to dust some of the flour out of it. "*After* you tell Daddy what you did," I added. "And in the meantime, how about we put you in the tub?"

Sara winked at me while Connor was otherwise occupied pouting, and then she headed back downstairs to continue Operation De-Flour the House. I got Connor in the tub. Cassidy wanted to climb in with him so badly she nearly pulled herself over the side of the bath still fully clothed, so I stripped her down and tossed her in, too. Giving her a bath wouldn't hurt anything. By the time I had them both clean, dried, and dressed, Sara had finished the bulk of the cleanup.

She turned on a Disney movie for the kids and flopped down on the couch, brushing hair and sweat off her brow. I was a bit more careful in taking a seat on Cam's recliner, not trusting I wouldn't end up covered in white. Then she raised her brows. "So? I have to help you?"

Right. The kids had been a fantastic distraction, but there wasn't a chance in hell Sara would let things go so easily.

"I think I screwed up," I said.

"What? Coming here? I thought you and Anthony were sure to be a great fit."

"No, the problem's not him!" I didn't know how much to tell her. There were some parts of the story I couldn't bear for Cam to know, but half the reason I'd settled on trying to partner with Anthony was because he was based out of Portland. That meant I could be here with Sara. If anyone would understand the things I was only now coming to terms with, it was her. But would she run straight to my brother and blab everything I told her? I wasn't sure. And then I'd been stupid enough to tell Levi Babcock I'd go out with him, which was merely one more complication. My life was already too complicated by half. I was in one hell of a pickle.

"It's not Anthony," Sara said dryly, after I'd been quiet for too long.

"Then what? Don't like the coach? Don't want to have Cam breathing down your neck all the time? Help me out here, Cadence, or I don't know what I can do for you."

"I told Levi Babcock I'd go out with him," I blurted out before I lost my courage.

She raised a brow. "Does your brother know?"

I nodded.

She let out a slow breath. "Well, it could be worse."

"How?"

"Cam actually likes 501. Or at least he doesn't hate him. 501's a good kid, and we know he comes from a good family. Everything will be okay. Cam might piss and moan about it for a bit, put up a good show, but he trusts you to make good decisions for yourself. He knows you're a smart cookie."

"But I'm not sure *I* trust me to make good decisions," I said.

"Back up. What?" Sara shook her head, perplexed. "Are you second-guessing things with Guy?"

Not in the least. I probably should have left him, broken off that partnership, almost five years ago. Definitely by a couple of years ago, once our relationship had morphed from being nothing more than partners on the ice to being a couple. That side of things never should have happened. All the warning signs about how he would treat me were already there, yet I'd allowed him to convince me he loved me. He'd sworn I was his princess, that he would cherish me and turn me into his queen.

Lies. All of it. And the worst thing was, *I'd known* before I'd ever gone out on a single date with him. It was obvious from how he would berate me in practice. How every time we lost points in a competition, it was my fault. How he would yell and scream horrible things at me, and then beg me to forgive him. He never berated me while anyone was around, of course. He saved all of that behavior for when the two of us were alone.

Why would I think things should be any different just because we were romantically linked? Yet I'd convinced myself it would all be better, and I'd suffered through his antics for years before I'd finally gotten the gumption to put an end to it. If only I'd found my courage sooner. Things could be very different now if I had.

But living in regret wasn't me, and I couldn't allow myself to wallow in it. I had to find a way to move forward.

At the moment, Connor was acting out the scene of the movie, pretending to be Lightning McQueen and racing circles all around his sister, who was cackling at his antics. Buster, my brother's deaf Pomeranian, was chasing Connor and barking at him. They were loud, which might be a good thing. It meant they weren't paying any attention and therefore wouldn't repeat anything we said. That little boy was a parrot if ever a boy was one, repeating everything he shouldn't.

I turned my attention back to Sara and chewed on the inside corner of my lips. "This isn't about Guy. Or...well...not like you think." I took another look over at the kids, found Connor still watching the movie while hanging upside down from a chair with his knees hooked over the seat to keep him in place. Cassidy was almost to the point of giggling herself asleep. Must be almost nap time. Buster thought so, too. He had stopped chasing Connor to snuggle up beside Cassidy on the floor, sighing contentedly.

"Are you finally going to tell me why you broke everything off with him?" Sara asked.

"He dropped me," I said, blinking back tears. I would *not* cry over this. Not again.

"Yeah, when you were practicing a lift," she said, narrowing her eyes at me like she was trying to read between the lines. "You hurt an ankle and needed some surgery or another to fix it. It was all over the news. Even here. But that can't have been the first time he'd dropped you, surely."

"No." I took another calming breath, attempting to fill my lungs with the peace that had been eluding me for years. "But it was the first time he dropped me intentionally."

"What the ever loving fuck?" she practically shouted, coming halfway up from the couch before she glanced over at the kids and realized what she'd done. For once, Connor didn't immediately repeat her. He looked over with worried eyes, likely sensing the very different tone coming from his mother this time. "It's okay, buddy," she said, visibly putting on a calm front for his benefit. Then she turned back to me. "Why the hell would he drop you purposely?" she hissed. "That doesn't make sense. You two were dating. You'd been partners for more than half a decade. You'd just won a fucking gold medal together a couple of months before." She held out her hands, either in question or defeat.

"He dropped me because I was pregnant. Because if I stayed pregnant and delivered a baby, we would lose almost an entire year of training and competition, right at the height of our careers."

She stared at me, blinking a few times. With every second ticking by, I watched comprehension dawn in her eyes, leading first to understanding, then to compassion, and finally to outright fury like I'd never seen in her. Her voice was as soft as I'd ever heard from her when she said, "So he wanted you to miscarry."

I nodded.

"The surgery wasn't for your ankle, was it?"

I shook my head. "My ankle was only sprained. A bad sprain, but nothing that would require surgery."

"You needed a D and C?" Sara had tears in her eyes.

"Yes."

"If I ever see that motherfucker again, I will rip him limb from limb, take his remains to Florida, and feed him to the alligators."

Never in a million years would I have expected to laugh so soon after revealing such a gut-wrenching thing, but I couldn't stop myself. A gale of giggles bubbled up from my belly and came out alongside the tears I'd been holding back.

"I'm not joking," Sara said. "And once Cam finds out—"

"He can't find out," I cut in. "I don't want him to know."

"But… He's your brother, hon. He loves you to bits. He needs to know."

"No, he doesn't. Because everything you want to do to Guy, he honestly *would* do. And worse. So he can't ever know."

"Why the hell did you tell me?" she demanded, throwing up her hands. "I'm not good at secrets. Not when it comes to keeping things about my husband's sister away from him. Especially not something like this. You're asking for a hell of a lot, Cadence."

"I asked you because you're the only person I know who understands what I've been through." At least with part of it.

Sara had miscarried before. She could understand at least that part of things, although I doubted she'd ever been in a relationship like I'd had with Guy. But I needed *someone* I could talk to, someone who could help me sort through all the insanity in my head. I couldn't go to my sisters or my mom. I'd fed them the same story we'd told the press about my ankle, and that was all they ever needed to know. They all believed I lived a charmed life, and I was perfectly content to let them continue thinking it. The same went for Cam. He couldn't know. But Sara could…and she could threaten to feed Guy to the alligators.

"Please?" I said, since she was still staring at me like I'd grown a few heads. "I just need someone I can talk to about it, but I don't want to turn it into a big *thing*, you know?"

"Honey, there's no turning it into a big thing involved. It *is* a big deal. Huge. Are you sure he dropped you intentionally? It wasn't an accident?"

I'd been dropped accidentally enough times to be able to tell the difference, and if Sara really thought about it, she would realize that. "I'm sure. One hundred percent positive. He meant to do it."

She scowled. She didn't flat out reject my pleas, but she didn't exactly agree to help me out with my brother, either. This was going to be harder than I'd hoped.

"And you're going on a date with 501?" she asked. "Are you ready to date after all of that? Oh, who am I kidding? There's no way."

"Tomorrow. And you're right, I'm not even close to ready." I was still trying to screw my head on straight again.

"Well… At least he's a good guy. Maybe you don't trust your own judgment about men right now, but you can trust mine and Cam's. It'll be all right. Just don't get in over your head, okay? Start out as friends or something. Is it too late to make it a double date? I bet Babs and Katie—"

Right then, the front door opened and my brother walked inside.

As soon as Connor saw his father, he raced over to hug him. "Daddy! We're gonna feed the motherfucker to the agilators!"

I turned panicked eyes to Sara, who was cool and collected as ever. "He means 501. If he tries anything with Cadence when they're on their date tomorrow."

Something told me she was constantly coming up with quick excuses as to why Connor said some of the things he said.

Cam narrowed his eyes at Sara, but he didn't try to argue about it. He let out a *hmph*ing sort of sound and picked Connor up.

I tried to remember how to breathe.

"CAN WE FEED him to the agilators, too?" Connor asked, looking up at Anthony with a toddler version of an evil grin.

"No, we can't." I had a hard time not laughing at this kid. I didn't know how either Cam or Sara could ever keep a straight face with him. "We're not feeding anyone to the alligators."

"Mommy said we could."

"Are there going to be alligators at the park?" Anthony asked, taking Connor's coat from me and holding it out to help the little boy into it. "I'm *scared* of alligators." He winked at me.

"You're scared?" Connor cackled while I busied myself with grabbing the diaper bag and lunch box filled with at least four times more snacks than we could possibly need for a two-hour trip to play.

Sara rolled her eyes and finished buttoning up Cassidy's coat. "Come on. I don't know about alligators…"

"They're gonna eat him," Connor said gleefully. "And I'm gonna watch."

Somehow, the three of us adults managed to load the two kids into Sara's SUV and climb in ourselves, along with all our mounds of *stuff*, and soon enough were on our way to the indoor park. No sooner had we arrived than Connor seemingly forgot all about alligators due to the massive ball pit waiting for him. I managed to pry his coat free before he sprinted away and dove in without waiting to see how deep it was.

Connor sunk in up to his head, but he had the biggest grin on his face. I doubted he would care if he went completely under. At least the pit was full of balls and not water.

Sara busied herself with taking Cassidy's coat off and finding a play area more appropriate for someone of her size, leaving me and Anthony to find a locker in the coat room to store all our stuff.

"He seems like quite a handful," Anthony said, taking the diaper bag and snacks from me.

I raised a brow and chuckled. "You haven't seen anything yet. He seems positively well behaved so far today."

Anthony snort-laughed. "Should make for an interesting afternoon."

Which would suit me nicely. The more interesting this afternoon became, the less time I'd have to worry about my date with Levi Babcock tonight.

With everything safely stowed for the time being, we headed back out to the main play area. Sara and Cassidy had found some blocks and another mother and baby, leaving Connor to the two of us. The holy terror himself was busy flinging his body through the balls toward some bigger kids, using his arms to make it seem like he was a gator trying to chomp them. I let out an internal sigh and tried to mentally prepare myself to go haul him off before he went overboard and hurt another child. I'd barely resigned myself to what I needed to do before Anthony kicked off his shoes and jumped into the fray himself.

Connor gator-chomped Anthony's arm and giggled.

Anthony let out a fake howl of pain. "You got me!"

"The agilators got you."

"I'm dying! Help. Help me, Cadence." He held out his arms, which allowed Connor to jump on his midsection and bury him in the ball pit until I could only see his feet.

"CayCay can't save you from the agilators."

In no time, half the other kids in the place had joined Connor in climbing all over Anthony, but he only laughed and egged them on. It only took him minutes to become the prime attraction of the day, a human jungle gym for their amusement. He laughed and joked with them, giving in to any punishment Connor and his newfound friends saw fit to give him.

I found a nearby spot on a bench where I could be sure Connor didn't cause any true harm. My cell phone buzzed in my pocket only a moment after I took my seat. I dug it out and swiped the screen to find a text message from Sara.

> *I like Anthony, too. Just in case you don't trust yourself in determining whether you should like him. Don't know him as well as 501, but there's no need to feed him to the agilators.*

I laughed out loud, which caught Anthony's attention. He flashed a grin in my direction—a distraction that lasted barely long enough for Connor and the other kids to pile on top of him again—and I did my best to sit back and enjoy the day without worrying about any of the men who were at the forefront of my mind.

Levi

AT TEN TILL eight, I parked behind Jonny's pickup in the driveway, my knuckles practically white as I gripped my steering wheel. There was no fucking good reason for me to be this nervous. Yeah, Cadence was Jonny's sister, but despite appearances, he was a reasonable guy. Besides, he'd married his coach's daughter. And my brother had married the daughter of one of the other coaches. The guy who used to be the captain of the Storm before Jamie had married a teammate's kid sister. It wasn't like any of this was unheard of or out of the ordinary, and especially not around this team.

But no matter what kind of pep talk I tried to give myself, I was anxious as all hell. And I didn't like it.

Dating wasn't exactly a hardship for me. Women tended to throw themselves at me, especially now that Jamie was well and truly taken. It tended to go with the territory when you had the trademark Babcock dimples and propensity for blushing. I'd even gone in for a spray tan a couple of times to see if darker skin would cut down on the blushing, but it didn't seem to matter. Blushing ran in the family. Plus, all the guys felt the need to rib me for it, which only made me blush worse.

Sitting in my car wasn't going to do me any good, so I cut off the engine and headed for the porch. I hadn't even gotten my finger on the doorbell when the door flung open, and a wet, naked Connor Johnson grinned up at me. "You're a motherfucker. Mommy's gonna feed you to the agilators."

Buster followed after him, barking at me.

"How about you don't jump on my balls first?"

"I wanna go back and jump in the balls again," he said, grabbing my hand and taking off down the steps toward my car. "Let's go."

"Whoa, buddy." I ushered him back inside so I could shut the door and keep the cold out. "I don't know anything about that…"

Sara came down the stairs with Cassidy wrapped up in a hooded bunny towel. "Hey," she said when she saw me. "I didn't hear the bell."

"I didn't ring it. Connor let me in before I could."

She scowled at her son. "What did we say about answering the door?"

"Only Mommy and Daddy and CayCay can." That kid didn't look the least bit contrite.

"Mm hmm. And what were you supposed to do before leaving the bathroom?"

"Dry off and put on my Batman underwears." He looked up at me, like he was searching for an accomplice. Then he grinned. "501 said balls."

"So did you, buddy," Sara said, trying hard not to laugh.

"Can I go to the ball place with him?"

"Maybe some other day." Sara gave him a stern look. "Go. Dry. Put on Batman."

The naked boy streaked up the stairs with the dog hot on his heels. When he got to the top, he flung himself at Cadence, who was making her way down, apparently using her clothes as a towel to dry himself off.

"Connor Allan Johnson," Sara warned, shaking her head in my direction.

"The ball place?" I asked.

Cadence flashed apologetic eyes in my direction as she headed down the stairs. "We took them to an indoor park today. He spent hours pretending he was an alligator eating Anthony in the ball pit. Are we doing anything outside? I'll need to go change into something dry if we are." She had on a gold sweater dress that hugged her curves and ended an inch or two above the knee, and some sort of strappy heels that made her legs look long and sleek.

"Not tonight," I assured her. "Indoor only. So as long as you think you'll dry off soon... I don't mind waiting if you want to change, though." Although, that would leave me subject to whatever tortures Jonny might have in mind if he came in from wherever he was hiding.

Not only that, but I hoped she'd stay in this dress. The material didn't leave much to the imagination, but that didn't stop my imagination from running overtime.

"Nah. I'm fine. Let's leave before Connor does something else to sabotage me." She took her coat and purse out of the closet and allowed me to help her into it.

"We'll leave the light on," Sara called as we headed out the door.

Cadence nodded and waved.

Once we were in the car and on our way to the Moda Center, she turned to me. "Cam hasn't been giving you a hard time, has he? I didn't mean for it to go down like that yesterday. In front of him and all."

I shrugged. He wasn't being any worse than I'd expect. "Why did you lie to him?"

She raised a brow.

"You didn't agree to go out with me when I asked you. I would have remembered. Trust me."

"Maybe my brother doesn't need to know everything."

"Maybe not. But maybe, if I'm going to be part of your lies, I should know what's going on."

"Maybe you should," she said. "Maybe you shouldn't."

We were at a red light, so I faced her for a moment. Her face was still lit up with the same gorgeous smile she usually bore, but it didn't reach all the way to her eyes again, taking me back to the moment she'd won the gold medal and should have been on top of the world. Seeing her like that crushed a bit of my heart. I didn't understand it. I didn't understand her.

But damn if I didn't want to know her well enough to figure out everything about her.

"You're a web of secrets, Cadence."

She ducked her head down and stared at her lap. "Only a few."

"A few big ones."

"Could be."

The light turned green. Soon, we were in the parking garage.

"There's no hockey game tonight, is there?" she asked.

I parked and flipped down my sun visor, grabbing the two tickets I'd stashed there. I handed them to her.

"The End of All Things?" There was a hint of awe in her tone.

"Katie hooked me up." I winked. "There are perks to having a famous sister-in-law."

I reached for her hand as we headed into the arena, not sure if she'd let me touch her or not. She didn't cringe or flinch away, so I wrapped her hand in mine and held on as we made our way through the crowd.

There was a war going on in my head, though.

A part of me was crowing like a rooster, because Cadence Johnson was on an actual date with me. She was even more famous than my famous sister-in-law, and now that she'd agreed to give me a chance, I had the opportunity to turn our relationship into something more. That was the asshole part of me, and right now his voice was becoming seriously loud in my head.

Another part of me simply wanted to figure out what secrets she was keeping…and find a way to make that smile reach her eyes. I didn't know what to call that part of me. His voice was quiet but persistent.

I had no earthly idea which side would win.

Chapter Four

 Levi

"CAM'S NOT GOING to bed until I get back," Cadence said. "You know that, right? It's one of those overprotective big brother things. I don't think he'll ever outgrow that. Even once all his little sisters are married off to men he approves of, he won't stop…he'll end up shifting all the focus to Cassidy."

She was smiling. A real smile, even. One that reached all the way to her eyes. There was something magic about her eyes. The hazel in them seemed to change color with her mood. When she was wary, they were almost brown, dark and intense like a cup of rich coffee. When she was focused on something and thinking hard, they turned to a light golden color. But now, when she was relaxed and enjoying herself, they were morphing into something soft and green. So far, I'd seen each of those colors tonight, only sparking my curiosity to learn how many other hues might be found in them at different times.

"Yeah, I know. Poor Cassidy." I stretched my hand out across the table at Shari's, a twenty-four-hour diner we'd come to after the concert, tracing my fingers over Cadence's upturned palm and memorizing the curvature of the lines and the softness of her skin. I knew how late it was—already well after midnight. We had a game tomorrow, so I had to be back at the Moda Center early for morning skate, and the last thing I needed to do was stay up all night talking to Cadence. But it was exactly what I wanted to do.

As the night had gone on, she'd gradually loosened up around me, visibly relaxing. The music had been the first thing to help her let go of whatever had her all bound up tight. Katie had hooked us up with tickets on the floor, only a few rows back from the stage, and the speakers were so loud that even now, more than an hour after we'd left, the drum beat was pulsing through my body. I could still *feel* it, but Cadence was practically vibrating with excitement and energy. It was as if her true self had been in hibernation, but the bass and guitar had spoken to her soul and brought her back to life.

"What's it like being teammates with your brother?" she asked, giving me a smile that was at once both sweet and coy. She took a sip from her coffee to hide it, but that didn't do anything to mask the teasing expression in her eyes.

"You realize that's a loaded question, right?"

She gave me a blatantly unapologetic wink.

"Jamie's been my best friend for twenty-four years. But he's also had two years on me through my whole life, so he's always been a few steps ahead."

"So you compare yourself to him?"

"Not on purpose. The comparisons simply happen. And he always comes out on top."

"It can't be always. There has to be something you're better at than him."

"Yeah? Like what? Help me sort it out."

"Well, there's that dimple you've got on your left cheek."

I shook my head. "They're a Babcock family staple. Jamie's got two of them, one on each side."

"Oh," Cadence said, deflating. "Well, maybe one is better for some people?"

"Some people?" I cocked my head to the side. Yes, I was fishing for the answer I wanted, and I wasn't too proud to admit it.

"I kind of like your single dimple."

"Only kind of?" I gave her an exaggerated pout. "So now you can see where I'm coming from."

"Well, who's taller?"

"Me, but only by an inch. Really a half inch or so. But he's got five pounds on me."

"You could spend some time bulking up in the gym this summer."

"So could he."

"Now you're just being contrary." She flashed a fiery glance in my direction.

I chuckled. "I think I like being contrary if that's all it takes to earn me looks like you're giving me now."

Cadence blushed, which only made her hotter to me. All night, she'd looked like some kind of golden sex goddess in that sweater dress, but the addition of the blush brought out something protective in me. I couldn't decide how I should think of her.

Considering Jonny was her brother, the safer course of action might be to avoid thinking about her at all. I definitely needed to move away from the whole golden sex goddess line of thought, no matter what.

"When you figure it out," I said, trying to redirect my thoughts to some safe area, "let me know. In the meantime, I'll be over here playing catch-up so I'm not completely left in Jamie's dust. Didn't you ever feel like that with your siblings?"

"Never. We were always close, but as different from each other as possible. Cam was quiet, determined, and completely focused on hockey. Corinne's the smarty-pants, so no one was surprised when she went into nursing. She tends to keep her thoughts to herself. Chloe was always playing school with her dolls and as many of her dozens of friends as she could gather together. She did a lot of babysitting over the years, as often as she could manage it, and now she's an elementary school teacher."

"And you were the life of the party," I said, since she left herself out.

Cadence shrugged. "I don't know. I guess so. I think Mom got me started skating because I had so much energy to burn. She needed something to help me focus, because I was all over the place, otherwise. Bouncing from one thing to the next in the span of a breath. I might be undiagnosed ADHD or something. With figure skating, I loved how I could have an activity of my own, similar to what Cam was doing, but still different. It was my own thing."

"Maybe I should have done that—looked for something of my own instead of doing what Jamie was already better at."

"Why didn't you?"

"I don't know. We all followed in Jamie's footsteps, right down to the seventh Babcock boy. I don't know if any of us will ever be able to hold a candle to what he's accomplished, though. Definitely not me."

"I wouldn't say that. You're still playing for one of the best hockey teams in the best professional league in the world, and it's not like you're a slouch out there."

I raised a brow. "You've been watching me?"

"I've been watching my brother's team," she clarified, but I didn't miss her blush. Maybe she had been paying some attention to me, not only paying attention to *her brother's team*.

"Still, Jamie's the golden boy. He's the cream of the crop."

"And what does that make you?"

"Cream of wheat?" I joked.

She pursed her lips in what appeared to be a determined effort not to laugh. "Defensemen take longer to develop. That's what they always say. Besides, he wasn't captain of the team and earning a spot on Team Canada the day he got drafted, you know. You're still coming into your own."

"Maybe you're right," I said, smiling despite myself, because she was so determined to be a cheerleader for me. I got the sense she was like that with everyone. Always rooting for them. Always finding the brighter side of things. Never allowing herself to get dragged down in the kind of self-defeating negativity I'd been living in for a while. But whether she did it for everyone or not, right now, she was doing it for *me*.

I could get used to having someone like Cadence Johnson in my corner.

"I got an idea during the show," she said, dropping her voice down to barely above a conspiratorial whisper, despite the fact that there wasn't anyone around us to hear. The place was a ghost town at this hour. She took another bite of the pie we were sharing.

"What kind of idea?"

"I want to see if Anthony and I can obtain the rights to use one of the songs from their new album. 'Sunset Wave.' It would make for a killer free program. I'm thinking strings. Only an orchestra, no winds or brass or whatever. But maybe it should be something like Trans-Siberian Orchestra, you know? With the full orchestra plus all the electric guitar and drums and stuff? I don't know. Won't matter if we can't get the rights, anyway."

"Why not use the original The End of All Things version?"

"I still prefer not to skate to anything with lyrics. Used to be a rule that you couldn't."

I grinned and forked the bite of pie she'd been going for. "Learn something new every day. So Anthony is the guy you were skating with yesterday? Big blond guy?"

"Yeah. We're trying each other on for size to see if we'd be a good fit as partners. Connor was practicing feeding him to the alligators today."

"Practicing?"

"For you." She winked.

I chuckled. Something told me Jonny had something much worse in mind for me if I fucked up. "So you only stay in Portland if that works out? Or are you staying here regardless, and finding some other partner here?"

"This is going to work out."

I didn't point out the fact that she hadn't answered my question, but I definitely took notice of the change in her eye color. They were darkening again, going back to that near-brown they'd been when I'd first picked her up. I was fishing too much. Time to back off.

How the hell was I ever going to convince her to tell me what I needed to know, though, if every time I got close to finding answers, she closed herself off? This back-and-forth between us was starting to feel like an episode of *Tom and Jerry*. Every time I thought I had her caught, she slipped out of my grasp.

"So you're sticking around, then," I said, brushing off my frustrations. I smiled, hoping to help her relax. "Maybe you'll let me take you out again?" I left the suggestion hanging as a question.

"Maybe." Her eyes were still dark. Cautious. She picked up the last bit of pie and chewed thoughtfully. "Levi, I—"

"Don't tell me no. Not yet. I mean, we've had a good time tonight, right?"

"Yeah, but—"

"And we're both going to be in Portland. Your brother is one of my teammates. We'll be seeing each other every now and then, surely."

"We will, but—"

"But you only came out with me because you felt the need to lie to your brother about something, and not because you actually wanted to be with me," I finished for her.

She didn't deny it, which was a step in the right direction. Truth was better than evasiveness and lies. "Putting it that way makes me sound like a jerk."

So now we were on equal footing. I might not understand what was behind it, but at least she wasn't trying to lie to me as well as her brother.

"I don't think you're a jerk," I said. More like the exact opposite, whatever that might be.

"Maybe you should."

"Never gonna happen."

She chuckled, gracing me with a wry smile. "I won't hold you to that."

"So will you let me take you out again?" The question had barely left my lips when she was already shaking her head, preparing to shoot me down, so I kept going. "As friends. Doesn't have to be anything more than that. We could do something with your family. Take your niece and nephew out or something, like you did today with Anthony. Anything you want." That was good enough to start, and we could feel our way out of the friend zone later.

"Friends?" she repeated.

I nodded, never taking my eyes from hers, watching for any sign of change.

"I suppose we could try that."

The color of her eyes remained unwavering, but at least now I had my in.

Cadence

LEVI BABCOCK MIGHT just prove to be more trouble for me than I'd bargained for. As soon as I'd met him, I'd realized he had the potential to be problematic. I mean, add a dimple to tall, dark, and handsome, and I'd always been a goner. But the better I got to know him, the deeper my problem became.

The guy had an addictive, self-deprecating sense of humor. Yeah, he probably got down on himself a bit too much, but he also didn't take himself too seriously. He would make a joke at his own expense a heck of a lot sooner than he would do something like that to anyone else.

So maybe Sara was right. Maybe he honestly was a good guy, and someone I could trust myself to be around. If nothing else, the more I got to know him, the less like Guy he turned out to be.

But was he truly different, or was I only trying to make him so in my head, in order to convince myself that starting up some sort of relationship with him—even a friendship—would be all right? I honestly wasn't sure.

That was the primary reason I scheduled an appointment for next week with the counselor my sports psychologist back in Winnipeg had referred me to, and I did it only a week after I'd arrived in Portland. I'd made a ton of progress with Dr. Trivedi back home, but I was far from being in the clear. I wished I could see this counselor sooner, but at least the appointment was already on the books. It was coming. I simply had to keep myself together long enough to reach it.

I was an emotional wreck, both on the ice and off it, when it came to trusting any man who didn't share my last name and genetic makeup. Not only that, but I was smart enough to know this was no way to go through my life, constantly on guard with every man I came into contact with. I couldn't live that way. Not for long. Someday, somewhere along the line, I would have to choose to trust again.

To start, I was choosing to trust Anthony as my partner. Sara liked him. Connor absolutely adored him. I wasn't sure their judgment was better than mine, but it couldn't be worse.

Ellen had talked to both Anthony and me separately after we'd spent some time together with Sara and the kids, and we were both on board with moving forward. As far as I was concerned, it was a done deal. Ellen was still moving slowly with it, though. She wanted us to keep skating together several days a week for about a month, on top of acquainting ourselves with each other off the ice, despite the fact that we already knew each other. Well, we were more than acquaintances, at the very least.

The delay left me frustrated. I wanted to move on with this arrangement. I'd made my choice. I wanted to put that decision into action before I could chicken out and let my fears and insecurities creep back in and sever the bit of trust I'd decided to give Anthony.

But he agreed with Ellen.

And neither of them were aware of the whole truth of why I'd left Guy.

Was it fair of me to keep them in the dark?

They knew only what the rest of the world did: Guy had dropped me while we'd been practicing an overhead lift, and I'd been injured badly enough that I'd required several months off; I'd never taken the ice with him again after that; and the personal relationship I'd had with him had ended at the same time as our professional relationship had come to a close. Surely that was enough for them to understand there were some deep-seated trust issues I needed to work through in terms of building any new partnership. Something kept nagging at me, pushing at the back of my mind, telling me I needed to give them more than that, though. But how could I broach it? When was the right time?

I wasn't sure, but I figured it would have to be soon.

Levi wanted more, too.

In the week since that first date, I'd seen him three more times. He hadn't been pushy in order to convince me to talk. If anything, he was the soul of patience when it came to letting me reveal what I was comfortable with in my own time. But damn if he wasn't persistent about finding ways to see me.

Following a Storm home game against the Predators, he'd been one of the first guys to reach the owner's box, where the families watched the game. I'd been talking to Katie Babcock all night, and he'd used that to convince me to go have a late dinner with her, himself, and his brother. We weren't out as late that night as we had been on our date, but he'd been just as charming as ever. He and Jamie had a special bond, very similar to the one I had with all my siblings. They were comfortable together and could tell jokes at one another's expense, but their teasing somehow only drew them closer instead of driving them apart.

I couldn't help but notice that Jamie never once said anything to make his brother feel less than. Maybe Levi felt he wasn't as good as his brother, but I doubted Jamie would agree. If anything, Jamie spent half the night listing off his brother's attributes and making sure I was aware of what a good catch he'd be. It was as if he were checking items off a list, lining them out for me so I couldn't possibly miss them. Had Levi told Jamie that I wasn't ready to jump in headfirst? Maybe Jamie sensed my apprehension all on his own.

The next day, I'd barely gotten home from a session with Anthony and was still in my grungy, sweaty workout gear when Levi and Cam had come in together. Levi claimed to be bored, and that he thought some time hanging out with the kids would help with that. Even if Connor and Cassidy hadn't seen through the lie, there wasn't a doubt in my mind that Cam, Sara, and I all had. Still, Levi had spent the entire afternoon with us, letting Connor jump all over him and cuss at him like Anthony had done in the ball pit, while Cassidy plucked out his leg hairs one at a time, all without a single word of complaint despite hissing in pain more than a few times. He ended up sticking around long enough that Sara invited him to stay for dinner, ignoring the funny look that Cam gave her and the uneasiness she must have sensed in my eyes. So he'd stayed. And despite myself, I'd been glad.

But today was the real kicker. Tomorrow, the guys were due to leave for a week-long road trip, and today was one of their mandated days off. No practice. No video sessions. No meetings or children's hospital visits. Nothing they had to do for the team at all. Cam and Sara had taken the kids to a bouncy house so Connor could burn off all his energy and would hopefully nap this afternoon, leaving me with all sorts of time to myself. I adored my brother and his family, but sometimes I needed a break from toddler time. This came as a very welcome reprieve.

Anthony had to work today, and I thought that was the perfect excuse for me to go out on the ice all by myself. I could have spent my time applying for jobs—which, now that I was 99.99% certain I'd be staying here in Portland, I ought to do—or I could have spent the day filling out the dozens of forms I needed to file in order to see if they could expedite my citizenship stuff due to my status as an elite athlete, but all I wanted to do was skate. There was no better way for me to be alone with my thoughts. To try to settle my mind and wash away all the insanity my life had become in the last few weeks.

So that was exactly what I did.

I took my iPod and speakers with me to the ice house. I paid for two hours at the rink Anthony and I had been using so I'd have it all to myself. I was still lacing up my skates when the door opened and I shot my head up, only to see Levi Babcock coming in with his hockey skates draped over his shoulder.

"What are you doing here?" I asked. "Why did they let you in? I'm supposed to have the ice all to myself."

"That's what Jonny told me. He texted me after you left. I let Steve up front know you were expecting me."

"I wasn't." I tried hard not to grumble it, but I don't think I was very successful.

"You weren't," he said, slowing his pace. "Why would Jonny tell me that?"

"No idea." This time, I definitely grumbled.

What had brought on this change in my brother? I didn't know, and I didn't like it. Why couldn't he be a growly papa bear, warning Levi away from me like he'd been at first?

"So does that mean you want me to go?"

I scowled, deep in thought as I debated my options. I'd told him we could be friends, but he was coming around an awful lot for someone who only wanted to be my friend. I honestly shouldn't encourage him, and letting him stay would definitely do that. Granted, it seemed like everyone in both of our lives was bent on giving the guy hope. Jamie had practically thrown his brother at me that night. And why else would Cam have let him come home with him the other day? He wouldn't have. Plain and simple. Sara should know better, after what I'd confided in her, but that hadn't stopped her from giving us a bit of a nudge. And Cam texting Levi to tell him I was here and expecting him? It was as if the whole world were conspiring against me and trying to persuade me to date again before I was ready.

"I guess I should go, then," Levi said, turning to leave.

"No, stay." The words were out of my mouth without my full permission. I'd almost settled on telling him to leave. If I changed my mind now, though, I'd look like a crazy girl. And maybe I was. It was hard to know sometimes. "Did you bring the rest of your gear?" Cam almost never hit the ice without at least his stick, and usually a heck of a lot more than that—pads and tape and all sorts of other paraphernalia.

"You mean it?" Levi hitched a hip against the boards, crossed his arms in front of him, and grinned at me—a cocky move if ever I saw one, but on him it came across as sweetly flirtatious. "I thought I should get some work in, even if we don't have practice today. Bergy's been kicking my ass lately about needing to improve my stride so I can be on the puck faster. I'm only skating today. If it's okay with you."

"It's okay as long as you don't gripe and moan about the holes in the ice from my toe pick."

"That's Koz, not me."

"That's every hockey player I've ever met who's had to share the ice with figure skaters."

"And every figure skater I've ever met who's had to share the ice with hockey players complains about how bad our pads smell, so we're even."

"If you say so." I had to fight off a grin, though. It was true. Hockey pads stunk as bad as Cassidy's diapers, only in a uniquely foul sort of way.

He winked. "Fair enough. My complaining lips are sealed."

I finished tying off my laces and got up, stripping off the sweatshirt I'd worn to the rink. I tossed it on the bench and grabbed my iPod and speakers to set on the boards. "My music won't bother you, will it?"

"Please tell me you're not playing Bieber."

"Nah. Michael Bolton," I said to torment him.

His eyes went wide.

"It's a mix of stuff. I won't swear there's no Justin Bieber, but I can promise a lot of variety. Rock, pop, rap, maybe even some country."

"You listen to country?" Levi climbed over the boards instead of bothering with the door. Typical hockey player move, and one that only emphasized how long his legs were compared to mine.

"Tell me how I was supposed to grow up in a house with Cam and not be exposed to some Carrie Underwood and Florida Georgia Line." I hit *Play* and headed out to the ice—using the door, like a civilized person.

The mix started with "Lose Yourself" by Eminem, and Levi nodded appreciatively.

I raised a brow and took off to skate.

"I learn something new about you every day," he called after me, heading toward the other end of the ice.

"Only seven thousand four hundred and twenty-seven days to go before I even think about revealing anything you want to know," I muttered to myself.

Chapter Five

"HEADS UP!" HAMMER'S shout came only a nanosecond before the puck flew straight for both the bench and my head. I was smart enough to duck, but that left Drywall Tierney, our head equipment manager, right in the line of fire. That frozen piece of vulcanized rubber hit him in the jaw, which spurted blood almost immediately.

The trainers rushed him down the tunnel to stitch him up, one of them holding a towel to Drywall's chin as they scurried away.

Bergy slapped one hand on my shoulder, the other on Hammer's. "Get out there boys. Let's keep the pressure on them."

We were in Denver playing the Avalanche, leading by a single goal in the third. The Avs weren't the best team in the Western Conference by any stretch of the imagination. At least not this season, although they had some pieces in place for the future. Right this second, those pieces were on the ice, meaning they had some firepower up front that we didn't want to face. Better to keep the puck in their end and not give their offense the chance to go to work.

Hammer and I headed over the boards, and he tapped his stick on my skates to gain my attention. "I'll pass it to you. You get the damn thing out of our zone. Clean fucking first pass, and we'll let the forwards have at it."

I nodded and took my position for the face-off.

Hammer had been my defensive partner for the last couple of

weeks. He was still new to the team, but he definitely wasn't new to either the game or the league. Our general manager had signed him right before Christmas since we had a lot of injuries on *D*. He might be getting up there in years compared to a lot of guys in the league, but Hammer was still a steady presence, and the two of us were learning to work well together on the blue line. He was more of a stay-at-home defenseman, playing solidly in our end but rarely showing up on the score sheet. I was penciled in as an offensive-minded, puck-moving defenseman. That was what they kept trying to groom me into being, at least, but so far in the NHL, I hadn't done so well with that role. Still, I was the better of the two of us when it came to passing the puck to our forwards. We had a plan when we worked together, and we stuck with it.

Koz lined up to take the draw with his two wingers, Nate "Ghost" Golston and Axel "Jo-Jo" Johansson. The puck had barely hit the ice before Koz won it cleanly back to Hammer. He backed up a couple of strides and waited for each of the rest of us to settle in place. Once he had a clear lane, he sauced the puck over to me. His pass hit my stick right on the tape. I was already in motion, heading out of our defensive zone. A Colorado winger tried to poke-check the puck away from me, but I stickhandled my way around him and passed it up to Ghost, who was waiting at the blue line.

Clean entry. We got in the zone and the forwards went to work.

The Avs backchecked like crazy, trying to force the puck out of the zone. No luck. Koz had always been a crazy motherfucker, but he was even more doggedly determined when he had the puck on the stick. Ghost was small but strong as an ox and faster than should be legal. Jo-Jo could play keep-away for what feels like hours. When Bergy had gotten the idea to put those three together on a line a couple of months ago, it was like magic. All three of them started to play up to their potential—except for the fact that they still didn't score as much as everyone hoped they would. They spent way too much time showing off their various skills and not enough time shooting the fucking puck toward the net.

That was what they started doing now. The game started to feel like a passing clinic. We had the Avs hemmed into their zone and exhausted from chasing those three around, but no shots on net.

Ghost got the puck down near the goal line, but that left him with a crazy angle to shoot from, and he had two big Colorado defensemen bearing down on him. Koz and Jo-Jo were both well covered. For some reason, the remaining Colorado winger was covering Hammer instead of me. Dumbass. I whacked my stick on the ice a couple of times to gain Ghost's attention. In no time, the puck was screaming my way.

One-timer. Right off the goalie's pads.

But all three of our forwards crashed the crease, and Ghost managed to tip the rebound high and tight, under the crossbar and in the net.

"Fucking right," Hammer shouted as he skated over and smacked his gloved hand on my helmet repeatedly. "That's what you fucking do, kid. That's why you're going to earn the big bucks one day."

BY THE TIME I finished showering and dressing after the game, Ghost had already been called out to do the post-game interview with Anne Dennison. Better him than me. I sucked on camera. Put a hockey stick in my hands, and I was fine. But shove a mic in my face, and all I did was blush and stammer and answer in two-word sentences.

The television and radio crews rarely requested me for interviews because it was next to impossible to get a decent sound bite out of me. Ghost tended to do well with them, though—especially when Anne conducted the interview. The two of them had been flirting with each other like nobody's business all season, which only led to the guys ragging on him even more than we already did. He was the smallest guy on the team—and practically a fucking midget out on the ice compared to the rest of us—so he always took a lot of heat for anything and everything. His crush on Anne was only the latest fodder he'd let slip.

I busied myself with tossing all my gear in my bag so the equipment guys could haul it out and tried not to pay attention to the pair of them. Ignoring them wasn't easy, though. The way they'd set everything up here in Denver, Anne was conducting her interview about three stalls away from me.

Ghost dragged a towel down his face and draped it around his shoulders, holding on to the ends of it in a way that caused his biceps to flex. Then he winked at her. Apparently he didn't care that the cameras were catching his every move, as long as Anne noticed.

She gave him a sly grin, which emphasized her exotic cheekbones. I had no idea what all ethnicities she came from. She looked partly

Indian, but there was a lot more in there, leaving her with dramatic features to go alongside her taller-than-the-average-woman stature. Add in some killer heels, and you couldn't honestly blame the guy for being smitten with her.

"Tell me what you all talked about heading into the third period, only up by a single goal against this dangerous Avalanche offense." She pushed the mic toward him.

"We just wanted to keep the pressure on them, not get caught thinking we were ahead and didn't need to do anything more. One-goal games can be a trap, especially when you're on the road." Still the pat answer all hockey players tend to give, but Ghost said it with feeling, not to mention with cocky smiles and a bit more muscle flexing than was entirely necessary.

But Anne absolutely ate his response up. "You and your line did exactly that. Nice goal there halfway through the third. You were so strong on the puck with the Avalanche double-teaming you."

"Gotta give the credit to my line mates and 501 over there," he said, winking and pointing in my direction. "He's the one who made the magic happen. Great shot to get some action in front of their net. It was a group effort. Everyone on the ice contributed to that one."

Anne flashed a smile in my direction, but the amount of time she spared me was very brief. After that, her attention was squarely on Ghost.

Drywall Tierney came up to take my gear from me.

"How's your chin?" I asked as I hoisted my bag over to him.

He lifted his head to show me. "Seventeen stitches, but at least I've still got all my teeth."

"Better than most anyone else around here can claim. Didn't fuck up your jaw?"

"It'd take a hell of a lot more than some stray puck to take Drywall out," Hammer said, coming back from the showers. He stripped off his towel and tossed it in the hamper in the middle of the room, leaving himself naked as the day he was born.

"You don't care that..." I trailed off, waving my hand toward Anne and Ghost. At least the cameras were facing them and not us, but Anne would get an eyeful if she turned around any time soon.

Hammer glanced over and chuckled. "She's not paying any attention to me. Not with her lover boy right there making googly eyes at her." He took his time getting dressed, and Drywall headed off with my bag.

I took a seat on the bench next to him. "So we did all right tonight.

You and me, I mean," I added when he arched a brow at me.

"I'd say we did a hell of a lot better than all right. That was your best fucking game since I've been here. By a mile. You were calm with the puck. You made good first passes to clear out of the zone. You got a fucking assist. Give yourself a bit of credit sometimes, 501."

I shrugged. "I do when credit is warranted."

"Bullshit. Never met a kid so hard on himself before. Give yourself a damn break every now and then."

"But it's only one game."

"It was a good fucking game. Take 'em one at a time. Build on it." He sat down next to me to put on his shoes. "Look, you're going to have bad nights. We all do. The thing is, you can't focus on them. You can't let the fuckups outweigh the good nights, or all you'll end up doing is fucking up even more. You've got as much potential as any defenseman I've played with in my career, and I've played with some of the best. That's why they drafted you. That's why you're here and not in the minors. You just have to start believing in yourself. No big deal. Take chances. You're bound to fuck up sometimes, but you'll probably also start to do things you never thought you were capable of."

HAMMER'S WORDS WERE still ringing in my ears hours later when we got to our hotel in St. Louis. We would have stayed in Denver overnight if not for the fact that we had a back-to-back situation, so it was about two in the morning when we headed up to our rooms.

Koz was my road roommate, but he veered off to the hotel gym before coming up. He spent time in the gym every night in every hotel we stayed at—another thirty-minute workout before bed. For some reason, he claimed the activity helped him sleep better. I wasn't so sure of the reasoning, considering how much he always tossed and turned all night long, but since it meant I had him out of my hair for the next half hour, I wasn't going to argue.

Because I wanted to talk to Cadence. I realized that what Hammer said, he'd meant it to be about playing hockey. But he was an older and wiser guy, right? There wasn't any good reason his words of wisdom couldn't apply to everything in life.

Take chances. Stick your neck out. Maybe take a risk or two. Yeah, I could strike out. But I might just hit a home run, too.

Not if I didn't try.

I couldn't call her now, though. It was after midnight in Portland, so she probably wasn't awake. I'd figured out she tended to wake up early for some sort of workout—whether it meant going to the gym or hitting the ice—and I didn't want to disturb that.

But I could send her a text message. She'd likely sleep right through the tone, and then she'd see my message in the morning. I still had to sort out what I wanted to say.

> *I know we said we'd be friends, but I need you to know I want our relationship to be more than that. If you're not ready for more now, that's fine. I completely understand. I do. I'm willing to give you time, but eventually I want this to be more. So if I don't ever stand a chance with you, I need you to let me know that.*

Less than a minute passed from when I pressed *Send* before my phone was ringing. *Cadence.*

"Hello?"

"How much time are you willing to give me?" Her voice sounded raspy, kind of husky, like she'd just woken up. Sexy as all hell.

That definitely wasn't what I'd been expecting. And frankly, I didn't know how to respond. "How much time do you think you need?"

"I don't know. That's the problem."

"Can you tell me what happened?"

"No. Not yet, at least."

Progress. Baby steps, but it was progress. "Does this have anything to do with your former partner?" I hadn't ever forgotten the way he'd nearly brought her to tears right after they'd won the gold medal.

Her answer was silence, which was as good as a *yes* in my book. Maybe she didn't want to tell me, but she *was*, a piece at a time.

"Okay," I said. "So does this mean I at least have a chance?"

"You have a chance. I don't know how much of a chance, but it's something."

"I can work with something."

"After you guys get back, are you doing anything on that Saturday?"

My jaw nearly hit my chest, because *she* was suggesting doing something with *me*. "No plans other than practice."

"Anthony's fiancé has the night off. He wants to get together and do something. He said I should bring someone with me, and if it's not you, it'll likely be Connor."

413

"Do Anthony and his fiancé mind being around cussing toddlers?"

"I'm not sure." She laughed.

"Well, I suppose it had better be me, then. Just in case."

"Is a cussing hockey player better than a cussing toddler?"

Since it meant I would have a chance to spend time with Cadence? "Yes. Absolutely."

"I guess I'll see you then. I'll text you once I know a time and place."

Cadence

THINK OF IT *as courting*, I reminded myself for at least the thirty-eighth time in the last hour. That was what my new counselor, Wendy, had suggested when we'd talked through my trepidations. This wasn't a date. Levi and I weren't going to be alone together. We would have Anthony and Jesse with us the whole time, to act as my safety net, and there wasn't a chance in hell that Anthony would let me out of his sight the whole day. The more time I spent with him, the more I realized he was made of the same cloth as Cam, in terms of their overly protective instincts.

When Wendy had first brought up the idea of courting, I'd almost balked. I mean, courting was such an outdated idea, right? Only the more she explained the general concept, the more it made sense. When a couple is courting, they're never alone together. They can get to know one another first using friends and family as a buffer before jumping into the modern world's idea of dating, which often ended up moving way too fast for what I was ready for right now.

Better yet, Levi didn't necessarily have to know he was courting me. He'd agreed to give me time, and in the interim we'd be friends. We could do things that friends do, without him ever needing to come to terms with what we were doing in that way. Calling it courting was more to help me cope and not freak out about *dating* again.

The doorbell rang. My blood pressure shot through the roof with nerves despite all my efforts at calming myself down. I headed downstairs to answer it, but Connor beat me to it.

"Who're you?" he demanded, the way only a four-year-old can do.

"I'm Anthony. Don't you remember me?"

"I 'member agilators eating you. Who's he?" Connor demanded, pointing.

"This is my friend, Jesse."

"Mommy says I'm not asposed to talk to strangers. Maybe agilators should eat him, too."

"Mommy also says you're not supposed to answer the door," I said, coming around the corner. "But lucky for you, these guys are my friends and not some men who are here to steal naughty little boys."

Connor gave me a devilish smile. "You won't tell, will you, CayCay?"

Jesse lit up like a Christmas tree. "CayCay? Oh my gorgonzola, that is almost as adorable as you are, Cadence. Please tell me we can call you that from now on." He had all the hand waving and lisping speech often associated with the stereotypical gay man, which was Anthony's exact opposite. I wanted to pinch Jesse's cheeks every time I saw him.

I wasn't so sure about anyone calling me CayCay other than my nephew, though. Once Cassidy started talking, she could, too, if she wanted. But that was where I drew the line. I was about to tell Jesse as much, but Levi pulled into the driveway, rescuing me from having to say anything. If I was lucky, maybe Jesse would forget all about that nickname soon, and it wouldn't ever become an issue. At any rate, I grabbed my coat and purse, sent Connor back to the playroom, where he was supposed to be, and headed out for my day with the guys.

Anthony had an SUV, so we all loaded in and left Levi's car at Cam and Sara's house.

Levi climbed into the back with me. "So what exactly are we doing today?" he asked, settling his seat belt into place over his lap.

"ChocolateFest," Jesse answered. "As much wine and chocolate as you can handle, all day long. But please don't get sick, because that isn't cute."

"Something tells me we might run into Laura Weber," Levi said quietly to me.

"Katie's mom?"

"If anything involves wine… And then you're adding chocolate to the mix? Hell, half the guys' wives are probably going to be there."

It wasn't far to the Oregon Convention Center. As we headed inside, Levi walked alongside me, so close his hand brushed against mine. That slight contact sent tingles of awareness skittering up my spine. They took root in my hair, making me feel like it might be standing on end. Well, it might give me a bit more volume, right? Had to find the bright side, or else I'd find myself caught up in hormones going bonkers. Now wasn't the time for that.

Come to think of it, maybe wine wasn't the best plan for today, either. I'd have to keep an eye on how much I drank.

The convention center was filled with rows upon rows of booths, each boasting their own specialty chocolates along with wines to pair with them. The booths went on as far as the eye could see in the main room, and the guides told us there were a few other halls with more to explore.

"Where do you want to start?" Levi asked.

"Dark chocolate." My answer came with no hesitation.

"By itself? Or do you want truffles with other flavors?"

"They've even got chocolate-covered bacon," Jesse said, practically hyperventilating up ahead of us by a few steps. "Honey, I'm going to drool over this."

"No need to drool. We'll buy you some chocolate-covered bacon," Anthony replied.

"What about you?" Levi asked. By some unspoken agreement, the two of us held back a bit, allowing the others to go on without us. "Do you want chocolate-covered bacon?"

I wrinkled my nose in response.

He laughed. "Because we could get you some. Might be good to try it at least once. Expand your horizons or something."

"That's a horizon I don't need expanded, thanks."

"So in general, you're not much of a risk taker, then?"

"I never said that. I just don't think I need to risk having a heart attack and getting diabetes all in one fell swoop."

"Fair enough." His hand kept brushing against mine, and then he curled his pinky finger around to lock with my pinky—not holding hands, exactly, but close.

Painfully close.

Heart-leaping-to-my-throat close.

Too close? I couldn't decide. I kind of liked it, but wasn't I supposed to be keeping some physical distance between us while I decided whether or not I could trust him? That was one of the aspects of courting that I'd latched on to when Wendy had suggested it.

The truth was, I liked the bit of contact too much to want to let go.

"So you never told me that Anthony's fiancé was a man," Levi said after a bit of wandering aimlessly through the crowd.

"Does it matter?"

He shrugged. "Not really. It only means I don't have to dream about throat punching Anthony every time I see him grabbing your ass anymore."

This time, I laughed out loud. "He has to touch my butt if he's going to hold me in some of the lifts we do, you know."

"I know. And it makes me all kinds of jealous."

There wasn't much I could say to that. I bit the inside of my lower lip.

Levi strolled up to one counter where they had dozens of handcrafted specialty chocolates. He scanned the case for a moment. He turned to me, grinning. "Do you trust me?"

I wasn't so sure I was ready to go that far in general, but I supposed there wasn't any real harm in trusting him to make this decision. "Sure," I said. "You pick."

When he'd found the ones he wanted, he flagged down a worker. "Two of those," he said. "And do you have any coffee instead of wine?"

"Espresso would go well with them."

"Perfect. Two espressos, too." He dug out his wallet and selected a few bills to pay.

"Coffee's an interesting choice, when it's all about chocolate and wine," I noted.

"Figured we should pace ourselves. There's a lot of wine to be had, but no reason we need to plow through it all at the beginning. We won't even be able to taste the chocolate after a while if we have too much wine."

The worker handed over our selections and Levi's change, and we carried them to an area with tables and chairs. He held out a chair for me and helped ease me into it. I glanced around and found Anthony and Jesse a few aisles over but still within my line of sight. Good thing they were both tall. Their heads bobbed above the sea of other people crowding the area.

"So you trust me enough to pick out your chocolate, but not enough to be alone with me," Levi said as he took his seat across from me.

There wasn't any point in denying it. I hadn't exactly hidden the fact that I was looking for the other guys, and it didn't take much to figure out the motive behind it. "Something like that," I said sheepishly. "Although, if this chocolate is bad, I reserve the right to change my mind about trusting you for future chocolate decisions."

He smiled. "Duly noted."

"That doesn't upset you? That I'm not comfortable being alone with you yet?"

"Why should it upset me?"

I shrugged. The idea of having to share our time with anyone else would have driven Guy bonkers. He had always expected me to go along with whatever he decided, no questions asked. According to him, he was older and wiser—not to mention, a man, although he never used that one to my face—and therefore knew better what I needed. Somehow that had also filtered down to him supposedly knowing what I wanted. I didn't have the opportunity to make many decisions, in all my years as his partner. Even fewer once we'd been a couple off the ice.

Now that I thought about it, maybe I shouldn't have let Levi dictate what chocolates he was buying for me. It's possible I should have told him what I wanted.

I didn't get the sense that he was trying to rule my life, but did I need to assert myself early on, so he wouldn't think I was going to let him steamroll over me all the time? I wasn't sure. One more thing I needed to talk to Wendy about the next time I had a session with her, I supposed.

Levi leaned back in his chair, crossing his feet at the ankles. The chairs and tables weren't designed for someone of his size. He seemed cramped in them, almost like they were meant for children. He took his chocolate out of the wrapper. "You gonna try yours?"

"Thought I'd wait to be sure it doesn't kill you first," I joked.

"I see. I'm the royal food tester." He winked at me before biting off half the chocolate. Then he groaned in pleasure.

Once he swallowed, I unwrapped my own chocolate. "Since you haven't keeled over yet…" The second the chocolate hit my tongue, there was an explosion of flavor. Salt, creamy caramel, and rich dark chocolate. "Oh my God," I said, my mouth still full. I didn't care about manners just now, though. It was too good.

He gave me a wry smile. "So I did okay, then?"

"Okay?" I licked my lips, noticing how his eyes followed the path of my tongue. "You scored bonus points with this one."

"So maybe I move up a step or two in the process?"

I sipped from my espresso, buying time. "Process?"

"The one where you decide whether you can trust me or not. Where you decide how much to let me in and how soon."

I couldn't stop myself from smiling. He was so persistent, but without being pushy. I wasn't sure what to do with him, but there was no denying I wanted to be around him. "A step or two… Yeah, sure."

"Any chance you can tell me how many steps there are and which one I'm on?"

I finished off my chocolate, taking my time savoring the flavor as I debated how to answer him. "To be completely honest, I don't know how many steps you're going to have to take. A lot."

"So basically I'm on step three of twenty, or something like that?"

"More like step three of two hundred."

But two hundred was a lot less than the seven thousand four hundred and twenty-seven I'd estimated before. Something else I needed to chew on for a while.

Chapter Six

Levi

IN OUR LAST game against the Coyotes, their goaltender had shut us out. At home, no less, which only made the loss sting worse than if we'd been on the road. We were already at the end of January, and not once all season had we lost two games in a row. In today's NHL, that didn't happen. But now, it was looking like we were about to drop two in a row for the first time all season long.

Needless to say, that thought didn't sit well with anyone on the bench. We'd come so close to capturing the biggest prize in the sport, the Stanley Cup, at the end of last season, but we'd fallen just short. And why was that? Because, once we'd gotten to the Finals, we'd lost twice in a row. And then it had happened again. And then our season had been over. Done. Kaput.

All season long, Bergy and the rest of the coaching staff had been drilling into us the importance of not letting any sort of a losing streak take hold like that. Not during the season. Definitely not once we got to the playoffs, but we had to treat the whole season like it was the playoffs. That was how it worked when you were in the thick of things in the Western Conference. There was no room for complacency. Only for excellence, for pushing yourself to the very brink of your limits and then finding some way to push further, harder, faster, stronger.

It didn't help that our defense was currently being held together with duct tape and silly putty. In a normal season, I was a third-pairing defenseman at best. We were all playing over our heads right now due to injuries to our top guys.

Andrew Jensen was out indefinitely with a concussion.

Keith Burns had been playing through a hairline fracture in his foot, but once Cole Paxton had returned from his emergency appendectomy, Burnzie had blocked another shot with the exact same spot on his foot. Now he was out for at least the next six weeks, possibly longer. We might be lucky to have him back in time for the playoffs.

Dominic "Bear" Medved, who had been my partner before all these injuries, had been dealing with groin issues all season that kept pulling him out of the lineup.

That was why Jim Sutter had brought in Hammer a few weeks ago. Better to have a guy with some experience than to call up some kid from the AHL who wasn't ready for the kind of pressure we were under. So now, we had a makeshift defensive corps.

Cody "Harry" Williams was up on the top pairing with Colesy. They'd both at least been in the league for quite a while, but neither was truly a number one guy. Or at least they hadn't been before. Harry had been surprising everyone with how well he was adapting to his new role, though.

I was with Hammer in the middle, definitely a step above where either of us had spent much time before in our careers.

Bear—as long as he was healthy—was with Ilya Demidov. Demi usually floated in and out of the lineup, filling holes when needed; now he was an every night player.

When Bear had to sit out for a game or two because of his groin, Jim was forced to call up someone from our AHL affiliate, the Seattle Storm. Several of those kids had potential, but none of them were ready for the NHL. If they were, they'd already be playing up with us.

So far, as a ragtag group, we were holding our own. But if one more of us went down with an injury or did something stupid to earn a suspension, we were royally fucked.

All of that was running through my head when, down three goals to one against the Sharks heading into the second intermission, Bear came off the ice limping. Harry and I each draped one of Bear's arms over our shoulders and practically carried him back to the locker room, where the trainers took over. It didn't look good as they herded him back into the training room and called for Doc to join them. The way he was wincing and grimacing with everything they did—not a chance in hell he was coming back on the ice tonight. That meant we were down to five *D* for the rest of the game.

After a few minutes, Bergy and Adam "Handy" Hancock, the assistant coach who handled the defense, came out of the trainers' room and made their way over to the corner of the locker room where the five of us were huddled together.

"Doc says it doesn't look good for him to come back tonight," Bergy said unnecessarily. "We're going to stick with the current pairs. Demi will rotate in to spell the rest of you sometimes. I think we'll go to a four-forward, one-*D* set for power plays to give you guys a breather where we can, plus it'll give us a bit more firepower to score a couple of goals."

That meant for the rest of the game, Hammer and I would be out on the ice essentially every other shift, unless somehow the refs decided to give us a hell of a lot more power plays in this game. Not likely. They'd only handed out one between both teams in the first two periods combined.

I reached for a bottle of water behind me in my stall, and I chugged. I knew I'd need it.

"Let's do this, boys," Hammer said once the coaches left us. "Just stay calm out there. Do what you know you can do. Keep it simple. Nothing fancy—the Sharks forwards will pounce on a bad pass in a heartbeat, and Nicky's already got enough rubber coming his way without us fucking him over like that."

Throughout the room, there were small groups like ours, with someone giving a quiet pep talk like Hammer was giving. It had to do with the way my brother led this team. He wasn't much of a talker, more of a doer. He led the team by example, doing everything the right way and expecting everyone around him would follow his lead. The other leaders in the room had picked up on Jamie's style. There wasn't any need with this team for big speeches or yelling. We got shit done.

Tonight, we weren't getting shit done, though. Which was why there were currently so many of our leaders around the room, calmly talking to the guys around them—Hammer bringing all the defensemen together, Jamie talking to a few of the high-end forwards, Jonny gathering his line mates in.

Hell, even Brenden "Soupy" Campbell had come down from the press box to sit with a few of the forwards who went out on the penalty kill. Soupy was on the injured reserve again, out for a few weeks with a hip injury, but the guy was as much a part of this team as ever. He might as well be a coach with those guys, the way they listened to him. I figured he held so much sway with them because he'd had to fight tooth and nail for everything he'd earned in this league. He was a warrior, never giving in, even when his body was fighting against him.

Bergy only said a few words before we headed back out for the third—reminding us that we needed to dictate the tone of the game. Play our way. Skate fast. Fight hard. Clean, crisp passes. Keep the pressure on them, and we could come out on top, because we were as good as any team in this league.

It seemed to be working. Shift after shift, our forwards were cycling the puck in the Sharks' zone, peppering the goalie with shots. The *D* all focused on keeping an eye on good defensive positioning and not overstaying our shifts. As short as we were on defense, the last thing any of us needed to do was get caught out there too long.

Four minutes in, I deflected Sharks forward Pavelski's shot away from the net, then corralled and settled the puck. Glanced up ice. Jamie was already streaking through the neutral zone, so I lobbed the puck up and over everyone's heads to land right at his feet. He stickhandled it, all alone even though the Sharks' *D* were racing after him. Two dekes and a backhand shot later, the puck soared over the Sharks' goalie's glove hand and in the net.

"Hell of a fucking pass," Jamie shouted in my ear when I caught up to him, slapping my helmet.

He was the one who'd made the play happen, though. Not me.

It didn't matter. The only thing that mattered was we were now within a single goal. One good shot was all we'd need, as long as no one did anything stupid. Now to tie it up.

The next several minutes turned into a track meet between the two sides, racing up and down the ice from one end to the other, with countless flurries of activity in front of the goaltenders, but they both kept the scoreboard the same.

I was huffing for air on the bench after one of those crazy shifts when Koz and Ghost broke out with the puck and none of San Jose's players within range to cut them off—especially when you considered Ghost's wheels. The guy could fly out there.

Koz waited until the goalie committed and pulled himself out of position. Clean pass over to Ghost, who tapped it in over the goalie's sprawling attempt to remedy the situation.

Tie game. Seven minutes left, and we had all the momentum.

The track meet didn't end there, despite Bergy's attempts to calm us all down on the bench. "We play fast but within control. Take your time out there, boys. Slow down and assess the situation."

Shots kept pelting the goaltenders. Someone would grab the puck and shoot it up ice to a streaking teammate. The race was on again. Turnover after turnover in the neutral zone.

It was utter chaos out there, and I was so winded I didn't know how to slow the game down.

Four minutes left. Still tied.

I chugged an entire Gatorade as soon as I came over the boards to prepare for my next shift.

The Sharks crashed in on Nicky, with Colesy trying to break up the play. He and two Sharks forwards collided, full speed, at the boards. Colesy came up and immediately raced to the bench holding his arm funny. A trail of blood followed behind him.

"Skate blade," he said. No further explanation required. The trainers rushed him back to the locker room to perform whatever repairs he needed…if they could even do that here. I wasn't so sure. That was a hell of a lot of blood coming out of him in a very short period of time. He might need surgery or something.

Play was halted so they could clean the blood off the ice. We were down to four *D*.

Bergy was busy with the forwards, trying to reiterate the fact that they needed to slow everything down and let the game come to them, reminding them that there were only four of us on defense now, so they needed to help us out as much as possible. While he was doing that, Handy sat down with the four remaining defensemen.

"I want Harry with 501, Hammer with Demi." He slapped us each on the shoulder, and that was that. We had a plan. We could do this.

Harry and I went out first, ready to set the tone for how the remaining few minutes of this game needed to be played.

Our top center, Riley Jezek, won the face-off straight back to me. I skated backward a couple of paces, waiting for the rest of the guys on the ice to get into position. RJ and Jamie were both well covered, but Aaron Ludwiczak had gotten free from his guy, so I saucered the puck up to him. Those three cycled a bit, and RJ got off a couple of nice shots at the net, but nothing went in. Each time, one of our forwards managed to dig the puck free and maintain possession. But the Sharks were circling. Each second that ticked off the clock, one of them got closer to poke checking the puck free.

Pavelski almost managed it, but I pinched in along the boards to pass the puck back to Jamie while Harry shifted over to cover my point and RJ cycled back to fill in Harry's point.

Or at least that was how it was supposed to work.

Communication breakdown.

Pavelski zipped past me, puck on his stick, and Harry had realized what I was doing too late. We were off to the races again, and I was gassed.

I dived for the puck.

Got my stick tangled up in Pavelski's skates, instead.

The ref's arm went up, and he signaled for a penalty shot.

Pavelski went out to center ice all by himself. Picked up the puck on his stick. Deked once. Twice. Roofed it, stick side, beating Nicky.

And once again, it was my fault. It was the first shift Harry and I had been out there together. He hadn't anticipated what I would do; I hadn't told him. That was on me, especially since I'd missed poking the puck away from the other guy.

We skated back to the bench, me mentally berating myself the whole way.

Hammer came over the boards and slapped his stick on my ankles. "Hey. Look at me."

I shot my head up.

"You took a chance. It didn't work out. Big fucking deal. Take another chance anyway."

THEY'D SCORED ANOTHER goal in our empty net in the dying moments of the game, so we lost five to three. Two losses in a row. It fucking sucked, but I was determined to not only listen to Hammer's words but to believe them. I couldn't let this sink into my head any more than we, as a team, could afford to let this losing trend become a streak.

I was about to head out and go home when Jonny locked an arm around my neck like he was going to give me a noogie and dragged me toward the concourse.

"What the fuck did I do to deserve that?" I demanded once I got free from his grasp. I couldn't think of anything I might have done or said to Cadence to have him ready to kill me, but that was exactly what I'd thought was going to happen once I realized who had hold of me.

He gave me a look that said I was the biggest fucking idiot in the world. "Are you trying to start a relationship with Cadence, or what?

Because it sure as hell seems like you are. And I can promise you, *she* thinks you are. So are you?"

Seemed like a trick question. "Yes?"

"Then get your fucking ass up to the owner's box and talk to her before you go home." He took off ahead of me, his long legs not showing any of the exhaustion I felt after tonight's game. "Fucking dumb ass," I heard him say under his breath. He stopped halfway down the hall and spun around to face me. "I swear to God, 501, I hate every second of this. But I refuse to hold your fucking hand through it. You're not a toddler. Figure it out. And if you fuck this up, if you hurt her, I will rip every digit from your hands and feet, along with a few other choice appendages, and let my son feed you to the alligators like he wants to do." Then he stormed off again.

So now Jonny was encouraging me in regard to his sister, not trying to murder me for even breathing in her vicinity? I'd assumed there had been some sort of miscommunication when Jonny had texted me about meeting Cadence at the rink that day, but now I wasn't so sure. I was starting to think there must be something in the Johnson family's genes to make them impossible to figure out.

Sara might have had something to do with it. That was the only thing that made sense, as far as I could tell. Different gene pool. She didn't confuse me. Sara was as direct as they came.

I followed Jonny's retreating form up to the owner's box again. This time, Cadence was hanging out with both Katie and her younger sister, Dani Weber, but as soon as I came through the door, she turned to me and flashed a gorgeous smile in my direction. Harry was up here, grinning and winking at Dani from across the room. She gave him a coy expression in return. I shook my head, trying to clear away the fog that came from Harry and Dani Weber flirting with each other, and headed toward those girls.

I didn't make it far, though.

"Levi!" Sophie Calhoun, Bergy's youngest stepdaughter, leaped up from her seat and gave me the biggest, tightest bear hug ever. That was par for the course when it came to Sophie. She was a twelve-year-old with Down syndrome. And she had a massive crush on me. The first time I met her, she'd raced through the concourse and hugged me, exactly like this, and immediately asked me to marry her. She ran at me so hard that time, I'd had to brace myself to prevent being tackled to the ground. That was a little over a year ago.

Her older sisters had crushes on me, too, so I was always careful around those girls. Not that I thought either Bergy or their mother would let them pull a fast one on me, but I couldn't be too careful. The Babcock boys—we were all fully aware of the effects our dimples had on young girls. I was always on my guard once the giggles started.

Sophie was different, though. She was sweet as could be, and not a danger to me in the least.

It was a Friday night. No school tomorrow. That was the only reason Paige would have brought her girls to the game. I should've thought of that before. I would have been up here in a heartbeat to see Sophie if I'd realized they were here.

Since I knew it would earn me one of her infectious laughs, I picked her up and spun her around a few times. She cackled with glee. For a few moments, the rest of the room disappeared. That was the power this little girl had over me.

When I set her on her feet again, I planted a kiss on the top of her head. "Hey, Sophie Bug. I've missed you."

"That was a nice pass, Levi." She had a death grip on my hand, but she was grinning from ear to ear. "I'm gonna be just like you."

"It's so like you to ignore all the times I messed up out there."

"You never mess up. You're the best."

As far as she was concerned, no one would ever be better at anything than me. If only I could see the world through her eyes someday. She never failed to give me a boost of confidence, though, and Lord knew I needed it tonight.

"Have you met my friend Cadence?" I asked her. This part might be tricky, especially since I hoped Cadence would someday become a hell of a lot more than just my friend. The last thing in the world I wanted to do was stomp on Sophie's tender feelings. But if I introduced Sophie to the idea that Cadence was a friend, first, she could potentially come to accept it when the relationship progressed further. That was my hope, at least.

Sophie shook her head.

"Come on. I'll introduce you." I kept a tight grip on her hand and led her to where Cadence, Katie, and Dani were huddled together. "Cadence, I want you to meet a special friend of mine. This is Sophie Calhoun."

Cadence's grin hadn't dimmed in the least. She held out a hand for Sophie to shake. Sophie had never been one for formality, though. Instead, she released her grip on me and wrapped both arms around Cadence in the same kind of bear hug she'd given me.

"I love you, Cadence," Sophie said.

Cadence raised a brow in my direction, but she took it in stride. "Well, I guess I love you, too."

"I know." Simple acceptance of the fact that she was loved—exactly what I would expect from Sophie. After a minute, she let go of Cadence and took a step back toward me. She grabbed hold of my hand and held on tight. "I'm gonna marry Levi."

I winked. "Unless someone steals her away from me before she's old enough. But Sophie, is it all right if Cadence and I are friends?"

She nodded. "Yeah. I love her, too."

"I know you do. You love everybody."

Sophie grinned again. "You can have girlfriends. But I'm your *best* girlfriend."

"You know it, Sophie Bug." I pinched her nose and got another giggle.

"Bergy said I can try to skate tomorrow without my sled."

The coaches and equipment guys had rigged up a walker specifically for her last year. It had skis on the bottom, and they strapped her into the contraption to help her keep her balance while she built her core strength.

"You skate?" Cadence asked, perking up. "So do I."

"Are you a hockey player, too, like Levi? I'm gonna play hockey."

"Nope. I'm a figure skater."

"She's not just any figure skater," I said. "She won a gold medal."

"Wow." Sophie's jaw dropped to her chest. "A real gold medal?"

"In the Winter Games. Same as where Babs got his." She knew most of the guys by their nicknames, not their real names, so I was careful to use them with her. She called me by my given name, but I was the only one.

"But his is for hockey," Sophie said.

"They have lots of sports you can compete in," Cadence said.

"You wanna come skating with me tomorrow?" Sophie asked her. "You can come with Levi."

"Yeah?" Cadence raised a brow in Sophie's direction. "You're sure that'd be all right with you?"

"It's okay. But don't help me skate. I wanna do it all by myself."

"Got it." Cadence winked at me. "I'll find out when and where, and I'll be there."

I supposed that meant I was going skating tomorrow, too.

Chapter Seven

Cadence

SOPHIE CALHOUN HAD to be about the most adorable thing in the history of ever, but I was quickly learning that her status on that list was followed close behind by how sweetly Levi treated her. I'd gotten a sense of their relationship last night, but hanging out with the two of them at the rink today had proven to be as illuminating about the man he truly was, deep down, as anything.

It wasn't only one thing; it was everything. He hugged her as fiercely as she hugged him. He always held her hand if she wanted him to, but he never tried to force his help on her, giving her the freedom to try things on her own. He gave her his full attention any time she demanded it, and he never once looked like he begrudged her for stealing his focus. Even though he probably had dozens of things he could be doing—things that most twenty-four-year-old millionaires would far rather spend their time on—he stayed out on the ice with Sophie as long as she wanted, and he never voiced a word of complaint.

Clearly, Sophie had stolen his heart.

And now that I was watching him with her, he was stealing a piece of mine.

"Do another jump!" Sophie called out to me. She was shuffling along next to Levi, but she wasn't holding on to him for support this time. "A big one."

It hadn't taken me long at all to figure out Sophie valued height and air time far more than the number of revolutions I made in the air. Sometime, I'd have to bring her along when Anthony and I practiced, so she could see the throws and lifts. She'd probably eat those right up.

I gathered some speed and did a single lutz, soaring through the air for a moment before landing on one foot, to Sophie's applause. Then I skated over and joined them, coming up on Sophie's free side so Levi and I were surrounding her.

"You liked that?"

"Yep. Now Levi do it."

He laughed. "I can't."

"Yes, you can," she said adamantly. "You're the best skater I know."

"I'm a good skater when it comes to hockey," he said. "But Cadence can skate circles around me with this stuff."

"You can teach us, can't you, Cadence?" Sophie wobbled, but she put her arms out for balance and steadied herself without either of us reaching in to rescue her.

"Well…" For a moment, I debated giving her excuses as to why I wouldn't be able to teach her, but the thought behind my indecision was a bunch of crap. Clearly, this girl could do a lot of things. Who was I to tell her otherwise?

Levi raised a brow expectantly at me.

"*You*, I bet I can teach," I said to Sophie. "I'm not so sure Levi can learn, though. Besides, he's not even wearing the right kind of skates."

"We got on our hockey skates," Sophie said, looking down at her feet quizzically.

"Yeah. To jump like I did, you need figure skates. They've got a toe pick." I came to a stop and showed her the one on my right foot. "Hockey skates don't have them."

She took a moment to compare the end of her blade to the end of mine. "Why do you got a toe pick?"

"It helps you get a grip in the ice so you can jump high."

"No jumping in hockey."

"Nope," Levi said. "No jumping."

She nodded thoughtfully. Then she turned toward the other side of the rink and started skating that way. We went with her, with the wordless acknowledgment that we should be close by in case she struggled. "Bergy?" she called out. "I need figure skates! Levi needs some, too."

Bergy's laugh rang out in the arena as we got close to the boards. "We'll see what we can do. Is Cadence going to teach you?"

"Yeah. She's teaching us."

"I'll have to work out some lesson times with her and see what she charges then," he said. He caught my eye. "Assuming you actually did agree to give Sophie some lessons?"

Lessons hadn't exactly been in my plans. But then again, I still hadn't found a job, and I'd have to start working at some point. The money from my endorsement deals was running low.

I wasn't about to ask Mom for anything more. She'd sacrificed so much for me over the years, paying for ice time and lessons and costumes when the money wasn't there. Then Cam had gotten into the NHL, and probably half the money he earned had gone to helping me. At least it had always felt that way to me.

Even now, Cam and Sara had been letting me stay with them while I sorted everything out. I couldn't keep relying on my family forever, and there wasn't a chance in hell I'd let Anthony foot the bill for all of our expenses. We were a partnership. That meant we both had to contribute, and not just on the ice.

Yeah, I had sponsorship deals, so there would be more money coming in eventually. I wasn't completely broke. But I needed a job with a steady paycheck so I could pay my own way. Besides, teaching figure skating might not be a horrible idea, especially if I could work with some kids like Sophie. If our lessons went well, there was no telling what else it might lead to.

"I think this sounds like a great plan," I said. "We can definitely work something out."

I sat and finalized some details with Bergy while Levi helped Sophie remove all her gear and bundle up to head home. Within ten minutes, I had my first steady client lined up, and some weight lifted off my shoulders. Not bad, for an afternoon of skating.

Once she was ready to go, she came over and gave me another big hug, squeezing my ribs almost to the point of bruising.

I squeezed her back. "I'll see you on Tuesday, okay?"

"Okay. I love you, Cadence."

"Love you, too." It was easy to love Sophie. To open up and let her worm her way into my heart. I only wished letting someone else in was so easy.

Someone like Levi.

Whether I wanted him in my heart or not, he was finding a way to get there. But while letting Sophie in felt like the warm summer sun hitting my face, letting Levi in felt like pieces of me were breaking off. Shattering. Splitting in half. The problem was, I wasn't sure if the pieces he was ripping open at the seams were really meant to stay where I'd put them or not. Maybe it was for the best, even if it hurt. How could something good cause so much pain? But then again, it was easiest to rip the Band-Aid straight off, right? That was the old wisdom.

As usual, when it came to this budding courtship between us, I ended up with more questions than answers.

"That was nice of you," Levi said as we watched Sophie bound out of the rink with Bergy following behind her, carrying her gear.

I took a seat next to him and started unlacing my skates. "It wasn't nice. It was the least I could do for your best girlfriend." I glanced up to see how he'd reacted to my teasing.

The skin around his eyes crinkled with a silent laugh. "Was that for her, or for me?"

"I don't know." I shook my head, somewhat surprised to realize that it was absolutely the truth. I wasn't sure who I'd done it for. "Maybe for both of you."

"If you don't mind, I'm going to pretend you did it for me. All for me." He cocked me a grin and winked.

I laughed. "Tell yourself whatever you want."

"I'm trying to let her down easy. The last thing I want to do is break that little girl's heart, you know?"

"Let her down easy?" I said, and something squeezed around my lungs. No, not my lungs—my heart. It was my heart that stopped working, which made it impossible to breathe. "Because of me?"

He shrugged. "I'm still waiting. Hoping."

If I wasn't careful, he wouldn't have to wait too much longer.

"Any chance you're going to be ready to let me kiss you sometime soon?" he asked.

And even though a piece of my heart was desperate to say yes, I nibbled on the inside of my lower lip and shook my head. "I don't think so. Not yet."

"Okay." He didn't sound too insanely frustrated, at least. But when I met his eyes, I could tell he saw more in mine than I'd hoped for. He could see I was wavering. That he was wearing me down with patience and persistence and charm, not to mention his kindness when it came to Sophie.

That realization would only give him more hope. And there was some small part of me that refused to believe it was bad to let him have hope.

In fact, I was starting to hope, too.

WITH ALL THE gentleness in the world, Anthony lowered me to my skates and put his hand on my waist, drawing me back into position following the star lift we'd just done—the first time we'd done one flawlessly together. Everything about the trick had felt right.

"Yes!" Ellen called out from the boards, cheering us on. "That's exactly what I want. Now do it again, and don't either of you change a thing."

Anthony squeezed my hand gently, and as one we inhaled and took off with our left foot. Everything we'd done in the last week had been to improve our synchronicity, learning to breathe in time with each other, to match our strides, to anticipate the other's actions two beats before they would happen. All our hard work was paying off. It was crazy to think that less than a month had passed since our first skate together.

It was all starting to come together. We had officially agreed to a partnership now, which meant I needed to start moving on the massive amounts of paperwork I needed to file. It wasn't unheard of for a government to push through citizenship for an athlete who could compete at my level, especially considering I'd already won gold once, because of the prestige of international competition. Anthony and I would definitely have to sit out this season, but we could potentially be ready to compete next year. That would give us two full years leading up to the next Winter Games. But none of this would happen if I didn't file all the appropriate forms and convince the U.S. President to push things through. That was next on my to-do list.

After three strides, Anthony's hands were at my waist, and in no time I was soaring high in the air above him, my arms and legs locked into position, my abs tight to keep me balanced. At exactly the same moment, we shifted my position in the air, easily finding a new center point. Three seconds until the dismount. *One, one thousand. Two, one thousand. Three, one thousand.* He changed his grip and brought me back to earth. My skate blades met the ice in a feather-light caress, not like the way Guy would sometimes plunk me down following a lift. Guy had never been overly careful with me. He'd expected me to look out for myself. Working with Anthony was a nice change of pace.

"All right," Ellen said, her enthusiasm bringing her face to life and erasing the lines around her mouth and eyes. "Do that three more times, perfectly in sync with each other, and then we can call it a day."

She had another pair of students—much younger than us, only in their early teens—coming in for their session, so she turned her attention to them, trusting us to do as she'd instructed. Anthony and I continued on our own. Once we finished and he set me down on the ice, there was a long, loud, slow clap coming from the opposite side of the ice from Ellen.

"Bravo," Guy said, sarcasm dripping from his tongue and turning my blood to ice. I didn't even have to turn around to realize it was him. His voice still echoed in my head, even though I hadn't seen him for months. Berating me. Threatening me. Begging me to forgive him, only to start in on me all over again the next day.

Anthony turned me in his arms and chucked me under the chin until I looked up to meet his eyes. "You okay? You went all stiff on me as soon as he showed up."

I couldn't speak. My tongue was thick with dread and fear and a bit of hatred, and bile was slowly climbing up my throat and making my eyes sting. I nodded. Lying. I always lied when it came to Guy. Anthony didn't look like he believed me, so I forced a smile to my lips. "Fine," I forced out. "Give me a minute, okay?"

"Want me to come with you?" There was a crease between his brows. Had to be from worry.

I shook my head, fully realizing my voice would betray me, and I skated over toward Guy.

"So what, he doesn't trust you to be able to get rid of me on your own?" Guy asked, laughing, when I reached him.

I kept a few paces between us, though. No chance was I moving close enough for him to touch me. Because he would. He would touch me like he owned me. And that touch would make my skin crawl more than it already was from nothing more than seeing his sneering face.

I glanced over my shoulder. Anthony was far enough away that he couldn't hear but close enough that he could intervene if needed. He had his eyes trained on the two of us. That helped calm the churning in my gut, but only so much.

"What are you doing here, Guy?" My voice cracked on the words.

Nerves were eating me alive. I'd come a long way since I'd cut things off with him, but I wasn't ready for this. To see him. To confront him. I wasn't anywhere close to ready.

"I miss you, baby. I'm a mess without you."

"You were always a mess with me, too."

"Because I don't know what to do if you're not right by my side." His voice had taken on the sickening tone he always used when he wanted to sweet-talk me into forgiving him. "This is a joke, right? Skating with him? You've got to come back to me."

"This is not a joke. Anthony and I are partners now. I'm not coming back."

"You have to." His eyes went dark, taking on the slightly crazed look he got if he didn't get his way. "I'll die without you. As my partner. As my girl."

I shook my head and backed up on the ice, putting more distance between me and Guy...less between me and Anthony. "It's not going to happen, Guy. Let it go, okay? Just let me go."

"I can't. You know I'm worthless without you."

I knew he was worthless, but that had nothing to do with me.

"I've seen you with your new boy toy. The Babcock kid. Hockey player."

My throat got tight. Dry. I couldn't swallow. "He's not my boy toy."

"No? Then you won't care if anything happens to him?"

My insides knotted. Twisted. Tightened. I broke out in a cold sweat. Clammy. "What are you saying?"

"You be sure he's not your boy toy, okay?"

"You need to leave," I forced out. "Go back home." But he wouldn't. He might never be out of my life. The reality of the situation was creeping in on me, turning everything in my head into a gray, foggy, sodden mess. I had to go. I backed up again, until I felt Anthony's warmth behind me. His hands landed on my arms, and he stroked them up and down, warming me. Soothing. A reminder that I wasn't alone. That I didn't have to live in Guy's world anymore, that his lies were no longer the reality I chose for myself.

Guy turned and left, but his veiled threats wouldn't go with him. They hung in the air, surrounding me. Suffocating me. I might not be his partner, his girlfriend anymore...but he still owned a piece of my mind.

Would I ever be free of him, once and for all?

"You okay?" Anthony asked. His voice calmed me down almost as much as the solidness of his body behind me.

I nodded. Blinking to keep myself from crying.

"Because you don't seem okay. What was he doing here?"

I shook my head. The last thing I needed now was for everyone else in my life to start freaking out about Guy. I was doing enough of that on my own for all of us. "He only wanted to stop by since he was in town," I forced through my teeth, tasting bile as the words left me. Because it was a lie.

I'd never been one to lie before—except where Guy was involved. But that appeared to be all I could do when it came to him.

"YOU LOOK LIKE somebody just ran over your dog," Sara said. "But you don't have a dog. What gives?" We were at the mall to go shoe shopping, along with both kids. She had Cassidy in her stroller, and Connor was running up ahead, but only as far as his leash would allow. Yes, she had her kid on a leash. Sadly, I understood all too well why such a thing was necessary. She took a moment to adjust his leash to prevent him from running quite so far ahead.

I couldn't explain why she thought she needed more shoes. She had an entire closet full of them. In fact, I was pretty sure that about half of the money Cam had left after helping me out all the time went toward buying Sara new shoes. Still, at least going shoe shopping together was a way for me to forget about the fact that Guy had showed up at practice today.

Or I was trying to. But Sara was digging, and she was the one person here in Portland, other than my counselor, who knew anything about what had happened with him.

"It's nothing," I said.

"I may not be the sharpest cheese in the fridge, but I'm not stupid. It's not nothing."

"Well, you tell me. What do you think it is?"

"Did Levi try to pull something?" She shook her head as soon as the words were out. "No, not his style. He's still trying to win you over. Anthony? Did something happen in practice that reminded you of Guy?"

I didn't say anything. I only bit down on my tongue.

"That's it. What'd that fucker do?"

"Mommy! You said *fuck*!" Connor screeched so loud it echoed through the entire mall.

"How did you even hear that?" I asked, laughing. He was easily a good five feet ahead of us, and it was jam-packed in the mall, people everywhere, music playing over the speakers.

"He has selective hearing," Sara said, drawing in his leash and giving halfhearted apologetic looks to everyone walking by with scandalized expressions. "Don't you remember the rule?" she said to Connor once he was inches away. "Just because Mommy says something, that doesn't mean you're allowed to repeat it."

"I'm telling Daddy on you," Connor said in a taunting voice.

"Well, goody goody. I'm telling him on you, too. And you can bet he'll probably spank you this time."

Connor grinned. "If he spanks me, he'll spank you."

"I'd like to see him try," Sara muttered under her breath to me. But there was a hint of a blush on her cheeks. Sara didn't ever blush. Never. I was pretty sure I'd just picked up on something about her and my brother that I'd prefer not to know.

Mind bleach. I needed mind bleach.

Then as quickly as the blush had come, it was gone, and she waved Connor ahead. "Go. Run. Burn off some of that energy."

He took off again, but with the shortened leash, he could only run wide circles in front of us.

I couldn't help grinning at her. "You do realize you act more like he's an annoying little brother than your son, right?"

"I keep waiting for him to grow out of this phase."

"Something tells me that won't happen any time soon."

"Something tells *me* you're trying to change the subject," she said. She gave me a side-eyed glance. "So are we taking body parts to feed to the alligators in Florida?"

I shrugged. "Not Anthony's."

"Levi?"

"No."

"Cadence Johnson, you'd better fucking tell me what the hell's going on, or I'm going to feed *your* body parts to the alligators."

This time, Connor turned to look, but he stared with wide eyes. Sara's tone had changed. At least he recognized that much. He might just make it to five years old, after all.

I smiled, hoping it would help calm him down so he'd think everything was okay. Once he started running circles again, I said,

"Guy showed up at practice today."

"He *what*? He's in Portland? Oh, you just wait until I get—"

"Calm down so you don't scare the kids."

"Cadence, this isn't a *calm down* sort of moment."

"How do you know that?"

"Well, let's think about this for a moment, hmm?" She kept her voice down this time, but the intensity was still ramped up. "What was he doing here? After he fucking *dropped* you, after he made you have a fucking *miscarriage*, what the fuck does he think he's doing here?"

I shook my head, trying to defuse her. Instead of coming home, I should have gone straight to Wendy's office and begged for a quick session. Something. Anything but let Sara see how much Guy's drop-in had upset me. But I hadn't, and now she was flying off the deep end. If I didn't calm her down and convince her I was fine, there was no telling what she might do. Like tell Cam.

"I don't honestly know what he wants," I said. "I mean, he was talking like he couldn't live without me. Stuff like that."

"He's going to have to live without you. I'm not letting that son of a bitch anywhere close to you." She stopped short, causing Connor to jerk against the end of his leash and stumble back a few steps until he landed on his butt. He laughed maniacally, but he didn't seem hurt at all. Sara stared into my eyes, hers a little wild. "What did Anthony do? And your coach?"

"Ellen was already working with her next class. Anthony stayed close."

"How close?"

"Close enough."

"Hmph." She started walking again, though. "Do you think Guy's leaving now? Is he done fucking with you, or will he come back?"

I shrugged. "No idea." Only that was a lie, just like everything I'd said to Anthony about what Guy wanted was a lie. There was one thing I understood without a doubt about Guy, and it was that he never gave up easily. If dissuading him were possible, he never would have shown up in Portland. He would have been out of my life as soon as I'd informed him I was done with him.

But that hadn't happened. There'd been weeks of phone calls, text messages, emails, notes left on the front door of my house or under the wiper blade of my car. He'd come by and pounded on the door, demanding that I let him in so we could talk. After a while, he'd let it drop, only to pick up with the obsessiveness again after a month of silence. That had repeated time and again until I'd left. Until I'd come to Portland.

And now he was here.

I had a very good idea about what Guy wanted and whether he would leave now. Once again, I felt myself being pulled under by a powerful tide, and I didn't understand how to free myself from it.

Sara scowled. "Other than trying to get you back, did he say anything?"

I shrugged. Again. It was my go-to defense mechanism. I had always done that around Guy, because he never wanted me to answer him. He only wanted to act like he'd asked for my opinion, like he was taking my feelings into consideration.

"Nothing?" she demanded.

"He knows about Levi," I said quietly. I wasn't certain why I'd said anything at all.

"Bet he can't stand knowing you've got a good man in your life."

"It's not like that with Levi," I argued. Too quickly. Even I heard the defensiveness in my response.

"You don't think he'll do anything there, do you?"

I shook my head. It was only me Guy would hurt. Wasn't it? But I'd never thought he would actually hurt me until the day he'd dropped me so I would miscarry. And it was all because, when he'd suggested I should have an abortion, I'd told him I needed time to think about it first. I hadn't wanted to run off the same day and have the procedure done. I'd needed to figure out how I felt about it, but Guy hadn't allowed me that. If he'd been able to so casually hurt me physically, what else was he capable of, given the right circumstances? I honestly wasn't sure anymore.

"We should tell the police," Sara said.

"Tell them what? That my ex-partner came to my practice and asked me to come back to him?"

"More like that your ex-partner who has fucking abused you before came to your practice because he's fucking stalking you," she said.

"You're seriously exaggerating what is going on here." Wasn't she? She had to be. Or was I actually trying to convince myself of that, but really, she was right?

Days like this, I couldn't decide if I would rather be an adult or a kid. Adults had to actually deal with things like this, but kids had to be told what to do.

Which was better now?

"I want to tell Cam," Sara said as she turned Cassidy's stroller into the first shoe store she came across. "Run it all by him and see if he thinks I'm exaggerating."

"No! You promised."

"I did," she said, dropping her voice well below her usual level. "But I think there are things you're not being entirely truthful about."

"I've told you the truth." I simply hadn't told her everything.

"Hmm," she said. Scowling. "You're killing me, Cadence. I'm worried about you. I appreciate that you're seeing a counselor and all, but I'm worried."

"But you won't tell him, will you?"

"I need to think about it."

There wasn't much to do but accept that and move on. And in the meantime, I needed to sort out what I should do about Levi.

Chapter Eight

Levi

"YOU'RE COMING TO my fucking birthday party whether you like it or not, numbnuts." Koz tugged on his tie, always uncomfortable wearing anything more elaborate than sweats, and looked down the concourse toward the exit for the parking garage. Then he glared at me as if daring me to contradict him.

We'd just finished beating the Habs in a shootout—Jamie had scored the game winner—and my feet were ready to move toward the escalator leading up to the owner's box, taking the rest of me along with them whether that was what I intended to do or not. I didn't exactly have plans with Cadence for tonight, but that didn't mean I couldn't make them with her. Did it? But then again, we weren't dating. We were *friends*. That was all. And *friends* shouldn't simply assume that the other friend would go along with anything and everything on the spur of the moment.

I shoved my hands in my pockets. "But it's a Saturday night." My complaint was feeble and I knew it.

"And you don't have a fucking date or anywhere more important to be than my birthday party, so don't pretend you do."

It was true. Cadence still hadn't given in and agreed to take our friendship to the next level, but that didn't stop me from wanting to see her tonight. If I dropped by the owner's box to see her... Maybe she'd give in tonight. If I didn't try, I'd never know.

Nicky streaked past us, bumping into Koz as he went. "Sorry.

Jessica's in labor!"

"Go," Koz shouted after him, actually grinning for once.

"Your birthday isn't even until tomorrow," I argued once Nicky was gone.

"My birthday starts in exactly forty-seven minutes. Clock's ticking. Maybe Nicky's kid will be lucky enough to share my birthday. But if you aren't at my place when the clock strikes midnight and we start celebrating, I will kick your ass from here to eternity."

Harry came out into the concourse this time, heading for the garage wearing one of his ridiculous bowties. No guy in the league but Harry could get away with wearing a damn bowtie all the time. Fucking ginger. No soul. If he had one, there was no chance bowties would work on him. Tonight, he even had on a vest as part of his suit.

Still, he'd been my defense partner for the last couple of weeks, and we were working well together after my first big blunder. Whether the guy had a soul or not, at least he and I were making a good team. Hell, he'd even scored tonight's game-tying goal off a one-timer from my pass.

Koz caught sight of Harry's bright red hair flashing in the lights and yelled at him across the empty space. "My place. You're coming, right? All the single guys are supposed to be there. Party of the year."

"I have plans already, Koz. Can't do it."

"Do your plans involve strippers? Because mine do."

Harry laughed. "Strippers don't come close to what I've got planned. Not gonna happen this time. I'll buy your dinner tomorrow to make up for it." With that, he disappeared down the corridor.

Better than strippers, huh? Did Harry actually have plans—and if so, did they involve Dani Weber, who was still in town—or was he simply uninterested in one of Koz's crazy parties? Harry always seemed so straight-laced, but sometimes he threw me for a loop with something that seemed completely out of character. Like flirting with Dani that night. Out of all the guys on the team, he might be the most private.

"What the fuck is he trying to pull off, thinking *anything's* better than strippers?"

I could think of a lot of things that were better than strippers. Like a night with Cadence. Hell, even if Jonny and Sara went out for a night without the kids and we spent the whole time babysitting Connor and Cassidy, and Connor jumped up and down on my balls, that'd be a lot better than strippers. But I didn't expect Koz to understand that. He lived in a world that was all his own. The rest of us could drop in and look around sometimes, but rarely did any of it make any sense to anyone but him.

I also knew without a shadow of a doubt that if I didn't show up at Koz's party, he'd hold a grudge the size of Mount Hood. I was his road roommate. His best friend on the team. One of the only guys who managed to put up with his shit on a regular basis.

So I headed back inside and up to the owner's box to make my excuses to Cadence. Only she wasn't there.

Sara saw me and headed over almost immediately, digging around in her purse for something. She handed me the folded piece of paper when she got it free from her bag. "She asked me to give you this."

"Thanks." I folded it over one more time and slipped it into my pocket. Whatever it said, I got the sense I should read it alone. "Is she all right?" Every single home game we'd had since her arrival in Portland, Cadence had been there. She hadn't told me she had anything else going on. Granted, she didn't owe me any explanations. We were still nothing more than friends, however much I might want us to be more. There was no reason she had to tell me anything at all. It was entirely possible she even wanted to stop being my friend. Something squeezed my chest at the thought, but there wasn't a hell of a lot to be done about it. She might never change her mind and give me the opportunity I wanted. Then where was I? All alone, same as always.

"She's fine," Sara said. But her eyes told me a different story.

"Did I fuck things up somehow? What did I do?" It had to be something I'd done. My brain couldn't process any other explanation for the worry in Sara's eyes.

She shook her head. "It wasn't you."

But the fact that she'd said it wasn't me meant I hadn't imagined things, and there *was* something wrong. But who had done something to hurt her?

Jonny? No, that couldn't be it. As far as Cadence was concerned, her older brother had practically hung the moon.

Maybe something was going on with their mother, though, or one of their sisters? But if there was a family emergency of some sort, Jonny would be aware of it, and he would have gone home to deal with it along with her. That couldn't be the problem.

Possibly there were issues with Anthony. But why wouldn't she be here, with her family, if she was struggling with something related to her new partner? And based on the way the guy had acted around her the day we'd gone to ChocolateFest, I couldn't dream that he'd ever do anything to hurt her. If anything, he was as protective of her as Jonny was.

None of the scenarios that came to mind made any sense at all, and Sara didn't seem inclined to fill me in. I thanked her for passing on Cadence's note and headed down to my car to read it.

> *Levi,*
> *I'm truly sorry to do it like this, but I think I need some space. Please don't come around anymore. I don't want to hurt you, but I never should have let things go this far.*
> *I'm so sorry. Please, if you can, try to forgive me.*
> *Cadence*

No real explanation at all. Just a fucking Dear John letter. She couldn't even bother to call me, let alone tell me to my face. I had to remind myself again that she didn't owe me anything, not even the courtesy of telling me to my face that she wanted to break off the bit of friendship that we had.

It still hurt like a motherfucker, though.

For a moment, I thought about calling her. But if she'd wanted to talk to me, she could have called. I thought about driving over to Jonny's house and trying to catch her there before Jonny and Sara got home with the kids. But, again, she could have come to the Moda Center tonight if she'd wanted to see me. Instead, she'd chosen to send a terse note with Sara and have that be the end of it.

So that was it. Right? It was over. Done. Whatever I'd thought was brewing between us was no more, and I was back to only being me, the guy who always fucked everything up.

I started my car and headed out of the parking garage, unsure where I was headed. In no time, I pulled up in the lot in front of Koz's place.

Strippers. He'd said there would be strippers. And there wasn't a doubt in my mind that he'd have plenty of beer.

Time to get shitfaced.

Cadence

CONNOR TACKLED ME when they came through the door after the game, attempting to tickle my ribs. He didn't have good tickle technique, though, so all he did was dig in with his fingers. At least his nails were trimmed. I laughed anyway and flopped back on the sofa to give him better access as Sara headed straight upstairs with a zonked out Cassidy to put her down for the night.

Cam crossed through the living room, tossed his bag in the laundry room, and came back to rescue me from his son, lifting the little boy up over his head. "Bedtime," he said. "You were supposed to fall asleep in the car."

Connor giggled in response.

Cam raised a brow. "Why are you still so wired?"

"Mommy bought me candy."

My brother rolled his eyes at me and groaned, slowly lowering Connor to the floor. As soon as his feet hit the floor, Connor started running in circles around the coffee table.

"Good game," I said once I caught my breath.

"At least we came away with two points. It wasn't a sure thing," Cam replied. "I told Nicky I'd come up to the hospital with him to wait. Jessica's in labor. Want to come?"

"I do," Connor said. He stopped running, grabbed my hand, and tugged to pull me up from my prone position. "Let's go, CayCay."

"Not you. You're going to bed," his father said, then turned back to me. "Come with me. Keep me company. We need to talk."

There wasn't a question in what he'd said this time around, even though he'd originally worded it as an invitation. It came out more like an order. Cam never tried to boss me around. That meant it was serious, whatever it was. Had Sara told him? Or had Levi said something after reading the note I'd sent with Sara?

My pulse slowed to a crawl.

Hanging out in a hospital waiting room wasn't exactly how I'd envisioned the rest of my night, but I didn't see that I had much choice. "All right," I said, hoping my wariness didn't come out in my voice. "Let me go grab a sweater."

Cam grunted and carried Connor upstairs to turn him over to Sara. I followed them and slipped into my room, closing the door and leaning against it. I needed a moment to settle my nerves. It wasn't any use, though. The more I tried to calm down, the more heightened my anxiety grew. After a moment, I took a sweater out of the closet and headed back out, only to bump into Sara.

She grabbed hold of my biceps to steady me and looked me over a few times, a slight scowl marring her otherwise movie-star perfect features. "You're pale."

"Did you say something to him?" I hissed. "You promised."

She shook her head. "Not yet, but I was seriously thinking about it."

"Levi, then?"

"Doubt it. He took off after I gave him your note. A bunch of the guys are going to Koz's place tonight. I'm sure that's where he is."

"Then what is this about?" I waved my arm in the direction of my brother and the living room, in case she wasn't clear.

"Cadence?" Cam called up the stairs before she answered. "You ready?"

Sara pulled me in for a brief, tight hug, then nudged me on my way. "Go. I don't know any more than you do, and there's no better way to find out what he wants than to let him get to the point."

"Fat lot of help you are," I muttered.

"It's always better to come straight out with the truth, you know. Even if it hurts."

"I can't." I blinked hard to show the tears threatening to fall who was boss as I headed down the stairs with my sweater draped over one arm. And it was the truth, as far as I could tell. There were some things in life that I simply wasn't capable of doing, and telling my brother any of this beyond what he'd already discerned on his own was definitely one of them.

Sara did have a point, though. Maybe I would have to find a way to come clean with some of it. But how much? I wasn't sure.

Cam winked when I reached him. His attempt to put me at ease didn't do a darn thing to calm my nerves. He already had my coat and purse out of the closet, and he held them out for me before opening the door and heading down to his truck. I quickly donned my coat and hurried after him.

"Confession" by Florida Georgia Line poured through the speakers when I climbed in.

He backed out of the driveway without saying anything. I glanced over at him, watching the street lights flicker over his face as I tried to figure out how much he'd caught on to and what I should force myself to tell him.

"So you've been here almost a month now, and we've hardly talked," he said, his tone conversational. "Things going all right?"

"Going great." However casual it was starting, this conversation wasn't going to be so light and breezy for long. I had no doubt about that. "I think I've spent more time with Sara and the kids than with you."

"Part of the deal, playing in the NHL. My time's not my own. You've been busy, too." He cocked his head in my direction for a moment, just long enough for me to catch the wary expression drawing his brows together. "You and Sara getting along all right?"

"We always have. You know I adore her."

His chuckle was loaded with sarcasm. "I do. I'm aware you're nuts about her mainly because I love her. I think you're stretching things to say you've always gotten along, though."

"It's not like we ever argued."

"Argued? No. Only because she bites her tongue all the time. You drive her up the wall. At least most of the time. The two of you are as opposite as it's possible for two people to be. I know she loves you even though you can be trying for her—for the same reason. You're my sister, and she loves me, so she's determined to put up with all your antics that drive her berserk. But you haven't been. Not since you arrived."

"What do you mean by that?"

He shrugged. "You're always so bubbly and energetic and over-the-top happy. She'd been bracing herself for your arrival. But you're as docile as ever."

"Maybe it's only that Connor's being wilder than usual, so she doesn't notice me as much." But I hadn't been myself lately. Cam was right, whether I wanted to admit it or not. If anything, I'd been practically morose, for me. Sara definitely hadn't seemed as annoyed by me as she typically did, but then again, we'd been distracted by everything I'd told her about Guy. Our relationship was evolving from where it had started, back when she and Cam had first gotten together. Now we were much more equal than ever before. On level footing. I was no longer the obnoxious seventeen-year-old kid sister.

Cam didn't even bother rebutting my suggestion. I hadn't fooled him at all, apparently. My heart sunk.

"Everything okay with Anthony?"

"Everything's great with Anthony. Better than expected." I tried to force the usual lightness into my voice and not let on how unsettling today's practice had been. It hadn't had a darned thing to do with Anthony, after all. My brother wasn't often able to tell when I was putting on a show for his benefit, thank goodness. "Why shouldn't it be?"

"Because you and Sara were both acting funny when I got home this afternoon, and the only thing I thought of that was different was you'd had practice this morning. I wondered if anything had happened to upset you. And because you faked being too tired to come to the game tonight."

"I was tired. I *am* tired."

"I bet. It's hard work, lying all the time."

My breath all left me in a flood. "What do you mean?"

Cam came to a stop at a red light. "Only that I'm aware you and Sara are keeping something from me. I've always been able to see straight through you, and I can't always tell *what* Sara is holding back, but I do realize when she's trying to keep me in the dark."

"See straight through me?" I fiddled with the buttons on my coat.

"Yeah. You've never fooled any of us. Not me, not Mom, not Corinne or Chloe. Yes, you're as happy as a clam a lot of the time, but we know there's a lot more to you than simply that. We know you use your smiles and personality to hide when you're hurt."

"I'm not hurt."

"Bullshit." The light changed, and he eased into the intersection. "Maybe you don't realize you do it, but you turn it on too much when you want people to think everything's fine. Try to shine too bright. You've been doing it for months. Since you cut things off with Guy, according to Mom. When you were injured."

"I just didn't want anyone to worry too much about my ankle. It wasn't like it was a serious enough injury to end my career or anything. No reason to let everyone get all worked up."

"And stop it with trying to convince us your ankle was the problem, all right?"

I chewed on my lower lip. How much had they figured out? Corinne wouldn't have dug into my medical records, would she? That was unethical. And illegal. My doctors couldn't tell her anything without my permission.

"If you don't think it was my ankle, what do you think it was?"

Sooner than expected, he was turning the truck into the parking lot at the hospital. He found a space near the Women's Center and came to a stop before speaking again. "I wish you'd tell me what it was. All I know is I think it has a lot more to do with what's going on inside you than with anything physical."

There wasn't a thing to say to that. If I even bothered trying to respond, he was bound to hear the truth, no matter what words I tried to feed him. I stared down at my hands in my lap.

"So I'm right," he said after a moment.

I shrugged.

"Is it helping to have Sara around to talk to? Is that why you wanted to come here?"

"I came because I wanted to skate with Anthony."

"Mm hmm." Cam turned off the engine and put his keys in his pocket. "So is 501 your rebound, then? You're with him so you can land on your feet after having your heart broken?"

"Guy didn't break my heart." More like my soul. "And I'm not with Levi, anyway. I told him I needed some space."

"Why'd you do that? I finally came to terms with the idea, and you give him the heave-ho?"

"I'm not ready," I said, evading reality. Because the reason I'd pushed Levi away had very little to do with me and even less to do with Levi. It had everything to do with Guy.

Cam stared at me the way he always had, where it felt like he was trying to see through all my smiles and laughter to reach what lay underneath. "I think you are ready," he said after a near-painful moment. "I think the problem is you're scared."

He had no idea just how right he was.

Chapter Nine

Cadence

NICKY HAD SPENT the entire time we were at the hospital in the room with his wife, so there wasn't any true reason for Cam to be here. His niece and nephews—he and Jessica were their guardians now—were too young to stay at home alone all night, but at the same time too old to need much supervision. Still, we kept an eye on the three of them. Elin, the oldest, kept her two younger brothers in check without our help.

By two in the morning, the boys were dropping off, dozing in their seats in the waiting room. Elin occasionally got up to go visit her aunt and uncle, giving us status updates when she came back. More often, she had her nose right up against her phone, texting like crazy.

"Who do you think she's talking to this late?" I asked Cam, dropping my voice so she wouldn't hear me from across the way.

"She's fourteen. I bet all her friends are up right now, whether school is happening tomorrow or not." He laughed, slipping his phone out of his pocket to check for messages. "Soupy's oldest is her best friend. Those two are almost inseparable. That'd be my guess." He scrolled through a few screens before settling on something and pausing to read. "Sounds like Koz's party was something else."

I yawned, stretching my arms overhead. These waiting room chairs were murder on my butt. "You wish you were there instead of here?"

"Sara would kill me if I was there, based on the pictures I'm seeing."

I raised a brow and stifled a laugh.

"Don't say a word," he grumbled, shoving his phone back in his pocket.

I drew my fingers across my lips, then tossed the pretend key over my shoulder. "Who sent you pictures, anyway? Is someone trying to land you in trouble with your wife?"

"Doubtful. They're just being guys."

His phone buzzed again, but he ignored it.

"You don't want to see more?"

"Not particularly."

"Liar."

"Look who's talking," he shot back.

Better not to go back there, since I'd gotten him to drop the subject when we'd arrived at the hospital. I bit down on my tongue to keep from putting my foot in my mouth. "What if it's someone else? Could be Nicky," I pointed out.

Cam scowled and dug out his phone, glaring at me. Apparently someone was calling, not texting. He swiped his thumb across the screen and answered it. "What?" he demanded. I couldn't hear the person on the other end well enough to make out what they were saying, let alone determine who it was. A couple of moments passed with Cam listening. "What the hell did you do?" He glanced over at me and shook his head, his expression not giving a darned thing away to me. "I'm at the hospital with Nicky and Jessica. The kids are here. I can't go off and leave them in the waiting room." Then silence again. "Because they're fucking kids, Harry. Try 501 or one of the other guys at Koz's party." A couple more beats passed by, and Cam got up to pace. "Well, what do you want me to do? I can't make those guys sober up in the next five minutes. I can't wake Babs or someone else up if you can't."

I found myself leaning forward in my seat to hear him as he walked, trying to figure out what sort of trouble Harry had gotten himself into.

"Call Bergy or Webs. That's what you should do." He walked back in my direction, not paying any attention at all to me. "Because if you're in jail, you've got to have someone bail you out. And they're going to find out eventually. Might as well let them know what the hell's going on now so you don't surprise them with it. Maybe they can start figuring out how to deal with the media…" His voice trailed off as he stalked down the hall.

Jail? Admittedly, the only things I knew about Harry were that he was one of Cam's teammates and his hair was as red as could be, but I never would have pegged him as one who'd do anything to land himself in jail. What on earth was going on?

I didn't have long to wonder because as soon as my brother disappeared down the hall, Levi came walking in, filling the space Cam had vacated only moments ago. He was staring down at his phone, not paying attention to where he was going until he practically tripped over my feet, crossed at the ankles.

"Sorry, wasn't paying attention to where I was going," he said, slurring the words slightly and glancing up from his phone. Then his eyes met mine. He reeked of beer, but he smiled at me, sweet and cocky all at once. That combination only lasted a few moments, soon dissipating into a pained grimace. "Cadence," he breathed. "Why are you at the hospital? Are you okay?" He felt my forehead with the back of the hand holding his phone, as if checking me for fever, of all the ridiculous things he could have done.

"I'm fine. Better than you are," I teased.

He raised a brow, like he doubted me, but that slight change in his position was all it took to make him sway where he stood. He had to be as drunk as I'd ever seen a person.

I reached up a hand to grab hold of his arm and steady him. "Maybe you should sit down."

"Maybe I should." So he did. Not very gracefully. He plopped down into the seat next to me so hard it nearly skittered backward across the floor. If it had been against a wall, he might have caused some damage from the force. "I'm a bit drunk."

"More than a bit, I'd say. Please tell me you didn't drive here." I had the awful sense that my note was behind it, too.

He shook his head. "Ghost has all the guys' keys. Took a cab."

That was a relief. "So why are you here?" Never mind the fact that he'd asked me the same thing and I hadn't answered. As drunk as he was, I doubted he could remember his own name for long, let alone anything more pressing.

"Because there aren't enough beers or strippers in the world to wipe your face from my mind."

Ouch. So I was the reason for it. Not a good feeling, even if I nearly cracked up at the way he'd said it. I bit down on my lower lip, trying hard not to burst a gut while laughing at the ridiculous honesty of that statement. Still, the pain behind it was evident, not only in how insanely wasted Levi was but in the lines around his mouth and eyes. That sobered me up quickly enough, even if it didn't come close to helping him sober up.

"Thought I'd keep Nicky company," he slurred. "Koz wanted to keep throwing strippers my way, having them give me lap dances and shit, so I'd stop being so depressed about you. But I don't want them. I want you. I want you way too fucking much, but you don't want me."

I blinked a few times, not sure if I was trying to fight off tears or if I was simply stunned by what I was about to do. "I do want you," I said before I spent too much time analyzing it. "That's the problem."

His head whipped around to stare at me with bloodshot eyes. "Why's it a problem?"

"Because I'm scared." There wasn't any point hiding the truth. Levi was so drunk, there was no chance he'd remember a single word I said. I could tell him everything without fear that any of it would sink in.

Heck, maybe I should. It'd be nice to tell *someone* in my life everything, or at least someone other than my counselor. I'd filled Sara in on some of it. Cam only knew the bare bones. Mom and my sisters were aware of even less than Cam. The thought of relieving myself of the burden, of ridding myself of the enormous lump that had settled in the center of my chest and refused to budge, was so tempting I doubted I could resist.

"You scared of me?"

I shook my head. "Not you." If anything, I was scared *for* him. And for me. There hadn't been too many times in my life that I'd even admitted to myself how much fear I lived with on a daily basis, but Guy showing up at my practice today had sent it all rushing straight back to my heart. Stopping my pulse. Stealing everything good from me in an instant.

There wasn't any good way to describe it other than fear. And it was debilitating.

"It's that asshole, Guy, isn't it?" Levi pressed. "He's still in your head."

"In my head?" I shrugged. "It's not as simple as that." Nothing was simple.

"Why not?"

I hesitated. Glanced across the waiting room to find that the boys were still fast asleep and Elin might as well be. She wasn't paying any attention to us. Cam still hadn't returned from dealing with whatever trouble Harry had gotten himself into. All of that meant there was no point in lying, no reason to tell him anything less than the truth. I bit down on my lower lip again and then I went for it.

"He showed up at practice today."

"What the fuck is he doing here?" Levi tried to stand up, but his foot slipped and he fell down again almost immediately.

I put my hand on his, hoping it would keep him where he was. We might be in a hospital, but that was no reason for him to go and hurt himself by doing something stupid. "Trying to get me back," I said. "Telling me how he can't live without me. Threatening me. And threatening you, too."

"What about me?"

"Guy knows about you. He didn't come right out and say he'd hurt you if I didn't stay away from you, but he might as well have."

"So that's what your note was about? Trying to warn me off? So, what, so you can fucking protect me?" Levi was practically roaring now, with no signs of recognizing he was in a public place and should keep it down. "That's fucking backwards, Cadence. Screwed up. I'm not the one who needs to be protected from this son of a bitch. I saw how he fucking made you cry back in the Winter Games. Maybe no one else did, but I did. I saw it. Fucking bastard."

Throughout his entire tirade, I kept trying to calm him down so he wouldn't wake the kids or cause a scene. There weren't any others in the waiting room at this hour, but there was no telling when someone else might come in. His eyes were flashing, so full of hurt and anger and booze that I could barely find the sweet, self-effacing, funny guy I'd come to care about underneath it all.

"Levi, please," I said, taking his hand in both of mine and drawing it to my lap.

"Has he threatened you before?"

I shook my head. "Not really. Or maybe. I don't know. Everything's a mess in my head."

"What *everything?* Tell me."

My shoulders started to go up in a shrug, almost involuntarily, but I stopped myself. "It started years ago. Not long after we first became a team. Things were going great. Our coaches and choreographers loved us and had high hopes for us. I thought I'd hit the jackpot because we seemed like such a perfect match. But before long, it started. He'd catch a rut with his skate in practice, and because of the way we'd be skating side by side, I would stumble or maybe fall. In the early days, he would glower at me and grumble about keeping my footing, and I'd apologize and promise to do better. There was never any point arguing that it hadn't been my fault, that he was the one who'd caused the mishap. He wouldn't hear a word of it.

"Before long, I started to believe it myself—because the rest of the time, he was as charming as ever. He was great in front of the cameras. He was personable. He went on and on to anyone who would listen about what a great team we made, how we were going to go as far as we could in figure skating. We were going to win the gold. Or we would, he'd tell me, as long as I got my act together and stopped screwing everything up all the time."

"Son of a bitch," Levi grumbled. He rubbed his thumb over the back of my hand. Although, he wasn't slurring his words anymore. My admission might have done the unthinkable and sobered him up somewhat. That could be dangerous. Maybe he'd remember some of this tomorrow... I couldn't exactly stop telling him now that I'd started, though.

"It really was my fault often enough that I took it all on myself. And the longer we were together, the worse it got. Early on, he was careful to only berate me when we were alone and no one else would hear. But once we started dating, that changed. I'm not sure if it was because we were together all the time or something else, but he forgot all about that filter. He'd do it quietly so the whole world wouldn't hear, but hearing about how inadequate I was quickly became a daily thing. And it spread to areas that weren't strictly related to figure skating. If I wanted to go out with my sisters, he gave me a hard time because I wasn't giving him enough attention. If I tried to start up a friendship with someone, he soon convinced me that relationship was bad for me, so I'd cut it off before it turned into anything substantial or lasting. He did his best to make sure he was the only person with any influence over me, the only one who held any sway."

"Why the fuck did you put up with that?"

This time, I couldn't stop myself from shrugging. "It started so small, but it kept building. Gradually. A bit at a time, he took over my life. I thought he loved me and was pushing me to be the best. That he was looking out for me. It wasn't until later that I realized he was cutting me off from everyone in my life who would put a stop to it."

"So what changed? I mean, you were still with him at the Games. And he was still being a bastard. That much was clear to me."

And now we arrived at the part I had such difficulty putting into words. "A few months later, I was pregnant. I told him as soon as I realized, before I'd had a chance to figure out what I wanted to do about it. He flew off the handle. Screamed bloody murder at me. He said I was trying to ruin our careers. That I'd gotten knocked up on purpose because I was trying to hurt him. Then he demanded I go in for an abortion."

"And did you? You must have," Levi said. There was so much sadness simmering beneath the anger in him. With his free hand, he tucked some of my hair behind my ear. Such a gentle and unexpected touch. Too much more of that, and he might just undo me.

I was both intrigued and frightened by the prospect.

I shook my head. I needed to let it all out. Now that I'd started talking, the urge to plow through and empty the whole clip was so strong I felt powerless to stop it. "I didn't have an abortion. I didn't think I wanted one, but no matter what, I wasn't ready to make a snap decision. Not about something like that. So I told him I needed some time to decide what I wanted. Guy sulked all night, telling me over and over again that I was doing this to hurt him and there was no other explanation that made any sense. The next day in practice, we were working on a lift, and he dropped me. He hadn't hit a rut or anything like that. It was a lift we'd done hundreds, maybe thousands of times before, and he'd never once dropped me. But this time he did. Hard. It was almost like he threw me into the boards more than dropped me."

"And you miscarried," Levi finished.

I nodded. "My ankle was sprained pretty badly, but I lost the pregnancy. Had to go in for a D and C. We told everyone it was all about my ankle, though."

Levi was calm. Too calm. It felt like the dangerous sort of calm that Cam tended to arrive at right before he went off the deep end in trying to protect someone he loved. I couldn't seem to stop shaking, worrying about what he might do.

"So this son of a bitch treats you like shit for years, knocks you up, then he hurts you bad enough that you lose the baby. Then you leave, and he follows you? And threatens you? Am I understanding this right?"

I wasn't shocked by hearing profanity, but Levi seemed to have lost some sort of filter over that. Likely because of all the alcohol in his system. In all the time we'd been together, he'd kept it in check a lot better than this. It knocked down a layer of my defenses, leaving me vulnerable. "There was more in between, but yeah. That's basically it."

"What kind of more?" Levi growled.

"Nothing too serious. He just wouldn't take the hint. He kept calling me, leaving me notes on my door or my car. That sort of thing."

"He stalked you."

"I wouldn't go—"

"He fucking stalked you. He abused you for years, and then when you tried to put an end to it, he started stalking you. And he's still doing it. He's trying to intimidate you into doing whatever the fuck he wants you to do, and that's why he's threatening me. Well, not to my face. I doubt he wants to do that. It's all about getting to you. But he followed you here to keep stalking you, Cadence."

I swallowed hard. When he put it like that, there wasn't much point in trying to argue with him. Maybe I'd never thought of any of it in quite those terms, but there was a sickening ring of truth to them. "Maybe," I said slowly, taking my hands from his and wrapping my arms around my middle.

"Instead of calling the police, you decided to take things into your own hands and break things off with me."

"Do you honestly think the police—"

"Yes, I damn well think the police need to be involved. And not because I'm scared for me. I'm scared for you. I'm scared for your brother and his kids. I'm scared for your fucking partner and your coach, and the barista who sells you your morning coffee. This guy's a fucking time bomb, from what I can tell."

The last thing in the world I would ever want to do was subject my niece and nephew to anything Guy might come up with. And now that Levi had mentioned them, all sorts of horrible thoughts swarmed my mind. To that point, I'd only been thinking of myself and Levi. There were way too many people Guy might hurt in order to get to me, though: Levi, my mother and sisters, Cam and Sara, Connor and Cassidy. He could even try to hurt Anthony, Ellen, or Jesse.

I blinked, wishing my pulse would slow down. The blood raced through me so fast, my veins might've ended up with whiplash.

"How the hell can Jonny be aware of all this and not insist on involving the police?" Levi demanded.

"He doesn't know."

"Didn't," Cam cut in from behind us, his voice quiet and seething with fury. "I *didn't* know. Now I do."

"I..." Words failed me as I looked back and forth between these two furious men. "How long have you been standing there?"

"Long enough," Cam clipped off.

"Why the hell didn't you tell him?" Levi asked. "I mean, I

understand why you didn't say anything to me. Sort of. We were only friends, or whatever the hell kind of bull you've got in your head about the two of us. But he's your brother. You're living with him and his kids."

Cam came around in front of us, his arms crossed in an intimidating posture that broke my heart. "How much of this is my wife aware of?"

I shook my head. "Don't blame Sara. I made her promise—"

"You made her promise not to say a word about this to me. When your safety was concerned. When *my family's* safety is concerned." His glare was enough to melt my bones. "I do blame her."

"No, please don't," I begged, blinking back tears. What had I done? The last thing on earth I wanted was for anything to come between my brother and sister-in-law simply because I had acted like an idiot. But that was exactly what appeared to be happening. And it was all my fault. "She was going to tell you."

"Oh, was she? When, exactly, was she planning to do this? Not soon enough." He shook his head in a cloud of disgust and disappointment. "She should have told me as soon as she knew anything. She should have—"

"Please, Cam. It was only because I begged her not to say a word to you." I blinked some more, but it was no use. Tears streamed down my cheeks. There were few things in the world that cut me to the core the way my brother's disappointment did.

"We'll go to the police in the morning," he replied. Not a word about forgiving Sara for doing as I'd asked.

What a mess I'd caused. My only consolation was in the knowledge that the majority of their anger wasn't directed at me. There was some, of course. Because I hadn't trusted my brother enough to tell him. Because I'd ignored the signs Guy had given me for far too long. Because I'd been stupid and hadn't thought about the very real threat he posed to everyone in my life, assuming he would limit his shenanigans to me. And that they'd merely be his usual tactics, not anything that would truly hurt me, despite the fact that he'd already done precisely that.

"I'm sorry," I said, but my voice cracked, coming out as barely more than a whisper. "I should have—" But my throat closed up before anything else would come out.

"Yes. You should have," he clipped out. Then he stalked across the waiting room and checked on the three kids, taking a seat beside Elin, who was now dead asleep, even through all the emotion pouring out of us on the other side of the space. Almost as soon as he sat, her head fell over to land on his arm. At once, he turned back to his usual teddy bear self, wrapping an arm around her and drawing her closer the way he used to cradle me when I was a little girl.

I tried to blink my tears away, but it was no use. All I could do was stare at my hands in my lap and rethink all the things I should have done differently. It went back for years, so I could easily spend weeks going over them all in my mind ad nauseam until I made myself sick with it.

Levi reached out a hand and brushed a tear from my cheek. "So is this the only reason you wanted space? Because you didn't want Guy to hurt me?"

I nodded, swallowing hard in the hope that I could move the massive lump away from my vocal chords.

"So if I don't care? If I refuse to let him intimidate me away from you? Then we can keep going as we have been?"

"I—" My tongue was thick and dry as I looked up to meet Levi's eyes. "Maybe we should see what the police say first?"

He shook his head. "I don't care what the police say. No one's going to keep me away from you. Not now. I'll only stay away if you convince me that's what you want and it has nothing to do with this son of a bitch. And I promise you, I won't be easy to convince of that. Because I think it's bullshit."

"I've never been a good liar," I said.

"Good." The corners of his lips quirked up in a cocky smile. "But Cadence?"

"Hmm?"

"I still want more. A lot more."

The lump in my throat grew so big I couldn't take a breath anymore because of the way he was looking at me. Like he wanted to wrap me up in his arms and hold on until I gave in. Like he wanted to take me somewhere private and do things that would make my brother want to kill him. Like he wanted to kiss me.

And I wanted to let him. I wanted it really, really badly. So much I almost tasted the wanting.

But Nicky bust into the waiting room, grinning from ear to ear. The slamming doors woke the kids, and he rushed over to their blinking faces. "It's a girl!"

Chapter Ten

I WOKE UP with a splitting headache, the urge to puke up my guts, and the knowledge that there wasn't a damned thing I'd done to cause Cadence to want to back away. Not only that, but it looked like things might be moving forward again. Soon, at least. Maybe not immediately.

I looked down at my phone and saw the shitload of text messages from Koz, calling me a pussy-whipped douchebag for wimping out on his party and leaving before it was over. There were a ton of missed calls and voice mails, too, probably all from him. For all I knew, the party was still going on, well after eight in the morning. I was way too hung over to deal with him right now.

Ignoring Koz for the time being, I dropped my phone on the nightstand, dragged myself out of bed, and climbed into the shower to wash off the stench of last night's excess. By the time I was clean, dressed, and trying to replenish my body with water to ease my hangover, I remembered that Jonny intended to go to the police station with Cadence this morning.

Should I volunteer to go with them, too? I wasn't sure. I'd done my best to make it clear to her how I wanted things to go between us, that I wanted us to be more than the friends we'd agreed upon, and sooner rather than later, but did that put me in the go-to-the-cops camp? Might be too big of a jump.

Even though it ate at me to do so, I decided to let Jonny and

Cadence handle this one on their own. I should stay out of it. If the police needed me for anything, I was easy enough to find.

The team had the day off. Since Koz and most of the single guys were hopefully sleeping last night off, they wouldn't be up and about any time soon. If I didn't start moving, I'd probably end up back in bed the whole day, burying my head under the covers to pretend drinking so much last night hadn't happened.

It *had* happened. In a devastated stupor, I'd allowed myself to get more wasted in a single night than I ever had before. No point in trying to hide from it. Besides, while parts of the night were all kinds of fucked up, other very good things had come from it.

With nothing better striking me, I called for a cab to take me over to my brother's house. My car was still at Koz's, and I was fairly sure Ghost still had my keys. I'd talk Jamie into helping me deal with all of that later. Didn't bother texting or calling first. Even if he had gone to the gym or something else equally responsible, I was sure Katie would be at home. She had turned one of the extra bedrooms into a recording studio, and most days she was in there working on her budding songwriting career.

The cabbie dropped me off in front of their house. I paid him and got out. Rang the doorbell.

Jamie answered wearing nothing but a pair of boxers. His cat, Blackbeard, was draped around his neck and shoulders. He gave me a disgusted look—Jamie did, not Blackbeard, although that cat was always suspicious of me. Still, I guessed my shower hadn't done enough to hide all of last night's excesses.

"You look like death warmed over," Jamie said.

"Not sure how warm I got it."

"A cold shower might do you some good. Hell, any shower might help."

"Already had one."

He looked doubtful, but he stepped back to let me inside. Katie's cat, Oreo, raced in to wind himself around my legs. Oreo had always liked me a lot better than Blackbeard did. Granted, Oreo liked anyone who would scratch behind his ears.

"You have breakfast yet?"

My stomach gurgled in response.

"Never mind. I don't want you puking on anything." He led me into the kitchen, where he was busy putting together something involving eggs in muffin tins. He finished adding all his ingredients and popped it in the toaster oven, Blackbeard supervising everything from his shoulder perch. "Coffee? Think you can handle that?"

I shook my head and took a seat at the breakfast bar. "Water would be better."

Oreo jumped up onto my lap and purred, so I scratched behind his ears like he always wanted.

Jamie grabbed a glass and filled it from the fridge before sliding it over to me. "How late did you stay at Koz's last night?"

"Late enough. Got wasted. Then I got the bright idea to go keep Nicky company at the hospital."

Jamie raised a brow.

"Took a cab. But I didn't spend too much time with him. He was busy with Jessica in the delivery room."

"So what'd you do all night? Hang out with the kids?"

"While I was drunk?" I raised a brow. "They were sleeping by the time I arrived. Jonny and Cadence were there."

Katie came around the corner wearing a towel, her hair wet and dripping. She took one look at me, blushed, winked, readjusted her towel to keep it in place, and left again before Jamie murdered me for seeing his wife in such a state. Like it was my fault! Haha.

My brother pretended he hadn't noticed. Bunch of horseshit.

"What's going on with you two?" I asked, hoping to turn the conversation away from me.

Jamie made a face, like he didn't want to talk about it.

"That doesn't look good."

"It's just… Katie wants to have a baby. We're trying to get pregnant, but…"

"But no luck so far." And there very well might not ever be. Twice already, Katie had gone through chemotherapy and radiation to treat different forms of cancer. "You both knew kids might not be possible."

"We did." He shrugged. "We do. She still wants them, though."

"What about adoption?"

"That's what I suggested, but she wants to keep trying for a while first. I doubt if she'll give up until they tell us she *can't* have kids, you know?"

"And you're taking that all on yourself, aren't you?"

He and I were a lot alike in some ways. Too much alike.

"Maybe." He poured himself a cup of coffee and joined me, giving Oreo a tail tug for good measure. "So…Cadence? How's that going?"

"Could be better," I replied. "Could be worse. About to be complicated."

"Yeah?"

"Yeah." But I wasn't ready to tell him or anyone else about the son of a bitch who was trying to fuck with her life.

"Good complicated or bad complicated?"

"Just complicated."

"Okay." He took a sip and stared at his cup the same way I was staring at my glass of water. Times like this, it was unnerving how similar we were, even though there were countless differences. This must be another Babcock trait. Now that I thought about it, I recalled a lot of times I'd seen Dad in this same posture. Scary thought.

"For what it's worth," Jamie said, "I hope you two are able to uncomplicate things before too much time passes."

"Why's that?"

He waited until I looked at him, then he grinned. "I don't know if it's all the time you've been with her, or if something else has gotten into you, but you're finally starting to play like I've always realized you're capable of. You're not beating yourself up constantly. You're finding your footing. You're regaining your confidence. So if Cadence Johnson has anything to do with that, I hope it continues for a hell of a long time."

All at once, Katie came back in with clothes on, the timer on the toaster oven dinged, and Oreo nipped my finger because I had stopped petting him. I sucked in a sharp breath, even though it hadn't hurt, and thanked the powers that be for saving me the need to respond right away. Because there was no fucking way I could come up with a reasonable response. Not yet.

"Morning," Katie said, beaming at me. She planted a smack on my cheek and stole Jamie's mug of coffee since he was busy dealing with taking breakfast out of the oven. "Didn't expect you up so early."

"Neither did I," I admitted.

"Any idea what's up with Harry?" Jamie asked me as he slid the omelet muffin things onto plates for himself and Katie.

I raised a brow. "Harry? He had big plans. Didn't come to Koz's party. Why?"

"What kind of big plans?"

"No clue. Better than strippers. That's all he said."

Katie snorted and took a sip.

"Hmm…" Jamie fixed himself another cup of coffee, since Katie didn't seem inclined to return the one she'd stolen.

"What's up?" I asked, curiosity stoking my appetite enough that I reached for one of the forks in Jamie's hand and cut myself a bite.

"Not sure. I had my phone off all night. Woke up to some weird voice mails from him."

"Weird how?"

He shook his head. "Never mind. I'm sure it's nothing."

If it was nothing, my brother never would have mentioned it. And I had never bothered to listen to all the voice mails on my phone. I'd assumed they were Koz bitching me out about leaving as early as I had, but I'd never confirmed my assumptions. They could have been Harry. I dug my phone out of my pocket and looked at the missed call log. Eight of them, all from the same unfamiliar number. "What did he say in the messages? And how many?"

"Only that he needed someone sober and awake to help him out. Wouldn't say what it was about. I called his phone this morning, but he didn't answer."

I held my phone out to him. "Was it from this number?"

He nodded and raised a brow. "He called you, too, huh?"

"Apparently so."

"I hope he got the help he needed."

So did I. And now, I felt like a shitty friend.

Katie's phone buzzed with a text message. She took a moment to read it, then glanced up at the two of us with surprise making her eyes wide. "He got help. Dad just bailed him out of jail."

Cadence

HARRY AND ONE of the team's coaches were on their way out of the courthouse across the street from the police station Cam and I were heading into. Cam slowed and called out to them.

"So Webs got you all sorted out?"

Harry nodded and ducked his head. With the way Webs was glaring at him, I didn't blame him. They went on their way, and we went on ours.

Three hours later, Cam and I left the police station with an emergency protective order against Guy, the promise that they'd serve him notice, and a court date in two weeks to have it finalized.

"Doesn't this seem like a bit much to you?" I asked Cam as we climbed back into his truck to head home.

My brother gave me one of his patented you've-got-to-be-shitting-me looks and backed out of his parking spot.

We'd listed Cam, Sara, and the kids on the order, as well as the address for the house, the rink, and even the Moda Center, since they were all places I tended to spend a lot of time. When the officer had asked about a significant other, I'd hesitated for a moment. Cam had cut in and given Levi's name.

It had been eating me alive ever since.

"Why did you tell them Levi is my significant other?"

"That son of a bitch threatened him, too, didn't he?"

I supposed that was a fair point, but that didn't make Levi my significant other. He might want to be, but that didn't mean he was. After that, I bit my tongue the rest of the way home.

When we got there, Cam gave Sara a copy of the protective order and put another on the fridge. "Be sure you've always got that with you," he said. Then he picked up Connor and stalked off to the backyard with Buster yapping and chasing after them.

Once they were gone, it was only the two of us. Sara went into the kitchen to clean up from Connor's snack, so I followed to help her out.

"Cassidy's sleeping?" I asked.

"Mm hmm." She shoved a couple of plastic bowls into the dishwasher rack with more force than necessary.

She was mad at me. And she had a right to be mad, in all honesty. I'd made her promise to keep a secret from my brother, and it had turned out to be a much bigger, more harmful secret than I'd anticipated. He'd barely said a word to either one of us today. I'd had to fill Sara in on what had gone down at the hospital this morning, before we'd left for the police station.

I took a rag from the sink to wipe down the table. "I'm sorry," I said. "I should never have asked you to—"

"You had every right to ask me for a favor. Don't go there, Cadence. You and Chloe and Corinne—you're always telling me I'm one of your sisters now, right? And that's something sisters do. They help each other out."

"But it wasn't fair of me."

"Bullshit." She slammed one of Cassidy's sippy cups into the rack. "You asked. It was on me whether I should keep your secret or tell him. If he's pissed at me for keeping your confidence, that's between the two of us. It's not anything for you to worry about. Cam and I are going to have to sort this out on our own. Once he'll listen."

Only that meant *I* was between the two of them. Almost literally. They weren't speaking, and it was all because of my stupidity. How could I possibly do anything but worry?

I finished helping her clean up, but then I had to prepare myself for practice. Anthony and I had an afternoon session scheduled. Maybe it would help me take my mind off everything else that had gone on in the last twenty-four hours. That was my hope.

As I should have expected, my hope was in vain. Now that I'd gotten a restraining order against Guy, I needed to explain the whole shebang to both Anthony and Ellen. That had taken up a good half of our ice time. We spent the other half eating ice cream at Ben and Jerry's, because I was an exhausted, emotional wreck, and I was supposed to give Sophie her first figure skating lesson after she got out of school.

Anthony took another bite of Cherry Garcia. "So if he shows up at the rink again, I'm allowed to call the cops and have his ass arrested, right?"

I laughed for the first time in way too long. "Yeah. Something like that, at least."

"You don't think he'll try that, though, do you?" Ellen asked. "I mean, not once they've served him with the papers."

I didn't want to think so, but Guy had proven time and again that he'd do the unexpected. "Let's hope not," I said. "It'll be much easier if he simply respects the court order and stays away. Maybe he'll go back home."

"Doubt it. I don't think he's that type." Anthony stole a bite of my Chunky Monkey.

I swatted his hand away. "If Jesse finds out you're having ice cream without him…"

"He'll what?" He raised a brow. "Buy more. That's what he'll do. I promise."

"And do you really need any more after this?"

"You can never have too much ice cream on a crappy day. That's Jesse's motto."

Ellen winked at me. "It's a good one."

I chuckled and took another bite before Anthony stole too much out of my bowl. Seemed like a good enough motto to live by for the moment.

After we finished, I promised them both I'd be very careful and take care of myself, that I'd report anything Guy did as soon as possible, and that I'd buy some pepper spray to carry around with me. This morning, Cam had already made me promise I'd let him teach me some kickboxing type of stuff for self-defense, but I figured pepper spray would be another tool in my arsenal. With the way they were all acting, the police officers I'd spoken to this morning included, I was starting to realize exactly how dangerous this could become.

It all added up to leaving me feeling like I was too stupid to live. Maybe I had been, but I couldn't afford to be any longer. I had to stop thinking Guy was harmless. I had to stop believing he would never do anything to hurt me, or anyone else. The absolute opposite was the truth, and there was no room for me to believe my own lies.

I headed back to the rink. Even though I was early, Sophie and Bergy were there ahead of me.

So was Levi. He was kneeling down on the floor in front of Sophie to help her lace up her skates, and he flashed a grin in my direction as soon as I came through the doors.

I waved at them, but Bergy headed me off before I joined them.

"Your brother filled me in on everything that's going on," he said, getting straight to the point. "I've already talked to the security guys here, and they've assured me they won't let the bastard in. I thought I'd stay for Sophie's lesson, though. Just in case."

I blinked and nodded, but it was quickly becoming apparent that the rest of the world was far more in touch with the danger of my present situation than I was. "You're...you're not rethinking this, then? You aren't worried—"

"I'm worried about you," he cut in, giving me a pointed look. "Jonny's been part of the Storm long enough that you should understand we're not only a team. We're a family. And that means his family is part of our family. And it means that 501's girlfriend is part of our family. We take care of our own. You should start getting used to that, especially since you're living here now."

What came out of my mouth then was the silliest, most superficial thing I could possibly say: "I'm not Levi's girlfriend."

Bergy cocked a grin in my direction, and he chuckled. "All right. Whatever you say. You're still part of the family because of your brother, so you're stuck with us. Everyone in the Storm organization is on your side. Whether you like it or not. Besides, Sophie has decided to adopt you."

"Adopt me?" At first, I thought he was being facetious, and I laughed.

"That's what she told me. She said she's 501's best girlfriend, but you can be his other best girlfriend. And then she asked me to adopt you."

That was enough to wipe all the negativity of the last twenty-four hours straight out of me. This little girl might as well be a magician, the way she warmed me through from head to toe. No wonder Levi doted on her.

I took a seat next to Sophie on the bench to lace up my skates. Levi sat on her other side and drew his skates out of his gym bag. Only they weren't hockey skates. They were figure skates. I'd thought he was only here to support Sophie, or maybe because he was as worried for my safety as Bergy was after all I'd told him last night. I hadn't expected that I'd truly be teaching *both* of them today. Hadn't that only been to play along with Sophie's idea? Wasn't it something meant to mollify her for the time being, and then cooler heads would prevail? There was no reason he couldn't come out there in his hockey skates. It wasn't like he would be doing spirals or jumps.

Levi caught my eye and winked. "Sophie told Bergy we both needed figure skates. Now we've got them. You ready for this?"

Not even close, but today was turning into a day I wouldn't soon forget.

TWO HOURS LATER, Sophie and Bergy were on their way out of the rink—Sophie beaming like I'd just given her a puppy—and Levi was waiting by the door to walk me out.

"My ankles feel all wobbly in those things," he said.

"Maybe you need to work on your ankle strength," I said, winking. "Do your trainers have any workouts designed specifically for that?"

"I'm sure I can find something."

He took my gym bag from me and carried it, along with his own, over his shoulder. We headed outside, prepared to be blinded by the late afternoon sun, but instead we were greeted by gloomy gray clouds.

Levi stared up at the sky as we crossed the parking lot. "Might have some snow tonight."

"I'm still not used to living where there isn't snow all winter long."

"Yeah." He grinned at me. "It's nice to not have to shovel the car out every morning, though."

I laughed and pressed the button on my key fob to unlock my car. When I looked up, though, I nearly fell over. Stopped cold. Guy was halfway across the lot, standing out in the middle of the aisle with his arms crossed. His all-too-familiar silver Honda Civic was parked a few feet behind him. After a moment, he waved and blew a kiss in my direction.

Levi stopped beside me, his hand settling on my waist. "What do you want to bet that's exactly how many feet he has to stay away from the building?" he murmured in my ear.

I was too stunned and too scared to move. All I could do was stare. Was this all to intimidate me? It was working. I had never felt so much fear in my life. My blood was ice, and I couldn't swallow.

But Levi nudged me toward his car. "Lock your doors again," he said once my feet were moving. "I'm driving you home. Jonny and I can come back later to pick up your car."

I pressed the button and watched the brake lights flash. Then Levi held the car door open for me and I sat. I wasn't sure if I could breathe again until he parked in Cam's driveway and helped me go inside.

Cam and Sara were both on the floor in the living room playing with the kids. Everyone was smiling, so that was a definite improvement. Maybe Cam had gotten over it and forgiven Sara, finally.

He jumped to his feet as soon as Levi and I came through the door, though. "What? What happened? You look white as a sheet."

"Guy was in the parking lot when we were leaving the rink," I forced out. Then, after a moment to let it all sink in, I added, "I think we should call the police."

Chapter Eleven

Levi

I WAS STILL at Jonny's house hours later. They'd invited me to stay for dinner after Cadence and I had given our report to the officer who'd come to the house. Even if they hadn't, I might have invited myself. The last thing I wanted to do was walk away from Cadence right now. The way I saw it, the more people she had around her, the better.

Yeah, the officer said they were going to immediately send someone to talk to Guy again. That said, the emergency order hadn't stopped him from showing up at the rink, so I doubted another visit from the cops would do anything to deter him. Not unless they were putting him in cuffs and taking him to jail. Didn't sound like that was going to happen, though. Apparently, waving and blowing a kiss from a distance wasn't quite enough.

It was entirely possible I didn't want to leave more for me than for Cadence. To calm my own nerves. Seeing how pale Cadence had gone the instant she'd realized the bastard was standing there had left me shaken and unnerved. I needed to be near her. To assure myself that she was safe.

But now, the kids had been put in bed and it was late enough I ought to go home. Especially after the debacle of last night. We had morning skate early tomorrow, followed by a game, and I needed to be rested and in top form.

Jonny's line of thought must've been headed in the same direction, because he stretched and yawned, glancing over at Sara. "Ready to call it a night?"

"You have no idea." She glanced over at me and Cadence with bloodshot eyes. "Get all your late nights in while you don't have kids. Everything changes once you do. It's like someone flips a switch and you go from twenty-five to eighty, just like that." She snapped her fingers to emphasize her point.

"I don't think we're planning on having kids any time soon," I said without thinking.

The glare Jonny shot in my direction was enough to melt my bones. Cadence stifled a snicker.

"You'd fucking better not be planning on making babies with my sister any time soon," Jonny growled. "Not if you plan on ever being able to make more of them. We're heading to Florida next week, you know. Lots of gators down there." But then he took Sara's hand and led her toward the stairs. "Be sure you lock up when he's gone," he said to Cadence.

Then Sara winked at me as they disappeared.

"You're probably exhausted, too," I said once we were alone.

"Yeah. It's been one heck of a day."

"So I should go?" I wasn't sure why it came out as a question, but I said it again with much more certainty. "I should. Go, I mean. I should go home." Okay, maybe there still wasn't a lot of certainty in it. In fact, I was still hoping she would want me to stick around for a bit longer.

"You don't have to. Not yet, at least."

"No?"

"No." She met my eyes. Hers had been all sorts of colors all afternoon and evening, mainly in the dark and intense brown realm since the incident with Guy. But now they were lightening. Shifting into something softer and almost green.

I remembered that night at the diner after the concert. They'd been green a lot that night. When she'd been relaxed with me. Not on her guard. They'd been golden during most of Sophie's skating lessons, with hints of green peeking out every now and then.

But now? They were as green as I'd ever seen them, kind of like moss.

We were both sitting on the couch, but there was still a big gap between us where Connor had been. For the longest time following his bath, he'd stretched out between us, his head on Cadence's lap and his feet bopping me in the nuts in time to the song he was singing about agilators. Wearing nothing but his Spider-Man Underoos, of course, because what else should a four-year-old wear at any point in the day? I hadn't been sure if Jonny had orchestrated it or if it had been Connor's idea, but it had very effectively kept me from trying to snake my arm around Cadence's shoulders or her waist, to draw her closer to me.

Now that we were alone, it was all I could think of, though. Touching her. Being close to her. Holding her and breathing in her scent.

"I wanted to thank you," she said.

I shook my head, baffled. "For what?"

"For thinking clearly this afternoon. For putting me in your car and driving me home, since my head had gone blank and I didn't know what to do."

"All I wanted was to take you away from that son of a bitch as soon as possible," I said. The thought of what might have happened if she'd been alone had been racing through my head ever since. Would he have tried to talk to her? To grab her? What if he'd had a weapon of some sort? The way I saw it—the way Cadence had reacted to his presence—the asshole didn't need a weapon. Simply showing up and surprising her was all it took. It left her shaken, terrified, unable to act.

She gave me a shy smile and ducked her head. "I'm just glad you were there." Then, before I was prepared for it, she reached across the empty space between us and took my hand. Hers was tiny, barely bigger than her nephew's, it seemed. Almost fragile. She twined her delicate fingers through mine, and my pulse jackhammered out of control.

This was the first time she'd been the one to make a move. Every other time, it had been me.

"I'm glad I was there, too," I said, trying to keep the words steady, despite the fact that all my nerve endings were going haywire. I rubbed my thumb over the back of her hand, and she tugged. Not away, though. She drew me closer to her by an inch or so, which seriously set me into overdrive. "I always want to be with you."

"I know you do."

There was something odd in the way she said it. Something that left me wondering what was coming next.

Cadence bit her lower lip, but she still didn't try to take her hand out of mine. "I'm sorry I tried to push you away, too."

"You are?"

"I am. Because it was the exact opposite of what I should have done. I realize that now."

All the hyperactivity going on in my body slowed to a trickle. I was fairly certain I knew where she was headed with this, but I didn't want to jump to conclusions. I needed to hear the words straight from her mouth. I needed it as much as I needed air.

"You do?" I said. "And what do you think you should have done instead?"

She started to shrug but stopped herself, visibly forcing her shoulders down. "I should have run to you, not away from you. I should have recognized that you're nothing at all like Guy, at least not in any of the ways that matter. I should have figured out that instead of pushing, you were letting me take things at my own pace. You were already giving me time. Giving me space. Letting me figure it all out on my own, even when I was being an idiot."

She inched closer to me, closing the space between us. Then she took my hand and lifted my arm up and over her, wrapping it around her shoulders. She burrowed into my side, letting her head drop back onto my ribs. If she were taller, she might fit against my shoulder. This felt right, though. It felt so damned right I thought I might burst.

"Cadence?" I asked, hesitant because I didn't want to spoil the moment.

"Hmm?"

"What does all this mean?"

"All this?" She lifted her head away from me for a moment, and I thought I'd gone and fucked everything up. I should have kept my mouth shut.

But I hadn't, so now I had to fix it. "This," I said, using my free hand to gesture toward the way she was snuggled up to my side. "What's happening here? Because to me, this feels like more than something we'd do if we were still only friends, like we agreed." A hell of a lot more, actually. I'd been very careful all along to keep my hands to myself. To avoid touching her even though it was one of the few things I was capable of thinking about when we were together.

Gradually, she nestled against me again. Then she lifted her chin to stare at me. Her eyes weren't moss green anymore. They were dark green with golden flecks making them appear to be on fire. Alive. There was so much life and energy flowing through them it floored me. Bedroom eyes—that was how I'd thought of them before. And that was definitely what they made me think of now. She was back to being the sex goddess of my dreams.

"You still want this to be more?" she asked. Slowly, but not like she was afraid of my answer.

"More than I could ever put into words."

"Then maybe we should be more than just friends."

Addictive warmth shot straight out of my belly and spread through to all my limbs in no time. "Like what? Are you ready to be my girlfriend?" Because Lord knew, I was a hell of a lot more than ready for that.

She bit that lower lip again, and my eyes were glued to that spot. I wanted to taste her there. If I had to guess, I'd think she tasted like fire, too.

"I think so."

Fuck me, that wasn't good enough. "You only think so?" Talk about a guy deflating like a flat tire.

But she smiled, and it lit up the entire room. A real smile. Not one of her fake, forced ones. It was like she was coming alive in front of me. Before I had an inkling of what to expect, she put a hand on my jaw and turned my face toward her. And then her lips were on mine.

They were like molten silk, heated and smooth and so fucking perfect. I breathed in the scent of her, clean and feminine, and held it deep in my lungs so long I might have passed out if not for her gliding her tongue along the seam of my lips, begging entry.

She tasted like sweet cinnamon candy. I wanted to devour her, but I forced myself to hold back. To accept what she was giving instead of taking what I wanted.

She twisted and tucked one leg underneath her. Almost greedily, she moved her hand behind my head and dragged me down. Down. Down still some more until I had to brace my arms on either side of her to avoid crushing her. She wrapped her thighs around my waist and tugged me closer, like she wanted to be crushed.

"Not so fast," I murmured against her lips. Not that I wanted to stop what was happening—I'd have to be a crazy man in order to avoid reveling in the sensation of having her beneath me, writhing against me—but this was taking things from one extreme to the other.

Cadence dug her fingers into my hair. "But I want—"

"Not so fast," I repeated. I pushed myself up to keep from continuing. "You've had a lot happen in the last couple of days. The last thing you need to do is jump into something without thinking it through."

"I have been thinking it through, though."

"I know. But one day we're only friends, then the next you need space and can't even be friends with me, and now you're mauling me on your brother's couch with his kids sleeping upstairs. Not that I mind being mauled." I couldn't stop myself from grinning. "I actually like it way too much. But I still think it's better if we take things one step at a time like we were before."

She pouted. It looked so damned cute I wanted to nip her nose.

"Fine," she said. "You're probably right."

"I know I'm right." I had to be. Otherwise, why the hell would every nerve ending in my body be screaming that I was wrong, that I should ignore all that shit? There was a part of me that wanted to carry her out to my car and take her home with me, and screw the rest. But I was smart enough to recognize that part of me was behaving like a fucking idiot.

"Don't get used to me agreeing with you, though," she said.

I chuckled and climbed off her—reluctantly as all hell, but it had to be done. Otherwise, I'd be the one doing the mauling. "I should probably head home. Come on and lock the door behind me." I grabbed my coat from the hall closet. When I turned around, she was standing there, her lips puffy and swollen and pink, which made it incredibly difficult to keep myself from pushing her back up against the door and kissing her again.

Instead, I opened the door. The snow I'd expected earlier had apparently been falling for a while. There was a thick blanket of the stuff all over my car that I'd have to clear off before I could leave.

"Let me grab my coat," Cadence said. "I'll help."

I started the car and put the defrost on high to help things along. With the two of us working, it didn't take us too long to clear the snow away. At least it was still soft and not packed down like it would be by morning. When I took the scraper from her, I couldn't resist drawing her in for another kiss—one that warmed me up in no time.

Breaking away from her wasn't easy. "Go back inside and lock the door. Get warm."

"I am warm," she said. "With you."

I pecked her on her nose. It was as cold as the snow. "Liar."

She grinned and ducked her head against my chest, drawing me into an embrace. "'Night," she said.

"'Night."

But she didn't move.

"You need to go in, you know."

"I do. But it feels too good to be standing here like this. With you."

I forced myself to nudge her toward the door. When she got to the top of the porch, she turned around and waved at me. Then I got in the car and waited until she was inside and the porch light went out before backing out of the driveway.

Moments later, as I turned from their street to another, I could have sworn I saw a man sitting in a car that wasn't running. Just sitting there. Not doing anything.

Once I was past it, I glanced in my rearview mirror. The street lights illuminated it enough that I could tell there wasn't anyone in that car.

Must have been my imagination.

MY HEAD HAD never been filled with such a jumble of things at once. I was scared out of my mind about Guy and what he might do, excited and a little nervous about the relationship I was building with Levi, energized by the progress Anthony and I were making, fulfilled from being able to put my skills and training to use in order to teach Sophie, and gutted that I'd come between my brother and sister-in-law—even if they seemed to be getting back on track now. On top of all that, I missed Mom and my sisters like crazy, and I felt like an absolute idiot for not speaking up about everything that had been happening with Guy, going back for years, when he'd first started treating me like garbage.

Yeah, I'd been young and stupid. Maybe I still was. But that didn't mean I had to stay that way.

Cam took me to the gym up at the Storm's practice facility with him early the morning after my first lesson with Sophie. Well, technically it had been the first lesson with Sophie and Levi, but I'd promised Levi my lips were sealed about that, at least when it came to being around his teammates. Yep, one more secret to keep from my brother, but at least this one didn't have anything to do with my safety. Those days were over.

The team had to be at the Moda Center for morning skate at ten, but Cam said there was no time like the present to work on self-defense, especially since the team was leaving for a road trip in a couple of days. "I used to work with Dana Zellinger on this stuff," he said, tossing me some sparring gloves before putting those boxing pad target things on his hands. "You can start working with me, and maybe take some kickboxing or Krav Maga classes when we're out on the road."

"Krav Maga?" I asked.

"It's a kind of self-defense they started up in Israel, I think. For their special forces guys. It's what they're encouraging women who've been victims of assault to learn to take care of themselves."

That didn't sound like the worst idea in the world. I nodded and focused in on the instruction he was giving me. We'd been at it for about twenty minutes when he got frustrated with me. I was becoming frustrated with myself, too, come to think of it.

"Harder, Cadence. You've got to put all your force behind it. Try to hurt me."

"I am putting all my force into it." I huffed, and it blew my hair out of my face. I stripped the gloves off and adjusted my ponytail holder, mainly to buy some time to catch my breath. Cam had been working me hard, and none of this was familiar to me.

"No, you're not."

"Maybe you've forgotten, but I'm all of five foot nothing and maybe a hundred pounds soaking wet. I seriously doubt I can do anything that will hurt you."

"Get him with an uppercut under his jaw," said someone with a deep voice. "While he's distracted, knee him in the nuts. That'll hurt him."

I spun around to see who it was.

Chris Hammond winked at me. "It'll work every time."

"But I don't want to kick my brother in the..." I couldn't even finish the thought. That was just plain wrong. It was on par with thinking about Cam and Sara's sex life. It belonged squarely in the do-not-go-there department.

"That much is clear enough." He came in closer, letting the door swing closed behind him. "Right now, he's not your brother. He's the son of a bitch who's trying to attack you. So you distract him with an uppercut, knee him in the nuts, and then you escape."

"But..."

"Here." He reached for the hand targets Cam had been using and put them on himself once my brother relinquished them. "Do it to me instead."

"I don't think I can do that."

"You can," Cam said. "If you hurt him, Hammer and I can sort it out later." He waited a moment, then crossed his arms. "Pretend he's

Guy."

"But he's not Guy." It was a great idea, in theory. I wasn't sure how great it was in actuality. I didn't think I could ever do the things they wanted me to do to anyone. Maybe not even the real Guy.

"Oh, I'm not?" Hammer lunged toward me, tossing the targets away. He grabbed at my waist with one arm and put the other hand over my mouth.

My brain went straight to panic mode. I screamed for Cam to help, but my voice was smothered in Hammer's hand. In seconds, he was dragging me across the room, no matter how much I flailed.

I kicked anything I could connect with, preferably something soft. But Cam still didn't come to my rescue. Was this a test? Were they trying to prove something to me? Must be. My brother wouldn't allow anyone to attack me while he was standing by and watching. I tried to calm down enough to remember what he'd told me to do. Distract him with something and then kick him in the nuts.

With the way he was holding me, I couldn't punch him under the jaw like he'd suggested, but I could sure as hell bite his hand. So I did. Hard.

Hammer shouted and ripped his hand away from me.

As soon as possible, I twisted around and kneed him.

He released me, holding both hands to his groin as he stepped back. I collapsed to the floor, thoroughly spent and sucking in air.

But then he laughed, and he winked at me again. "See? I knew you could do it."

Cam came over and helped me to my feet. "You okay?"

I nodded, trying to reassure him. But then I thought better of it and punched him as hard as I could in the stomach.

"Oof! What was that for?"

"Heavy-handed tactics," I said, and Hammer only laughed harder.

"At least we know she can do it," Hammer said, as I stalked out of the gym.

"YOU SHOULD'VE PUNCHED him in the nose," Anthony said later, when I filled him in about everything that had happened since yesterday's non-practice. Ellen had a family emergency to see to, so we were on our own today. Whether we'd been partners for long or not, the two of us both knew exactly what we needed to work on, so it wasn't the end of the world for us to have a practice without our coach every now and then.

The bigger problem for the two of us was simply staying on task.

Now was a prime example of that. We should be working on our combined spins or our split twist. Instead, we were shooting the breeze. Yes, I needed to be sure he stayed abreast of the situation, but that didn't mean we should waste our ice time.

Yet that was exactly what we were doing.

"My arms are too short," I explained. "I can't reach Cam's nose to punch him there."

He grinned at me. "Good point." Then he skated over next to me and stretched my right arm as high as it would go.

"What are you doing?" I demanded.

"Measuring to be sure you can't reach mine."

I punched him in the belly with my free hand, for good measure, although not hard enough to do any damage.

He laughed and skated away, so I'd have to chase him if I wanted to cause him any true pain. He was as bad as Cam, only in his own way.

"You need to hit harder," he called out over his shoulder.

"You need to work on your abs," I shot back. "They're soft."

Anthony chuckled. "Your man wasn't there to help with the lessons?"

I couldn't stop myself from blushing. Good thing he wasn't looking. "What do you mean, *my man?*" I started skating until we were doing spirals across from each other.

He automatically mimicked my posture, trying to match me. Yes, we were talking and teasing each other. That didn't mean practice was over, especially since we'd completely bailed out yesterday.

"Levi Babcock," he said, dry as ever. "Who else would I be talking about?"

"He was probably sleeping. It was earlier than the butt crack of dawn." I intentionally avoided saying anything about whether he was my man or not, or how it made me feel. Since I hadn't sorted out my thoughts on the matter, I definitely didn't need to be talking to Anthony about it. Or anyone else. No one but maybe Levi.

"Was he up late with you last night? Is that why you're blushing?"

Now I blushed even harder, which didn't help matters any.

"Give me details. I need to know everything so I can fill Jesse in later. He'll eat this up."

"There's nothing for him to eat up."

"There is. You said he stayed after the cops left. Was he still there for dinner? Maybe you played footsie under the table?"

"Footsie?" I rolled my eyes. "What, are we twelve?"

"So it was better than footsie. Please tell me you made out."

"I'm not telling you anything." But the fierce heat in my cheeks was probably all he needed to know.

"Mm hmm," he said.

The longer we were out there, the closer together we moved on the ice. In no time, we were touching again. Anthony took me into a hold, and we started spinning, gradually shifting positions to experiment with what worked well for the ways we each moved.

I lifted a foot, stretched my head and arms back, and let Anthony's momentum spin me at high speed.

"For as tiny as you are, you get some incredible extension like that," he said. "You're like a cat. Weird spine or something. How do you do that?"

"Lots of stretching," I said when we slowed to a stop. "Maybe you should try it."

"Maybe." He waggled his eyebrows at me. "You think Jesse'll like it as much as your man does?"

"He's not my man."

"Whatever. You keep telling yourself that, honey."

"I will," I said, laughing. "At least for as long as you two are just fiancés. If you finally set a date, maybe I'll change my mind."

"Is that all it'll take?" Anthony gave me a Cheshire-cat-worthy grin. "Nothing more than setting a date?"

Something told me I might have to eat my words. "Why? Don't tell me you finally made plans."

"Valentine's Day. I was going to give you your invitation after practice. So..." He reached for my hand and pushed off, so we were skating side by side. "He's your man. Give me deets to give my man."

I couldn't stop myself from smiling as big as he did. "Fine. Be that way. There might have been some making out."

"Only some?"

"Not enough," I admitted. "He thinks we need to take it slow. Because of Guy and all."

"I think," he said slowly, "he might just be good enough for you. Even if he wasn't helping you learn self-defense."

Chapter Twelve

Levi

"SHOULD'VE PUT ON a cup first," Harry said to Hammer, and half the guys in the room cracked up laughing.

Hammer included. "Maybe so. But at least she knows she can fucking knee a guy in the balls and it'll work."

"Which means 501 has officially been put on notice," Harry said.

Another chorus of laughter and lighthearted ribbing followed that, and Jonny winked at me. He fucking winked. What the hell was that about? One of these days, I needed some time alone with him. Figure out where his head was. I knew where mine was, and I was almost positive he knew, too, but I hadn't figured him out in terms of whether he intended to murder me the next time I fell asleep on the team plane or if he was on board with the relationship Cadence and I were building.

Hammer met my eyes once the rest of the guys quieted down and went back to preparing for tonight's game against the Blackhawks. Winked at me, like maybe he was trying to reassure me.

I tossed him a roll of stick tape. "You're a crazy motherfucker, you realize that?"

"Took a risk," he replied.

It was all he needed to say, taking me back to his earlier advice for me. *Take chances. Stick your neck out. Maybe take a risk or two.* I nodded my understanding and finished tying my skates as Harry came to his stall beside mine and pulled on his pads.

I glanced around to be sure no one was paying us any attention. They weren't. Everyone was busy doing his own thing to get ready for the game. Nicky was showing off the newest baby pictures of little Molly, and Ghost was telling stories about Koz's party to anyone who'd listen—mainly telling stories about how shit-faced drunk most of us had been. He'd be aware, since he'd been the only sober guy of the bunch that night.

Then I turned back to Harry. "So what happened?" I asked, keeping my voice down.

He cast his eyes around the room before answering. "Nothing anyone needs to worry about. My lawyer's sorting it all out."

"You're not in any trouble, are you? Because we can—"

"I'm fine," he cut in. "It was only a misunderstanding. Not a big deal. Jim and the coaches know everything they need to know. My lawyer's handling it. Shouldn't slip out in the public, but if it does..."

"What kind of misunderstanding lands you in jail overnight?"

"I was at a party. Someone called the cops. Disturbing the peace, whatever the fuck that means. I don't know. They ended up arresting everyone in the place, but I wasn't part of the problem. I was...um...in the back. I wasn't around where they were being loud and giving the cops problems. Didn't know what was going on until they busted into the back and arrested us all."

I raised a brow. "Sounds like your party was even more out of hand than Koz's." I wasn't convinced that meant it was absolutely better than strippers, though. No one at Koz's party ended up in jail.

"Never mind all that. Let's get out there and beat these fuckers."

GETTING OUT THERE and beating those fuckers was exactly what we did, too. The Blackhawks were perennial Stanley Cup favorites these days, one of the teams that ended up on the preseason lists of who was most likely to win. We were on those lists, too, these days. Especially after last season, when we'd come within a few games of accomplishing our goal.

Every guy in our locker room intended to make sure all those talking heads knew we belonged on those lists every bit as much as the Blackhawks, and this game would go a hell of a long way toward accomplishing that goal.

We beat them two to nothing. Nicky came away with the shutout, despite facing forty-seven shots. And that only accounted for the shots that got through to him. Apparently fatherhood agreed with him. The whole team was black and blue after the game from all the shots we blocked, Harry and me in particular. Ghost scored both goals. Koz got a crazy hair and decided to fight Shaw in the third; he came away bloody, but not as bloody as the other guy. Jamie had hit every Blackhawk he could line up, playing like a human battering ram all night. It didn't matter that he hadn't scored. He'd done everything possible to prevent the other team from landing on the scoresheet and had dug his way under their skin with his physicality.

In the end, it was a statement game, and maybe our best game all season long. We had served notice to the Blackhawks and the rest of the league that we meant business—and that if anyone but us was going to win the Cup, they were going to have to go through us.

It felt amazing.

We headed back to the room in high spirits, with "Uptown Funk," our celebration song for the season, blaring from RJ's iPod and speakers. Winning games like this one always seemed to make aches and pains hurt a lot less.

I stripped off my jersey and tossed it in the laundry bin as I danced my way to my stall. Harry held out a hand for everyone to fist-bump on our way past him. They all did, until Webs came into the room. Webs glowered at Harry like I'd never seen him glower before, but Harry didn't even duck his head. He stared straight back at Webs, almost daring him to say something. What I wouldn't give to find out what had really happened that night... Maybe I could get him drunk some night and see if he'd talk then. It was worth a shot.

Once everyone was in the room and changing, Bergy said a few words. He focused on how we'd stuck to our game plan, played a solid team game, and no one had shirked his responsibilities in either zone. It was a real team win, and an important two points.

Then Ghost stood and fished the obnoxious purple umbrella hat out of his locker. It was a stupid thing we awarded to the best player of the night each time we had a win. He'd gotten it last game, so it was his responsibility to decide who got it tonight. No chance he'd select himself, even if he'd scored both goals. That wasn't how it worked.

I was all ready to go pat Nicky on the head again once he had this abomination on his melon, but then Ghost threw me for a loop.

"Hell of a win tonight, boys. And like Bergy said, it was a true team effort. Everyone chipped in and played their parts. Nicky held down the fort with a monster game in the net. But there's someone I think deserves this tonight more than anyone else. We all know the boys on D have been playing above their heads all season long. Each of those guys is being asked to fill a role bigger than he's ever filled before, and they're kicking ass and taking names while they do it. But tonight, 501 blocked probably as many shots as the rest of the team combined. Every time I looked out there, he was dropping to the ice and absorbing rubber. Then he'd limp over to the bench, walk it off in the tunnel, and go right back out for his next shift. The guy never complained even though he's probably purple from head to toe tonight. Not only that, but he and Harry did it while shutting down the Blackhawks' top line, which is no small feat. So 501, this is for you."

He crossed the room and placed that fucking thing on my head, then opened the umbrella top.

I looked like a fucking idiot. Didn't need a mirror to realize that.

The rest of the boys hooted and hollered, and Hammer slapped me on the back. "Too many more nights like tonight, and those other guys are going to have a real fight on their hands to reclaim their spot on the top pairing."

I wasn't so sure about that, but I wouldn't deny it felt damn good to do something right. Not only that, but it was something I felt like I could do again and again. Maybe it wasn't a one-time thing. Maybe I was starting to find my stride at the NHL level, finally.

It'd taken long enough.

I passed Ghost doing a post-game interview with Anne Dennison on my way up to the owner's box. She was making googly eyes at him, and he was eating it up with the biggest shit-eating grin I'd ever seen. I had to fight down the urge to tell him they should get a room. They were on live TV. Not the right time for that.

Besides, I was hoping to collect Cadence and take her out somewhere. Not to do something of the get-a-room variety, although that thought had merit, and I hoped we were heading in that direction and would arrive sometime in the not-too-distant future. But for now, I simply wanted to be with her for a bit before we had to leave town again.

She looked up and smiled at me as soon as I came through the door, warming me all the way down to my perpetually cold toes. She'd been sitting with Katie again—no Dani, this time—but once she saw me she came over and rose onto her tiptoes to give me a peck on my chin.

It wasn't quite the kiss I wanted from her, but at this point in our relationship I'd take whatever she'd give me. Pecks on the chin were still a hell of a lot better than being only friends.

I took her hand and led her into a quieter part of the room to give us some semblance of privacy. Not that I was deluding myself. No doubt every ear in that room would be on high alert, trying to figure out what was going on between us. Sometimes it seemed like that was all the Storm WAGs did all the time—try to hook up all the single guys. Hell, they'd gone above and beyond their usual level of interference at Christmas with the general manager, going behind his back to set up a profile for him on a dating website. It had all worked out in the end, but that was a ballsy move if ever I'd seen one. These women could be relentless when it came to being sure every guy involved with the team ended up just as happy and settled as they were, preferably with a boatload of babies on the way sooner rather than later.

If all went according to plan, though, they wouldn't need to interfere with what Cadence and I had going. We were managing just fine on our own, thanks. Not that anything would keep these women out of it if they thought they might need to help. They hadn't ganged up on me yet, but something like that could happen at any time, whether their interference was necessary or not.

Cadence wrapped her arms around my waist and rested her cheek on my chest. "You had a good game tonight," she murmured, her voice muffled against my suit.

"You noticed? I thought I was nothing more than a guy on your brother's team," I teased.

"You are a guy on my brother's team. But you're also…" She shook her head and burrowed closer.

The sensation of having her pressed up against me like that was too much. Despite the layers of clothes between us, I felt every curve of her body. The soft mounds of her breasts and the hard peaks of her tits. The gentle slope of her waist and the smooth flare of her hips. My thoughts were heading south, fast. Needed to redirect my thoughts.

"Also what?" I prompted.

She shrugged. "According to Anthony, you're also my man."

There wasn't any point in trying to stop myself from grinning. "What do you have to say about that? Am I your man?" Because I sure as hell wanted to be.

"I don't know. What would that mean?"

"Well, to start, it'd mean I can kiss you. And hold you, like this. Maybe take you out sometimes."

"So basically like before but with kissing and all that other yucky stuff that Connor doesn't like, hmm?" There was a definite teasing quality to her voice.

"*All* that other yucky stuff?"

She went rigid in my arms as soon as the words left my mouth. But then she laughed. "Not right away."

"Right. So not tonight, but tomorrow is a new day."

"Watch it," she said, laughing. "I'm getting pretty good at punching guys in the belly."

"And kneeing them in the nuts," Jonny said as he came into the owner's box.

Hammer was right behind him. "Amen to that."

Cadence whirled around, blushing. She was too fucking hot when she blushed. Made me think all sorts of things I had no business thinking with her brother standing three feet away. Still, I didn't care. She was gradually letting down her walls and welcoming me in.

Slow and steady, I reminded myself. *One step at a time.*

"Come out with me tonight?" I asked once the guys made their way past us and we were as alone as was possible surrounded by all the WAGs and kids, not to mention half the team.

Still blushing, she turned back to face me. "Come out with you where?"

"Your choice. We can go with the big group to dinner and be surrounded by people. Or we can go, only the two of us, back to Shari's and share a slice of pie." I tried hard not to let my preference show too much. Either way, I'd be with her.

"Shari's," she said, grinning. "But only if you agree to the coconut cream."

"It's a deal." And a date.

She hurried over to fill in Jonny and Sara about our plan, and then we headed out before anyone could stop us.

Cadence

"I WISH WE didn't have to head out on the road so soon," Levi said, taking another bite of our shared pie.

"But you do. It's part of the job."

"I know. But I don't like the idea of your brother and me both being gone right now."

I fought to keep from rolling my eyes, but I barely succeeded in that battle. "It'll be fine. Sara and I will be careful. We'll call the cops if anything fishy happens. Anthony and Ellen are both fully aware of the situation, and they're going to be looking out for me, too."

"But what if it isn't enough?"

I started counting items off on my fingers. "I've got pepper spray. I can kick a guy in the balls. I'm signed up to take Krav Maga classes starting in a few days. The security guys for every facility I'll be spending much time at have been informed."

Levi grabbed my fingers to stop me, and I shot my eyes up to meet his.

"I know all this," he said. "But I'm allowed to worry."

"You are?" The knots of annoyance in my belly gave way to butterflies because of the look in his eyes.

"I am. Because you said I'm your man, right?"

I wasn't sure I'd said it exactly, but I might as well have. "Right," I croaked.

"I'm your boyfriend." He sounded a lot more confident about it than I was.

"You are." My heart squeezed when the words came out.

"So you're my girlfriend. I'm allowed to worry about my girlfriend when I'm away. That's part of the deal."

"Who made up these rules?" I asked, cutting off another bite of pie to try to hide the fact that my face had rapidly filled with heat.

"Someone, somewhere, a heck of a long time ago." He speared most of the bite I'd been going for.

I gave him the evil eye.

"You snooze, you lose." He popped my pie in his mouth and winked at me.

"You're as bad as Anthony."

"Are we as adorable as Anthony and Jesse are together?"

I laughed. "You think they're adorable?"

"What, you don't?" He raised a brow. "Come on. The way they were at ChocolateFest…" He reached for the last bite, but I snagged it before he got there.

"Speaking of Anthony and Jesse," I said, popping it into my mouth, "they've finally set the date. Valentine's Day. I can bring a date."

Levi scraped up the last dregs of the coconut cream. "Does this mean you're asking me?"

"I suppose so. If you want to come."

"I can think of worse ways to spend my day."

"Gee, what a compliment," I said, laughing.

"I'll be there with bells on."

"I won't tell Jesse that last part, or he'll try to hold you to it."

He paid our bill and left a tip for our waiter before we headed back out to his car. He opened the door for me, but before I could climb in, he leaned in for a kiss. Not a wild and crazy one like the first had been. This one was slow and hot—scorching, almost—with the kind of heat that bubbled up from my belly and left me desperate for more. One of his arms slipped behind my back, holding me close to him, but not as close as I wanted to be.

"What was that for?" I murmured against his lips when he broke it off without backing away.

"Because, since I'm your man now, I can kiss you and all that other gross stuff." He trailed the tip of his finger over my lips a few times, leaving me panting. Breathless. Then he pressed his lips against mine again, hard and fast and hungry. "I could get used to this, Cadence."

"So could I." Every time he kissed me, I felt a bit tipsy. Almost drunk, but from lust instead of alcohol. It was addictive. I bit my lower lip, and his eyes went straight there.

"Every time you do that, I think about biting you."

"Do you?" I could barely speak, because my lungs weren't working anymore.

"I do. Like this." His lips pressed against the side of my jaw. His tongue followed, and then he nipped me, sharply enough to make me gasp for air, but not hard enough to cause true pain. "Only I want to do it everywhere," he said.

"Everywhere?" My head was swimming, and I felt dizzy, so I grabbed hold of his biceps to keep from falling back into the car. It was too soon to back away from him, too soon to lose that contact. His touch steadied me even as it left me lightheaded.

He brought his hand forward until the backs of his knuckles brushed the side of my breast, making me shiver. "Everywhere."

It sounded like a promise. I latched on to it, determined to hold him to his word.

"Get in the car, Cadence," he said, his forehead bent down until it pressed to mine. "I need to take you home before I forget everything about how I've told myself this has to go."

"Do you always follow the rules?"

"Usually." He grinned at me, but his eyes were still dark with the same heat surrounding and filling me. "But you make me want to break them."

I laughed as I lowered myself into the car. Levi closed the door and went around the front to climb in on the driver's side. After he started the ignition, he froze, staring out the window on my side.

"What?" I asked, turning to follow his gaze.

"Doesn't that look like Guy's car? The silver one under the light. I remember it from the parking lot at the rink."

My heart stopped. "It does." It didn't simply look familiar. There was no doubt it was Guy's car. Which meant Guy was here.

Levi pressed the button to lock his car doors. "It was parked down the street from your brother's house last night when I left, too." He put the car in reverse. "Take out your phone and call the police."

Chapter Thirteen

Cadence

KRAV MAGA CLASSES WERE no joke. Neither was my determination to learn how to protect myself. Seeing Guy's car in the Shari's parking lot had left me more shaken than I'd ever been in my life. By the time the cops had arrived at the diner, he and his car had been gone.

They told us they were going to stop by wherever he was staying today and give him another warning, but so far he hadn't done anything to warrant his arrest. Right now, I wasn't sure I wanted him arrested. Deported back to Canada would be much better. Nothing short of at least having him in jail would help me feel safe again, though, and it didn't matter how many people I had surrounding me or how many weapons I had with me. I wanted Guy out of my life, once and for all.

Aside from all that, even if I wasn't fond of Cam and Hammer's tactics the other morning, they'd proven one thing—something I'd already realized but maybe hadn't been ready to admit to myself. If Guy decided to physically attack me in some way, I was going to have to fight tooth and nail to escape. He could easily overpower me. Nearly any man in the world could, for that matter. Which meant I needed to learn ways to fight back that he wouldn't expect.

So, even though I was spending hours every day on the ice with Anthony and working out in the gym like I always did, then spending several more hours teaching Sophie and the handful of other figure skating students I'd picked up along the way, I was giving it everything I had in Krav Maga.

Especially now, while the Storm was out on the road. I didn't have my brother and Levi here as distractions, so I was able to fully devote myself to my training.

Not that I was doing it alone. Anthony and Jesse came with me sometimes, taking the classes alongside me. One night, Sophie's mom, Paige Bergstrom, suggested that she and her daughters should all join me. That had been quite the adventure, but Sophie had proven to all of us exactly how strong she was. She actually took me down a couple of times, and not because I was going easy on her. Katie had tagged along a couple of times, dragging her mother with her. Some of the other players' wives and girlfriends were starting to pop in on the classes, all saying it was a good idea for each of us to understand how to protect ourselves in case anything were to happen since the guys were on the road so much. Sara had even left the kids with one of the other guys' wives on a few occasions to come with me, not that I understood why any of them would agree to keep an eye on Connor. None of them were related to the tiny terrorist.

By the time I got home at the end of each night, all I wanted to do was soak in a hot bath and melt into bed, but my nephew typically had other plans. He liked to jump on me, especially since Levi wasn't around to be used as a jungle gym.

That was how Jesse and Anthony discovered me when they came over for wedding planning one night after the team had been gone for almost a week. But at least I hadn't seen any signs of Guy stalking me in that time. Maybe the additional warning from the cops had been enough.

"All right," I said as Connor dug his toes into my ribs and flung himself across my shoulders. "Venue for both the service and the reception are taken care of. Officiant has been arranged. What's next on the agenda?" I did my best to hold on to my pen and note pad, despite Connor's efforts to get all my attention on him.

Three voices answered at once, each with a different response.

"Flowers and photographer," Sara said.

"Wardrobe," Anthony insisted.

"Cake," Jesse said with way too much enthusiasm.

"Flowers and photographer are two separate items," I replied.

"Not necessarily." Sara tossed a platter of fruits, veggies, meats, and cheeses on the coffee table between us. "Mia Quincey offered to shoot the wedding for you at a very fair price. And she's got a friend she works with sometimes who's a florist. They'll give you a package deal. She gave me a quote, based on everything you've already decided." She dug a couple of flyers and a price list out of her purse and passed it over to the guys.

"Not bad," Anthony said a moment later.

"Not bad at all," Jesse put in. "In fact, it's good enough that we can splurge a bit on the cake."

I held up a hand. "Hold on. One thing at a time. Are you two happy with using Mia and her friend for photography and flowers? Or at least happy enough to set up a meeting to talk with them?" There were only a couple of weeks left before their date, so we didn't have any time to waste on jumping from one thing to the next without settling on anything.

They looked at each other for a moment, then turned back to me and nodded. "Yes," they said simultaneously.

"Done." I marked a few things down on my note pad before looking up at Jesse again. "The cake? What are you thinking? Did you go sample—"

"I didn't. Because I have a better idea."

"This sounds like trouble," Sara said.

"This sounds *expensive*," Anthony corrected her.

I waved a hand at the two of them to be quiet. "Go on," I said to Jesse. "What's your idea?"

"Well, you two remember the chocolatier from ChocolateFest, the one who made the chocolate-covered bacon?" He ignored his fiancé's groan and kept going. "I grabbed her business card while we were there, and I gave her a call. She said she can make chocolate-covered-bacon roses to use as decorations on an ice cream cake. All of our favorite things! All together!"

"I'm not quite sure chocolate, bacon, and ice cream were meant to go together," Anthony said warily.

"Honey." The single word came out as a whine. "Please. Do it for me."

"What's she going to charge?" Sara asked, bringing us back to the details.

"I'm glad you asked," Jesse said, whipping out a scribbled note on a used napkin covered with coffee stains. He passed it over to Anthony, who made some faces. After some hemming and hawing, he gave in so we could move on to the next item on the agenda.

Half an hour later, all the details for the wedding had been settled upon. Everyone knew who was responsible for arranging which services. Sara excused herself to take the kids up to bed, thankfully relieving me of my small-but-deadly-to-my-kidneys burden.

"So what are you doing this weekend while we're gone?" Jesse asked me once Connor's bedroom door thumped closed upstairs. He had a skating competition in Cleveland, and even though Anthony and I weren't ready to start competing yet, Anthony was traveling with him for moral support.

"I've got lessons with Sophie and a couple of other students, and Krav Maga classes. Katie invited me over to her place with a few of the girls to watch the Saturday afternoon game."

"Keeping busy," Anthony said.

"As busy as I can." It was the only thing that kept my mind off of the two men who otherwise consumed it. Levi would be back in town on Monday, at least. That would help. Or at least it would mean I could see him. Maybe kiss him some more.

A lot more.

And, maybe, we could do a lot more than just kiss.

I understood why he wanted to take things slowly—he was trying to be sure we followed through with what I'd said I needed—but something had clicked for me. Levi was funny and patient, humble and outrageously kind. He was everything that Guy could never be, and he'd shown me time and again exactly how right for me he was. I didn't have to trust Cam's and Sara's judgment any longer. I saw it for myself.

Once all that was clear to me, I didn't see any more need to keep putting Levi off.

Now I just needed to convince him of that.

Jesse picked up an apple slice and dunked it in caramel dip. "You could come with us," he said, crunching. "Your man's not here. It might be good to get away for a while."

"Tempting as that may be, I think you two will be better off without a third wheel." Besides, I wasn't convinced that Guy had given up. If he tried something while I was away from home and all the safeguards we'd put in place so far… That wasn't something I wanted to think about. "I think I'll pass."

Jesse pouted. "No midnight pizza-and-PJ parties?"

I tossed a throw pillow in his direction, laughing. "Not this time."

He knocked the pillow aside, his eyes crackling to life. "Ooh. Next time you come, we're doing a pizza-PJ-and-pillow-fight party."

"I'LL SEE YOU two next weekend," I said to Devyn and Kaetlyn Griggs, sisters who'd just completed their third skating lesson with me. They giggled and waved as they rushed out of the rink with their mother.

Usually, I left with my students, but they were in a big hurry to get to their older brother's basketball tournament, which was all the way across the city and due to start in ten minutes, and I wasn't quite done sorting myself out.

I finished putting all my gear in my gym bag. Then I slipped my feet into my boots and tugged on my coat. I took my phone out of my pocket before heading out into the cold. There was a text message from Levi. Simply the thought that he was messaging me before his game sent warmth spreading through all my limbs. I slid the bar to read it.

> *I think about you nonstop. Can't wait until I can see you again.*
> *In person, not only on Skype. I'm falling hard for you, Cadence.*

He was falling for me. That was probably a good thing, since I was almost positive I'd already fallen for him, whether I'd been intending to do that or not. I jotted off a quick response, trying to keep my thoughts to myself for the time being—telling him something like that would be much better done in person—and then headed out myself.

Gord, one of the guys who worked at the front desk, smiled when I got to the entry hall. "Why don't I walk you out?" he suggested.

"Oh, I…" This wasn't normal, but then again, I wasn't often all alone when I left. I smiled at him and nodded. "That would be really nice of you, Gord. Thanks."

"Just making sure you're all right," he said, taking my gym bag from me and holding the door open. He was an older man, probably past retirement age, and always behaved like a true gentleman, even though they were rare in today's world. "Gotta jump-start that Zamboni, now that you and those girls are gone. There's a midget hockey game in a few hours."

"Jump-start it?" I laughed, fishing for the sunglasses buried in my purse.

Gord winked at me. "It's almost as old as I am. Needs a good jump to start up in the morning." He glanced out into the parking lot and slowed his pace enough to catch my notice.

"What is it?" I followed his gaze. Guy's car was parked in the same spot it had been before, but I didn't see him in it or anywhere else.

"That the car of the man who's bothering you?" He inched closer to me and put a knobby hand on my elbow.

I nodded.

"Thought so. You get in your car. Lock your doors and go. I'll call the police as soon as I get back inside. Tell them he's here."

"Not yet," I said. I wanted evidence this time. "Come with me. I want to take a picture of his plates with the building in the background as proof that he's here and shouldn't be." I shifted the keys in my hand until my pepper spray was in position and ready to be fired.

"I could do that," Gord argued. "You just go on home and let me—"

"Not this time."

He stayed with me as I took pictures and emailed them from my phone to the officer in charge of my case. The whole time, he kept scanning the lot, looking for Guy to return. Thank goodness that didn't happen. Then I dutifully walked beside Gord back to my car and got in as directed.

I locked the doors and started the engine, waving Gord back into the building so he'd be aware I was fine.

I wasn't fine, but I didn't need him to worry. That wouldn't help anything.

He turned and headed back into the building, and I put my car in gear.

But then I froze.

There was a piece of paper shoved underneath the wiper blade, fluttering in the light wind.

I climbed out and ripped it free, getting back into the car and locking the doors again before I did anything else. My pulse battered its way through my veins and my hands shook as I unfolded it.

Guy's familiar scrawl covered the sheet from a hotel note pad. At first, I couldn't read it. Then I realized I was crying, and my tears had obscured my vision. I brushed the tears away with the sleeve of my coat and tried again.

I saw your boy toy kiss you outside the diner. I saw you making out with him that night at your brother's house. I've seen you with your fag friends, too. Not to mention all those bitches and the kids. I've seen you trying to learn how to fight. I've seen you with your fucking pepper spray. Like any of that will help you. But you know what else I see, Cadence? I see when they're all gone. When it's only you.

Like now.

When I finally looked up from the note, Guy was standing halfway across the lot, directly in front of me. He waved and blew me another kiss, exactly like last time.

Without another thought, I picked up my phone and blindly dialed, then put the car into gear and hit the gas, heading straight for him. He jumped out of the way right before I would have otherwise hit him, falling to the ground and rolling.

"Hello? Cadence?" It was Levi's voice on the other end of the line, which instantly helped to calm me.

"Hi." My voice cracked.

"What's wrong?"

Everything. Everything was wrong, because I was alone, and this bastard wouldn't leave me be, and the thing I wanted most in the world right at this moment was to fall into Levi's arms, for him to hold me until I stopped shaking, but he was all the way across the country. "I'm going to the police," I forced out, turning my car in that direction, clutching the note between my hand and the steering wheel so I couldn't possibly lose it.

I didn't look in my rearview mirror. Couldn't stand the thought of seeing Guy any more than was absolutely necessary.

"Okay," Levi said. "Good. Why? What'd he do this time? And are you all right? He didn't touch you, did he?"

"No. I'm fine." I wasn't. That was about as far from the truth as possible. "He was at the rink again. Left a note on my car."

"A note? What kind of note?" His voice was clipped. Angry. But not at me.

"Threats. More threats." A tear fell down my cheek.

"Take it to the police. You've got evidence this time. Maybe now they can do something about the son of a bitch."

"I am." Despite my better intentions, I sniffled. "Driving there now."

"You're crying. Try not to cry while you're driving. That's never good."

I knew that all too well. "Trying." Then I sniffled again.

There was a sound like he'd slammed a door or punched a wall. "Fuck, I wish I was there."

"I do, too."

"A couple more days. Two more days, and then we'll be home. When do Anthony and Jesse get back?"

"Monday. Same as you." Too long. I was starting to think maybe I shouldn't go back to the house. Was it safe for Sara and the kids if I was there? Wouldn't Guy leave them alone if I wasn't with them? I wasn't so sure.

"Cadence?" Levi's voice was rough and strained.

"Yeah?"

"Promise me you won't go anywhere alone once you're done at the police station."

How could I promise him that when I'd just been thinking the best way to protect the people I loved was to stay as far away from them as I could?

"Promise me," he repeated. "Don't go doing something stupid. I need to know you're not alone."

I turned in at the parking lot across from the station. "I'm here," I said. "I have to go take this in."

"Don't be stupid," he repeated as we hung up.

I hadn't made him any sort of promise, but his words echoed in my head the whole way into the building. *Don't go doing something stupid.* Wasn't that exactly what I'd been saying to myself? If I were alone, that would be the easiest way for Guy to get to me. He wasn't making himself known when I was surrounded by people. Usually only when it was just me, or if I only had one other person with me.

Alone, I was an easy target. Surrounded, I wasn't.

Truth and fear didn't mesh well in my head.

Levi

KEEPING MY HEAD together on this trip had been difficult in the best of times, considering how worried I was about Cadence and her stalker. But before our Saturday matinee game against the Rangers, when I'd gotten that call from her, it had gotten to be about a thousand times more difficult than before. I'd filled in Jonny with what I'd learned as soon as I hung up with her, but now we were both worried sick.

Here we were, stuck in New York and unable to protect her. Anthony and Jesse were in Cleveland all weekend. Yeah, the cops were there, but so far they hadn't done much but give her a piece of paper. We didn't like it. Neither of us. Not one bit, but what could we do short of skipping out on the team? Nothing.

Right before warm-ups, Jonny came stalking over to my stall in the locker room, looking ready to rip my head off.

"What?" I asked, sure it had nothing to do with me and everything to do with Cadence.

He glared at me, shook his head, and stomped off.

"Go," Hammer said. "Follow him. Figure out what's up."

So I went, finding him in a quiet corner in the bowels of Madison Square Garden, not too far from where Koz and several of the other guys were kicking around a soccer ball.

"Sara just called," he said once I caught up with him. He ground out the words, like he'd swallowed gravel.

"That doesn't sound good."

He shook his head. "She's having a hell of a time convincing Cadence to stay at the house. Cadence seems to think it would be safer for Sara and the kids if she wasn't there."

"Fuck," I muttered.

"Yeah."

The worst part of it was that there might be some truth to Cadence's fears. I wasn't sure. Would Guy leave the other people in Cadence's life alone if she wasn't around them? Maybe or maybe not. It was too soon to tell.

"She's not leaving yet, is she? She needs to stay at least until we return home. I don't like the thought of her being alone."

"If she leaves, she'll be alone whether we're there or not."

"Not if she comes to stay with me."

Jonny glowered at me for a long time. Long enough that most guys would immediately back down from whatever it was they were doing.

I didn't, though. I couldn't. Not on this. "She's scared for you and your wife and kids. I get it, but she can't be alone."

"She's scared for you, too," he finally said. "What happens if she won't stay with you?"

"I'll find a way to convince her."

"And when we're out of town the next time? What then?"

I shook my head. "We'll figure it out. I don't know yet."

Jonny grunted and nodded. "All right. So we convince her to stay until we get back to Portland, then she stays with you. But I swear to God, 501, if you put one toe out of line…"

"You don't need to threaten me. I'm as worried about her as you are. I'm not going to hurt her."

He grunted in response, and his glare didn't lighten up at all. But he wasn't acting like he was about to rip me limb from limb so his son could feed me to the alligators. That had to be a good sign, didn't it?

Holy hell. He wasn't going to murder me over my suggestion.

"How do we convince her to stay put for now?"

"Sara can manage it," he said. Then he turned around and stalked back to the locker room.

Chapter Fourteen

THE RANGERS HAD been one of the best teams in the league all season, and today, we were quickly learning why. They were relentless on the puck. Their forwards were constantly coming at us, and the *D* typically joined the rush. Henrik Lundqvist was no slouch in goal, either. Not a surprise, since he and Nicky tended to fight for that position for Team Sweden every time it came to international competition.

Today, they were having a goaltending dual.

Partway through the third period, shots were coming at each of them almost nonstop, despite both teams actively trying to block the puck before it snuck through.

Marc Staal, one of their *D*-men, wound up for a slapper. I went down without even thinking about it. The puck got me on the inside of the knee, right where there's no padding.

"Fucking son of a bitch, that fucking hurts," I shouted, trying to get myself up so I could return to the bench and walk it off.

Lucky for me, our forwards gathered up the puck and skated out of the zone, and Harry gave me a shove, putting his stick in my back, to help me get off the ice.

"You break anything?" Archie, our head trainer, asked.

I shook my head, grimacing. "It's only a stinger."

Bergy glanced in my direction. "Walk it off, 501. Need you in this game."

"I'll be fine," I insisted as I made my way to the tunnel behind the bench, limping around until the worst of the pain dissipated into a dull throb. That was much more manageable. I headed back and took my spot on the bench between Harry and Hammer.

We were defending against the Rangers' attack again, with Koz, Ghost, and Jo-Jo doing their damnedest to get the puck back in our possession. Koz finally got a stick on it, and that black rubber motherfucker squirted out into the neutral zone.

Ghost turned on his afterburners and shot out to catch up to it. The Rangers' defenseman covering that point lost an edge and fell to the ice, leaving Ghost all alone. He picked up the puck on his stick and skated in all alone against Lundqvist. High, glove-side. That was what Ghost needed to do if he was going to have any chance against this guy, and everyone on our bench knew it.

He didn't elevate the puck enough with his shot. Straight into the glove. Would've been a bull's-eye if Lundqvist had a fucking target on him.

Ghost skated back to our bench for a change. "Sorry, boys. Didn't put enough mustard on that one." He took a seat, and Webs bent over his shoulder, telling him something like "You've got to elevate to accumulate," as Harry and I headed over the boards for our next shift, along with the third line of Austin Cooper, Otto Raita, and Dylan Poplawski—a speedy trio who frustrated the hell out of the opposition, even if they didn't tend to score a lot.

Coop won the draw to Lundqvist's left, and we went to work. Pops set up camp directly outside Lundqvist's crease, providing an excellent screen and absorbing a ton of slashes and crosschecks that the refs chose to overlook. Otter and Coop played keep-away with the puck, every now and then passing it back to me or Harry while they tried to free themselves of their cover.

Harry wound up and shot it toward the net, and Pops tipped it just wide. Coop beat the Rangers to the rebound and sent it back to me.

I didn't have a good look at the net. No clear lanes. I passed it back to Otter before shifting myself into a better position.

By now, we'd had the Rangers chasing us for longer than the average shift, and they were tired. The forwards cycled the puck some more, but it got trapped in the corner and two of them went in to dig it out. Once it finally popped free, the puck shot up my side of the boards, so I pinched in to keep the play alive.

The next moment, I was behind the net with the puck on my stick. Pops and Coop both went straight to the paint in front of the net.

I passed it out toward them, and it bounced off a skate. Lundqvist tried to change directions, but it was too late. The puck slipped under his pads and past his attempt to contort his body into a position that might stop it.

"Fucking right," Coop screamed, leaping into my arms as the other guys rushed to join the celebration. In no time, they were all pounding me on the top of the head and slapping me on the back.

"Did it hit your skate?" I asked Coop. If it did, he'd get credit for the goal. Hell, the Rangers might even challenge it, saying he'd kicked it in.

"Not me, man. It was one of them."

Huh. Maybe this time I was on the right end of an own-goal situation.

I skated in front of our bench, holding out my glove for fist bumps as I went. When I reached the end, Hammer grabbed me like he was going to give me a noogie.

"Hell of a risk you took, kid. See what happens?"

Yeah. I saw. And I kind of liked it.

The lights over the penalty box came on, signaling a TV timeout, and Jamie skated over to stand in front of me. "Hell of a redirection. Tell me you planned it to happen like that."

I started to shake my head, but he punched my shoulder.

"Lie to me. Tell me you planned it, because now I want to practice doing that. Need to show my kid brother how it should be done." Then he winked.

"Yeah," I said, drawing the word out. "I knew exactly what I was doing. Good luck repeating it." Because I sure as hell didn't think I'd ever be able to.

"Gotta have something to work toward, right?" Then he skated back to center ice to set up for the next face-off.

"Watch it, 501," Webs said, coming up behind me. "If you're not careful, he'll have the whole team trying to learn how to steal your move."

I ENDED UP scoring the only goal in that game against the Rangers. Sunday night, I had another good game against the Islanders. Didn't end up in the goal column, but I had two assists and three blocked shots, not to mention what might have been the biggest hit of my career, when I'd lined up Clutterbuck and caught him with his head down. Usually, he was the one on the other end of hits like that, so it felt good.

But now, the only thing on my mind was getting home and making sure—for myself—that Cadence was all right.

We spent Sunday night in New York instead of flying cross-country in the middle of the night and arriving home in the wee hours of the morning. Any way you looked at it, we were going to lose Monday for practice anyway.

By the time we landed at PDX, it was late afternoon. Jonny caught my eye as I was leaving the plane.

"You following me to the house?"

No point in putting things off. I nodded. "As long as you're okay with that."

"Sara got her to agree to stay until we returned home, but that's all she agreed to. I think it's better for everyone if we sit down and hash it all out. Anthony and Jesse should be back by now. I'm sure we can convince them to come over, too."

"You mean you think it's best if we gang up on her."

He shrugged and grunted.

I did exactly as he suggested and followed him home. It turned out Anthony and Jesse were already there. Connor was jumping on Jesse's balls when we came through the door, so I decided to do as little as possible to draw the little boy's notice. The less he jumped on mine, the better my chances of ever being able to father children, if that was in the cards. A quick look around revealed Cadence was nowhere to be found.

Sara kissed Jonny and passed Cassidy into his arms almost as soon as we got there. "We ordered pizza," she said. "Seemed easiest, with this many people."

"Good," he said. "I'm starving. Where's Cadence?"

"Here," Cadence said from the stairs. Then she saw me, and her eyes lit up. That was all it took to shake off all the cold from the outside and warm me all the way through. She rushed down and straight to me, wrapping me up in a hug.

I put my arms around her and held her close, breathing the scent of her hair.

"I missed you," she said, her voice muffled in my coat.

"Not as much as I missed you."

"All right, you two lovebirds," Jesse said. "Now that everyone's present and accounted for, can we get to the business of sorting out what we need to do about Guy?"

"Feed him to the damn agilators!" Connor squealed, jumping on Jesse's balls so hard the man let out an "oof."

Not that I had any intention of letting Cadence go any time soon, unless she wanted me to release her. I was perfectly content to stay exactly as we were, and besides, I didn't want to give Connor any excuse to start jumping on me instead of Jesse. Thanks, but no. I liked my balls exactly how they were.

She didn't move to pull away, thank goodness. I needed the comfort of being able to touch her. To reassure her I was here.

"Don't use Mommy's words," Jonny admonished his son, carrying Cassidy to his recliner and taking a seat. She fussed for a moment, so he rocked until she settled down again.

Sara gave Connor an eye-rolling sort of look and shook her head, not that it would do any good. "I think the bigger order of business is figuring out where Cadence is going to stay, since she seems to think she's putting all of us in danger by being around us."

"Which is absolute bullshit," Jonny said. He turned to us and waited until Cadence peeked out at him. "You're in more danger if you're alone than we are if you're with us. You should stay here, exactly like you have been. He hasn't tried anything while you've been here. He's only coming after you in public when you're alone or might as well be."

"Just because he hasn't done anything yet, that's not a good enough reason to assume he won't ever."

"Just because he's threatening you, that's not a good enough reason for you to do something stupid and go off all on your own," her brother countered.

"But you didn't read that note." She started shaking against me as soon as she mentioned the stupid message he'd left for her on her car. "You didn't see. He threatened all of you. Every single person in this room. If anything happened to Connor or Cassidy—"

"He'd have to be an idiot to try anything with one of the kids," Anthony cut in. "Or any of the rest of us, for that matter. I don't think that's his game. He wants you to be scared something will happen to one of us so he can trap you alone. That's what he's been doing all along, and I don't think there's any reason we shouldn't assume that's what he's going to continue to do until he's finally arrested or deported."

"But what if he's even more off his rocker than we think?" she argued.

"Then you come and live with the two of us," Jesse said. "Then you're away from the kids but not all alone. You'd have me and Anthony to look after you."

"I'm not... You're about to get..." Cadence spun around to face the rest of the room, staying in my arms, though. "The last thing the two of you need is a third wheel."

"Oh, hush now," he replied.

Sara plopped down on the arm of Jonny's recliner, rolling her eyes. "So you forget all the crazy ideas in your head about protecting everyone else and stay put. The cops are going to arrest him. One of these days—and probably soon—he's going to do something dumb enough that he'll get caught, and they'll throw his ass in jail—"

"Mommy said *ass!*" Connor shouted.

"—and then they'll deport him. You can be done with him for good." Sara finished it without even paying her son's outburst any attention.

"Not for good, though. What if he goes after Mom? Or Chloe or Corinne? He can find all of them easily enough and torment them to get to me."

"You can't protect the whole world, Cadence," Jonny said. "And who says getting away from us will be enough to make him leave us alone? If he'd go after Mom, what's to say he wouldn't try to attack someone you care about here, whether you're around or not?"

"Would you stop being reasonable?" she said, throwing up her hands. I rubbed her arms, trying to calm her down, but she was so worked up I doubted it would help much, if at all. She leaned back into me, though. "Everyone needs to stop making sense, because Guy doesn't. He just doesn't make any sense at all. He's gone off the deep end, and I'm trying to be sure if he's going to hurt anyone, it'll be me and not one of you. Because I can't handle that." She shook her head adamantly. "I can't. If he did anything to—"

"Then come and stay with me," I said, cutting her off before she went any further into panic mode.

She went completely still against me. Silent.

Well, fuck. We'd gone straight from everything progressing nicely to now she might want to run away. I should've eased her into the idea instead of tossing it out there like I had, but it was too late to take it back.

Now I had to pick up the pieces.

Cadence

STAY WITH LEVI? Was that honestly what he'd just suggested?

I glanced at Cam, who raised a brow.

Maybe I'd misheard him. Because if Levi actually *had* suggested I move in with him, surely Cam would be shouting threats at him or something similar, but instead he was looking expectantly at me.

Levi had stopped rubbing my arms, and he'd gone kind of rigid after asking me. So maybe I'd heard him right, after all.

"You don't have to go live with him if that's not what you want," Sara rushed to say, after a prolonged silence. "But I don't think anyone in this room is going to sit back and tell you we're fine with you not staying with *someone*. You can stay here. You can go live with Anthony and Jesse. You can move into Levi's apartment. Hell, I think half the other wives and girlfriends with the team would invite you to come live with them if it comes down to it. But you can't go off somewhere all by yourself with no one else around. Not gonna happen."

"I've got a guest room at my place," Levi murmured in my ear. "I'm not suggesting... I mean, only if that's..." He sighed. "This is not easy to talk about with your brother glaring at me."

I nodded and reached for his hand. "Come with me." Then I led him up the stairs, away from the insanity that had started the moment he and Cam had returned from their road trip.

"What the hell do you think—"

"We need to talk in private, Cam," I said, cutting my brother off and not slowing down at all. "Ten minutes. We'll be back."

"If she goes to live with him, they'll be alone a lot of the time, you know," Sara admonished him.

"Not in my house," Cam grumbled.

When we got to my room, I closed the door behind us and took a seat on the edge of the bed.

Levi stood there looking uncomfortable as all get out, shifting from foot to foot.

I patted a spot on the bed beside me. "Sit down."

He shook his head. "I just don't want you to think this is about me trying to rush you," he said, staying put. "I've got a guest room. You could have your own space. Bathroom. Privacy. I'm—I'm not trying to get you in my bed."

"I never thought you were."

"I mean, I *want* you there. In my bed. But not until you're ready." His dimple popped out on his cheek, and he dragged a hand through his hair.

I grinned and ducked my head. He was so embarrassed that I was embarrassed for him. It was kind of sweet. How on earth had I ever thought Levi was even remotely like Guy? The thought of Guy being embarrassed about anything was laughable.

"I know what you mean, Levi," I said, once I got myself together again. "I know what this is about."

"I swear, I'm not going to try anyth—"

"Would you please stop making me promises like that?"

He raised a brow.

"It's kind of flattering to think there might be something more to you asking me to come and live with you than you simply wanting to protect me from a psychotic stalker ex-boyfriend."

"You can't honestly believe there's not a hell of a lot more involved than that, can you? Cadence, I've been pursuing you since you first showed up in Portland more than a month ago. Only I've been trying to play by your rules and give you the time and space you need to come to terms with the fact that we're supposed to be together. And I'm *still* trying to play by those rules. If you're not—" He broke off for a moment, crossed over to sit beside me. He took my hand, sending tingles racing up and down my spine. "I don't want to move too fast. You've been through hell, and you're still in hell. I'm trying to be a good guy and put your needs above mine, but it's not easy when all I can think about is you. Making sure you're safe. Doing whatever I can to make you happy. Being with you in every possible way."

I slid the pad of my thumb in lazy circles over the back of his hand.

"I've got to be completely honest with you," he said, taking me by surprise.

"You haven't been?" I blinked a couple of times, trying to figure out what he could have been lying about.

"For the most part. But I've never told you the whole truth about why I started pursuing you."

"You mean it wasn't the spread in *ESPN: The Body*?"

He licked his lips and grinned. "That might have had something to do with it. But seriously... It was really shitty of me. That night, at Burnzie's house when I first saw you? I was beating myself up again over being less than my brother, and I wanted to find something—anything—where I was a step up on him."

"I know that. We talked about it that first time we went to Shari's. How you're always comparing yourself to him."

"But I didn't tell you all of it. The thing is, these days, you're more famous than Katie, so I thought…"

"You wanted to date me because I was more famous than your brother's wife?" I spluttered, trying not to laugh. Only, maybe I didn't try too hard. Or not at all.

He gave me a sheepish look. "I know. It's ridiculous, right?"

"It's kind of funny. Did you seriously think that could somehow make you believe in yourself more?"

"Nah. Not *me*. I just thought maybe some people would be more likely to take me seriously. But I think that was all in my head."

"Seems to me you're finally starting to take yourself more seriously—at least if I'm focusing on how you're playing these days. You're not hesitating out there. You're only doing what you know you need to do."

He shrugged. "Maybe."

"Something tells me Bergy wouldn't say *maybe* about that. Or your brother. Or anyone."

"I know. I'm too hard on myself. It's not an easy habit to break when you've been doing it for twenty-four years."

"But you realize being with me isn't going to do a darn thing to make you any better or worse than Jamie is, right?"

"Yep. And I'm starting to come to terms with the fact that even though I've felt like I'm in competition with him in everything I've done my whole life, he hasn't got a clue."

"No?"

"No. He only wants the best for me. Like I do for him, to be honest. It's all been in my head." He quirked a grin at me, letting that dimple come out again. "Kind of like you. You're the starring attraction."

"I'm not just in your head, though. I'm as real as it gets," I said before I thought better of it. Then I nibbled on my lower lip, watching as his gaze lowered there.

"Trust me." Levi took a long breath, lingering on it like he was trying to brace himself. "I'm very much aware of precisely how real you are. Too aware."

My heartbeat was pounding so hard I thought my chest might

explode. "So you're serious about this? About me coming to stay with you?"

"Serious as Jesse's chocolate-covered-bacon obsession. I'm not scared of what Guy might do to me, but I'm fucking terrified of what he might do to you if he got you alone."

"So what happens when you guys go back out on the road?"

"Come back here. Go stay with Anthony and Jesse. Katie would love some company, I'm sure, or maybe the two of you could go stay with her mom and have a week-long slumber party. Whatever you want—I just don't want you to be alone. Not until we're sure that son of a bitch is out of your life."

I couldn't stop chewing on my lip. "I still don't like the idea of him coming after me while I'm with you."

"Better than him coming after you when you're with Connor and Cassidy, though, right?"

I nodded.

"I solemnly swear I'll keep my hands to myself—unless you don't want me to."

Laughter burst free without my permission. "Thought you were going to start quoting the Weasley twins on me."

"I'll save that one for when you're ready." He winked. "Because at that point, I *will* be up to no good."

Something in the general vicinity of my heart fluttered. "All right."

"All right?"

"I'll come to stay with you. We can work out the keeping-your-hands-to-yourself part once we're away from my brother's house."

"That sounds like a plan I can live with."

Surprisingly, it sounded like a plan I could live with, too. "Mischief managed?"

"Not yet, it's not." He nipped my nose.

I laughed again as we got up and headed back down the stairs to fill everyone else in on what we'd decided. The smell of pizza nearly knocked me over. Or maybe it was Levi picking me up and carrying me over his shoulder so we could go downstairs to the pizza faster.

As soon as he set me down, Connor demanded his turn to be carried by Tarzan.

"Looks like that one backfired on you," I said.

The way he looked at me, I got the impression he was more than okay with that.

Chapter Fifteen

Cadence

"WHAT DO YOU wear to a wedding for two gay men?" Levi asked me from down the hall. "I mean, I know that probably sounds like a stupid question, but…"

"Just wear whatever you'd put on for any of your teammates' weddings," I called out in return. "Any of the suits you'd use for going to or from a game should work out fine."

"You're sure?"

I sighed. "You don't need to put on a tux, but I'm not taking you with me if you come out with a tracksuit on."

"Okay. Got it."

I looked myself over in the mirror, checking to see if there were any holes in my hairdo after all the curling and hairspray and whatnot. It looked all right, from what I could tell. I wished Levi had a handheld mirror, or that I'd thought to bring one of Sara's over with me when I'd moved in a little over a week ago. But I hadn't, and he didn't, and so far I hadn't found the time to run to the store and buy one.

There hadn't been a single peep from Guy in all the time I'd been living here. No more creepy notes on my car. No sign of him showing up in parking lots at any of the places I tended to go. He had gone silent enough it was tempting to forget all about him.

I couldn't, though. The last thing I needed to do was let down my guard. He'd pounce the moment he thought I wasn't expecting him to do anything.

I'd kept up going to Krav Maga classes and had otherwise gone about my life as though nothing were wrong.

If only that were the truth.

The most natural, normal thing about life since moving into Levi's apartment was learning to be around each other so much. I wasn't certain why I'd pushed against him for so long. We were good together.

Insanely good, actually.

Most nights, when he didn't have a game, we curled up together on the couch for hours, our arms wrapped around each other, watching whatever show was on that night—*Black Sails* and *Impractical Jokers* were his two favorites, but he didn't put up any fight at all when I asked him to watch *Downton Abbey* with me. Sometimes we kissed. Sometimes we went quite a bit further than kissing, but we never ended up going to bed together. Not yet, at least. It was becoming more and more difficult to go down the hall to my bedroom at the end of the night without trying to drag him along with me. Not only that, but I could tell it was taking every ounce of patience he could muster to take things as slowly as we both realized we needed to take it.

I wasn't sure how much longer we'd be able to hold out.

For that matter, I wasn't sure how much longer I *wanted* to hold out.

My one saving grace was that the team was due to leave for another road trip in a few days, so then we *couldn't* jump each other's bones. Not while he was gone. That trip would also coincide with me needing to be more on my guard again. With Levi and my brother out of the picture, it was far more likely that Guy would strike again. I had to be ready.

With my hair as good as I could manage and my makeup looking decent, I shimmied into the dress I'd picked out to wear today—a soft, coral pink, since that was the color Jesse requested I wear to go with their Valentine's Day theme—and slipped into my shoes.

I glanced at the clock. We should've left five minutes ago. "You ready?" I called out again as I rushed into the living room.

Levi was standing there looking sexier than should be legal in a soft gray suit, striped pale violet shirt, and a teal tie. I stopped short, just to look my fill.

"Shit. Should I have worn pink? I know you told me they were doing pink for everything. I should've thought of that. I can go chan—"

"No time to change. We're already late. You're fine like this."

He grabbed both of our coats and helped me into mine. "Only fine?"

"If you ask Jesse, he'll probably say you're *fine*." I snapped my fingers and head, mimicking Jesse's move. "And I agree with him."

Levi pecked me on the nose, his dimple making an appearance, and then ushered me out the front door.

By the time we arrived at the courthouse, the parking lot was jam-packed. We had to find pay parking off the street and hike a short distance to make our way inside. We found seats near the middle just in time.

Anthony came out first, in a black tux with pink cummerbund and bowtie. Then Jesse came out in an insanely fabulous white tux with matching pink accents, including a top hat. The justice of the peace brought everyone to order, and the guys said their vows. It was a quick, tasteful service.

In no time, it was over, and we were all headed back to Anthony's house for the reception. Or really, since Jesse had put it together, I supposed we should call it a party.

Sara and Cam were there—they'd left the kids with Sara's dad for the afternoon, although I wasn't sure how they'd convinced Scotty to keep the two little hellions. Since she'd been such a big part of the planning, Sara basically ran the show after everyone was inside. She was good at bossing people around and making sure everything was done the way Anthony and Jesse wanted it.

Levi and I found the happy couple and gave them our presents. Jesse made a big show of kissing both of us on the cheeks to thank us, which made Levi blush and stammer.

"Never been kissed by a gay man before?" I asked, teasing him once we were alone again.

"There's something I can check off the bucket list."

"Just be glad he didn't kiss you like this," I said, stretching up on my tiptoes and sealing my lips over his.

I kept it short because today was not about the two of us. Apparently I didn't keep it short enough. Cam caught my eye once I'd broken off the kiss, and he ground his jaw in the distance.

Behave, I mouthed at him across the living room.

Tell him to behave, he mouthed back.

I laughed and shook my head, then tucked my hand into Levi's arm and led him off to talk to some other acquaintances from the world of figure skating.

Before long, it was time to cut the cake. A woman who was so hot she made me look like a bum came out with the aforementioned ice cream cake with chocolate-covered-bacon roses for decoration. I'd never seen anything less appealing in my life, but it was exactly what Jesse wanted—and Anthony would never deny Jesse anything if he could manage to avoid doing so.

Mia Quincey got herself into position and choreographed the two of them cutting into the cake. I blinked, and then ice cream was flying. Literally.

"Um" —I looked at Levi, wide-eyed— "ready to skedaddle?"

"It's okay for us to sneak out early?"

"Unless you really want to get hit with ice cream and bacon?"

He took my hand, and we made a mad dash for the front door, laughing and grabbing our coats on the way. We were still laughing by the time we were in the car and moving.

At a stoplight, Levi turned to me and brushed something off my cheek, then put it in his mouth. "Hmm. Bacon and ice cream isn't half bad. Who knew?"

I was about to tell him that apparently Jesse did, when he leaned over and kissed the same spot on my cheek, flicking his tongue against my skin. Then I couldn't say anything. Heck, I couldn't even breathe anymore, not after my initial gasp from the contact.

He straightened away from me and started driving again when the light turned green.

The rest of the way to his apartment, my ability to concentrate was nil. All I could think about was the soft touch of his lips and tongue against my skin and how I wanted more of it.

Once we got inside, Levi came up behind me and helped me out of my coat. The warmth of the material had barely left me when the heat of his lips replaced it. He kissed me right where my neck melted into my collarbone, and I shivered. That was one of the spots he'd discovered early on—one of the ones that made me melt into a puddle of goo and had me willing to do almost anything he suggested.

"Cold?" he murmured, his lips still making contact with my skin. He wrapped his arms around my waist and drew me back against him.

I shook my head. "Not cold. If anything, I'm hot."

"You don't have to tell me that," he teased.

I was tempted to elbow him in the ribs, but I was too short to reach him there. I might accidentally hit him somewhere that might cause damage, or at least put a quick end to what I hoped we were starting.

Instead, I linked my hands with his, threading our fingers together.

"I got you a Valentine's Day present," he said, his mouth so close to my ear that his voice sent reverberations through my whole body. "I hope that's allowed at this point in our relationship."

"A present?" I asked, both elated and upset at the same time. "I didn't think to get you anything."

"Good. Because I want this to be all about you right now." He took a moment to hang our coats in the closet, then reached for my hand and led me into the living room. "Sit here and close your eyes," he said, nudging me onto the couch.

"I'm not good at keeping my eyes closed."

"No, you've got too much of Connor in you. Can't do what you're told." He winked. "Close them, or I'll blindfold you."

I bit my lip to suppress a grin. "You could blindfold me if you want."

He stared for a minute. Then he shook his head. "Don't give me ideas. Close your eyes."

I closed my eyes and waited until I heard him doing something in his bedroom. Then I opened them again. He was right. There was a bit of Connor's devious streak in me. Maybe that was where he'd gotten it, because that little boy's nature was about as different from Cam's as possible.

A moment later, Levi came back carrying a small box, big enough to hold a stack of index cards. "You're supposed to have your eyes closed," he said accusingly.

"Should've gone with the blindfold. Here." I patted the seat next to me. "Let me see."

The expression on his face was a combination of amusement and annoyance. I figured that meant good things to come. He sat next to me, putting an arm around me the way he almost always did, and passed the box into my hands.

"Go on, nosy," he said.

The lid was labeled *Cadence's Daily Treat*. I lifted the top off the box and set it aside. Sure enough, it was filled with note cards. The first one said *Present this card to redeem one romantic afternoon walk at the International Rose Test Gardens followed by dinner of your choice*. I flipped through the box, scanning the different cards. They were good for all sorts of things: a kiss to be delivered even when one or both parties were angry, a dinner prepared by him, an authentic and heartfelt apology (whether he felt like he'd been wrong or not), a bubble bath, a thorough cleaning of the kitchen, a candlelit massage, a day spent babysitting my niece and nephew so I could hang out with my brother and sister-in-law without the kids getting in the way, a weekend getaway to the beach (schedules permitting), a foot rub, and even a few labeled *Lady's Choice*. Some were clearly meant for when he was on the road or when I had to travel for competitions, since they offered things like an uninterrupted hour of Skype time, flower delivery, or travel arrangements to wherever the team was playing.

I set them all back in the box and returned the lid to its position. "I don't understand."

"It's not difficult. Every day, you pick a card, and I give you whatever's on the card. I'll restock it whenever it starts running low, so there are always plenty of options."

"But…" No one had ever done anything like that for me before, let alone doing something for me every single day. With Guy, it had always been about what I needed to do for him.

"But nothing," Levi said. "Every day, no matter what, you get to pick a card. And you get whatever is on the card, no questions asked, no arguments, no hesitation."

"No matter what?" I asked. Because the wheels had started spinning in my mind.

"No matter what."

"And I get to start today."

"I hope you will."

"All right." I opened the box again and fished through it until I found one of the *Lady's Choice* cards.

"Going for one of those to start with, hmm?"

"Yes." I pressed it into his hand. "Because I have something very specific I want."

"I'm all ears."

I looked up, meeting his eyes full on. "I want you to take me to bed."

Levi

I WASN'T SURE what I'd been expecting her to ask for, but sex was definitely not it.

And that was what she meant, wasn't it? Maybe I was reading too much into it, putting my own desires into her words when she hadn't intended anything of the sort. I needed to be sure before I did something stupid.

"You want me to take you to bed?" I repeated.

"Yes. Your bed."

That was all it took to have me salivating. "You're sure?"

We'd been making out a lot over the last week, so much that I tended to lie in bed awake at night afterward, jerking off to the memory of her taste, her scent, the firmness of her body beneath my hands mixing with the softness of her curves. Every time I was around her, I had to fight off my inner teenager. I wasn't sure I was ready to be with her in a way that would be good for her, not only good for me. Sheer terror swamped me that I might blow my load the second I came into contact with her naked flesh.

"Positive." She didn't look the least bit deterred. "Absolutely one hundred percent positive." She took my hand in both of hers and held it still for a moment before placing it flat against her ribs.

The tips of my fingers brushed the underside of her breast, and I groaned.

She set the box of cards on the coffee table and straddled me, rising up on her knees so we were on the same level. Her eyes had gone dark green again with those fiery golden flecks making them come to life. I wanted to drown in them, to let the flames consume me.

"Remember?" she murmured before her lips pressed to mine in a teasing, taunting kiss. "No questions asked. No arguments. No hesitation. Take me to bed, Levi."

"You're sure you're ready for this?"

She rabbit-punched my shoulder. "That's a question."

"It's an important question."

She kissed me again, sucking my lower lip between hers and flicking her tongue against my skin. "I solemnly swear that I am making trouble, and you're going to like it or else."

"That's not even close to the quote."

"It's close enough. Besides, I don't care about that at the moment. What I care about is you gave me a box of cards, and you're letting me pick what I want from you, and this is what I want. And if you don't stop asking questions and take me to bed, I'll start twisting quotes from the Dowager Countess of Grantham, instead."

"Oh, God. Not *Downton Abbey*. Please, don't torture me like that."

"Levi…" She had the most adorable warning tone in her voice, like

I'd heard her use several times with Connor when he was misbehaving.

I was tempted to peck her on the nose again, to further infuriate her, but I held back. "I'm done. No more." I stood up, holding Cadence by the waist. She wrapped her legs around me, and the skirt of her dress inched upward until it was barely covering her at all. Her gorgeous, bare thighs squeezed tight around me.

She worked on undoing my tie as I carried her to my bedroom. By the time I set her on her feet in front of me, she had the knot undone. It slipped free from my collar and remained in her hand.

"You planning to use that for something?" I asked in a teasing tone.

She shrugged, her eyes sharpening while a devious smile came to her lips. "I don't know. I'm sure there are a lot of things we could do with this."

"Maybe some other time." I slid my fingertips up her rib cage and over the length of her arm, then took the tie away from her and tossed it to the floor. "Not this time. I don't want anything between us this first time."

"Okay." She lowered her eyes until all I saw were lids and lashes, and she bit her lower lip in a move that was equally innocent and sultry. Then she slipped her hands up my chest and started undoing the buttons of my shirt.

I had to suck in some air to be sure I kept breathing through whatever she had in mind. "Okay?" I repeated.

She nodded, dragging my shirt free from my waistband to finish getting it open. "You can have what you want if I can have what I want."

"And what do you want?"

"I don't want you to be careful with me. Everyone's constantly trying to be sure I'm not hurt, that no one's done anything to me." There was a fire burning in her eyes that would melt me if I wasn't careful. "Tonight, I want you to do things to me. Dirty things. Messy things. The kind of things you could never talk about in front of the guys without turning bright red from embarrassment."

"But...I thought the first time should be sweet and romantic." Hell, it was Valentine's Day. Wasn't I supposed to be doing the whole flowers, chocolate, and candles thing? Not mauling her like a piece of meat. Don't get me wrong—mauling her sounded seriously fucking good, but it wasn't how I'd envisioned any of this would go. Especially since I was falling so hard for her. Hell, I never thought I'd be taking her to my bed so soon. The wild and crazy part, with her adorable-one-minute-turning-to-sex-goddess-the-next eyes, might do me in and make it official.

The *L* word. How could I have possibly gone from trying to one-up my brother to falling in love in the blink of an eye? But I clearly had.

"We've got lots of time later for slow and sweet. Right now, this first time? I want it hot and fast and loud. Frantic, like I am." She undid my belt buckle and the fly of my slacks, never removing her eyes from mine. Then she dropped her hand lower until the tips of her fingers barely grazed my straining cock.

My heart was about two solid beats shy of bursting through my ribs, simply from the thought of all she was asking of me. But then I stopped thinking entirely. There was no room for thought in this. Only for action.

"You're sure that's what you want?" I asked.

She nodded, delving lower to wrap her hand all the way around me.

I groaned, but then I spun around so Cadence's back was against the wall. I picked her up by the waist, pinned her in place with my hips and thighs, and kissed her as hard as I'd been dreaming of.

She let out a tiny sound, and I backed off a bit in case I'd hurt her. She pulled me closer, putting both arms around my neck and nipping at my lower lip the same way she always bit her own. Then she squeezed me with her thighs and ground against me.

"Oh, fuck, baby," I said on a groan.

I fumbled with the zipper in the back of her dress, but it was no use. Couldn't get it to budge, so I caressed her breasts through the fabric. Her nipples were hard nubs, even through all the fabric. I slid my hands up her thighs, lifting the skirt out of the way until it bunched at her waist. She was so slick and hot that her panties were soaked, and I'd barely touched her.

She shoved my shirt and suit jacket over my shoulders, and they pooled at my feet while she worked on lowering my pants. "Condom," she panted.

"Hell." Wasn't thinking. Not at all.

I carried her with me to the bathroom, kicking off my pants as I went, and pressed her against the door frame for stability. Then I ripped open the top drawer, where I had a small stash. Fumbled around until I got my hands on one. I tried to get the stupid thing open, but I was too hot and sweaty and frustrated to get the job done.

"Give it to me," she said, ripping it from my hands. In no time, she had the foil wrapper open. I slipped the condom into place as she tugged her panties to the side.

Then I was inside her.

Her eyes went wide. Fucking hell, I should've taken at least a little more time to be sure she was ready for me, but it was too late now. Her pussy was as small and tight as the rest of her. I'd never felt anything like the way she squeezed me. This might as well be heaven, because I couldn't think of anything better than the way I felt right at this moment.

I tried to move slowly, to give her time to adjust, but Cadence dug her fingernails into my upper back and buried her head in the space between my neck and my shoulder, and she said, "Fuck me, Levi."

So I did. It was hard and fast and loud—all the things she'd demanded of me. I pounded into her, thrusting so hard it knocked her back against the doorjamb repeatedly. Somehow we ended up on the bathroom floor, my head banging against the toilet seat on my way down. I didn't care how bad it hurt because it was the best fucking sex I'd ever had in my life. Maybe the best I ever *would* have.

Because this time, it mattered. Cadence mattered more than I was prepared for.

She rose up over me, riding me while I let my hands explore her petite body. Her pink dress was drenched in our sweat and wrinkled beyond belief, and I was only making it worse by manhandling her through the fabric. I couldn't seem to stop myself, not with the sounds she was making. Soft moans mixed with sharp cries that echoed in the bathroom, all of them urging me on. But we'd started out so fast and hard I didn't know if I could hold on much longer.

"Baby, I need you to come," I ground out, trying to hold back my own release.

"I'm close."

"I'm *too* close," I insisted.

Keeping her eyes on mine, she grabbed a handful of my hair and tugged me up and over her, leaning back until I was on top. She hooked her ankles over my shoulders and locked them together behind my neck. I held on to her hips and tipped them forward just enough that I had to be hitting her G-spot.

After a few more thrusts, her eyes rolled back and she cried out, while I rode the wave of her release. The tremors squeezed my cock so much that I lost the thin rein of control I'd had to that point, shouting "I love you," as I came.

Her hands stroked my face, my neck, my shoulders, both of us panting and trying to come back down to earth. After a moment, I realized she had to be insanely uncomfortable being crushed beneath me with nothing but the cold, hard tile floor to cushion her. I rolled off her, but she came with me, straightening her limbs as we adjusted.

I was about to suggest we get up off the floor and maybe take a hot shower together when she propped herself up on her elbows to look down at me and said, "You love me?"

"I…" I blinked a couple of times, trying to figure out if I should pretend I hadn't said it or if I might as well admit it. But it didn't matter. It was the truth, and there wasn't any good reason to lie about something as important as that. "Yeah," I said, grinning at the dumbstruck look on her face. "I do. I love you, Cadence Johnson. So get used to that."

She bit her lower lip again, but she was smiling. "Okay. But only if you get used to the idea that I love you, too."

Just when I thought things couldn't get any better, she went and flipped the script on me. I tugged on her hair until she came down and let me kiss her, long and slow.

She broke off the kiss after a minute and giggled. Straight back to the cute and adorable version of herself. How on earth could she switch back and forth like that? I didn't have the first clue, but I intended to spend as much time as necessary studying her to figure it out.

"What's so funny?" I asked.

Cadence shrugged with a devious grin that would put her nephew to shame. "Mischief managed."

At least she got that quote right.

Chapter Sixteen

ONCE AGAIN, I leaned forward on those damned figure skates Bergy had bought for me—the ones he insisted I wear for these lessons—and once again, I caught the fucking toe pick on the ice and fell flat on my face.

"Ow!" I shouted, barely stopping myself from shouting a bunch of less acceptable things in front of Sophie.

She giggled, and Cadence skated over to offer me a hand.

"So, what does Levi need to do, Sophie?" Cadence asked. "What's he doing wrong?"

Sophie put her hands on her hips, taking up a posture I'd seen her mother use countless times. "Don't just bend the knees. Bend the ankles."

"Hockey skates don't allow you to bend the ankles," I grumbled.

"But figure skates do," Cadence said. "Which is why you're wearing them and not those stiff old hockey skates."

"I like my stiff old hockey skates."

Cadence shrugged. "You can learn to like these, too."

With that, Sophie skated away from us, trying to perform a spiral move she'd been working on with Cadence for a while. The way her eyes lit up when she finished it, I couldn't help but nod. "Yeah. I suppose I can." For Sophie's sake, at least.

The twinkle in Cadence's eyes told me she understood exactly where I was coming from. She took off to follow her true student, and I had to try to catch up to her without falling on my ass. "You're as messed up over Sophie as I am over you, aren't you?" I asked her once I reached her side.

She grinned. "Sophie is far and away my favorite student. And it has nothing to do with the fact that she's your best girlfriend."

"Mm hmm."

"Hey, Sophie," she said, ignoring me. "You're doing great with that spiral on your right leg. What about trying it while leading with your left. Think you can do that?"

"I can do it," Sophie insisted. And no one who had ever watched her try would ever doubt it. This little girl could do anything she set her mind to.

Her first several efforts weren't successful. Sophie ended up on her butt even more often than I did, but she never stayed down, and she never cried. She simply got back onto her skates and tried again.

"Why don't you try it, too, Levi?" Cadence suggested after helping Sophie to her feet. She winked at me, ignoring the evil eye I was sending her direction.

I picked up some speed and then pushed off, and almost instantly tipped forward. I probably came close to breaking the fall with my nose.

"Try it again, Levi," Sophie shouted at me.

"Yeah, try it again, 501."

I whipped my head around when I recognized Koz's voice. "What are you doing here?" Fucking hell, none of the guys knew I was doing this. Bergy did, of course, since I was doing it for Sophie's sake. We had an understanding, though. He wasn't going to spill my secrets. I supposed Jonny might be aware, if Cadence had told him. But that was it. I hadn't even told my brother about these lessons. The last thing I needed was for any of the guys to find out I was taking figure skating lessons. I especially didn't need them to find out I was falling on my face constantly because of these stupid skates or my inability to use them properly.

But now that Koz had seen me in these skates… I would never hear the end of it.

"Bergy wanted me to meet some speed skating instructor here," Koz said. "I wasn't too happy about it. Not until I saw this."

The son of a bitch had a grin on his face that likely wouldn't go away for months. This had just made his fucking day. Hell, maybe his whole year.

I glanced at my watch. Our ice time should've been over about twenty minutes ago, but the guys up front hadn't kicked us off yet. Old Gord had a thing for Cadence. I couldn't blame the guy, since I definitely had a thing for her, too, but that didn't mean he needed to let her go long with these sessions. Either Bergy or Paige would be here any minute to pick up Sophie, and she wasn't anywhere near ready to go home.

"Come on, Sophie Bug. Need to get you out of those skates so you can go home."

"Time's already up?" she said, pouting.

"Time's up," I replied.

She skated over to the door I held open for her, and Cadence and I helped her get her skates off.

"Are you coming to my next lesson?" she demanded. "You need to practice. You fall down too much."

"Wish I could," I said, winking at Cadence. "But you know I've got to go with the team. We're leaving tomorrow."

"Yeah." She gave me another practiced pout. "I'm gonna skate better than you soon."

I slipped her skate off and put it in her gym bag. "I don't doubt it. You're improving fast."

"Score lots of goals, then," she said. "And make sure Harry is a good boy."

I tried not to bust up laughing. What on earth did she know? Maybe more than I did. "Harry?" I asked innocently, ignoring the way Cadence was shaking her head at me.

"Bergy said he was bad and went to jail. Tell him to be good, like you."

Cadence snickered, no doubt thinking of how very bad the two of us had been last night, but Sophie didn't pay her any attention.

The doors down at the other end of the ice opened, and both Bergy and Paige came through.

"Will do, Sophie Bug" I said, tying her shoelace. Cadence had already finished the other shoe, so I picked up Sophie's coat. "Now let's get you all bundled up, okay?"

"Okay." She let me slip her arms into the sleeves, but then she turned and gave me her serious face.

"What's up?" I asked.

"You should take your skates with you. You need to practice."

"Yeah, 501," Koz called out from the ice, where he was already warming up. "Bring your figure skates so you can practice for *The Nutcracker on Ice.*"

I was about ready to crack his nuts, but I bit my tongue to keep from saying anything I'd regret. No chance was I going to slip up and curse in front of my Sophie Bug.

I could take care of Koz later. Or maybe, if I was lucky, he'd forget all about it.

Not likely, but a man could hope.

Cadence

SURELY ONE OF these days, Levi and I would get around to taking our time and enjoying sex with each other. That hadn't happened yet, though. Every time we started off heading toward his bed, we somehow ended up getting all sorts of random bumps and bruises from various pieces of furniture, and we typically ended up on the floor in a sweaty tangle of limbs.

I couldn't say I minded in the least, and it didn't seem like he did, either.

That said, there was zero chance I'd ever look at the rounded corner of the kitchen counter the same way again. Even now, as I said as much in hushed tones to Katie and her sister, the small of my back ached something fierce. I rubbed it while they busted a gut laughing.

"Keep it down or someone else will come over here," I said, laughing just as hard as they were. I glanced around the owner's box, where we were hanging out after the Storm's game, waiting for the guys to finish cleaning up. No one seemed to be paying the three of us any attention, thank goodness, but that could change at any moment. Especially if we kept it up the way we were now. "If my brother gets word of this, I'm blaming both of you."

"Lips. Sealed." Dani dramatically pretended to zip and lock her lips, then tossed away the imaginary key. It was a Thursday night, and she'd driven down from Seattle for a long weekend away from her fashion school, to coincide with the team heading out of town. The plan was for me to stay with the two of them for the weekend, since the guys would all be gone, and since Anthony and Jesse were still gone on their honeymoon, so I'd brought a duffel bag with me.

"So how, exactly, do you get into the right position for that?" Katie asked. "I mean, you're tiny."

"Not on my own," I said, blushing. "He's so much taller than me that we're always having to make adjustments."

"Good thing you're flexible," Dani said. "I sincerely doubt I could last like that for longer than three seconds. He'd have to be strong enough to hold me up like that."

"Good thing you're single and don't have to worry about it," Katie shot back at her.

"Just because I'm single, that doesn't mean I'm not—"

"Doesn't mean you're not what?" her father asked ominously from behind us. We hadn't been paying much attention, so none of us realized the guys were starting to make their way up to join us. If we had, no doubt we would have changed the subject well before now.

"Nothing, Daddy," she said, trying to pull off a sweet, angelic note.

"Mm hmm. Let's keep it that way, hmm?" He stalked off to collect his wife, and the three of us burst out laughing.

We looked around to see which of the guys had made it upstairs so far. Nicky Ericsson and Keith Burns had already come up to give their families good-bye hugs, but Levi and Jamie still hadn't joined us. I caught a glimpse of Harry, with his flaming-red hair and matching bowtie, hanging out in the corner and keeping a wary eye on Katie and Dani's father.

"Your dad still hasn't said anything about what happened with Harry?" I asked them, dropping my voice.

"Nope," Katie said. "He's not saying a word."

Dani rolled her eyes. "Other than to tell me that I'm to steer clear and not even think about it."

"But you don't want to steer clear?" I asked.

She shrugged. "I don't know. I mean, I've got to go back to school, and I'm not into the long distance thing. But there's not any harm in some minor flirtation, right? And a quick fling never hurt anyone."

Katie chuckled and shook her head. "Be careful."

"Careful of what?"

"I don't know. I just don't think Harry's the kind of guy you have a quick fling with."

"Maybe so, maybe no," Dani said, crossing her arms.

I didn't miss the fact that she kept making eyes at Harry. Or that he was returning them, when he wasn't otherwise occupied with watching her father.

Cam came through the doors and stalked straight over to the three of us. "You're all set? Have everything you need?"

"My bag is in the trunk. We'll all leave together."

"Cadence is going to be perfectly fine," Katie told him. "Dani and I are both going to be with her all weekend. Mom's coming over some, too."

"Babs told me he made sure you two both have pepper spray."

"Got it," Katie said. "We're going to be fine. *All* of us will be."

He gave her a curt nod, and then he hauled me up into a bear hug. "You call me if you need anything. Doesn't matter what time, day or night."

"I will," I promised, mainly so he'd let me go. He was squeezing the air out of me.

Once he put me down, I realized Dani had snuck off to go flirt with Harry up close. Apparently her father was distracted enough for her to take the chance. Either that or she honestly didn't care if he saw. I had a feeling Harry cared a bit more than she did, based on the way he kept glancing over in the coach's direction.

Cam gave me a worried look. "No practice, since Anthony's still gone, right?"

"Right. I do have a couple of sessions with my students on Saturday, though. Gord and the guys will be on alert, and my kids almost always have a parent at the lessons with them. Especially on the weekends. It'll be fine."

He scowled, but he nodded. Then he gave me a quick kiss on the forehead. "Text me every day."

I gave him an exaggerated salute. "Sir, yes sir."

Then he rolled his eyes and crossed the room to Sara and the kids.

At about the same time, Levi came in and wrapped me up in his arms. Tension melted away as soon as he touched me. I couldn't get over how easy it was to let myself fall further in love with him, without worrying about what might happen if I let down my guard. I didn't need any sort of a protective wall with him. Only with Guy.

Levi rested his chin on the top of my head. "I don't want to go."

"I don't want you to go."

For a long time, we stayed exactly as we were. There wasn't a need to speak. Nothing between us was uncomfortable, and the simple act of touching each other was more soothing to my nerves than anything. But time was running short, and he had to head back down with the rest of the guys to fly up to Vancouver tonight for a game tomorrow. Eventually, he drew back enough to tip my chin up.

"You're going to be okay with Katie and Dani?"

"Girls' weekend," I said to keep him from worrying. "We're giving each other pedicures and all sorts of things like that. I've even got plans to finagle Dani into designing some skating costumes for me and Anthony. Don't tell her that, though. She thinks the weekend is all going to be fun. She's got no idea I intend to make her work."

Levi laughed and kissed me, still laughing. Everything around us melted away when our lips touched. I definitely hadn't had my fill of him yet, and he was already leaving. At least this trip was short. They were due back in town on Tuesday, but that seemed like a very long time from now.

"Don't forget to pick a card every day," he said softly.

A wicked thought struck me, and I motioned for him to bend down so I could whisper in his ear. "If I pick the hour of uninterrupted Skype time, can you *make sure* you're alone? Because I might want to manage some more mischief during that time."

He cracked a grin. "I'm sure I can come up with a way to get rid of Koz for an hour."

"Longer wouldn't be a bad thing."

"Are you going to get away from Katie and Dani for that?" he asked.

"I'm sure I can arrange that. I can have time alone, even if we're doing a girls' weekend."

"You have a wicked streak. Is your brother aware of that?"

"Probably. Just wait till Connor hits puberty. Cam can think of me as training, to prepare him for dealing with that boy."

"I doubt anything could prepare someone for dealing with your nephew."

"Probably not. Still…" I gave him another quick peck on the chin. "I'll pick my card in the morning and text you with what I want."

"I doubt I'll sleep from the anticipation."

"Maybe we can both stay up…"

"We'd have Koz for company," he said.

I pouted. "That doesn't sound as good."

"Know what having to leave you now is making me realize?"

"Not a clue. But I'm desperate to know."

His eyes roamed over every inch of my face, as if he were trying to memorize how I looked at exactly this moment. "It's that I don't ever want to be without you. We haven't been together all that long, and it's way too soon to be talking about getting married or anything. But when I'm with you, it's easy to think about forever."

That wasn't even remotely what I'd been expecting. My lips formed an O, but nothing came out, and this amazingly warm sensation spread from my belly all the way out to the tips of my fingers and toes.

"I only want you to know I'm thinking about it. With you." Then he kissed me again, a long and lingering one, before being dragged out of the owner's box with the rest of the team.

I headed back over to see if Katie and Dani were ready to go, surprised to find Dani grinning like a loon—much the way I suspected I might be, after what Levi had just said to me.

"What?" I asked, dropping down into my seat to gather up my purse and coat.

Katie shook her head, laughing. "Dad's going to murder you. Not to mention Harry."

"Seriously," I said. "What happened? You're killing me."

"I kissed him." Dani beamed. "He's a very good kisser. And his hands! Oh my God, his hands are huge. And so strong. And he understands how to use them. The thought of what he could do with those hands if we were alone... But Dad came up before I was done, and I think Katie's probably right. It looked like he was going to murder the poor guy. And *Harry* looked like he wanted to murder me. I probably shouldn't have done that with Dad around..."

"It was way worse than the way Dad ever reacted with me and Jamie. *Ever.* Even when I was still only seventeen."

"Now I *really* want to find out what Harry did to end up in jail," I said.

"I couldn't care less," Dani said. "I just want him to kiss me again. And maybe try that move you were talking about. The one on the kitchen counter? Yeah. I think if I was with Harry, I could totally manage that one. He's more than strong enough."

"You're a mess!" I said.

Katie rolled her eyes. "And you're going to get him killed before you ever get to try it."

"Maybe not," Dani said. "They kind of need him on *D* right now. I doubt Bergy'll let Daddy kill him."

"And you're heading back to Seattle before they come home again." Katie gathered up all her things and waved to her mother and a few of the other wives as we headed out the door.

"Yeah." Dani sighed. "But I'll be back for spring break. Not to mention all summer long."

"Good thing for Harry he doesn't stay in Portland for the summer," Katie said.

"True." Dani turned to me with a wicked grin. "But my semester ends mid-May. With any luck, they'll still be in the playoffs at that point."

I didn't even try to stop myself from laughing. There wasn't a chance I could succeed.

FRIDAY PASSED WITH a lot of laughter and no cause for concern. Dani and Katie's mom, Laura, came over for dinner and brought wine and Riley Jezek's fiancée, Amanda Morris, along with her. Dani technically wasn't old enough to legally drink, but since we were sticking around the house and her mother was the one giving it to her, I figured it wasn't the end of the world.

Since it was a full house and we were busy giving each other makeovers, I chose a card for Levi to order delivery for our dinner. We sat around eating Chinese food, drinking wine, and watching the guys crush the Canucks.

The next morning over a late breakfast, Katie brought up the idea of her and Dani coming with me to the rink while I taught my students.

"I've got three hour-long sessions. You'll both be freezing and bored out of your minds."

"But you wouldn't be alone," Dani said.

I rolled my eyes. "I won't be alone. Gord will be working up front. I'll have my students, and I should have at least one parent sitting in the stands and observing. Besides, Guy hasn't tried anything in weeks. I think he's forgotten all about me, or maybe he's gone back home." Although, if he'd gone home, the police would have informed me about that. I decided not to mention that part to these two sisters, because they appeared to be giving in. No reason to alter circumstances against myself.

After a couple more minutes of debate, they gave in and agreed to let me teach my students without the two of them tagging along.

Running later than I'd intended, I headed out to my car and froze. There was a large envelope stuck under the wiper blade. Running my fingers over the pepper spray on my keys, I glanced up and down the street. No sign of Guy's car, or anything that seemed out of the ordinary. So maybe he knew I was here, and just wanted to remind me that he hadn't forgotten about me.

I took the envelope and got into the car. The whole way to the rink, I debated whether I should cancel my classes for the day and go straight to the police with this or not. But I didn't want to let the girls down. And besides, Guy hadn't done anything but try to scare me. There was no reason to think he'd do otherwise now.

Once I parked, I took a moment to open the envelope. No note this time. It was just pictures.

Of me.

And Levi.

Having sex on the floor of his bathroom.

They'd clearly been taken by some sort of camera with a zoom lens, so it wasn't like Guy had managed to set anything up in Levi's apartment. Still, the violation of it clawed at me from the inside.

Someone knocked on the window of my car, and I might as well have jumped out of my skin. But it was just Devyn and Kaetlyn Griggs and their father, arriving at the rink for their lesson. *Calm down*, I told myself. I could do this. I could get through these lessons, then go to the police. And maybe this time, it would be enough evidence for them to arrest Guy.

My heart was pounding so hard I could practically hear it, and I could barely see through my tears to shove the pictures back into the envelope. I slammed them into the glove box and forced myself to smile as I got out of the car.

"Sorry," I said. "Running late."

We hurried inside and got started. Their father sat in the stands watching attentively as we worked through some very basic mechanics. From what I could tell, he didn't realize anything was wrong. All the better. The last thing I needed was to freak out so badly I scared anyone else.

We got through their hour, and I ushered them on their way. And, as expected, Guy hadn't shown up or done anything else. I took a few minutes to head up front and talk to Gord. He seemed to think everything was as it should be, which was very reassuring.

Next up was Rachel Allan, whose mother had come along, as usual. Rachel had proven to be a challenging student for me, as she was dealing with both ADHD and a bit of autism. Skating gave her something to focus on, though, and she was just as determined as Sophie. By the time I finished with Rachel's lesson, I was finally starting to calm down and breathe normally again. It was just Guy trying to get to me again, and it had worked all too well. I couldn't keep letting him bother me like this.

Rachel and her mom were on their way out when Sophie and Paige rushed in.

"I'm sorry we're late!" Paige said. She set Sophie's gym bag on the bleachers and started getting her dressed. "It's been a crazy day. Always is with four girls. I forgot that Zoe has dress rehearsals today for her next dance recital, and she doesn't have her costume. So I've got to race back home, grab it, and rush it up to the studio."

"No problem," I assured her, even though I felt more nervous than I hoped I was letting on. But honestly, Guy hadn't done anything other than put a freaking envelope full of photographs on my car this morning. That was all he'd done. There was no reason to think he'd do anything now. I forced a smile to my lips, determined to remain calm. "Sophie and I'll be just fine on our own, won't we?"

Sophie nodded emphatically. "We're doing spirals today, Mom."

"You're sure?" Paige asked me, trying to get one of Sophie's skates laced. "Because Mattias said I should stay with you two. I tried calling the girls' father—"

"I'm sure. Sophie and I will be just fine, and if we need anything, Gord can help us out. Right, Sophie Bug?"

She'd recently given me permission to call her that, too, just like Levi did. Only the two of us were ever allowed to call her that.

"Right," she said, tugging her arms out of her coat. "Cadence and I are just gonna skate, Mom."

"Go," I said, shooing her on her way. I took over working on Sophie's skates because the activity would surely help me calm down. "I've got everything under control here."

"You're an angel," Paige said. She kissed Sophie on the top of the head, and then she headed out with the same brisk pace as she'd come in.

I made sure Sophie's laces were tight and then grinned at her. "Ready?"

"Yep. But I wish Levi was here."

"Me, too." For more reasons than I cared to explain at the moment. I held out my hand to help her up, but she pretended she didn't see it and got up on her own. We headed out to the ice and got started.

Twenty minutes into our session, the doors banged open.

"That was fast," I said, without bothering to look over my shoulder.

I'd thought it would take Paige nearly the full hour before she returned. "I wasn't expecting you back so soon."

"Weren't you?" Guy said.

Every ounce of blood in my body froze.

Chapter Seventeen

Cadence

"WHO'S THAT MAN?" Sophie asked, always full of sweetness and light and all the good things Guy wanted to suck out of my life.

I tried to breathe, but the air got stuck halfway down my throat. Wouldn't reach my lungs. I needed to calm down enough that I could breathe and figure out what to do. This was for real this time. He was actually here, and he intended to act, not just threaten me. Didn't he? Why else would he be here? No reason I could fathom.

Think. Think! By now, Guy was already closer to my phone and my pepper spray than I was. No time to go get them.

I didn't have the first clue what Guy intended, but if he was deliberately going against the protective order and coming closer to me than he should, I had to get Sophie to safety, to make sure she understood how serious the situation might be, but not scare her—all at once. That was my first order of business. Everything else had to come later. But how? No clue.

She was skating toward me, thank goodness, so I waited until she came to a wobbly stop in front of me. Then I put an arm around her shoulders and started guiding her toward the opposite side of the rink from Guy, who had almost reached that door.

"Sophie Bug, I need you to do me a favor," I said quietly.

"What favor?" she asked.

At the same time, Guy shouted out, "Where do you think you're going, Cadence? I need to talk to you. I came all this way for you. You can't just skate away from me like that."

Sophie looked up at me, her big, caring eyes filled with concern. "He's the bad man, isn't he? Bergy told me about him."

There wasn't a chance in the world I'd lie to her about this. Getting her cooperation was too important. I nodded, a thousand thoughts racing through my head at once.

"I can help you fight him."

"Not a chance."

It was true that she'd gone to a couple of self-defense classes with me, but I couldn't handle it if anything happened to her. As it was, I was worried sick about Gord. There was no way he would have just let Guy walk past him. Something awful must have already taken place, and more seemed to be on the way.

How stupid had I been? I should've gone straight to the police as soon as I'd seen the envelope on my windshield this morning. Instead, I'd fallen back into my old habits, and I'd convinced myself it was no big deal. Nothing more than Guy pulling the same things he'd been pulling.

No more stupidity. It was time to act decisively. To get this asshole out of my life once and for all, whatever it took.

"He's not going to hurt you, though, okay?" I said, trying to ease both of our minds. "He's going to leave you alone. I'm going to make sure of it. But I need you to go up to the office and tell Mr. Gord that we need help. And if you can't find him at the front desk, or if anything's happened to him, then pick up the phone on the desk and call nine-one-one. Can you do that for me?"

She nodded. "Yep. Mom taught me how to call nine-one-one."

"Good girl." I opened the door and helped her steady herself, glancing behind me to find that Guy had already come through the other door and was halfway across the ice. "Hurry, Sophie. Go as fast as you can. And stay out at the desk after you call, okay? Do exactly what they tell you."

Once she disappeared, I stayed on the ice, hoping to keep him as far away from that little girl as I could, and I spun around. Guy was only ten feet away from me, fast-walking across the rink. How the heck was he moving so fast in his shoes? He'd clearly spent way too much time on the ice in his life. Shaking but determined, I did my best to assess the situation. That was one of the first things I'd learned in my Krav Maga classes. I needed to think calmly and clearly about what he could use against me and, just as importantly, what *I* could use against *him*.

This wasn't just self-defense. I had to be ready to attack.

He was bigger and stronger than me, but I wasn't at a total disadvantage. He was in shoes on ice; I had on skates with sharp blades. I didn't see anything close by that would make a good weapon, so that was out. It was going to be me and my wits.

"I don't know what you're so scared of," Guy said, gradually inching closer. He'd slowed down once he was almost within striking distance, after wobbling a couple of times. "I've never treated you like shit the way your boy toy does. You let that punk fuck you up against the wall, toss you on the floor, spread you out on the kitchen counter… He's a fucking animal, the way he treats you. But you're living with him and issuing protective orders against me. Doesn't make any sense, Cadence."

With every step he took toward me, I backed farther away. I didn't say anything. Something told me Guy wanted to hear himself a hell of a lot more than he wanted to hear anything I might have to say, unless it was along the lines of, "Yes, you're right, I'm coming back to you right this second."

No way would I tell him anything of the sort.

"Is that what you wanted from me? I was always gentle with you. Didn't fuck you like a beast. Maybe I should have, since it seems to get you off." He smiled in a way that made my stomach churn with fear. "We could do that right now if you want. I could bend you over the boards and fuck you raw."

Had Sophie found Gord yet? Was she on the phone with nine-one-one? God, I hoped so.

Guy took another step, and I pushed back, never taking my eyes off him. Didn't look like he had any sort of weapon on him, but there was no telling what might be under his coat. He hadn't reached for anything yet, though.

"Would you scream for me the way you scream for him?" He chuckled, and my insides curdled. "I'd like to hear you scream again. It'd make me think of the sound you made when you fell that last time we skated together."

"You mean when you dropped me," I shot back. Couldn't stop myself. The more he spoke, the closer I got to being ready to fight back—to *really* fight back.

"Falls happen in figure skating," he said, brushing it off. He was still moving. Closer to me all the time.

I was paying too much attention to him and not enough to the rest of the situation. My butt bumped into the boards, and that was when Guy lunged for me.

His feet slipped on the ice, but he caught both hands around my neck as he went down, dragging me with him.

I squirmed to get myself in a better position, fighting to breathe with his hands making that complicated, but it was no use. He used his leverage and got himself above me, his knees shoving between my thighs to get a better grip on my throat. I couldn't spare the energy required to scream, not that it would do me any good if I did. It might scare Sophie, and that was the last thing I needed.

Don't panic. Stay calm. Think!

My arms weren't long enough to hold him back, but I remembered what I'd learned. I crossed my arms up over the top of his and grabbed hold of the outside of each of his wrists. Raised my hips as high as possible. Brought them down again with as much force as I could muster, and my arms at the same time. That was enough to break his hold on my neck. I bucked a hip out and got a skate in the bend of his hip. The other followed a moment later. I inched my skate blades closer to his crotch, and I kicked with everything I had in me.

My head slammed hard against the boards, leaving me dazed, and he let out an animal-like scream of pain. But I was free of him, at least for now. I scrambled to my feet and took off toward the other side of the rink as fast as I could, but I was woozy and kept stumbling every few feet. He tackled me halfway there, one hand catching my ankle. I hit hard when I went down. Hot, red blood stained the ice below me. Maybe I'd hit harder than I'd thought.

My other foot was free. I kicked. Made contact with something. Kicked again and again and again until he released my foot.

Then I was up again, skating as fast as I could. Threw myself over the boards, tumbled to the concrete floor. I crawled to the bench and grabbed my keys. I hit the button on the pepper spray before I'd fully spun around, holding down the button as he screamed in agony and fell, covering his face with his hands. Even then, I didn't let go.

Not until the doors banged open and cops rushed inside, guns pointed at the two of us, shouting, "Nobody move!"

I dropped the pepper spray and kept my hands in the air where they could see them.

"Fucking bitch!" Guy screamed.

Two of the officers hurried closer, their weapons still aimed in our general direction.

Dizzy. So dizzy. I swayed in place, and one of the policemen lowered his gun and put an arm on my shoulder.

"Sit down. Looks like you've lost a lot of blood." He lowered me to the nearest bleacher while one of his partners dealt with Guy.

"I think—" I stopped, shaking my head. It was too difficult to think.

"What do you think?" he asked.

I blinked at him. Couldn't bring him into focus anymore. My head hurt, and I reached up to scratch it. Came away with more blood than I'd ever seen in my life.

He put a cloth or something on my head and held it there. "Why don't you lie down?" he suggested.

That sounded like a very good idea. I let him lower me until I was stretched out on the aluminum bench. But then I shot straight back up, instantly wishing I hadn't. Couldn't tell which way was up and which way was a quick way to a concussion. Which I might already have, come to think of it.

I held my hand to my head and wished the world would stop spinning. "Sophie! And Gord. Are they okay?"

"Everyone's going to be just fine," he said, gently easing me back again. "Including you, if you'll let us do our jobs."

I nodded. Immediately regretted it. Nothing would come into focus, not in my vision or in my mind. Except—"Am I under arrest?"

The cop laughed, which confused me.

"Let go!" It was Sophie's voice. "Let me go. I'm gonna take care of her for Levi."

Then I felt her small, strong hand gripping mine.

"I did it, Cadence. I called nine-one-one."

"You sure did," I said, doing my best to stay calm and coherent for her sake. "You did great, Sophie."

"They said the ambulance is coming. I'm going to ride with you."

I nodded again, but the more she talked, the less I understood. Then she faded. Faded. Faded away.

Levi

"WRONG SKATES, PECKERWOOD." Koz tossed a roll of stick tape in my direction.

I caught it just before it hit me upside the head. We were in Calgary, getting ready for morning skate before our game against the Flames. I glared at him, ready to rip his head off if he said a fucking word about me figure skating, but Hammer spoke up before anything else happened.

"Look like the same skates he always wears to me." He grabbed the tape from me and sat down beside me to work on prepping his stick. Then he glanced over at Koz. "Looks like you could use a new pair, though. How long have you worn the same skates? They're as beat up as your face was after scrapping with Shaw."

Ghost snorted in laughter as he passed between us.

"What's so fucking funny?" Koz demanded.

"Just remembering how your nose got rearranged," Ghost said. "That was a good day. Hey, you should go with Engelland tonight. I bet he can rearrange the rest of your face."

"How about I just rearrange your face right now?" Koz shot back.

"How about we all try to remember what we're doing here," Hammer said.

Koz sat back in his stall and shoved his headphones in his ears, sulking. Then he took out his book of Sudoku puzzles and started solving one. I'd never understood why, but puzzles and games like that always calmed him down. At least he had a trick for getting past things.

And at least he'd shut his trap before saying anything about me figure skating.

I taped up my socks and went back to getting myself ready for morning skate. Not even two minutes passed, though, and Jim Sutter came into the locker room.

That wasn't normal.

At all.

He might drop in after a game every now and then, and he stopped by during morning skate or practices all the time. But in the time before a game, he was busy doing his thing, and he always left it to the players and coaches to get ready.

That couldn't be a good sign, him being in here.

He headed over to Jonny, who was quietly putting on his gear in his corner of the room, the way he always did. Head down, focused on the task at hand, no joking about. Jim said something to him, and Jonny's head shot up. Then they both looked over at me.

It had to be Cadence.

In no time, I was standing in front of Jonny's stall next to Jim. "What is it? What happened?"

"I need the two of you to come into Bergy's office for a minute, okay?"

That made it sound even worse. All the blood drained out of my head. I had to be white as my fucking jersey.

We got up and followed him into the coach's office, and Jim shut the door. Bergy looked as worried as Jonny and I were. He was up and pacing behind his desk instead of sitting there like the perfect picture of calm he so often presented.

"Why don't we all have a seat?" Jim suggested. The three of us glared at him, so he shook his head and kept talking. "Or not. I just got off the phone with Rachel. It seems that Cadence was attacked by the guy who's been stalking her. Guy? Is that his name? He used to be her skating partner."

I nodded grimly.

"It happened at the rink when she was giving Sophie a skating lesson."

Without listening for more, Bergy pulled out his phone and started dialing, and Jonny punched the wall, sending a whiteboard and markers clattering to the ground.

"Hold on," Jim said, holding up his hands. "Everyone's going to be fine."

"Going to be?" I croaked out. "Meaning they're not fine now."

"Sophie is completely unharmed. Scared, but that's all. Cadence got her out of the rink and had her call nine-one-one while she took on the bastard on her own."

"By herself?" Jonny repeated. "Where the fuck was the guy who works at the rink?"

"Guy hit him over the head with something and knocked him out. They said he was an older man, and likely couldn't have put up much of a fight, anyway. He's got a hell of a headache and might have a concussion, but he's fine, otherwise."

"Where was Paige?" Bergy demanded. "She's supposed to be there during the lessons if I can't be."

"She'd forgotten something for one of the other girls and left to go deal with that. Guy waited until it was just the old man, the little girl, and Cadence."

So Cadence truly had been all on her own against the son of a bitch.

"And Cadence?" I asked, dreading the answer.

"She's in the hospital," Jim said. "But she's going to be fine."

That wasn't good enough for me. Not even close to good enough.

I felt like I was going to be sick, but I needed to know everything. "Tell me what he did. Tell me what he did to her."

"I will," Jim said. "But first, I need you to tell me if you think you can play tonight."

Play? A stupid fucking game? My girlfriend had just been attacked by a psychotic ex, so the last thing in the world I wanted to think about was hockey.

Before I answered, Jonny said, "No. We need to go home. Both of us."

I raised a brow at him, but he glowered in return. I supposed that was a good thing, and there wasn't much positive to take from this this other than the news that Cadence would be all right.

Jim nodded. "I thought as much. Rachel's already working on it. We'll get you out of here as soon as possible."

"But you can't play tonight with only five *D*," I argued.

"Just got word from the doctors," Bergy said. "Colesy's cleared to play. Get your ass out of here before I change my mind."

Cadence

LAURA WEBER'S FACE and the glare of fluorescent lights met my eyes when I came to again.

I squinted and held an arm over my face to block out some of the brightness, groaning.

"Too much?" she asked. Then she turned to someone else in the room. "Can we turn the lights down?"

"Got it," said someone who sounded an awful lot like Katie.

The blinding quality of the lights faded, until it didn't hurt too much to keep my eyes open.

"Katie?" I said. My voice croaked over the word, and I realized how dry and scratchy my mouth and throat were. I tried to swallow, hoping it would aid the flow of my saliva so at least that part of me would stop hurting.

"Yeah. I'm here. Mom and Dani are here, too." She came over and took my hand, and I blinked a few times to bring her into focus. She and her mother looked almost like twins with the fuzziness clouding my vision, except for the fact that one had long hair and the other had short.

"What…?" I couldn't even finish the question.

"Guy is in prison. He's most likely facing deportation, following the stalking and physical assault charges. You're in the hospital. You cracked open your skull and have a concussion. Got a few staples in your head, but it's not too bad. They had to cut away a bit of hair to clean you up, but there's plenty to hide it while it grows out again. There's some bruising on your throat from where he tried to strangle you, but the concussion is what the doctors are worried about more than anything. The bruises will heal."

"So it's nothing horrible that'll keep me down for too long?" I asked.

Katie gave me a look. "Concussions are a pretty big deal. You might not be able to skate for a while."

I brushed that off. Compared to what could have happened, that was nothing. "And Sophie? What about Gord?"

"Sophie finally agreed to go home with her mother once the three of us got here to stay with you," Laura said. "She didn't want to leave your side. Gord, too, but he's in excellent condition. More a precaution than anything. It seems Guy hit him over the head with something off the desk. He's got a mild concussion, too, but he should be back on his feet in no time."

"Well, I suppose that's a relief." I'd imagined all sorts of awful things about what might have happened to Gord. And Sophie. The knowledge that they'd come away relatively unscathed was a blessing.

Katie nodded. "Your brother and Levi are on a flight back to Portland as we speak. In fact, they might already have landed. Could be here at any time."

"Don't they have a game tonight?" My brother had never missed a game unless it was for a reason out of his control, like an injury or a suspension. He just didn't do that.

"Game's on as we speak," Dani said. "They're still coming home. Bergy would be with them, too, if not for Paige convincing him that Sophie was completely unharmed."

Laura pulled up the chair next to my bed and sat. "I got off the phone with your mother a little bit ago. She and your sisters are looking into flights."

"They shouldn't bother," I said, swallowing some more. Everything to do with using my voice hurt. Maybe there wasn't any permanent damage from when he'd strangled me, but it definitely didn't feel good at the moment. "I'll text Mom and tell her I'm fine."

"You're not fine," Laura replied, raising a brow. "And even if you are, it's a mother's right and responsibility to overreact when one of her babies is hurt—and you're *always* going to be her baby, no matter how old you grow up to be. Overreacting is part of what we do."

"I just left Sara in the waiting room," Dani added, easily changing the subject to something equally painful for me. "She was in here with you for a while, but she had to go sort out some trouble that Connor was getting into. I can go take over for her, though."

I shook my head, then wished I hadn't moved that much. "Don't. Trying to watch that little boy will put you off ever having kids of your own." And I wasn't sure I was ready to face Sara after being as stupid as I'd been today. And it wasn't just today, either. It had started from the moment I'd first arrived in Portland at New Year's Eve. What if I'd been alone with the kids, instead of with Sophie? What if Guy had attacked when I'd been at the house with all of them instead of at the rink? Any of those things could have happened. I'd put them all in terrible danger, and if Sara didn't light into me, then no doubt Cam would.

"So now what?" I asked.

Laura poured some water into a cup for me and passed it over.

"It *is* water, not wine," Dani said with a grin and a wink. "Already checked."

Laura rolled her eyes. "What you do now is you stay here until the doctors decide you can leave. At some point, you'll have to give a statement to the police about what happened. There's video, though. The rink had security cameras rolling, so it's all been captured. That should mean you won't need to be involved too heavily in whatever legal proceedings take place."

"Or at least that's the hope," Katie said.

I nodded and took a sip from the water because Laura was giving me a mom sort of look. Everything I did and everything they said made my head hurt worse, though, so I rubbed my forehead.

"Do you want us to leave you alone?" Dani asked. "We should. Come on, Mom." She took her mother by the arm and dragged her toward the door. "Katie, you coming?" she said, stopping to look over her shoulder.

"I'll be out in a minute," Katie said.

The door closed behind them, and then Katie looked down at me with kind eyes. "Jamie told me he'd never seen his brother such a mess before. Levi's pretty torn up over you."

"I'm a mess over him, too. I mean— Not that there's anything—"

"Good," she cut in, saving me from trying to explain. "We're both behind you, Jamie and I. We want to see Levi happy. I think you can help with that. You *are* helping with it."

The door to my room banged open, and I winced up at Levi and my brother. Sara and the kids were right behind the two of them, with Sara trying to grab on to Cam and calm him down even as she wrangled the kids.

"Shh!" Katie hissed in their direction. "She's got a concussion."

I couldn't do anything but stare at Levi as he rushed in and took the seat Laura had left vacant, taking my hand in both of his. He lifted it and kissed my knuckles.

A smile crept to my lips. "Amazing. I think I feel a bit better." The words croaked out, and I forced myself to take another sip from my water.

"You should kiss her on her booboo," Connor demanded. "Kiss it and make it better. That's what Mommy always does."

"I'm not sure it works that way with this kind of booboo," Levi said, chuckling without taking his eyes from mine.

Connor climbed up onto my bed on the other side and let out a beleaguered sigh, rolling his eyes. "You don't know nothin', do you?" Then he inched up higher on my bed and kissed me on the top of my head. "There. Now CayCay will be all better."

"Just like that?" I asked.

"Yep. Now can we go feed the agilators?"

"Not tonight, buddy," Sara said. "The bad guy's in jail."

He gave me a devious grin. "We could bring the agilators to jail." Then he cackled.

Suddenly, my head didn't hurt quite as much as it had before. Maybe the kisses really could make it all better. Just in case, I had every intention of demanding that Levi kiss me all over, as soon as they let me leave this hospital.

Chapter Eighteen

LATER THAT NIGHT, they discharged Cadence from the hospital with instructions on how to take care of the staples in her head and when to follow up on the concussion with her doctor. Jonny and I both agreed that we wanted her to see the same head specialist that Jens had been working with since being out of our lineup for the last few months, dealing with the same thing.

What we didn't agree on was where Cadence should go once they let her leave the hospital. He seemed to think that now that Guy was effectively out of the picture, she should go back to living in the spare room of his house. I wasn't on board with that—not at all—so I enlisted help from Katie and Dani.

"The last thing Cadence needs right now is to be surrounded by kids and chaos," I argued within the sisters' hearing.

"There's not chaos at my house," Jonny replied.

At that very moment, Connor cackled as he made an attempt to climb his father.

I gave him an oh-really sort of look.

"Levi has a point," Katie said.

Dani nodded. "But honestly, shouldn't it be up to Cadence where she goes? I'd think she should have some say in this."

"They said she shouldn't make any big life decisions," Jonny grumbled.

Both sisters rolled their eyes at the same time.

In the end, we got him to admit it should be up to Cadence. She agreed with me.

Katie and Dani came with us back to my place to help me settle her in and make sure she had everything she needed. They had packed up the duffel bag she'd taken with her to spend the weekend with them, but they didn't stick around too long. All Cadence wanted to do was snuggle against me on the couch, resting her head on my shoulder with her eyes closed. Needless to say, I was more than all right with that arrangement. It meant she was in my arms, right where she belonged.

The next day, there were more visitors at my apartment than I'd ever had in all the time I'd been living here combined. Cadence put on a robe and a smile, but I knew better than to trust the smile. I made it a point to keep a close eye on her for signs of fatigue, ready to kick everyone out at a moment's notice.

Midmorning, Paige brought all her girls over because Sophie needed to see for herself that Cadence was going to be fine. Her sisters kept their giggling to a minimum, thank goodness.

"Cadence?" Sophie said, holding tight to her hand.

"Hmm?"

"You can be Levi's best girlfriend now."

The other girls got quiet, and their expressions clearly said *awwwwww*, even if they didn't voice it aloud, but Cadence sat upright too fast.

She closed her eyes and waited a moment, probably hoping the shooting pains or nausea, or whatever it was this time, would quit. Then she gave Sophie a very serious look. "I can't be, because you are, Sophie Bug."

Sophie shrugged. "It's okay. I'll let you. And you can kiss him and stuff, too, as long as I can be his other girlfriend."

Cadence spluttered and looked over to me for help.

I got up and dragged a hand through my hair, studiously avoiding her gaze. "I need to...uh..." I didn't have the first clue what I needed to do other than get the hell out of Dodge, so I did exactly that, disappearing down the hall to my bedroom.

Because the direction of this conversation was making me think of one thing—marriage. And the more I thought of it, the less it sounded like a bad idea. Whether I wanted to pursue that or not, though, now wasn't the time to broach the subject.

I waited about ten minutes and then headed back out, hoping they would be on a different topic by now. As soon as I reached the living room again, someone was knocking on my door.

"We should go," Paige said, giving each of her girls a meaningful look. They blushed when they glanced up at me, so I headed over to answer the door while they busied themselves gathering their coats and purses, not to mention prying Sophie's grip away from Cadence's hand.

A few of the other guys' wives were waiting on my porch. I ushered them in, and Paige herded her daughters out so they could exchange places.

The day continued in that fashion for a long time. Nearly all of the Storm WAGs dropped by, some of them bringing food and others with flowers or books to keep Cadence busy while she recovered. Soupy, Burnzie, and Jens all stopped in, since they were in town recovering from injuries. Jens and Cadence sat together in the dining room, quietly talking about concussions, while the rest of us hung out in the living room.

Early in the afternoon, Anthony and Jesse showed up to fawn over her. They hadn't even stopped at their place after returning from their honeymoon in Hawaii. Anthony had a nice tan, but Jesse was as red as a lobster.

"Even with SPF 100," he said. "That sun's no joke."

I had to fight not to laugh at him, because the guy winced with every tiny movement.

"So I guess I'm skating on my own for a while," Anthony said.

"For a while," Cadence agreed. "I'm hoping it won't be a long while, though."

"We're not messing around with a concussion, though," he said, ignoring her pout.

They hung around for a while but excused themselves before I was ready to kick them out.

Then Jonny and Sara came over—sans kids, thank goodness—late in the day.

"They're with Daddy," Sara said.

"How'd you manage that one?" I asked.

"He's wrapped around my little finger," she replied. "Cassidy is quickly learning how to convince her Pops to do anything she wants, too."

Cadence raised a brow. "How's that?"

"Kisses and giggles."

Jonny took a seat in the recliner and stretched out his long legs. "I convinced Mom the last thing you need while you're recovering is for all of them to come down from Winnipeg."

Cadence let out a sigh of relief. "Thank you. Today has been more than enough, and that's without Mom getting in the middle of it."

"You look tired," he said.

All she did to respond was nod. She *felt* tired to me. Once again, she was curled up against my side on the couch, resting her head on my shoulder. Usually, she kept more of her weight off me than this, but right now she'd completely collapsed into me. I didn't mind in the least, other than recognizing just how worn out she was in order to let go like this.

"I told Jim I could rejoin the team," he said slowly. "Play in the next game."

Shit. I wasn't ready to leave her again. Not yet. Why hadn't Jim talked to me about this?

"He's had Rachel book me a flight to join the team in Edmonton tomorrow morning."

"Just you?" Cadence asked, inching closer to my side. I rubbed my hand up and down her arm. There was no chance I'd be allowed to miss another game now that we knew she was going to be all right. Especially not if Jonny was going back already.

"Just me. We'll be home again the next day."

"I don't understand," I said.

Jonny fixed me with a stare. "I told him that even though she's going to be fine, my sister is in no condition to be left alone. That she needs you."

I had to fight off a grin at understanding what that meant.

Jonny wasn't going to kill me. He'd decided to accept me as part of Cadence's world.

GRADUALLY, CADENCE WAS starting to get back to everyday life.

For the first couple of weeks after Guy's attack, she'd spent a lot of time in dark, quiet rooms with her eyes closed. Jens, Jonny, and I had ganged up on her about going to see the concussion specialist, and she'd eventually given in. Now that spring was in the air, she was starting to act more like her normal self.

They still hadn't cleared her to resume skating again, but some lighter exercise was allowed. On my days off when the team was in town, I tried to spend every possible moment at her side, at least as long as she wasn't growling at me to back off.

She was a lot like Sophie, in some ways. Cadence wanted to do everything for herself and not be coddled along. I found it difficult to avoid helping her more than I should. It killed me to see her struggling to do everyday things, or becoming exhausted from what she could have handled with ease only a month ago.

Still, Cadence's concussion had turned out to be great for me on one score—it got me out of the Light the Lamp Foundation's annual fundraiser that had been moved back to St. Patrick's Day, due to Noelle Kallan's and Jessica Lynch's pregnancies. Most of the rest of the guys were being forced to dress up as leprechauns and carry around pots of gold, but I got to spend the night at home on my couch, making out with my girlfriend in between bouts of equally silly and serious discussion.

"Do you want to have kids?" Cadence asked me, staring up into my eyes. Hers had taken on that deep, mossy green tint again.

I quirked up a grin. "With you?"

She punched my shoulder. "I mean in general. Do you see kids in your future?"

"I don't know. Not any time soon." Then I remembered the day the previous weekend when Sara had brought Connor and Cassidy over, and Connor had proceeded to empty every cabinet in my kitchen. "I don't suppose there's any way to control what sort of personality they'll end up with, is there?"

"We've already got one Connor in the family. No idea if that means we're likely to end up with another just like him, or if the opposite is true."

"We?" I said. "In the family? You realize you're the one saying these things, right?" Not that I minded. I kind of liked the thought that she wanted me to be part of the family. That she was thinking about kids with me in the picture was a definite bonus.

"Hmm," was all she said, and she cut me off from making any other points by kissing me. Her tongue glided along the seam of my lips, not that I needed much prodding to open for her.

When we broke apart a bit later, she asked, "What about Jamie and Katie? Do you think they want kids?"

"Want them? Yeah. Very much so. They've been trying to get pregnant, but I kind of doubt if it'll happen."

"Because of the chemo and all?"

"The doctors tell her it isn't likely," I said.

"So will they adopt if they can't do it on their own?"

"No idea." We'd talked about them trying to get pregnant, but this wasn't a subject I felt comfortable broaching with him. Maybe he would bring it up with me, when he was ready to talk about it again.

Cadence fell silent for a minute. She leaned back against me and we watched some of the pranks the guys were pulling on each other on the newest episode of *Impractical Jokers*. In no time, we were both laughing so hard she could barely breathe, and I definitely snorted a time or two.

"How'd you find this show?" she asked me when it went to commercial break.

"Koz. He thinks it's the best thing ever. He even tried to convince me to start up our own version of it—not for TV, just for fun."

"But you didn't want to?"

I shook my head. "Koz's idea of fun things to do to me would equal torture. No doubt about it. He doesn't recognize when he takes things too far. Social cues don't click for him."

"Yet you're still friends with him…"

I shrugged. "I understand him. I mean, he's not good in social situations. He doesn't realize how he comes across. But he's a good guy underneath it all. A jackass, sure. But he's a good guy."

"Seems to be a common thread between you two."

"What do you mean?"

She tipped her chin up to look at me. "You don't see yourself the way the rest of the world sees you. He doesn't understand how he presents himself. I get it. That's all."

"You don't mind that I'm friends with him, do you? I swear, I won't let him pull something with you." Not that it was easy. I was constantly reminding the guy that he was behaving like a jerk, and that he couldn't say certain things to people because it was rude. He just had no clue.

Cadence shook her head. "I think I love you more because of it. The same as I love you more because of how you are with Sophie. You see the good in people, even when no one else can. I only wish you could see it in yourself more often."

"I do, though."

"Do you?" She looked skeptical.

"I'm starting to, at least. You've helped with that. And Hammer. He's constantly reminding me that I'm doing exactly what I should be, but I need to believe in myself more. It's sinking in, a bit at a time."

She kissed me again. This time, we both lingered over it, not wanting to separate at all.

After a few minutes, we settled back against the couch and returned our attention to the show on TV. At the next commercial break, though, I knew it was time.

I picked up the remote and muted it.

"What?" she asked.

"You never picked your card for the day."

"Oh." She smiled all the way up to her eyes.

I got up to collect her box, then brought it back to her. "It was running a little low. I restocked it earlier, so you might want to look through all of them before making your choice."

"But I already know what I want," she said.

"Just look through them." I handed her the box and headed into the kitchen to kill a few minutes. This wouldn't work if she didn't pick through the cards and read all of the new ones. Once I thought enough time had passed, I slipped into the hall to retrieve the ring from my coat pocket.

Sure enough, when I returned to the living room, she'd dropped the entire box, and the cards had spread all across the floor. She had one in her hands and was staring at me with tears in her eyes.

Cadence turned the card around for me to read, not that I needed to see it to know what it said. Her mouth kept opening and closing.

"So will you?" I asked after what felt like an eternity had passed. My heart was in my throat, and I felt like I was being poked with a thousand thumbtacks in all my most sensitive places, because the wait was killing me. I opened the ring box and held it out for her.

She looked through her tears, letting one fingertip trace the stone. Then she looked up at me again. "I can't give you an answer yet. I need to talk to Sophie first."

"What?" That answer felt like a punch to the gut. Had I read the signs wrong? Maybe Cadence didn't want to marry me. I could be right back to being the guy who always fucked everything up, just like that. "But Sophie already told you she's okay with us," I said.

"She did. I can't explain it yet. It's only— I need to talk to Sophie first, and I need you to be okay with that. Paige is bringing her to your game tomorrow night. And I think I've recovered enough I can handle being at the arena through a game."

I thought I might puke up the contents of my stomach at any moment, but I agreed. After all, at least she hadn't said *no*. That had to be a good sign. Didn't it?

Cadence

EVEN THOUGH I'D texted Paige this afternoon to be sure she was still planning to bring all of the girls to the game tonight, I spent about the first twenty minutes after arriving at the arena up in the owner's box, anxiously chewing my fingernails. Then some of the other wives and girlfriends started showing up. Several of them had been trying to distract me and calm me down, but it was no use.

"You're going to say yes, aren't you?" Katie asked, settling into the chair next to me and giving me a kind but hopeful smile.

Dani brought over a few bottles of water and joined us. She had just come home for spring break, and there wasn't a chance she'd pass up an opportunity to sneak another kiss with Harry. Or whatever she was planning for tonight. Who knew what it might be?

She screwed off the lid of her water and took a sip. "You're not supposed to be making any important life decisions for a while, you know. They told you that in the hospital. Not until you're relatively concussion-free or something."

Katie rolled her eyes. "She was already living with him before the concussion." Then she turned to me. "I mean, I'm not saying it isn't a big decision. Just that you'd already made part of it well before all of this."

"I want to say yes," I said, hoping it would be enough for them to stop hounding me. "I need to talk to Sophie first."

A happy softness came into Katie's eyes. "You know she adores you, right? She's going to be fine with this, so stop messing up your manicure."

"Too late for that," Dani said, giving my hands a once-over.

"They're here." I bounded out of my seat and caught Paige's eye as she ushered her girls inside.

"Go do your thing so we can enjoy the game," Katie said, shooing me away.

As it was, the guys had already finished their warm-up, and they'd be back for the national anthem and other pregame stuff any time now. I knew I'd lose all of Sophie's attention once they skated out—she'd be too focused on Levi to pay me any mind—so I needed to get this done.

I crossed over to the girls, and Sophie flung herself into my arms.

"Are you all better now?" she demanded, squeezing so hard it was difficult to breathe. "Mom said you were coming tonight, but I didn't believe her."

"Not all better, but I'm getting there." I hugged her back. "Listen, I was hoping I could talk to you for a minute before the game."

"Okay." She smiled and put her hand in mine.

I led her to a quiet corner, completely aware that two of her older sisters were discreetly following a few steps behind. They found somewhere to sit not far from the two of us, and both of them no doubt had their ears trained on me.

I could appreciate that. Being the baby in my family, I'd spent years with Cam and my sisters constantly hovering to be sure I was all right. Sophie certainly needed it more than I did. Still, I had no intention of hurting her, and I hoped they knew that.

"Sophie Bug," I said, sitting across from her. She grinned from ear to ear when I called her that. I only hoped she was still smiling when we were done talking. "There's something I need to ask you."

"Shoot," she said.

"Well, you know I love Levi, right?"

"Yep. We both love him."

"We do. We absolutely do." This was becoming far more difficult than I'd hoped.

"We're his best girlfriends. But you're the one who does all the yucky kissing stuff."

I laughed out loud. "I am, that's true."

"Zoe kissed her new boyfriend. I saw her last week. He put his tongue in her mouth. It was gross!" Sophie used her hands to emphasize exactly how gross she thought it was, which kept me in stitches.

"So no kissing for you," I said. "At least not any time soon."

"Nope. No kisses. Yucko."

Zoe snickered behind me, but Sophie seemed oblivious to it.

"So here's the deal," I said, trying to bring the conversation around. "I wanted to know how you'd feel about it if I married Levi."

"You're gonna marry Levi?" she said so loudly that half the heads in the room turned to stare at us. Then she stood up. "Mom! Cadence is gonna marry Levi! We get to go to the wedding."

"I guess that means you're all right with it?" I said, laughing as she threw herself into my arms again.

"We can come to the wedding, right? 'Cause I just told Mom we could." Then she let go of me and pulled back enough that she could look in my face. She dropped her voice low. "Zoe told me that when you get married, there's lots of kissing. I don't wanna kiss Levi. I just want to love him. You can do all the kissing."

"Well, in that case"—I pinched her nose until she giggled—"I guess we'd better go ask your Mom if you can be my junior bridesmaid. If you want to be, of course."

"Mom!" she shouted again. "I'm gonna be a bridesmaid."

I supposed that settled that. Now all I had to do was tell Levi, and convince Sophie to bite her tongue about it long enough for me to be the one to tell him. Sophie and secrets were a complicated equation, but I had a feeling she would do her best.

BY THE TIME the guys made it upstairs after the game, my head was definitely pounding. I probably shouldn't have come to the game tonight. Watching it on TV at home would have been much more sensible. Still, I was glad I'd come, since it had given me the opportunity to speak with Sophie face-to-face.

It didn't matter how glad I was of it, though. The second Levi walked in and saw my face, he said, "You look miserable."

"Thanks," I said, trying to laugh it off. "Here I was, about to tell you that you look good enough to eat, and you tell me I look miserable. Really gives a girl a jolt of self-confidence."

He reached for my hand to help me up. Then I thought he was going to draw me in for a hug or a kiss, but instead he lifted me into his arms. "I'll take you home and make it up to you," he said softly in my ear.

"Is that a promise?"

"Mm hmm. Now let's get you out of all the noise, okay?"

I didn't complain. Not even when he carried me over to Sophie and Paige to collect a hug from his other best girlfriend, and then proceeded to carry me out of the owner's box, through the corridors, down the elevator, into the parking garage, and all the way to his car.

He opened the door and set me in the passenger seat, pecking me on the nose before closing the door behind me.

I pouted when he climbed in on his side.

"What's the pout for?"

"Don't I deserve a better kiss than that?"

"I don't know." He started the car and backed out of his space. "Have you done anything to deserve a better kiss?"

I shrugged and nibbled on my lower lip, doing my best to look innocent. "Well... I had my talk with Sophie tonight."

He gave me a questioning look. "And?"

I fiddled with the zipper on my purse, drawing out my response as long as I could. "And she's agreed that I should be the one who does all the yucky kissing stuff with you, and she knows that when you get married you do lots of yucky kissing stuff, so she'll be my junior bridesmaid at our wedding as long as she gets to love you still."

About halfway through my answer, Levi slammed on the brakes in the middle of the parking garage to turn and stare at me. Now his jaw was hanging slack, but his dimple was out alongside a huge grin.

"So what are you saying?" he asked.

"I guess I'm saying yes, I'll marry you. Is that worth a better kiss?"

In answer, he leaned over, cupping a hand behind my head and drawing me in to kiss me senseless. With the way he was kissing me, if we hadn't been in a car in the middle of the Moda Center's parking garage, I might have straddled him and insisted he make love to me right then and there.

Good thing someone behind us laid on their horn, shocking us back to our senses.

Barely in time, too. Levi slammed his foot back down on the brake right before he hit a car that was parked along the wall. "Shit! I lifted my foot, I guess."

My heart was about to pound through my chest, both from the exhilaration of telling the man I loved with all my heart that I would be his wife and from the adrenaline of nearly crashing into a parked vehicle.

Levi put both hands on the steering wheel and took a couple of deep breaths. The car behind us—the one whose driver had honked—pulled around to pass us. Levi rolled down his window and waved in thanks.

It turned out to be Koz, who rolled down *his* window and flipped us the bird. "Get a room, fuck face," he shouted before zooming off ahead of us.

"I think that's an excellent idea," Levi said. He rolled up his window again and drove us back to his apartment as fast as he could without breaking too many laws.

We were barely inside before he had me pinned against the wall, kissing me with an intensity that cleared my headache and melted any resistance I might have otherwise felt. It had been a long time since we'd had good, frantic sex—ever since my trip to the hospital, Levi had been treating me as carefully as ever—but I was ready for it. I wanted him any way I could have him right now. Maybe even on the kitchen counter again. I was due for a new sex injury or two.

I started ripping at my clothes, but he put his hands on mine, stilling me.

"What?" I said, searching his eyes.

"My turn to ask for what I want."

The way he said it, staring at me with such heat and desire turning his baby blues to the same color as the midnight sky, left me shaking with the need to do whatever he wanted from me.

"Okay," I said, my voice quivering. "What do you want?"

"You." He twirled a strand of my hair around his fingers. "Naked. In my bed. Letting me make slow, sweet love to you and watching you come again and again."

I would have had to be out of my mind to argue with that suggestion.

Needless to say, I didn't.

Later, still spooning, with Levi's arm draped heavily around my waist, I twisted around in his arms until I could tease the few bits of hair on his chest. He kissed me, as slowly and languorously as he'd made love to me, and I fell a little deeper in love with him.

"I forgot something," he said, rolling away from me.

I instantly felt the loss of him—his heat, his strength.

He rolled back almost immediately, with the ring box in his hand. "You ready to put this on?"

I grinned and took the ring out. Even in the moonlight coming in through the window, the diamond glinted. "It's beautiful," I said, sliding it onto my finger. Then I kissed him again, coming around to fully face him.

He wrapped both arms around me, drawing me deeper into his embrace. "Mischief managed?"

"And then some."

Epilogue

Levi

"EVERYONE SETTLE DOWN for a few more minutes," Bergy said at what we'd all assumed was the end of our meeting. We'd had an optional skate today, as it was getting close to the end of the season, and we were still really banged up. At this point, rest was easily ten times more important than practice. Still, we'd just had a long film session, and most of us were restless to get away from the team facilities and enjoy the rest of the day off.

I shifted in my seat, itching to get home and see what card Cadence had selected from her box today. I hoped she wanted to go for a walk in the rose gardens or something like that. Spring had arrived, along with all sorts of new life. Not only that, but the weather was amazing today. I was itching to get out in it, and I had no doubt she must be, too.

The doctors had cleared her to start skating again late last week, so she'd been easing her way back into the everyday. Instead of rushing home to find out how I could spoil her today, now I had to stay until Lord only knew how late.

"We're not going to keep you boys too much longer, but Jim has something to announce that you all need to hear."

I sat up straighter in my seat as our general manager came into the room. I wasn't the only one suddenly shifting and trying to look more alive.

He'd loosened his tie but otherwise looked the same as we ever saw him, complete with the bifocals perched halfway down his nose. He smiled when he came into the room. Anne Dennison followed him in, which was particularly odd, along with Rachel Campbell, which wasn't odd in the least. Rachel had a stack of manila folders in her arms, which Soupy rushed over to take from her. He set them on the table up front and grabbed a quick kiss before returning to his seat.

Out of the corner of my eye, I caught Ghost winking at Anne. She looked to be intentionally avoiding making eye contact with him.

Must be serious, then, whatever was going on here.

"Bergy's right," Jim said. "I'm not going to keep you long, but I've got a very important announcement to make, and there's no better time than when everyone's gathered together like this. I asked Anne to join me because she's going to play a big role in what we've got in store for all of you. As you're probably already aware, close to half the other teams in the league already have behind-the-scenes web series that they produce and air on their websites. We've decided it's time that the Portland Storm join that trend. It's a great way for our fans and season ticket holders to see more of the inner workings of the organization. It's also a way for their families to become part of our family. We've brought Anne on board to produce the series, so she's going to be far more involved in your lives than she's ever been before. She'll be traveling with the team when we go on the road. She and her crew will be filming practices, film sessions, time spent with the trainers and doctors. She might ask for permission to follow you home some days to see what your life is like away from the team. She'll be involved when we participate in charitable events. Anne is going to be the fly on the wall as far as everything to do with this organization, and I fully expect each of you to cooperate as much as possible.

"Rachel's brought in all the consent forms that need to be read and signed. Your contract with the Portland Storm organization obligates *you* to participate as we see fit. However, if we're going to include your families, we'll need consent to use that footage."

Hammer shifted in his seat up front. "So if my ex won't consent to my kids being involved...?"

"If we don't have consent from all required parties, then we won't use it," Anne assured him. "That said, we're hoping that as many of you who are willing and able will allow us to involve your friends and families. What Jim said is exactly what I'm hoping to show the world. I want them to see that this team is a family. Maybe a big and sometimes dysfunctional family, but it's all a big unit. Everyone comes together."

Hammer nodded that he understood.

A few of the other guys asked questions about whether this meant they needed to be sure they were fully clothed when the cameras were around, and what would happen if they cursed in the middle of an interview. Anne answered all of their questions to the best of her ability.

"This isn't about changing who you are or what you do," she said in closing. "It's about capturing each of you as you already are. So be yourselves."

Jim took off his glasses and folded them, holding them in his left hand. "If that's all the questions you all have right now, I'll let you get out of here. Except for 501," he said, catching my eye. "I need a word before you go. Can you join me up in my office? As for the rest of you, Rachel's got the forms she needs from each of you."

What the hell was this about? I didn't have a clue why Jim needed to see me, and I wasn't sure whether it would be something good, bad, or indifferent.

Most of the guys got up and flooded toward the front of the room so they could collect their paperwork. Ghost headed straight for Anne to flirt with her some more. The guy couldn't seem to help himself.

"The fuck did you do wrong?" Koz asked from behind me, kicking the back of my chair. "Heading to the principal's office."

"Might be he did something *right*," Hammer said. He winked at me. "Go on. Go find out."

There wasn't any point in sitting around and wondering, so I headed out and met Jim on the way up the stairs.

"You're due for a new contract this summer," he said, smiling.

"Oh. Yeah." That was the last thing I'd expected this to be about. "I thought you'd just call up my agent and talk to him about that, though." I was still a restricted free agent. Basically, that meant I had almost zero negotiating power and had to take what they offered me or else not be eligible to play. Jim usually handled all the RFA contracts directly through the agents, and almost never while the season was still in full swing.

Jim opened the door to his office and let me precede him in. He took a seat behind his desk and set his glasses down in front of him. "I will be calling him, but I wanted to see where your head is first. I assume you like playing here in Portland."

"Love it. I don't want to be anywhere else." Especially not now that

Cadence and I were an item.

"That's good. The coaches and I have been talking a lot about you lately. We've all noticed how much you've improved this season. You're starting to become the player we all knew you had it in you to be, and we want to make sure you stick around for a long time."

"A long time?" My tone was half-skeptical, half-hopeful.

"We'll have to work that part out with your agent, but I was hoping you'd be amenable to a long-term deal. Something in the six-to-eight-year range, with pay that would reflect the fact that we'd be eating into your unrestricted free agency years. Is that something you'd be open to?"

Open to? I was about to jump out of my chair, that was how much I wanted what he was saying to be real. "I think that sounds like something we can probably work out," I said, though, trying to maintain my cool.

"Excellent." Jim folded his hands into a steeple and gave me an appraising look. "I know you've struggled with believing in yourself sometimes, but I think you should know that none of us has had that same difficulty. We want you to continue your growth here. We want to see you become one of the cornerstones of this organization for a long time to come."

We talked for about five more minutes before he shook my hand and ushered me out of his office with the promise that he'd be getting in touch with my agent sometime in the next week so they could start hammering out the particulars.

I thought about veering back toward the locker room to share the news with Jamie or Hammer, but changed my mind. There was no one I wanted to tell more than Cadence, so I headed straight home instead. When I opened the front door, I was greeted by the smell of banana bread that had just come out of the oven. That wasn't even the best part. Cadence was in the kitchen wearing nothing but a T-shirt she must have dug out of the bottom of one of my dresser drawers. It was huge on her, almost like a dress, and her wet hair had darkened some of the fabric. She had headphones on and was humming along and dancing in the kitchen, oblivious to the fact that I'd caught her like this.

I snuck up behind her, careful not to alert her to my presence, and grabbed her by the waist.

Bad move. Seriously bad move. I should've thought that one through a bit more, but I was too caught up in my own excitement.

She used one of her Krav Maga elbow jabs and got me right under the ribs at the same time as she spun around, readying her leg to kick.

"It's just me!" I backed away and dropped my hands in front of my balls for what feeble protection they could provide.

She stopped just barely in time to avoid kneeing my nuts, eyes as wild as her hair. Then, once I saw the recognition filter into her eyes, she followed it up with a sound punch to my ribs. "You scared me." She ripped the earbuds out and flung her iPod on the counter.

"So I noticed." I rubbed the places she'd just left bruised.

"I guess I should kiss you and make it better, then, shouldn't I?" She'd flipped that switch again, only this time, instead of going from adorable to seductive, she went from fierce to sex kitten. She licked her lips, and I imagined that tongue landing on me.

I was half tempted to let her go ahead and kick me in the nuts if it meant she intended to kiss me there and make it better. Probably a bad course of action. That didn't mean I shouldn't take her up on what she'd already suggested, though.

"How about we start there?" I said. "And then I can fill you in on the new contract Jim wants to offer me. We can work our way around to how your day's been, and finish up with you picking a card from your box."

"Hmm…" She slipped into my arms and stretched onto her toes so she could put her arms around my neck. "So it sounds like it's been a good day all around."

"Oh, has it?" I dropped my head to steal a kiss, letting my hands roam all over her back and firm ass. I'd been right when I'd guessed there wasn't anything under that shirt.

"Mm hmm," she murmured against my lips. "Anthony and I just booked our first competition for next season, and we got the rights to use that song I told you about. The one by The End of All Things."

I nipped her nose. "So all systems are go for skating again, then?"

"Yes. And Dani Weber agreed to design our costumes for next season." She slid her hands along my abs and tugged the shirt up from my waistband.

"Did she?"

"Mm hmm." Cadence got her hands under my shirt and splayed them over my ribs, exploring in a way she had to know would drive me wild. "And that's not all."

"No?" I followed her lead and tugged up the hem of the T-shirt she was wearing. "What else?"

"She's going to make me a wedding dress. She said once she finishes this semester at school, she's moving back to Portland to start up her own fashion line, and she wants to dress me. Free advertising or something."

I picked her up and set her on the kitchen island, tugging my T-shirt off her as she worked on the fly of my jeans.

"Just promise me something," I said.

"Anything."

I reached up and pulled my own shirt over the top of my head, tossing it on the floor to join the other items we'd already shed. "Swear you're not going to let Jesse take over the planning of the wedding."

She laughed as her hand wrapped around me, her eyes dancing like flames. "Do you really think either of us is going to have any say in it, other than the date? Sara, Katie, Laura, and Dani have already dug in their heels about the venue. Mom and my sisters are setting up Skype calls with them to talk details, leaving me out of it. Your mother is emailing them constantly with suggestions and questions. Jesse's the last thing we need to worry about with all of this going on."

"Hmm. I see your point."

She put her hand on the back of my head and dragged me down for a kiss, her tongue delving inside my mouth to dual with mine. When she backed away, she said, "I don't care, though. You know why?" Her hands both went beneath the waistband of my boxers, and she shoved them down my hips to get me as naked as she was.

"Why?"

"As long as I'm married to you, the rest doesn't matter. The wedding is one day. The marriage is forever."

I dug a condom out of the drawer we'd stashed them in, since we tended to end up having sex everywhere but in bed most of the time. "Forever's a long time," I said, rolling it into place.

Cadence drew me between her thighs and welcomed me in, holding me right where I belonged. "It's a long time. But not nearly long enough."

Roster

Name	Position	Nickname	Number
Dominic Medved	Defense	Bear	2
Cole Paxton	Defense	Colesy	3
Andrew Jensen	Defense	Jens	4
Levi Babcock	Defense	501	5
Chris Hammond	Defense	Hammer	6
Keith Burns	Defense	Burnzie	7
Cody Williams	Defense	Harry	8
Luc Vincent	Center	Vinny	10
Brenden Campbell	Left Wing	Soupy	11
Blake Kozlow	Center	Koz	14
Radek Cernak	Center	Radar	15
Austin Cooper	Center	Coop	16
Ilya Demidov	Defense	Demi	18
Jamie Babcock	Right Wing	Babs	19
Axel Johansson	Right Wing	Jo-Jo	20
Dylan Poplawski	Right Wing	Pops	21
Otto Raita	Left Wing	Otter	27
Cam Johnson	Left Wing	Jonny	28
Mitchell Quincey	Right Wing	Q	29
Nicklas Ericsson	Goal	Nicky	30
Sean Roberts	Goal	Bobby	35
Aaron Ludwiczak	Left Wing	Luddy	43
Jiri Dvorak	Right Wing	Devo	44
Nate Golston	Left Wing	Ghost	83
Riley Jezek	Center	RJ	91

Game Breaker

by
USA Today bestselling author

Catherine Gayle

Chapter One

Anne

"THIS IS FANTASTIC footage, guys. Really excellent work," I said, somehow focusing on all the screens in front of me at once. The adrenaline coursing through my body seemed to be in overdrive, more so than at any other point in this new adventure so far.

My eyes flipped back and forth as I tried to determine exactly where our focus needed to be. Nate Golston had already scored twice in this game, and he was out on the ice again with the rest of his line, with only a little over a minute left on the game clock. No doubt the Blackhawks would be pulling their goalie soon for an extra attacker, which meant the Portland Storm players on the ice would surely try to feed Golston and help him score a National Hockey League hat trick for the first time in his career.

We were nearing the end of my initial week of filming for *Eye of the Storm*, a behind-the-scenes web series focused on the Storm, and I hadn't yet decided on how to focus the premiere episode. As the producer, it was on me to find the story we wanted to tell and bring it to life. Since I was one of the only women in the world of sports broadcasting and journalism to be given this level of responsibility, I had no intention of screwing up my chance.

Golston was a good story. Or he could be, depending on how we framed it. Smaller guy in the NHL. One of the few black players in the league, finding his footing in a sport that boasted very little diversity.

From my days working as part of the television broadcast team, I knew the coaches and management were hot on him. He had a ton of potential, but he'd only recently been starting to fulfill it. Over the last couple of months of the season, he'd found his offensive touch and started using it to develop what should be a very promising career.

We could frame the struggles and fortunes of the team around his story if we did it right. The team had gotten near the pinnacle of the sport a decade or so ago. Then tough times hit, and they missed the playoffs several seasons in a row before a resurgence. Fresh blood. Now they were climbing toward the top again, and it was up to me to chronicle this resurrection as best I could.

They'd been in the Stanley Cup Finals last season. If all went according to plan, they could win it this season. If they did, it would be because of players like Golston finally playing up to their potential.

I might be wrong about this, and I could always find a new angle once I was editing the webisode together, but everything in my gut screamed that Golston needed to be my focus.

"Dave, can you zoom in tight on Golston for me?" I said into my headpiece. "You, too, Ben. Stick with him, no matter what happens."

"Got it, Anne."

Within moments, the views on Camera Two and Camera Four had gone from wide shots at different angles, covering much of the ice, to isolations on Golston—one capturing his face head on and the other coming in from the side.

The teams lined up on the face-off dot to the right of the Blackhawks goaltender. I kept my eye primarily on those two cameras, although I flickered my gaze around to each of them every few seconds, as well as down to the ice, just to be sure we weren't missing anything important.

The linesman squared up to drop the puck, but something else hit the ice first, right at Golston's feet. One of the other officials skated in, putting a stop to the action before play resumed.

"What is that?" I demanded, straining my eyes to make out what had been tossed from the crowd. "Dave, go in tighter on that, whatever it is."

With my other views, the ref was getting in the way as he bent to collect the debris. When he came up with it in his hand, I finally recognized it.

"No freaking way," I said, my stomach clenching.

Someone had tossed a banana peel at Nate Golston's feet.

"I got it, Anne," Dave said, reminding me that we had an obligation to capture the story as it unfolded in front of us, whatever that story might be. We had a show to produce, and like it or not, the story was unfolding in front of us.

Fighting down waves of nausea, I snapped back into action. "Right. I want Five to get shots of the crowd, particularly the parts of the crowd close enough to have seen what happened. Dave, stay with the ref and that fucking banana peel until it's gone. Three, I want reactions from every player on the ice. Four, don't you dare lose Golston for the rest of this game or I will murder you in your sleep. One, give me the team benches. I want to see the coaches' reactions, the other players. Even the equipment guys. Got it?"

My camera crew did exactly as I instructed them. The ref took the banana peel over to the timekeeper's bench and dropped it off there. Within moments, the PA announcer came over the loudspeakers with a reminder that nothing was to be tossed on the ice, and breaking this rule would result in expulsion from the arena and a minor bench penalty assessed to the home team. Then everyone lined up again to resume where things had left off.

Through my disgust, only two things truly registered in my mind.

The first was a shot of a man in the crowd, angrily shouting things in Golston's direction. Things I couldn't hear, but I could sure enough read the man's lips. Things that left me shaken, angry, and hurt. Things that left me scared for the world in which we lived.

The second was the look of utter shock that had come over Golston's face and refused to budge.

The puck dropped. The game resumed. The Storm players fought hard and kept the Blackhawks from getting a tie, and with eighteen seconds left on the clock, Nate Golston zipped the puck up the ice and into the empty net, scoring his first hat trick.

I should have been elated, because—like it or not—I had a definite focus for the first episode of my web series. Instead, I wanted to find the nearest bathroom and puke up my guts.

This was not what I thought I'd signed up for.

Nate

I DIDN'T WANT to wear the stupid purple umbrella hat, so as soon as the boys let me, I took the fucking thing off and tossed it in my stall.

That ridiculous hat was tradition for us this season. When we won a game, the guy who'd been awarded it after our last win selected someone else to give it to—typically the player who'd been most instrumental in the win that night. Apparently, tonight, that was me.

But right now I didn't care that I'd scored a hat trick. I didn't even care that we'd won the game. This win didn't have any effect on our positioning heading into the playoffs, so it didn't factor into the big picture beyond us starting the postseason on a roll.

The only thing I wanted to do right now was get the fuck out of this arena so I could have a few beers and try to forget about what had happened at the end of the game. Only we were on the road and flying back to Portland tonight, so I couldn't escape so easily. It'd be hours before I got home and could drink enough to numb all the insanity racing through my mind.

I stripped off my jersey and tossed it in the bin in the center of the locker room. I ripped off my pads, hurrying through the process of changing. The bus wouldn't leave for the airport until all the guys were ready to go, which would be a while since the media would want to come in and interview a few of us and the coach, but maybe I could slip out sooner, catch a cab to the airport. At least there, I wouldn't have to look at the rest of the boys while so many of them were busy studiously avoiding looking at me at all. Not to mention these cameras that had been following us around for the last week. Two of those cameramen had joined us in the locker room, and if I wasn't mistaken, one of those two had been zoomed in tight on me since the final horn had sounded.

None of my teammates had said a word to me when we'd come off the ice. No doubt they didn't know what to say. I didn't either, so I couldn't blame them. Never, not once in my life, had I been up against such blatant racism. I'd read about it. I'd seen it on the news. But it had never been directed at me before.

I didn't know how long ago that banana peel had come over the glass to land at my feet, but I was still vibrating. Not just because of the symbolism, either. The words they'd shouted at me before arena security guards escorted them out hadn't stopped echoing in my ears.

"Get on the bus and go back to the projects. You have no business on the ice."

"Fucking monkey, finally learning to perform tricks. At least you're good for something more than fighting now."

"Don't you know niggers are supposed to play basketball, not hockey?"

Yes, the three of them had been drinking, and yes, the rest of the crowd had given them hell over what they'd said and done. But drunk or not, they'd said it. And they'd done it.

Somehow, I'd had it in my head that people only said those things in books and movies. Or maybe only in the South, where racial tensions still seemed to be so heightened. But Chicago wasn't in the South, and while the cameras had filmed every bit of it for both the TV broadcast and this web series the team had commissioned, this was still my real life, not some piece of fiction.

It had really happened.

To me.

The more time that passed since that moment, the more I felt suffocated by everything surrounding me. My lungs were trapped in a vise that kept squeezing tighter and tighter, forcing the air out of me by degrees.

There was a part of me that wanted to let the vise finish me off. It would hurt less than the realization that there were people out there who hated me *that much*, but not for anything I'd done. It was because of who I was.

No, not even that. It was because of who my ancestors were, if anything. Because of my DNA. The color of my skin. Because of something I couldn't change even if I wanted to.

But right now, I wanted to. Something else I'd never experienced before. It was seriously starting to fuck with my head.

"Ghost." It was the head coach, Mattias Bergstrom, standing right behind me.

That was what the guys all called me—Ghost—a play on my last name, Golston, and maybe a bit of an inside joke, too, since I definitely didn't look like anything close to Casper. But Ghost was just my nickname with my teammates, something meant in good fun, the same as me being officially listed as five foot ten and a hundred eighty-five pounds, even though that was only close to true when I was in all my gear. Five foot eight and one seventy was a lot closer to reality. Guys had started calling me Ghost so long ago that I didn't even remember who was responsible for it, back when I was a kid playing hockey in Toronto. I'd never thought anything of it until I was older, and by then the name had stuck. Ghost was simply who I was to everyone I played with or against.

A couple of months ago, Bergy had pointed out a new side of that nickname to me. He'd said I tended to be a ghost on the ice, sneaky and elusive, slipping past guys twice my size before they knew what to do about it. He wanted me to find ways to use that to my advantage instead of thinking of my size as a disadvantage. He'd even had me come to work with him one-on-one several times on days off, me trying to slip past him. The guy may have retired as a player several years back, but he'd been a strong-as-fuck defenseman in his day with a hell of a nasty streak, and he still had all the size and strength he'd been known for. Working with him like that meant taking a beating. But lately, I'd been slipping past him untouched, and now I was finding a way to do it in game situations, too. Like tonight.

I grunted to acknowledge him, swallowing hard. I didn't trust my voice. Hell, I didn't trust myself not to throat-punch someone right now for looking at me wrong. I wouldn't throat-punch Bergy, but I couldn't make any promises about anyone else who might come along.

I didn't like this side of me. I hated that it had been so easy to bring it out. Ten seconds' time, with ignorant asswipes revealing their hatred, and I'd been reduced to a pressure cooker ready to explode at the tiniest provocation.

"Kurt just gave me the word from communications," Bergy said. "The media specifically wants to talk to you tonight."

Of course the press wanted to talk to me tonight. They came to me after just about every game, mainly because I tended to give a good sound bite. Add in the fact that I'd scored three goals, had a banana peel thrown at me, and had things shouted at me I'd never heard a human being actually say out loud before, and there wasn't a chance in hell that every sports reporter in this damn city wouldn't be closing in around my stall and suffocating the life out of me for as long as they were allowed to stay.

I nodded that I understood.

"I could send you to the trainers' room," Bergy said. "Tell them you're being treated for an injury and aren't available. Buy you some time so you can figure out what you want to say."

"I'm not hiding," I bit off. The temptation to take him up on it was definitely there, but burying my head in the sand and pretending nothing had happened wouldn't solve anything. It'd only make facing their questions worse once I finally got around to it, because they'd think I'd been running.

I'd never been a fan of avoidance, and I wasn't about to change my mind about that now, even if I'd been debating hopping in a cab only moments ago. I doubted I'd ever have actually done it. That wasn't me, even if it's nice to fantasize about being someone else occasionally.

"It wouldn't be hiding," Bergy said. "You did get banged up in the third blocking that shot."

I took a seat on the bench and tore through the laces on my skates, pulling them free. "I'm fine, so unless you're planning to force me to go to the trainers' room—"

"No one's forcing you to do anything. That's just it. If you don't want to talk to the press yet, you don't have to."

If I wasn't so hot already, I knew I'd have no problem seeing the truth in what Bergy was saying. The guy was a hard-ass, but he was as fair as they came. He just wanted to give me options.

I took a breath and willed myself to calm the fuck down. "I'm fine. I appreciate what you're doing, but I'm fine. Send them in."

He gave me a tight nod, crossing his arms. Then he gestured toward Kurt Yarbrough, the head of the Storm's communications department, before returning his attention to me. "Fine. But Kurt's going to be right by your side the whole time they're in here. If anyone asks you something you don't want to answer, or if you're ready to be done, you just nod at him, and he'll take care of it."

I had no intention of fighting Bergy on that one, but I also didn't plan to send out an SOS in front of all those cameras. I could fight my own battles, something I'd been striving to prove to Bergy, my teammates, and the rest of the damned league all season long. This was just one more battle in the war. One more mountain to climb.

I'd be damned if I'd let anything or anyone get in my way.

Bergy headed off to talk with the other coaches, and Kurt took up position near me but not all the way in my grill. The security guard outside the locker room opened the doors, and a flood of reporters swarmed inside—far more of them than was normal during the regular season. I caught a glimpse of Anne Dennison among them, but she walked over to one of her camera guys and whispered something in his ear as the crowd converged on me, and I lost track of her.

Too bad. She was probably the only one out of the lot of them who'd be completely safe from me losing my temper. Granted, she wasn't a reporter anymore, now that she'd taken over the production of this web series.

In no time, a few dozen mics and other recording devices were shoved in my direction. I couldn't see anything beyond the glare of lights shining in my face.

Mike Polanski, the Storm beat writer for the *Portland Tribune* and the absolute bane of my existence, stood directly in front of me. "Nate, what's your reaction to the banana peel incident?" he demanded.

"Have we already whittled it down to that?" I groused. "*The banana peel incident?* Sounds like a case to put Sherlock Holmes on. Someone get Cumberbatch on the line."

A few of the media guys chuckled, but Polanski wasn't one of them. "So you're just going to laugh it off?"

"I'd rather laugh than react in a way that would land me in jail," I bit off, and everyone sobered. "And I'd rather be talking about the game than the fact that three buffoons in the crowd decided to let the world see just how ignorant they are. Why aren't you asking me about scoring my first ever hat trick in the NHL? Why aren't you asking me about the fact that the Storm just soundly beat a team we might be facing again in only a couple of weeks in the playoffs? Why aren't you asking me if we're ready to take on the Sharks in a few days and how we think we'll handle the way they throw their weight around, or if our skill can outperform their skill?"

"Sorry to say it, Ghost, but that isn't the story. Considering what happened this afternoon with Marcus Jameson and after what happened tonight—"

"Hold up. Who is Marcus Jameson?" I wasn't following. At all.

"You haven't heard about that?" Polanski asked. "This afternoon, a man named Marcus Jameson was pulled over by Chicago PD for a routine traffic stop. They shot and killed him. Everyone's saying it's racially motivated, and then this..."

"I'm sorry to hear that about Marcus Jameson, but I don't know what he has to do with the game tonight. As far as I'm concerned, the story you should be asking me about is the game. That's what I know about. And if you ask the other nineteen guys in this room right now, I think they'd all agree with me that it's the story that *we* think is important."

"So Marcus Jameson's death isn't important, Nate?" one of the other reporters asked, and I wanted to kick myself.

"That's not what I'm saying at all. His death is very important. But I didn't have anything to do with it, and he didn't have anything to do with this game. Frankly, *this game* is the only thing any of us is focused on, so if you want some other story, you're going to have to get it from another source. Because here's some truth for you. The guys who were behind *the banana peel incident* aren't worth my time."

At that point, half a dozen of the other reporters tried to jump in with questions at once, but the only thing that registered with me was the sight of Anne pushing her way forward—the only woman in a mob of men, the only flash of color in an ocean of white faces much like I was the only minority among my teammates—with her cameraman at her side.

Kurt held up his hand and tried to regain control of the session, getting them to stop talking over each other. Once they shut up, I nodded at Anne, giving her the floor. I'd rather talk to her any day than the rest of these guys, and not just because she was hot as hell and we'd been flirting outrageously with each other for the last couple of seasons, either.

Her cameraman shoved his boom mic forward and she smiled, putting me at ease.

"How are you going to make sure this doesn't become a distraction for you and your teammates heading into the playoffs, especially if you do end up playing against the Blackhawks in the second round?" she asked, and I felt a hell of a lot less at ease.

I'd thought Anne, at least, would be willing to focus on what really mattered right now. I'd expected her to realize that the press making this incident out to be a bigger deal than it was would only cause it to blow up and *become* a distraction. There'd been some part of me that had been counting on Anne to be on my side.

At least now I knew she wasn't. Flirtation or not, she was still part of the press. Maybe she worked for the team in some small way, but she was still out to get her story, trying to sell her angle on it, whatever that might be.

I ground my jaw, apparently hesitating for so long that Kurt got nervous. He inched closer to my side and nudged my elbow, but I wasn't going to let anyone rush to my aid and rescue me from a situation I didn't need rescuing from.

I looked straight in Anne's eyes, hoping she got a full sense of the betrayal roiling through my gaze, and said, "The only people making it a distraction are all of you. My teammates and I have bigger things to worry about. Like San Jose, since we've got Game One to prepare for, and it's coming up in a few days. If no one has any questions about hockey, I think we're finished here."

Without checking to see if Kurt was satisfied with my response or not, I grabbed a towel from my stall and pushed my way through the throng.

Chapter Two

Nate

FOR THE LAST two days, I hadn't been able to escape the fucking banana peel incident other than in the middle of the night, once I finally managed to shut off my brain and get some sleep. By the time we'd gotten back to Portland after that game, it had blown up all over Twitter, Snapchat, Facebook, and every other social media platform in existence, including a few I'd never heard of before. The media kept flogging it, and not just the sports media, either. This story was hitting the mainstream news. I'd even seen it on CNN last night while flipping channels.

More racial tensions in Chicago, the headlines blared. *Black hockey player subjected to slurs. Discrimination is alive and well in the Midwest. Marcus Jameson murdered at the hands of white police officer.* Everywhere I turned, I kept running into it. At bars. At the gym. On the radio every time I got in my car. On newspapers and magazines at the grocery store. I couldn't escape it, no matter how hard I tried.

And trust me—I was trying. All I wanted was for the distraction to go away so I could get back to focusing on improving my game and being the kind of player Bergy was determined I could be. That was what I needed to have happen, especially with the playoffs starting tomorrow.

He seemed to think I could be a game breaker, the kind of player who could get on a scoring streak and almost singlehandedly destroy another team in a seven-game series. I wanted to find out if he was right about that. Back in juniors, I'd been able to, but it hadn't ever translated to my game in the pros. But with the way things had been clicking for me lately with my line mates, Blake Kozlow and Axel Johansson…

"How you holding up?" Riley Jezek asked me after practice, getting in my way and preventing me from making my escape.

I'd been trying to hurry up and get my ass out to my car before someone could stop me, and especially before Anne and one of the guys from her camera crew could try to tag along with me like they'd attempted to do yesterday. I'd managed to slip out while the coaching staff distracted them, but it had been a close call. Apparently RJ had other plans for me today.

"How do you think?" I replied, glaring.

"I think you're about ready to blow, based on the way you've been griping at everything that moves just about every chance you get. You just about bit Coop's head off out there for passing you a bouncing puck. Not the kid's fault the ice was shit after we'd been on it for a solid hour."

Even as he spoke, I noticed one of the camera guys heading our direction. Jamie Babcock, the team captain, got in his way and held him up. I made a mental note to buy Babs a steak dinner as thanks the next time we were out together.

I gave RJ a significant look, angling my head toward the jackass who wanted to capture my every movement to broadcast for the whole world to see. "Is it any wonder I'm about to snap?"

"Nope. But that doesn't mean you need to take it out on Coop. Or any of the rest of us, for that matter. It's not our fault there are asswipes in the world. We had nothing to do with all the shit you're having to deal with. And in case you hadn't noticed, we're all on your side."

He was right, and I knew it, but that didn't make it any easier to stop myself from behaving like a son of a bitch. If my mother were here, she'd be giving me a serious earful about how she'd raised me and the way I should conduct myself around my colleagues. And she'd be right. I didn't need her here to say the words—just like I didn't need her here to hold my hand while I tried to get through this ordeal with the media. She'd threatened to fly in from Toronto, although I was sure she didn't see it as a threat. Moral support, she'd called it. It had taken both me and Dad to convince her I was a grown man and could sort this out on my own.

Hell of a job I was doing with that, though.

"I'm sorry, man," I said, wishing like hell I could get my head back under control.

"Don't apologize to me. Or at least not *just* to me."

"I'll say something to the boys tomorrow." Once I'd had a chance to figure out what the hell I wanted to say. Besides, half of them had already split today. It'd be better to do it when I knew they were all present and accounted for.

The truth was, they'd all been standing by me through every bit of this—sticking up for me, trying to help me escape the media any time they could like the coaches had done a couple of days ago and Babs was doing now—and I'd been acting like a douchebag with a major case of PMS.

"And I'll take Coop aside to apologize to him personally," I added. Austin Cooper was the youngest guy on the team, called up from our minor league affiliate as an injury replacement. The kid was just trying to fit in and find his role on the team. He didn't need me ripping him a new one, especially when he hadn't done anything wrong.

"That's good," RJ said. "It's a good start, at least. I think your mom would say you could do better."

He knew he could talk to me like that and get away with it, especially since he actually knew my mother.

RJ was my closest friend on the team. We'd grown up about three blocks away from each other in Toronto. My older sister had been in classes with his older brother for as long as either of us could remember. I'd been a year ahead of RJ in school. Didn't matter much that he was a year younger than me, though. He'd always been a step or two ahead of me on the ice and at least a few inches taller than me. We'd played against each other just about our entire lives, right up until the moment when I'd been traded to the Storm a few seasons ago and we became teammates.

"She would," I admitted. "You're right. I'm trying not to lose my shit, but right now I think that's the best I can do."

He gave me a look that said he thought I was full of shit, but he let it drop. "Listen, Amanda and I were planning to take the dogs out for a walk this afternoon. She wants to take them to the Rose Test Gardens. I told her it's probably too soon, they aren't blooming much yet, but she's insisting. Why don't you come with us?"

Amanda was RJ's fiancée, and they had two enormous two-year-old

Mastiffs that seemed to think they were still puppies, along with all the exuberant energy to show for it. Amanda claimed they were her dogs, but she didn't do a very good job of taking care of them without some muscle around to assist her. They were each almost twice her size, so there was no way she could walk them on her own. If they wanted to get away from her, it wouldn't be very difficult at all.

"So basically you want me to control one of the beasts, huh?"

He grinned. "Something like that. But don't call them beasts to their faces. You'll hurt their feelings."

"They could stand to have their feelings hurt if they're going to try to climb on my lap again. My balls still haven't recovered."

"Doubt that's solely due to my dogs. Might help if you got laid."

"How am I supposed to get laid if your dogs mash my balls?"

"Lola is an angel. She can't help it that she loves you. Or that she's bigger than you. Not the dog's fault you're a shrimp."

"Well, try to teach her that she's not a lap dog, then."

"You teach her."

"She's your dog."

He shook his head. "Nah. They're Amanda's."

"Since when have you been agreeing with that load of shit?"

"Since it suits my purposes. They're Amanda's dogs when they're bad."

"Does that mean you're giving me Lola?" I asked, hoping against hope I was right. Max, RJ's other dog, easily had thirty pounds on Lola, and she weighed as much as I did.

"Max loves you, too, even when you're an ass."

"He might love me better when I'm an ass. He likes stinky things."

"Then you're all set."

"This is quality cologne I'm wearing," I shot back at him. "Not like your Axe body spray. When are you gonna realize you're an adult?" It was better than the Old Spice he used to wear, but not by much.

He sniffed his arm. "Smells fine to me. Amanda likes it well enough."

I rolled my eyes and glanced over to see Babs still had the cameraman distracted. "Maybe that's why Max likes you as much as he does. Come on. Let's get out of here before we have more company watching your dogs drag my ass through the gardens."

RJ laughed, but he didn't argue. In no time, we were heading out of the practice facility on our way to the parking garage…only to run headfirst into Anne Dennison as we walked through the double doors.

"Nate," she said, looking up at me and smiling, her hand on her chest. Damn, but she had a gorgeous smile, and when she was this close, I could see the hints of green in her light brown eyes that always did a number on me.

I didn't smile in return. Couldn't. The way she'd joined in with the other media guys that night still stung too much. The last thing I needed right now was to forget that she was on the other side of things. She wasn't my friend, and definitely not anything more than a friend, even though we'd been flirting way more than was good for either of us since she'd been around the team. She was part of my problem right now, no matter how hot she was.

"I was hoping we could get some time with you sometime today," she said, not taking the hint that I didn't want to have anything to do with her right now. "I've got Dave all set up and ready—"

"I've got plans," I cut in. I jerked my head in RJ's direction. "*We* have plans, actually."

She nodded. "It's fine if we have some of the other guys from the team involved. Or even some of your friends outside of the team. Dave and I could come with you."

"I don't think that's going to work." I took off again, and RJ came with me.

"Going somewhere you can't bring extra people with you?" She kept pace alongside me, her legs as long as mine. Not even her heels slowed her down. "You sure we couldn't sneak in? We could stay in the background, just filming without interfering. We really want to get some footage of you doing whatever it is you do in your time off. Trying to get the bigger picture of who you are."

The woman didn't let up. No wonder she'd been given such a big assignment already. There weren't many women in sports broadcasting, in general. But she was young, and other than spending a few seasons working with the Storm's broadcast team, she was relatively inexperienced. I hadn't been able to figure out how she'd finagled such a prime gig, producing a web series about the team. Now it was starting to make sense. She'd probably hounded whomever was in charge until they'd given in just to get her off their back.

It couldn't be easy to be a woman in this industry—one more reason I'd wrongly assumed Anne would be on my side when it came to wanting to ignore everything that had happened a couple of nights ago.

One more reason to never assume anything.

"I really don't think that's a good idea," I finally bit off as we reached my car. "This isn't something—"

She stopped and scowled at me. "I didn't want to have to do this, but I'll remind you that based on the contract the Storm has with my production company, and your contract with the Storm, you can't keep brushing me off forever. You're contractually obligated to cooperate, whether you're happy about it or not. Your friends and family don't have to be part of this series, but everyone involved with the team does."

I jerked open my car door and leaned on the frame, thinking through my options. They seemed to be slim and growing slimmer by the moment. "So what happens if I brush you off again today?"

"I'll take it up with Jim Sutter," she said without hesitation.

Jim was our general manager—someone who could make my life hell if I made Anne's life hell.

I ground my jaw and looked at RJ for help. He frowned and shrugged, which meant he was as lost as I was when it came to coming up with anything better. Damn it.

"We're walking dogs at the International Rose Test Gardens," I bit off. Then I climbed into my car and slammed the door.

"Got it," Anne said, taking off into the building at a run. She spun around, jogging backward on those heels. "We'll meet you there! Thanks, Nate."

Lucky me.

"If they're bringing the cameras along, you need to be on your best behavior," RJ said.

"I'm always on my best behavior," I grumbled.

"You know your mom's going to be watching this. Just...try to act like you normally do around Anne."

"Meaning?"

"Meaning why don't you flirt with her again or something?"

"I don't want to flirt with her right now." I wanted to give her an earful about how I felt about her turning this into a bigger deal than it was.

But RJ was right. If I gave in to the temptation, I was stooping to her level. Time to put on a brave face and convince the world that I hadn't been fazed by all the shit being thrown my way. Even if it was a fucking lie.

Anne

I KNEW THE reasons Nate had been avoiding me. Hell, I'd avoid me, too, if I were in his shoes. But that didn't change the fact that I had a job to do and a show to produce, and at the moment, everything surrounding him was the focus of the story I had to tell.

I'd spent the morning and early afternoon holed up in the cutting room with my editor and a couple of assistants, poring over hours and hours of footage from the last week so we could meet our deadline. The first webisode was scheduled to go live tomorrow evening, about an hour before puck drop for the first game of the playoffs.

We had a ton of film to sift through. Maybe too much, to be honest. But now we had to determine which angles to use from the game sequences and how to combine it with interviews and other behind-the-scenes moments in order to present a sound narrative arc, making the determination of which pieces were important and which could be left behind without losing impact.

On top of that, the story we'd *thought* we were telling the whole time we were filming? It had been turned on its head in the final moments of the last night of filming, so now we were in a panicked rush to reframe everything to fit the new story line.

Yes, story line. That wasn't me using the wrong word in terms of this journalistic endeavor. I had to remind myself that *Eye of the Storm*, the web series I was producing, wasn't strictly news. It wasn't pure journalism. There was a bit of a documentary feel to what we were doing with this, which meant we had to pull from the world of fiction in order to properly present it for our audience.

We were presenting what had happened in the world of the Portland Storm, true, but doing so in a way that made it entertaining for the viewer. The episode needed a beginning, rising action, a climax, falling action, and a denouement. There had to be a narrative arc, taking the viewer from the opening moments all the way up to the end, and it needed to leave them wanting more so they'd tune in again next week. That meant we had to take some creative license in the way we pieced everything together.

We weren't changing facts; we were simply sorting out the best way to present it to the people who watched, in order to keep them riveted. Not an easy task.

At the moment, my editor and his assistants were still hard at work putting together the first episode, using the guidelines I'd given them before leaving, but I had to shift my focus to what we had in front of us for the second episode. The playoffs starting tomorrow would certainly get a lot of attention, but we couldn't ignore what had happened in the first week.

Which meant I had to get Nate Golston to talk to me.

Which was why I'd pulled rank and threatened him with taking things to the general manager if he didn't cooperate.

It irked me to stoop to that level, but the guy hadn't left me much choice. And that was how I'd ended up at the International Rose Test Gardens, attempting to keep my heels from sinking into the soft ground while I fitted Nate, Riley Jezek, and Jezek's fiancée, Amanda Morris, with mic packs, at the same time as two dogs the size of small horses tried to climb me.

Did I mention I'd always been afraid of dogs, even the small yappy ones? Just being in the same vicinity of these two had me shaking uncontrollably. At least no one seemed to have noticed. And once I had the mics in place, they could go about their business, and Dave and I could keep our distance to film them without interfering.

One of them—the bigger one—gave a happy bark and put his front paws on my shoulder, further pressing my heels into the grassy earth.

"Down, Max," Jezek said, laughing.

I noticed there wasn't a whole lot of authority in his tone. The guy was amused by his dog's antics. Nate didn't seem too bothered by them, either. In fact, he wasn't doing much to keep the dog on his leash under control. I bit down on my tongue to keep from saying anything I'd regret and hurried to finish getting them situated.

One more mic to go—the one for Nate. "Turn around for me," I said.

He winked, the first hint I'd seen since that final game of the regular season of our former flirtation. "You just want to check out my ass." But he passed the leash into Jezek's hand and turned around like I'd instructed him to do. "Don't get me wrong," he added. "I don't mind you checking out my ass. I'd check it out, too, if I could."

"If you were a contortionist," Jezek added, trying to keep both massive animals under control. They probably each weighed as much as he did, though, and it looked like they were all muscle.

"As long as I'm not an extortionist," Nate replied.

"I wouldn't make any promises on that score," Jezek said with a snort-laugh.

I bit down on my lower lip to keep from joining them in inappropriate laughter since I was trying to keep everything professional. Finally, Nate lifted the back of his shirt the way I'd had Jezek and his fiancée do moments before. Only he lifted it a lot higher than was necessary, giving me a nice glimpse of his muscled back. I handed him the mic pack and quickly strung the wire up and over his shoulder, my fingertips accidentally brushing his skin. It was soft, damn it. Not what I needed to be thinking about. I dropped my hands to my sides like he'd burned me. "There you go. Just hook that into the waistband of your pants—"

"You could do that for me," he cut in, with a definite hint of laughter in his tone, which left me struggling to keep my composure. He'd always done that when I was with the Storm's broadcast team, too, trying to throw me off my game by flirting with me. Outrageously. And I'd flirted back, because he'd made it so easy to do.

Even though it felt a lot better to be treating each other the way we'd always done before instead of going at each other, I knew it was a bad idea. I had to keep this aboveboard. I had way too much riding on this job, and I couldn't afford to jeopardize anything by getting too personal with one of the players. My boss had made that abundantly clear when he'd reluctantly given me the assignment, and he'd only done that due to not having anyone else on staff who had any experience whatsoever doing the sort of work I was doing. Because of the Storm's timeline for getting this series going, there hadn't been time for him to do a massive search for a producer and bring in someone from the outside.

He'd have more than enough time to do that over the team's summer break, though—which served as a constant reminder to me that I could have *Eye of the Storm* ripped out of my hands at any moment. Right now, it was my baby. But for how long?

"—and we're all set once we pop the mic through a buttonhole in front," I finished firmly, not taking Nate's bait. I took a step back, trying to get both some distance and some perspective. "In fact, you can handle that part yourself. Then you three can go about your business and forget all about the two of us."

"I don't think that's going to be possible," Nate said.

Dave smirked at me, but he was smart enough to keep his mouth shut.

"All right," I said, brushing my hands on my thighs because they were sweating. Nerves. Getting that close to him, touching him ever so slightly, had brought out my inner geeky teenager. Bad timing for that. "You're good to go. Just pretend we're not even here."

I took another step backward, but my heel plummeted through a soft spot in the grass, and I fell on my ass. As soon as I was on the ground, both dogs took that as a sign that they should pile on and wrestle with me. Jezek tried to hold them both back, but it was no use. They were too big, too strong, the pair of them overpowering him and leaping onto my chest.

Out of instinct, I screamed like a petrified little girl and put my arms over my face to protect myself. Didn't do any good. Two enormous canines shoved my hands out of their way with their noses, and then they started licking my face, holding me down with their front paws. Both Jezek and Nate tried to drag the overly exuberant dogs off me, adding their weight to the mix, and then Dave dropped his camera and joined the fray, leaving only Amanda standing off to the side, watching with a dazed expression.

I giggle-shrieked. Couldn't help it. This was the most bizarre, hilarious, painful thing to have happened to me in months. Maybe years. My adrenaline shot through the roof, and I was fully in self-preservation mode. It was a sad realization that my natural gut reaction when presented with one of my greatest fears was to laugh my head off in a psychotic panic. That didn't bode well.

Finally, they got the dogs off me, Jezek manhandling the bigger one and forcing him back while Dave—who was easily as big and strong as most of the guys on the team—practically laid on top of the smaller dog to keep her off me.

Nate reached out a hand to help me up, with a sexy-as-sin curve of his lips. He was probably trying not to laugh as maniacally as I was. "Unless you'd rather stay in the dirt," he said when I sat there a little too long staring at him. "Too bad you didn't get any of that on film. That'd make a much more entertaining show than anything you got on me last week."

He was wrong on that score, but I still reached up and took his hand, allowing him to drag me to my feet. As soon as I was standing, I wished I was back on the ground again. My ankle felt like I'd done a serious number on it, one of my heels had broken off the shoe, my tan suit was covered in dirt and grass stains, and I didn't think I'd be able to fix the rat's nest of my hair until I could dunk my entire head in a vat of shampoo. That sobered me up pretty fast. If I wasn't careful, my laughter would turn to sobs of pain—both real, physical pain and the sort that rips you apart from the inside when you're embarrassed in front of a crush.

"Please tell me they didn't hurt you," Jezek said, cutting through the fog of humiliation eating me alive.

I shot my gaze over to him, taking my hand out of Nate's before I got too comfortable with holding on to him. "I'm fine," I forced myself to say, brushing some debris off my butt.

Nate dropped his gaze down to my hips, just long enough that it was obvious, before bringing his eyes up to meet mine again. "Yeah. Fine."

I kicked off both my shoes since they weren't going to do me any good as they were. "You came to walk the dogs, right? So walk the dogs." Then I tossed my shoes in my purse, slung the strap over my shoulder, and turned to Dave, trying not to put too much of my weight on my right foot. Unsuccessfully, I might add, but I did try. "Come on. Get your camera set up. We have a job to do."

All the flirtatiousness drained off Nate's face in an instant. "Yeah, you sure do." He grabbed the dog's leash from Dave, and he and his friends took off without us.

"You're not fine," Dave said once they were gone.

"I'm as fine as I have time to be." I could put my foot up and have a good cry when I got home. Until then, I had to grin and bear it, even if it was the last thing on earth I felt like doing.

Chapter Three

Nate

RJ HAD BEEN right. It *was* too early for many of the roses to be blooming, which led to Amanda's disappointment—and pouting. Her histrionics didn't stop Max and Lola from having the time of their lives, though.

We didn't walk them so much as *they* walked *us*. The pair of them spent the afternoon racing from stranger to stranger, from one new scent to another, dragging me and RJ along for the ride while Amanda hung back and alternated between laughing her head off and remembering that she was supposed to be sulking.

Anne and her cameraman kept up with all of us well enough, which was impressive in Anne's case, given that she was limping around in bare feet and nursing an obviously sprained right ankle. At least I hoped it was only a sprain. It seemed to me she was stubborn enough that it could be worse. If so, she was likely causing herself more damage by continuing to hobble around on it.

I had to remind myself that I hadn't done anything to hurt her, and I hadn't been the one to invite her along. This was all her. She'd insisted on coming, and she hadn't bothered to put on sensible shoes. All her fault, even if Max and Lola had probably been responsible for at least some of the damage.

I felt bad for her, which was stupid considering all the crap she was putting me through. Earlier, I'd only flirted with her because of RJ's reminder that my mother would be at home glued to her computer, watching every moment of this show Anne was producing. But then it had started to feel natural again. Comfortable. Like there was no other way we ought to be together than overly playful, cracking jokes and making each other laugh.

Anne and I had chatted each other up far more than was good for either of us over the last couple of years, and now that we'd started it up again, I wasn't so sure I wanted it to stop. Lord knew I enjoyed the way we were together like this a hell of a lot better than how we'd been the last couple of days—even though that was all on me. I was the one avoiding her at every possible opportunity, not the other way around.

That said, I couldn't let myself forget that she was *not* my friend, no matter how I looked at it. Letting something as important as that slip my mind would be setting myself up for a world of hurt. Since the banana peel incident, I'd already had enough crap to deal with to last for years. Anne Dennison was determined to do her job, to get her story, and it didn't matter one bit to her if she destroyed me in the process. I had to remember that. Always. Even if I'd rather forget it.

Still, watching her limp around in the grass as she followed us, her pain overly apparent, I couldn't stop myself from feeling sorry for her.

The worst part of it all—at least for Anne—was that I doubted she'd gotten any useful footage all afternoon. All we'd done was get dragged all over the place by these two beasts, laughing our asses off. How the hell was that going to fit into the story she was trying to present of me being this poor SOB getting picked on by racist bigots everywhere I went? I didn't have a clue.

Finally, it seemed Max and Lola had worn themselves out. They plopped down on a stretch of grass in the middle of the gardens and lay on their sides, breathing heavily. Looked like a good plan to me. I collapsed next to Lola and rolled onto my back, looking up at the few wispy clouds dotting the otherwise perfectly clear sky. Lola took that as an open invitation to drape herself across my belly, forcing all the air out of my lungs.

"Oof," I said, trying to shove her off. It was no use. She was right where she wanted to be and had no intention of moving again until she was good and ready. "Seriously, RJ, you've got to find a way to convince them they're too big for this shit."

"She can't help it that she loves you. We don't choose who we love." He took a seat next to Max and rubbed his belly. Amanda looked at the grass, then at the light-colored shorts she was wearing, and remained standing with her nose crinkling ever so slightly in distaste. She couldn't stand getting dirty. Lord only knew why she'd wanted to come to the gardens today, because the chances of her getting dirty increased by an enormous degree outside the house. I still hadn't figured out what RJ saw in her other than the fact that she was hot as hell, but oh well. Maybe he really believed what he'd said, that he couldn't choose who he loved.

On the other hand, I wasn't going to fall into that trap. "You sure about that?" Because I'd definitely decided I *wasn't* going to even like Anne Dennison any more, and I had no intention of ever doing more than that. Wasn't going to happen. I couldn't let it.

Out of the corner of my eye, I noticed her slipping into position next to her cameraman, giving him silent instructions as he filmed us. Couldn't even lie here basking in the sun without them trying to capture every inane moment of my life.

"Pretty sure," he said, rubbing Max on the belly. That was apparently the right thing to do in Max's opinion. He rolled and writhed around like a puppy, four paws flying through the air in glee and barking like he was possessed.

"He's going to need a bath when we get home if you keep that up," Amanda griped.

RJ rolled his eyes and kept doing what he'd been doing. "He's going to need a bath when we get home anyway. He's sweaty, smelly, and covered in dirt and grass. So is Lola."

"Well, have fun with that," Amanda said.

"It wouldn't kill you to help me out with them."

"I feed them. I take care of them when you're gone."

"You *feed* them when I'm gone. You don't walk them. You don't clean them or clean up after—"

"How do you expect me to walk them when the two of you can barely handle them?" she cut in.

"They're your dogs!"

"I do the best I can," Amanda bit off, the camera absorbing every bit of this—which might actually prove to be a good thing for me. Not that I wanted RJ to suffer the same kind of scrutiny I'd been under, but it would be a relief to have the focus shifted. Amanda seemed to remember that we were being filmed, shifting her eyes over to Anne and her crew of one. Then she ripped off the microphone and jerked the mic pack free from her waistband, tossing them in Anne's direction. "I'm ready to go. Let's go." Then she stalked off, leaving us on the ground as she headed toward RJ's enormous SUV.

He gave me an exasperated look, but it slipped away as soon as it came on. I was tempted to remind him that he was the one who intended to marry her, not me, but I bit my tongue. Not the kind of thing I needed to say in front of Amanda, let alone in front of anyone and everyone who decided to tune in and watch this show online.

"I'd better go," he said, dragging himself to his feet and tugging on Max's leash to get him up. He reached for Lola's leash, which I gratefully handed over. "Thanks for giving me a hand with them."

I shrugged now that I could move again, no longer pinned to the ground by Lola's exuberant affection. "You know me. Glutton for punishment."

He laughed. "Yep. Always have been." Then he tugged on the dogs' leashes and started to follow his fiancée. "See you in the morning, Ghost," he called over his shoulder.

I was still on my back, basking in the sun and momentarily oblivious to the fact that I was now all alone with Anne and her cameraman, when she limped over and took a seat next to me.

Well, shit. I draped an arm over my eyes to block the sun.

"Hiding from me?" she asked.

More like hiding from the camera. But that wasn't like me, at least not until lately, so I put my arm back down on the ground at my side. "You'll get your pants dirty," I pointed out.

"Too late, they're already ruined."

"You can probably get the grass stains out."

"Maybe my dry cleaner can, but not me." She winked. "I never learned the art of doing laundry. One more way I failed in my mother's eyes."

The sun was behind her like a halo, and I squinted to see what I could make out in her expression. There wasn't any irony in her tone— only resignation. Which meant she actually believed what she'd said. That had to be one of the most ridiculous things I'd ever heard. Anne Dennison was making her mark in a career where few women ventured.

"How on earth could your mother think you're a failure?" I demanded.

"It'd be easier to list the things I've done that she approves of."

"Which are?"

"I have a college degree. The *wrong* college degree, but still. I graduated."

"And?" I coaxed when she didn't continue, sitting up so I could see her better. I draped my arm over my knee and searched her eyes. Definitely no irony in her look. Good grief.

"That's about it."

"You're joking." She had to be.

"Nope. I went into journalism and minored in radio, TV, and film. She wanted me to get a degree in math or science—something useful, she said—and marry an Indian doctor so I could make Indian babies and let my degree go to waste. I wasn't supposed to still be single at this age."

"How old are you?"

"Twenty-four. By now, she thinks I should have popped out at least my first two Indian babies. I should spend my life barefoot and pregnant, don't you know? That's what a good Indian girl is supposed to do. Be smart, but never use her smarts other than to snag an Indian doctor and make Indian babies."

I rolled my eyes. That sounded like the last thing she would want, based on what little I knew of her. "I didn't realize you're Indian." Never would have guessed it, based on her name, but now that she said it, I could see it in some of her features—her lighter skin and curly hair, not to mention the shape of her face. She had high cheekbones that gave her an exotic look.

"Half-Indian. My dad's half-black, half-Irish. He's a doctor. Mom got that part right, she says, but their marriage was always rocky. They divorced when I was ten. Mom has been trying to brainwash me into getting everything *right* that she got *wrong* ever since. That's one of the reasons I don't spend as much time with her as I do with my dad."

I didn't have any difficulty imagining what it would be like growing up with animosity between divorced parents. Not that mine were like that—they were still happily married more than thirty-five years later. But RJ and his brother had spent a ton of time at our house growing up because his parents were constantly fighting. Even after they'd divorced, he'd continued coming to my house because it was a refuge for him. Mom and Dad had treated him like he was one of their kids, loving him in ways his own parents seemed incapable of doing. We hadn't ever really talked about what happened at his house. I'd never wanted to push him into it. I just knew that he needed somewhere to go, and we were always happy to be that *somewhere* for him.

But I did have a hard time imagining a life with a parent who was trying to get you to do all the things they felt they'd done wrong. Shouldn't they want their kids to chase their own dreams, to go after the things they loved? My parents had never played hockey in their lives. Hell, Dad couldn't skate and refused to even try, claiming he wasn't fond of falling down and breaking his ass. But they'd taken me to every practice and tournament, watching from the stands and cheering me on. My sister, Nicole, had wanted to become a teacher, so they'd gotten her into babysitting and enrolled her in early childhood development programs so she could get a head start and be sure it was the career she wanted to pursue. They did everything they could to support both of us in reaching our goals, never attempting to force their own dreams on us.

"You've known Jezek for a long time?" Anne prompted after a long silence.

"Since I was probably nine or ten? RJ and I've known each other for what feels like forever. I barely remember a time before he was around."

"Seems like you two are good friends."

"You could say that," I replied, trying to figure out what she was fishing for. These felt like leading questions. But leading up to what?

"And your family? You're close to your family?"

"Yeah. I spend time with Mom and Dad every chance I get. My sister's a teacher, so her summer breaks tend to coincide with the time I have off from hockey. It works out well." I remained intentionally vague, not giving away too much, because in the back of my mind, I knew the camera was still rolling. "RJ's kind of like family to me. Hell, the whole team is like family to me. We're a bunch of brothers, teasing each other, giving each other a hard time, but when it comes down to it, these are the guys watching my back. They're the ones I'm going into battle with. We take care of our own."

One thing we learned early in my world was that hockey was a team sport. It should never be about individual achievements or failures. We tended to answer questions about the team as a whole, lauding teammates and pointing out areas where our personal game needed improvement. The focus was almost never on an individual, though, which was one more reason the entire situation with the banana peel had made me uncomfortable. It was about *me*, and only me. Not about the team. And all this time with Anne was forcing me to look at myself even more. She wanted me to talk about myself. I wanted to put the focus back on the team.

"I've noticed that," Anne said dryly. "Every time I've tried to get you alone like this to talk to you, someone else has tried to get in the way or distract me. They've wanted to talk to me about anyone and anything else. No one has given me anything more than pat answers when it comes to what happened the other night."

"Because that doesn't matter."

"Doesn't it?" She raised one of her eyebrows, drawing my attention to how thick and perfectly arched they were. "Can you really say that and believe it? In this day and age, the fact that someone threw a banana peel at your feet and shouted racial slurs at you doesn't matter?"

"It doesn't," I ground out.

"How can it not be a huge deal?"

"It's only a big deal if you decide to make it into one. But me? I'm not giving it that much power. Neither are my teammates. There are ignorant people everywhere. Racists, homophobes, sexist assholes, perverts, people who are scared of other religions… But I don't think that's what most of the world is like. I choose to believe that most people are good. Most realize that hatred based on someone being different is truly just fear of what they don't understand. So you can make this into something bigger than what it is if you want, but I'm not going to play along. I'm going to go about my life like I always have. We've got our first game of the playoffs tomorrow. That's what I'm focused on. And only that."

To Anne's credit, she didn't blanch at anything I said. She kept a straight face. Interested. Intrigued, maybe. "I was talking with your coaches about you yesterday," she said. "Coach Bergstrom seems to think that final game of the regular season might have been the beginning of your coming-out party. He seems to think you've got the talent to become a real game breaker, something you've shown hints of in the last few months."

I shrugged. "I was always an offensive threat growing up. Took me a while to figure it out at this level."

"You're seriously going to downplay that?" Anne shook her head and laughed. "That's an amazing compliment, and you're going to shrug it off like it's nothing."

"It is nothing unless I back it up. Let's see what happens in the playoffs."

"Yeah, let's see. Thanks for agreeing to do this, by the way. I know you didn't want to, and I can't say I blame you."

"Well, like you reminded me before we left... I don't really have a choice, do I?" As soon as I said it, I wished I hadn't been so short with her. Everything had been smooth between us, but now it was like a cold front had blown in. "Sorry. It's not your fault."

"No, but it isn't yours, either. I get it, Nate. I really do. I'm not trying to make your life difficult. I hope you know that." When I didn't respond, she let out a sigh. "Well, I think that's good enough for now. Dave, you can pack up to go," she added, glancing over her shoulder at the cameraman. She got to her knees and made to stand, but her ankle twisted beneath her again, and she flopped back down to the ground with a pained squeak.

I tugged her ankle toward me for a better look. "That's a lot of swelling. You shouldn't have been traipsing around on it all day."

"I had a job to do. It wasn't that bad until I sat down."

"It's always worse once you get off it." I scowled. "You have no business walking on this right now. Not until you get some X-rays and we can be sure what's going on."

"We?" she asked, drawling the word and arching one of those gorgeous brows.

"Figure of speech." I wasn't sure why I felt the need to cover my tracks there.

She struggled to an upright position again. "I'll be sure to keep that in mind."

When she tried to stand, I had to push on her shoulders and keep her down. "You don't listen very well, do you?"

"Well, how do you propose I get back to my car and drive myself to a doctor without walking?"

"I could carry you." Then I saw that Dave had finished putting away all his equipment, slinging the strap of a carrying case over one shoulder. "Or you can put an arm around each of our shoulders so you can use us like crutches. Honestly, I don't care which, but I don't want to let you walk on that any more right now."

She huffed, the breath blowing her bangs out of her face for a moment as she frowned. "To be honest, I don't know if I can manage it, anyway."

"You're too stubborn for your own good."

"Something else my mother is constantly reminding me of," she said, but this time when she spoke of her mother, she did it with a laugh.

Chapter Four

Anne

I SPENT THE majority of the next day holed up in the cutting room with my editor, a writer, and Carson, the local actor we'd chosen to be the narrator of the series. They kept nagging me to elevate my foot, and an assistant continually ran errands for me instead of allowing me to get up and do things for myself—fetching ice packs, food, and drinks, bringing me more ibuprofen, running messages back and forth between me and other members of my crew, and a thousand other things at once.

The whole time we were piecing the episode together, I was also fielding what felt like a thousand calls, texts, and emails from different members of my crew, from people involved in the Storm organization, and a couple from my father, who reminded me to take it easy today. Just a sprain, I told him repeatedly, and a couple of the Storm's trainers intended to monitor me occasionally to be sure I was doing what I was supposed to be doing. That part might have been a slight exaggeration, as they were only providing me with ice packs and wraps for my ankle, but my father didn't need to know that.

Besides, Dad wasn't my doctor. He wasn't even the sort of doctor anyone would go to over a sprained ankle. He was a bariatric surgeon. He worked with severely obese people, helping them to lose weight and live a healthier lifestyle, which had next to nothing to do with sprains. Still, I was his little girl, and he was determined to worry about me. There were worse things he could do, so the least I could do was put up with his meddling and worrying.

With barely more than an hour to spare before the first webisode went live, I sent Carson and the writer off to the sound studio to record the narration we'd discussed so it could be cut in over the footage we'd selected. While they were gone, Bill the editor and I both worked at a feverish pace alongside each other, both of us occupied by a different sequence, to edit the remaining few scenes and cut them together.

They raced back in with the audio with only twenty minutes to go. I hadn't intended to cut things so close—we really ought to have a final run-through of the whole thing so we could make a few tweaks before it aired—but there wasn't time for that.

We uploaded and crossed our fingers that there weren't any issues. I sent off a quick message to the Storm's Internet guys so they knew to put a link about it on the home page of their website and have their social media department post about it. Then I took a moment to post about it on our own *Eye of the Storm* social media accounts so the world would know it was available. Once all of that was done, we sat down and watched it through for the first time, along with everyone else in the world who decided to check it out before the Storm's first playoff game of the season.

I don't think I took a breath through the entire thirty-minute webisode, and especially not when it got to the banana peel incident. Even though I'd seen it happen live, and I'd watched all of our footage countless times over the course of the last few days as we'd painstakingly selected what to use and what to leave behind, I still choked up when it hit the ice in front of Nate, and I saw the pained expression come into his eyes while Carson's words trailed off into nothingness.

We'd settled on using only the true audio for that moment. No exposition. We weren't going to tell anyone how they should feel about it as they watched Nate's dawning comprehension, or the explosive anger that lit a fire in the eyes of some of his teammates, or the hatred revealed in the faces of the men who were behind the moment. We wanted everyone to make up their own minds as to how they should respond to such a disgusting display.

Watching it through like that, I was left with chills racing up my spine.

Somehow, it went off without a hitch. All the men in the room high-fived each other, and I sucked in a breath, finally filling my lungs with air.

"Great work, Anne," Bill said, slapping me on the back like I was one of the guys.

"Same to you. *All* of you." I removed the most recent ice pack from my ankle and grabbed my crutches. "But for now, I have to run." The camera crew was at the Moda Center already, filming what I'd instructed them to, but I needed to get out to our control center so I could keep an eye on everything going on in this game. One episode down, but now we needed to start thinking up the narrative for the second.

"Car's waiting for you out front," Bill said. He grabbed my bag for me and held open the door for me to crutch my way through. When we reached the car we'd arranged, he tossed my bag inside and shut the door behind me once I had the crutches situated.

The driver pulled out. Bill winked at me as we drove off.

Since I was just along for the ride, I took out my phone and pulled up Twitter to see if people were posting reactions to the first webisode.

Then I wished the driver would pull over, because I felt like I might toss my cookies.

@EyeoftheStormShow is just glorifying racism. No surprise with @AnnePDennison at the helm. Someone should rape her to shut her up.

How many people did @AnnePDennison fuck to get this @EyeoftheStormShow gig? Women don't know sports. #stupidcunt

Why is @StormNHL letting @AnnePDennison run @EyeoftheStormShow? #rapethebitch

Those were just the first three reactions I came to, but scrolling through my feed revealed hundreds more along the same lines.

This wasn't anything new, of course. I'd been facing the same sort of hate since my first day on the job as part of the Storm's broadcast team. I'd faced it throughout my college days, working for the university newspaper and radio departments and taking on the hockey coverage. I knew there was bound to be more to come, and I'd thought I was prepared for it now. But it washed over me like a torrential downpour, drowning me under its weight.

The Moda Center came into view, and I forced my face into a calm, neutral expression. Now wasn't the time to give in to the negativity threatening to swamp me, and I needed to have my game face on; I had a job to do, whether the world thought I was capable of doing it or not.

Nate

OUR HOME-ICE ADVANTAGE against the Sharks didn't seem to be working out in our favor so far. Granted, it was only halfway through the first game of a seven-game series, but they had a two-to-nothing lead and had been drowning us with constant, smothering pressure in our own end. Nicky Ericsson, our goaltender, had been standing on his head to withstand their assault, but the man was only human. He'd been calm and steady for us, and he'd even made a few miraculous saves that would play on highlight reels for the duration of the playoffs. One of the goals that had gotten past him had been on a three-on-none breakaway when we'd been caught on a bad change. The other came on a Sharks power play just a few moments ago when they converged on the net, and Pavelski banged in a garbage goal that deflected off Brenden "Soupy" Campbell's ass in his first game back after a long stint on the injured list.

Soupy wanted to impact the game, but I didn't need to look at the thunderous expression in his eyes to know this wasn't the kind of impact he'd been hoping for. He slammed his stick against the boards, splintering it in two before taking his spot on the bench.

"Not your fault, Soupy," I said. He was one of our best penalty-killing forwards and had been since before I'd joined the team. As long as he was healthy, at least. I knew this had to rankle him like nothing else, though. No hockey player liked being responsible for scoring on his own goaltender, but especially not the guys known for being defensive specialists.

Soupy glared at me.

"We'll get it back," Koz added. Blake Kozlow was the center on my line. About the only time I could stand the guy was when we were playing hockey. He was a jumped-up spaz the rest of the time, and one of the biggest assholes I'd ever met on a good day. On a bad day? Better to stay the hell away from the guy. But he seemed to chill out when he got out on the ice. I wasn't sure what it was—the activity, the competitiveness—but whatever was behind it, he seemed to focus in a lot better in a game, and his asshole-ish tendencies drifted away.

Except for when it came to the opposition. Koz never stopped talking trash. At least he was starting to back it up more often than not.

Pissed me off, though, when I was out there with him and he started shit that he wouldn't finish. That left me and Jo-Jo to clean up his messes—and Jo-Jo was just a twenty-one-year-old kid. A skinny blond Swede, no less. Not a fighter. I was scrappy, but that didn't change the fact that almost every guy in the league had at least half a foot and thirty pounds on me. Besides, Bergy didn't want me fighting. He wanted me on the ice, setting an example for those two and trying to somehow take over games like he seemed to think I could.

Bergy slapped a hand down on top of my shoulder. "Koz, Ghost, Jo-Jo... Get out there and give 'em hell."

"That's what I do best," Koz said, jumping over the boards with more energy than should be legal.

I tamped down my annoyance and followed him and Jo-Jo out to take the face-off at center ice. The guy hadn't done anything to deserve it. Yet. Sounded like he was planning to stir up a crap ton of shit, though.

The Sharks left Pavelski's line out there for this shift. They had the momentum, so it made sense, even if they were more winded than we were.

Levi "501" Babcock and his new defensive partner, Leif Sorenson—a trade deadline acquisition who'd been with the Oilers most of the season, and a guy we all called Thor because of his godlike build and long hair—joined us on the back end.

"God, suck on a fucking breath mint, would you?" Koz said to Pavelski. "I might pass out from the fumes before this guy ever drops the fucking puck."

Pavelski just put his stick on the ice and readied himself for the face-off.

Koz managed to get his stick under Pavelski's and win the draw back to Thor. My guy tried to tie me up, but I ducked past him and barreled my way toward the Sharks' zone, sure that Thor and 501 would get the puck up to me in no time. Sure enough, as soon as I reached the blue line, the puck hit my stick. Sharks defenseman Brent Burns and his caveman beard were all that stood between me and the goalie, and Jo-Jo was streaking down the other wing with Paul Martin covering him hard and tight.

Head up, I surveyed the scene before me. Burns had his eyes locked on me. The guy always seemed to read things exactly right. I had to fake going one way and convince him to bite or I'd never get free from him. Time to use the moves I'd been working on with Bergy.

I made like I would go left, but at the last second, I shifted my weight and powered my way to the right with my thighs.

Burns took the bait, and in his effort to change directions the same way I had, he fell down. Clear path to the goal.

I deked once, glanced across to see Martin had Jo-Jo tied up, deked one more time to convince the goalie to take himself out of position, and shot the puck high, glove side. It clanged off the crossbar and in the net. The goal horn sounded and the crowd went wild.

Jo-Jo and the rest of the guys converged on me, and Thor lifted me up in the air.

"Fucking right," Koz shouted in my ear. I couldn't make out all the rest of the things the guys were saying. Because, despite myself, I'd frozen with an unfounded fear. I didn't want to look out into the crowd. I didn't want to see if there were any people out there screaming things at me instead of shouting in elation.

I'd never reacted like this before to something that should be positive and exciting. I should be on top of the world, but instead, I was shaking in my skates.

I didn't like this new side of me. I wanted to bury it. Six feet under didn't seem deep enough.

Bergy gave me an odd look when we skated over to the bench, but it was gone before I could try to figure it out. He slapped me on the back. "That's what I'm talking about, boys. Let's get some more of that going. Keep it up." Then he leaned over my shoulder. "Hell of a fake on Burns. Told you."

I nodded and stared out at the ice. No one needed to know how bad that shit had gotten into my head, and I was going to have a hell of a time hiding it if Bergy was already giving me strange looks. The only thing that needed to be in my mind right now was this game. Period.

Everything else was just a distraction, and I didn't need any more of those.

THE PRESS CONVERGED around Koz instead of me, Babs, or any of the usual suspects after the game, for once, since he'd not only scored the game winner, but he'd also assisted on my second goal and fought two different Sharks players in the third period. My knuckles thanked him for dealing with the shit he'd started instead of leaving it all to me.

Commenting on Pavelski's breath had only been the start of it. By the end of the second period, every guy on that team wanted to rip Koz's head off, and I couldn't say I blamed them. I was just glad he was on my side. Playing against him would drive me batshit crazy in about 0.12 seconds.

I gave him a warning look from my stall, hoping he'd interpret that to mean he shouldn't say anything stupid that he'd have to retract later, but it didn't seem as though he'd noticed. His problem, not mine, I reminded myself. No matter what kinds of idiotic things Koz said, it was on him. Kurt Yarbrough and the other guys in the communications department could help him sort it out. I was just glad they weren't all over me tonight. I'd had enough of that in the last few days to last a lifetime.

I stripped off all my gear and headed for the showers, hoping they'd be finished with all of their interviews by the time I got back. Out of the corner of my eye, I caught a glimpse of Anne ditching her crutches and hobbling over to say something to one of her camera guys. She really shouldn't be doing that. I had half a mind to tell her as much before I took a step back and reminded myself it wasn't any of my business if she fucked up her ankle worse than it already was. Not my show; not my monkeys—same as with Koz.

When I returned to the room a while later, fully dressed and ready to get the hell out of there, most of the media had left. Anne and her guys were still around, though, camera trained on Koz and a mic shoved in his face. I inched past and hoped she wouldn't notice, but as I walked by her, I couldn't help but hear what he was saying.

"...not going to let anyone do or say shit about Ghost." He cut himself off and grimaced for a moment. "Sorry. Shouldn't have used that word, but I think you catch my drift. We're not going to just sit by and let people get away with that stuff. He's one of us. He's our brother. We're all sticking by him."

"So are you saying that one of the Sharks players made a comment about Golston and that's why—"

"I'm not answering that," Koz cut in dismissively. "What happened on the ice stays on the ice. That's how it's always been and how it's always going to be."

"Because wouldn't that be something the league would want to look into?" Anne continued. "I know there have been penalties handed out in the past when players have used derogatory language—"

"Not answering that," he said again. "And unless you have

something else to ask me, I think we're done here." He didn't give her the opportunity to ask him anything else, shoving past her and the cameraman and heading for the showers.

I ducked my head down and tidied up my stall, hoping beyond hope she wouldn't try to start anything with me next. I sure as hell hadn't heard anyone out on the ice saying anything like what Koz had hinted at. If anyone had said anything to him, I figured it had a hell of a lot more to do with him being a son of a bitch who couldn't shut the fuck up than anything about me. Lord only knew what he was thinking, because I sure as hell didn't.

"That's good enough for tonight, guys," Anne said to her crew behind me. She sounded weary, like she was overdoing it. Which she probably was, considering she still hadn't picked up her crutches again. Not only that, but there was no telling how many hours she'd been working lately with producing this show.

I grabbed my phone out of my stall and shoved it into the pocket of my suit jacket alongside my wallet. If she was telling them to shut off their cameras, she wasn't going to hound me tonight.

Or so I thought.

When I turned around, she gave me a curious look and arched a brow. "Did you hear anything like what Kozlow was talking about?"

"No," I bit off.

"Would you tell me if you had?"

This time, I chuckled. "Nope."

She shook her head with laughter in her tired eyes. "First episode is up. You can watch it when you get home."

"I doubt that'll happen."

She deflated a bit, disappointment drawing those gorgeous brows together over her nose. "You're not curious how it went?"

"I lived it. I don't need to watch it on repeat."

She nodded thoughtfully. "I wish you'd watch it. I'd like to know what you think."

"Why does it matter what any of us think?"

"I didn't say anything about an *us*. I want to know what *you* think. And I think you know why."

The only reason my opinion would matter was something I'd already determined wasn't a possibility—that she cared what damage she might have inflicted on me on top of the sons of bitches who'd started it to begin with.

Not a possibility. She was doing her job, and that was that. She didn't care about me, and I'd be an idiot to think otherwise.

I might be many things, but an idiot was not one of them. "I've got to get out of here," I said. "Practice in the morning."

"Yeah." Anne's voice sounded strained. "I've got a lot to do, too." She hobbled away without looking at me again.

I couldn't stop myself from calling after her, "You should get off that ankle!"

"That's what my dad tells me, too." She turned her head toward me and winked. "But like you said, I'm too stubborn for my own good."

Damn if I didn't like it too much when she smiled at me like that.

Maybe I was a bigger idiot than I wanted to believe.

Chapter Five

Anne

AFTER THE STORM'S second game of the playoffs—a one-to-nothing loss—we were getting close to finishing up with filming the second week's footage for *Eye of the Storm*. Several of the guys on my crew and I were up well after midnight at a bar, drinking a few beers and debating the angle we should take as we edited the episode together.

I'd been studiously avoiding looking at social media, instead turning that responsibility over to my assistant, Tim Wilmington, who had signed on as an intern. He'd been given instruction to ignore the nasty comments about me but to pass on anything constructive about the show, and to respond to as many of those tweets and other posts that were positive as he could. We wanted to present a good image to the world and not get caught up in the nastiness that tended to come out in crashing waves when people could hide behind the anonymity of the Internet.

"We could continue to keep the focus on Golston," Dave put in, taking another swig of his beer. "I mean, he's not giving us much, but you've gotten a few good sound bites out of several others. The guys want to stick up for him. You could paint it as the whole team, even the whole organization, rallying around him."

"He wouldn't like that much," I said. And I wouldn't blame him. Granted, I didn't think he'd bothered to watch the first episode, so I doubted he would be very keen on watching the second one any time soon, either. Maybe I didn't need to worry too much about how Nate would feel about us continuing to harp on this one incident.

"It's not about what he likes," Bill said. "You can't make your decisions based on if you're worried about hurting his tender feelings. You've got to put together the best show you can using the material you've got—and right now, he's the best material you've got. Or at least the way they're closing ranks around him is."

I scowled down into my empty beer glass, wishing I'd asked for another the last time the waitress had come by. "I still don't like it. We can't keep pushing the same story repeatedly with only minor changes. The audience will tune out fast if we do. It'll get stale. We need a fresh angle on it."

"This is a fresh angle," Ben said. "In the first episode, it had barely happened. There wasn't much exposition on it. We left them drowning in the muck and mire of how awful it felt with nothing but Golston's initial response to ease the sting. In a way, it was a cliffhanger. You need to resolve that story arc, and that could take a few episodes to tie up neatly."

"I'd rather it become a side plot instead of the main focus, though."

"It will," Bill said. "With time. You can't push it to the side right away, even if Golston would prefer for you to."

"I'm not doing things based on what Nate wants!" I argued. Maybe too forcefully.

The guys all gave me looks that said as much before taking another sip from their beers.

"So maybe you're doing it based on your own feelings," Tim said, and the other guys nodded.

"Don't you dare start with the whole Anne-is-a-female-with-too-many-hormones-so-she-can't-be-objective bull," I snapped.

Tim blanched, but he said, "No, that's not what I mean. I just meant maybe you're sympathizing with him right now. He's up against people who think he shouldn't be doing what he's doing because of his race. You're dealing with something similar right now because some jerks think you shouldn't be working in this field because you're a woman. So maybe you're getting too close and can't look at the situation objectively right now."

He might have a point, but I wasn't inclined to give in to it.

"Objective or not, I don't like the idea of harping on the racism issue any more than we have to. I'd rather we find another angle and start veering the audience into that territory sooner rather than later. So let's see what direction we can shift the focus in this episode. We have a couple more days to film and then two days to piece it together. I want all your best ideas as soon as possible."

"You've *got* our best idea," Bill insisted, and a couple of the other guys—the older ones, who had more experience, nodded in agreement.

"You know we're on your side, Anne," Dave said.

"It doesn't sound like it at the moment," I shot back.

"Well, we are," he said. "But here's the thing. You've got to give the guys who make decisions what they want. And what they want is the story that is all over the headlines. They want you to get the inside scoop from the people closest to what's going on, and deliver *that* in a way that keeps viewers riveted, keeps their asses in their seats, and makes them want to come back for more. If you don't—"

"I'm not pandering to what they want just because they think they want it," I cut in. "I'm producing the show that I think we need to produce, focusing on what's important overall."

"Then you might not have this job for very long," Dave said. I knew it wasn't a threat. He worked for me and not the other way around, and he didn't have any sort of say as far as whether I got to keep my job or not. He was telling me this more as a warning than anything, which, in a way, I could appreciate.

And I wasn't stupid enough to think that he was wrong. I still wasn't sure how I'd landed this job. There weren't many women in this field in any position, but even fewer who were entrusted with such big responsibilities. The kinds of responses I'd gotten on Twitter? It wasn't just nameless, faceless people on the Internet who thought those kinds of things, and I was sure some people actually said them in real life— just not to my face. They were said in men-only meetings, in passing when those few women in the business like me weren't around. Dave was very much right.

But I still couldn't produce this show while worrying about the possibility of losing my job if I didn't do it the way they wanted it. I had to maintain my integrity. I had to do it the way I saw it, even if it meant losing my job. I'd be doing everyone a disservice otherwise, myself most of all.

"So be it," I said, looking Dave straight in the eye with as much conviction as I could muster. I needed these guys on my side, because there were enough other people out there hoping to see me crash and burn. "We're still doing this my way for as long as it *is* my job."

The guys muttered, "Got it," and other similar words of assent, but they sounded less than enthusiastic. I understood their reluctance. The easy thing to do would be exactly what they were suggesting. I didn't want to take the easy way out. I had never been one to travel the path of least resistance. If I had been, I'd have a physics degree and would be popping out Indian babies like my mother thought best.

I shook my head, brushing all the negativity aside. If I allowed myself to dwell on that, I'd be swallowed up in it in no time. "Let's call it a night, guys. We've all got a lot to do tomorrow." Not the least of which was figuring out how to frame the second episode.

This job might well be the death of me, but at least I'd go out doing something I could be proud of.

"ANIKA, YOU SHOULD talk to your mother," Padma said into the phone. "She's driving us all up the wall with how her only daughter has banished her from her life, how you're shaming her with the work you do."

"Will you ever start calling me Anne like everyone else does?" I demanded of my cousin, trying to deflect the conversation from the direction she wanted to take things.

"Everyone? Who is this everyone? The whole family has always called you Anika."

Not *my* whole family, I thought to myself. Only the Indian half of it. The rest of my family called me by my real name, Anne. "Only because Mom calls me Anika."

"Because it's how we know you."

"But it's not my name."

"It should be your name."

"But it isn't. If you doubt it, have a look at my birth certificate." I shoved the phone between my shoulder and my ear so I could keep packing my suitcase. I'd already thrown in my toiletries and my undergarments. Now I needed enough suits to get me through the four days I'd be with the Storm in San Jose. It was definitely warm weather there now, in late April, so lightweight suits would be best. Too bad I'd completely ruined that tan suit. It had been my favorite, but the dry cleaner hadn't been able to get all the grass stains out of it. Even if they could, I'd ripped it open in a couple of places—not along the seams, either, since that would be too easy to repair—when I'd fallen, so I'd ended up tossing the whole thing in the garbage.

"Your mother said she wanted you to be named Anika," Padma insisted.

"Then she should have named me Anika when I was born. She didn't."

"Because your father wanted you to have an American name even though you're Indian."

"Half-Indian," I corrected her. "But regardless, that was between the two of them."

"And he won. Just like he always wins."

He always won where I was concerned because he loved me as the person I was, not the person he wished I was, but that was neither here nor there. Padma wouldn't want to hear it, anyway. My mother's family was always on her side in all things, and since I didn't share those sentiments, I was continually on the outs with half my relatives these days. Black sheep, thy name is Anne.

Not bothering with my crutches since I was dealing with the phone and needing to fill my hands with clothes, I limped to the closet and grabbed the first three suits I could find that weren't made from a hot, thick wool. Before going back to the bed, where my suitcase was thrown open, I grabbed one more suit for good measure. Then I loaded a few colorful shells and blouses to wear beneath the jackets, so I wouldn't have to make another trip to the closet on my aching ankle.

"You're not denying it, Anika."

"There's nothing to deny. My name is Anne. And I will talk to my mother when she apologizes to me."

"Why on earth would your mother need to apologize to you? She carried you for nine months. She gave birth to you. She raised—"

"She berates me at every opportunity she gets for not being her version of an ideal Indian daughter. And you know what? She wasn't the ideal Indian daughter, either, and she was and is as far from being the ideal American mother as possible. She made her choices, so I don't know why she can't respect the fact that I need to make my own choices, as well."

"But her choices were wrong!" Padma insisted.

"They were wrong for her. I'm not making the same choices she made, though. She needs to accept the fact that I am not her, and I will never be her, and she can't turn me into something or someone I'm not. It can't and won't happen. So until she can apologize—"

"For what?" my cousin cut in, and I ground my jaw, tossing the suits into the suitcase without even bothering to fold them.

I slammed the top closed and seethed silently for a few moments, trying to calm myself through deep breathing before I went off on Padma. It was really my mother who deserved to be on the receiving end of my ire, not my cousin.

"Don't you remember that farce of a wedding?" I finally bit off.

"She was just trying to be proactive."

"Proactive?" I nearly shouted into the phone. "How is my mother planning a wedding for me, buying the dress, inviting every member of her family but no one from the other half of my family—including my own father—and even picking out the groom, an Indian doctor who was more than twice my age, no less, all of this without saying a freaking *word* to me until I showed up after graduation, simply being *proactive*? How is it not majorly overstepping?"

"Arranged marriages are common in India," Padma said feebly, feeding me the same line every member of my mother's family had been reciting in the two years since that disaster.

"Well, we aren't in India, are we? This is America. And they're not common in America. Good grief, I've never even been to India," I added, almost as an afterthought. A very important afterthought, though, if you asked me. Granted, my mother didn't seem to think that was necessary. She wanted to marry me off to a fifty-two-year-old Indian doctor who could barely speak English, and the only non-English language I could speak was geek. "I can't even speak the language, other than a couple of phrases."

"She was only trying to help."

"She didn't help. At all. And until she can recognize that what she did was wrong and hurtful, and apologize to me for it, there's nothing else I have to say to that woman. And there's no amount of pleading and guilt-tripping the rest of you can do to change that. My mother is the one in the wrong here. If you can't see that—"

"What, are you going to cut the rest of the family off, too?" Padma cut in.

"At this point, it feels to me as if it's all of you cutting me off, because you refuse to accept the truth of the situation."

"I'm not going to sit here and listen to this anymore," she said. Then the line went dead.

When I heard the dial tone, the only thing I felt was relief.

Nate

WE WERE A team built on skill and speed, which was why I was able to fit in reasonably well despite my obvious lack of size in comparison to almost every guy in the league. The Sharks boasted an intimidating combination of the same skill game we played along with a lineup full of big bodies. As a team, we might be a bit faster and have a few more players who could pull off crazy skill moves than they did, but they were a team designed to bang and bruise.

And they'd been doing plenty of that.

After every game so far in this series, almost every guy in our locker room had a bag of ice strapped to at least a few choice body parts. We were taking a serious beating, even though the series was tied at two wins apiece heading back to Portland for the fifth game in this seven-game series.

As for me, I'd tweaked an old knee injury when I'd been trying to dig the puck out of the boards tonight, with two big Sharks defensemen banging away at it, as well. It wasn't anything that would keep me out of the next game, but the trainers had me keeping ice on it even during the flight home and elevating it as much as I could. They'd stacked a couple of carry-on suitcases on top of each other and instructed me to put my foot up on it. Good thing my legs were shorter than most of the guys', because mine were almost too long to make this kind of setup work, even though we had a lot more room on this private jet than we would on any commercial plane.

Anne and two of her cameramen were on the flight with us, and they were moving around the cabin, filming segments with various guys. For the most part, they'd left me alone during the few days we were in San Jose, which felt like a blessing. Maybe all the bullshit about the banana peel was finally starting to die off. I hoped that would be the case, at least.

RJ had been sitting next to me, his nose buried in his phone as he messaged back and forth with Amanda, an ice pack strapped to his shoulder. But about halfway through the flight, 501 and Cody "Harry" Williams dragged him to the back of the plane to play poker, leaving the seat beside me empty.

Anne was in it so fast it seemed like she'd been watching for her opening. She propped her bad ankle up on the suitcases beside my foot and let out an audible sigh. I took a quick glance down. The leg of her slacks hid quite a bit, but not enough.

"Your ankle is the size of a watermelon," I pointed out.

She gave me an annoyed look, then followed my gaze. "More like a cantaloupe."

"Why aren't you using your crutches?"

"Have you tried using crutches on an airplane?" she shot back.

"More times than you have."

She just rolled her eyes.

"You should put some ice on that."

To that, she didn't respond at all. My knee was already feeling a lot better, so I reached down and took the ice pack off, then bent over to strap it around her ankle. She shuddered with the chill, but she didn't do anything more than give me a nasty look in complaint. I kept my leg elevated so the trainers wouldn't yell at me too much if they strolled back to check on things. Besides, I was in much better shape than she was at the moment, so I figured she needed it more than I did.

"It'd be nice if everyone would stop trying to tell me what to do," she grumbled after a moment. But she didn't seem quite as grouchy as she had when she'd first sat next to me. No doubt the ice was already starting to numb some of the pain.

"You'd rather be in charge, wouldn't you? Like with your minions."

"Minions?" Anne's perfect eyebrow arched so high it was almost comical.

I found one of the camera guys and nodded my head in his directions. "Your crew."

"They're hardly my minions. And they seem to think they know how to do my job better than I do. At least some of the time. They've all got more experience, you know. And they're *men*. So clearly they know better than I do."

I didn't miss the bitterness in her tone.

"Having some issues with insubordination?" I asked, trying to keep my tone light.

She shook her head and shrugged. "They're just trying to help me keep my job."

I sat up straight. "You think you might lose it?" That seemed crazy to me. She'd just gotten started with this new project, and from everything I'd heard from fans, and from the guys who'd checked out the first episode, she was putting together an excellent program.

"They only gave it to me because it was put together at the last minute, and I was the only person who qualified and who could start right away. They'll almost definitely replace me with a man before the next season starts, though. I'm only temporary, and everybody knows it even if no one's actually *saying* it."

"Why do you think that?"

"You haven't looked at Twitter lately, have you?"

"Never." I almost shuddered at the thought. Some of the guys stalked Twitter, looking for trade rumors with their names floating around, seeing what people had to say about the way they were playing. Sounded like torture to me. Not my idea of a good time. I had never been one of those guys who read articles written about me, searched out blog posts about myself, or anything else like that. I watched the hockey highlights, but I got up to do something else once the focus was on how I'd played. That kind of thing only served to screw with my head. Hell, 501 had spent most of the season with his head stuck up his ass, all because the so-called fans on Twitter had started up a #DamnIt501 hashtag, and it trended just about every time we'd played for the first half of the season. All the more reason to avoid that shit like the plague, if you asked me.

"Probably better if you don't," Anne said somberly. "I've recently sworn off of all social media for a while."

"Do I want to know what they're saying?" I wasn't sure why I even bothered asking, because I was one hundred percent positive I would rather gouge out my eyes with a rusty spoon.

"Nothing worth wasting your time reading." She cracked a grin. "Unless you're of the mind that women working in sports media should all be drawn, quartered, raped, and left tied to a tree for anyone who comes along to do with as they will. You know, the typical *Game of Thrones* treatment for women. Oh, or if you wanted to weigh in on any side of the Marcus Jameson event. There's a lot of that right now."

I wasn't surprised that Marcus Jameson was still dominating social media, but what she said about women in sports media hit a nerve. She had to be exaggerating, didn't she? No one would go so far as to post about raping a woman, and definitely not just because of the job she did. Right? I had to believe that. "How can you even joke about that?"

"It's either make a crack or hate the world. I'd rather laugh it off. Same as you'd rather go on about your life like nothing happened a week ago."

Maybe the two of us were more similar than I'd like to think. Not a good thought when I'd spent the better part of the last week being pissed off at Anne because she was determined to do *her job* even when doing it was like a slap in my face. "So what are your guys trying to tell you? What do they think you need to do to perform your job better?"

"Nothing to bore you with," she said, shifting her weight slightly and wincing when it changed the position of her ankle.

"Bore me anyway."

She scowled over at me.

I raised a brow and settled back in my seat.

"They want me to keep the focus of the show on you right now. Because you're the big story that's all over the news, and you tie in well with the national story line, too."

"Because racial tensions are high all across the country."

"Exactly. They think if I give the higher-ups exactly what they want, I'll have a better chance of keeping my job after the end of this first season."

"But you're not?"

"You still haven't watched, have you? The second episode went live yesterday. You should see for yourself." She glanced at me, then chuckled, probably because the look on my face had to be one that said *fat chance.* "Well, even without watching, you should have noticed that I haven't been hounding you lately. We haven't left your story line in the dust, but I refuse to glorify that kind of hatred. Reporting on it when it happens is one thing. Beating it into the ground is something else entirely. I'm not going there. Not when there are so many other important things going on within the team right now."

"Not even if it means losing your job?"

"I'd rather lose my job than my integrity," Anne said.

"If you lose either, it'll truly be a shame," I said. And I meant it. Sticking to her convictions, even with everyone around her telling her that she was making a mistake, took a hell of a lot of courage. I had to admire her for it.

She gave me a self-deprecating smile, and before I had a clue what was about to come out of my mouth, I said, "You're so damn gorgeous."

Her grin became flirtatious in a flash. "You're not too bad to look at yourself. Thanks for bullying me into putting ice on my ankle. It's helping, even if I don't like letting someone else be right."

I winked. "I don't need to be right all the time. Just some of the time."

"I'll keep that in mind. How often? Once a week or so?"

"Maybe twice a week."

"You might be pushing your luck with that…"

The way I saw it, I was pushing my luck enough already by allowing myself to flirt with Anne, when the guys on her crew were probably right, even if I wished they were wrong. If she didn't play by their rules, she could lose her job. On top of that, our flirtation could lead to other problems for her.

Maybe there was a double standard in place, but that was the way of this part of the world. Not much I could do about it.

We were walking a tightrope with this, and I'd never been much of a daredevil. I had to wonder how adventurous she wanted to be. Because if we weren't careful, this could easily become more than a simple flirtation.

I didn't want to be the one responsible for putting her job in jeopardy. But she was an adult, too, perfectly capable of making her own decisions.

The question now was…what choice would she make if given an option? And did I want her to choose me?

Chapter Six

Nate

RJ STOWED HIS skates on the lower shelf in his stall and looked over at me with massive brown puppy-dog eyes. They had always been his primary weapon with girls when we were in our teens, but the guy had never been stupid enough to try using them on me.

Did he honestly think that would make any difference in whether I'd do what he wanted or not? Hardly likely. I'd never been one to fall for that shit, not even with my sister. Maybe for my niece, but she was only one year old. *And* she had the ultimate trump card, being my niece. RJ, though? Dumb ass. I rolled my eyes.

"Please," he said. "It's just for an hour."

"An hour of your beast dogs trying to drown me," I shot back, even though I'd already made up my mind to go along with him. There wasn't much heat in my words. Hell, to be completely honest, I *was* curious about this whole thing. That didn't mean I needed to give in too easily, though. Especially not with him trying to guilt me into it. "You know black men can't swim, right?" I tossed out to egg him on.

"And white men can't jump if you believe the movies, but I can still get a three-pointer past you any day of the week."

"And twice on Sunday," I finished. "But only because you have half a foot on me." Depending on whether you believed the *official* numbers they had on me or not.

He rolled his eyes. "More like because you can't shoot hoops to save your life. Doesn't matter. Don't try to pull that shit on me. Your mom was the one who taught *me* to swim when we were growing up."

"That doesn't mean I can swim with a dog that weighs as much as me trying to slobber all over me in the water," I pointed out. If they both decided to jump on me at the same time? I might as well be a dead man.

Sounded like it would be a fun day for the dogs, but...

Amanda had booked time for Max and Lola to go swimming at a dog pool. She said they needed to burn off their energy because they'd been driving her up the wall the whole time the team had been gone to San Jose. If she could take them out for a walk, of course, that would help immensely with their hyperactivity, but if RJ and I could barely handle the two of them together, there was no way Amanda could manage them both on her own. Don't ask me how she thought she was going to deal with taking them swimming when she'd booked the session, because I couldn't tell you, but together, RJ and I could manage it.

Which, now that I thought about it, was probably her plan all along—getting the two of us to take care of things so she wouldn't have to.

Even if she was being lazy and expecting us to do everything for her dogs, it didn't sound all bad.

Besides, spending some time in the pool might actually be soothing for my knee. It felt worse than it had last night, not that I intended to say a thing to the trainers about it. Based on my past experience and the way it kept trying to give out on me every now and then, I'd likely strained a ligament. I hoped it wasn't anything worse, but whether it was or not, the last thing I needed was for the trainers to get wind of the severity and decide they needed to send me to the hospital for a bunch of tests. They might find an injury bad enough that they'd pull me from the lineup.

So as long as I could play through the pain, you could damn well bet I was going to do it. This was the playoffs. We had a legitimate shot at winning the Stanley Cup this year. I'd have to be on my deathbed to come out of the lineup without putting up one hell of a fight. I didn't know for certain what this knee injury was, but it wasn't bad enough for me to be sitting up in the press box and watching the boys take care of things down below.

That meant I needed to do as much self-care as possible—staying off it when I could, icing it every day, and that sort of thing. The pool sounded like a good way to get a bit of a workout in without putting any unnecessary pressure on the joint and muscles.

RJ grabbed his gym bag and raised his brow. "You gonna help me or not?"

"Yeah, I'm coming."

Anne and one of her camera guys hustled into the room—this time she was using her crutches, at least—and took a quick look around to see who was still here...and an idea struck me.

An idea that probably meant I'd lost my mind.

Still, I'd rather she get more footage of me and RJ being goofballs with Max and Lola than trying to pick my brain on the state of the world considering that racism was still so rampant in this country. Surely she could find a way to use the footage.

"Okay with you if I invite Anne to tag along?" I asked him, never taking my eyes off her.

The laugh he let out said he agreed with my earlier assessment and I must be crazy. But he said, "Sure. Whatever you want to do."

"You need my help getting them there, or what?"

He followed my eyes over to Anne, then he shook his head. "Nah. You just get whatever you're swimming in and meet us there." Then he rattled off the address and left, saying he'd be there with the dogs in forty-five minutes.

Anne and her cameraman were still surveying the almost empty room. Most of the guys had taken to clearing out fast since they'd been filming us. I wasn't the only one who wasn't keen on having my life put under the microscope, but the Storm organization hadn't exactly given us any say in that matter. I crossed over to them, shoving my hands in my pockets.

"Hey," she said with a genuine smile.

"Hey." I shrugged, trying to look casual even though this felt anything but casual. It almost felt like asking her out on a date, only I had the sense that I'd be a lot more comfortable doing that than this. "RJ and I are taking his dogs out again. To a place called Doggy Paddles this time. If you guys wanted to come with us..."

"Doggy Paddles?" she repeated, stifling a laugh. "Is that what it sounds like? A pool for dogs?"

"Yeah, I don't know. Something Amanda booked for them. She thinks it'll help with their over-exuberance."

"You promise they won't sprain my other ankle?" Anne asked.

"I don't think it's possible to contain them enough to make any promises like that." I winked. "Try to look mean or something. Maybe they won't like you so much then."

"I don't know, they seem to like *you* just fine."

I tried to pull off an offended look, sure I failed miserably even though I put a hand over my heart and everything. "You think I look mean?"

"I think you look like you're *trying* to look mean a lot of times. Mainly on the ice, though."

"When you're the shortest guy in the league…"

"Nice try, but nope. Gerbe is shorter than you. I've interviewed him, and I was taller than him even in flats."

"Might have been a slight exaggeration."

"A slight exaggeration, kind of like that look you get right before a face-off."

She wouldn't give in. Which was kind of hot, in its own way. I chuckled. "You're determined to wound my pride, aren't you?"

"If that's enough to wound your pride…"

"So are you coming? Or do you have something better to do?"

She glanced at her watch, then took out her cell phone and scrolled through a couple of screens before her eyes—gorgeous, honey-colored eyes with flecks of green that seemed so out of place yet so perfect—flashed back up to meet mine. "I'm all yours. Give me an address and we'll be there."

Anne

FORTY-FIVE MINUTES LATER, Dave and I pulled up at Doggy Paddles, which turned out to be exactly what it sounded like: an indoor pool that catered solely to canine clientele and their human masters. I'd Googled it on the way, but I was still trying to process just what, exactly, we were getting ourselves into. Doggy Paddles worked with dogs of all ages, breeds, and sizes. They helped rehabbing injuries, held play therapy sessions, and offered any number of other amenities for their canine clients. Their humans could get in the pool with the dogs, but it wasn't required, as one of the Doggy Paddles staff members would always be involved.

Required or not, something told me Nate and Riley Jezek would be in the water today. Those two dogs were going to be way too much for any one person to handle by themselves, no matter how much experience the staff here might have.

Dave parked and started unloading all his gear while I headed for the main doors, since I saw Nate and Jezek already in the lobby with Jezek's two enormous dogs.

Nate held the door open for me while Jezek tried to hold both dogs back. They were barking up a storm and looked like they were either happy to see me or hoping to eat me for lunch, one of the two. On second thought, they might be happy to see me *because* they were planning to make a meal out of me. I tried to push that thought away and focus on the job at hand.

In *Eye of the Storm*'s second episode, I'd started to focus the show on some of the relationships between the people involved with the team. The idea had come to me after tagging along with Nate and Jezek that day at the International Rose Test Gardens. I'd taken it further than that by spending some time with other groups of friends and family within the team.

I'd started with Jamie and Levi Babcock, two brothers playing for the Storm. Jamie was the team captain and married to Katie, who was the daughter of one of the coaches—David Weber. Levi was engaged to Cadence Johnson, who was the youngest sister of one of the older players on the team, Cam Johnson. Cam just so happened to be married to Scotty Thomas's daughter, and Scotty had been the Storm's coach once upon a time, but these days he was part of the scouting staff.

That was just one of the tangled groups of relationships on the team. Another grouping started with Brenden and Rachel Campbell. Brenden was a veteran player, and Rachel worked as the assistant to the general manager, a man who used to play with Brenden's father. Brenden's sister was married to the former Storm captain who was now playing for the expansion Tulsa Thunderbirds.

So far, that was as far as I'd delved into the inner dynamics among the players, but I knew there were many other layers to explore in future episodes.

Not only was it more interesting to me to explore the guys' dynamics away from the rink and witness how that played out on the ice, but it made the story we were telling that much more personal. It gave the show a heartbeat. This wasn't just about hockey; it was about everything that made these men tick.

A woman who looked like she worked at the doggy pool nodded at me as I came in. "Right. They told me you wanted to film today, which is fine as long as you and your crew stay out of our way. Safety is our biggest concern, so if we tell you to move, you've got to move. And we won't be responsible for any damage to your equipment because of the water, so that's on you." Then she turned to the two guys. "You're welcome to come into the water with us, but it's not required. We'll be fitting Max and Lola with water harnesses so I can assess their swimming ability. After today, they might not need them any longer. Is everyone ready to go?"

Max and Lola responded by barking and jumping around like they were puppies being unleashed into a pile of autumn leaves.

"I think that's a yes," Jezek said.

The woman laughed and glanced up as Dave came in with his cameras. "I'd say so. Off we go." She nodded in my direction, then angled her head toward Dave. "You'll fill him in?"

"I'm already on it."

We followed her into the pool area. She took over putting the harnesses on the dogs while Nate and Jezek stripped down to their swim trunks. I scoped out the area and found a corner where we should be out of the way of anything but tidal-wave-sized splashes and still have good light and angles on the action. I nodded toward that spot. "Over here," I said to Dave.

He came with me and took a minute or two to set up all his equipment while I gave him the bullet points. He'd barely started filming by the time the dogs were running along the edges and dipping their front toes into the water along the ledge, unsure what to think. This must be a new experience for them.

The woman in charge and the two guys got straight into the water. Lola seemed to think the fact that Nate was already in the water was good enough reason to believe that she wouldn't die if she joined him, so she made a flying leap into the water, sending up a huge splash that drenched Max and nearly reached us. He barked indignantly, but a moment later, he followed her into the water.

For two dogs that had never gone swimming before, they took to it in no time.

The humans threw balls and other toys for the dogs to fetch, and within minutes, both dogs were paddling up and down the length of the pool, climbing out of it, jumping back in (and taking no notice whatsoever of whether a human or another dog was in their way while doing so), and otherwise having the time of their lives.

Nate and Jezek kept up a steady stream of banter, of the sort that would have to be bleeped out if this were to air on network television. Good thing we hadn't been saddled with those restrictions for this web series, although, since it was meant for viewing by all ages, I'd be careful to select footage with a limited amount of cursing.

It was great, seeing these two hanging out together so far away from the pressure cooker of the playoffs, just being themselves and having a good time. In fact, I was pretty sure they forgot we were filming them after a bit—at least I thought they had until Nate turned his head and looked right at me, waggling his eyebrows only a nanosecond before Lola leaped on him and dunked him underwater with her front paws on his shoulders. He came up spluttering, and I grinned and shook my head.

It wasn't just the dogs' playfulness that had me enjoying myself, either. Nate and Jezek were hamming it up and having a grand old time. I had extreme difficulty not bursting out laughing at their antics, especially when Nate clearly sought me out and flexed his muscles with a wink. But I couldn't allow myself to do that. Dave's boom mic would pick me up. This wasn't supposed to be about me but about the men in the water having a good time with the dogs.

There was so much laughter that they were getting out and drying off, the dogs shaking and spraying water everywhere, well before I expected the time to be up. I couldn't help but stare at Nate as he tried to corral Lola so he could rub her dry with a towel, the beads of water glistening on his skin and emphasizing his chest and arm muscles. In fact, I might have even licked my lips before remembering I was supposed to keep this professional. At least he hadn't seen me. I wasn't quite so lucky with Dave if the twinkle in his eye was any indication.

I'd seen Nate half-naked plenty before over the last couple of seasons, when I'd gone into the locker room after practices and games to get a quick interview, but there was something special about seeing him like this, completely free and not being careful about what he did or said. We had a camera trained on him, but all indications pointed toward him starting to feel more like himself in front of it, less self-conscious and aware that everything he did and said was being recorded for posterity.

I finally ripped my eyes away from him, turning to Dave. "I think that's good enough for today. We've got enough to work with."

"Want me to head back up to the offices and see who I can scrounge up for an interview?" he asked me, starting to pack things away.

I shook my head. "Take the rest of the day off. Lord knows you've earned it. I've arranged for us to head back to Jamie Babcock's house with him after morning skate tomorrow. I'll take both you and Ben. Katie's supposed to be there, and maybe her sister, too. I bet we can get some decent footage then."

"You're the boss," he said.

I slung my backpack that was doubling as a purse onto my shoulders so I could easily crutch out of there once he was ready to go, but Nate looked over his shoulder and grinned.

"You're already leaving?" he said.

I shrugged. "I think we've got enough for today."

"Oh." He sounded disappointed, which sent a tingle racing through my belly and up to wrap around my heart. "I was just hoping I could take you out for coffee or something. So we could talk some more. But if you've got—"

"I don't have any other plans," I said a little too enthusiastically. "But I came with Dave. My car's back at the practice facility."

"Don't use me as an excuse," Dave muttered in my ear. "If you want to fuck up your career before you get too far into it, be my guest."

I shot a glare in his direction.

"I could take you back to your car later," Nate said.

"Good," Dave said, loud enough for the guys to hear this time. "Because that'll save me a ton of time. I can just go straight home."

"Traitor," I whispered.

He chortled. "This has been building up for way too long. Don't even bother trying to deny it. No one who's been watching the two of you in those interviews would buy it."

"Not denying it." I was just sulking because he was right. Nate and I had been building our flirtation for two years, so it felt almost inevitable to take things a bit further. Coffee was relatively safe in terms of our next steps, even if it might be dangerous in terms of my career.

Might be? Who was I kidding?

But then again, I doubted I'd have this job much longer anyway. Would I really be hurting anything by crossing this line? Probably not.

I smiled across at Nate. "Go put some clothes on. I don't mind the view, but food establishments have strange rules about shirts and shoes."

He winked. "Damn rules."

Indeed.

Chapter Seven

Anne

THE LATE-AFTERNOON SUN was just starting to drop in the sky, warming me through the massive coffee-shop windows. We'd been sitting here nursing our coffees and flirting outrageously for a couple of hours, if not longer.

It'd been so long since I'd taken an afternoon off, or even more than an hour off here and there, that I wasn't quite sure what to do with myself. That alone was enough to leave me giddy, but the floating sensation was amplified by how much I truly enjoyed being in Nate's company. It felt as easy and natural as breathing. At least it did until he smiled at me again. Then I started soaring, and had to drink more coffee to ground myself.

I was now working on my third nonfat, decaf cappuccino, and Nate had just started on an Americano after finishing off two caramel macchiatos. Watching him drink that caramel goodness had done a real number on me, in more ways than one. I couldn't understand how he could drink something so full of sugar without putting on twenty pounds, because I could barely look at the syrupy goodness without feeling my hips get wider. But then again, he worked out all the time, and his body was built to burn energy. Even if I was in the gym twenty-four seven, I doubted I could look half as good as he did.

And all this thinking about sweets wasn't doing me any favors in another area. My stomach was starting to rumble with hunger noises, even though I wasn't in any big hurry to leave; I'd rather sit and talk.

The whole time we'd been here, it was as if the world had melted away and it was just the two of us. No enormous dogs trying to jump all over either of us or eat us alive. No deadlines to meet. No high-stakes games to play. No reminders of all the crap we'd both been facing with the general public.

I could get used to this if I allowed myself.

But that was a big if. And a dangerous one if my job wasn't already hanging in the balance like everyone knew it was. Nate probably wouldn't face any major consequences for starting up a personal relationship with me, but I had to play by a different set of rules. Arbitrary rules, true. And sexist ones. Archaic, even. But none of those arguments changed the fact that this was the field I'd chosen to work in, and I'd known going in that it would be an uphill climb with roadblocks to maneuver myself around at every step.

Still... I might as well enjoy the rest of the time I had with Nate. Everyone knew there was no chance I'd keep this job after the first season of *Eye of the Storm* was officially in the books, so why pretend otherwise?

"I don't know how you could drink those macchiatos," I said, blowing on my coffee to cool it off before taking a sip. "They're so sweet." Never mind the fact that I had a sweet tooth to rival the product tasters at Hershey's and was jealous as all hell that he could have them.

"Just like me. Strong, dark, and sweet as your grandma's pie."

I shot my eyes over to find his full of laughter.

"Couldn't go with the tall, dark, and handsome line," he said, winking. "No one would ever buy the tall part."

"You think I'm going to believe you're sweet?"

"Maybe someday you'll be ready for a taste so you can see for yourself."

Maybe seemed to be too wishy-washy for the state of things, considering a warm, tingling sensation had started in my belly and jolted through my body like a flash of lightning. I bit down on my lower lip to keep from saying anything at all before I'd thought through every possible consequence of any potential response.

"Maybe you're ready now," he said, leaning back and draping his arm over the back of the chair like he could read my mind. His lazy posture made me wish I was next to him, his arm wrapped around my shoulders, instead of being seated on the other side of the table.

"Tell me what it was like for you growing up," I said, desperately needing to change the subject.

He shrugged, but there was a bit of disappointment in the move. "I could say it was all hockey, all the time, but that wouldn't exactly be true. Mom and Dad wouldn't let me be quite so single-minded about anything."

"No?"

"Not unless it was my education." He grinned, and my insides melted. "My parents were—actually, they *are*—both working-class. He's a plumber, and she runs his office. They make good money, considering what they do, but they wanted better for their kids. My sister, Nicole, went to college like they wanted her to. Now she's a teacher, and she married an engineer, so they're solidly middle class and moving ahead in the world, the way Mom and Dad wanted. I was always a good student, but I wanted to pursue a hockey career even if it was a long shot for me to make it in the NHL. They tried to get me to play college hockey. I insisted I had a better chance of making an impression if I went into juniors."

"They seem to be fairly equal in scouts' eyes these days," I said.

"They are." Nate winked. "But I did my damnedest to convince my parents otherwise."

"Don't you usually start in juniors in high school?"

"Yeah. It meant leaving home with two more years of high school to go, and forgetting about college. Let's just say that my parents weren't too keen on the idea."

"But you did it anyway?" I asked.

"I did. But the only way they'd agree to it was if I made them a promise."

I raised a brow. "What promise?"

"I told them that if I didn't get into the NHL by the time I was twenty-four, I'd come home and start college in earnest. And if I did make it by then, I'd take a couple of courses every semester and do summer school, too. It might take me a long time to get my degree, but I'd get one. They weren't thrilled with the idea of me waiting so late to get started, but they agreed in the end."

There wasn't any point in denying I was impressed. Coming from a family like mine—even if my mother didn't want me to *do* anything with my degree once I got it, both of my parents had been adamant that college was an absolute necessity—I had an appreciation for the kind of dedication it took to put such a priority on higher education.

"So did you keep your promise? Get a degree?"

"I'm *keeping* it," he said, taking another sip. He winked. "I'm on the ten-year plan at Portland State. I started once I made it to the AHL level, even though that was sooner than I'd said I would. I'd thought about getting started while I was in juniors, but I needed some more stability than I had back then. Logistically, it wasn't exactly a piece of cake figuring out how to make it all work."

I nodded, completely enraptured. Smart men were a heck of a turn-on for me. "So you're taking classes now?"

"I'm technically a junior, but it'll probably take me two to three more years to finish since I'm still playing full time. Business management major."

"Business?" That one took me aback. I shook my head. "Not what I imagined."

"What, did you think I was going to be a nutrition science major? Or maybe kinesiology? Something that makes more sense for an athlete?"

"Not really. I'm not sure what I expected, but not business management." My stomach rumbled again, but I didn't get the impression that Nate heard it. At least I hoped he hadn't. I took another swallow of my coffee, wishing there was more substance to it so we could keep talking like this for hours to come. My inner geek was getting off on this conversation as much as my superficial side was enjoying staring at him. "So, are you going to use it to help your parents out after you retire as a player? Find ways to help the plumbing business grow?"

He scrunched up his nose. "Plumbing's not my thing. I figured I could find a way to use it to continue in the hockey world. Get into upper management or something with a team. Maybe."

"You could also go into broadcasting," I suggested. He gave me a look that said I had lost my mind, but I wasn't going to give up so easily. "You're good on camera. Some guys, you can hardly get a decent sound bite out of them, but you've always got something interesting to say. You don't clam up. Plus, you're easy on the eyes," I added with a wink.

"It's a possibility, I guess." He shrugged. "I don't know if I'd really like it."

"Why's that?"

"I'm not keen on the idea of getting *the story* when it's something I don't think should be a story." He didn't sound angry, but there wasn't any point trying to convince myself he wasn't thinking about how I'd jumped right in with the rest of the media after the night of the banana peel incident. How I hadn't let it go for most of a week. How I'd put the job ahead of what was right.

"You don't always have to get *the story*," I said. "Sometimes, you can tell them what the true story ought to be."

"Can you really?" he asked, sarcasm dripping thick, like molasses.

"That's what I'm doing now. You might know that, if you'd bother to watch."

"But aren't all your guys telling you they know better than you do how to do your job? Or was that all a figment of my imagination?"

"I'm still doing it my way," I pointed out.

More than ever before, I was determined to produce this show the way I thought it should be, not the way everyone else seemed to think I should. Because, whether the powers that be liked it or not, *Eye of the Storm* was my baby. At least until they took it away from me. But I had no intention of producing a show I wasn't proud of in the hopes that I could somehow save a job that was already essentially a lost cause.

Nate passed appraising eyes over me and nodded. "You are. I wouldn't take that away from you."

"I wouldn't let you, anyway," I said. Then my stomach made itself known in the most undignified way possible, and I groaned.

"Hungry?" he said, grinning.

"You could say that."

He finished off his Americano and leaned forward across the table, making like he was reaching for my hand before he stopped himself. "I'll make you a deal."

I narrowed my eyes. "What kind of deal?"

"I'll watch your show. Really watch it, even though I hate watching anything that's about me."

"If?" I added when he didn't finish.

"If you'll let me take you out to dinner tonight."

"Doesn't seem like much of a hardship on my part."

"Good. Then you'll come?"

Even with the warning bells clanging in the back of my mind, reminding me that dinner was a hell of a lot closer to a date than coffee was and that if I had any intention at all of keeping my job I needed to stay the heck away from dating any of the players on the team I was responsible for covering, I nodded. "Yeah. You can buy me dinner. I'm starving."

I only hoped I wasn't committing career suicide.

Probably an unfounded hope, but still.

THE NEXT DAY, as Dave and Ben set up their cameras, microphones, and lights in Jamie Babcock's living room, I couldn't seem to stop myself from yawning. Often. Repeatedly. Loudly, too. It didn't even matter that we were surrounded by organized chaos. Jamie invited his brother along, who brought his fiancée, who brought her brother, sister-in-law, niece, and nephew. Then there were Jamie and Katie's two cats, one of which was currently circling my legs and doing its best to trip me at every turn while it studiously avoided the two children. And Katie's sister was still due to arrive at any moment.

None of that was doing a thing to wake me up. I either needed a stiff cup of coffee or a dunk in a basin of cold water.

"Late night?" Dave asked with a knowing wink after I yawned for at least the eighth time since we'd walked through the front door and started getting ready for whatever was to come.

"Not for the reasons you seem to be implying."

"Whatever you say, boss," Dave said, but he smirked over at Ben, who laughed out loud while he adjusted the height of a light rig.

In truth, Nate and I *had* been out until the wee hours of the morning...but we hadn't done anything more than talk, laugh, and tease each other. Dinner had been an extended version of our afternoon over coffee. Lots of making eyes at each other. Even more getting to know one another. Not even a hint at anything that went beyond flirtation.

I wasn't sure who felt more anxious about taking things further, him or me. It seemed odd to think about Nate Golston being nervous, considering he came across as ridiculously full of confidence and more than merely sure of himself in most of our interactions. But every time I'd gotten the sense that a kiss, however innocent, was imminent, he'd backed off.

And me, being the bookish and awkward nerd I'd always been...well, I'd never been the one to make the first move with someone I was interested in, no matter how much I might want to. I could hang out with guys all day long, trading barbs with the best of them. But when it came to anything in the realm of one-on-one relationships with a man, anything in the love-and-dating world, I turned into a giant chicken.

So nothing had happened.

Yet in some ways, everything had happened.

Because I wanted him to kiss me, even knowing exactly what that would mean for my career once word got out. And it *would* get out. There wasn't any way of hiding it. His life was too public, and my life revolved around my job these days.

I wanted a heck of a lot more than just kisses, too. The more time I spent with Nate, the more I came to realize he wasn't just a sexy-as-all-get-out athlete with an amazing smile. He was confident, intelligent, driven, loyal, and he had a sense of humor that wasn't too far from my own.

The problem was it might not just be nerves on his part. In fact, nerves might not even be part of the equation on his side of things. I could just be reading that into it because that was what I felt.

What if he still saw me as the enemy? As someone who was only trying to get *the story*, as he'd put it earlier. Yeah, he'd invited me out for coffee and followed it up with dinner, but maybe he was just trying to deflect my professional attention away from him by showering me with personal flattery.

No matter how many times I tried to work it all out in my head, I couldn't settle on a single answer. For all I knew, he might not have come to that conclusion himself.

The doorbell rang, snapping me out of my ruminations.

I whipped my head over to see if the guys were ready to start filming, but they'd beaten me to the punch. Ben already had a camera over his shoulder, and Dave had his set up on a tripod. With a nod from me, they both pressed their buttons to start filming.

Katie Babcock raced down the hall with Cam Johnson's little boy, Connor, trying to climb her and Cam attempting to drag Connor down. Katie, grinning from ear to ear, flung open the front door to let her sister in, oblivious to the chaos surrounding her.

"You're late," she said without any preamble.

Dani Weber came in, nearly a mirror image of her older sister. Dani's brown hair was long and slightly curling, with a hint of red highlights. Katie's was growing out, cut in an adorable bob. They were the same height and had identical faces. The only difference other than their hair, as far as I could tell, was that Dani had a few more curves.

"Only late because I stopped to hug Mom and Dad before coming over." Dani came through the door and tossed a duffel bag and her purse on the floor at the front of the hall. She pried Connor's sticky fingers free from Katie's hair to help Cam extricate the boy. The sisters came into the living room and plopped down on the couch next to each other, acting like there was nothing more natural or normal than the cacophony in this house.

I took a seat on the floor in a corner of the room where I could spy on everyone and observe. I had a mic of my own, which allowed me to quietly give instructions to Ben and Dave, letting them know who I wanted them to focus on and when.

Jamie, Levi, and Sara Johnson went into the kitchen to prep some steaks to go on the grill. They started talking about Sara's father, Scotty Thomas, and whether or not he was dating a woman who worked in the Storm's travel department.

Cam got down on the floor in front of Katie and Dani. He dragged Connor down there with him, who then decided to climb him like a jungle gym, cackling like a loon. His daughter, Cassidy, was already on the floor crawling around. She giggled at everything her brother did, especially if it was something that hurt Cam. The two cats got in on the act, too. Filming a bit of that wouldn't be bad at all. It made Johnson seem like an ordinary dad, not some millionaire athlete.

The two sisters started talking like there weren't any cameras around, catching up on the things sisters who hadn't seen each other in months would do. *How's school? What have you heard from Luke? Why is Dad so grumpy today?*

I sent Ben in to catch the kitchen talk, just in case it turned into something as juicy as the steaks might be, and I directed Dave to film the action on the floor while I eavesdropped on Katie and Dani's conversation.

"I'm taking an independent study this summer," Dani said. "They don't usually let students do this one until they're seniors, but I nagged my prof until he agreed to let me."

The talk of college and professors automatically sent my thoughts back to Nate, which didn't help me at all. I shoved the thought aside.

"So you aren't coming home for summer break?" Katie replied, sounding wounded. "I had all sorts of plans, and Mom wanted to get us all together to go to the Bahamas…"

"Do they have wine in the Bahamas? I only think of fruity rum drinks."

Katie scowled at her sister. "Don't change the subject."

"I'm still coming home." Dani rolled her eyes. "I'll need somewhere I can set up a studio and do my work, and I'll have to shoot up to Seattle a couple of times to meet with Dr. Schlesinger and show him what I've done, but otherwise I can do it all from here."

"What kind of independent study is this?"

Dani tucked both feet underneath her, sitting cross-legged on the couch. "A makeover challenge. I'm supposed to find a woman—a *real* woman, not some supermodel type—who has a hard time finding clothes that flatter her because of whatever problem area. And then I have to design a wardrobe that not only flatters her but that fits her aesthetic."

"Are you going to have time to go to the Bahamas?" Katie asked.

Dani winked. "For that, I'll make time. Especially if she lets me have some of those fruity rum drinks."

"I'll sneak you a few if you don't let Dad know."

"Seriously, though, why was he so grumbly with me when I was there?" Dani asked with a pout. "He hasn't seen me in almost a month. I come home for a long Easter weekend, and all he wants to do is glare and grumble about staying away from asswipes."

"He saw you kiss Harry."

Harry. I did a quick mental rundown of the team, trying to remember which of the players the others all called Harry. Big, redheaded defenseman named Cody Williams who looked kind of like the British royal. Scruffy facial hair that had nothing to do with being a playoff beard. He tended to wear bowties, and he actually pulled the look off. He was like a sexy physics professor off the ice but a mean SOB on the ice.

Dani didn't exactly blush, but it came close to it. "None of Dad's business who I kiss."

"Mm hmm. You remember how many *years* it took him to be okay with me being with Jamie? And you're his baby."

"But still a grown-ass woman who can make her own decisions when it comes to who I kiss."

"It's not like Harry is even close to your age, either."

"He's close enough."

Katie rolled her eyes. "Not going to make a difference to Dad. Not when it comes to you being with one of his players. *Especially* not if the player in question is that much older than you."

Dani rolled her eyes, and I made a mental note to further investigate whatever was going on between her and Cody Williams. Before I could get too far with that, though, Cassidy Johnson toddled over and climbed into my lap. She reached up and shoved something sticky into my mouth.

I scanned the room quickly to see if there was anyone to come to my rescue without disturbing everything that was happening, but no luck. I was on my own.

At least it was kind of sweet, whatever it was. Applesauce? With a hint of yogurt.

Shouldn't kill me, in any case.

I was so distracted by the little girl in my lap, though, that I lost track of the conversation between the sisters. By the time I looked up again, Dave had switched to filming the pair of them instead of Johnson and his son. I tuned out all the noise and focused in on their words. They were talking much more quietly than before, so it wasn't easy to make them out. Especially not with the toddler's babble right by my ear.

"Dr. Oliver keeps stressing that we shouldn't get our hopes up," Katie said. "And I'm not, honestly. I mean, if we can get pregnant, awesome. But if we can't, it's not the end of the world. But I don't think Jamie sees it that way. He seems to think it's going to happen."

"Probably because there's something in the water with his teammates," Dani murmured. "Every time I come home, someone else is knocked up. They're breeding like bunnies. You'd think they're all old enough to know what's causing it..."

Both sisters laughed, but Katie quickly sobered. "But he's known all along that it wasn't likely for us. After all the chemo, there's just not much chance."

"Apparently that isn't enough to stop him from dreaming."

"Apparently not," Katie said. Her eyes flickered over and landed on me. She blinked a couple of times, then seemed to realize that her conversation wasn't private. She stared at me for a moment.

"So now what?" her sister asked. "Fertility specialist? Will you talk about adoption?"

"The last thing I want is to go to more doctors."

Dani reached over and squeezed her sister's hand.

I glanced up to be sure Dave was capturing every moment. Then, one more time, Nate's words from earlier fluttered through my mind. *I'm not keen on the idea of getting* the story *when it's something I don't think should be a story.* Was I about to turn what should be a private moment, something that should stay within the family, into my latest story? This wasn't news. This wasn't something that the public had a right to know, unless Jamie and Katie Babcock decided to tell the world about their struggles.

Oh, sure. In my head, I knew all the arguments the guys would give me about why I had to use the footage. I needed to save my job. They'd signed off on all the releases, and they'd invited us into their home with the knowledge that we'd be filming and potentially using anything that we witnessed. Legally, we had every right to use the footage in any way we saw fit.

But was that enough?

Maybe Nate had more of a point than I'd like to concede.

With every day that passed of working in this job, I questioned myself and my motives more than the day before. I'd known when I took this job that I was either setting myself up to fail spectacularly or succeed beyond my wildest dreams.

I'd never imagined I was walking into a crisis of conscience, but here it was, staring me in the face. Laughing at me.

Now what?

Chapter Eight

Nate

WE'D ONLY BEEN home for a few days—just long enough to take Max and Lola to the dog pool, take Anne out for coffee and dinner, for me to catch up on the first two episodes of Anne's behind-the-scenes production about the team, and to beat the Sharks in Game Five to go up three games to two in the series—and already we were on our way back to San Jose.

With any luck, we could take complete control of Game Six from the drop of the puck and not have to worry about playing the seventh. We could all use a couple of extra days to rest before the next series started. Almost every guy on the team was playing through some injury or another, large or small. My knee hadn't gotten any worse, but it hadn't gotten any better, either. I still had no intention of talking to the trainers about it. Hell, Babs had broken two toes in Game Three, but he refused to come out of the lineup. They shot him up with some stuff to kill the pain before each game, and he forced his foot into his skates without a word of complaint. If he was playing through that, I would play through anything that didn't kill me.

No one on this team cared whether we ended up facing Chicago, who had snagged one of the Wild Card spots in the Western Conference, or LA, who had finished first in the Pacific Division. No one but me, at any rate, but my reasons were entirely selfish—especially now that I'd heard there was a demonstration planned in Chicago for next week. A bunch of people were going to march through downtown, protesting the fact that the cop who'd shot Marcus Jameson had only been put on probation and wasn't even being formally charged. I just wanted to stay the hell away from all the racial tensions, and there wouldn't be much chance of that if we had to play against the Blackhawks in the next round.

Game Six in that series was ongoing as we boarded our plane, with Chicago putting on quite a show in front of their home crowd in an effort to tie the series and force a seventh and deciding game. They'd scored three goals in the first ten minutes of the game. The boys and I had all been watching on a big screen in the locker room before they'd ushered us out to a charter bus bound for PDX.

As expected, Anne and several of her guys were coming with us to continue filming her show. She was up ahead of me, climbing the stairs on her crutches. She looked like an old pro at it now. Must have been using them like she was supposed to lately. I couldn't stop myself from grinning.

In fact, I seemed to do that almost any time I saw her or thought about her lately. Couldn't help it. She brought that side of me to the forefront and kept any thought I might have had of pushing her away well outside of my mind.

Koz bumped into my shoulder—intentionally. "Playing poker on the way. Sit by me and I'll try not to take all your fucking money."

"Doesn't sound like much of a deal." It also didn't sound like how I wanted to spend the flight.

RJ gave me a knowing look, rolled his eyes, then turned to Koz. "I'm in. Lover boy here is going to be too busy making fucking googly eyes at Anne to play."

"Which means he won't be paying fucking attention and we can get all his money," Koz argued, starting the climb to our chartered plane.

RJ laughed and followed him, putting some distance between me and my obnoxious line mate. Once I got inside the cabin, I spotted Anne in a window seat not far behind the coaches, her laptop out and headphones covering her ears. The seat next to her was empty.

Not for long, though. As soon as the guys ahead of me got out of my way, I snagged it.

She whipped her head around and removed the headphones from one ear, looking slightly annoyed. "I've got about seven hours' worth of work to get done and probably only forty-five minutes to do it in, since they're going to make me put this away for takeoff and landing."

"Anything I can help with?"

She blinked at me like I was an idiot. "No. How could you help?"

"I don't know. You tell me." I glanced at her screen. She'd paused video footage of Katie Babcock and Dani Weber hanging out at what appeared to be Babs's house. "More focus on the guys' lives away from hockey for this next episode, then?"

"You watched?" she asked with a skeptical raising of one of those perfect brows.

"Promised you I would. We made a deal. You let me buy you dinner, I watched your show."

"And?" She removed the headphones completely, letting them rest on her shoulders, draped around her neck. "What did you think?"

I didn't miss her anxious tone, and I couldn't stop the smile from coming to my lips. "Impressive. The first episode wasn't as hard to watch as I feared it would be. The second gave a more complete picture of the team as a whole, what the guys are about, and didn't focus on me so much. Other than hanging out with RJ and his dogs. Which, I'm guessing, there will be more of in the third episode."

A softness had started to come over her, gradually replacing the stressed-out, frazzled look of annoyance she'd given me when I'd first sat next to her. "We've already pieced that section together. My editor's pulling an all-nighter here in Portland to work on tonight's game while I finish off a couple of segments with the other guys away from the game. Then tomorrow, we've got to put the whole thing together, write and record any narrative bits, and upload the completed webisode."

That sounded like a hell of a lot of work, and I wouldn't have the first clue how to do any of it. Good thing I had no intention of ever trying to do her job or anything like it. "And you think you can get your part done on this flight?"

"If you'll stop flirting with me and let me do it."

I chuckled, but I reached over and settled her headphones over her ears again. "Get to work, slacker."

She winked at me.

I reached into my carry-on bag and took out my textbook for Financial Accounting and Analysis and flipped to the right chapter. I had finals coming up in the middle of the next round, and some of the accounting concepts I knew would be involved still made my eyes cross and my head throb every time I had to look at them.

Ten minutes later, the whole team had boarded and the flight attendants started their safety spiel. Instead of paying attention to them or working on editing her film, Anne's eyes kept straying over to me and my textbook.

There wasn't any point in denying it. I was paying a hell of a lot more attention to the fact that she was checking me—well, technically, checking my *book*—out than I was to reviewing the Going Concern Principle. Like it or not, Anne was more into me now than she had been before.

I, for one, definitely liked it.

ONLY A MINUTE and twenty-three seconds remained in regulation. We were up by a goal, but the Sharks had already pulled their goalie in a last-ditch, season-on-the-line move. They had my line hemmed into our zone, along with 501 and Thor on *D*, and the five of us were completely gassed.

I could hardly move, let alone take a good breath.

Former Sharks captain Joe Thornton had the puck on his stick. He passed it back to Dillon, one of his teammates, on the blue line. Dillon hesitated just long enough for me to close the gap between us. He still hadn't decided—shoot or pass—so I had half a second to make a move. I lunged for the puck.

Missed it and fell flat on my face.

By the time I got to my skates again, Dillon had sent the puck toward the net. Our goaltender, Nicky Ericsson, had stopped it, but he didn't control the rebound. Now half the guys on the ice were converging on him, and it was a mad scramble.

I raced as fast as I could to get over there. Nicky was down in a full split and trying to reposition himself, 501 was literally inside the net, and Thor was bashing everything in teal that came within his considerable reach. I'd barely joined the fray when the puck squirted free from the pile, heading out toward the right-side face-off dot.

It had taken every bit of juice I had to get back into the play, but there wasn't a single teal jersey between me and that little black piece of vulcanized rubber. I dug in and found another gear, zipping over to pick up the puck and race toward the other end of the ice with it.

Grabbed it with the tape on my stick and shuffled out toward center ice, with Dillon right behind me. Not a surprise. The guy had half a foot on me and a powerful stride. I was speedy in general, but this shift had gone on way too long.

Still, I gave it all I had. Got close to the blue line. Felt him gaining on me, but there was a gorgeous, wide-open net at the other end calling my name. Inched past the blue line, but now his stick was whacking at my skates. Needed to get past the red line at center before shooting, in case my aim was off. We couldn't afford an icing call right now. Not when my guys were this tired.

But then Dillon was almost completely alongside me, and his stick was longer than mine. And he poked at the puck, nearly knocking it away from me.

Red line or not, I had to shoot.

So I did, putting so much behind my wrister that I fell over in the process.

Dillon dived for it, but he missed.

The puck rolled on its end, bouncing around and acting like it might just squeak inside the goal post. But at the last second, it angled to the left and stayed out.

Another Sharks player was racing in an attempt to stop it. Even though he wouldn't get there in time, that was enough for the refs to call icing. Now the Sharks could get a line change and put out fresh players, but the five of us had to stay on the ice.

I got to my feet and skated back to the circle to Nicky's left as slowly as I could without the refs calling a penalty for delaying the game or some other bullshit. Koz and Jo-Jo were both bent over at the waist, their hands resting on their knees as they tried to suck in as much oxygen as possible. Thor tapped me on the back of the calves with his stick and nodded, which was as close to him saying, "Nice effort," as he'd ever come. The guy hardly ever said a word since his arrival at the trade deadline.

No matter how bone-tired the five of us were, though, I knew that Nicky was the one who would truly be tested here. I glanced back at him long enough to see that his eyes were sharp and focused. Hell, he even winked at me. The guy was fine. Confident to the point of bordering on cocky, which was about as close to perfect as you could get as a goaltender. I sure as hell knew I wanted a goalie back there who believed in himself even if no one else did, and that was exactly what Nicky was giving me. His body language said he had this in the bag, as long as none of us did anything to fuck it up for him.

That alone was enough to get the oxygen flowing more freely through my body. I took my position at the face-off circle with one goal in mind.

I was going to put this game—and series—away, whether my lungs wanted to cooperate or not.

Anne

THE WHOLE TEAM leaped over the boards as one as soon as the final horn sounded to end the game, racing out to tackle Nate. He ended up at the bottom of a massive, sweaty dog pile of his teammates. Once they dug him out, he came up with an enormous grin.

As he should. He and his line had been out on the ice for the final two-plus minutes of the game, unable to get off for a change while the Sharks had thrown everything they had at them. Through it all, Nate had managed to score not one but two empty-net goals. To call him a hero in his teammates' eyes right now would be putting it mildly. The other guys on the ice with him hadn't been slouches, either, but Nate was the one to put the game completely out of the Sharks' reach.

I made sure the guys on my camera crew were all well positioned to get the shots of the handshake line I wanted. It was a tradition in hockey, and one I had no intention of neglecting in the show, especially since this marked the end of the first-round series against the Sharks. In a couple more days, the Portland Storm players would find out who they would be facing in the second round, but for now, they could relax in the knowledge that they were moving on.

Apparently, I didn't have enough control over myself to watch the whole team as they shook hands with the Sharks players. My eyes stayed rooted to Nate, so I didn't miss the fact that, when he reached for Brent Burns's hand, the big Wookie-esque Sharks defenseman picked him up in a bear hug, lifting him a foot or two off the ground. I busted out laughing and couldn't get myself under control again until Ben said in my ear, "Got that for you, Anne."

"Great work, guys," I finally said once I sobered. "Everyone knows where to go once the team clears off the ice, right? Dave, make your way to Golston's stall. I'm sure that's where the reporters will want to start."

They all gave me murmurs of assent. Now that we'd been at this for a few weeks, I didn't have to direct them too much. My team almost always knew what I wanted, and they gave it to me, frequently before I asked.

Jim Sutter, the team's general manager, poked his head into my control room once most of the players were heading down the tunnel. "Coming down to the locker room?" he asked.

I reached for my backpack and shoved a couple of items inside it. "On my way."

Before I could sling it onto my shoulders, Jim took it from me. "You bring yourself," he said. "I'll get everything else."

I didn't want to waste the time it would take to argue with him that I could do it all on my own. Instead, I grabbed my crutches and followed him, allowing him to hold doors open for me on the way. "Your team did well for you tonight," I said as we arrived at the elevator bay.

"The boys always do."

I couldn't help but smile as the elevator doors opened and he ushered me inside. "You sound like a proud papa."

He winked without confirming or denying my assessment. "Rachel tells me you want to set up some time with me. Maybe involving her and Brenden, too."

"I would." I leaned back against the wall, thankful to allow my aching armpits a reprieve, even if only for a few moments. Getting around on crutches wasn't for the faint of heart. "I'm trying to highlight some of the relationships on the team. I understand you used to play with Campbell's father."

"That I did. I owe Mark Campbell more than I could ever repay. I have to say, I'm impressed that you haven't focused on the hoopla surrounding Golston any more than you have."

"In my opinion, there's a lot more going on with the team than just that. I'm trying to give a bigger picture."

"And I'd say you're succeeding." The doors opened again, and he pressed the button to keep them open while I made my way off into the bowels of the arena. In no time, he was walking alongside me. "I think we could work something out getting us all together. In fact, Rachel said that Eric and Dana Zellinger are planning on a trip to Portland during the next series so all the cousins can spend some time together. I bet we could even get the two of them to agree to be involved."

"Yeah?"

Jim nodded at the security guards standing outside the locker room, and one of them opened the doors to allow the two of us to pass, even though the rest of the press wasn't being given access just yet. "I'll see what I can do. I'll have Rachel set something up with you in the next few days."

I could hardly believe my luck with how it was all starting to come together. "Thanks, Jim. That sounds amazing."

"Just keep doing what you're doing," he said. Then he veered off to join the coaches in Bergstrom's office—I glanced inside long enough to see Ben with his handheld camera trained on Adam Hancock, the assistant coach who was currently speaking—and I made my way in to see the team's reaction and make sure Dave and the rest of my guys had repositioned themselves already.

Sure enough, Dave had his tripod set up not far from Nate's stall, and the other members of the crew were scattered throughout the locker room with their equipment ready to go.

Most of the guys were quietly taking off their uniforms and equipment, but Nicky Ericsson was standing in the middle of the room with their ugly purple umbrella hat in his hands.

"There are a few guys who deserve this fucking thing tonight," he said, flipping it around so it spun in the air almost like a top. "I could give it to Ghost, for basically putting the game away when they were trying like crazy to tie it up."

Several of the guys clapped or made murmurs of assent. I glanced over and caught a slight hint of embarrassment in the way Nate ducked his head as he unlaced his skates.

"I could give it to Harry, because I have to tell you—I haven't seen a defensive game like that in so long I don't remember it. How many fucking shots did you block, anyway?"

Harry looked down at his left leg, which appeared to be turning purple from top to bottom. He shrugged. "A few."

"Maybe next time, let me handle a few more of those," Nicky teased. "At least I've got the right gear on for it."

The team laughed, and a few of them said some things that I might end up bleeping out if we used this footage because of the young fans watching at home.

Out of the corner of my eye, I saw Ben and most of the coaching staff making their way out of the coach's office and into the locker room.

"But there's someone else that I think deserves to wear this umbrella more tonight," Nicky said. "Harry wasn't the only one who saved my bacon tonight. I got myself out of position during that scramble at the end, and 501 didn't even think twice when he took my place. He didn't have the mask or the pads. Hell, he didn't even have a goalie stick. But the son of a bitch planted his ass on that goal line, and there wasn't anything getting past him. By my count, he had four saves before I was able to get back into position. Whoever tracks the stats is probably giving those saves to me, but I didn't touch that fucking puck. That was all 501."

"Damn it, 501," Jamie Babcock said, winking at his brother.

"Don't forget to fucking hashtag it," Levi said, taking the umbrella hat and putting it on his head while the rest of the team applauded and ribbed him.

With that out of the way, Riley Jezek turned up the volume on his iPod, letting the strains of "Uptown Funk" fill the room while the guys finished changing out of their gear. A few minutes later, the coaches let the media in. The room was swarmed with the biggest crowd I'd seen around this team outside of the Stanley Cup Finals last season.

Sure enough, the majority of them headed straight for Nate. A few stragglers scattered around to talk to Jamie Babcock and Nicky Ericsson, and one went for Levi Babcock before he was able to hide the purple umbrella hat among his things.

My guys slipped into position, virtually unnoticed by anyone but me.

Since everything seemed to be going according to plan, I thought it would be an excellent opportunity for me to find somewhere quiet to get off these stupid crutches and put my ankle up. I headed into the hall, well away from all the press, and found a bench not far from the recently vacated coach's office.

At least, I'd assumed it was recently vacated and I was away from all of the press. One reporter was in Coach Bergstrom's office, with a handheld voice recorder shoved into David Weber's face.

"So you don't have any idea at all about what sort of announcement your son is planning to make?"

"None," Weber said. "Maybe some NHL team offered Luke the opportunity to sign on as a free agent, so he's electing to forgo his senior year. If that's it, I can tell you it wasn't the Storm. I don't know, though. You'll have to ask him."

"But if he was signing with an NHL team, surely he would have said something to you about it. To his family."

"Well, that could be why he's waiting until next week to announce whatever it is," Weber said, exasperation coming through in every word. "Maybe he wants to speak to me and his mother first, before it becomes official."

"So you don't think it's anything…" The reporter trailed off.

"Anything what?" Weber demanded. "Why don't you save us both some time and get to whatever it is you're hinting at?"

"There are rumors floating around campus at the University of Minnesota."

Weber raised a brow and crossed his arms, taking on a posture that should have left the reporter quaking. Lord knows I would have been if I were on the other end of that glare. "You're seriously standing here and grilling me over some rumors about my son right now? *This* team just won a playoff series. We're getting ready to face our next opponent, whoever that may be. I don't have time to play around over some silly rum—"

"They're saying that your son, Luke Weber, has been seen at some gay clubs in Minneapolis," the reporter cut in.

"*They're* saying," Weber repeated darkly. "Who's they? Or is it just you?"

I wished I'd had Ben remain in the coach's office instead of heading back into the locker room among the players once he'd finished filming the coaches' discussion. Or that I had a camera of my own. Something. Anything. But I didn't, and there was no time for me to rectify the situation, because now that he'd gotten started, this guy rushed to get the rest of it out before he lost his nerve.

"That's been the big talk on campus since early last semester," the reporter said, not bothering to answer Weber's pointed question. "Everyone's speculating that he's going to come out next week, that he wants to put an end to all the rumors and admit that there's truth to them."

Within the span of a few seconds, the initial shock that registered on David Weber's face evaporated, to be replaced with an expression of utter disdain. "And?"

"And what do you have to say about that?"

Stone-cold glare. It went on for so long I was shocked the reporter didn't give up and excuse himself or move on to something else. But the guy stood there, handheld recorder pressed up next to Weber's face, and waited him out.

Despite myself, I was impressed. That took some serious guts.

Finally, Weber said, "I don't have anything to say. I don't know why my son is holding a press conference next week, and even if I'm lying to your face, even if I *do* know, and even if you're right, there's not a chance in hell that I would tell you so. Because if that's what my son is holding a press conference to tell the world next week, then it's his news to tell. Not mine."

Then without another word, Weber pushed past the reporter and left the coach's office, giving me a curt nod as he left. To let me know he knew I'd heard every word of it? Or to give me the go-ahead to use what I'd heard?

But it didn't matter. I hadn't gotten it on film. I couldn't use it. I could only do my best to prepare my team to capture whatever might be on the horizon next week, if these rumors turned out to be true.

There was a part of me that was glad I hadn't had a camera on him then.

Maybe I wasn't cut out for this job after all. Maybe my guys were right.

I was still mulling it all over a few minutes later when Nate sat next to me. When I glanced over at him, he grinned, making me wish I could talk to him about my predicament. But since he was one of the reasons behind the dilemma, it didn't exactly seem fair to dump it on him. I needed to figure out someone else I could talk to about it, but I didn't have the first clue who that would be. Maybe I could call Dad tomorrow. He should have the day off since it was Easter Sunday.

"How's the ankle?" Nate asked.

I shrugged. "Better than my armpits."

He burst out laughing. "They really need to figure out something better for when you hurt a leg. Crutches are a bitch."

"Nice couple of minutes at the end, there," I said.

He shrugged. "All in a day's work."

"Yeah, sure. All in a day's work if you're a super-elite athlete giving everything he has…"

"So, are you working on the flight home tonight?"

"Maybe. Are you studying?"

"Maybe. Mind if I steal the seat next to you?"

I shook my head.

"Would you be offended if I tried to casually put my arm around your shoulders on the plane? I'm pretty damn smooth. You might not even notice me doing it until it's too late."

This was one of those moments I was glad my skin wasn't as fair as some of my cousins. My blushes didn't show up very well, so he might not realize I was thoroughly embarrassed and excited. I tried to keep cool. "I wouldn't be offended by that as long as you wouldn't get upset if I let my head fall on your shoulder."

He nodded, his lips pursed in thought. "I think we could work something like that out."

"Yeah?"

"Yeah."

No matter how calm and collected I might appear on the outside, inside it was like the butterflies in my belly had started a conga line. I had no idea where this was heading, but I had every intention of seeing it through to whatever end.

Chapter Nine

Anne

"YOUR COUSIN TOLD me you're being unreasonable," Dad said over our Easter brunch. We were doing brunch instead of breakfast because the team plane hadn't landed at PDX until about three in the morning, and there was no chance I was getting up before ten at the earliest. He reached for his mimosa and winked, not that I needed confirmation that he was teasing more than admonishing me.

"Padma?" I asked. Not that it really mattered which cousin, but I assumed it was her since she'd been on my back recently.

He nodded.

"Why are you talking to Padma about me?"

"She called me. I have no idea why she thought it would help, but she seems to be under the impression that I could—or would—attempt to convince you to do the *right thing*, whatever that may be."

While a mimosa sounded great, I'd settled for coffee. Not decaf this time, either. I'd asked our waitress to brew a fresh pot extra strong...and to leave the pot. "I'm sure she did."

"Do I want to know what you did this time? She never filled me in on that part of it, and I never asked."

"Only the same as always. I refused to apologize to my mother when she's the one who should apologize again."

"Padma seems to think you're cutting off the entire family."

"Padma *needs* to see that it's the family cutting me off and not the other way around. But I doubt that's ever going to happen. Not while my mother continues to spread her woe-is-me garbage among her relatives."

Dad studied me for so long it left me squirming, but then he reached for the salt shaker and doused his eggs without saying a word.

"You should really try to eat more like you tell your patients they need to eat, you know," I muttered. He raised a brow and pointed to his plate that was filled with proteins and not many carbs. I pointed at the salt shaker. "You want them to cut back on salt and eliminate caffeine and alcohol. Oh, and let's not even bother to think about how much fat is on your plate right now. Probably as much as you allow them in a day."

"It's not about what I allow or don't allow. It's about them learning to eat in a new way that their bodies can handle after the changes to their digestive tract. They can't handle much fat because of the surgery. Besides, fat isn't what makes people fat. Carbs are. But after surgery, too much fat will make them sick. Their stomachs can't process it. I haven't had bariatric surgery, so I eat a generally healthy diet for someone whose digestive tract is normal."

"Plus ten times as much salt as you should have."

"My cardiologist says my heart is perfectly fine and I don't need to worry about my salt intake."

"Mm hmm. For now," I said, but I dropped it. For the most part, Dad took really good care of himself, so I shouldn't nag him about those few things he did that were unhealthy. We all had faults, and he was no different. "Just be glad your patients don't watch you eat. They'd be all over you about it, I bet you anything."

"I know one of them would, for sure."

"Yeah?" I raised a brow, scooping up some oatmeal. "Who's that?"

"Beatriz Castillo. Bea's a little over a year out from bypass. Lost about 140 pounds so far. She's a firecracker. Every time she comes in for a checkup, she spends half the time telling me all sorts of things I could do to get my staff to be more efficient and offering to bring in some of her students so they could teach us."

I raised a brow, refilling my mug of coffee. "Her students?"

"She's a special education teacher for one of the local high schools. She's always trying to find ways to get her kids out into the community, but I'm not sure volunteering in a bariatric surgeon's office is ideal."

"I don't know," I said, shrugging. "Might help teach them empathy for other people, or maybe show them they aren't the only ones who're different. Those things can be problematic for kids with autism and whatnot."

"Which Bea is all too happy to point out at every opportunity she gets." Dad winked. "Along with anything and everything else that comes to her mind, usually as soon as the thought strikes her."

"She sounds like a woman who knows what she wants."

"She does. And right now, what she wants is something I have no idea how to give her. Clothes that flatter her new body."

I raised a brow, my mind racing back to that conversation I'd overheard between Katie and Dani the other day. "I suppose she's got lots of problem areas after losing so much weight?" I said.

"They always do. Some of my patients have surgery after their weight loss to remove the excess skin, but a lot of them can't afford it. Insurance doesn't cover it. Even if they can, they have to live with the excess until their weight stabilizes." Dad studied me. "Your mind is going a thousand miles an hour. What's going on in there?"

"Just an idea."

He frowned.

"All right. Fine. I might be able to hook Bea up with someone who can design her a new wardrobe. If I can, will you put me in contact with her?"

He reached for the salt shaker again and doused the sausage patty he was about to eat. "I can do that. On one condition."

"What kind of condition?" I asked warily. My father wasn't the manipulative one out of my parents, but if he had any thought of forcing me into doing something with Mom…

"I want to meet your new man."

That was the last thing I'd been expecting. It took me so thoroughly by surprise that I dropped my fork, and it clattered against my plate.

Then it was Dad's turn to raise a brow. "You didn't think I knew, did you?"

"Knew what? What new man?"

"Nate Golston. That hockey player. The one who had a banana peel thrown at his feet a couple of weeks ago."

"Why do you think he's my man?"

"Just something I saw on Twitter."

Now he'd really thrown me for a loop. "What are you doing on Twitter?" I couldn't wrap my head around the idea of my father doing anything on social media. He abhorred using the computer, and he only did because it made life easier in his practice. He didn't own a tablet of any sort. Somehow, he still had a flip phone instead of a smartphone. The man was as technology-phobic as they came, unless it involved a new medical advance in his field.

"Trying to figure out how many of those assholes who post things about you are people I really need to worry about," he said matter-of-factly. "I've been talking to my lawyer to see if there's anything we can do about all the threats being made against you."

I was pretty sure my jaw would be sore tomorrow, it had dropped so hard and fast. "They're not real threats."

"How can you be sure?" He took another bite of bacon, going about his meal as though he hadn't just dropped a bomb on me.

"Because they're just idiots who think they can say anything they want because they're protected by the anonymity of the Internet. The police won't bother looking into it. It's too complicated to try to track someone down over what are almost always baseless threats just meant to scare someone."

"But sometimes these people really act on their threats," he insisted. And he was right, even if I'd rather not admit it. There'd been enough reports in the news for me to know the truth of the situation. Reports of women—often journalists in traditionally male-dominated fields or outspoken feminists—who'd been subjected to online threats, which were then acted out. My father was right, darn it. "Who's to say that next time, instead of some racist buffoon throwing banana peels on the ice, it's not going to be some sexist ignoramus following you to your car? These things happen, you know."

"Not *that* often," I said, with full knowledge of the feebleness of my argument. The fact that it happened at all was enough to convince my father to worry. Admittedly, the idea of Dad being concerned enough to check Twitter to see what people were saying about me and had been talking to a lawyer meant he was an awesome dad. Maybe he was a bit intrusive, but his curiosity was forgivable in the long run. Especially because it meant he cared enough to delve into this part of my life.

"Often enough," he said. "Anyway, my lawyer is keeping a close eye on a few of them and talking to the police to see if we can file any sort of official reports against the worst offenders. Online harassment or something. I'll let you know what he says. But, in the midst of all my research, I stumbled on some tweets between Golston's teammates about the two of you."

"What kind of tweets?" Maybe I should break my own rule and take a look at what was happening on social media more often instead of leaving it all to Tim. If I had, I might have known what my father had found. It wouldn't have prevented this conversation, but it could have prepared me for it, if nothing else.

"The kind where they talk about him being, and I quote, your *lover boy*. So I want to meet him."

"He's not my lover boy."

"So you didn't fall asleep with your head on his shoulder on the plane last night?" Dad asked, his tone full of teasing. This was worse than him attempting to pull off Dad Jokes. "And before you try to lie about that, one of them posted a picture."

"Who did?"

"Riley Jesus or something like that."

"Jezek," I corrected him.

"That's the one. So when am I going to get to meet this Golston?"

"I don't— We're not—" Augh, this wasn't at all what I'd intended to talk to my father about this morning. And if the guys on the team were posting pictures of me and Nate all over social media, then any chance I might have once had of keeping my job—however slim—was now gone. No doubt, my boss would be calling me first thing tomorrow morning to tell me I'd been fired. Or at least that I would be as soon as the season came to a close, one of the two.

"Looked like you two were nice and cozy," Dad said.

"I don't know what we are."

"Has he taken you on a date?"

"Coffee. And dinner," I amended. And hours of talking.

"Has he kissed you yet?"

Again, I was grateful that my cheeks didn't really turn pink when I blushed. At least he'd only asked about a kiss and not anything beyond that. "Not yet."

"But you want him to," Dad said with a great deal of certainty.

"Maybe."

"That could prove to be problematic with your job, couldn't it?"

I shrugged. "There's no chance I'll still have this job next season, anyway, so does it really matter?"

"You tell me. I was under the impression that you wanted to prove you could do this as well as any man. That you wanted to make your mark in sports journalism. You were all gung-ho about paving the path for other women to follow, but I don't know how that can happen if you throw it away."

"I'm not throwing anything away! And to hear that coming from you, of all peop—"

"You know I don't think that," he cut in, hands up in surrender. "But that's the picture they'll paint. That's the story they'll try to sell."

"Well, I have my own story to tell."

Dad nodded thoughtfully. "I know you do." Total and complete acceptance, without a moment's hesitation. That was how Dad had always been with me—the complete opposite of my mother. It was nice to know some things didn't change, even if I wished so many others would.

"I just don't know if I'm doing the right thing," I whined.

"What do you mean? With Golston?"

"No. Not exactly." I reached for my coffee, but apparently I'd already drained the whole thing.

Dad picked up the pot and refilled my mug, patiently waiting for me to continue.

"It's just…" I sighed, wishing it were easier to put into words. "If I get involved with him, how can I present an unbiased picture of him for this show? I don't think that's possible. And the closer I get to him, the closer I'm getting to his friends on the team, so there's no way I'll be able to be unbiased in how I'm editing them. And it *is* editing them, not just putting things out there like it's strictly journalism. This is more of a documentary. There has to be a story—a beginning, middle, and end, rising action, climax, and falling action, all of the things they talk about in fiction and screenwriting. So I can't just present the events as they unfold, can I? I have to put some sort of narrative twist on everything that happens, which has left me trying to find other stories to follow beyond Nate and the racist stuff, but now I'm running into the issue of things cropping up that should be private. They shouldn't be filmed and shared with the whole world. I know these people all signed release forms and whatnot, but were they counting on me breaking the news of their infertility or a family member maybe coming out of the closet? I don't think they were, but I'm still leaning toward using that kind of footage when I get it, because it'll take the heat off Nate. But is that right? And am I only doing it in a sick, twisted effort to salvage a job that I'm probably going to lose anyway?"

I finally stopped speaking only because I was about to choke up and start crying, and the last thing I wanted to do was cry in public. The only times I'd ever broken that rule had been stupid, academic things, like when I'd lost the spelling bee in the fifth grade after misspelling *errand*, one of the simplest words offered in the whole event.

I tried to settle my nerves by sipping from my coffee. When I looked up at Dad again, he was just staring at me. Not in judgment. Not in disappointment. Just staring.

"What?" I asked.

"Did you get it all out yet?"

I nodded. "I think so."

"Okay."

"So?"

"So what?"

"So what do you think I should do?" I demanded.

"I think you need to follow your gut. It's always led you down the right path before."

"Not with—"

"Even with your mother, it's led you to the right answer *for you*. It might not be the right answer for her or for your cousins. But it's the right answer for you and your sanity. Your gut led you to your college major. It led you to your first job after college. It got you this position, which, as you've said before many times, no one your age gets offered, and definitely not a woman. You've got the job. It's yours. Maybe not for long, but for now, it's yours. So what story is it you think you need to tell while you've got the platform? That's what I think you should do. Tell *your* story, and tell it the way you think it should be told. Ignore all the rest."

"But what if…?"

"What if you get fired? Sounds like that's already going to happen anyway. Might as well make the most of the opportunity in front of you."

Nate

ANY TIME SOMEONE asked if we'd rather face the Kings or the Blackhawks in the next round, there was a *correct* reply. Both teams would be worthy opponents, and we were more concerned with making sure we were rested and ready, no matter who we faced—something along those lines. In other words, a non-answer was the only appropriate response to the question.

In truth, those two teams *were* both formidable opponents, in many of the same ways. They'd each won the Cup in recent years, and the core of their Cup-winning teams remained intact, meaning they had the skill and experience to do it again. Not only that, but those guys knew what it felt like to reach the ultimate pinnacle in our sport, which gave them the drive and urgency to get there again.

The Blackhawks might have struggled more during the regular season, but that was only because they were part of the Central Division, which, to oversimplify matters, was the toughest division in the NHL right now. In that way, the Blackhawks might prove to be a more difficult adversary for us. They also played a more similar style to ours, as a team built around speed and skill more so than size and brute force.

The Kings were more of a hybrid. They could play our way, but they could also push us into playing a more physical game, which would surely give them an advantage. And, as the top seed in our division, they would have home-ice advantage over us, whereas we would have that benefit in a series against the Blackhawks.

But on a personal level, I would much prefer for the Kings to win Game Seven. I wasn't keen on dealing with the inevitable return of the attention if we had to go back to the same city where the banana peel incident had taken place…where Marcus Jameson was killed by a cop…where protests and demonstrations were heating up. The drama around me had finally started to die down, and the press was beginning to focus on the fact that we'd come together as a team and beaten the Sharks, and the press in Chicago was focusing more on the bigger picture of the racial tensions in the city and the nation.

I'd prefer to keep things moving in the current direction.

Maybe it was a ridiculous reason for me to hope for one opponent over another, but there was never much logic to be found in emotional responses—and if anyone deserved to react emotionally, it was me right now.

When we got home so late from San Jose, Bergy had announced he was giving us the full day off on Easter Sunday. We had at least a few days before the first game of the next series, and he said he wanted us all to get some rest. No practice. No film sessions. The guys who wanted to go in for treatment for their various ailments were welcome to do so, but otherwise we were free to spend the day with our friends and family. He wasn't requiring anyone to show up at the practice facility for any reason.

Briefly, I'd thought about hitting the gym, if nothing else, but then I thought better of it. My knee was killing me, so the more rest I could get, the better. But that meant I had no plans for how to spend my day.

RJ's brother had come into town, and so RJ and Amanda invited me to spend the day with the three of them. I wasn't keen on the idea of being slobbered on by Max and Lola all day, so I passed.

Koz was getting a few of the younger, single guys together at his place, too, but I wasn't in the mood to play designated driver or be the guy who made sure Koz didn't get arrested for groping a stripper. I turned down that invitation, too.

To be honest, I wanted to spend the day with Anne, but I hadn't thought to ask her before we'd said good-bye after getting back to PDX. And besides, she had family in the area. She'd probably want to spend the day with her father.

If she even celebrated the holiday. I didn't have any idea if she was Christian, Buddhist, Muslim, atheist…or just one of those people who celebrated holidays regardless of the religious meaning behind them. Any of the above was possible.

There was also a good chance she might spend the whole day working. The more time I'd spent around her lately, the more I realized she was a true workaholic, not to mention a perfectionist. As an NHL player, I devoted a lot of time and effort to the team and to bettering myself as a player, but she put me to shame in that regard. I'd never seen someone who was so devoted to her career.

For a couple of hours, I lounged around the house and debated whether I should call her up anyway to see if she wanted to get together. I *should* spend the day studying for finals, not that I wanted to. But before I could make up my mind to do either of those things, my phone buzzed with a text message from Harry.

Bored as hell. Hanging out with Hammer and Thor. Their kids are with their exes this weekend. Colesy's on the way. You coming too?

Colesy was what we called another of our teammates, Cole Paxton. After a momentary private chuckle over the juxtaposition of Thor and Hammer, which I doubted Harry had noticed when he'd plugged it into his phone, I tapped out a response.

Me: *Sounds like the over-the-hill, overpaid defensemen's guild meeting. Why would I want to be part of that?*

Harry: *If you come, we can be the overhyped, underperforming, short-as-fuck jackwads league. You coming or not?*

Me: *Your place?*

Harry: *Yes. Bring beer. We've got food.*

I grabbed a couple of six-packs and headed out the door with my phone pinging at me again. Assuming it was Harry with another request for booze or something, I swiped my thumb over the slider and stumbled into a message from Anne.

Actually, it was just a picture—of the two of us, her head resting on my shoulder while we both dozed on the flight home last night.

Fuck.

I tossed the beers on the passenger seat, climbed in, started the engine, then sent her a response.

Me: *Do I want to know how you got that?*

Anne: *My dad let me know it's on Twitter. Apparently, Riley Jezek posted it. Called you "lover boy." Now Dad wants to meet you.*

Yeah, *fuck* didn't even begin to cover it.

Me: *Do you want me to meet him?*

Anne: *I don't know. Are we at the meet-the-parents stage? We've barely been on a date, and we haven't even kissed yet.*

Good question. And one I didn't have a ready answer for. I wouldn't deny that the idea of moving things into that territory sounded great, even if I didn't know the first thing about her father or how he would react to me, but I doubted he'd be as bad as Webs had been when Babs started dating Katie.

If Anne wanted me to meet her father, maybe that meant we could move things along more quickly than we had been.

Me: *So if I kiss you next time I see you, will you be ready for me to meet your father? Because I'm game if you are.*

It seemed like an eternity passed before she responded. I almost gave up and started driving over to Harry's place, assuming I'd pushed too hard, too soon. But finally, my phone buzzed again, with a single-word response: *Yes.*

Chapter Ten

Nate

SPENDING EASTER WITH the guys turned out to be more fun than I'd anticipated. There was something about getting together with some of the older guys on the team, with no wives, girlfriends, fiancées, or kids around, and just shooting the breeze. I didn't do that often enough. Most of the time, I either hung out with RJ and Amanda or I stuck to myself and hit the books. When I did get together with a big group, it was usually with the younger, single guys—Koz's crowd, even though they all complained about him nonstop—but those guys wanted to party and goof off, which wasn't very appealing to me anymore. Maybe I was becoming an old fuddy-duddy.

I'd sure as hell been called worse things before. Everyone knew that after what had happened in Chicago a couple of weeks ago.

Anyway, we spent the day lounging around Harry's pool. It was the warmest it'd been so far this spring. He started up the grill. We ate, drank, and spent hours poking at each other like guys tend to do when there aren't any women around.

Harry's skin was turning pink and the sun was starting to set. About an hour ago, he'd put up an umbrella to block the sun's rays and put on more clothes and sunscreen to protect himself, but by that point it was too late to do any good. He was well on his way to lobster-ville when his phone buzzed for what had to be the tenth time since he'd made the changes. He glanced down at the screen briefly, but then he tugged his ball cap down over his face and ignored whoever it was trying to get in touch with him yet again.

"You ever going to answer that?" I asked.

"It's a text message, not a call."

"And? You could respond."

"Not if I want to still be alive after next time I see Webs, I can't."

Colesy and Hammer both busted up laughing.

"What?" I said. "What am I missing?"

Harry poked his head out again to stare at me. "Last time Dani Weber was home from school, she cornered me in the wives' room after a game and kissed me."

"And she's home again for the holiday weekend, I suppose."

"He's leaving out the best part," Hammer said, reaching into the cooler for another beer. He leaned across the table and grinned at me. "Webs saw the whole thing go down. *And* it was right after the big hushed-up arrest incident, so you can imagine Webs wasn't a happy father."

"Oh, shit," I said, trying not to burst out laughing. A few months back, instead of coming along with most of us to help Koz celebrate his birthday, Harry had gone off on his own. He still hadn't filled any of us in on exactly what he'd been doing that night, but he'd been arrested…and we'd all been too drunk to go bail him out. He'd ended up getting Webs involved, and the team's legal department had made sure nothing serious ever came of it, but there'd been more than just a hint of mystery surrounding Harry ever since that night. Not only that, but he seemed to have found a permanent spot on Webs's shit list. Surely seeing his youngest daughter kissing the guy hadn't sat well at all. Webs had taken a long time to give in on Katie, his older daughter, hooking up with Babs—and there weren't many who came more clean-cut than Babs. Harry couldn't even hope to come close.

"She kissed me, not the other way around," Harry argued. "Which is exactly what I fucking told Webs. I didn't encourage her in any way."

Colesy seemed ready to be done with the direction of our current conversation. He turned and asked me, "Did you see what RJ put on Twitter yet? Doesn't seem like him. I don't know why he would have done that."

"Ghost doesn't do Twitter," Harry said.

Hammer set his beer down on the table between us and raised a brow. "You don't do Twitter? How the hell, in this day and age, do you not do Twitter?"

"Hammer's got a point," Harry said, peeking at us from under his hat again. *"He's a fucking dinosaur, and he's on it. Why aren't you?"*

"Watch it," Hammer said. "I might have T-Rex arms, but if I catch you..."

"You won't have any problem catching him," Colesy said. "He'll be burned to a crisp."

"Hammer's only on Twitter to watch videos about how to braid his daughters' hair," I shot back. "Why would I need to see those? I don't want to see all the other shit that gets posted about me."

"They have hair videos?" Thor asked, ignoring me. Those had to be the first words out of his mouth in over an hour.

"You might have a little girl someday," Hammer replied, nodding in my direction. "Then we'll see how much you need hair videos. When my girls are with me, their mom's not here to help, but someone still has to do their hair. And trust me, if it's bad, I'll hear about it from all the moms at the park." Then he dug out his phone and pulled up some app or another. "YouTube's better than Twitter for hair tutorials. I'll show you which feeds to follow. And you can get good stuff on Pinterest, too."

Thor took out his phone, too, leaning over to follow along with what was on Hammer's screen.

I rolled my eyes. "See what I mean? But to answer your question, yes, I saw what RJ fucking posted. Anne's father saw it first, actually, and he pointed it out to her. Haven't talked to the asswipe yet. Thought it would be better for me to calm down before I rip his throat out or do something else just as stupid."

"You should tell him to delete it," Colesy said, like it was as simple as that. Maybe in his world, it was. He never seemed to get caught up in all the drama that sometimes took place around the locker room, like with the way he'd changed the subject away from Harry's dilemma just now. He kept to himself a lot, other than hanging out with Burnzie.

"Deleting it won't do much good now," I pointed out. "Her father's already seen it, and now he wants to *meet* me."

Harry let out a slow whistle, and the rest of the guys laughed. "At least I'm not the only one with daddy drama," he said.

I shrugged it off. That was just how it went when you got a bunch of the guys together for any reason. "If he's seen it, you know the higher-ups in her production company have, too. It's too late to change anything." Too late to change things for the better, at least. Things could definitely get worse, and they *might*, depending on how meeting Anne's father went. Or what her boss thought. No point in worrying about that until it happened, though.

But I could at least make sure RJ didn't do anything as stupid as that again. I didn't exactly need him fucking things up for me with Anne before we really got started.

MONDAY MORNING, I hit the trainers' room early before practice, hoping for some relief. Despite all my efforts to stay off it and hope whatever was wrong would heal on its own, that wasn't happening. When I rolled out of bed, my knee was more swollen than it had been since the injury. And it was stiff. Not a good sign.

I was still wary of walking in and telling them I needed to have it checked out, because they might decide to prevent me from playing through it, but the fact remained—with as swollen as it was right now, there was no chance I'd be able to hide it from them for long. Better to be up front about it than to lie and try to hide it. If I got lucky, they could give me a few treatments and I wouldn't have to sit out any games at all, or maybe only a handful.

I wasn't expecting to walk in and see Anne sitting on one of their exam tables, though. She had her injured ankle up and unwrapped so Ken Archer, the head trainer, could take a look at it.

Archie held her leg in one hand and her foot in the other, putting pressure on it at various angles and rolling it around. "No pain when I do any of this?"

She glanced up and saw me, then bit her lip and turned her attention back to him. "Nope. I think it's good."

"You just saying that because you're sick of the crutches, or do you really mean it?"

"I'm done with the crutches whether you think I should ditch them or not," she said. "I've got blisters on my underarms and my palms. Not worth it."

"Hmm," Archie said, scowling as he continued to manipulate her foot.

She didn't wince or try to pull away, so either she really didn't feel any pain or she was a good actress.

"All right. No more crutches, but you should keep it wrapped while you're on your feet for at least a few more days. And try not to be on your feet as much as you usually are."

"Ha. Good luck with that one," she said.

He gave her the same kind of stern look he always gave us when we tried to come back too soon from an injury. "It's healing, but it's not fully healed. Unless you want to set yourself back, you'll do what I say."

The look she gave him in response was one that rivaled his, but she reached for the ACE bandage and started rewrapping it. "I've never been very good at doing what I'm told."

"I got that impression already, strangely enough." But Archie left her to take care of herself and came over to me. "What's going on with you? That knee acting up?"

"You could say that." I hopped up on the nearest table and pulled the leg of my pants up so he could see.

"How long's it been that swollen?"

"Woke up with it this way this morning. And it's stiff. A little better now that I've been moving around on it some, but it's not great."

Archie started poking around, moving the joint and whatnot to see what he could learn. I glanced over to find Anne putting on her shoe but peeking at me. I winked at her, but then Archie pressed a finger into a certain spot, and I hissed in a breath.

"Has it still been bothering you since that night you hurt it?" he demanded.

"Yes."

"And you were scared I'd make you sit."

"Yeah. That about sums it up."

He scowled, but he didn't seem surprised. I was surely not the first pro hockey player he'd ever dealt with who'd tried to hide an injury, and I wouldn't be the last, either.

"Did you hear a pop when it happened?"

"Nope."

Out of the corner of my eye, I caught a glimpse of Anne picking up her backpack and a few other things, but it appeared she was taking her time about it. So she wasn't in any big hurry to leave? Fine by me. I kind of hoped we'd be able to talk for a minute or two, now that we were in the same place.

"Are you having any problems with stability?" Archie asked, still working the joint so much I was tempted to kick him.

"None. It just hurts. And it's swollen and stiff."

"Where does it hurt, specifically?"

"I don't know," I said, trying to pinpoint it in my mind. But to be honest, the pain was just kind of all over the place, not in any one spot.

"It's just the whole knee."

Archie nodded and finally let go of my limb. "All right, so here's the deal. My guess is you've at least strained or sprained your ACL, but we're going to have to do an MRI to determine that for sure and understand just how bad it is."

"And once we know that?" I asked, dreading his answer.

He sighed. "If it's just a sprain and not a tear, Doc will probably let you keep playing on it because we're in the playoffs. He might have you sit for a couple of games to rest it, but after that, he'll probably leave the ultimate decision up to you."

"Which means I'll be playing."

Archie chuckled. "Sounds like it."

"But if it's a tear?"

"I don't know what'll happen if it's a tear. You'll need surgery to correct it, but you've still been playing on it, so…" He shook his head. "I'm not the doctor. It might not even be your ACL. I don't know. You'll have to take it up with Doc, no matter what the diagnosis is. But for now, I'm putting in a call to him, and then I'm sending you over to the hospital for an MRI. And don't keep shit like this from us, dumb ass," he said, knocking me lightly on the side of the head. "You could have been making a small problem worse this whole time."

Then he walked out, and Anne gave me a sheepish look.

"Didn't mean to walk in on you like that," I said.

She shook her head. "I don't care. It doesn't matter." She shrugged. "I probably should have left when I was done and not listened in."

"That's your job. To listen in." I winked.

"No cameras here, so I should be minding my own business."

"Listen," I started, not really sure how to say what was on my mind, "I just wanted to say I'm sorry about that picture. I'm going to have it out with RJ. He knows better than to post things like that—"

"Don't worry about it."

"But I *am* worried about it. That's the thing. I mean, I don't give a rat's ass if the whole world sees that I'm into you. Because I am." I angled my head toward her to emphasize my words. "I'm *really* into you, even if it would be better for me—well, better for you, I guess—for me to stay away from you. But I know things are different for you. With your family, maybe. Definitely with your job…"

"Don't worry about my job. Let me worry about that." Anne took a seat next to me on the exam table, and her arm brushed against mine. She shivered.

I turned so I could see her eyes. "Are you? Worried?"

"Not exactly. I mean, yeah, I'm expecting my boss to call me in for a meeting sometime today, but if it wasn't this, it'd be something else."

"What do you mean?" I couldn't wrap my head around the fact that she sounded so completely resigned, like it was inevitable for her job to be in jeopardy.

"Just that if it's not this, it'll be something else. They'll find some other reason to replace me." She punched my upper arm. "Hey. No sad faces. I've known all along that I didn't have long in this position. It's not like it's any big surprise."

"It's bullshit, that's what it is."

Her smile was enough to ease the ache in my knee. "Glad you think so, at least. But seriously, the picture's not a big deal, even though I didn't know about it up front. Don't do anything to ruin your friendship with Jezek over that."

"RJ's the one who made the decision to post it."

"And you can be the one who decides to take the high road. Be the bigger man."

I laughed and winked. "At least this once, I can be bigger than him."

She just shook her head, her lips pursed to keep her from laughing out loud.

"I know I basically promised to kiss you next time I saw you," I said, glancing around the trainers' room. It felt like a doctor's office, only there was a permanent stench of sweaty hockey pads instead of the typical cold, sterile scents. "I wasn't counting on this being that moment, though."

"Not too romantic, huh?" she said, stifling a grin. "Good thing I've never been the romantic sort."

"No?"

"I spend too much of my time around men."

"Some men can be romantic."

"Sure they can." She narrowed her eyes to sarcastic slits and nodded slowly.

"Should I take that as a challenge?"

"I wouldn't know what to do with you if you went all romantic on me."

There was no chance in hell I could stop myself from grinning…and from considering myself duly challenged, whether she thought she wanted it or not. "I might like to see that."

"Hmm."

We were still alone. A glance over my shoulder confirmed it. And I *had* promised to kiss her. I leaned in, my lips close enough to hers that I could feel her warmth. She had a cinnamon scent on her breath, strong and spicy. Seemed fitting.

Those honey-gold eyes stayed on mine, reflecting both desire and surprise.

But Archie threw open the door before I got my kiss in, interrupting us and destroying the moment.

Probably for the best, anyway. Stale hockey pad stench wouldn't make for a good memory to go with a first kiss.

Anne

DAVID WEBER SKATED over to me as the team was leaving the ice after practice. Nate hadn't been out there with them—he'd gone to the hospital for his MRI, and there hadn't been any further update since he'd left—but otherwise, most of the team had been involved, other than a couple of the older guys who were nursing injuries that would have kept lesser men completely out of games as opposed to simply missing a few practices.

It had been a relatively upbeat session, the guys proving to have a lot more energy than I did, despite the fact that they'd already completed an eighty-two-game regular season and a tough six games in the first round against the Sharks. The meeting this morning with my boss had drained almost every ounce of gumption out of me, and all I wanted to do was crash in bed and not come out for a week.

In short, I wasn't fired—yet—but only because they didn't have anyone in line to replace me. Yet. Oh, and because my guys had all threatened to walk out if they kicked me to the curb. In short, if I left, they'd have no film crew, no editor, no footage… They wouldn't have anything. So they were stuck with me. But more than ever before, I knew I was living on borrowed time.

Too bad Archie had walked in on us before Nate had kissed me. A kiss would have done a world of good in terms of boosting my ego right now. But that hadn't happened, and I didn't know when it would, so all I wanted to do was sulk.

In fact, going home and digging into a vat of ice cream covered in chocolate and caramel syrup sounded like an excellent idea. With a banana. I could make it a banana split. That would make it *healthy*, or at least healthy enough that I wouldn't feel any guilt about it.

I couldn't do any of that until I figured out what David Weber wanted from me, though.

He'd seemed to be in a good mood, relatively speaking, throughout the team's practice, but that didn't give me much reassurance. I still remembered the glare he'd given that reporter in San Jose, and in my current state of sulking, I didn't think I could handle being on the receiving end of one of those.

"You planning on working tonight?" he asked. "Or are you taking time off?"

Not what I was expecting. At all. "The guys and I were going to get together in about half an hour to discuss what we could film tonight, so I'm not sure yet." My hope was that they could each figure out somewhere to go, something to do, that wouldn't require my presence. Sometimes, a person just needed a night alone.

Weber nodded thoughtfully. "Well, if you and one of your guys want to come over to my house tonight, you'd be welcome. My youngest daughter's still in town until tomorrow morning. We're going to watch Game Seven in the Kings-Blackhawks series together."

I nodded, but there wasn't anything about that to interest me more than my enormous banana split, so I doubted I'd take part in it. I could send Ben, though…

"And we're expecting a call from Luke," he added with a meaningful look. "His press conference is scheduled for tomorrow afternoon."

There wasn't any mistaking the fact that he was fully opening himself and his family up to me this time, no matter what this call might be about. "You're sure?" I asked. "Because I know you signed the releases and all—"

"We're sure. I've talked it over with Laura, Dani, and Katie. Luke's opening up to the press tomorrow, whatever it's about, so there's not really any difference where he's concerned."

"But shouldn't it be a private thing at first? Just the family?"

"Isn't that what *Eye of the Storm* is all about? Showing the world what it's really like to be part of this family?"

Well, then. There wasn't much I could say to that.

Chapter Eleven

Anne

LAURA WEBER HAD been nursing the same glass of red wine for the last thirty minutes, taking nervous sips that I was sure Ben's camera was picking up while her focus was supposedly on the television. She'd been perfectly friendly toward the two of us, offering food and drink and acting more like a hostess than someone having her personal life invaded for other peoples' entertainment, but now that her husband's focus had switched to the game, her nervous tics were starting to make themselves known.

During the first intermission, they'd shown coverage of the protest in downtown Chicago from this afternoon. Tensions had been very high, but thank goodness there hadn't been any violence—just a lot of yelling on both sides. But no one had taken out a weapon. I was honestly worried about that, especially with the possibility that the Storm would be heading to Chicago soon for the second round of the playoffs.

The Blackhawks and Kings were tied at two in the second period, and David Weber was oblivious to everything going on around him.

Dani had gone between halfheartedly watching the game and passing surreptitious glances in her mother's direction, clearly worried but seemingly unsure how to make things better for her. I doubted there was anything to be done. Until Laura learned what this phone call and the impending press conference were about, she was going to behave like a Nervous Nellie.

Normally, I didn't interrupt when we were filming unless we were doing a segment that was more like an interview or confessional. Otherwise, I did my best to stay out of the way. Tonight seemed like an excellent opportunity to help someone out, though, and we were in a holding pattern until Luke Weber decided to call his parents, so I decided to break my own rule.

I waited until Dani got up to refill her drink, and I followed her to the kitchen. Ben gave me a questioning look, so I shook my head, letting him know to stick with the parents. This wasn't anything he needed to get on film.

"I hope you don't mind me coming to you like this," I said once Dani turned around and saw me. She smiled slightly, even if it looked like she was putting on a show for my benefit. I hoped what I wanted to bring up would help. "But the thing is, I couldn't help but listen in on your conversation with your sister the other day, and I've got an idea I wanted to run by you—about your independent study for this summer."

Suddenly, she got a lot more interested, perking up and raising a brow. "Yeah? What's that?"

"See, my dad is a bariatric surgeon. He does weight loss surgery," I added, since most people didn't get it at first, and she was giving me a questioning look. "So a lot of his patients have lost a hundred pounds or more, but they're still kind of lumpy in places, or they have loose skin that gets in the way. It's really hard for them to find clothes that fit right and look good. He's got one patient who's a little over a year out from her surgery. She's lost a ton of weight and is holding steady, but it's still too soon to get any sort of plastic surgery to deal with it, and she might not be able to afford it...so she needs clothes that work with her body, not against her."

The longer I talked, the more excited Dani became. Her eyes lit up like a fireworks display. "And you think she'd let me do a makeover for her? I mean, I'm still just a design student. I don't have my own line or anything."

"I think she would. If you want to talk to her—"

"*Yes*, I want to talk to her. I'm supposed to go back to Seattle tomorrow, but I could call her in the morning. Or better yet, I can meet her in person. Take some measurements. Get a feel for her style and what she's looking for. Oh my goodness. This is the best thing *ever*."

I frowned. "Not sure that'll work. She's a teacher. She's got to go to work, and I don't know when her planning period is…"

"Then I'll wait until after school tomorrow to meet with her, and I'll drive back to Seattle after that."

"Won't you miss classes?"

"Yeah, but it'll be worth it for this," Dani insisted. "And besides, that'll give me the chance to… Well, never mind that." She shook her head and grinned. But it wasn't any normal grin. It was the sort of look that said her plans to take over the world were clicking into place, and we'd all better watch out.

Whatever else she was thinking of sounded more than just a bit devious, based on her tone, but I didn't get the chance to try to deter her from doing anything she might regret later—because the phone rang.

We both looked at each other, with understanding flowing through the space between us. Without another word, we headed back into the living room, where her father was muting the television with his cell phone pressed to his ear. Dani took a seat on the couch between her parents.

"Hey, Luke," he said before falling silent for a moment. "Yeah, your mom and Dani are with me. We've got a camera crew from *Eye of the Storm* here, too. Is it all right if I put you on speaker?"

Luke must have given his agreement, because his father lowered the phone and pressed the button. I glanced over to be sure Ben was catching everything, my gut clenching in anticipation. I'd never witnessed anyone coming out to their family before, and the emotional side that I tried to always keep in check when I was working was going haywire. I couldn't imagine being in any of their shoes. The way they reacted in the beginning would have such a huge effect on all their lives going forward.

"Hi, Mom," Luke said. It sounded like he had a cold, but my guess was that he'd been crying. In fact, he might be crying right now.

"Hi, baby," she replied. She gripped her wineglass tighter, but everything about her seemed unsteady. Dani took the wine from her mother and set it on the coffee table, where it would be out of harm's way.

"So I just wanted you guys to hear it from me first, because I'm sure it's going to blow up as soon as the press conference happens tomorrow," Luke said. He started to go on, but his father interrupted him.

"I just have to say something before you say whatever it is you called to tell us. We love you. You're our son, you're Dani and Katie's brother, and we love you. We're behind you, no matter what. And there's nothing you can do or say to change that fact. Okay?"

About halfway through her husband's speech, Laura started crying, silent but uncontrolled. Dani took her hand and squeezed. Based on the sounds coming from the other end of the line, she wasn't the only one crying. Heck, I was about to lose it, myself, and I had never met Luke before.

"I know that," Luke said, but those few words came out in fits and starts.

"Good," David replied. "Because if this is some ploy to run us off, you're shit out of luck. You got that?"

And everyone laughed, including me and Ben.

"So I guess you've figured out I'm trying to tell you I'm gay," Luke said, choking on some of the words but still powering through.

"So you're saying I have more competition with the cute guys," Dani teased, earning an eye roll from her father.

"I'm being serious here!"

"So am I," she countered. "Because, damn it all, you're a hottie."

"Oh my God," Luke said, but he was still laughing. "You're really turning this into a fight over guys?"

"What, did you want me to treat this like it's a big deal? It's not. You're still my big brother. Nothing's changed."

"I know, but—"

"But nothing. That's what we're all saying." Dani shrugged, not that he could see it through the phone. "Do you have a hot boyfriend? When do we get to meet him?"

"I don't— I'm not—"

"You just be sure that any guys you date aren't asswipes," their father said. "And if they are, they'll have to answer to me."

"Oh God," Luke said, an eye roll evident in his tone. "Dad, give it a rest with that. We're all adults now."

"If I'm gonna run the asswipes off from my little girls, it's only fair for me to do the same if some asswipe decides to chase after you."

The next few minutes passed with a lot more laughter than tears, although the occasional sniffle made itself known. But Laura hadn't said a thing. In fact, she hadn't been laughing as much as the rest, even if her tears had slowed and she appeared to be much calmer than she'd been before the phone rang...but Luke apparently noticed.

"Mom?" he said in a lull in the conversation. "You've been awful quiet."

"Have I?" she replied, reaching for a tissue.

"Yeah, you have. You okay?"

All the laughter died off while they waited for her to answer.

"I'm fine." But she didn't sound fine.

"You're lying," Luke said. "If you're not oka—"

"I'm just worried about you," she cut in.

"Worried about me? Why?"

"Because this isn't just you coming out to your family and friends. This is you making an announcement to the whole world—in a world that doesn't necessarily already love you. You've seen all the things that happen just because someone's gay. Our world isn't kind to anyone who's *different*, for whatever reason. And it's not like there's a huge community of other gay hockey players out there for you to lean on."

"I've got support, Mom. Not just my family, either. My team's standing beside me for this."

"I'm glad to hear that, but do you have any idea how big a mantle you're picking up with this? There's not a single *out* player in the NHL. You'll be paving new ground."

"If I even make it to the NHL, which right now, that's not looking good."

"Yeah, but if you do?"

A couple of moments passed before Luke said, "Someone has to."

"But why you?" Laura asked with a worry-filled ache in her voice. "Why not someone else?"

"That's the problem. Everyone keeps hoping someone else will do it. Someone has to be the first, Mom."

"And you're determined it has to be you," she said, sounding resigned.

"It has to be me because it's time for me to be myself, no matter what the fallout might be because of it. I'm tired of hiding. I'm tired of keeping secrets."

"Well, then..." Laura steeled her spine, like she was preparing to do battle. "I guess that's all there is to that."

They kept talking for a while, but I stopped paying such close attention. My focus strayed to thoughts of how it must feel to have a mother like Laura Weber. She might want different things for her children than they wanted for themselves, but she was ready and willing to fight for them, no matter what decisions they made. It was clear to me that her concern was because we lived in a world that could be less than accepting of anyone who was different…something I knew all too well. If only all mothers were cut of the same cloth.

After another ten minutes or so, Luke said he needed to call Katie so he could fill her in on the same thing, and they hung up. David went back to watching the game, with the Blackhawks pulling ahead while it had been muted. Laura headed into the kitchen to get more wine. Dani came over to me to continue our conversation about my proposal, and I left Ben filming in case anything else of significance took place. An hour later, when Ben and I packed up our gear and left the family in peace, I knew three things: the Storm would be facing off against the Blackhawks in the next round, I'd done at least one good deed with my day, and I had the beginnings of what could make for an incredibly powerful episode—and the blessing of the Weber family to use it—if only I could figure out the right context to present it.

By the time I crawled into my bed at the end of the night, I was as bone-weary as I could remember being. To say the day had been eventful would be putting it mildly. I was more exhausted than ever before on every front—physically, professionally, and especially emotionally. All I wanted to do was sleep for the next week.

Before I could fall asleep, though, my phone dinged with a text message. I was tempted to roll over and ignore it until tomorrow, but I'd never been able to do that any more than I could leave emails unread in my inbox at the end of the day. I swiped my thumb across the screen and found a message from Nate.

> *Thinking of you. Can I tear you away from your work tomorrow night? I want to follow through on what got interrupted this morning.*

Despite my exhaustion, my heart started racing just from reading those words, and I was right back in the moment when Archie had walked in and stopped us from kissing. It'd taken me almost an hour to get over my disappointment, once they'd sent Nate off to the hospital for tests, and my day had gone downhill fast after that, before coming to a climax at the Weber house.

I keyed in a response.

> Me: *I can be finished by six.*

Nate: *Pick you up then. Wear something nice.*

Nice? How nice? Suddenly, this was sounding a whole heck of a lot more like a date and less like a quick kiss. I did a quick inventory of my closet, but the only things I could think of that would qualify as *nice* were the usual suits I wore for work, and I somehow doubted that was what he had in mind.

I really needed someone to give me lessons on girly stuff. That was so not my forte. I hoped he didn't expect me to have on some cute dress or a flirty skirt, because I couldn't even remember the last time I'd worn something like that.

Although, a quick trip to the store on my lunch break might not be out of order. If such a thing could happen in such a short amount of time.

For a moment, I debated responding again and backing out, because that would be so much easier than trying to find something to wear on short notice.

But before I could do that, he sent me another text.

> It kills me that I have to wait that long to kiss you. I'm tempted to come over right now and take care of that, but I figure you've already changed for the night, and I'd have a hard time leaving. And I took your challenge for being romantic, so I'd better wait. Barging in like that wouldn't be very romantic of me.

It might not be romantic, but I wouldn't turn him away…a thought that warmed me through and left me tingling in all the right places.

I could find myself falling for Nate Golston if I wasn't careful.

I'd never been one to be overly careful when it came to making decisions that could impact my life. If I were, I'd be married to an Indian doctor and popping out babies like my mother wanted. Instead, I was treading water encouraging a relationship with a man that would almost definitely end my career.

Nate

THE MRI HAD shown a mild to moderate sprain to my ACL. Doc agreed to let me keep playing since I wasn't experiencing stability issues, with the understanding that I could potentially make the injury worse, and it might then require surgery. He told Bergy and the rest of the coaching staff to let me rest as much as possible, and he put me in a knee brace that I had to wear off the ice and was fitting me for one to wear during games. In addition to that, I had to ice it as much as possible and go in to see the trainers for treatment anytime I sat out of practice. Bergy then informed me that I would not be participating in practices until further notice, but only in game-day skates to get the blood pumping.

Since I intended to keep playing, Doc warned me to expect that it wouldn't fully heal until after we'd finished our playoff run, whenever that might be. Hockey was hard on a body—something we'd simply come to accept as a reality of our lives.

That said, this injury definitely wasn't proving to be the end of the world, and if I was lucky, it would heal up on its own before too long.

In my opinion, the fact that we were facing the Blackhawks in the next round was a much more difficult pill to swallow. I wasn't looking forward to the return of the media attention that had finally started to shift away from me in the last week or so, but I couldn't delude myself that it *would* do exactly that.

Unless something or someone else came along to take the attention off me.

I was in the trainers' room with Archie working on my knee when one of the other trainers flipped the TV from CNN's coverage of the protests in Chicago over to NHL Network, which was airing Luke Weber's press conference. The guy was still in college, not in the NHL, but that didn't seem to matter. The fact that a hockey player at this level was coming out—the son of a former NHL player and current NHL coach, no less—meant it was big news. Huge, even. The number of reporters who'd gone out to be part of it was astounding, given that the guy hadn't been drafted and had yet to sign with any NHL team as a free agent.

It was the sort of news that *might* deflect some attention away from me, but that was my selfish side talking.

It was also the sort of news that might keep Anne busy.

Again, with my selfish side rearing its ugly head. I needed to get that under control.

The other guys came off the ice after practice at about the time that the press conference was coming to a close. I caught sight of Anne and a couple of her camera guys shuffling down the hall past me on their way to Bergy's office—following Webs, it seemed—and hoped that maybe this was a sign that I was right.

She glanced back over her shoulder before heading into the office, and her gaze met mine. She winked in the moment before ducking inside.

Damn, but I couldn't wait for tonight.

ANNE CAME OUT wearing a soft green dress made of some fabric that practically floated on her skin, along with some strappy heels that I doubted Archie would approve of, given her barely healed ankle sprain. I didn't particularly care if he approved or not, at the moment, because the complete package was enough to nearly have me drooling.

I'd never seen her in anything that wasn't a business suit of some sort, usually in black, navy, gray, or brown—all bland and lacking in personality, even if she wasn't. The only real pop of color came in with whatever top she wore under the jacket. But in this, she looked like spring turned to human form.

"This okay?" she asked, sounding tentative as all hell. "You just said to wear something nice, but you didn't say what we were doing, so…"

"This is better than okay." I didn't understand how she could be so uncertain of herself. In some things, she was the epitome of confidence. Apparently not when it came to dating, though. It was kind of cute, in a way that made me want to kick the asses of any guy who'd ever overlooked her, or whatever it was. "You look amazing. Makes me think you should wear dresses more often. I didn't realize you had legs under there," I teased.

That only made her look even more self-conscious than before, wrapping her arms in front of her in a protective sort of gesture.

"Just trying to help you relax," I said. "I'm not giving you a hard time."

She shook her head. "I'm probably overreacting. I do that. When it comes to this kind of thing."

"This kind of thing?"

"Dating," she clarified. "I'm okay hanging out with guys when there's a bunch of them and we're talking about sports or whatever, but this is just…"

"Different," I finished for her when she trailed off.

"Right." She gave me a sheepish look.

"I get that. But I'm still the same guy I've been all along. I don't expect you to change anything about who you are. I'm into you already, exactly how you are."

"Yeah, but you like me in dresses…"

"I think it would be safe to say I'd like you in anything. Or nothing." I winked.

She bit her lower lip, which made me want to kiss her just there. But I had plans for that first kiss, and those plans didn't involve us still standing just outside her apartment.

"Come on. Let's get out of here." I held out a hand for her.

Anne hesitated for a moment, but then she placed her hand in mine and let me lead her out to my car. "Where is it we're going?" she asked as I held open the passenger-side door for her.

I waited until she'd safely settled the fluttering fabric, then closed the door and walked around the front to get in. "Will you kill me if I keep it a surprise until we get there?"

She gave me a look that said she might, but in the end, she consented.

I drove us to the waterfront park along the Willamette River and found somewhere to park.

"Here?" Anne asked. She looked around at all the office buildings and businesses. "I'm confused. What's going on down here?"

"We're taking a dinner cruise on the river."

"Oh." She sounded both surprised and awed. Her gaze traveled over to the Portland Spirit, which was docked and waiting for us to board.

I shut off the engine. "Not what you were expecting?"

"Not even close, not that I could tell you what I thought we were doing."

"It's okay, though?"

She smiled. "Better than okay. Much better."

"Good."

I reached for her hand as we crossed to the dock. She took it, and the soft fabric of her dress tickled my arm as it fluttered in the breeze. I handed in our tickets, and an employee guided us on board.

"Would you like to sit inside or out?" he asked.

"Out?" I asked Anne. The weather was nice enough, and sitting up top would give us a great view of the city at sunset.

"Outside is perfect," she agreed.

The worker led us up a couple of flights of stairs and seated us at a table for two. The candles were fake, but everything else was exactly what you'd expect at an upscale restaurant.

Another employee came along to give us menus, take our drink orders, and make sure we had everything else we needed as the other tables started to fill in around us, although there were several empty spots, as well. They must not have sold out tonight. Not a bad turnout for a weeknight, though. A few minutes later, a jazz trio started playing live music. When we left port not long before sunset, the waiter returned with our drinks and took our food order.

"I was afraid you were going to try to back out on me," I said after everyone left us on our own.

Anne blinked a couple of times. "Were you? Why?"

"Because of that press conference with Luke Weber this morning. I thought it was going to mean a lot more work for you, and you were going to choose that over me."

She smiled as she reached for her glass. "Well, you're in luck. I actually got a head start on the fallout from that."

I raised a brow.

"David Weber asked me to bring one of my guys over to his house last night, since Luke was going to call and fill the family in on whatever the presser would be about. So we got their immediate reactions already, and I had a plan in place with my team before anyone got to work this morning. My editor is already piecing some of it together as we speak."

"Sneaky," I said with a wink.

She laughed. "I prefer to think of it as being efficient. There's still a lot of work to do along those lines. We have to sort out the narrative arc of the episode. To do that, I'm going to have to somehow tie it in to you guys winning your first series, and the beginning of the next series. But that's something we'll work on as a team over the next few days."

"So you could come out with me tonight," I finished for her.

"So I could come out with you tonight." Anne bit her lower lip again, hiding a smile. "So... Your knee? How bad is it?"

"On the record or off the record?" I asked, then immediately wished I'd thought that through before speaking.

She didn't even bat an eye, though. "Off the record. No cameras here tonight."

"I didn't mean—"

"It's a fair question," Anne interrupted. "And it's probably good to get that out in the open. If any of my guys are around with their cameras, then assume things are on the record. If I'm with you in a social situation and not tagging along to film something, then it's safe to say we're off the record."

"I think it's easier to understand that when it comes to you and your guys than it is with my friends."

"Jezek didn't mean to cause any trouble. I'm sure he didn't."

"He says he didn't even post it to Twitter himself," I said—an answer that only pissed me off more. Why the fuck wasn't he keeping a closer eye on his phone than that? There'd been enough guys in the league to get into trouble over their friends getting hold of their phones and doing stupid shit as pranks. "He took the picture, but he claims he was just going to use it to tease me with. He thinks Amanda did it while he was napping, or something. He's deleted it now. Not that it did any good, I imagine."

Anne shrugged, brushing it off a hell of a lot more easily than I had. "You still haven't told me about your knee."

"ACL sprain. I get to wear a brace all the time and go in for treatments if the coaches don't need me in practice."

"No surgery?"

"No surgery." Unless I fucked it up worse than it already was.

"Good," she said, flashing the most amazing smile I'd ever seen.

The waiter brought out our appetizers. We kept talking as we ate, barely looking out at the amazing view. Looking at each other seemed to do the trick, instead. And once we'd gotten past the initial discomfort over RJ's stupidity, everything between us seemed to flow, with our natural flirtation coming back in full swing.

At one point, while she filled me in on how she'd set Dani Weber up with one of her father's patients for a school project, I reached across and teased the tips of her fingers with my own. It should have been a casual touch, but there was nothing casual about the electricity that seemed to flow back and forth between us in that moment.

We talked for what felt like hours, paying far more attention to each other than to our food. They brought out dessert and coffee not long before sunset. Most of the other tables around us had already been cleared off, the people who'd been sitting at them heading over to the railings to look out.

I still couldn't look anywhere but at Anne. Didn't want to. I couldn't care less how gorgeous the city skyline looked from the river at sunset. Not when she was looking at me like there was nowhere else she'd rather be.

Anne took a small bite from her crème brûlée, leaving the spoon in her mouth longer than was truly necessary. Savoring it.

And I couldn't wait any longer. She set down her spoon. I leaned across the table and cupped her cheek in my hand. She met me halfway like she'd been expecting it. But instead of the perfect kiss I'd been hoping to give her, our noses bumped, she jumped, our faces collided in such a way I worried she'd have a fat lip, she yelped, and the table collapsed underneath us.

Everyone on the top deck spun around to stare.

Anne looked at me, eyes wide.

And we both busted up, laughing so hard it hurt.

Chapter Twelve

Anne

DAD TEXTED ME on a break between surgeries the next day, telling me about the call he'd received from Bea Castillo and how she couldn't stop gushing about her meeting with Dani Weber. Apparently, I'd been right to set the two of them up. It left me with a smile, even if the rest of my day was hectic and stressed.

The first game of the Storm's second-round series was scheduled for tonight, but hockey was far from the only storyline my guys and I were suddenly covering. In fact, it was starting to feel secondary to everything else.

Luke Weber's press conference yesterday afternoon was completely dominating not only the typical sports media coverage, but it was trickling over into the mainstream media, as well, mingling with all the coverage of racial tensions around the nation. Suddenly, the media outlets trying to get time with the Storm—or more specifically, with David Weber—had quadrupled. It felt like a circus anytime I walked into the locker room, once the rest of the media had been allowed in. So many swarmed around him that there was no chance most of them could get the sound bites they wanted. Before long, a few of them started trickling over to the players and asking them for their take on gay hockey players.

As I made my way through the crowd to get to Ben and make sure he was ready to go, I overheard Chris Hammond nearly shouting at a few of the reporters in front of him that he didn't care who a guy went to bed with as long as he could skate—only his language was a bit more colorful than that. Then Keith Burns nearly punched one of the media guys in front of him, shouting about how his brother was gay, too, before a couple of his teammates got in the way and led him out of the locker room to cool off. I'd rarely seen anything so out of control as the spectacle surrounding this team right now. I didn't know how the guys were going to maintain their focus in order to keep it on what truly mattered for them right now—their matchup against the Blackhawks.

A little while later, Jamie Babcock told me they were hounding his wife just as much, if not more, than the way these people were cornering her father. Only it was a different sort of media chasing after her. With all her Hollywood connections and the history of being followed by the paparazzi, suddenly her life was looking much like it had back when she'd starred on the TV show *The Cool Kids*. He told me she could hardly leave the house without being trailed. In fact, she was debating not coming to the game tonight, because she didn't want to detract from the game itself.

As if that weren't enough, all sorts of unusual media folks seemed to have followed the Blackhawks, and it didn't take me long to figure out the reason behind it. Most of them flocked to Nate's stall after the team's morning skate as soon as they were given the green light to enter the locker room. The look on his face told me everything I needed to know about the questions they were asking him, but there wasn't anything I could do to help.

When I wasn't making sure my camera crews were getting through the throng to film what I needed, I was busy fielding emails from my editor in the cutting room. Bill and Tim were holed up in Bill's office working on splicing together the Weber family footage in the way I'd asked them to. This particular piece was so important to the overall production, in my opinion, that I'd turned Tim over to Bill's care. That way, they could work as a team and be sure they got every moment of it exactly how I wanted it. Tim's social media responsibilities could be put on hold for a while.

In the middle of all that—as if this wasn't already more than enough for a single day—Cody Williams waylaid me to ask for a favor.

"A favor?" I repeated, confused but more than a little curious.

We were in a corner of the overly crowded locker room. He'd already changed clothes and looked like he was ready to make his escape.

So far, my guys and I hadn't spent much time focusing on him—he'd only been in the periphery of a few segments we'd aired, and we'd never presented him in any sort of a negative light. My initial assumption had been that he wasn't happy with the way he'd been edited, but that didn't make any sense once I thought it through.

"Maybe somewhere with a bit more privacy?" he suggested. He glanced around at the masses of people holding cameras and other sorts of recording devices, then jerked his head toward a quieter hall in the underbelly of the Moda Center.

I nodded, then followed until he came to a stop in an equipment room that was currently unoccupied.

"Look," he said, dragging a hand through his still-wet red hair. "I don't exactly know how to put this, and I know you've got a lot more you need to cover right now with things happening for some of the other guys, but if you could— It's just— I made Webs a promise, and his daughter's not making it very easy for me to keep that promise."

"You mean Dani?" I asked, and suddenly, the unexplained parts of our conversation from the other day started to click into place. Whatever it was that sticking around Portland for an extra day would allow her the chance to do, it must have had something to do with Cody Williams.

"She's not taking the hint," he said, nodding. "I've tried flat-out telling her that I'm not interested. I've tried ignoring her. She won't give up. She even showed up at my place yesterday. I'd thought she was going back to Seattle sometime on Monday, but there she was at my house…"

I bit down on my lip to keep from laughing, because the picture in my head was more than simply amusing. There was no doubt Dani could be a handful and then some, and I doubted she took being told no lightly. That girl was a firecracker, and it seemed Williams didn't have the first clue how to handle her.

"But how can I help?" I asked, thoroughly at a loss. To me, this seemed like something that was between the two of them. And maybe Dani's father.

"You just… You haven't shown me much on the show yet. I was thinking maybe you could send one of your camera guys out with me one night. I've got a friend who's agreed to play the part of my girlfriend, and—"

"You want to present a lie," I cut in, again trying not to laugh.

"It's not a huge lie."

"Big enough," I said. "What happens when your teammates see it and reveal the truth?"

Williams shrugged. "I keep to myself a lot. Don't really let on too much about my private life. They're always saying I've got some girlfriend hidden away from them. Too ashamed of them to bring her around or something. Or maybe the opposite. I don't know what they think."

"And you want to perpetuate the rumors?"

"Are you saying you won't do it? Because it's not like this show is nothing but the facts or anything."

I scowled. "But it's not an outright lie, either."

"This lie's for a good cause."

"Breaking Dani Weber's heart is a good cause?"

"No," he said, the word coming out as a frustrated grumble. "I don't want to hurt her feelings or anything. I'm just trying to keep my promise to Webs."

"Is the promise that important?"

"This one is. And I don't know how else I can convince her to leave me be."

Going along with his request rubbed me wrong in all sorts of ways, but there was something in his eyes—an odd combination of determination and desperation—that compelled me to do it. "Is tomorrow night too soon?" I asked, racing through my mental calendar.

"I can make it work."

Then I supposed I could make it work, too, even if it felt as though I would be compromising my journalistic integrity to do so.

But if I was already losing this job soon, anyway, I might as well do what I wanted, not what I felt as if I was supposed to do. Right now, I wanted to help Cody Williams. In the process, I might even end up helping Dani, too, although she likely wouldn't see it that way at first. If he was willing to go to these lengths to drive her away, though, then she was better off without him.

That said, I couldn't help but notice that he'd never actually said he wasn't interested in her. Only that he'd made a promise to her father.

Very, very interesting.

I finished making plans with him to send a crew out with him tomorrow, and then we both headed back into the locker room. Once there, I did a quick scan to see what was going on. There was still a large crowd around David Weber, along with smaller groups of reporters surrounding a few of the guys. Nate had the second largest gathering, and he looked miserable. And there still wasn't any way I could help him out, other than send him a text message that might make him smile when he saw it later, and wait for a time when we could talk without all the cameras around. So, once I was certain that my guys still had things well under control, I took out my phone and tried to think up something funny or otherwise helpful to say.

Bad knee or not, Nate turned out to be the best player on the ice in Game One of the Storm's series against the Blackhawks. He'd only scored a single goal, but he and his line mates had put so much pressure the other team that the Blackhawks' top line had been incapable of generating any momentum. Between the way Nate used his speed and lack of size to swerve away from the defenders' reach, Johansson's stick-handling, and Kozlow's ability to get under the skin of even the calmest players, they'd controlled the play in almost every moment they spent on the ice.

I didn't know if they'd be able to keep this same sort of dominance up throughout the series, and particularly not once the games were played in Chicago and the Blackhawks would have the final change. If they could, this might turn out to be one of the more dominant performances of any line in recent playoff memory.

As expected, dozens of reporters gathered around Nate's stall in the aftermath, so many of them that Dave could hardly get in there with his camera. I kept my distance—something I was attempting to do more and more when it came to filming anything to do with him for *Eye of the Storm*. I wasn't anything close to unbiased, so I needed to let my guys do their jobs and keep myself out of it as much as possible.

There were still a large number of unexpected journalists among the ranks, due to Luke Weber's announcement, but not as many as earlier. It seemed they were far more interested in covering the gay hockey player angle than actual hockey.

Later, once the press had cleared out and the guys had finished cleaning up after their dominating win, Nate sought me out. "Too late to take you out for coffee tonight? I know you've got a lot on your plate tomorrow." He looked determined to convince me, even if I didn't immediately jump on the idea.

I had every intention of spending the majority of the day tomorrow holed up in the cutting room putting the final touches on the next webisode, but the lure of spending some time with him tonight was far too enticing to ignore.

"I suppose you can," I teased. "Although I might prefer a meal over coffee."

"Stomach growling again?" He winked. "Good, because I'm starving. I was so worked up before the game because of all the press garbage that I didn't eat like I should have."

Ten minutes later, my guys were packing up their gear to head home for the night, and Nate and I were on our way out to his car. He reached for my hand, even though there were still a ton of people around. I hesitated for a moment, but not very long. Any damage that could be done to my career had already been done when my boss had seen that tweet from Jezek—or whoever it was that had gotten their hands on his phone. Besides, I hadn't been concerned about people watching us last night on that river cruise, and we'd made quite a spectacle of ourselves.

"Do I make you nervous?" he asked me when we reached the parking garage.

I narrowed my eyes and tried to give him a glare that said *you wish*, but my laughter ruined the effect. "Maybe a little."

"Why's that?"

"I just… I've never been the girl who dated the jocks, you know? I dated the other geeks and nerds. I reported on the jocks. So I feel out of place being with you."

"Yeah, but I'm a nerdy jock," he said with a wink, and I laughed.

"More jock than nerd."

"Maybe. Depends on who you ask. Koz is always telling me I spend too much time with my books and not enough time with the guys."

"Do you care that much what he thinks? I doubt Jezek would say the same."

"RJ knows why I'm doing it. He gets it. He knows my parents."

"Then I'd say that his opinion matters more, wouldn't you?"

"Hmm…" he said, but it sounded more like he agreed than wanted to argue.

"What about me? Do I make you nervous?"

"More excited than nervous. It's like I'm always trying to figure out ways to be with you. To get you alone." He squeezed my hand gently.

"That hasn't been easy lately."

"Not at all. Something tells me it won't be easy for a while. But I've never been one to shy away from a challenge, and I don't get the impression you are, either."

The corners of my lips curled upward. "My father would certainly agree with that. Speaking of him, he wants you to come to his house for dinner some night. I pushed him off until next week, but…"

"But he won't be put off forever," Nate finished for me.

"He'll like you," I felt compelled to tell him. "He won't give you a hard time. He's never been like David Weber, trying to run guys away from me."

Nate turned and raised a brow. "Who's Webs running off this time?"

I'd said something I shouldn't have. If I wasn't careful, I'd give Cody Williams and his plan away before he'd ever had a chance to execute it. It wouldn't matter if things turned out the way he hoped or not if I couldn't manage to keep my mouth shut. "Never mind that," I said, shaking my head. Then I remembered what Weber had said to Luke during that phone call. I made a mental note to be sure that part was included in the cut we aired. I figured I could use that to explain what I'd meant if Nate ever brought it up again.

Not that I thought he would, but it was hard to be certain. I hadn't exactly done a great job of explaining myself.

We reached his car, and he spun me around until my back was against the passenger door. My eyes went wide, flashing across to meet his. They'd gone dark and hungry, much like they'd been last night when he'd started to kiss me…before the debacle that had followed.

"I'm going to do this right this time," he said, just before he inched his face closer to me.

Nate's lips were soft and full as they matched up with mine. He braced his hands on either side of me, not quite pressing his body weight against me but still leaning enough that I felt every inch of him. I raised my arms, unsure what to do with them. Finally, I settled my hands on his biceps, which flexed beneath my touch.

He was all muscle, and still warm from so much exertion in the game even though he'd showered and changed into a suit. There wasn't an ounce of tension in him, but as for me? I was taut from head to toe, wound up tight and ready to spring into him as soon as he released my trigger. He shifted his head, his nose brushing lightly against mine as he changed the angle, and the breath I'd been holding slipped free. It fluttered out as a sigh, and I closed my eyes to lose myself in him. His lips parted, and he glided his tongue along the seam between mine until I opened for him. My hands dug into his biceps, fisting of their own volition. I tried to inch closer to him when he took my lower lip between both of his and suckled, his breath mingling with mine. It was tender and sexy as all get out, and I couldn't get enough.

Then, almost as soon as I began to stop overthinking things and simply enjoy the moment, he pulled away with a cocky grin that melted my insides like a Bunsen burner had been placed in my gut and turned up to high. "That was much better."

That was putting it mildly. This kiss was so much better that my knees were weak.

Nate backed up and nudged me away from the door so he could open it, but I wobbled to such a degree that he put an arm around my waist to steady me. "Your ankle?" he asked, his voice filled with concern.

I shook my head. "Just a little light-headed."

"Are you getting sick? Should I take you home and make you some soup? You're working yourself into an early grave."

Lovesick? Maybe. But there was no way around it... I had to stroke his ego and give him the truth. "I'm fine. It's just because of how good that kiss was."

He chuckled and guided me into the passenger seat. "There's plenty more where that came from."

I was counting on it.

Nate

WHEN HARRY WALKED into the locker room late in the morning after our Game Two loss to the Blackhawks—a loss that came in overtime during one of the craziest thunderstorms I'd ever experienced, no less—Burnzie wanted answers. It didn't matter that we were all busy getting ready to leave for Chicago, either. He wanted them now.

"Why the fuck haven't you brought Jasinda around at all?" he demanded, tossing a towel in Harry's direction to get his attention.

Jasinda? I didn't have a clue who that was or what was going on. No doubt it had something to do with the latest episode of *Eye of the Storm*. It had been scheduled to go live on the Internet shortly before the game last night, but I hadn't found time to watch it yet. I'd had better things to do—like taking Anne out for a late-night dinner at a twenty-four-hour diner again, even though the storm had still been raging, plus longer and longer study sessions with finals just around the corner.

"Didn't feel like letting all you fucking buffoons give her a hard time," Harry responded. He tossed the towel back at Burnzie and kept heading for his stall.

"You're with a girl long enough that you're comfortable letting the whole world know she's your girlfriend on that show, but you're not comfortable bringing her around your teammates?" Burnzie actually sounded pissed off, which wasn't something that happened often. He typically let things roll off his back. Not this time, though. "What the fuck do you think that says about how you feel about us? You should bring her to the games. Introduce her to the other WAGs."

"Maybe she doesn't want to be part of all this," Harry replied sheepishly.

"You have a girlfriend?" I asked, but no one was paying any attention to me.

"If she's going to be part of your life, she's going to be part of *all this*," Hammer pointed out, always a voice of reason and experience. "Whether she wants to be or not. And whether you want her to be or not. That's just how it works. Might as well get her used to it now."

Mitch "Q" Quincey walked through the middle of the room before taking a seat on the bench to tape up a stick. "If it's too much for her to take in at once, maybe introduce her to one or two of them, just so she's got someone to lean on. Not trying to fit in on her own. Mia could help with that. She wouldn't mind."

"It's not—" Harry let out a sound of pure frustration.

"Hell, you could hook her up with Ghost's girl," Hammer suggested. "They could stick together."

"*My* girl? Anne already knows everyone," I spluttered. And besides, was she my girlfriend? I mean, yeah, I wanted her to be, but we hadn't exactly put it in so many words as of yet. "She's hanging out—"

"She's working," Q said, raising a brow. "She's doing a job. That's not the same as hanging out, even if she knows who the WAGs are. It's not like they're getting a chance to know her. And she's not taking part in all the fundraisers they do."

"Katie would love some more help with the fundraisers," Babs put in.

"At least I'm not trying to hide her," I pointed out, hoping to shift the focus back onto Harry instead of me. I'd had more than my fair share lately. Time to dump some of it on someone else.

They went back to ragging on Harry again, so it seemed to do the trick.

RJ came in, looking like death warmed over. His stall was immediately next to mine. He plopped down on the bench, more so than taking a seat, and raked a hand through his hair.

"Rough night?" I asked, keeping my voice down so it could be just between the two of us.

"Lola is apparently terrified of thunder."

"Apparently? You didn't already know this?"

"We haven't had many thunderstorms since I've had the dogs, have we?"

Come to think of it, he was right.

"Anyway, when she gets scared, it gets Max riled up. You ever try sleeping with three hundred seventy pounds of so-scared-they're-shaking dog trying to crawl in your lap?"

"You should have shoved one of them off onto Amanda, at least."

"She wasn't even home to help me with them last night. Went out for one of her girlfriends' birthdays. She was too drunk to drive home, so she spent the night there. It was just me and the dogs."

No wonder he looked like shit. Didn't mean I needed to take it easy on him, though. "Yeah, she *says* she was too drunk to come home. She's probably secretly bisexual, and she wanted a hot night with a chick."

"She would've invited me along if that's what she was doing."

"You sure about that?" Because I sure as hell wasn't. In fact, I probably should've picked something else to poke at him with. It was too late to take the words back, though.

"Sure enough." He grabbed a roll of tape and started working on one of his sticks. "You look at Twitter lately?" he asked, sounding far too casual. That couldn't be a good sign.

"You know I haven't. Why? Who's posting shit about me now?"

"Not you," he said darkly.

"Anne?" I didn't need to hear his answer to know it had to be. "What kind of things?"

Before he could answer, she walked into the locker room along with a couple of her cameramen and started pointing out where she wanted them to go, effectively putting an end to the conversation. We weren't going to talk about that shit if it might be caught on film, that was for sure.

She caught my eye and smiled. I winked to let her know I'd seen her, and then she went back to ordering her guys around like a sexy-as-hell drill sergeant.

Most of the guys headed out to the ice for a short practice, but I went to the trainers' room along with Soupy, Hammer, and a couple of the other guys to get treatment on our various ailments. While I iced my knee and let Archie work on it, I took out my phone and decided to set up an account on Twitter, after all. It wasn't my idea of a good time, but it seemed necessary if I wanted to know what was going on.

Once I'd set up my profile, I found RJ and a few of the other guys so I could scroll through the people they followed. That seemed as good a way as any to find Anne.

Sure enough, I stumbled onto her profile in no time. Nothing bad was there. In fact, she hadn't posted to her profile in almost a month. I seemed to recall that she'd sworn off social media recently, so this made sense to me.

It took me a couple of minutes to figure out how to search for what people had been posting about her, but that was when I understood RJ's concerns.

No wonder @AnnePDennison got the @EyeoftheStormShow job. She's fucking everyone she can to get it and keep it. #slut #whenisitmyturn

A picture of the two of us about to kiss on the dinner cruise the other night was included with the tweet. And that was just one of what had to be dozens of similar messages posted within the last few days. Some had pictures of us together, like the one that had been posted on (and subsequently deleted from) RJ's account. Others had links to gossip sites that went on and on about her supposedly selling herself to everyone from me to her boss to Jim Sutter, and even Mr. Engels, the team owner.

It made me sick to my stomach.

I wanted to punch something.

More than anything, I wished I'd listened to my gut and backed off once I realized all the possible implications a relationship between the two of us would have on her career. Getting involved with Anne wasn't problematic for me—but there seemed to be no end to the type and number of problems she was facing because of it.

There wasn't any way to convince myself otherwise anymore: if I didn't put an end to this, I would be one selfish son of a bitch.

Anne deserved better than that.

Chapter Thirteen

Anne

NATE HAD WINKED as he'd walked past me in the aisle, heading toward the back of the plane with Jezek instead of taking the open seat next to me.

While more than simply disappointed, I hadn't thought too much of it at the time. He was still part of this team, after all, and he had responsibilities to fulfill and friends to spend time with. Those things hadn't changed just because we'd gone out on a few dates. Besides, we'd never officially said anything about being a couple. There wasn't any reason he should drop everything in order to hang out with me, especially if we would just end up spending the flight like we so often did—me working and him studying.

It still stung, though. I couldn't deny that.

It stung even worse now that we'd arrived in Chicago for Game Three. In fact, it now felt as if he was actively avoiding me.

Once we got to the hotel, he'd disappeared with Jezek and a few of the other guys while I was still giving instructions to my crew about when and where I needed them next. After I got settled in my room, I had texted him to see if he wanted to grab dinner somewhere. No response. I ended up poring through the footage Bill had sent over while we'd been in the air over room service, since the guys on my crew had all broken up and tagged along with various groups of players and team executives, as I'd instructed them to do, filming everything they could.

I briefly checked in on Facebook, but wished I hadn't. There was something going on between a group of black teenagers and the police in some suburb of Chicago. I set aside my work and turned on the news to learn as much as I could. I'd been watching for a few hours when my phone buzzed on the desk.

Nate. Calling me. The clock read 9:48, so it had sure taken him long enough.

I dropped everything and answered. "Hey. I was starting to get the feeling you'd been avoiding me."

"You were, were you?" he asked, sounding distant. And he didn't immediately try to put my mind at ease by telling me it had all been in my head or explaining why he hadn't bothered to at least respond to my earlier message.

This couldn't be good.

"Yeah…" I said, drawing the word out as I racked my brain to figure out what to do and how to respond. Because, while I may be inexperienced when it came to being with seriously hot guys who seemed way too good to be true, this sure felt a lot like he was dumping me.

Could he dump me if we weren't officially a couple? I mean, we'd only kissed a few times and gone out on a couple of dates. There wasn't anything more official than that.

"I just…" He let out a ragged sigh, which more than confirmed my fears.

My gut started churning. I shouldn't have ordered pizza for my dinner. Really bad choice, in more ways than I could count. And I should have stopped eating it a long time ago instead of continuing to graze on it long after the point it should have been tossed in the garbage. Now I was going to have to pay the price for my poor decision-making.

"Where are you?" Nate asked after a protracted silence.

"In my room."

"Can I come up and talk to you?"

If he intended to dump me, I'd rather have him do it over the phone. Because I didn't want him to see me fall apart. I wasn't a pretty crier. I didn't cry often, but when I did, it was all ugly crying. Worse yet, I could already feel the beginnings of it starting. If we could get it over with right now, then I could cry my eyes out all alone, and I could curse him and throw things and bury my emotions in the cheesecake that I'd popped into the mini-fridge for later. And then by the time I saw him tomorrow, I could pull myself together again and act like he hadn't completely crushed me.

Because that's exactly what it would be. An act. A show. It would be me putting on a front for all the world to see so he wouldn't know how deeply he'd hurt me.

Which meant I already cared about him more than I'd realized before now. I might have fallen for him just a bit. Stupid move, really, but it was too late to stop it from happening.

"Anne?" he said, because I hadn't responded to him yet. I'd been too busy dumping myself in my head.

I swallowed hard, hoping that would be enough to keep my voice from cracking when I spoke. "Can it wait?" I finally asked. *Wait?* Why, other than the fact that I was a glutton for punishment? Waiting would be the worst idea ever, because then I'd only obsess over it all night long. I wouldn't get a lick of work done, and there wasn't a chance I'd be able to sleep. But now that I'd started down that path, I figured I might as well keep going. "I've got a lot on my pla—"

"It really can't wait," he said. "I know you're busy. I should've done this earlier, but I couldn't figure out how to say what I need to say. It won't take long, but please, can I come up?"

No, it wouldn't take long for him to tell me he didn't want to be with me. We might as well get it over with. I still wouldn't sleep tonight, but it would be for a different reason entirely.

"Sure," I forced myself to say, even as I felt my throat closing. "Room 2318."

"Be right there." Then the line went dead.

I turned off the news, tossed the remainder of my pizza in the trash can, and raced around to tidy up. At the last second, I realized I'd already changed into my pj's—a ratty T-shirt with holes I hadn't realized were in it when I'd packed, and a pair of men's boxer shorts that I'd bought as soon as I'd moved out for college and which had seen better days. No bra. I threw open the dresser drawer and grabbed the first bra I could get my hands on. I ripped the shirt off and squirreled my way into the bra, but then he was already knocking on my door. Flinging open the door of the closet, I somehow knocked the ironing board off its hooks. It smacked me in the head before clattering to the floor, barely missing my toes.

I let out a stream of curses.

"Anne?" Nate called from the hallway. "You okay?"

Not in the slightest, but I replied, "Fine! Just... Just gimme a second." I managed to pick up the ironing board, but I couldn't get it back on the hooks, so I angled it against the wall of the closet. It started to fall again, dragging my clothes off their hangers. They fell to the floor. Frustrated, I tried to right the stupid thing again, but it was all I could do to shove the door closed with everything inside the closet. The ironing board clattered around in there again for a moment.

But I still hadn't taken out anything else to wear.

I tried to tug the door of the closet open, but it appeared to be wedged closed now. There wasn't anything I could do but put on my ratty, hole-riddled T-shirt again and get rid of Nate as fast as possible. I tugged it back over my head and glanced at myself in the bathroom mirror. Not good enough. At all. I raced back into the main part of the room, grabbed a pillow off the bed, and held it in front of me to open the door so I'd at least have *something* covering me.

He looked me over with concern at first, but then his eyes dropped lower. He burst out laughing. "What on earth are you doing in here?"

I scowled at him, rubbing my temple with one hand. It hurt worse than I'd initially thought. "Are you coming in or not? Because I'm not standing here with the door open all night."

He came through the door and closed it behind him, so I scurried into the room and took a seat on the couch. Nate sat next to me. Belatedly, I wished I'd thought to sit in the desk chair, because I wasn't sure how I felt about being this close to him when he was about to break my heart.

"You'd already changed for the night," he said, sounding almost apologetic if not for the hint of laughter coming through in his tone. "You should have said..."

"But you said it couldn't wait," I pointed out.

"Sounded like you were doing battle with something."

"The ironing board in the closet." I shrugged. "But that's not why you're here."

"No, it's not." Still, he didn't rush to get to the point. Instead, he passed his gaze over me again, until I shifted away from him and held the pillow tighter to my body, as if it could somehow protect me.

I didn't know how much more of this I could take. "Can you just tell me why you're up here? You said it couldn't wait, so..."

He dropped his eyes to his lap for a moment, and I prepared myself for the hammer to fall. It couldn't hurt too much worse than the blow to my head moments ago, could it? Probably not.

"I was on Twitter this morning—"

"You don't have a Twitter account," I cut in, completely thrown. "You told me you don't like reading what everyone's saying about you, so you avoid social media like the plague."

"I didn't have Twitter. Now I do."

"Why?"

"Because RJ told me I needed to see something."

The awful churning in my belly only got worse. There wasn't anything *good* he could have found on Twitter, at least not if it was something his friend was telling him he needed to go look at. Jezek knew why Nate avoided it, the same as I did.

"And?" I asked tentatively.

"And he was right. There were a lot of things I needed to see. So I could understand—*really* understand—the sort of effect I'm having on you."

I blinked and shook my head. "The effect you're having on me? Why not ask *me*? Why bother signing up for Twi—"

"On your job," he clarified. "Your career."

"I already told you not to worry about all that. Yeah, my boss saw that picture, but he doesn't have anyone to repl—"

"I'm not talking about the picture RJ posted. Or at least not *just* about that. There's more. A lot more."

I shook my head. "So some other people saw it and saved it before he delet—"

"Someone got pictures of us on that dinner cruise," Nate said.

"Oh." That part took me by surprise, but it didn't change anything, as far as I could tell. There still wasn't anyone ready to replace me tomorrow. My boss had been very clear about that part.

But now I was more confused than ever. Was this all because Nate had just figured out that people on the Internet were jerks? Had he been avoiding me because he couldn't figure out how to break the news to me? Because our relationship was more public than we might have wanted it to be, at least at such an early juncture?

Maybe I'd been getting myself all worked up for no reason, and he wasn't about to dump me. Now I had at least a glimmer of hope.

"They're saying all sorts of things about you that I won't repeat."

"That's not new," I said, shaking my head to reassure him, uncertain what direction this conversation was heading. "It's not anything to worry about. People say all sorts of things when they think they're anonymous. You shouldn't look at that stuff. It'll get in your head, the same as seeing what the press is saying about you. It'll only make you mad."

"Mad?" Nate said with a lot more force than I'd ever heard from him before. He was usually even-keeled, as calm and collected as they came, always thinking things through before letting them fly out of his mouth. In that moment, he was the exact opposite. "It made me a hell of a lot more than mad. It made me scared for you and ashamed of myself for being so selfish—"

"Wait a second," I interrupted, angling my body so I was facing him but keeping the pillow between us so he wouldn't see all the holes in my shirt. "Back up. There's no reason for you to be ashamed, and you've been anything but selfish."

"Ignoring the fact that the two of us having any sort of relationship that goes beyond being strictly professional would be putting your career in danger isn't selfish? How do you make that one out?"

"It's my decision," I insisted. "I went into this with both eyes open."

"And I went in with blinders on."

"Doesn't matter now. Any damage that could come from this is already done."

"Not exactly," Nate insisted, eyes flashing.

I shook my head. "Meaning what? I already know the consequences I'm facing with my employer."

"Yeah, you're probably losing this job. That's already been established. But what happens when you try to get your next job and all these rumors and innuendo follow you?"

"I point out that they're nothing more than people being idiots on the Internet, which, by the way, is as good as an epidemic. I admit where I went wrong. And then I hope my prospective employer is able to see past the stupid people tweeting at me to find the truth. But seriously, I doubt they'll see any of this stuff—"

"Seems like an awfully big assumption. Especially if nothing happens to quash it all now."

I frowned at him, hugging my pillow closer. "My father's already doing what he can on that score. He's got his lawyer working on going after the worst offenders."

"But what if that's not enough? What then?" Nate raised a brow. "And that doesn't have anything to do with how future employers will look at all the things that are floating around about you."

"What things?" I demanded, my frustration leading to the words sounding snippier than I intended. "I don't see how any employer could refuse to give me a chance simply because a bunch of idiots think I need a good rape, just because I'm a woman trying to make it in a man's world."

"Rape?" Nate practically roared. "Who said anything about rape?"

"A few hundred men on Twitter, last time I looked. Could be a few thousand by now, though. I told you about it before."

"Yeah, but I thought you were exaggerating."

"Not exaggerating. At all. But I doubt the lawyers have gotten very far with making them stop. And frankly, the police have a lot more important things to worry about, given the state of the world right now. Have you seen the news tonight?"

But clearly, the rape threats weren't what he'd seen, and whether he'd seen tonight's news or not, he wasn't in any mood to be deterred from the conversation he'd started… Not if the utter fury causing a tic in his jaw was any indication.

I rolled my eyes. "It's not like you haven't been up against the same and worse."

"No one's threatened to rape me that I know of," he grumbled.

"Maybe not, but they've certainly made unfounded comments about you based on nothing more than the color of your skin. And things are getting worse out there."

"That's not the same."

"Isn't it? Tell me how it's different. Tell me how it's not all a bunch of ignorance and hatred and idiocy, because I don't see it. You've had to face racism. I've had to face sexism. Big whoop."

"How can you be so blasé about something like this?"

I threw a hand up in annoyance. "What else do you want me to do?"

"I don't know," he shouted.

"It's not like you've been fighting back with everything you've got, either. You're just pretending like it didn't happen. Wishing it would go away, even though it isn't. Two black teenagers got shot and killed by the cops tonight, not too far from here, you know. This city's about ready to explode with tensions."

"You've been helping me with pretending it wasn't happening," Nate pointed out. "And what am I supposed to do about kids getting killed? I'm just trying to do my job. That's it."

"I have been helping on that score! That's absolutely right. I've been focusing my show on anything and everything else, to try to draw some of the focus off of you. I admit it. So how is this any different?"

"Because all that happened with me was a couple of assholes

throwing a fucking banana peel on the ice and shouting a few slurs. No one threatened to fucking hurt me."

"They're just threats! What better way is there for me to fight back other than to go on about my life like they don't have any effect on me?"

Nate glowered, but he didn't immediately spout off a comeback. "But maybe—"

"Maybe nothing. Like I said, Dad has his lawyer on it. There's not anything else I can do about it if all they're doing is offering up vague threats on the Internet. No one's acting on them. In a lot of ways, what happened with you was more real. They were physically *there*. In the building. You could see them, and they could see you. And there *are* real, physical things happening right now, in this city, related to the racial tensions. That's a hell of a lot more real than anything I'm facing online. With this stuff, it's all just..." I shrugged. "They don't see me as a real person, you know? Someone with feelings. As long as they can hide behind the Internet, I don't think there's anything to worry about."

"I hate this," Nate said, his jaw tic intensifying. "I hate everything about this."

"I know. So do I."

"Noted," he grumbled.

"So what kinds of things did you see if it wasn't that?" I half dreaded hearing his answer. But I wanted to move the conversation well away from the anonymous threats that I hadn't thought about in weeks. "What are they saying now?"

He shook his head a couple of times, an internal war going on in his head. "They seem to think that the only way you got your job is by sleeping your way into it. They think you're sleeping with me, with your boss, with Jim Sutter...with all sorts of people, just so you can keep your job."

"Oh. Well, that's not anywhere near as bad as I was assuming based on the way you're acting."

"You don't care about that?"

I shrugged. "When you've seen all the threats I've seen, this isn't all that bad. It's just gossip. It's not anything to worry about."

"It is for me," Nate said. "Which brings us to why I wanted to see you tonight."

In the midst of our argument, I'd forgotten all about my fears from earlier, but now they came rushing back like a tidal wave, threatening to tow me under. I swallowed, barely managing to get the sudden excess of saliva past the huge lump in my throat. "Why is that?" I croaked.

The intensity in his eyes spoke of a dozen different emotions at once: anger, sadness, fear, lust, and countless others I couldn't differentiate. And determination. That one, I could make out.

"I can't be the one responsible for your career being ruined," he said after what felt like an eternity.

"But you're not—"

"I think we've already established that the kinds of things being spread around about you right now *can* and *will* destroy your career. Maybe not the job you have now, but it'll follow you forever."

Every word he said sucked more air out of the room, leaving me fighting for each and every breath I could get.

"So that's it?" I demanded. "You're done? You want out? It's not like we were really a couple or anything, any—"

"Bullshit we weren't."

"That's still what you're saying, though, isn't it? Whatever we might have been, you want to end it."

"That's *not* what I want. At all."

"Then what?"

"You," he shouted. "I want to be with you."

"Well, great. I want to be with you, too."

"Good."

"So what are we even fighting about?"

"This isn't a fight," Nate insisted. "We aren't fighting."

"Sure seems like a good imitation of it."

"We're not fighting. We're having a discussion. Maybe an argument, but not a fight. I've seen people fight, and that's not what this is. I'm telling you that it doesn't matter what I want, because I can't be with you. Not if it's going to—"

"Shouldn't I have some say in this?" I demanded. "I mean, it's my damn career we're fighting over."

"We're not fighting."

"It's still *my* career," I said, rolling my eyes. What the hell was it supposed to be like if we really *were* fighting, in his opinion? I didn't want to see that. But, in a way, I was kind of glad we were getting a good argument in now—before things went too far between us. This way, either we would know that we could disagree and still move on as we were before, because we cared enough about each other to keep it from coming between us, or it would be too much and we could make a clean break.

He gave me a pouting sort of look and crossed his arms. "Fair enough. But I don't want to—"

"To tell me what I should and shouldn't do with my career, right?" There was no hiding my sarcasm. It was dripping through my pores and invading every inch of the space between us. "Because you're not the kind of guy who would try to tell a woman how she needs to go about her business just because you're a man."

Nate scowled, but he didn't try to argue his way out of that one. Good thing, too, because I was ready to jump all over him if he tried it.

"I just think," he said slowly, "that you've worked so hard and given up so much in order to even *have* a career, so maybe you shouldn't throw it away so easily."

"What do you mean by that? What have I given up?"

"Your relationship with your mother and her family." He didn't even hesitate when he said it, just laid it out there like it was a fact.

In a way, he was right. Absolutely right. But... "Don't you think that's even more reason I shouldn't walk away from something like this?"

"Like your job?"

"No. Like us. Like what we're building, whatever it is." I sighed, because he didn't immediately jump on board and agree with me. "There's a lot more involved in my relationship with my mother than her not approving of my choice of career. That's oversimplifying things to an insane degree. But I'm not willing to let my job ruin what we could have."

Nate stared at me a long time, his dark eyes scanning every inch of my face, like he was trying to see into the depths of my soul. "Then I think we're at a bit of an impasse."

"We don't have to be."

"We don't?" He raised a brow.

"Nope. Look, we both want to be together. Isn't that enough for now? We can figure out the rest later. It's not like we can solve the issue of my job tonight, let alone my entire career, while we're sitting in this hotel room."

"With you in your pj's," he said, winking.

I snuggled the pillow closer to my lap, but he grabbed hold of a corner and tugged it away, leaving me with nothing but those boxers and that holey T-shirt to cover me.

"That's not fair," I complained, but my laughter ruined the effect of my argument.

"Why not? You've been coming into the locker room for years with me in next to nothing. Besides, you look hot like that."

Hot? I bit my lower lip and looked down, hoping to understand what he was seeing. All I could see were my clothes that needed to be trashed, not worn, and skin that I never let anyone see. I tucked my knees up to my chest and wrapped my arms around my legs, hoping to cover as much as possible in lieu of racing over to the bed and burrowing beneath the blankets in an effort to disappear.

"Someday," he said, not seeming to notice how uncomfortable I was, "some *morning*, I want to see you in my shirt and boxers, your hair all messed up, maybe borrowing my toothbrush."

"I want my own toothbrush." And a lot more clothes than what he wanted to see me in, but it wouldn't do either of us much good to argue over that right now.

"Okay. You can have your own toothbrush, but I want you in my clothes. My bed."

My stomach fluttered again, but this time from an entirely different sort of nerves. "So does that mean you're done trying to get rid of me for my own sake now?"

The corners of his lips quirked up in a grin. "At least for now. But I'm not done worrying about you."

"I suppose I can live with that."

"And I want to talk to your father to see if there's anything I can do to help."

I sighed, but there were worse things in the world than having men in my life who cared enough to involve themselves, even if getting involved was bound to be a hopeless cause. "You free Wednesday night for dinner?"

Nate leaned in, his lips hovering over mine so close I could feel the warmth of his breath. "With your father?"

My breathing stopped. My heartbeat, too. "Yes."

"Wouldn't miss it for anything," he said. Then he closed the distance between us and kissed me so well I felt it all the way to my tingling toes.

Chapter Fourteen

Nate

AS WE LEFT the ice at the at the end of the second period of Game Three—still scoreless—my eyes drifted up into the lower bowl and landed on a sign that was clearly meant for me. No words. Just a crudely drawn monkey and an enormous banana peel.

The sign disappeared only a moment after I saw it, remaining just long enough for me to register what I was seeing. I swallowed the bile that had gathered in my throat and forced my legs to keep moving until I reached my stall in the locker room.

I'd barely taken a seat before Archie was on the floor in front of me, trying to get my breezers up enough that he could take a look at my knee.

"It's fine," I said. Which was a lie. My knee wasn't fine at all, especially not after I'd taken an awkward fall behind the net when I was trying to dig the puck out against two Blackhawks defenders about ten minutes ago. It also appeared that someone involved with the Blackhawks had been watching *Eye of the Storm* and knew I was playing on an injury. The Storm hadn't made any sort of announcement to that effect, and we definitely hadn't stated which knee was the problem. But every time I turned around out there tonight, some guy on the other team was taking a good, solid whack at the injury.

I'd probably be doing the same thing if the tables were reversed, so I couldn't blame them. But it wasn't helping with my pain level, to say the least.

Archie didn't listen to me and kept shifting my gear around so he could take a look.

"Might be quicker and easier for me to strip," I drawled.

But too late. He'd reached my knee brace and was poking around in there. "Pretty swollen," he said. "Doc said we can give you a shot, if you nee—"

"I don't need a shot in it."

"Well, you're getting a shit ton of ice on it as soon as this game's over. And I think I want you to wear a wrap on it all night."

"Fine." I shrugged. Right now, I didn't care about my knee. All I cared about was getting my head back on straight after what I'd just seen. Plus, I was worried that someone else had seen it. Or that cameras had captured it. If so, all signs pointed to my entire world being about to blow up all around me again.

He made a few adjustments to my brace before the coaches came into the room, then headed over to Soupy's stall to perform a similar inspection.

Bergy took a quick look around, taking stock. We were banged up, but that was nothing new. He'd never been one to give rousing speeches, though, so I doubted that was what he had in store. "This one has the feel of a game that's either about to get broken wide open or one that's going to keep going until the wee hours of the morning," he said. "I, for one, know which I'd prefer. Let's get back out there and take care of business."

Short and sweet, much like I'd been expecting.

After the coaches went back into Bergy's office, RJ elbowed me in the ribs. "You okay?"

"Fine." Total lie again. But I got the sense he already knew I wasn't, anyway, so it wasn't a big deal to lie to him. I shot him a look that I knew he'd be able to interpret without explanation.

"I saw it," he said, sending ice through my blood.

"You think anyone else did?"

He shrugged. "Not sure."

But if RJ had seen it, there was little doubt that plenty of others had, too. In fact, when I glanced up again, it was to see one of Anne's cameramen focusing in on me.

Son of a bitch.

He didn't say anything else the rest of the intermission. Didn't need to. I knew he had my back, the same as the rest of my teammates did. I knew that whoever it was out there in the audience with that sign, they weren't worth my time or energy. Nothing mattered but getting back out there and taking care of business, like Bergy had said.

Bergy sent me, Koz, and Jo-Jo out to take the first face-off of the third period. I didn't bother looking up at the crowd. No need to see any more signs like the one I'd already witnessed. It'd only serve to piss me off worse than I already was, and that wouldn't help me focus on the game. Didn't need anything to grab my focus.

Koz won the draw and sent it back to our *D*. Not wasting any time, I barreled past my guy and headed straight for the blue line. Sure enough, 501 sent a pass straight to the tape on my stick. Jo-Jo was flying down the other wing, making a beeline for Crawford in the Blackhawks' goal, and I could feel Koz's presence not far behind me, coming up through the middle.

Koz and Jo-Jo both had defenders bearing down on them, but I was in the clear. I waited for Jo-Jo to cross in front of the goalie, creating a screen. I faked a pass to Koz, and the *D* tailing him bit, diving to the ice to prevent it.

I spotted a hole over the goalie's stick-side shoulder and took my shot. He just got the butt end of his stick in the way in time, but the puck bounced onto Jo-Jo's backside and trickled past Crawford into the goal.

I barely had my hands in the air to celebrate when Thor lifted me off the ice and spun me around, yelling some unintelligible Swedish gibberish in my ear. The rest of the guys on the ice joined in, slapping my ass, my helmet, and every other part of me they could reach.

Bergy winked at me when we headed back to the bench for a line change. He gave me a good smack on the shoulder once I took a seat next to RJ. "Let's keep it going, boys," Bergy called out. "Keep the pressure on them."

"Nice one," RJ said.

I grinned at him, but then I saw another sign in the crowd over his shoulder. Only two words and a single image from the sign registered before it disappeared: *faggots* and *niggers*, and a picture of a gun. Any thought of laughter fizzled away.

SO MANY REPORTERS had gathered around my stall after the game that

I couldn't take a full breath. They'd left a slight gap between me and them, but there wasn't any air in the room. It had all been sucked away like a vacuum system was in play. With the masses of lights blinding me, the hordes of cameras and microphones being thrust in my direction, it was all I could do to keep from suffocating beneath the weight of it.

I glanced around for Anne or any of her camera guys, but I couldn't find them in the throng. Didn't mean they weren't there, though. With the mass of humanity in front of me, my family could have been in there, and I would be none the wiser.

Kurt Yarbrough stood behind my left shoulder, not that his presence made anything better.

"Nate!" they were all shouting, spouting off their questions, each trying to have his voice heard above the rest. Finally, only one voice kept going—one of the men in the front.

"Nate, tell us about the penalty shot. When did you know the puck went in?"

That was probably the easiest question I'd face all night, and I knew it. "I was just trying to watch Crawford and wait for him to bite first. Everyone talks about his glove side being his weak side, but honestly, he's worked a lot on that lately. He bought a deke to his glove side, and I got off a backhand shot on the stick side. I didn't realize it was in until the goal light lit up."

I'd barely finished speaking before they were all shouting over each other again. The next question wasn't anywhere near as safe.

"Nate, several of the cameras picked up shots of less-than-complimentary signs in the crowd tonight. Did you see any of them?"

I'd been grinding my teeth together so much for the last couple of hours that my jaw was sore. I forced myself to relax. "I saw some," I bit off. "Didn't pay much attention to them. Next question."

"Did those signs add any fuel to the fire for you?" another guy asked.

I leveled him with a stare. "Did they upset you?"

He stammered for a moment, and Kurt inched forward. "Does anyone want to ask Mr. Golston about the game? About his goal and two assists that he scored tonight? Maybe about his thoughts on how the rest of the team played, especially his goaltender, who had a playoff shutout? Those are the things he's here to talk about tonight."

"So he'd rather hide from questions about the racism he's facing?" some other voice from the crowd put in.

"I'm not hiding from anything. I'm just focusing on what's important right here and right now, in this moment."

"You don't think it's important that two black teenagers got killed yesterday?" another called out.

"Again, that didn't have anything to do with me. And frankly, anyone who would go to the trouble to make signs like those just to pull me off my game isn't important. Not in the least."

There was a rumble rolling through the locker room coming from somewhere across from me. I glanced over to see if I could sort out what was going on, and several of the reporters surrounding me followed suit.

A smaller group of media was huddled around Colesy, but it was his voice that had risen above the hubbub.

"You all just need to get over it," he said, almost in a shout.

Colesy wasn't a shouter. He wasn't a fighter. Hotheaded wasn't a word anyone would ever use to describe the guy, yet right now...that was the shoe that seemed to fit best. If anyone needed Kurt or one of the media guys to rescue him tonight, that was Colesy.

I glanced back at Kurt, trying to tell him exactly that without using words. He seemed to be of the same mind, trying to shove his way out of my maze so he could get to the other side of the room—but the crowd didn't give way very easily. He hadn't made it very far when Colesy responded to another question.

"No, I don't give a fuck that one of my teammates is black. I don't give two shits if they're brown, yellow, red, orange, or green, either."

I couldn't believe he was using that kind of language in front of reporters. That was completely out of character for Colesy. Kurt was apparently having the same sort of reaction I was, as he pushed harder to dig his way through the sea of people who'd shifted from my stall to Colesy's.

"Does it bother you to see signs in the crowd about having people of color on your team? And what about the one that cast aspersions on the character of this organization because of the sexual orientation of David Weber's son?"

"I think it says a hell of a lot more about the character of the person who held up the sign than it does about anyone involved with this organization. What does that even mean, doubting the *character of the organization* because there's a homosexual in the family? What kind of family would this be if—" He broke off, dragging a towel down his face. "We're all behind Ghost in this room, and we're all behind Luke

Weber, too. Every last one of us."

"What if one of the guys on this team *is* gay?" someone I couldn't see asked.

"Why the hell would I care if a teammate is gay? That's as stupid as thinking Ghost can't play because he's black. Can the guy still play the game? Is he part of this team? Those things are all that matter to me, and I think they're all that matters to any guy in this locker room."

"A lot of players would care—"

"Who the fuck is this *a lot of players* you're talking about? Because that's news to me. And if anyone on this team has a fucking problem with someone being gay, then they have a problem with me. Because I'm gay. Okay?"

What? Colesy was gay? Granted, I'd never seen the guy with a girlfriend, but I never would have guessed the reason behind it, either. But like he had already said—it didn't matter. Because he was Colesy. He was part of this team—this family—and he had been for a long time, and that was that.

Except, I hated that he was coming out like this. It didn't feel right to me. Colesy hadn't said a word to the guys on the team, as far as I knew. That meant there was a reason for keeping his silence. I didn't know what his reason for secrecy was any more than I knew why he was coming out with it now, but I hated that they'd goaded him into revealing such a personal thing in this way. I wanted to punch someone. Something. Anything.

The glare on Colesy's face when he was looking at one of those reporters was unlike anything I'd ever seen from him before in my life. All of the media in front of him started talking at once, trying to force their questions forward as the story suddenly took a shift no one had expected. But he didn't let them pick up any steam, pushing through before they could ask him anything else. "Yeah, that's right, I'm gay. Do you have a problem with that? Do you think you're going to catch it from me? There must be something running rampant in hockey locker rooms lately, now that there's a whopping two of us who've come out. Maybe you should go f—"

But Kurt reached him and grabbed his arm before he could finish the thought and put his foot in his mouth worse than he already had. "That's all for today, folks," Kurt said, much calmer on the exterior than I knew he must be on the inside. "We're done here." A few of the reporters tried to stop Kurt, hoping to ask more questions, but he didn't give them the opportunity. "There will be an official statement from the Portland Storm offices tomorrow, but not before," he said. Then he dragged Colesy out of the locker room, heading for the coach's office.

Colesy caught my eye as they went past. He winked in my direction. *Holy shit.* I don't know what sort of reaction I'd been expecting when he went by, but a wink was definitely not it.

What the hell just happened?

Several of the media guys still surrounding me started murmuring among themselves, and a couple of them turned around and tried to thrust their mics back in my face.

I shook my head, having none of it. "You heard Kurt, the same as I did," I said, shoving past them before any of the others could get any bright ideas about foisting questions about having a gay teammate on me. They'd been after the rest of the guys ever since Luke Weber's press conference, but so far, they'd left me out of it. There were enough other things to harp on me about, I supposed. But either way, I'd had enough. "That's all for today. I'm done."

Before they could try to get anything else out of me, and particularly before I said something they could take out of context and twist around into another thing entirely, I tugged my jersey over my head, tossed it in the bin in the middle of the room, and followed Kurt and Colesy to Bergy's office. Webs opened the door when I knocked. He nodded and jerked his head toward the middle of the room to invite me in, closing the door behind me.

"What the fuck were you thinking?" I demanded as soon as I made sure we were alone—no reporters, not even any of the guys from Anne's crew.

Colesy rolled his eyes. "I was thinking I was sick and tired of the way they're beating you over the head with that shit, so I wanted to give them something else they can flog to death."

"But you— You're not—" I stopped, shaking my head, not even sure what to say to that.

"Yes, I'm really gay. Not exactly how I intended to come out, but whatever. My family already knows. My father will be furious that this is how the world finds out, but that's his problem. Hell, he still thinks he should be able to beat the gay out of me or something." He closed his eyes and shook his head. "I just couldn't stand the way they keep digging at you, solely because there are some racist shits in the world."

All I could do was stare at him, trying to find a way to turn everything running through my head into words. "You just came out to take the heat off of me?"

He shrugged. "Something like that. Not a big deal."

Big deal didn't even come close to covering it. No one had ever done anything like that for me before. I didn't know how I'd ever thank him enough to cover it. I started by doing the only thing that felt right. I crossed over, grabbed his hand, pulled him in for a hug, and slapped him on the back.

Anne

"SORRY I DIDN'T get in there before they shut the door," Ben said, packing up his equipment now that the press had left the locker room and we were getting ready to ride the bus back to the hotel with the team. "There were too many people in the way."

I shook my head. "Don't worry about it. You got plenty in the locker room, and I'm sure we can get anything else we need over the next few days."

To be completely honest, there was a part of me that was glad Nate had those moments alone with Paxton and the coaching staff after what had gone down following the game. I got the sense that they all needed to process it first, before they were ready to comment on it in any way.

For that matter, I hadn't fully wrapped my head around everything that had happened tonight. The Storm had won the game, taking a two-to-one lead in the series. But that felt minor in comparison to everything else—the racist and homophobic signs that had kept popping up around the United Center, the way the media had gone on the offensive with Nate, and how Paxton had come out as being gay.

It didn't matter how far the world had progressed in terms of acceptance. The truth was, there weren't many professional athletes who were officially *out*. For that matter, there were none, until tonight, in the NHL. Luke Weber's coming out as a gay college athlete last week had been a huge event in the hockey world, but Cole Paxton's revelation would prove to be the ultimate trump card. Now that he'd made his revelation, the doors would be open for others to come through.

How soon that would happen remained to be seen—there were still a ton of barriers to be crossed, and I couldn't imagine it would be an easy decision for many players to make due to locker room culture—but Luke Weber and Cole Paxton had, in the last week, bulldozed a path for others to follow.

But right now, my concern was for Nate. Our cameras had landed on at least four different racist signs in the arena, and I knew he'd seen some of them, as well. Add that to the way the media hadn't been able to let the story go after the more recent events, and I wasn't sure where his head was.

I sent my guys out to load their equipment on the truck, since I'd made the executive decision not to film any more tonight, then made my way out to the bus. Nate was already there, with a book in his hands and an empty seat next to him. It was a regular paperback this time, not one of his textbooks, and he was holding it open in such a way that he wasn't creasing the spine.

I took the seat next to him and tipped the book back so I could see what he was reading. *The Hunger Games.* Not at all what I would have expected.

I raised a brow in question when he looked up.

"You have a problem with me reading this?" he asked, but he did it with a wink.

"Just surprised. Never pegged you for being the futuristic dystopian love triangle sort of guy."

"I tried *Twilight*, but I couldn't get into it. The vampire thing just didn't work for me."

"But alternate realities are fine?"

"Depends on the alternate reality. I tried *Divergent*, too, and I was okay with it until the last book, where everything was explained."

"Didn't like the ending?" I asked.

"Didn't like any piece of the explanation about everything in the world. I was mad. Got all invested in what seemed like a really cool thing, and the answers were stupid."

"Stupid is bad."

"Stupid is worse than bad. It's awful. I had to fix a hole in a wall because I threw the book."

I laughed.

"It was the hardback," he explained.

"So what happens if you don't like the ending to this series?"

"I already know the ending, or at least I assume I do. Saw the movies first, so unless they changed a ton because of it being Hollywood, I have a good sense of it. Seemed like a safer plan, so I wouldn't have to fix any more holes in the walls."

"A lot cheaper, at least."

"You have no idea. Drywall. Paint. We had to repaint the whole room, because we couldn't match the original color exactly, and that led to doing the entire house." He gave me a meaningful look. "It was my mom's wall. I was visiting my parents over the summer. Turned into a massive redecorating project. Dad wanted to murder me before she was done. New paint wasn't enough. She ended up remodeling the entire kitchen and both bathrooms before he finally put his foot down and insisted she had to stop."

The bus pulled out into traffic. I hadn't been paying attention to see if everyone had gotten on board, too caught up in talking young-adult fiction with Nate.

"You know those books are all essentially romances, right?" I pointed out. "Written for teenagers, too."

"You have a problem with the fact that I read romance?"

I shook my head. "No problem at all. Just surprised, I guess." Again. He *kept* surprising me.

"I need a few tips in the romance department."

I rolled my eyes. "From teenagers?"

"I'll take them from anyone and anywhere I can find them."

"Hardly. You did well enough on your own with that dinner cruise." I'd never been treated to anything as romantic as that before. With most of the guys I had dated over the years, ordering pizza and playing a few rounds of *Dungeons and Dragons* was as romantic as it got. "Or have I missed the book you got that one from?"

He wrapped a strong arm around my shoulders and drew me in against his side. It was all I could do not to let out an audible sigh of contentment.

"That was one date. It takes more than one night of romance to be considered a romantic."

"Hmm," I said, snuggling closer. "So what kind of tips are you getting from this book?"

"Well, it's too late to throw burned bread to you in the rain while you're starving as a child, so I'm hoping I run across some better tips once I get further in. Were you ever starving as a kid?" he asked, raising a brow. Then he shook his head. "Probably not."

"Definitely not," I said. "Dad always made a good living. We never wanted for anything. You seem like you're in a good mood."

"You surprised after everything that happened tonight?"

"A bit." No point in lying about that.

"I *was* in a shitty mood. But then Colesy did what he did, and everything changed."

I lifted my head so I could raise a brow at him. "Everything?"

He shrugged, grinning. "Enough. At least when it came to my mood."

"Guess I should be glad he opened himself up to be the next media whipping boy, then."

"Oh yeah? And why is that?"

"Because I thought I was going to have to spend some time putting you in a better mood."

"No reason why you shouldn't do that anyway," Nate murmured, waggling his eyebrows.

I laughed and curled into his side as he marked his page—using a sticky note as a bookmark instead of folding down a corner and desecrating the book, I couldn't help but notice—and we stayed like that until the bus pulled up in front of the team's hotel.

A bunch of the guys immediately headed out in groups to get a late-night dinner. I assumed Nate would want to do the same, but he surprised me by taking my hand once I followed him off the bus and leading me inside, heading straight through the lobby and making a beeline for the elevator bay.

"You're not hungry?" I asked after he pressed the up button.

He glanced around, making sure no one was within earshot, then put his mouth next to my ear. "Different kind of hunger," he whispered, moments before his lips closed over the lobe of my ear.

A shiver raced up my spine as the elevator doors opened. We went in together. Alone. As the doors closed again, Nate pressed the button for his floor.

I didn't press the button for mine.

Chapter Fifteen

Anne

BY THE TIME we reached Nate's room, my pulse was at a full sprint from a combination of nerves and excitement. We'd managed to keep our hands to ourselves in the elevator, but an unspoken agreement of what was to come filled the space between us.

His hand holding tightly to mine, he flipped on the lights and closed the door behind us. He leaned back against it, his eyes passing over my face in a way that heated me from the belly out in every direction. He looked as calm and unflappable as I felt out of control, especially when he smiled at me. His smile could always do that to me. There was something confident and maybe just a little bit cocky about it. He had an utter and complete belief in himself that I envied. It didn't matter how successful I might be in anything—I'd never been so self-assured. And right now? I felt as uncertain of myself as I ever had in my life.

How could he be keeping it together like this? He was supposed to be wild and angry and falling to pieces because of those signs in the crowd and the way the press had tried to flog the racism angle to death again, and I was supposed to let him lose himself in me. That had been my plan. I was going to be there for him on a physical level, to let him vent whatever frustrations he needed to vent into me.

Instead, he was acting like nothing out of the ordinary had happened tonight, and I was the one falling apart at the seams. He seemed to be gathering all my loose ends together, too, keeping them safe until I was able to stitch things together again. Still, it annoyed me to no end that our roles were reversed from what I'd been expecting.

"You're breathing hard," he said, raising our joined hands. He set mine against his chest, and my fingers curled in toward him.

The whole way back to the hotel, I couldn't wait to get my hands on him. I'd been thinking about it for so long—longer than I should have been. He was right in that the two of us should be off-limits for each other. We both knew it in our heads. Too bad no one bothered getting that message through to our hearts.

I felt my own chest rise and fall, much harder than his was at the moment. He'd said I was breathing hard? That was putting it mildly. "I suppose I am." I took a step closer to him, my pulse drowning out all sounds other than our unsteady breaths. There was one sign, at least, that he wasn't quite as cool and collected as I'd imagined at first—his ragged breathing. His heart beat hard and fast beneath my fingertips. Another sign of his struggles. Maybe I wasn't the only one losing my grip on reality because of lust.

Was it just lust, though? I wasn't so sure of that anymore. For my part, I was well and truly beyond the lust stage and verging on falling hard. After the way we'd argued last night... All signs pointed toward us both being in the same place, which was both exhilarating and startling. I couldn't say that I'd ever been in love before. There'd been plenty of infatuations over the years, and I wasn't immune to a healthy crush. But was this how love felt? Aching need, mixed with a calming sense of *rightness* settling over me, and a good dose of aggravation to balance everything out?

With my pumps, we were the same height. He reached behind my head and released the clip that had been holding the mess of my hair captive all day. My hair was long, thick, and curly, an unruly mass that had always been the bane of my mother's existence. She'd spent years cursing my father for his DNA and lamenting the fact that I wasn't fully Indian, with the sleek, easily restrained hair that ran in her family.

As an adult, I went back and forth between cursing my hair as much as she had and reveling in the ways I was different from my mother and her family. Nate combed his fingers through my tangled ringlets, and it was all I could do to keep from sighing and falling into him.

"You wore it down like this that night on the cruise," he said. "I can't tell you how hard it was to keep from running my fingers through it."

"Why didn't you?"

He shrugged, but he didn't take his hand away. Thank goodness. I couldn't handle it if he stopped now, which only proved I was more of a lost cause than I'd realized. "Thought I should kiss you first," he said with a half shrug.

"Do you have a list of steps to follow for everything you do?" I let my other hand rest on his chest, too, a smile working its way to my lips. My fingers itched to loosen his tie and undo his buttons, but I didn't want to rush into anything. If I did, we might both end up with broken limbs or concussions, given the way I always seemed to be hurting myself around him.

"Is it a problem if I do?"

"Not a problem, exactly, no. But does that mean you've got a formula in place for how this next part is going to go?"

"Why?" He laughed. "You want a rundown? Let me think... Step one: kiss Anne until her toes curl. Step two: grope Anne until *my* toes curl."

I halfheartedly punched him on the shoulder.

"Sorry. Groping isn't the romantic word I should be using if I'm paying attention to *The Hunger Games*. Peeta would never talk about groping Katniss. He might think about it, but he'd be a gentleman."

"Just don't tell me that step three is *bump and grind*, and I think I'll cope well enough."

"I was thinking more along the lines of *bump uglies*."

I rolled my eyes. "Either way."

He gave me an exaggerated pout. "You mean we aren't going to get to that step tonight? Because if not, I'll have to adjust my schedule to account for not making it all the way to home base yet."

"Please tell me we're not going to have to use sports analogies for everything."

"I'm happy to use any form of pop culture references you prefer, and especially those that rank high in the realm of geekdom."

"You'd do that for me, hmm?"

"I'd do just about anything for you," he said, sounding as serious as ever. Like he meant it. Like he wasn't just exaggerating because that's what you do when you're flirting. He couldn't mean any such thing, could he? *Anything* was an incredibly broad term.

I rolled my eyes, deciding to take it as a simple flirtation, but he stopped me from arguing with him by kissing me. A few torturously long moments after his lips pressed to mine, his tongue traced the seam of my lips. I welcomed him in, taking hold of his jacket lapels to ground myself because I felt ready to float away otherwise. Somehow, gravity ceased to exist. I had to wonder what other basic laws of human life were going to be turned on their heads before this came to a conclusion. He stopped teasing his fingers through my hair, instead sliding them down the column of my neck.

"That's a lot better than groping," I murmured when he nipped my lower lip and then broke away.

"You sure about that?" He trailed his other hand down my back until he could grab a palm full of my bottom and squeeze. He winked. "Because I can give you both."

I laughed out loud, which only led to a deeper kiss. All the sweetness of the first one was gone. This was so much more intense. Harder. Hungrier. It was wet and raw, with teeth and tongue, our bodies rubbing together in a heated frenzy.

But we both had far too much clothing in the way. With shaking hands, I tugged at his tie until I got the knot loose. Nate appeared to be of the same mind. He jerked the tie free from his collar and tossed it on the dresser, then walked me backward into the room, undoing the buttons of my jacket as he went.

Within moments, we were a tangle of limbs and clothes, both partially undressed as we tumbled onto the bed. Our jackets were gone. One of my shoes was still on my foot, but the other was missing. He'd stripped his belt and pants away before we fell on the bed, leaving his powerful thighs bare other than the bands of his boxer-briefs and the bandage on his leg.

Nate rolled us over until I was on top of him. I steadied myself, bracing my knees on either side of his hips and resting my hands on his shoulders. My hair hung down between us, the long ends of it dusting his chest. He freed my shirt from my waistband, shifted the fabric up, and tugged it over my head.

Out of nowhere, panic hit me. I scrabbled to grab my shirt again, or anything at all I could use to cover myself with, but he caught my hands in his, trapping them between us and willing me with his steady gaze to calm down.

I tried. Took deep breaths. Focused on his eyes, like they were my safe space. Couldn't stop thinking about how no one had ever—*ever*—seen me this naked before, not since I was a little girl and my parents had bathed me. I'd had sex before, sure, but never with the lights on. Even in high school gym class, I'd gone into a private bathroom stall to change clothes. I wanted to free my hands and cover my body, but Nate's grip, while gentle, was unrelenting.

"What's wrong?" he asked.

I shook my head, trying to get free from him, but he held me still.

He tucked some of my hair behind my ear with his free hand, his fingertips teasing me with a light, gentle touch. I wanted more of that, but...

"I just want to look at you," he said. As if to prove his point, his gaze roved from my face to my neck. My shoulders. The space between my breasts. *I* didn't even spend any more time than necessary looking at my own body in the mirror, covering up as soon as possible. How could I allow him to? But he kept staring. "Is that all right? If I spend some time looking at you? God, you're so fucking beautiful."

My breath formed a knot under my breastbone. His touch was soothing, but his gaze had the opposite effect on me. I needed to cover myself, and I needed to do it *now*. But I was frozen beneath his stare. Couldn't move, even if Nate wasn't trapping my hands in his grip.

"What's wrong?" he asked. He trailed his fingers along the same path his eyes had just taken. Everywhere he touched, my skin jumped. Goose bumps popped up along each inch of his journey, warming me even though the air in the room suddenly felt cold enough to turn my breath to frost—if I had any breath, which, of course, I didn't. Everything about this moment was a war inside my body, and one I couldn't understand, let alone explain.

I shook my head. I convinced myself I could tell him nothing was wrong even though it was a lie. But that wasn't even close to what came out of my mouth.

"Can we turn out the lights?" I spluttered, wishing I could force the words back inside, but it was too late. There they were, out in the open, laughing at me. The most ridiculous part of it was that I *wanted* to see Nate's body with everything that was in me. I'd seen him nearly naked so many times before, and he was a gorgeous specimen of a man. Rock-hard abs. Smooth, dark skin that I wanted to taste. A chest like Hercules. A butt like a Speedo model.

I'd been thinking about getting him undressed for longer than was good for me.

But now *he* was looking at *me*. And I didn't think I could cope, which was beyond pathetic. I couldn't stop thinking about covering myself again. Not only that, but it was all my mother's fault. She'd gotten so deeply into my head that she was invading my thoughts even now, at a time when she was the last person on earth I ought to be thinking of.

I'd only started wearing shorts and T-shirts to sleep in once I'd moved out of my father's house to live on my own—once there was no one else around to see my bare arms and legs, or anything else that might be hanging out there. It was one of the vestiges of all the years living with my mother, even if I'd done my best to shake free of her influence in every way possible. Apparently, I'd never been able to rid myself of her voice in my ear anytime I attempted to wear something that was common in America.

My recognition of that fact didn't do anything to ease the discomfort of the current situation, especially with Nate looking at me like I'd lost my mind.

"You want to turn the lights out," he repeated, sounding as full of dismay as I'd ever heard him.

"Never mind," I insisted, shaking my head and trying to convince myself that I could get through this with the lights on. "It's ridiculous. I'm being—"

"No," he said, as calm as ever. "If you need the lights off, we'll turn the lights off. You're sure you want this, though? Because I don't want to rush you. If you need more time…" He released my hands, letting me reach for the blankets to cover myself. The way he was looking at me, his gaze so filled with concern, nearly broke me.

"I don't need more time. I want this. I want *you*. More than anything." Even more than my next breath. "I just—" Couldn't find the words. Definitely couldn't explain.

"You just need the lights out."

I nodded, hating myself because of the momentary flash of disappointment that swept through his eyes.

Men were visual creatures. I knew that. But here I was, asking Nate to give up that part of the experience just because I couldn't deal.

He sat up and eased me off his lap before crossing to flip the switch, leaving only the lamp next to the bed burning. I clutched the blankets to my chest as he took a moment to remove his shirt and retrieve a foil-wrapped condom from a box on the nightstand. Then he turned off the lamp, as well, and sat on the edge of the bed.

"Better?" he asked, stretching out a hand for mine.

I put my hand in his, letting his calmness seep into me as the blankets drifted back down to the mattress. "Much."

"You're sure?"

My breaths came more regularly. The uncomfortable jumping sensation in my belly was starting to ease. "Positive," I said.

"Good. So any chance I can get back to the groping part of the proceedings? Because I was getting really close to the toe-curling stuff."

I laughed and inched closer to him. Once again, he'd surprised me by simply accepting whatever was thrown at him and moving forward, as though nothing was standing in his way. "I don't know about yours, but mine were already curling."

"Not curling anywhere near enough yet." There was a hint of a smile in Nate's tone. He caressed my cheek and drew my face toward his, but he didn't kiss me even though our mouths were only a hairsbreadth apart. He slid his other hand up and down the side of my arm. "You're sure this is okay?"

I nodded, trusting that the movement would be enough with his hand on my face.

The thumb of his other hand slipped across to tickle the side of my breast. "You'd tell me if I did something that's not, wouldn't you? You'd stop me?"

I hated how worried he sounded, especially because I was the reason for it. "Promise. I'll tell you. But this is good. I want this. Just not…"

"Not with the lights on," he finished for me.

"Right." I couldn't get over the fact that he was going along with it, not trying to figure out why I couldn't allow him to see me.

His touch was still so tentative, though—not groping like he'd promised only moments before. Lifting up onto my knees, I reached behind my back and unclasped my bra. When the straps fell forward, I took Nate's hand and guided him to touch me. He palmed my breast, and I sucked in a breath at the surge of energy racing through me.

"That's better," I said.

He kneaded gently, and I felt the pull all the way in my core.

Not trusting my legs to hold me up for much longer, considering the amount of adrenaline surging through my veins, I undid the hook and zipper of my slacks. I hooked my thumbs under the band of both my pants and my underwear, lowering them past my hips as Nate started exploring my body with his hands. He used them the way a blind man would, learning how I looked through the sense of touch.

I steadied myself with my hands on his shoulders. He helped me free myself of the last of my clothes, tossing them to the floor. He kissed me again, and I lost myself in sensation. His hands—strong and sure—teased me to a frenzy, until I was aching to be closer to him. He had amazing hands. Skilled hands. Loving hands. Before long, he started using his mouth to torment me in new and delightful ways.

"Nate," I begged, arching into him as he shifted us, placing me on my back.

He took a moment to remove the rest of his clothes and put on a condom, but then the bed shifted with his weight as he settled between my legs. I raised my knees and drew him toward me, so ready to be with him I thought I might burst.

He let out a groan as he slipped easily inside, his head coming down to rest beside mine. I rocked my hips against him, urging him to move with me. He held himself above me, his powerful arms preventing him from crushing me as we crashed into each other repeatedly.

It was all I could do to hold on, both arms around his shoulders, my legs locked behind his waist, riding the cresting waves caused by sensation and emotion colliding inside me. I held on and knew I couldn't let go even if I'd wanted to, because no one had ever made me feel more accepted than Nate did in that moment. My crazy panic about him seeing my body and all, he took me as I was and left me feeling cherished.

It all came together in my mind at the same time as my climax struck. Every muscle in my body clenched, and I clasped Nate tightly to me until the tiny tremors came to a stop. He whispered things in my ear I couldn't make out, driving his hips against me a few more times. His body tensing, his back flexing, he came and rolled off me, drawing me to his side almost in the same movement.

I laid my head on his chest, rising and falling with his breaths, his heart pounding out a rhythm against my ear.

"I could stay like this forever," he said once his breathing started to settle into a more normal pattern. "Never move another muscle. I'd be fine with that."

I'd be fine with it, too. Until the sun came up, and he could see every bit of me. I decided to keep that thought to myself.

"You're awfully quiet," Nate said after a moment. He stretched his arm around my shoulder and drew me closer to his side. "Not having second thoughts now, are you?"

"No regrets," I insisted.

"But? Are you still worried about whatever had you freaking out with the lights?"

I shook my head again and slipped away from Nate, dragging a pillow with me and holding it over my chest and abdomen. Not that he could see me with it pitch black in here, anyway, so it shouldn't matter. But I couldn't seem to face this without covering myself.

Moments ago, *he'd* been what had covered me. It seemed crazy that I could have been so close with him—the two of us touching one another in every way people could touch—but I couldn't bear the thought of his eyes falling on my naked body.

He rolled over so he was facing my back, but this time, he didn't take the pillow away. Not like he had last night. He didn't attempt to make me face him, either. He just rested his hand on my elbow, letting me know he was there. That he wasn't going anywhere.

"Why don't you want me to see you?" he asked.

I tried to shrug it off, but a massive sense of shame was welling up inside me, choking me with its intensity. There was no way to get rid of the sensation other than to spit it out. "It's stupid," I said.

"That's one word that doesn't ever belong anywhere near you."

"No, but… There's no good reason for me to be like this. Except I am."

"Like what?" he asked, so calm and patient, just like always.

"I just— I can't handle anyone looking at me. Seeing me undressed. Seeing me without something covering every single inch of me."

"But you're beautiful. You know you're gorgeous, right? I've never been as turned on as I am when I look at you."

I shook my head. "It's not that, even. It comes down to all my mother's ideas of what's acceptable and what isn't. When I was a girl, she forced me to wear traditional Indian clothes, even though I was living in America. Everything had to be covered all the time—and I do mean *everything*. My neck, face, and hands were just about the only parts of me that ever saw the light of day, all the way through high school. I had to swim in full clothing, so I chose not to swim. I couldn't participate in sports if I wasn't in long pants and long sleeves, so I didn't participate—I just reported on them, instead. She even made me go to my prom in a sari."

"Saris are pretty," he said.

"Pretty, but they're not like regular prom dresses."

"You don't dress like that now," Nate pointed out.

"I wouldn't even if you paid me to. Except, if I'm being completely honest, I still dress like that in some ways."

He made a sound of disagreement.

"No, I'm being serious!" I said. "I wear business suits that cover everything but my neck and my hands. You pointed out yourself that I never wear dresses, and you weren't sure I had legs under there…"

"I was teasing you. Because I like to tease you, not because I think you need to change anything."

"But I do need to change things, because my mother's still in my head. I don't know how to handle anyone seeing me if I don't have every available inch of skin covered in some way."

"Even though I was just inside you?" he asked.

"Even then."

"But you don't have a problem with me touching you?" As if to test the theory, he slid his hand down my side until it settled on my hip.

"No," I said, but the word came out on a puff of air.

"Just with me seeing you."

"I told you it was stupid."

He didn't say anything for so long I thought he might have fallen asleep. But then he curled his arm around my waist and drew me back against him. "Don't say things like that," he murmured, his face buried against my hair.

"Why not?"

"Because I don't like hearing anyone attack the woman I love."

All of those emotions that had been crashing into each other a bit ago? In that moment, they smashed together all at once and caused an explosion.

In my heart.

Chapter Sixteen

Nate

SOMETIME BEFORE SUNRISE, after spending most of the night in my arms, Anne kissed me, found her clothes in the dark, and made her way back to her own room.

There'd been a selfish part of me hoping she'd keep sleeping until the sun lit the room, but I had no intention of pushing her for something she wasn't ready to give me. I might want to deliver her mother a piece of my mind, but the kind of shame Anne felt about her body wasn't something she would break free from overnight. She needed time. And acceptance. And I intended to provide her with as much of both as she required.

With the playoffs in full swing, Bergy and the rest of the coaches weren't holding too many practices these days. We needed rest a hell of a lot more than we needed a refresher course in the systems we'd been using all season long, so that was exactly what they gave us. Instead of a needless practice the day after Game Three, Bergy had us all come in for a brief film session so we could talk about all the things that had gone both right and wrong the night before. Then he gave us the rest of the day off to spend in whatever manner we preferred, with a warning to be very careful if we were out and about in the city, considering the heightened state of tensions.

I wanted to spend it with Anne, of course, but while I had the day off, she still had a job to do. She and some of her crew tagged along with Koz, 501, Coop, and Jo-Jo. I wasn't sure where they were headed, but since Koz was involved, I hoped he wasn't going to get Coop and Jo-Jo in over their heads with anything. They were the two youngest guys on the team, and they were definitely still impressionable. Coop hadn't even been with us the whole season, only getting called up a few months back due to some injuries. I couldn't say that Koz would be a good influence on them, but they were grown men and could do what they wanted…even if what they wanted wasn't good for them. At least 501 was going, too. Maybe he could rein Koz in.

It was probably for the best that Anne had other things to do, anyway, because I needed to write a final essay for one of my classes, and the day off would give me a perfect time to do that.

So, after we finished with the film session, I went to lunch with RJ and Babs before heading back to the hotel alone to break out my laptop and start writing. Hours later I was still working on my paper, going through my notes, and looking things up in textbooks, when my phone buzzed, alerting me to a text message.

Anne: *You busy?*

Me: *Depends on your definition of "busy."*

Anne: *Okay, let's try this again. Are you hungry, do you already have plans for dinner, and/or are you too busy to go grab a bite with me? If you still want to have dinner with me, after last night.*

Me: *I know how you get hangry, so let's get some food.*

Anne: *Meet you in the lobby in ten minutes?*

Me: *Done.*

She was already waiting for me when I got down there, still wearing the business suit she'd had on earlier—pale gray, with a bright green top under the jacket that made the green flecks in her eyes dance. I planted a kiss on her as soon as I reached her side, grinning when she blinked a few times in surprise.

"Hey, gorgeous," I said.

"Hey, yourself." Her expression was filled with a combination of excitement and nerves, much like last night when we'd gotten up to my room. I loved the excitement but hated the nerves. I wanted to help her get past that, but I wasn't sure what she needed from me. No matter what, it would take time—something I needed to remind myself of again. In fact, I might need the reminder a few times.

But there was no rush.

I reached for her hand and headed out front to have a cab hailed. Twenty minutes later, after a bunch of flirting and laughing in the back of the cab, we were seated for dinner at a swanky steak place.

Anne sat across from me as the waiter handed over a wine menu and filled our water glasses. But then she started fidgeting with her suit jacket, like she couldn't make up her mind about something.

"You all right?" I asked.

She nodded, but she didn't stop messing with the jacket. The next thing I knew, she undid the buttons and took the whole thing off, draping it over the back of her chair. The shirt she had on underneath was sleeveless. Two wide straps covered her shoulders, but her arms were bare—and absolutely nothing to be ashamed of. They were toned and shapely, much like the rest of her. Absolutely perfect, if you asked me.

I raised a brow. "You don't need to do that if you're not comfortable."

"I know." She nodded resolutely. "But I *do* need to do this. It's just my arms. There's nothing scandalous about showing off your arms, especially when it's as warm out as it is right now. I can do this."

Her determination was one of the things I loved the most about her. When she made up her mind to do something, she did it no matter how much might stand in her way. We were a lot alike in that way.

"One thing at a time, right?" she said, arching one of those gorgeous brows. With more of her shirt showing, her eyes looked almost fully green.

I was captivated. Completely.

I knew I probably shouldn't draw any more attention to the fact that I could see her arms, but I couldn't resist, just this once. "If you're not careful about how much you show off, I'll get the urge to grope you again."

She narrowed her eyes and gave me a little kick under the table. "Watch it. No public groping."

"But private groping is all right?"

"Depends on how you behave the rest of the night until we're in private again."

"Fair enough."

She took a sip of water. "What'd you do today?"

"Worked on one of my final papers. And what were Koz and the guys up to?"

She gave me a mischievous look but didn't answer.

"Oh God. Tell me he didn't corrupt Coop."

"Corrupt? I wouldn't say that, no."

"But you aren't denying that he dragged them into something."

"Cooper and Johansson got their first tattoos," she said with a shrug.

That definitely could have been worse. But then again... "What did they get? And where?" And how much influence had Koz exerted over their decisions?

"Maybe you should ask them." Anne winked, and the waiter came back for our wine orders, effectively putting an end to that conversation.

Anne

TWO MINUTES INTO the second period of Game Four, Brenden Campbell had been out killing a penalty when he crashed awkwardly into the boards, and a few players from both teams fell on top of him. When he came out from the bottom of the pile, he was carrying his arm in a crazy position, which couldn't be good news.

Turned out he had pulled his shoulder completely out of socket. He was done for the playoffs.

Coach Bergstrom double-shifted a bunch of other players the rest of the game, especially those who normally played left wing—Nate's natural position. In fact, the coach sent Nate out with the third line more than any of his other players. Nate came close to scoring a goal with Cooper's help, but the Blackhawks goaltender snagged it at the last second.

He ended up being the one with the shutout that night, sending the teams back to Portland for Game Five tied at two games apiece.

I spent the flight home sleeping, my head resting on Nate's shoulder while he read more of *The Hunger Games*. He started on the second book in the series before I drifted off. Neither of us had gotten much sleep over the last couple of nights, but he had at least taken his pregame nap this afternoon. I'd been busy editing film for *Eye of the Storm* while the team had their downtime—something I'd been doing more and more of in my so-called time off. There seemed to be no end to things to be done with this job, and it didn't help anything that I was constantly changing my mind about things I'd thought I'd settled on already, as the narratives in front of me shifted. I was at once invigorated by my work and exhausted from it, but I wouldn't have it any other way.

Nate woke me as we landed, shaking out his arm once I straightened away from him. "It's been asleep for the last hour," he said in explanation.

I yawned, covering it with my hand. "You should have shoved me off."

"Not a chance," he said with a wink. "I only get so much time to hold you. Not going to give up even a minute of it if I have anything to say about it."

There wasn't any good reason I could come up with to argue that point.

He picked up my carry-on as well as his own as we left the plane. But instead of taking it to my car, he headed straight for his.

I slowed down enough that he stopped and turned.

"What? You've got a toothbrush in here, right?" He winked.

"I do, but—" It was one thing to spend most of the night in a hotel room with him, when the lights were all out and I could sneak back to my own room before the sun came up. It was something else entirely to be with him all night at his house.

My pulse skipped a few beats.

Nate set our suitcases on the ground and closed the distance between us, cupping my face between both hands. He kissed me, soft and sweet, in the way he tended to do to calm my nerves. "Bring your car. You can leave whenever you're ready to go. I just want to hold you for a while longer."

That was all the encouragement I needed. I headed for my car and followed him to his house. Once there, he carried our bags inside. I debated asking him to go ahead and put mine in my trunk, but stopped myself. I could take it out later, so there was no reason to pick an argument with him now over something so minor.

Then we spent far too long wrapped up in each other, making out on his couch while we watched *The Hunger Games* together. I fell asleep with my head resting on his lap, his fingers combing through my hair.

When I woke hours later, I didn't have it in me to wake him up only so I could go home. He was spread out on the couch, his head lolling back against the cushions. He might be more comfortable in his bed, but I got the sense he needed the sleep more than comfort. Instead, I rearranged the throw blanket he'd draped over me so it covered him, too, and adjusted my position in the hope that we'd both be more comfortable. The lamp was still on, though, so I stretched to turn it off.

Despite my efforts to keep from waking him, his head popped up before I reached the lamp, and he gave me a sleepy smile. "Going home?" he asked, blinking a few times.

"Trying to make you more comfortable."

"No such thing as more comfortable as long as I'm touching you."

I rolled my eyes.

"We could move to the bed," he suggested. "To *sleep*," he added before I could start to panic. "You could go home, too, but I'd like you to stay."

I wanted to stay, too, so I nodded. "Let's do that."

A few minutes later, he'd stripped down to his boxer-briefs and was offering me a T-shirt and some shorts to change into. I refused, still not ready for him to see that much of me. It wasn't exactly comfortable to sleep in all my clothes, but it was a choice between doing that or going home, the way I saw it.

When we crawled into his bed, he curled up behind me, one arm around my waist keeping us tucked in together like spoons in a drawer. All thought of my discomfort over sleeping in my clothes slipped away. Being so close to Nate all night would far outweigh anything like that.

Maybe it was a good thing he'd brought my suitcase in rather than transferring it to my car, after all. That toothbrush would come in handy in the morning.

THE NEXT DAY, Jim Sutter and his assistant, Rachel Campbell, took the day off entirely—something that was as out of character for either of them as I'd seen in the time I'd been working around the Storm organization. They took the time off for me. Or for my show, to be more precise.

Ben, Dave, and I were set up to film at Mr. Sutter's house by midmorning, before the Campbell and Zellinger families were due to arrive. It was quiet while it was just me and my crew along with the general manager and his wife, Elaine. I took the opportunity to focus in on the two of them, seating them on the couch while I asked a few questions.

"So you two were married once before, but then you were divorced for a number of years. Is that right?" I asked.

"A couple of decades, actually," Elaine said.

"I made some big mistakes," Jim added. He winked at his wife and took her hand. "Really big."

"But even after all those years, we still loved each other."

"How did you get back together again after so much time had passed?" I asked.

"It came down to Laura Weber and a bunch of my players' wives," Jim said before delving into the story.

I'd picked up on bits and pieces of it last season, when I'd been covering the team for the local sports network, but the full story was even more fascinating than what I'd already gleaned. The Storm WAGs had placed an ad for him on a dating site. Elaine had run across it and responded. Then she flew halfway across the country to surprise him at Christmas, and the rest was history.

She'd gone back to Minnesota for a few months, preparing to pack up her life and make the move to Portland. A couple of weekends a month, she'd flown back to be with him here, so they could go through the process of getting to know each other again. Then last summer, they'd remarried during the few days between the NHL draft and the opening of the free agency period.

"Elaine was forgiving enough to take a rain check on the honeymoon," he said, winking at me.

"But only because he promised to take me to Europe this coming summer. *Before* the draft, so I can have all his attention."

"And your son?" I asked after hearing the full story, unable to stop from putting myself in his shoes. I couldn't imagine I'd be happy at all if my parents decided to get back together again now. But then again, they hadn't loved each other for most of the time they'd been married. They'd only stayed together because of me, which was in some ways worse than it would have been if they'd split up while I was still in school. But since these two still clearly loved each other... "How's he dealing with the reunion? Is he thrilled to have his parents back together?"

"He's…coming around," Elaine said cautiously.

Ouch. I must have hit on a sore point.

"Dillon blamed me for a lot of things," Jim said. "And he was right to do so. I've had a lot of wrongs to right, and he has every reason to be angry with me."

"But he's starting to let Jim back into his life, a bit at a time. We even went—as a couple—to Dillon's wedding a few months ago."

Before I could delve any deeper into Mr. Sutter's strained relationship with his son, the doorbell rang. All hell broke loose when Elaine opened the door and let the Campbells and Zellingers in. In no time, the living room was filled with four more adults and seven kids—five of them under the age of five—plus toys, food, drinks, laughter, tears, and the insanity of family.

I took a step back and let my cameramen do their jobs, situating myself on the brick hearth by the fireplace so as to be well out of the way. This was about filming the day as it happened, messes and all.

And there were plenty of messes.

Three-year-old redheaded twins Sidney and Peyton Campbell were constantly into everything. Tuck and Maddie, their older siblings, did their best to keep them out of harm's way, but Rachel was constantly following behind her toddlers with wet wipes and a garbage bag, trying to keep the mess contained, even if she couldn't completely prevent it.

Eventually, Tuck gave up since his mother was tackling the job of toddler wrangling. He took out an iPad and started playing a game, oblivious to everything around him.

Maddie also stopped chasing after the kids before long. She buried her nose in her cell phone, but it didn't look like she was playing a game. Probably texting a boy, based on the way she was blushing.

Brenden took a seat in the dining room so that the little ones would stop trying to climb him like a jungle gym. That was where Elaine took it upon herself to wait on him. She brought him food and drinks, homemade cookies, and anything else she could, until he complained that while his shoulder had been dislocated, his legs still worked perfectly well, thank you very much. That slowed her down in terms of spoiling him rotten, but it didn't stop her completely.

Eric Zellinger—the former Storm captain, current Tulsa Thunderbirds captain, and Brenden's best friend—sprawled out on the floor in the living room and let his little ones crawl all over him while he caught up with Mr. Sutter. Eric's wife, Dana, alternated between changing diapers as needed, refilling snacks and drinks for the kids, taking the toddlers to the bathroom every three minutes, and trying to convince Mrs. Sutter to stop babying Brenden—who happened to be Dana's brother.

Having been an only child, I found this whole situation to be as wonderful as it was unfamiliar. Not to mention slightly uncomfortable. I'd been somewhat overwhelmed with the two Johnson kids that day a few weeks ago. This was more than I'd been prepared for.

I definitely wasn't ready for Dana to deposit her infant son with Elaine before coming to join me on the brick hearth. "You've been putting together a great show," she said, but I could barely hear her above the cacophony surrounding us.

Still, I swelled up a bit with pride. It was nice to have my hard work acknowledged. "You've been watching?"

"Wouldn't miss it! Eric and I tune in every week as soon as it goes live, as long as we've already got the kids down for the night. We spent so many years here that it's kind of like being back with the family."

"Well, that's nice to hear." Especially since I'd been focusing so much on the family aspect of the team. She was taking from it exactly what I had hoped would come across. It was hard to believe in my judgment, though, when my boss was so completely against the choices I'd made.

"I was kind of worried," she admitted conspiratorially. "Before we started watching, that is. I mean, we all follow the news, so everyone knows about all the things going on around the team lately. We've been dealing with enough of that on our own, lately, after what happened with Eric and Drew Nash in the last game of the season."

Nash had taken a skate blade to the neck and, rather than let him bleed to death on the ice, Zellinger had immediately used his own hands to put pressure on the wound. In the aftermath, it came out that Nash was HIV positive, so the Thunderbirds had been dealing with their own hullabaloo over that.

"He's okay, though, right?" I asked.

"Tests are normal so far, but sometimes it doesn't show up for a long time. So we have to keep testing and taking precautions. Anyway, I was sure you were going to focus the show more on the external stuff, which would have been a shame. We get plenty of that just from turning on the news. That's not what the show should be about, you know?"

"You could have taken those words right out of my mouth when I met with my boss the other day," I said. Then I wished I hadn't said so much. It was one thing to talk to Nate about how I would be losing my job. It was something else entirely to bring someone from the outside in.

"Well, like I said…I'm glad. You're showing exactly what I want to see." Then she grinned. "My brother tells me you and Ghost are an item lately. I had a feeling that could happen from watching the way you two flirted all the time whenever you interviewed him. It's good to know my radar still works, even though I've got mommy-brain. You should have brought him along today."

I felt heat rush to my cheeks. Good thing my skin would hide the blush. "I'm working today," I pointed out.

"Yeah. And? No one here would've cared if there was one more person around."

"He's coming to dinner tonight with my father, so this might have been too much for him for one day, anyway." But then again, he might be more used to being around all these kids than I was, considering about half his teammates had little ones.

Maybe I should start to get used to them.

Just then, Brenden let out a pained sound, and we all turned to find both of his little redheaded twins trying to climb his arm—the same arm that he'd injured yesterday.

"Damn," Dana said, jumping to her feet, but Rachel and Mr. Sutter beat her into the dining room to pry the little girls off their father's arm.

My guys leaped into action, shifting the focus of their filming without me giving them any direction. I followed, keeping my distance as I observed the action. Maddie and Tuck hauled their little sisters away to play in the living room with their Zellinger cousins while Dana and Eric worked together to resituate Brenden's arm in his sling. Elaine bounced the baby and moved him out of the way. Mr. Sutter went into the kitchen and came back with an ice pack.

But my eyes landed on Rachel and wouldn't leave her. I slipped up behind Ben and whispered in his ear to be sure he was filming her, preferably at an angle where he could capture Brenden's reactions, too.

Fat tears rolled down her cheeks as she took the ice pack from her boss and strapped it to her husband's shoulder with an ACE bandage. "I know you're not ready, but will you *please* consider retiring this summer? Because I don't know how much more of this I can take."

Brenden didn't respond, but his eyes said everything: he wasn't ready to call it quits, even if his body already had—but he didn't want to torment his wife anymore, either. Or his kids.

My heart broke for them both.

Dana got up and came back over to me. "Did you get all that?" she asked quietly.

I nodded. "I think so."

"Good. Because this is the story you're telling. The human story."

She was right about that.

Chapter Seventeen

Nate

MY PALMS WERE sweating. Completely cliché, and I knew it, but I couldn't stop it from happening as we pulled into the driveway at Anne's father's house for dinner.

"Promise he won't bite," she teased. She was wearing a dress again—a soft pink thing that showed off a bit of arm and a bit of leg, but not too much of either. Hell, there was even some chest showing, although not anywhere near as much as I'd like to see. We definitely weren't entering cleavage territory, but that did nothing to negate the fact that she had a heck of a lot more skin showing than I was used to seeing. And I liked it.

"Does he have a dog that'll do the biting for him?"

"Nope, and no cats, either." She grabbed her purse from the floorboard and climbed out of my car, not giving me any more time to delay the inevitable.

I opened my door to follow her. "You do realize this would be a hell of a lot less awkward if we hadn't—" *Already had sex* died on my tongue as her father opened the front door, and she rushed ahead to hug him.

"Dad, this is Nate Golston," she said when she backed away. "Nate, my father, Brian Dennison."

I climbed the steps, still nervous as hell. "Dr. Dennison. Nice to meet you, sir."

"Brian's fine," he said, holding out a hand for me to shake.

I wished I weren't sweating, but I wiped my hand on my pant leg as discreetly as possible before taking his.

In no time, he had whisked us both inside the house, which smelled deliciously of steak and potatoes, and was offering me my choice of beer or wine. Maybe it wasn't going to be so bad after all.

He opened a beer for himself, too, and headed into the kitchen to flip the steaks on his grill pan. Anne followed him and started putting together a salad, both of them looking much like this was something very familiar to them.

"Tough game last night," Brian said.

"You were watching?" I wondered if it was just because of Anne dating me, or if he was actually interested.

He winked in his daughter's direction. "I like to stay on top of things when it comes to my little girl. But I also needed to know what happened before I went in to work this morning. My nurses are all diehard Storm fans. One of them is half in love with the one... Oh, what's his name again?" He looked over at Anne for help. "I told you before."

"The one Lacey has a crush on? Or do you mean Brenda?"

"Lacey. He's the new one."

"Leif Sorenson," Anne said, winking at me.

I laughed. "I'd say I could introduce them, but I don't think his wife would like it too much. Or his little girl."

"Probably better to pretend you don't know about her crush, then, if you ever meet her," Brian said.

To my complete surprise, the night progressed much along the same pattern. Anne had been right—there was no reason at all to be nervous about meeting her father. He was as normal and down-to-earth as they came, very similar to my own parents, as far as I could tell. He might be a doctor and be much better-educated than them, but I saw a lot more similarities than differences. He made me feel right at home.

Halfway through dinner, though, the doorbell rang.

Anne looked over at her father. "Were you expecting someone else?"

He shook his head, wiped his face with a napkin, and pushed his chair back. "Probably someone going door to door for one of the candidates. I'll get rid of them." Then he turned to me. "Sorry about this."

"Don't be sorry on my account," I insisted.

He disappeared down the hall, but he wasn't gone long. And he wasn't alone when he returned.

"Anika," a woman with a heavy accent said. She was wearing a colorful sari and head covering, and she set a purse down on the table.

Anne dropped her knife and fork on the table, eyes furiously wide. "Mother," she said coldly. "What are you doing here?" She passed accusing eyes over in her father's direction.

"She called me over the weekend," he said. "Apparently I let it slip that you'd be here tonight without realizing it, and she thought that would be her best chance at intercepting you. I'm sorry."

"What are you wearing?" the mother demanded, sounding scandalized. "All that skin showing. It's indecent."

"It's as far from indecent as she could get," Brian said, rolling his eyes. "She looks beautiful." I wanted to give him a fist bump or a good slap on the back. Anne's father was definitely someone I could get behind.

"She looks like a slut," the mother said, and Anne recoiled.

"Now stop right there," I put in. "You're way out of line with that. She might not dress in a way you approve of, but that doesn't make her a slut, and it doesn't make her inappro—"

"And why?" the mother cut in, glaring in my direction. "Why must you go on with this man? Going all over the place with him. Kissing. Touching. Disgusting and brazen, the way you're behaving in public. But what should I expect from this athlete? He doesn't even have a college education, but you think—"

"Don't do this, Mother," Anne said. "Just don't. I think it's time for you to go."

"How can you think he's good enough for you?"

Anne stood and picked up her mother's purse. "I don't think it. I know it. And I know you don't understand, and that's perfectly all right. Your opinion doesn't matter to me. I don't care if you approve, because I love him. I do. I love Nate, and that's all that matters, okay? When I'm with him, I'm happy. He wants me to have what *I* want, not what he thinks I need because of some twisted values. He doesn't try to turn me into something I'm not. He doesn't expect me to do a thousand things because he supposedly knows what I need better than I do. So whether you understand or not, he's perfect for me. And you need to leave."

I was so proud of Anne for standing up to her mother that I was shaking with it. Add in the fact that she'd said she loved me, and I was a mess inside. I wasn't even sure she realized she'd said it, but she had, and that was all that mattered.

"Anika!" her mother shouted. "How dare you speak to your mother this way."

"I'd say it's about time she did," Brian said. "And like Anne said, it's time for you to go."

Anne carried the purse toward the front door, but her mother didn't budge—not until Brian put a hand on her arm and gently but firmly guided her in the same direction.

I waited in the dining room for them to come back, partially because I thought Anne and her father might need a father-daughter moment, but also because I seriously wanted to give her mother a piece of my mind and wasn't sure I'd be able to bite my tongue. This wasn't my moment; it was Anne's, and she'd done brilliantly.

A few minutes later, they returned. Anne walked straight into my arms and buried her face against my neck, which was exactly where I wanted her to be. I held on to her, stroking her back until she stopped shaking.

Brian went back into the kitchen to get another beer, winking at me on his way. I supposed I'd passed his test, whatever it might have been. But that didn't matter. The only thing important right now was that Anne wanted me.

"I love you, too," I said quietly in her ear.

She backed away and blinked at me a couple of times. "You what?"

"I love you, too." I kissed her cheek and winked. "You told your mother you loved me. You said it twice, actually."

"I suppose I did, didn't I?"

"Mm hmm. But I have to warn you."

"What?" she said cautiously, a wary expression drawing her eyebrows together.

"If she ever barges in like that again and tries to tell you anything about how you're not good enough, I'm not going to hold back. I'm going to give her a piece of my mind."

Anne laughed quietly. "If she tries that again, I'll cheer you on."

"Good. Because I think I told you once before... I don't like hearing anyone attack the woman I love."

FOR GAME FIVE, Bergy moved Q up to play left wing on the third line, filling in for Soupy. Jiri Dvorak took Q's usual place on the right wing on the fourth line, instead of sitting in the press box with the other healthy scratches and guys who were injured. That meant he had no need to double-shift me, which was just as well.

I had what was probably my best game of the playoffs that night, scoring two of the team's four goals and nearly scoring a third in the second overtime period. We still ended up losing that one, though. Patrick Kane did what he almost always did in overtime during the playoffs for the Blackhawks, and he scored a crazy goal near the end of the third overtime period.

For the first time, we were behind in the series. It didn't sit well with any of us. Now, we knew we had to win the next two games in a row, or else we would be heading out to the golf course a lot sooner than we wanted to be.

We had two days off before Game Six, thank goodness, so we didn't have to fly to Chicago in the wee hours of the morning after that one finally came to an end. But there were protests planned across the country for Saturday—including in both Chicago and Portland. The people of Chicago were actually planning multiple protest marches throughout the city all day long. After the higher-ups for both teams talked it over, it was decided we'd all fly out on Friday. They weren't keen on having us all in the city while the protests were ongoing, but there was no telling what would happen with the airports and traffic if we waited. Better to already be there and ready to go, apparently.

After arriving in Chicago on Friday, Anne was busy with her guys, filming a session with the coaching staff, so I holed up in my hotel room to take the last of my finals for the spring semester. By the time I finished with that, Anne had gone up to the United Center with Drywall Tierney and the rest of the equipment staff. Her text message to me said she didn't expect to be back until late, so I should find someone else to have dinner with.

I texted a few of the guys to see who was around. RJ was already out with Burnzie and Harry. Babs and 501 were already eating. Hammer, Thor, Jonny, and Vinny appeared to be having a meeting of the Older-Than-Dirt Fathers Club, but they offered to let me tag along. I passed, since I wasn't in the mood to watch hair videos all night.

Finally, though, I found a couple of takers in Aaron Ludwiczak and Dylan Poplawski. I met Luddy and Pops down in the hotel lobby. After talking to the concierge for a few minutes, we decided to head out to an Italian restaurant within walking distance of the hotel. We wanted somewhere close enough to walk since traffic was unusually heavy and we weren't in the mood to sit in a cab for an hour to travel only a few miles.

"Why aren't you out with Anne tonight?" Luddy asked on our way. "Hardly ever see you without her these days."

"She's with Drywall tonight."

"You've got competition," Pops said, laughing his ass off. "Better watch out, or he'll be stealing your girl."

I rolled my eyes. "I don't doubt he's flirting with her, the son of a bitch. But I'm not so sure she'll fall for it."

"She fell for it with you," Luddy pointed out. "Drywall might be missing some hair—"

"All his hair," I cut in.

"—but at least he's not a fucking shrimp."

The ribbing went on like that throughout the night, all three of us joking around and picking at each other for our various flaws, real or perceived. The food was good, and the break from all the stress of the playoffs was more than welcome, so we ended up staying for a few hours, our waiter coming back to bring us more drinks a few times. Once we finally decided to return to the hotel, we left him a hefty tip and made our way back out to the street.

Less than a block from the restaurant, we came into a thick crowd of people—so thick we were forced to slow down and take notice. Most of them were black, but there were a few white, Hispanic, and Asian faces among them. Many were carrying signs.

"I thought the protests around the city were all supposed to be tomorrow," Pops said.

So had I, but apparently we were either mistaken or misinformed. "Come on," I said, trying to shove my way through the sea of bodies. "Let's get out of here." Most of the protests I'd seen on the news in the last few days had been peaceful, but you never knew what might happen when so many people came together over such a heated issue. We would *probably* be safe out on the streets, but we'd *definitely* be a hell of a lot safer back at the hotel.

Pops and Luddy helped me push through the bodies around us, but people didn't want to let us through. It seemed like a big crush on all sides, like one of the New Year's Eve parties I'd been to years ago, where everyone wanted to be somewhere other than where they were, but they all just did their own thing, not following along with any sort of flow or traffic pattern.

Speaking of traffic, the cars on the street were all at a standstill. I caught a glimpse of a few uniformed police officers blowing whistles and trying to direct people with arm-waving directions, but no one was doing what they were told. In fact, there were dozens of people sitting in the street, blocking traffic completely and refusing to move. With every minute that passed, more people sat down.

This was getting worse by the moment. I pushed harder, trying to create any sort of opening in the crowd, but without much luck. We were only moving by inches, when we should have been moving by feet.

Where the hell was Anne? Was she caught up in a mess like this, too? With any luck, she'd already finished up with whatever they were filming today and gotten back to the hotel before this shit started.

I took out my cell phone, holding it as tightly as I could so I wouldn't lose it, while I typed out a quick text message for Anne, asking where she was. No response right away, but I wouldn't expect her to look at her phone if she was still working.

The noise in the crowd started to climb, raised voices chanting the names of Marcus Jameson and the two teenagers who'd been killed.

I glanced over my shoulder to be sure Luddy and Pops were still with me. They caught my eye and nodded, a silent confirmation that they were ready to get the fuck out of there, and the sooner, the better.

Finally, I saw a bit of a clearing ahead—not much of one, but enough to give me hope we would be able to move more freely soon— and I fought my way through to reach it.

A police officer was trying to get people to cooperate, but there was a man standing right in his face and screaming about how the fucking murdering cops needed to watch their racist asses, and no one was doing what he told them to do.

I caught the eye of another officer nearby and pointed toward the other end of the street, trying to show that we just wanted to get out of there. There was no point in trying to say anything from this distance. No one would hear me over the insanity.

He blew his whistle and waved us through. "Keep on moving, guys," he said as we reached him. "Keep on moving and get out of here."

"Yeah. Thanks," I said. *Stay safe* was on my lips but got swallowed by the sound of gunshots and screams and the sight of the officer falling to the ground, while someone collapsed on me from behind.

Chapter Eighteen

Anne

"THANKS FOR LETTING us tag along," I said to Drywall Tierney as his crew and mine both worked on putting away all of their equipment.

He winked at me and put a cover over his skate sharpener. "Any chance I get to spend time with a pretty lady like you, you know I'm going to take it."

"Just don't let your wife hear you talking like that," one of his guys said, and everyone laughed.

Drywall's guys had been doing some prep work at the arena to get ready for tomorrow's practice and Sunday's game, and I'd brought Ben and Dave along to get some time filming them. I wanted to show all the work that's involved with a professional hockey team, and not simply focus on the players. Since we'd already spent some time with Jim Sutter and some of the coaching staff, I was starting to delve a bit deeper. I wanted to meet with the trainers, maybe even follow some of the scouts around as they prepared for the upcoming draft.

The family atmosphere surrounding the Portland Storm went well beyond the players and coaches, encompassing everyone involved with the team. The more time I spent with them, the more I *wanted* to spend with them.

Once everything was situated, we headed for the exits.

Before we got there, though, a security officer stopped us and shook his head. "Can't let you leave right now. There's an active shooter situation at a protest not far from here, only a few blocks away. Police are asking us to keep everyone inside."

My blood froze in my veins. "A few blocks away?" The hotel was within a few blocks, too. Most of the team, the coaches…they could all be out and about right now.

Nate could be out there.

"There's a television in the locker room," Drywall said. "Let's go put it on CNN so we'll know what's happening."

Everyone nodded in agreement, and we headed back in that direction.

While we walked, I tore through my backpack to find my cell phone. All the guys who'd been with me did the same, immediately looking to see who had been trying to reach them and to tell their loved ones that they were safe. The wait for my phone to power on seemed interminable. I cursed myself for my habit of turning it off instead of just silencing it while I worked, but finally the screen came to life at around the same time as Drywall got the TV on and found the news coverage.

I had half a dozen messages waiting for me. One was from Nate, sent about ten minutes ago, simply asking where I was.

I replied that I was still at the arena and was safe, but that they were keeping us there until further notice, then asked where he was.

No reply.

While I waited, I responded to the messages from my father, Ben, Bill, Tim, and the other members of my crew who weren't with me, keeping one eye on the news.

Everyone but Nate replied almost immediately.

I felt like I might vomit.

Once I'd contacted everyone I could think of, including my mother, to let them know I was safe, I set my phone aside and tried not to worry about Nate. His phone might be dead. He might be somewhere that he couldn't use it. He might not have heard it at all. For all I knew, he was out with some of the guys at a bar, and they were all none the wiser about the situation going on in the city.

Other than the news reports, the only sounds in the locker room were the message alerts on our cell phones or occasionally one of the guys answering a call to calm a loved one. But the more I watched the news, the more I worried about Nate.

Because he still hadn't responded. And because what I saw was awful.

A protest in the streets that started out peaceful but quickly got out of hand. People sitting in the roadways. Drivers threatening to run them over. Citizens getting in the faces of police officers and screaming bloody murder at them. It was utter chaos, and that was before someone opened fire with semiautomatic weapons.

The first shots were fired about thirty minutes ago, but there were already reports of at least three deaths and close to a dozen injuries. Not only that, but shots were still ringing out on the live footage.

It appeared the shooters were targeting the police officers. The first reports said there were two gunmen. Then three. Now they were saying they suspected at least four were involved, and they wouldn't rule out the possibility of more than that. Some people were calling 9-1-1 and reporting bomb threats. It was impossible to know just exactly how bad the situation was. Only that it was horrific.

If he was out there, would I ever see him again? What if he was one of the people who'd been caught in the crossfire? He could be dead or dying at this very moment.

Despite the gravity of the situation, the one thing slapping me over the head repeatedly was that even though I loved him, and even though I knew I wanted nothing more than to be with him, I still hadn't ever let him see any part of my body other than a bit of forearm and calf. How unbelievably selfish was it of me to keep any part of myself from him? And how ridiculous was it that I was so concerned about modesty when it came to being with a man who clearly loved and respected me?

I hoped beyond hope that Nate wasn't out there on those streets. But if and when I ever saw him again, things would change between us. I wouldn't hide from him anymore. I wouldn't allow my mother's voice to stand between the two of us. That was a promise I was making to myself, here and now, and I would damned well keep it.

But amid the chaos, the live cameras captured acts of true heroism.

A woman was caught in the middle of the pandemonium with her three small children, one she was pushing in a stroller. When others saw that she couldn't carry them all and the two walking kids couldn't run to safety fast enough, they dropped what they were carrying to help her protect her children.

A police officer had two men screaming in his face, but when the first shots rang out, he knocked them both to the ground and covered them with his own body, drawing his weapon so he was ready to take on whatever threat came their way.

A restaurant employee raced out into the streets and ushered dozens of people inside the restaurant, providing them with cover from the gunshots.

There seemed to be no end to the stories of humanity shining through this act of wanton hatred.

The news anchor announced they were going to cut to another bit of amateur footage that had been posted to social media, so I took out my phone one more time to see if I'd somehow missed a message from Nate.

Nothing. Nothing at all. I wanted to cry, but I knew that once I broke down and started, I wouldn't be able to stop any time soon. Becoming a blubbering mess wouldn't help anything, so I forced my tears back.

"Shit, that's Luddy," Drywall said. "Isn't it? Looks like Luddy."

I jerked my head up to see two men, one with his arm draped over the other's shoulders and limping along, with blood staining one leg of his jeans as he walked.

"It is. And Poplawski," Ben said. "That's Poplawski carrying him."

The tears I'd been trying to hold inside stung the backs of my eyes. But then any attempts to keep myself from crying fell apart, because the camera panned over to show Nate dragging along a police officer, who had a hand pressed to his belly, in much the same way Poplawski was helping Ludwiczak.

The four men were going as fast as they could away from the shots in the background, but they couldn't move very fast. Then more shots sounded in the distance, and the grainy cell phone video came to an end.

I dropped my phone onto my lap. Dave moved to sit beside me, putting an arm around my shoulders. All I could do was let him hold me, because there wasn't any chance my tears would stop for a long time to come.

Nate

A COUPLE OF EMTs raced over to us, taking the officer I'd been dragging. They helped him onto a gurney. About a block ago, he'd completely passed out from blood loss or shock or something. I'd picked him up onto my shoulders and carried him as far as I could that way, but he was almost as big as I was. He weighed too much for me to get very far like that, so I'd just done what I had to do.

They whisked him off and loaded him into the back of an ambulance. He was gone before I realized I didn't even know his name.

Two more EMTs rushed over and, checking out the blood all over me, tried to help.

"Not my blood," I said, waving them off. "I'm fine. But my buddy…"

Pops had been pretty much dragging Luddy along the whole way, too, and I knew they weren't far behind me. I turned and pointed them out.

One of the EMTs nodded and they wheeled their gurney back to where I'd indicated. Within minutes, they had Luddy strapped in and were rushing him toward another waiting ambulance.

"You two coming?" they asked.

I looked over at Pops, and we both nodded at the same time. "We're coming," I said. For one thing, I didn't want Luddy to be alone right now. And for another, the sooner I could get the fuck off these streets, the better. We knew we'd been moving away from the gunshots, but we could still hear them in the distance. Being out on the streets seemed like a bad idea, especially since we didn't know who was doing the shooting, how many were involved, or where they were set up.

They sent Pops up to the passenger seat and I climbed in the back. In no time, the siren was wailing, so loud as to be deafening, and the ambulance was in motion.

The EMT in the back immediately started assessing Luddy, asking him where it hurt and how many shots he thought he'd taken while she took his vital signs.

"Think I just got hit once," he said. "In my left thigh."

She cut open his jeans and took a quick look, then tossed me a box of gloves. "Put those on. I need your help, since you're here."

I dug out a pair and slipped them into place, then looked over at her.

"Put pressure on the wound," she ordered me. Then she set to work on inserting an IV into his arm.

"If you wanted to cop a feel, there were easier ways to do it, you know," Luddy joked.

I breathed a hell of a lot easier since he felt up to making jokes.

"Maybe I should've been the one in the back," Pops called out from the front.

"Wanna trade places?" I asked. "Because he's not anything to write home about."

We kept up a steady stream of jokes the whole way to the hospital, which helped to keep Luddy calm. I figured that was a good thing. The last thing he needed right now was to start panicking.

Once they wheeled him into the emergency room, Pops and I found seats in the waiting room and took a breath for the first time in what felt like hours.

A woman who had seen us come in walked out for a moment. When she returned, she had bottled water for each of us. "We've been watching on the news. It's horrible."

Horrible was putting it mildly.

"Thanks," I said. We took the water. I downed half of mine in a few swallows. Then I turned to Pops. "You still have your phone?" I'd dropped mine when the first shots rang out, and it got lost in the shuffle. But one of us needed to let people know we were all right.

He blinked a couple of times, the shock of what we'd been through still coursing through him. But then he nodded. "Yeah. Yeah, I do." He took his phone out and got to work.

"Let Jim and the coaches know once you've talked to your family."

"Gimme your parents' numbers, too. I'll send them a message. And Anne."

"Shit." Anne's number. I didn't know it. I'd saved it in my phone, but I didn't have the first clue what it was.

"You don't know them?"

"I know my parents' numbers." I rattled them off, and he shot them a quick message, his phone going crazy with responses coming in.

"I'll see if Jim or one of the coaches can get word to Anne for you," he said. "Surely someone has her number."

I only hoped that she was safe and sound, somewhere well away from what we'd just gone through. And I wished she was with me now, because there was nothing I wanted more than to wrap her up in my arms and tell her how much I loved her, as many times as she could bear to hear it.

Even then, it wouldn't be enough.

IT WAS WELL after midnight by the time Pops and I got back to the team hotel, both of us still covered in the caked-on, dried-up blood of the guys we'd carried.

Luddy had needed surgery. He'd taken two bullets in the thigh. One had gone straight through; the other had to be removed. He was in the clear now, though. He'd be perfectly fine once everything healed. They were keeping him in the hospital overnight as a precaution, and he wouldn't be back on the ice for a while, but those were relatively minor concerns.

The cop I'd carried hadn't fared so well. The bullets had pierced an internal organ or two, so he was still in surgery when the two of us had climbed into the car Jim had taken to the hospital. He wanted us to go back in it and get some rest while he stuck around with Luddy.

Anne was in the lobby when we walked in, surrounded by RJ and a bunch of the rest of my teammates, looking like she'd been through the wringer. As soon as she saw me, she was on her feet and running. I caught her in mid-leap and wrapped her up in my arms.

I never wanted to let her go again.

Another couple of hours later, I'd finally reassured all of the guys that I was fine, that Pops was fine, and that yes, even Luddy would be fine. Sleep wasn't on any of our minds. Being together was.

Through it all, Anne hadn't left my side. For that matter, I couldn't make myself let go of her hand. I needed the physical reassurance of her presence in a way that I'd never felt before. I wasn't sure I'd ever feel anything quite so profoundly as that again, no matter how long I lived or what else I experienced.

But now, she and I were in my room. Just the two of us. Once we came in, I'd collapsed on the small sofa, and she had curled up next to me, and neither of us had moved an inch. I put an arm around her shoulders. She rested her head on mine, the way she had on the plane that night when RJ had snapped the photo of us.

"I should get in the shower," I said after a long time.

She nodded. "You should."

But neither of us got up. I didn't want to let her go for long enough to wash the blood away, but I couldn't spend the whole night like this, either.

Finally, I forced myself to straighten away from her and stand. She reached for my hand so I could help her up.

"You going back to your room?" I asked, dreading her answer. Tonight, of all nights, I wanted her to stay with me. I needed her to keep me grounded.

She shook her head but didn't explain. Still holding my hand, she walked toward my bathroom, bringing me along behind her. Once we were in there, she turned on the water in the shower before turning to help me out of my clothes. My pants came off easily enough, but my shirt was stuck to my skin. It wouldn't come free without potentially ripping out a bunch of chest hair in the process.

"You'll have to soak it under the spray," she said.

I was too bone-weary to argue. Still in my boxer-briefs and the shirt, I climbed into the shower and let the water do the work. Closing my eyes, I put my head under the spray.

But then I felt Anne climbing into the shower behind me.

"What are you doing?" I asked.

She didn't answer. Not with words, at least. Soapy cloth in hand, she scrubbed the places on my back where the dried blood was causing the most problems. Her touch soothed my nerves more than I'd imagined possible.

From the way her body brushed against mine, I could tell she'd taken off all her clothes before joining me. She was behind me, true, but the lights were still on. This was a huge step for her. So huge it felt like I might have her heart in a vise, much like she had mine. One wrong step, and I could derail everything.

"Turn around," she said after a few minutes.

But I hesitated. "I can take care of the front."

She rested her forehead against the back of my arm, wrapping one of her arms around my waist. "Let me."

"You don't have to do this, Anne."

"I know that." Then she inched around in front of me since I hadn't turned. "Let me."

I was too deep in shock to resist her gentle ministrations, too touched to do anything but stand beneath the warm spray of water and allow her to tend to me.

After working silently for a while, she dropped the cloth and attempted to slip her hands beneath my shirt, testing to be sure all the stuck-on places were now loose before dragging it over my head.

"Thank you," I said, but it felt so completely inadequate for all that had happened.

Anne shook her head, on the verge of tears. Then she came into my arms again, burying her face against my chest. Shaking. God, she was shaking so hard. I squeezed her to me, hoping to soothe her nerves and my own at the same time.

"I was so scared," she said. "I sent you messages, but you weren't responding, and we saw what was happening out there, and I didn't know where you were, and I was terrified. I didn't know if you were okay, and all I could think was that I'd never see you again. That it would all be over, and I had been so caught up in my mother's ridiculous thinking that I hadn't ever let you see me. I'd barely told you that I loved you, but even that's not enough. Those are just words, you know? But I'm not going to let her have that kind of power over me. Not anymore. Life's too short to spend it worrying if the things I do or say or wear would meet with her approval. So I thought I needed to put some action behind the words. If I really love you, then I can't hide any part of myself from you. Not ever again."

I might have been holding myself together well enough up until that point, but her words shattered me.

Chapter Nineteen

Nate

THE MEDIA CIRCUS had been bad before, or so I'd thought. The way the press had reacted—or overreacted, in my opinion—to the banana peel incident had been nothing in comparison to the way all the news outlets wanted a piece of me now. They wanted to talk to Pops, too, since he'd been involved, but more of them wanted me. Because I was black, which supposedly made me more qualified to comment on the trauma we'd experienced on Friday night. If Luddy had been made available to the media, I knew he would be getting more attention than he would ever want, since he'd actually been shot. But now he was on the injured reserve, so he didn't have to deal with the media. Only Pops and I did.

They surrounded me every chance they could, always wanting to get more out of me than I'd been willing to give before.

"Surely now, after being involved in one of the protests, you've got something to say," one of them insisted, shoving a microphone in my face after the morning skate before Game Six.

It turned out I did have something to say, after all. "To start, I wasn't *involved* in one of the protests. The guys and I were just trying to walk back to the hotel after having dinner, and we got caught in the mess. But beyond that, yeah, I do have something to say." I felt Kurt's tension as he stood next to me, ready to jump in and come to my rescue in case I started to say something I shouldn't. But I didn't need him tonight, and I refused to be reined in now. "Black lives matter. Absolutely, and I don't think there are many people out there who don't agree with that statement. Maybe a few buffoons who think throwing banana peels at my feet or spewing hateful words somehow makes them better than someone whose skin is a different color than their own, I don't know. But recklessly going out there and killing cops, who were trying to *protect* the people who were protesting against them... That isn't the answer. We're never going to stop the cycle of violence by adding more violence on top of it. We've got to love each other. Period. We need to go back and listen to the words of Dr. King. What was it he said? Hate begets hate, but love begets love? Something like that. He was right then, and he's still right now. We're breeding hate. And it has to stop. We have to start loving each other. That's what I have to say."

Before they could ask me anything else, I walked out. Colesy and a few of the other guys winked at me on my way.

Luddy had been released from the hospital and was in good spirits, even though he was in a decent amount of pain. The bullets had torn through muscle in the outside of his thigh, so it'd take a while to heal enough for him to get back on skates. At least, that was what the doctors were telling us. There was the distinct possibility that the healing process could take longer than expected, but we weren't going to let ourselves think or talk like that, especially when we were around him. Everyone wanted to keep his spirits up.

In fact, instead of taking a pregame nap like we usually did, most of the guys got together in Luddy's room to hang out. Anne brought a couple of her cameramen along to film, but at this point, most of us didn't even notice the intrusion.

I, for one, was *glad* to have Anne with us. I wasn't keen on letting her out of my sight, now that we'd experienced firsthand the evil that existed in our world. The people who left threats for her online might not ever choose to act on them, but I'd rather have her with me, all the same.

It didn't need to be said—we were playing for Luddy now. As a team, we would be using him as our motivation for the rest of the playoffs.

With Luddy officially out of the lineup, Bergy put me on the top line with RJ and Babs for Game Six—a game we won by a healthy five-to-one margin. We flew home in good spirits, considering all that we'd been through in the last few days, ready to take on the Blackhawks in an all-or-nothing Game Seven situation. But we'd be doing it on our home ice. In *our* arena, surrounded by *our* fans.

We'd waited to fly home until Monday morning. Usually when we got back from a road trip, the guys' families were waiting for them at home. This time, almost all of them had come to the airport. Emotions were running high, as was to be expected in the fallout of the shooting. As soon as a guy made his way off the plane, his family raced into his arms. Since my parents were still at home in Toronto and I'd been able to wrap Anne up in my love while they hadn't had the same opportunity with their loved ones, I took it upon myself to help Luddy off the plane. Besides, Anne and her guys were filming the homecoming, so she was otherwise occupied.

Harry joined me, which seemed odd, considering the circumstances.

"Isn't Jasinda here to meet you?" I asked.

"Jasinda?" he repeated, giving me a blank look. "Why would— She's at work," he finished suddenly.

I didn't have a chance to think much of it, as Luddy's fiancée and parents rushed over with a wheelchair for him, and Dani Weber stalked up to Harry and shoved him hard in the chest with a look of utter fury in her eyes.

He backed away from the rest of us, until they were well out of hearing distance, Dani advancing on him with every step of his retreat. I watched them for a moment, fascinated beyond belief. I had no clue what was going on between those two or how Jasinda fit into the picture, other than the bit Anne had included in *Eye of the Storm*, but I would love to be a fly on the wall. In fact, there was a part of me that wished Anne would send one of her guys over to capture whatever was going down between those two at the moment, but they were all otherwise occupied with filming the more tender reunions taking place.

That did seem to fit the type of story line Anne had been telling, I supposed, but there was no point in denying my disappointment.

Anne

In shaping the narrative of the next webisode, I decided I wanted to follow the same path I'd been following all along. I chose to veer away from the horrors we'd all experienced in Chicago, instead keeping the focus on the Storm family as a whole.

During Game Seven, I had a couple of my cameramen filming game footage, but I set up Dave and Ben—my two guys who'd done the most work with the more intimate pieces—in the owner's box with the players' families, and in the press box with the injured players, respectively. I split my time between the two areas, keeping one eye on the action of the game while I alternated between observing and interviewing the various subjects of focus.

In the owner's box, everyone was on edge because of what was at stake in the game, but also relieved because their men had come home relatively unscathed following a harrowing experience.

Dani Weber had finished her semester at fashion school and was home for the summer. She wasn't the only new addition to their ranks, either. Luke had also returned to Portland now that the school year was at an end. I did my best not to pry into the discussions going on between those two and Katie Babcock, but I couldn't help but hope Dave managed to capture a bit of it.

There was a sense of quiet focus in the press box when I joined Brenden Campbell, Aaron Ludwiczak, Dominic "Bear" Medved, and Andrew Jensen, particularly since the game was still scoreless. It was starting to take on a feeling of first team to score wins. Usually, when I was around a group of the players, they spent most of their time ribbing each other. Not these four. Their focus was fully on the action down below. Every now and then, one of them would make an observation, like "Hjalmarsson is trying to pinch down the wing earlier than normal, don't you think?" or "Everyone but Coop is cheating on face-offs and getting away with it, so he needs to start cheating, too," and someone would send a text message to one of the coaches, relaying their information.

During intermission, most of the injured guys went down to the locker room to talk to the rest of the team. Jensen stayed put, though, so I took the opportunity to talk to him, catching Ben's eye to be sure he was filming.

"We haven't seen you around much lately," I said, leaving my comment open-ended.

He shook his head slowly. "Concussion symptoms haven't made it easy. Still can't handle being in a big crowd. That's why I'm not down there with the boys now."

"You seeing any improvements yet?"

He gave a mirthless laugh. "Maybe? Some days, I think I'm finally getting better. Other days, it's worse than ever before. The blinding headaches. The inability to focus. Nausea, dizziness… Some days, all I can do is sit in a dark room." He shrugged. "I'm just in a waiting game now. But I try to hang out around the boys when I can. It's tough to do, though, other than maybe the other guys who're injured."

"So it must be nice to have some company right now."

"It is, even though I wouldn't wish it on any of them."

"No. No, I'm sure you wouldn't. Do you still want to play? Or are you over it at this point?" As soon as I asked the question, I realized I probably shouldn't have. Especially if he was over it and wanted out. He was still under contract, so this wasn't the time for that sort of honesty.

But he looked at me and said, "I'd give my left nut to be down on the ice with those boys right now. It kills me that I can't play. That I can't do much of anything right now. I used to know who I was and why I was here. Right now, all I have are questions."

Down at ice level, they were holding a game of human bowling for the fans, to keep everyone entertained during the break between periods. For every pin a contestant knocked over, the arena set off the goal horn.

After a few of those, Jensen gave me an apologetic look and shook his head. "This is why I tend to stay home. Can't handle this." Then he got up and walked out, taking out a pair of sunglasses and putting them over his eyes, reminding me once again that these men were very much real men. They put their bodies on the line to play the game they loved, but sometimes it could have devastating consequences.

Those consequences didn't stop many of them from playing, though. Or wanting to play, even long past the point when they shouldn't anymore.

Like Andrew Jensen and his concussion that had left him alone in dark rooms for months.

Like Brenden Campbell and the string of injuries that had plagued his career and had his wife begging him to retire.

Like Nate, playing through a knee injury that would put the average person out of commission for weeks, at the very least.

After the tense few days in Chicago, I'd needed some perspective. About what I was doing with *Eye of the Storm*. About what I *wanted* to do with it.

Andrew Jensen had just given me a poignant reminder of my plan. The story wasn't about black or white, gay or straight, good or bad, right or wrong. It was about life, in all its imperfect glory.

Now I needed to follow through with the plan.

THE STORM WON Game Seven against the Blackhawks, with Nate scoring the only goal in the game. That meant they would move on to face the Stars, who'd been waiting to learn their opponent for the better part of a week, in the Western Conference Finals. The Stars also had home-ice advantage, due to having a better regular-season record than the Storm, so we'd be starting this round on the road.

Despite the best efforts from Nate and his Storm teammates, the Stars won both of the first two games in their home building. We headed back to Portland with them behind two-to-nothing in the series, but full to the brim with determination to change that as soon as possible.

Once back at home, I spent hours on end holed up with my editor and the other guys on my team, making sure we shaped the next webisode to give exactly the message I wanted conveyed. It was painstaking work, particularly since there were so many *big* stories surrounding the team.

I didn't want to tell the big stories, though. They'd already been covered ad nauseam by the mainstream media. I wanted to tell the little stories: the decision as to when it's time to hang up the skates and retire; the loneliness of going from being a core part of a team to being stuck on the sidelines due to injury; the bond of brotherhood; the fear of acceptance faced by a player whose native language isn't spoken by anyone else on the team; the hijinks that happen when a group of young men are away from their families with more money than they'd ever dreamed of having before; the joy that comes from fulfilling a lifelong dream; the mixed emotions that resulted from a phone call, when the family of the police officer Nate had carried through the streets of Chicago called to thank him for his efforts and, at the same time, let him know that the officer had passed away.

I'd already been telling this story throughout the playoffs, but the newest episode would follow that pattern more than ever before. There would be *no* coverage of the big issues, beyond delving into how they touched the personal lives of these men. Not only that, but I'd drawn a hard line. If a couple was struggling with something off the ice, unless they specifically invited me to delve into their struggles, it was out of bounds for my show. That meant no tackling the issue of Jamie and Katie Babcock's fertility issues, and no exploration of whatever was or wasn't taking place between Cody Williams and Dani Weber.

Making a decision like this was a big step to take, but, as I was already all too aware, I had nothing to lose.

I'd taken to going home with Nate each night instead of heading back to my place, and staying all night with him in his hotel room when we were on the road. In fact, I'd started to leave a few items at his house so I wouldn't have to go without or borrow from him too much. I had a toothbrush that stayed there, along with a few other toiletries. A couple of times, I'd left some clothes there. He always pulled out one of his own T-shirts and a pair of shorts for me, though. He liked seeing me in them, and I couldn't deny they were insanely comfortable.

I more than liked the way he looked at me when I wore them, too. He always appeared ready to devour me whole when he came into the kitchen while I was fixing a cup of coffee, wearing his clothes. And when he looked at me like that, I wanted to let him. It wasn't uncommon in those moments for us to end up back in his bed for a while.

But the way it made me feel to find Nate looking at me with such intense desire only served as further proof that my mother had messed with my head in ways that I would likely be dealing with for the rest of my life. Especially since, following the shootings in Chicago, she was trying harder than ever before to convince me to go along with her plan. She had three more Indian doctors at her beck and call, each of them ready to marry me as soon as I came to my senses, stopped dressing like a slut, left my line of work, and agreed to the arrangement.

I hadn't stopped taking her calls. I couldn't seem to make myself draw that line completely, always hoping that somehow, someway, she'd realize she was causing more harm than good. She was my mother, after all, and she always would be. But I was still waiting for her to make the next move.

Back on home ice, the Storm pulled out a win in Game Three, largely due to Nate and Jezek playing like they'd grown up on the ice together. Which wasn't all that surprising, I supposed, since they had done exactly that. No matter how much of a show those two put on in Game Four, though, it wasn't enough for the team to come away with a win, setting up a do-or-die situation for the next game back in Dallas. Win and live to play another day. Lose and go home.

The day before Game Five, I gave my guys time off. There were any number of things I could have sent them off to film, but I wanted them all fresh, rested, and relaxed for the game the next day. Beyond that, I got the strong sense that Game Five might be the end for this season. There wasn't a chance that any of the men on this team would throw in the towel, but they were exhausted—mentally, physically, and emotionally. This season, and in particular, the last couple of months, had drained them in any number of ways. I wasn't sure how much more they had to give.

I was preparing to wind things down. Most of my crew hadn't taken a full day off in well over a month. I hadn't taken more than a few hours here and a few hours there to myself. I knew I needed it as much as anyone, even if I was likely to have more time off than I knew what to do with soon.

Nate and I spent the evening in his hotel room, wrapped up in each other's arms. Some of the time, we talked. Other times, we made love. For a while, we lay in bed, each reading a different book. He was now reading *Eleanor & Park* by Rainbow Rowell, and at Nate's urging, I'd started *The Fault in Our Stars* by John Green. Those books led both of us to getting weepy, so we set them aside and held each other instead, content simply to be together.

LESS THAN TWENTY-FOUR hours later, I was sad to learn I'd been right. The Storm just didn't have enough juice left to beat the Stars.

Watching Nate and his teammates skate out to shake hands with the Dallas players tore at my heart. These guys had all the motivation in the world, but apparently, in the end, it wasn't their year. Or maybe they had *too much* motivation. Maybe there were simply too many other things going on, stealing away their focus.

If so, my crew and I had been part of the problem. Not a happy thought. But the silver lining in that idea was that any part I might have played in their demise was now almost at an end. This meant I could wrap up the introductory season of *Eye of the Storm*, officially be fired, and move on to whatever the next stop in my career might be. In the process, it would eliminate all the problems I was experiencing with presenting a biased view in my coverage of the team. I could be Nate's girlfriend, hang out with the other WAGs, and not worry about any of them being concerned I might use something they say or do against them simply in order to further my own career.

I felt like a huge weight had been lifted off my shoulders.

I headed for the locker room after the handshakes had been completed, but I still got there before the team arrived. My crew positioned themselves on their own, not needing any direction from me, so I stood off to the side to observe, as was my custom.

Nate found me as soon as he came into the room, though. And instead of heading for his stall to begin taking off his equipment and changing clothes, he headed straight for me. He had me off my feet and in his arms in no time, kissing me like his life depended on it.

I wrapped my arms around his neck and held on for all I was worth.

When he broke off the kiss, he asked, "Is that the end of it, then?"

I didn't have to search my brain to understand his meaning. The end of my job. The end of the media being so hyper-focused on him because of events outside of his control. The end of all the things that had kept us under a microscope for so long.

I nodded, a laugh trying to bubble up within me. "I think so, yeah."

"Thank God."

My sentiments, exactly. Because now, we could just be *us*—whatever that ended up meaning. Now we had the time to figure it all out, in our own time and our own way.

Together.

Epilogue

Anne

"I DON'T SEE any reason to beat around the bush," my boss said on the other end of the phone. And yes, he was doing this over the phone. He couldn't even bother to have me come in so he could fire me in person. What a jerk.

It was the Monday morning following the final webisode going live. My crew and I were gathered around a box of Blue Star donuts and coffee, celebrating the conclusion of our initial season of working together.

"Despite repeated reminders that we wanted you to cover the big ticket events surrounding the team during their playoff run, you continued to avoid those subjects and focus instead on making *Eye of the Storm* into a soap opera. You knew this was coming, and now it's here. You're fired, Anne. You'll have a month's severance. We wish you well."

"Understood," I replied, feeling both relieved and disappointed at once. "Good luck to you and whoever you bring on for the next season. And thank you for the opportunity."

Ben and Dave both rolled their eyes from across the table.

I exchanged a few more *pleasantries*, if you could call them that, and then hung up.

"Fuck that," Dave said. "Thank you for the opportunity? That's bullshit."

"Even if we all knew I was only in this for the short term, they *did* give me an opportunity," I pointed out. "And I got some great experience out of it that I can use in whatever's next."

"So, the rest of us give them notice today," Ben said, looking around the table.

"Now hold on a minute," I said. "You guys aren't throwing your jobs away over me. We *all* knew this was coming, but that doesn't—"

"We told them a month ago when they first threatened to fire you," Bill cut in. "You go, we go, too."

"But I don't have anything lined up. I can't promise you guys another job right away or anything. I don't even—"

"Doesn't matter," Dave insisted. "We've all been working in this business for a long time, and we won't have any problem getting more work. We'll be fine. They need to know that they can't get away with that. They had Internet gold with the show you produced for them, and they're tossing you for a bullshit reason. That's not someone I want to keep working for."

Ben held up his coffee, like he was making a toast, and the other guys followed suit.

"I'm going to be really pissed off at all of you if you don't have jobs again within a couple of weeks," I said. "You got that?"

They laughed, but they agreed.

A COUPLE OF hours later, I arrived at the Storm's practice facility. I'd promised to meet Nate there so we could go out for lunch together to celebrate the end of my job and the end of his season. It was clean-out day for the team. They were all clearing out their lockers and having exit interviews with the coaches, things like that.

I walked into the locker room to find a few of them giving out what I called guy hugs—the sort where they were slapping each other on the backs. In my time working around this team, I knew that was normal for a day like today. Some of these men wouldn't ever be back as members of the Storm. They'd retire or get traded or not be offered a new contract with the team. Changes were always taking place. It was hard to see, though, because I'd gotten really attached to all of them over the last couple of months. It felt like a part of *my* family was leaving.

In an effort to keep from getting teary-eyed, I looked around for

Nate, but he was nowhere to be found.

"Ghost's in Jim's office," Jezek told me. "You can go up. They won't mind."

I nodded my thanks and made my way up the stairs.

Rachel grinned at me when I came around the corner. "Another season in the books."

"So it is." In more ways than she likely knew.

She angled her head toward Mr. Sutter's office. "Go on in. They're expecting you."

They were? I couldn't help but wonder why Mr. Sutter would be expecting me, but it wouldn't take me long to find out.

I knocked on the open door as I poked my head inside.

"Anne!" Jim said, coming to his feet. He smiled and took off his bifocals, folding in the earpieces and setting them on the desk in front of him. "Come on in. I was just going over some possibilities for a new contract with Nate, but we're done with that for now, and I was hoping to talk to you."

I crossed over and shook his hand before taking a seat next to Nate.

"I've been talking to Mr. Engels and the coaching staff about you and the work you did on *Eye of the Storm* this season."

This couldn't be good. I glanced at Nate, who gave me a reassuring smile and reached for my hand to squeeze it. I needed to explain that I'd just been fired before Mr. Sutter got much further. "About that, I—"

"We loved it," he cut in, not letting me get any headway. "We loved everything about it, actually. When we first hired your production company, we wanted the show produced as an experiment, to see how it would help to bring the team into the public a bit more, before we decided on whether or not to take it on again. Now that we've seen the way it's played out, though, we're excited to talk about next season. Not only that, but we want to produce it in-house going forward. We'd post it directly to the Storm's website instead of only linking to it, which will hopefully get even greater reach for your work. But we want you to come on board. Now, I know that would mean changing employers, and I completely understand if that's not something—"

"Are you serious?" I interrupted, gawking.

"Completely serious. If you agreed to this, we'd give you complete creative freedom, as long as you comply with the rules and regulations the NHL has in place for these kinds of productions. I don't think that should present any problem for you, though. And we'd need you to bring on a team to work under you… Human Resources can give you all the specifics on that, of course. I'll understand if you need some time to think about it. This would mean a big change for your future."

It would mean the best change possible for my future. But I'd never been one to jump into things headfirst without knowing all of the details. "I'll go talk to HR, then, and give you my answer next week."

"Excellent. Nate, can you show her the way?"

"You've got it, Jim."

We all stood, and Nate and I both shook Mr. Sutter's hand. Once we were out in the hall together, Nate pulled me into a corner and kissed me like we hadn't seen each other in weeks, even though I'd been in his bed with him this morning.

"How perfect was that?" he asked when he came up for air.

"Beyond perfect. Did you know?"

He shook his head. "No idea. But that's not even all. He wants to offer me six more years. He'll have to work out the money and other details with my agent, but seriously. Six years! That means I won't be going anywhere anytime soon."

"That's fantastic news. We've got even more to celebrate than we thought."

"Speaking of which…" Nate said slowly. "I know we were going to have lunch, but now you need to go talk to HR. And there's something else I need to go do, anyway. Let's do dinner instead. And is there any chance we can get your father to join us?"

I narrowed my eyes at him. He and Dad had gotten along well on the previous occasions they'd met, but I wasn't sure why he'd suggest bringing my father to dinner when initially our plan had been a day of celebration involving only the two of us. In fact, I'd been hoping our festivities would end up in the bedroom sooner rather than later.

"I think he can probably come along. But why?" I didn't do a darned thing to hide the suspicion in my tone, either.

"There's just something I need to ask him, is all."

"Something you need to ask him," I repeated.

Nate winked. "What can I say? I'm an old-fashioned kind of guy. I need his blessing for something. Been taking lessons from the books I'm reading…"

And I had a feeling I knew exactly what that something was, too. Beaming, I bit my lower lip. "Is that so?"

"Very much so."

"I'll make sure he comes, then. But for now, you need to take me to

HR."

He rolled his eyes. "All business, all the time." But he put an arm around my waist and guided me down the hall. "Any chance you'll give me a hint what your answer might be?"

"Nope. You're just going to have to wait and see."

Because some things in life were worth waiting for. And he wasn't getting an answer until I got my question.

Roster

Name	Position	Nickname	Number
Dominic Medved	Defense	Bear	2
Cole Paxton	Defense	Colesy	3
Andrew Jensen	Defense	Jens	4
Levi Babcock	Defense	501	5
Chris Hammond	Defense	Hammer	6
Keith Burns	Defense	Burnzie	7
Cody Williams	Defense	Harry	8
Luc Vincent	Center	Vinny	10
Brenden Campbell	Left Wing	Soupy	11
Blake Kozlow	Center	Koz	14
Radek Cernak	Center	Radar	15
Austin Cooper	Center	Coop	16
Ilya Demidov	Defense	Demi	18
Jamie Babcock	Right Wing	Babs	19
Axel Johansson	Right Wing	Jo-Jo	20
Dylan Poplawski	Right Wing	Pops	21
Otto Raita	Left Wing	Otter	27
Cam Johnson	Left Wing	Jonny	28
Mitchell Quincey	Right Wing	Q	29
Nicklas Ericsson	Goal	Nicky	30
Sean Roberts	Goal	Bobby	35
Aaron Ludwiczak	Left Wing	Luddy	43
Jiri Dvorak	Right Wing	Devo	44
Nate Golston	Left Wing	Ghost	83
Riley Jezek	Center	RJ	91

About the Author

Catherine Gayle is a *USA Today* bestselling author of more than thirty contemporary hockey romance and Regency-set historical romance novels and novellas, with over half a million books sold. She's a transplanted Texan living in North Carolina with two extremely spoiled felines. In her spare time, she watches way too much hockey and reality TV, plans fun things to do for the Nephew Monster's next visit, and performs experiments in the kitchen which are rarely toxic.

Visit her website at www.catherinegayle.com. Join her mailing list at http://eepurl.com/GXcwr to receive news about new releases, sales, and pre-orders, as well as to receive a free Portland Storm short story titled ICE BREAKER, which is not available for sale through any outlet.

Other Books by Catherine Gayle

Breakaway

On the Fly

Taking a Shot

Light the Lamp

Delay of Game

Double Major

In the Zone

Holiday Hat Trick

Comeback

Dropping Gloves

Bury the Hatchet

Home Ice

Smoke Signals

Mistletoe Misconduct

Losing an Edge

Ghost Dance

Dreaming Up a Dare

Game Breaker

Twice a Rake

Saving Grace

Merely a Miss

Wallflower

Pariah

Seven Minutes in Devon

Flight of Fancy

Rhyme and Reason

Thick as Thieves

An Unintended Journey

To Enchant an Icy Earl

The Devil to Pay

A Dance with the Devil

Wanton Wives

CPSIA information can be obtained
at www.ICGtesting.com
Printed in the USA
LVHW05s0755171018
593879LV00009B/516/P

9 781541 050419